THE TENANT OF WILDFELL HALL

broadview editions
series editor: L. W. Conolly

THE TENANT OF WILDFELL HALL

Anne Brontë

edited by Lee A. Talley

broadview editions

Library and Archives Canada Cataloguing in Publication

Brontë, Anne, 1820-1849
    The tenant of Wildfell Hall / Anne Brontë ; edited by
Lee A. Talley.

(Broadview editions)
Includes bibliographical references.
ISBN 978-1-55111-508-5

    I. Talley, Lee Allen, 1964-   II. Title.
III. Series: Broadview editions

PR4162.T4 2009   823'.8   C2009-902933-2

Broadview Editions

The Broadview Editions series represents the ever-changing canon of literature in English by bringing together texts long regarded as classics with valuable lesser-known works.

Advisory editor for this volume: Martin R. Boyne.

Broadview Press is an independent, international publishing house, incorporated in 1985. Broadview believes in shared ownership, both with its employees and with the general public; since the year 2000 Broadview shares have traded publicly on the Toronto Venture Exchange under the symbol BDP.

We welcome comments and suggestions regarding any aspect of our publications—please feel free to contact us at the addresses below or at broadview@broadviewpress.com.

North America   PO Box 1243, Peterborough, Ontario, Canada K9J 7H5
                    2215 Kenmore Ave., Buffalo, New York, USA 14207
                    Tel: (705) 743-8990; Fax: (705) 743-8353
                    email: customerservice@broadviewpress.com

UK, Ireland,   NBN International, Estover Road, Plymouth, UK PL6 7PY
and continental Europe   Tel: 44 (0) 1752 202300; Fax: 44 (0) 1752 202330
                    email: enquiries@nbninternational.com

Australia and New Zealand   NewSouth Books
                    c/o TL Distribution
                    15-23 Helles Ave, Moorebank, NSW, Australia 2170
                    Tel: (02) 8778 9999; Fax: (02) 8778 9944
                    email: orders@tldistribution.com.au

www.broadviewpress.com

This book is printed on paper containing 100% post-consumer fibre.

PRINTED IN CANADA

Contents

Acknowledgements • 7
Abbreviations • 8
Introduction • 9
Anne Brontë: A Brief Chronology • 34
A Note on the Text • 35

The Tenant of Wildfell Hall • 37

Appendix A: Other Writings by Anne and Charlotte Brontë • 409
 1. Anne Brontë, Letter to the Reverend David Thom (30 December 1848) • 409
 2. Anne Brontë, "To Cowper" (1846) • 410
 3. Anne Brontë, "A Word to the 'Elect'" (1846) • 412
 4. From Charlotte Brontë, "Biographical Notice of Ellis and Acton Bell" (1850) • 413
 5. Charlotte Brontë, Introduction to "Poems by Acton Bell" (1850) • 417

Appendix B: Contemporary Reviews • 418
 1. *Athenaeum* (8 July 1848) • 418
 2. *The Examiner* (29 July 1848) • 419
 3. *Fraser's Magazine* (April 1849) • 422
 4. *The Literary World* (12 August 1848) • 426
 5. *North American Review* (October 1848) • 433
 6. *Rambler* (September 1848) • 435
 7. *Sharpe's London Magazine* (August 1848) • 437
 8. *The Spectator* (8 July 1848) • 439

Appendix C: Women's Education • 441
 1. From Mary Wollstonecraft, *A Vindication of the Rights of Woman* (1792) • 441
 2. From Hannah More, *Strictures on the Modern System of Female Education* (1799) • 445
 3. From Sarah Lewis, *Woman's Mission* (1840) • 447
 4. John Cowie, "Noble Sentiments on the Influence of Women," *Howitt's Journal* (March 1847) • 449

Appendix D: Wives • 452

  1. From Hannah More, *Coelebs in Search of a Wife* (1808) • 452
  2. From Caroline Norton, *A Letter to the Queen on Lord Chancellor Cranworth's Marriage and Divorce Bill* (1855) • 456

Appendix E: Childrearing • 461

  1. From Hannah More, *Strictures on the Modern System of Female Education* (1799) • 461
  2. From John S.C. Abbott, *The Mother at Home* (1833) • 462
  3. From John S.C. Abbott, *The Child at Home* (1834) • 463
  4. From Sarah Lewis, *Woman's Mission* (1840) • 464
  5. From Berthold Auerbach, "Every-day Wisdom, Plucked from the Garden of Childhood," *Howitt's Journal* (January 1848) • 467
  6. From Anonymous, "The Moral Discipline of Children," *British Quarterly Review* (April 1858) • 468

Appendix F: Temperance • 472

  1. From Joseph Entwisle, "On Drinking Spirits," *The Methodist Magazine* (July 1804) • 472
  2. J.P. Parker, Lecture on Temperance and Slavery, *Howitt's Journal* (24 April 1847) • 474
  3. From Anonymous, "Temperance and Teetotal Societies," *Blackwood's Edinburgh Magazine* (April 1853) • 476
  4. Thomas Buchanan Read, "What a Word May Do" (1868) • 479

Appendix G: Women and Art • 480

  1. Anonymous, "Let Us Join the Ladies," *Punch* (July 1857) • 480
  2. From Ellen C. Clayton, *English Female Artists* (1876) • 483

Select Bibliography • 487

Acknowledgements

This edition of *The Tenant of Wildfell Hall* owes a great deal to a host of scholars and institutions whose generosity helped shape it. I would like to thank Broadview Press, and D.L. Macdonald and Kathleen Scherf, for permission to reprint portions of their edition, *The Vindications: The Rights of Men and the Rights of Woman* by Mary Wollstonecraft (Appendix C1); Ann Dinsdale and Kathryn White of the Brontë Parsonage Museum for sharing important Brontë books and papers with me; the Department of Rare Books and Special Collections, Princeton University Library, for permission to reprint Anne Brontë's letter to the Reverend David Thom (Appendix A1), and for access to and information about the Author's Own Copy of *The Tenant of Wildfell Hall*, as well as other important nineteenth-century editions of Brontë's work; Yale University's Sterling Memorial Library for supplying me with a photocopy of the crucial Newby edition of the novel, and the Department of Rare Books at the Beinecke for providing the photograph of the original title page. I am grateful to the previous editors of Brontë's work as well: especially Stevie Davies, G.D. Hargreaves, Herbert Rosengarten, and Margaret Smith; their editions of *The Tenant of Wildfell Hall* illuminate my own.

I am also appreciative of the inter-library loan librarians at California State University, Dominguez Hills, and Rowan University, who were able to secure copies of numerous obscure Victorian texts for me. Both C.S.U. Dominguez Hills and Rowan University provided me with occasional course releases to carry out the research necessary for this volume, and Rowan University also funded two student assistants, Cindy Best and Jennifer Fassolino, who, under the guidance of Georgette Sahm, carefully converted the copy of the novel into a computer-readable text.

At Broadview, Leonard Conolly thoughtfully responded to myriad questions on every aspect of this book, Martin Boyne skillfully copyedited it, and Tara Lowes expertly oversaw the production and proofreading of this complicated text. Others deserve special mention as well: Jane Rynex's biblical detective work provided a sturdy foundation for most of the religious footnotes; and Michael Grove's patient and nuanced responses to my numerous biblical queries were invaluable. Many others also generously gave of their time: Ellen Brinks, Jacqueline Falkenheim, Ann Jurecic, Julie Pfeiffer, Patricia Melzer, Wendy Weinberg, and Shelley Wilcox provided constructive feedback on early drafts of the introduction. Lastly, countless colleagues shared information with me on subjects ranging from ancient Greek and medieval humoral theory to Victorian philanthropists and nineteenth-century theology. I am particularly grateful to Margret Aldrich, René Boatman, Ellen Brinks, Maria Davidis, the members of the VICTORIA-List discussion group moderated by Patrick Leary, Mical Moser, Bill Tipper, Cindy Vitto, and most especially Wendy Weinberg.

Abbreviations

AOC	Author's Own Copy of *The Tenant of Wildfell Hall*
DNB	*Dictionary of National Biography*
OED	*Oxford English Dictionary*
OTWH	*The Tenant of Wildfell Hall*, edited by Herbert Rosengarten with an Introduction by Margaret Smith (Oxford: Oxford UP, 1998)
PTWH	*The Tenant of Wildfell Hall*, edited by Stevie Davies (London: Penguin Books, 1996)

Introduction

Upon its publication in 1848, *The Tenant of Wildfell Hall* received immediate, sustained, and controversial reviews because of its subject matter: alcoholism, the promotion of women's rights, hard-hitting criticism of domestic abuse, and an exploration of the possibility of universal salvation (the belief that everyone, even sinners, will eventually get to heaven). In fact, some Victorian reviewers even warned their "lady readers" to avoid the novel because of its bold and realistic depictions of human passions and the unflinching descriptions of drunkenness and the debauched behavior often associated with it (Appendix B7). Despite concern about its moral content, however, many reviewers found the novel gripping and recognized it as a powerful and important literary work.

Yet many twenty-first-century readers have never heard of *Tenant* and are surprised to learn there was "another" Brontë sister in addition to the better-known Emily and Charlotte. Although scholars have been paying more attention to Anne Brontë's work over the past thirty years, she is still the Brontë sister about whom most readers know the least, for a number of reasons. The literary worth of her novels *Agnes Grey* (1847) and *The Tenant of Wildfell Hall* (1848) was overshadowed at first by their controversial subject matter and the confusion surrounding the identity of their author. Over time, the extraordinary success of Emily's *Wuthering Heights* (1847) and Charlotte's *Jane Eyre* (1847) also worked to occlude Anne's work from view. Within contemporary popular culture, for example, her sisters' novels have had very successful incarnations as Hollywood and made-for-television films. While a 1996 BBC production of *Tenant* briefly brought Anne's work into the popular limelight, along with a new movie-edition of the novel, her work is still eclipsed by her sisters' in the public's imagination.

Initially there was a great deal of confusion surrounding the identities of the three Brontë sisters, who wrote under the gender-neutral names of Acton, Currer, and Ellis Bell in order to hide their feminine names of Anne, Charlotte, and Emily Brontë, respectively. In her "Biographical Notice," appended to the 1850 edition of *Wuthering Heights* and *Agnes Grey*, Charlotte Brontë explains that "we veiled our own names under those of Currer, Ellis, and Acton Bell ... [because] we had a vague impression that authoresses are liable to be looked on with prejudice" (see Appendix A4, where all subsequent quotations from the "Biographical Notice" can be found). While fear of discrimination based on their gender motivated the women to adopt "ambiguous" pseudonyms, Victorian readers at first were unsure not only of the sex of these authors, but also as to whether there were even three distinct writers.[1] Anne's publishers, for example, fraudulently advertised *The Tenant of Wildfell Hall* in the United States as written by the same author of *Jane Eyre*,[2] and the New York Harper edition of the novel credited Acton Bell with *Wuthering Heights* (Ruff 145). Even after Anne's death, when *Agnes Grey* was published in the United States, it was advertised as written by "the author of *Jane Eyre* [and] *Shirley*," as well as *Tenant* (Ruff 144). Ultimately, Charlotte and Anne journeyed to London from distant Haworth to meet Charlotte's editor in order to prove that there was more than one Bell brother (or Brontë sister) who wrote.

The Brontës' reputations as writers were secured with the publication and acclaim they received for their first published novels (*Jane Eyre, Wuthering Heights*, and *Agnes Grey* in 1847), but they had also self published a collection of their poetry in 1846 (*Poems by Currer, Ellis, and Acton Bell*); Anne's *The Tenant of Wildfell Hall* was released in 1848. Each novel was greeted with passionate reviews as they challenged both literary and social conventions of the time: all three Brontës fictionally represented the situation of women in mid-Victorian England and explored human passions. Anne and Emily, in particular, examine violence in their fiction. Anne's two novels, however, present the brutal realities of women's lives and the difficulties of family life with more realism than her sisters' gothic *Wuthering Heights* or romantic *Jane Eyre*. This also accounts for a great deal of Anne's status as the more neglected Brontë sister: she was speaking an "unpalatable truth" that many would have liked to ignore (40). Until the rise of feminist scholarship in the 1970s and 1980s, it was easier for critics to overlook a novel about a bad marriage that highlighted the problems of Victorian women under an oppressively patriarchal society.

Readers have also had a more difficult time learning about Anne Brontë because, aside from her poems and some juvenilia, only a handful of letters remain in addition to her drawings, diary papers, and marginalia in published works. Perhaps even more significant than the paucity of materials is Charlotte's shaping hand in how our predecessors read Anne's work. After Emily's and Anne's deaths to tuberculosis in December 1848 and May 1849 at the early ages of 30 and 29 respectively, Charlotte had an edition of *Wuthering Heights* and *Agnes Grey* published along with several of their poems in an attempt to salvage their reputations as virtuous women—as well as talented writers. In this volume she provided a preface and "Biographical Notice of Ellis and Acton Bell," along with short introductions to their poems. In ad-

---

1 See Appendices B2 and B4–7 for questions about whether there were three authors; see Appendices B3, B4, B6, and B7 for questions about the sex of the author.

2 Charlotte Brontë's letter to Mary Taylor of 4 September 1848 explains Newby's dishonesty at length. See Smith 111–17.

dition to editing their poetry substantially, however, she selected poems that would write Anne into the role of a depressive Christian zealot. For example, of the nine poems of Anne's she selected to include, seven are religious, and she chose twice as many poems of Emily's to appear in the collection. Charlotte's selection implies that Emily was the more talented writer and Anne the religious one. While her choices could have been motivated solely out of grief—by age 33 she was the only surviving sibling of six—or an unselfish desire to protect their reputations, she could also have been motivated by competition and sibling rivalry.[1]

Charlotte took a more visibly active part in shaping Anne's reputation in her influential "Biography of Ellis and Acton Bell," in which she tried to "wipe the dust from their gravestones, ... leav[ing] their dear names free from soil." Unfortunately, her words there had a deleterious effect on Anne's reputation as well. Charlotte describes the motives dictating the choice of subject matter for *Tenant* as "slightly morbid," and goes on to depict Anne as of a "naturally ... sensitive, reserved, and dejected nature," deeply affected by her witnessing "near at hand and for a long time, the terrible effects of talents misused and faculties abused." Here, Charlotte is referring to the disastrous events that occurred when Anne was a governess at Thorp Green and their brother, Branwell, invited to work there as well as a violin instructor, embarked upon an affair with the married Mrs. Robinson. According to Charlotte, *Tenant* is the result of a traumatic witnessing; it is a fictional response from the horrified bystander who watched her brother be tempted by a married woman. She goes on to describe Anne's writing of the novel as an obsession, since Anne hated the subject matter yet continued to write, viewing others' attempts to reason with her as "a temptation to self indulgence." Charlotte attributes Anne's single-minded focus on this "morbid" topic as the product of her belief, explaining how "the tinge of religious melancholy communicated a sad shade to her brief, blameless life," assuming that Anne's Christian faith held her to this subject matter. This portion of the "Biographical Notice" presents *The Tenant of Wildfell Hall* as the production of a gloomy Christian who obsessively copied from life, not someone who, as Anne publicly wrote in her preface, wanted to "contribute [her] humble quota towards ... [helping] reform the errors and abuses of society" (39). Later, in the 1850 edition of *Wuthering Heights*, when Charlotte introduces Anne's poetry, she describes Anne's faith as a "sorrowing piety," the reason for her "perpetual pensiveness," ultimately describing Anne's life as a type of "martyrdom" to her faith. Charlotte's more negative focus on Anne's faith and deeply felt religious views inadvertently alienated Anne's potential reading audience: Victorians had a deep suspicion of anything that smacked

---

1   For more information on specific alterations of text, see Barker 655–57.

of fanaticism or, as they termed it, "enthusiasm," despite being profoundly shaped by a religious worldview.

Charlotte's other tactic to try to save Anne's and Emily's reputations from charges of immorality—brought upon them because their novels depicted passion, violence, desire, drunkenness, and abuse—was to paint them as isolated, rustic geniuses. Here, Charlotte describes Anne as the lesser of the two:

> Anne's character was milder and more subdued; she wanted the power, the fire, the originality of her sister, but was well-endowed with quiet virtues of her own. Long suffering, self-denying, reflective, and intelligent, a constitutional reserve and taciturnity placed and kept her in the shade, and covered her mind, and especially her feelings, with a sort of nun-like veil, which was rarely lifted.

Charlotte's reference to Anne's faith—conflated here with her personality— is not complimentary, given the pervasive anti-Catholic sentiment of the times and the Protestant suspicion of those who lived a cloistered life.

Charlotte also claims that her sisters' geographic isolation assured their innocence. She writes that "they were two unobtrusive women; a perfectly secluded life gave them retiring manners and habits." This "fact" of their seclusion is one that several critics have documented as untrue, since, despite their location in a tiny town in the north of England, the Brontë children were encouraged to read widely and had access to countless books and periodicals. Charlotte, however, strategically presents them as untaught, writing that "Neither Emily nor Anne was learned; they had no thought of filling their pitchers at the well-spring of other minds; they always wrote from the impulse of nature, the dictates of intuition, and from such stores of observation as their limited experience had enabled them to amass." Presenting her sisters as innocents who wrote intuitively and naturally may well have helped salvage their reputations for Victorian readers, who were shocked by their novels' coarse materials; yet these descriptions falsely imply that Emily and Anne just happened to write powerful novels and conceal that they were skilled writers who labored at their craft for years. Although we can only speculate about why she presented such a narrow view of Anne, it is undeniable that her influence helped shape how later generations of readers and critics understood her sisters' work.

Privately, however, Charlotte admitted to disliking *Tenant*, an opinion that doubtless influenced how she crafted her "Biographical Notice." When Charlotte wrote her editor, W.S. Williams, about reprinting *Wuthering Heights* and *Agnes Grey*, she asserted that

> *Wildfell Hall* ... hardly appears to me desirable to preserve. The choice of subject in that work is a mistake—it was too little consonant with the char-

acter—tastes, and ideas of the gentle, retiring, inexperienced writer. She wrote it under a strange, conscientious, half-ascetic notion of accomplishing a painful penance and a severe duty. Blameless in deed and almost in thought—there was from her very childhood a tinge of religious melancholy in her mind—this I ever suspected—and I have found, amongst her papers mournful proofs that such was the case. (Smith 463)

Even in confidence she paints her sister as religiously excessive, and she views *Tenant* as the product of a self-punishing faith and a depressive zeal. Asserting that Anne's work is the product of a mind tainted by "religious melancholy" further dismisses it as a type of religious enthusiasm. Similarly, presenting Anne as a Christian who wrote the novel "under a strange, conscientious, half-ascetic notion of accomplishing a painful penance and a severe duty" in order to explain why her sister chose such dark material, Charlotte downplays her sibling's literary talent, reduces her artistry to mere imitation, and compresses a rich novel within the narrow confines of psychobiography. Anne Brontë did indeed witness horrors as a governess and as a concerned relation of their brother Branwell, whose own talent was never fully realized before he drank and drugged his life into dissipation and then death. Although a few scholars believe *Tenant* is indeed a fictional rendering of Branwell's disastrous affair with Mrs. Robinson, the mother of the children Anne was instructing when she worked as a governess at Thorp Green, to contemplate *Tenant* solely as an obsessive reproduction of "real life," rather than a carefully plotted artistic production, detracts from the work's force, purpose, and originality. The text itself seems to work against this reading as well, since its central aesthetic focus is how to render experience in an artistic production. The heroine of *The Tenant of Wildfell Hall*, Helen Huntingdon, an amateur artist who is forced into professionalizing herself, muses repeatedly on how to render what she sees into art, not being willing merely to copy what she sees directly onto the canvas.

Reviews of *The Tenant of Wildfell Hall*

Realism and questions surrounding which events to depict and how to present difficult incidents to the reading public form the central thread that runs through most of the reviews of the novel. Nineteenth-century reviewers' concerns about the realistic way in which "coarse" behavior is depicted in this novel provides us with important insights into how Victorian ideals about propriety shaped and reflected class and gender roles. Reviewers were concerned about who should—and would—be reading this novel, believing that, for their own good, women especially needed to be protected from witnessing debauched behavior. For example, the first reviewer approached by *Sharpe's London Magazine* (see Appendix B7) found

> so revolting ... many of the scenes, so coarse and disgusting the language put into the mouths of some of the characters, that [he] ... returned it to [the other editors], saying it was unfit to be noticed in the pages of *Sharpe*; and we are so far of the same opinion, that our object in the present paper is to warn our readers, and more especially our lady-readers, against being induced to peruse it, either by the powerful interest of the story, or the talent with which it is written.

While this reviewer grudgingly praises the book, noting how well written and interesting it is, he objects to the scenes recounted in Helen's diary because "each revolting detail is dwelt on with painful minuteness, [and] each brutal or profane expression chronicled with hateful accuracy." For this reviewer, like several others, the incidents recounted in the book reflect the moral life of the author and are seen as threatening, especially to women. The novel seems a bit too real, as the reviewers cannot imagine how someone could create these scenes without intimate acquaintance with them. *Sharpe's* most shrilly denounces *The Tenant of Wildfell Hall* for its realism, concluding that "the profane expressions, inconceivably coarse language, and revolting scenes and descriptions ... disfigur[e] ... its pages."

Many reviews also reflect the gendered double standard for moral behavior against which Brontë was writing. For example, Charles Kingsley, in his review for *Fraser's Magazine* (Appendix B3), hopes "every man in England might read and lay to heart that horrible record" recounted in Helen's diary to learn by example what not to do. But Kingsley also believes it was a "great mistake" to "fill such a diary with written oaths and curses, with details of drunken scenes which no wife, such as poor Helen is represented, would have the heart, not to say the common decency to write down." Kingsley cannot imagine even a fictitious woman writing an account of depravity solely because of Victorian ideals about feminine propriety. He concludes that *Tenant* is "utterly unfit to be put into the hands of girls." It was against reviews like this one that Anne Brontë wrote the preface to the second printing of the novel, asserting that "it is better to depict ... vice and vicious characters ... as they really are than as they would wish to appear," firmly holding her ground when she states, "if I have warned one rash youth from following in their steps, or prevented one thoughtless girl from falling into the very natural error of my heroine, the book has not been written in vain" (39–40).

Despite her assertions, the novel's realism was clearly deemed threatening to "lady readers"; yet it also piqued reviewers' curiosity about the mysterious

Acton Bell, causing many to read the scenes of violence for clues about the author's sex. Kingsley concludes in a footnote to his review that it "is just such as a woman, trying to write like a man," while the editors of *Sharpe's* assert that "it may be the production of an authoress assisted by her husband, or some other *male* friend." Because of their narrow Victorian constructions of womanhood, reviewers were very uncomfortable imagining a female author writing these scenes.

It was not just the sex of the author that puzzled the reviewers, though; many remarked on *Tenant's* resemblance to the other Brontë novels. The reviewer for the *Athenaeum*, for example (Appendix B1), describes "the three Bells ... ring[ing] in a chime so harmonious as to prove that they have issued from the same mould." The review in *The Examiner* (Appendix B2) determines that "the authors of *Jane Eyre*, *Wuthering Heights*, *Agnes Grey* and *The Tenant of Wildfell Hall* are evidently children from the same family....We have, once or twice, entertained a suspicion that all the books that we have enumerated might have issued from the same source; sent forth at different seasons, in different states of mind or humour, or at different periods or elevations of the intellect."

While questions surrounding the identity of the author and the imagined effects of the novel on female readers dominated discussion, issues of class also played a significant role in reviews. Critics were so shocked by the bald depictions of passion and drunkenness that they presumed "Bell" must have used criminals as her characters' models. (Prevailing classist beliefs located criminality predominantly in the lower classes.) E.P. Whipple in the *North American Review* (Appendix B5) asserts, "The reader of Acton Bell ... is confined to a narrow space of life, and [is] held down, as it were, by main force, to witness the wolfish side of his nature literally and logically set forth." He then warns "Bell" that "the criminal courts are not the places in which to take a comprehensive view of humanity, and the novelist who confines his observation to them is not likely to produce any lasting impression, except of horror and disgust." Like many readers, Whipple found Huntingdon and his friends' debauched behavior horrifying, and surprising too, as an example of upper-class behavior—something he could not fathom being "wolfish" or "criminal." Brontë's progressive social vision is clear: she locates the bad behavior that destroys Helen's family *not* in the lower or working classes, but in the most powerful, "respectable" parts of the patrician class.

It was not, however, just the violence of Huntingdon and his set that upset readers' understanding of social order. While many found the novel's depiction of violence in the upper classes revolting, they were equally perplexed by Brontë's cross-class love story. Some reviewers found Helen's attraction to Gilbert Markham unbelievable on class grounds. They could not understand how "the beautiful tenant of Wildfell Hall, the heiress of parks and villas, and the belle of a London season" could be attracted to "this caitiff[1] ditcher,[2] who should have been passed out of the window with a farm-yard fork" (Appendix B4). Charles Kingsley also appears baffled and "cannot see any reason why Gilbert Markham, though no doubt highly attractive to young ladies of his own caliber, should excite such passionate love in Helen, with all her bitter experiences of life, her painting, and her poetry, her deep readings and deep thoughts" (Appendix B3). Even within the realm of the novel, Gilbert freely acknowledges the problematic class difference between Helen and himself, explaining that "there was a wide distinction between the rank and circumstances of [Helen] Huntingdon, the lady of Grassdale Manor, and those of [Helen] Graham the artist, the tenant of Wildfell Hall" (378).

Despite the reviewers' class-based questions about Gilbert Markham's suitability for Helen Huntingdon and their concerns about the novel's violence, several reviewers admitted the novel's strengths.[3] At least one ordinary reader felt moved enough by the novel to write Charlotte Brontë directly with concerns that she would not have the book reprinted. This reader, who calls himself "A Mountaineer of the Wild West,"[4] while speculating that "the subject [of the novel] was not of natural growth in Acton Bell's mind," as Charlotte affirms in her "Biographical Notice," asserts that "it is not the less true that the book throughout tells of a mind whose productions we cannot afford to lose" (Smith 580–81). The "Mountaineer" particularly notes the religious progressivism of the text with Helen's belief in universal salvation,[5] imploring Charlotte to keep this book in print, since

> there are many thoughts of Helen's that must not be lost—her burst of mingled enthusiasm & irony when she utters her 'heretical opinions' upon the meed meted out to men ... bears the stamp of great genius—The close of the book is instinct with deep feeling—To me the book seems full of quiet reflective power, that the titanic energy of Ellis Bell did not admit of, & that is very different from the profound & perfect reasoning that Jane Eyre calls to her aid in her mental wars.... (Smith 581)

The "Mountaineer" also astutely notes the humor in the novel, an aspect of the book reviewers overlooked, describing this "vein of humour" as "kind,

---

1 "Expressing contempt and often involving strong moral disapprobation: A base, mean, despicable 'wretch,' a villain" (*OED*).

2 "One who makes and repairs ditches" (*OED*).

3 See especially Appendices B1, B3, and B4.

4 Margaret Smith explains in her edition of Charlotte Brontë's letters that "Wild West" could mean "the West coast of America." See note page 581.

5 See Anne Brontë's letter to the Reverend David Thom for information about her own belief (Appendix A1). See also her poetry (Appendices A2 and A3).

perfect, [and] akin to, & yet distinct from, the humour of Jane Eyre herself" (Smith 581). Significantly, this writer closes the letter requesting that *Tenant* be republished by describing himself (or herself?) as "not one of those 'who dread the effects of such strange books'" (Smith 581).[1] Here, "the Mountaineer" embraces, even as he summarizes, the fear surfacing in so many of the reviews: could one be changed or possibly contaminated by reading?

Narrative Structure of *The Tenant of Wildfell Hall*

The Tenant of Wildfell Hall begins with a letter from one man, Gilbert Markham, to another, J. Halford, recounting his fascination with and courtship of the mysterious new tenant of Wildfell Hall, Helen Huntingdon. Although the reader does not learn the precise nature of Markham's relationship with his friend until the end of the novel, Gilbert Markham regularly intrudes upon the main storyline to remark upon and ask J. Halford rhetorical questions about the action. Part way through the story, however, Markham includes a lengthy transcription of Helen Huntingdon's diary where she tells the story of her past in her own voice. The result is extraordinary as Helen hijacks the narrative, telling of her young adult life, courtship, and marriage to the reprobate, Arthur Huntingdon. Despite the chapter titles Markham has invented to divide up her story, his interruptions to "talk" to his friend, and the framing letters that contain Helen's diary, the reader is swept up with Helen's account of the events of her very troubled marriage. The story about the difficult realities of her marriage overpowers Markham's lighter tale of an awkward bachelor's romance and challenges the social conventions of Brontë's time.[2]

While the diary functions as the all too realistic testament to Helen's youthful hubris in believing that she can reform her husband, and tells of her subsequent suffering in a very troubled marriage because of Arthur's alcoholism, narcissism, and debauched behavior, the external frame of Gilbert's correspondence to J. Halford intrudes regularly on her words and works to shape how readers interpret her diary. His interruptions also enable readers

---

1 The Mountaineer writes in an aside that he (she?) is quoting "the respectable Mrs. Grundy" in this line. Margaret Smith explains that while the "allusion is not traced," Mrs. Grundy was believed to be "the personification of propriety, [and] is named after Dame Ashfield, in the comedy by Thomas Morton [1764–1838], *Speed the Plough* (1798): see e.g. I.i" (581 note).

2 The diary's realism works deliberately against the more fanciful tales of wives reforming their husbands. Such tales were popular in religious periodicals, but also familiar to many in novels such as Hannah More's (1745–1833) best-selling *Coelebs in Search of a Wife* (1808) and, later, Thomas Buchanan Read's popular poem "What a Word May Do" (see Appendices D1 and F4).

to think more consciously about what they have learned, as the action starts and stops repeatedly. The addition of Gilbert's chapter titles shapes, in part, how readers interpret chapter contents as well. For example, the first two segments of her diary are given the chapter titles "Warnings of Experience" and "Further Warnings." While Helen may indeed read the incidents recounted therein as "warnings" about her future husband, Gilbert's chapter titles ensure that readers interpret these incidents with a sense of foreboding, looking for the danger about which Helen is being warned. Further, his periodic interruptions of her diary with comments to his friend consistently remind the reader that Gilbert is reading this diary for information about the woman who interests him. Thus, his friendship with Halford and his romantic interest in Helen regularly interrupt the account of the more difficult world of Grassdale. It is clear from nineteenth-century reviews of the novel, however, that contemporary readers found Helen's account far more powerful than Gilbert's external frame. While some reviewers felt the narrative shift of the enclosed diary to be clumsy, its stark realism was the recurring focus of their reviews—not Gilbert's presentation of those events within the context of his courtship of Helen.

Most later twentieth- and twenty-first-century critics have pointed out numerous, compelling reasons for this structure.[1] The multiple layers and protracted account of Helen's marriage produce a feeling of entrapment for the reader that mirrors Helen's own (O'Toole). Enclosing Helen's first-hand account of the atrocities of married life with Arthur Huntingdon makes that experience more immediate and accessible to Brontë's readers (McMaster), while also making the reader believe her husband's behavior in London is so depraved it cannot be relayed to the reader at all (Jackson). Encasing an unconventional story within the frame narrative, traditionally associated with the courtship plot, also "calls into question the viability of the courtship frame" (Gruner 309), yet Brontë "uses the transgressive possibilities of narrative exchange to *write* her transgressive story, a story of female desire" (Langland 112). The novel's structure reveals Brontë's "commitment and resistance to the language of salvation encoded within patriarchal ideology" of Victorian womanhood as well (Frawley 133). While the epistolary form of the book locates the novel within a tradition harkening back to Samuel Richardson's eighteenth-century novels *Pamela* (1740) and *Clarissa* (1747), it also calls upon Puritan spiritual autobiographies that rely on first-hand accounts of conversion (Davies xii–xiii). The novel's layered narrative calls attention to the artistic production of this work and reveals the importance of reading and the exchange of stories (Gordon). One can see how reading

---

1   The following summaries of critics' arguments are necessarily narrow; I have focused only on the part of their work that relates to narrative structure.

could change behavior and beliefs; further, passing the diary to Gilbert forces Helen's lesson to be deliberately disembodied (Talley) and moves attention away from the woman (artist) as object of the gaze to the woman (artist) as subject and creative producer in her own right (Losano). Additionally, by handing Gilbert her diary, Helen "seems to be positioning an aesthetic production between her body and her male viewer or reader" (Losano 23).

But there are important political ramifications to this structure as well. The contrast between the diary and the external framing letters calls attention to the stark divisions between the domestic sphere allied with women and the public sphere allied with men—a split that the novel presents as potentially dangerous indeed (Jacobs). Brontë's critique of public and private spheres is more than a Victorian critique, however. Rachel Carnell persuasively argues that the novel yearns for "the classical liberal model of bourgeois public debate" and invokes an eighteenth-century enlightenment model of the public sphere, asserting that the ruptured narrative reflects the "inherent contradictions between the different levels of discourse—literary, political, scientific—within the public sphere itself and the complex ways in which these levels are both accorded and denied cultural power" (Carnell 4). Yet another critic sees the text's critique of patriarchy grounded in narratives of religious testimony, not in Enlightenment discourse, reading the diary as a witnessing that uses Helen's understanding of the Bible to bolster both her critique and Gilbert's new understanding of British patriarchal structure (Morse). Containing the critique of patriarchy between two male correspondents and having the primary, external narrator be male makes the novel's project of "teach[ing] patriarchy the value of female rebellion" palatable and powerful (Shires 160). Lastly, the novel's form of several different types of narratives that compete for readers' attention and belief (e.g., letters, diary, town gossip) also forces readers to contemplate how they know something to be true and challenges the very idea of truth and its relationship to power (Gordon).

Tenant is thus centrally concerned with learning and ideas of virtue, and the diary within the novel, functioning as a written testament of Helen's education through experience, becomes a type of witness to her suffering and helps the reader see how difficult her studies of passion, alcoholism, universal salvation, family, and marriage are. The novel seems to assert the possibilities of some type of transformation through reading, because reading Helen's testimony in her diary makes Gilbert Markham more aware of how difficult the patriarchal structure of society could be for Victorian women. Some readers, however, could argue that he does not change nearly enough, since Helen gives Gilbert her diary asking him not to "breathe a word of what it tells you to any living being"—a wish he clearly violates (130). Helen's account, designed to testify to the horrors of alcoholism and, to use a more Victorian expression and concept, the danger of being "unequally yoked" (married to someone who is not your spiritual equal), does teach Gilbert about these issues, although it is uncertain how much he is transformed by this knowledge. While it is clear that the novel's formal innovations are rich and deliberate, the content of *Tenant*, and Helen's diary in particular, sheds light on a host of social issues to which we will now turn.

Women's Legal Status in Nineteenth-Century England

Bringing to life a particularly nasty marriage, Brontë examines Victorian women's predicaments in a patriarchal society where the legal system was designed to privilege the men in power. Laws that defined women to be men's property or parts of their persons after marriage, a belief called coverture, were especially difficult.[1] The laws of coverture during both the 1820s action in the novel and 1840s writing of *Tenant* saw wives only as the extension of the husband in marriage. Thus, a wife could not sue (or be sued), control her own property, or enter into a contract (Wright 178, n.10). The lack of individual legal status for women was a particularly serious issue for a woman in an abusive marriage, as husband and wife were viewed as a single person under law: a man with "property." Since one cannot sue oneself or charge oneself with a crime, the abused wife was left with no legal recourse either. Even monies earned independently by the wife were considered the husband's. In social terms, ideas of coverture affected reputation as well, since the husband's bad behavior automatically reflected upon the wife.

Like wives, children, too, were believed to be the husband's property. Not until 1839 with the passage of the Infant Custody Act did women have access to their children after separation. Specifically, the act granted mothers "a limited right to petition the courts for access to their children over age seven and custody of children under age seven"; even this, however, outraged some who called it the "Robbery of Fathers Act" (Wright 213). And, although this act was overruled later by the divorce law of 1857 which granted women far more rights than this act, conventional wisdom asserts it was the passage of the Infant Custody Act that began to chip away at the laws of coverture. Practically speaking, however, this was not the case. Through the 1850s, "physical violence to wives and children, neglect leading to illness or near starvation, irreligion, much less alcoholism, gambling, adultery, and swearing did not bring down on an errant father the state's moral censure necessary to deprive him of contact with his children" (Wright 233). A father could even be imprisoned and still retain custody of his children. It was not until the end of the nineteenth century that women began to obtain custody of their children (Wright 180).

---

1   See the excerpt from Caroline Norton's (1808–77) *A Letter to the Queen on Lord Chancellor Cranworth's Marriage and Divorce Bill* (1855) in Appendix D2.

Brontë's novel makes abundantly clear the perilous nature of Helen's situation, as Helen flees her marriage with her son in 1827, years before the passage of the Infant Custody Act. It was not until 1870 and 1886, long after *Tenant* was published, that the Married Women's Property Acts were passed, granting women control over their own money and enabling them to keep familial inheritances, which under coverture were also considered the husband's property.

Victorian Motherhood

Although married women had no legal rights as individuals, married women who were mothers were construed as having a great deal of power according to Victorian ideals of motherhood. Childrearing was deemed by both liberals and conservatives as one of the most important—and potent—things a woman could do. *Howitt's Journal*, a progressive Quaker publication of the nineteenth century, for example, published a piece by John Cowie on women's influence that echoes popular sentiments about women of the time (see Appendix C4):

> Woman's mission and influence constitute a subject of the most imperative and vital interest. Her position and relations are the most important and attractive in life. The mind of the young generation is molded by her plastic hand; she is the source and directress of the elemental statesmen, poets, philosophers, philanthropists, and producers of futurity; and it has become an axiom that there are few great men who do not either owe their intellectual or moral excellence to their mothers. It is on the knee and at the fireside that we imbibe the bias of afterlife.

The belief in the importance of motherhood to shape the young is neatly articulated in Cowie's description of the mother's "plastic hand," as she is given the credit for shaping "statesmen, poets, philosophers, philanthropists" and the more elusive "producers of futurity."

While this understanding of the powers of motherhood is remarkable, this belief also had its negative side, since mothers were held responsible for their children's failure. John S.C. Abbott's popular book *The Mother at Home; or the Principles of Maternal Duty Familiarly Illustrated* (1833) (see Appendix E2) lays bare the type of blame cast upon mothers.[1] Comparing the relative virtue of the mothers of president George Washington and poet Lord Byron, Abbott finds that Byron's mother falls short and roundly criticizes *her* for *his* life of vice.

---

1 Abbott was an American minister and writer (1805–77); the success of *The Mother at Home* led him to retire from the ministry and write full time.

It was the mother of Byron who laid the foundation of his pre-eminence in guilt. She taught him to plunge into that sea of profligacy and wretchedness, upon whose agitated waves he was tossed for life. If the crimes of the poet deserve the execration of the world, the world can not forget, that it was the mother, who fostered in his youthful heart, those passions, which made the son a curse to his fellow men.

Like Abbott, the fictional Helen also views her husband's bad behavior as the result of an overindulgent mother. While she finds fault in his "harsh yet careless" father, she writes, "If ever I am a mother I will zealously strive against this *crime* of over indulgence—I can hardly give it a milder name when I think of the evils it brings" (207). She blames Arthur's mother as utterly culpable, branding maternal indulgence a "crime."

Although Abbott's language appears hyperbolic to twenty-first-century readers, with his description of Byron's "plunge in that sea of profligacy and wretchedness," he, like many Victorians, believed that maternal care shaped children's preparation and behavior not just for this life, but for their afterlife as well. Language that seems shrill to today's readers was used to impress upon readers the magnitude of the situation, as the type of maternal care one received could have lasting, eternal effects. Therefore, it was believed imperative for Christian children to have good mothers. Sarah Lewis's immensely popular *Woman's Mission* (1839) states, "What is a child in relation to a mother? An immortal being, whose soul it is her business to train for immortality" (Lewis 22) (see also Appendices C3 and E4).

Helen understands motherhood through the lens of Christianity and describes her son for the first time in her diary as "a soul to educate for heaven" (216). She views herself as her son's "shield, instructor, friend—to guide him along the perilous path of youth, and train him to be God's servant while on earth, a blessed and honoured saint in heaven" (217). In fact, Helen is so concerned about the possibility of his becoming a "slave of sin, the victim of vice and misery, a curse to others and himself" that she would prefer him to die in childhood as a "guileless, unpolluted lamb" than to grow up a sinner (217). From Helen's fervent and terrifying prayer to God, today's readers can begin to understand the force of Victorian beliefs regarding a mother's duty to raise her child properly.

Gender and Education

During the Victorian era, ideas about how to raise children so that they would grow up to become virtuous adults were sharply divided along gender lines. Most people believed that girls and young women should be shielded from the realities of the world, whereas boys and young men should be exposed to them in order to make them strong and manly. *Tenant* takes issue with these approaches to raising children by advancing the controversial line of argument that *both* boys and girls should be taught about the difficult realities of the world. In her preface to the second printing of the novel, Brontë, disguised as Acton Bell, argues that "the snares and pitfalls of life" should be revealed to both sexes (39). Brontë further asserts that revealing the facts of life would result in "less ... sin and misery to the young of both sexes who are left to wring their bitter knowledge from experience" (40).

Brontë appears to be echoing Mary Wollstonecraft's earlier argument against educating men and women differently in *A Vindication of the Rights of Woman* (1792) (see Appendix C1). Wollstonecraft also believes that women should not be shielded from reality to keep them innocent. She writes, "Purity of mind ... is something nobler than innocence, it is the delicacy of reflection, and not the coyness of ignorance" (Appendix C1). In other words, the truly pure-minded woman will know about and comprehend the nature of transgression but will avoid it because she understands it—not because she is ignorant of it. This belief in the possibility of a knowledgeable purity helps explain how Brontë could give her protagonist another chance with a second husband. Brontë still sees Helen as fundamentally innocent, even though she has observed quite a bit of debauched behavior by her husband Arthur and his friends; indeed, Helen epitomizes the "purity of mind" that Wollstonecraft writes about. Further, Brontë assumes that readers—both male and female—can read about corrupt behavior and learn from it, without becoming damaged or "fallen" because of it.

Brontë imagines this novel as a setting straight of "facts," a warning to "rash" young men and "thoughtless girl[s]" about the "pitfalls of life" (39–40). Her preface emphasizes Helen's belief that sons should not be forced to "prove all things by their own experience, while our daughters must not even profit by the experience of others.... [B]oth [should] ... benefit by the experience of others, and the precepts of a higher authority, that they should know beforehand to refuse the evil and choose the good,[1] and require no experimental proofs to teach them the evil of transgression" (60).

Echoing Wollstonecraft, Brontë's Helen asserts that armed with an understanding of morality from a higher authority—either a parent or possibly the higher authority of God's word through the Bible—the young can make informed moral decisions.

Helen works to raise her son according to these principles, but her teaching him to dislike alcohol is viewed by the community as a direct threat to little Arthur's manhood, so deeply engrained were ideas about needing to

---

1 Isaiah 7:15: "Butter and honey shall he eat, that he may know to refuse evil, and choose the good."

"toughen up" boys as they grew.[1] For example, Gilbert's mother laughs until she cries when she learns of Helen's practices. She claims that "The poor child will be the veriest milksop[2] that ever was sopped" (57) and further recommends that Helen speak to the vicar, who will explain the consequences of treating her son "like a girl" (59). In a telling (and common) use of extended metaphor, Mrs. Markham asks whether, "if you were to rear an oak sapling in a hothouse, tending it carefully night and day, and shielding it from every breath of wind, you could not expect it to become a hardy tree, like that which has grown up on the mountain-side, exposed to all the action of the elements, and not even sheltered from the shock of the tempest" (60). Although she admits she would never raise a girl this way, Mrs. Markham believes that in order for boys to grow up strong they need to be exposed to harsh reality. Both the novel's plot and Brontë's preface to the "second edition" extend this debate about the relationship between virtue, knowledge, and ignorance. Brontë clearly calls attention to how gender is linked to understandings of health and advances a strong case for the importance of an informed purity for men and women, boys and girls.

Victorian Womanhood, Art, and the Public Sphere

While a gendered double standard of behavior called attention to Helen's childrearing methods and forced Brontë to defend her novel's appropriateness for young women, *Tenant* also significantly examines a more specific area of gendered experience: the woman artist. Helen writes a great deal about her artistic process in her diary, describing her paintings and both her frustration and satisfaction over rendering scenes on her canvas. These comments, enhanced by the details about the type of materials Helen has in her studio, mark her as a serious painter, and an unfeminine one at that, since oil painting was regarded as more appropriate for men. (Watercolor and drawing were seen as more appropriately feminine mediums.) For example, an 1834 issue of *The Lady's Magazine and Museum of Belles Lettres* asserts that "Oil painting, for many reasons, will never find superior female professors; there is that sort of squalid discomfort in its pursuit that makes it exceedingly repugnant to elegant women" (qtd. in Casteras and Peterson 11). *Tenant* makes it clear that this woman does not mind getting her hands dirty, and that Helen (like Brontë herself) thinks seriously and intelligently about her craft.

---

1 Anne Brontë's novel *Agnes Grey* (1847) is a full-length assault on this idea, where she lays bare the repercussions of raising boys with this ideal of "manhood."

2 "An effeminate spiritless young man or youth; one wanting in courage or manliness" (*OED*).

Being a professional artist was rare for women both at the time Brontë wrote the novel and during the 1820s, when the novel takes place. While women were encouraged to draw as part of their education as accomplished women, they were not encouraged to draw or paint professionally and were barred from attending the Royal Academy of Arts—the institution that trained professional artists in England. In the *Athenaeum* on 30 April 1859, Barbara Smith Bodichon[1] and several other Victorian women published a petition to the Royal Academy "to open that institution to women" (reprinted in Cherry 224–25). Women were finally admitted in 1861, but it wasn't until 1903 that ideas of feminine propriety had changed enough for women to be permitted to work with nude models—an absolutely crucial part of art education to learn the correct proportions and possibilities of the human form.

Before the 1870s, women artists from well-to-do middle- and upper-class families wrote of serious resistance from family members to their desires to professionalize themselves, and many cited financial reasons as the reason for taking up art. Ellen Clayton's 1876 *English Female Artists* describes many women artists' struggles with their families and explains that many of them professionalized themselves only after a father or husband became unable to support the family.[2] *Tenant* echoes these realities when Helen changes the way she thinks about the financial possibilities of her craft once she realizes she needs to leave her husband, Arthur.

Victorian ideas of proper femininity circumscribed what women could do artistically, and they also shaped women's economic position since these ideals prohibited middle- or upper-class women from playing an active role in the business world. Thus, while Helen's brother sells her paintings because of her wish to remain hidden from her husband, some man would have had to sell her work regardless. A woman of Helen's station would not have engaged in that kind of exchange.

Elements of these ideas about women and art and women's presence in the public sphere also shaped the Brontë sisters' need to write under male pseudonyms. Even though Charlotte describes the Brontë sisters as having only a "vague impression that authoresses are liable to be looked on with prejudice" (see Appendix A4), it is clear from the reviews of all three novels, where many speculated on the sex of the authors, that this issue did matter. Further, both Anne's need to defend her work in the preface to this novel and Charlotte's need to safeguard the reputations of her sisters after their deaths as "blameless" virtuous women speak volumes about the difficulties women faced entering the public sphere.

---

1 A feminist and painter (1827–91).
2 See Clayton's description of Mary Harrison, for example, in Appendix G2.

Temperance

Helen Huntingdon becomes a professional artist, selling her paintings to support herself and her son, because of her husband's alcoholism. And while some Victorian readers may have been curious about women's entrance into the art world, most would have been interested in issues related to alcohol, as temperance—the belief that one should drink very little or not at all—was a hotly debated topic when *Tenant* was published. The temperance movement began in Bradford, an industrial town in the north of England near the Brontës' home in Haworth, in 1830, and in its early days would have preached moderation in drink. (In 1834 Brontë's father, the Reverend Patrick Brontë, "along with other local ministers and clergymen, met to form a temperance society" [Shiman 48].) By the late 1840s, however, when the novel was published, the proponents of moderate drinking were a minority within the movement, which now preached total abstinence (Shiman 1, 30–31). *The Tenant of Wildfell Hall* directly addresses drinking from a number of perspectives: the characters in the external framing narrative debate the pros and cons of drinking, while Helen's diary provides evidence of the potentially ravaging effects of excessive drinking on one's body and family.

Contemporary reviews of the novel found its depiction of drunkenness to be too much, however. Critics were responding both to ideas about what should be discussed in fiction and to class-bound beliefs about the nature of alcoholism. Drinking was seen as a problem for the "lower orders" that the middle (and upper) classes were working to reform. Therefore, Brontë's depiction of problematic upper-class drinking habits was unusual. In fact, so ingrained were classist beliefs about which portion of the population had drinking problems that some people had an aversion to the temperance movement just because of the close contact it could afford one with the working classes. One pro-temperance writer in the 1840s challenged those "who are so terribly afraid of the coarse language and vulgar demeanour of teetotalers,"[1] and asserted that he had "never heard such vulgar language as we have been condemned to be present at when at the dinner-table of the rich,—even members of Parliament" (Carpenter 315). This writer's point of view, like Brontë's novel, makes it clear that class is not always a guarantee of seemly behavior.

Beyond issues of class, debates about temperance revolved around people's aversion to imagining not drinking or not appreciating part of what they believed was God's creation. What is missing from Brontë's novel is the

---

1 A teetotaler is someone who does not drink at all. Given that the working classes were the majority of people swearing off drink, this comment reflects a classist aversion to spending time with those believed to be less refined.

shrill tone of many teetotalers that countless Victorians found grating. For example, one article Brontë likely read[1] refers rather dramatically to those who drink: "The drunkard turns his body to a sty; ... drunkenness not only makes vices, but makes them manifest without shame[;] ... [and] [d]runkenness makes room for all other sins. It is the root of many evils and the rot of all goodness" (Anonymous 384).

Instead of denouncing drink with the stridency of a zealot, Brontë's novel advances a moderate point of view. Like the novel's exploration of other social issues, Helen's diary echoes and amplifies the understanding advanced by the external narrative frame that sets up the debates surrounding drink, becoming the testament to the facts. Both Gilbert's letters and Helen's diary support an understanding of drinking with moderation as its goal, acknowledging, however, that there are some people, who "may be naturally prone to intemperance—by the fault of [their] parents or ancestors, for instance" (66), who should never drink.

Because of Helen's understanding of the importance of motherhood and her deeply held belief in the power of maternal care to shape a child's personality well into adulthood, she works hard to train her son to hate "spirits." Brontë has her protagonist use the most recent understandings of associationist psychology (which later became behaviorist psychology) to do this when Helen admits early on in the novel to placing a small amount of tartar emetic in wine and to insisting that young Arthur drink alcohol whenever he is sick, so that he will associate illness with drink. While many wonder at the latent sadism involved in this type of aversion therapy—especially when the subject is such a young child—Helen's methods speak to her desperation, and to her understanding of the grave importance of the lessons she needs to impart to her son. Although the novel's overall tone lacks the zeal of classic temperance literature, Helen's manipulation of her son's habits and desires testifies powerfully to the horrors she witnessed with her husband.

Universal Salvation

The issue most likely invisible to contemporary readers that was very controversial to Anne Brontë's Victorian audience, and probably the most important one for Brontë herself, was universal salvation: the belief that sinners would not spend eternity in hell, but that after purification even they could ascend to heaven. This doctrine was controversial and hotly debated, spurring (and spurred by) discussion about the translation of key words and interpretation of certain passages in the Bible. A central part of this debate, which still exists

---

1   See Talley for information about the Brontës reading their mother's copies of *The Methodist Magazine*.

today, involves a New Testament passage where Jesus distinguishes between those who "shall go away into everlasting punishment [and] the righteous into life eternal" (Matthew 26:46). How one translates the Greek word *aionios* (in the King James version of the Bible "everlasting") makes the difference between that punishment occurring "for a long time" or "for eternity." Debates about the afterlife also centered on apparently contradictory passages in the Bible, in addition to translations and interpretations of single words. In the Matthew passage above, if "everlasting" does mean eternal, Jesus is condemning some to hell forever, apparently contradicting portions of the Bible which make it clear that He "will have all men to be saved, and to come unto the knowledge of the truth" (I Timothy 2:4).[1] Although the debates about universal salvation did not reach their peak until the 1850s and 1860s after Anne's death, *Tenant* squarely addresses both the issue of biblical translation and the hope of spiritual resurrection.

Brontë's poetry and one of her few remaining letters make her beliefs clear. In "A Word to the 'Elect,'" for example, she writes,

> That even the wicked shall at last
>   Be fitted for the skies;
> And, when their dreadful doom is past,
>   To life and light arise. (37–40; see Appendix A3)

Brontë asserts that the Christian beliefs that could have changed people's lives on earth can still be learned after death, thus making even the "wicked" fit for heaven. Eventually, she continues, they will "cling to what they once disdained,/ [a]nd live by Him that died" (47–48). The crucial element of those last lines is the acceptance of Christian principles. Theologically, these lines are vital because they stress that while salvation is available to all, it is not automatic; the individual must come to accept Christ's teaching. The lines are significant for the novel because they anticipate Helen's hope about her husband (discussed further below) and because they reflect the novel's central lesson about both the importance and possibility of learning and growth. Learning does not end in this life, since the doctrine of universal salvation provides opportunities for understanding—and growth—even after death.

Brontë's poetry advances yet another principle in favor of the doctrine of universal salvation that she incorporates into her novel: the idea that "God is Love" ("To Cowper" 21; see Appendix A2). This belief, which she promulgates with even more fervor in "A Word to the 'Elect,'" where she calls attention to the sacrifice Christ made for humankind (33), makes it impossible to

---

1   These debates are rich and complex. For more information, see the works by Wheeler and Thormählen.

believe that God, a benevolent divine being beyond human understanding, would deny some people's entrance into heaven since, by definition, He is love. Brontë and others who are opposed to the Calvinist doctrine of Election in particular cannot understand how God would "[choose] to pass the *many* o'er, / and only bring the favoured *few* to Heaven" ("Elect" 11–12). She scathingly attacks Calvinist faith, arguing that the "grace unsought, which made your black hearts pure, / ... fits your earth-born souls in Heaven to shine" ("Elect" 3–4). Her description of the elect's "black hearts" and their "earth-born souls" emphasizes the superficial nature of their perceived heavenly transformation. By contrast, later on in the poem when she imagines what happens to sinners who do go to hell, she acknowledges that we cannot know how long they will be there, or

> ... what the sinners' woe,
> Before their dross is purged away;
>   Enough for me, to know
>
> That when the cup of wrath is drained,
>   The metal purified,
> They'll cling to what they once disdained,
>   And live by Him that died. (42–48)

Her speaker makes it clear that there will be real suffering, yet by virtue of her fiery, metallic metaphors, one understands that their souls' transformations will be genuine and lasting.

Brontë does not confine her progressive theological views to her poetry; her letter to the Reverend David Thom boldly claims that she has "given as many hints in support of the doctrine [of universal salvation] as [she] could venture to introduce into a [novel]" (see Appendix A1). Earlier in her letter to Thom, she muses on the positive benefit were people to understand that "Eternal Death" might not be inevitable but could be "a limited season of punishment, far distant and unseen,—however protracted and terrible it might be." She understands people's need for some sort of hope and does not support a belief in eternal punishment for one's sins—although she also admits to not speaking a great deal about these beliefs for fear that some people might behave badly without the threat of an eternal hell.

The Tenant of Wildfell Hall provided readers with more than just "hints" in favor of this belief, though. While many reviewers chose to ignore this aspect of the novel, focusing instead on the more worldly issues it examines, a few reviewers found *Tenant*'s theological radicalism unnerving indeed. The *Rambler* describes "the religious sentiments which the authoress puts into the mouth of her heroine [as] ... false and bad" (Appendix B6), while the reviewer from *Sharpe's London Magazine* asserts that "the dangerous tendency of [universal salvation] must be apparent to any one who gives the subject a moment's consideration" (Appendix B7). He goes on describe this belief as a type of "madness of trusting to such a forced distortion of the Divine attribute of mercy," concluding that "this doctrine is alike repugnant to Scripture, and in direct opposition to the teaching of the Anglican church."

Understandings of and debates around hell and God's mercy centered on a few key biblical passages, many of which are discussed by Helen and her aunt during their argument about Helen's interest in Arthur Huntingdon. (Their fight also provides astonishing evidence of how well most people in the nineteenth century knew the Bible, since these family members argue by hurling biblical quotations at each other [see chapter 20]). Helen and her aunt quarrel about a host of issues surrounding involvement with a sinner. Her aunt, for example, is worried about what will happen to Helen and Arthur after death, "when you see yourselves parted forever; you, perhaps, taken into eternal bliss, and he cast into the lake that burneth with unquenchable fire" (168). Helen's aunt also believes that Arthur will likely be in hell "for ever" (168), a fact Helen quickly contradicts with biblical readings based on approximately seven different passages that hold out the possibility of universal salvation—although she claims her beliefs come from "nearly thirty passages" (169). When her aunt responds with horror, wondering if Helen had found "no passages tending to prove the danger and falsity of such a belief" (169), Helen replies with a discussion of the translation of the Greek *aionios*, which she believes means "for ages, and might signify either endless or long-enduring" rather than "'everlasting' or 'eternal'" (169).

Tenant returns to the issue of universal salvation much later in the novel, when Helen is older and Arthur is dying. She no longer reads the Bible as impetuously as she did in her youth, with the passion and hubris that enabled her to believe that she could "deliver [Arthur] from his faults" (167). Brontë creates moving and realistic assaults on both Helen's faith and her attempts to change her husband's drinking habits. She withholds the unrealistic power granted to concerned wives in works such as "What a Word May Do" (Appendix F4) and denies Helen the easier, unquestioning faith exemplified, for instance, in *Jane Eyre*'s Helen Burns. Further, Arthur's physical and spiritual torment is presented as exhausting and agonizing. After his death, Helen wonders,

> How could I endure to think that that poor trembling soul was hurried away to everlasting torment? It would drive me mad! But thank God I have hope—not only from a vague dependence on the possibility that penitence and pardon might have reached him at the last, but from the blessed confidence that, through whatever purging fires the erring spirit may be doomed

to pass—whatever fate awaits it, still, it is not lost, and God, who hateth nothing that he hath made,[1] *will* bless it in the end! (376–77)

Helen Huntingdon reflects the beliefs that Anne Brontë shares with the Reverend David Thom in her letter, and she echoes the hope of salvation found in Brontë's earlier poetry. Yet, as Marianne Thormälen aptly points out, Helen is much more than a mere projection of Anne's "keenest desire onto her heroine" (94); she is a richly crafted, religious character.

Helen's belief in the doctrine of universal salvation, however, provides hope for change even in this difficult chapter and serves a narrative function as well. It extends the central theme of the novel—that learning or growth is always possible—to yet another arena, one beyond the material world: Arthur may become penitent *after* death. Brontë provides readers with layers of characters reflecting upon their own and others' behavior (Gilbert; Helen; Gilbert on Helen's lessons; Helen on Lowborough, Hattersley, Millicent, Esther, etc.), even adding a preface by "Acton Bell" to defend the morality of the text's lessons that earlier readers found too shocking. Readers witness Gilbert Markham's growth as well as Helen Huntingdon's, as both characters mature through learning experientially and through a removed—and easier—growth by reading or witnessing others' situations. Gilbert's reading of Helen's diary and letters transforms without harrowing him, modeling for readers how we can learn without "wring[ing] ... bitter knowledge from experience" (Preface 40). The novel is designed to promote reflection, tempering the incorrect, hasty judgments Gilbert and others make about Helen early in the story with worldly lessons, while also making clear, through Helen's speedy courtship, how passion can disrupt or impair thinking. Although both Gilbert's and Helen's lessons are presented through the lens of romance, the novel's protagonists repeatedly reflect on the afterlife, and with Arthur's death they muse upon the nature of salvation. How twenty-first-century readers respond to the issues of faith, feminism, class, narrative structure, alcoholism, or art depends upon their political and intellectual orientation. Most will agree, however, that *The Tenant of Wildfell Hall* is a gripping tale, powerfully recounted, whose pedagogical power has not diminished over time.

Works Cited

Anonymous. "An Admonition to Youth. A Sermon on II Timothy 2:22. 'Flee Youthful Lusts.'" *The Methodist Magazine* 24 (Sept. 1801): 380–88.

---

1   Helen is quoting Ezekiel 33:11 and the Collect for Ash Wednesday in *The Book of Common Prayer* here. See n. 1 on page 377 for more information.

Barker, Juliet. *The Brontës*. New York: St Martin's, 1994.

Carnell, Rachel K. "Feminism and the Public Sphere in Anne Brontë's *The Tenant of Wildfell Hall.*" *Nineteenth-Century Literature* 53.1 (June 1998): 1–24.

Carpenter, Philip P. "On the Evils Indirectly Connected with the Temperance Reformation." *Howitt's Journal* 1.23 (May 1847): 313–16.

Casteras, Susan P., and Linda H. Peterson. *A Struggle for Fame: Victorian Women Artists and Authors*. New Haven, CT: Yale Center for British Art, 1994.

Cherry, Deborah. *Painting Women: Victorian Women Artists*. London and New York: Routledge, 1993.

Davies, Stevie, ed. Introduction. *The Tenant of Wildfell Hall*. By Anne Brontë. London: Penguin Books, 1996. vii–xxx.

Gordon, Jan B. "Gossip, Diary, Letter, Text: Anne Brontë's Narrative *Tenant* and the Problematic of the Gothic Sequel." *ELH [English Literary History]* 51.4 (Winter 1989): 719–45.

Gruner, Elizabeth Rose. "Plotting the Mother: Caroline Norton, Helen Huntingdon, and Isabel Vane." *Tulsa Studies in Women's Literature* 16.2 (Fall 1997): 303–26.

Jackson, Arlene M. "The Question of Credibility in Anne Brontë's *The Tenant of Wildfell Hall.*" *English Studies: A Journal of English Language and Literature* 63.3 (June 1982): 198–206.

Jacobs, Naomi. "Gender and Layered Narrative Technique in *Wuthering Heights* and *The Tenant of Wildfell Hall.*" *Journal of Narrative Technique* 16.3 (Fall 1986): 204–19.

Langland, Elizabeth. "The Voicing of Feminine Desire in Anne Brontë's *The Tenant of Wildfell Hall.*" *Gender and Discourse in Victorian Literature and Art*. Ed. Antony H. Harrison and Beverly Taylor. Dekalb: Northern Illinois UP, 1992. 111–23.

Lewis, Sarah. *Woman's Mission*. Boston: William Crosby & Co., 1840.

Losano, Antonia. "The Professionalization of the Woman Artist in Anne Brontë's *The Tenant of Wildfell Hall.*" *Nineteenth-Century Literature* 58.1 (2003): 1–41.

Morse, Deborah Denenholz. "'I speak of those I do know': Witnessing as Radical Gesture in *The Tenant of Wildfell Hall.*" *New Approaches to the Literary Art of Anne Brontë*. Ed. Julie Nash and Barbara A. Suess. Aldershot, UK: Ashgate, 2001. 103–26.

O'Toole, Tess. "Siblings and Suitors in the Narrative Architecture of *The Tenant of Wildfell Hall.*" *Studies in English Literature* 39.4 (Autumn 1999): 715–31.

Ruff, William. "First American Editions of the Brontë Novels: A Complete Bibliography." *Brontë Society Transactions* VIII (1934): 143–50.

Shiman, Lilian Lewis. *Crusade against Drink in Victorian England*. New York: St Martin's, 1988.

Shires, Linda M. "Of Maenads, Mothers, and Feminized Males: Victorian Readings of the French Revolution." *Rewriting the Victorians: Theory, History, and the Politics of Gender*. Ed. Linda M. Shires. New York: Routledge, 1992. 147–65.

Smith, Margaret, ed. *The Letters of Charlotte Brontë: with a selection of letters by family and friends*. Vol. II: 1848–1851. Oxford: Oxford UP, 1995.

Talley, Lee A. "Anne Brontë's Method of Social Protest in *The Tenant of Wildfell Hall*." *New Approaches to the Literary Art of Anne Brontë*. Ed. Julie Nash and Barbara A. Suess. Aldershot, UK: Ashgate, 2001. 127–52.

Thormählen, Marianne. *The Brontës and Religion*. Cambridge: Cambridge UP, 1999.

Wheeler, Michael. *Heaven, Hell, and the Victorians*. Cambridge: Cambridge UP, 1994.

Wright, Danaya C. "The Crisis of Child Custody: A History of the Birth of Family Law in England." *Columbia Journal of Gender and Law* 11 (2002): 175–270.

Anne Brontë: A Brief Chronology

1820	17 January: Anne Brontë born in Thornton
1821	15 September: Anne's mother, Maria Brontë, dies
1825	6 May: Anne's sister, Maria (aged 11), dies; 15 June: Anne's sister, Elizabeth (aged 10), dies
1826	5 June: Patrick Brontë, Anne's father, returns from Leeds with a set of toy soldiers that the Brontë children use to act out their plays and help create their imaginary worlds of Angria and Gondal
1835	October: Anne attends Roe Head School
1839	April: Anne becomes a governess at Blake Hall, near Mirfield
1840	May: Anne becomes a governess at Thorp Green
1842	29 October: Anne's aunt, Elizabeth Branwell, dies
1843	April: Anne's brother, Branwell Brontë, arrives at Thorp Green as a violin instructor
1845	June: Anne resigns her position at Thorp Green; 30 June to 2 July: Anne and Emily journey to York to see the York Minster; Autumn: Charlotte Brontë discovers her sisters' poetry
1846	May (?): *Poems by Currer, Ellis, and Acton Bell* published
1847	Early December: *Agnes Grey* published
1848	June: *The Tenant of Wildfell Hall* published; July: Anne and Charlotte travel to London to prove there are three "Bell brothers"; August: "Second Edition" of *The Tenant of Wildfell Hall*, with a Preface by Acton Bell, published; 24 September: Branwell Brontë dies; 19 December: Emily Brontë dies
1849	28 May: Anne Brontë dies
1850	Charlotte Brontë has Smith, Elder and Co. publish a posthumous edition of *Wuthering Heights* and *Agnes Grey* along with a selection of Anne's and Emily's poetry

A Note on the Text

I have used as my copy text the "second edition" of *The Tenant of Wildfell Hall*, published by T.C. Newby in 1848. As G.D. Hargreaves points out, however, this "second edition" is really another first edition, since the text type of the novel was not reset.[1] Although this edition is infamous for its errors in spelling and punctuation, it is a complete version of the novel that contains Brontë's important preface to the work. Alarmingly, many subsequent versions of the novel were published without the external framing letter from Gilbert Markham to Halford. In fact, as late as 1977, scholars were lamenting the lack of an accurate and affordable version of the novel.[2]

Significantly, one copy of this "second edition" also bears what is believed to be Anne Brontë's changes and corrections to the novel. That copy, now in the Princeton University Library and known as the Author's Own Copy (AOC), was consulted for this edition. The changes Brontë made in spelling and punctuation are confusing though, since she did not correct all of the obvious mistakes, and she only marked up the second volume of the three-volume edition. In a few other places, she made changes to the wording of the text, which I have noted in footnotes. The editors of the Oxford edition of *Tenant* point out that only four of the changes Brontë made were incorporated into later editions of the novel. Because of this and the puzzlingly selective nature of her changes, they consider the AOC to "lack independent authority."[3] Yet the AOC comes with a letter from the nephew of the Brontës' servant, Tabby, claiming that this copy "was given to me by my Father who got it from the Brontés [sic], on the occasion of his marriage to my Mother, Mary Brown, sister to Tabitha (Tabby), who was servant to the Bronte's [sic] ...."[4] Further, the changes to the text in her marginalia add new insights into how Brontë may have imagined Helen's character and the significance of the doctrine of universal salvation.[5]

---

1   G.D. Hargreaves, "Further Omissions in *The Tenant of Wildfell Hall*," *Brontë Society Transactions* 17.87 (1977): 115-21.

2   For information on the history behind this, see G.D. Hargreaves, "Incomplete Texts of *The Tenant of Wildfell Hall*," *Brontë Society Transactions* 16.82 (1972): 113-17. See also his article in n.1, above.

3   *OTWH* xxvii.

4   Letter from H. Jopling, dated 3 April 1938, accompanying the AOC of Brontë's *The Tenant of Wildfell Hall*, Parrish Collection, General Rare Books Division, Department of Rare Books and Special Collections, Princeton University Library.

5   See Lee A. Talley, "The Case for Anne Brontë's Marginalia in the Author's Own Copy of *The Tenant of Wildfell Hall*," *Brontë Studies* 32 (July 2007): 132-37.

I have used the AOC to support some of the corrections I made to the 1848 Newby edition. Throughout this edition, however, I have silently corrected obvious errors of spelling and punctuation (for example, "did'nt" and other similar contractions become "didn't"). I have also updated spelling and hyphenation that could distract contemporary readers, unless the older version of the word adds to the text's meaning. Thus, "to-day" becomes "today," but "some one" and "any one" remain as Anne originally wrote them. Similarly, "canvass" remains unchanged to reflect the way Brontë's characters would have spelled this word, which is central to Helen's art. When I have changed a word that is not the obvious error of the Newby editor or typesetter (e.g., "hall" rather than "ball"), I explain the alteration in a footnote. In general, I have kept Anne Brontë's eccentric use of dashes and commas as they appear in the Newby edition. I have deleted commas only when they are clearly incorrect and do not appear to serve a stylistic function (e.g., when one occurs between a subject and a verb). I have preserved Brontë's use of exclamation marks, including those instances where they are followed by a dash and then a word that begins with a lower case letter—Brontë's way of signalling a character's emotional rush of speech when he or she uses run-on sentences. However, when a character is clearly introducing a new thought, or when that next word begins with a capital letter, I have silently inserted periods, so that readers will not be distracted by grammatical inconsistencies, but will instead appreciate the emotion Brontë worked to convey in the scene.

THE TENANT

OF

WILDFELL HALL.

BY

ACTON BELL.

IN THREE VOLUMES.

VOL. I.

Second Edition.

LONDON:

T. C. NEWBY, PUBLISHER,

72, MORTIMER STREET, CAVENDISH SQUARE.

1848.

PREFACE TO THE SECOND EDITION

WHILE I acknowledge the success of the present work to have been greater than I anticipated, and the praises it has elicited from a few kind critics to have been greater than it deserved, I must also admit that from some other quarters it has been censured with an asperity which I was as little prepared to expect, and which my judgment as well as my feelings, assures me is more bitter than just. It is scarcely the province of an author to refute the arguments of his censors and vindicate his own productions, but I may be allowed to make here a few observations with which I would have prefaced the first edition had I foreseen the necessity of such precautions against the misapprehensions of those who would read it with a prejudiced mind or be content to judge it by a hasty glance.

My object in writing the following pages, was not simply to amuse the Reader, neither was it to gratify my own taste, nor yet to ingratiate myself with the Press and the Public: I wished to tell the truth, for truth always conveys its own moral to those who are able to receive it. But as the priceless treasure too frequently hides at the bottom of a well, it needs some courage to dive for it, especially as he that does so will be likely to incur more scorn and obloquy for the mud and water into which he has ventured to plunge, than thanks for the jewel he procures; as, in like manner, she who undertakes the cleansing of a careless bachelor's apartment will be liable to more abuse for the dust she raises, than commendation for the clearance she effects. Let it not be imagined, however, that I consider myself competent to reform the errors and abuses of society, but only that I would fain contribute my humble quota towards so good an aim, and if I can gain the public ear at all, I would rather whisper a few wholesome truths therein than much soft nonsense.

As the story of *Agnes Grey* was accused of extravagant over-colouring in those very parts that were carefully copied from the life, with a most scrupulous avoidance of all exaggeration, so, in the present work, I find myself censured for depicting con amore, with "a morbid love of the coarse, if not of the brutal,"[1] those scenes which, I will venture to say, have not been more painful for the most fastidious of my critics to read, than they were for me to describe. I may have gone too far, in which case I shall be careful not to trouble myself or my readers in the same way again; but when we have to do with vice and vicious characters, I maintain it is better to depict them as they really are than as they would wish to appear. To represent a bad thing in its least offensive light, is doubtless the most agreeable course for a writer of fiction to pursue; but is it the most honest, or the safest? Is it better to reveal the snares and pitfalls of life to the young and thoughtless traveler, or

---

1   *The Spectator.* See Appendix B8.

to cover them with branches and flowers? O Reader! if there were less of this delicate concealment of facts—this whispering "Peace, peace," when there is no peace,[1] there would be less of sin and misery to the young of both sexes who are left to wring their bitter knowledge from experience.

I would not be understood to suppose that the proceedings of the unhappy scapegrace with his few profligate companions I have here introduced, are a specimen of the common practices of society: the case is an extreme one, as I trusted none would fail to perceive; but I know that such characters do exist, and if I have warned one rash youth from following in their steps, or prevented one thoughtless girl from falling into the very natural error of my heroine, the book has not been written in vain. But, at the same time, if any honest reader shall have derived more pain than pleasure from its perusal, and have closed the last volume with a disagreeable impression on his mind, I humbly crave his pardon, for such was far from my intention; and I will endeavour to do better another time, for I love to give innocent pleasure. Yet, be it understood, I shall not limit my ambition to this,—or even to producing "a perfect work of art:" time and talents so spent, I should consider wasted and misapplied. Such humble talents as God has given me I will endeavour to put to their greatest use; if I am able to amuse I will try to benefit too; and when I feel it my duty to speak an unpalatable truth, with the help of God, I will speak it, though it be to the prejudice of my name and to the detriment of my reader's immediate pleasure as well as my own.

One word more, and I have done. Respecting the author's identity, I would have it to be distinctly understood that Acton Bell is neither Currer nor Ellis Bell, and therefore, let not his faults be attributed to them. As to whether the name be real or fictitious, it cannot greatly signify to those who know him only by his works. As little, I should think, can it matter whether the writer so designated is a man, or a woman as one or two of my critics profess to have discovered. I take the imputation in good part, as a compliment to the just delineation of my female characters; and though I am bound to attribute much of the severity of my censors to this suspicion, I make no effort to refute it, because, in my own mind, I am satisfied that if a book is a good one, it is so whatever the sex of the author may be. All novels are or should be written for both men and women to read, and I am at a loss to conceive how a man should permit himself to write anything that would be really disgraceful to a woman, or why a woman should be censured for writing anything that would be proper and becoming for a man.

July 22nd, 1848.

---

1   Jeremiah 6:14: "They have healed also the hurt of the daughter of my people slightly, saying, Peace, peace; when there is no peace," and Jeremiah 8:11: "For they have healed the hurt of the daughter of my people slightly, saying, Peace, peace; when there is no peace."

TO J. HALFORD, ESQ.

Dear Halford,

When we were together last, you gave me a very particular and interesting account of the most remarkable occurrences of your early life, previous to our acquaintance; and then you requested a return of confidence from me. Not being in a story-telling humour at the time, I declined, under the plea of having nothing to tell, and the like shuffling excuses, which were regarded as wholly inadmissible by you; for though you instantly turned the conversation, it was with the air of an uncomplaining, but deeply injured man, and your face was overshadowed with a cloud which darkened it to the end of our interview, and, for what I know, darkens it still; for your letters have, ever since, been distinguished by a certain dignified, semi-melancholy stiffness and reserve, that would have been very affecting, if my conscience had accused me of deserving it.

Are you not ashamed, old boy—at your age, and when we have known each other so intimately and so long, and when I have already given you so many proofs of frankness and confidence, and never resented your comparative closeness and taciturnity?—But there it is, I suppose; you are not naturally communicative, and you thought you had done great things, and given an unparalleled proof of friendly confidence on that memorable occasion—which, doubtless, you have sworn shall be the last of the kind,—and you deemed that the smallest return I could make for so mighty a favour, would be to follow your example without a moment's hesitation.—

Well!—I did not take up my pen to reproach you, nor to defend myself, nor to apologize for past offences, but, if possible, to atone for them.

It is a soaking, rainy day, the family are absent on a visit, I am alone in my library, and have been looking over certain musty old letters and papers, and musing on past times; so that I am now in a very proper frame of mind for amusing you with an old world story;—and, having withdrawn my well-roasted feet from the hobs, wheeled round to the table, and indited the above lines to my crusty old friend, I am about to give him a sketch—no not a sketch,—a full and faithful account of certain circumstances connected with the most important event of my life—previous to my acquaintance with Jack Halford at least;—and when you have read it, charge me with ingratitude and unfriendly reserve if you can.

I know you like a long story, and are as great a stickler for particularities and circumstantial details as my grandmother, so I will not spare you: my own patience and leisure shall be my only limits.

Among the letters and papers I spoke of, there is a certain faded old journal of mine, which I mention by way of assurance that I have not my

memory alone—tenacious as it is—to depend upon; in order that your credulity may not be too severely taxed in following me through the minute
details of my narrative.—To begin then, at once, with Chapter first,—for it
shall be a tale of many chapters.—

CHAPTER I
A DISCOVERY

YOU must go back with me to the autumn of 1827.

My father, as you know, was a sort of gentleman farmer in ——shire; and
I, by his express desire, succeeded him in the same quiet occupation, not very
willingly, for ambition urged me to higher aims, and self-conceit assured me
that, in disregarding its voice, I was burying my talent in the earth,[1] and hiding my light under a bushel.[2] My mother had done her utmost to persuade
me that I was capable of great achievements; but my father, who thought ambition was the surest road to ruin, and change but another word for destruction, would listen to no scheme for bettering either my own condition, or
that of my fellow mortals. He assured me it was all rubbish, and exhorted me,
with his dying breath, to continue in the good old way, to follow his steps,
and those of his father before him, and let my highest ambition be, to walk
honestly through the world, looking neither to the right hand nor to the left,
and to transmit the paternal acres to my children in, at least, as flourishing a
condition as he left them to me.

"Well!—an honest and industrious farmer is one of the most useful
members of society; and if I devote my talents to the cultivation of my farm,
and the improvement of agriculture in general, I shall thereby benefit, not
only my own immediate connections and dependants, but in some degree,
mankind at large:—hence I shall not have lived in vain."

With such reflections as these, I was endeavouring to console myself, as
I plodded home from the fields, one cold, damp, cloudy evening towards
the close of October. But the gleam of a bright red fire through the parlour
window, had more effect in cheering my spirits, and rebuking my thankless
repinings, than all the sage reflections and good resolutions I had forced my

---

1   Markham is referring to the parable of the five talents recounted in Matthew 25:14–20,
    where a man gives his servants talents and rewards the ones who invested the money to
    make more and punishes the one who merely hid it. Read metaphorically, this bibli-
    cal story exhorts its readers to make the most of what they are given—a message the
    conceited Gilbert uses to justify his dissatisfaction with being a gentleman farmer.
2   See Matthew 5:15: "Neither do men light a candle, and put it under a bushel, but on a
    candle-stick; and it giveth light unto all that are in the house."

mind to frame;—for I was young then, remember—only four and twenty—and had not acquired half the rule over my own spirit, that I now possess—trifling as that may be.

However, that haven of bliss must not be entered till I had exchanged my miry boots, for a clean pair of shoes, and my rough surtout[1] for a respectable coat, and made myself generally presentable before decent society; for my mother, with all her kindness, was vastly particular on certain points.

In ascending to my room, I was met upon the stairs by a smart, pretty girl of nineteen, with a tidy, dumpy figure, a round face, bright, bloom-ing cheeks, glossy, clustering curls, and little merry brown eyes. I need not tell you this was my sister Rose. She is, I know, a comely matron still, and, doubtless, no less lovely—in *your* eyes—than on the happy day you first beheld her. Nothing told me then, that she, a few years hence, would be the wife of one—entirely unknown to me as yet, but destined, hereafter to be-come a closer friend than even herself, more intimate than that unmannerly lad of seventeen, by whom I was collared in the passage, on coming down, and wellnigh jerked off my equilibrium, and who, in correction for his im-pudence, received a resounding whack over the sconce, which, however, sustained no serious injury from the infliction; as besides being more than commonly thick, it was protected by a redundant shock of short, reddish curls, that my mother called auburn.

On entering the parlour, we found that honoured lady seated in her arm chair at the fireside, working away at her knitting, according to her usual custom, when she had nothing else to do. She had swept the hearth, and made a bright blazing fire for our reception; the servant had just brought in the tea-tray; and Rose was producing the sugar-basin and tea-caddy, from the cupboard in the black, oak sideboard, that shone like polished ebony, in the cheerful parlour twilight.

"Well here they both are," cried my mother, looking round upon us with-out retarding the motion of her nimble fingers, and glittering needles. "Now shut the door, and come to the fire, while Rose gets the tea ready; I'm sure you must be starved;—and tell me what you've been about all day;—I like to know what my children have been about."

"I've been breaking in the grey colt—no easy business that—directing the ploughing of the last wheat stubble—for the ploughboy has not the sense to direct himself—and carrying out a plan for the extensive and efficient draining of the low meadow-lands."

"That's my brave boy!—and Fergus—what have you been doing?"

"Badger-baiting."

---

1 Man's overcoat.

And here he proceeded to give a particular account of his sport, and the respective traits of prowess evinced by the badger and the dogs; my mother pretending to listen with deep attention, and watching his animated countenance with a degree of maternal admiration I thought highly disproportioned to its object.

"It's time you should be doing something else, Fergus," said I, as soon as a momentary pause in his narration allowed me to get in a word.

"What *can* I do?" replied he, "my mother won't let me go to sea or enter the army; and I'm determined to do nothing else—except make myself such a nuisance to you all, that you will be thankful to get rid of me, on any terms."

Our parent soothingly stroked his stiff, short curls. He growled, and tried to look sulky, and then, we all took our seats at the table, in obedience to the thrice repeated summons of Rose.

"Now take your tea," said she; "and I'll tell you what *I've* been doing. I've been to call on the Wilsons; and it's a *thousand* pities you didn't go with me, Gilbert, for Eliza Millward was there!"

"Well! what of her?"

"Oh nothing!—I'm not going to tell you about her;—only that she's a nice, amusing little thing, when she is in a merry humour, and I shouldn't mind calling her——"

"Hush, hush, my dear! your brother has no such idea!" whispered my mother earnestly, holding up her finger.

"Well," resumed Rose; "I was going to tell you an important piece of news I heard there—I've been bursting with it ever since. You know it was reported a month ago, that some body was going to take Wildfell Hall—and—what do you think? It has actually been inhabited above a week!—and we never knew!"

"Impossible!" cried my mother.

"Preposterous!!!" shrieked Fergus.

"It has indeed!—and by a single lady!"

"Good gracious, my dear! The place is in ruins!"

"She has had two or three rooms made habitable; and there she lives, all alone—except an old woman for a servant!"

"Oh dear! that spoils it—I'd hoped she was a witch," observed Fergus, while carving his inch-thick slice of bread and butter.

"Nonsense, Fergus! But isn't it strange mamma?"

"Strange! I can hardly believe it."

"But you may believe it; for Jane Wilson has seen her. She went with her mother, who, of course, when she heard of a stranger being in the neighbourhood, would be on pins and needles till she had seen her and got all she could out of her. She is called Mrs. Graham, and she is in mourning—not widow's weeds, but slightish mourning[1]—and she is quite young, they say,—not above five or six and twenty,—but *so* reserved! They tried all they could to find out who she was, and where she came from, and all about her, but neither Mrs. Wilson, with her pertinacious and impertinent home thrusts, nor Miss Wilson, with her skillful manoeuvering, could manage to elicit a single satisfactory answer, or even a casual remark, or chance expression calculated to allay their curiosity, or throw the faintest ray of light upon her history, circumstances, or connections. Moreover, she was barely civil to them, and evidently better pleased to say 'good bye,' than 'how do you do.' But Eliza Millward says her father intends to call upon her soon, to offer some pastoral advice, which he fears she needs, as though she is known to have entered the neighbourhood early last week, she did not make her appearance at church on Sunday; and she—Eliza, that is—will beg to accompany him, and is sure *she* can succeed in wheedling something out of her—you know, Gilbert, *she* can do anything. And *we* should call some time, mamma; it's only proper, you know."

"Of course, my dear. Poor thing! how lonely she must feel!"

"And pray, be quick about it; and mind you bring me word how much sugar she puts in her tea, and what sort of caps and aprons she wears, and all about it; for I don't know how I can live till I know," said Fergus, very gravely.

But if he intended the speech to be hailed as a master-stroke of wit, he signally failed, for nobody laughed. However, he was not much disconcerted at that; for when he had taken a mouthful of bread and butter, and was about to swallow a gulp of tea, the humour of the thing burst upon him with such irresistible force, that he was obliged to jump up from the table, and rush snorting and choking from the room; and a minute after, was heard screaming in fearful agony in the garden.

As for me, I was hungry, and contented myself with silently demolishing the tea, ham, and toast, while my mother and sister went on talking, and continued to discuss the apparent, or nonapparent circumstances, and probable or improbable history of the mysterious lady; but I must confess that, after my brother's misadventure, I once or twice, raised the cup to my lips, and put it down again without daring to taste the contents, lest I should injure my dignity by a similar explosion.

The next day, my mother and Rose hastened to pay their compliments to the fair recluse; and came back but little wiser than they went; though my mother declared she did not regret the journey, for if she had not gained much good, she flattered herself she had imparted some, and that was better:

---

1 Helen Graham's mourning clothes ("widow's weeds") are not black, but another color signifying a later stage in the mourning process; she could be wearing gray or some shade of purple or lavender.

she had given some useful advice, which, she hoped, would not be thrown away; for Mrs. Graham, though she said little to any purpose, and appeared somewhat self-opinionated, seemed not incapable of reflection,—though she did not know where she had been all her life, poor thing, for she betrayed a lamentable ignorance on certain points, and had not even the sense to be ashamed of it.

"On what points, mother?" asked I.

"On household matters, and all the little niceties of cookery, and such things, that every lady ought to be familiar with, whether she be required to make a practical use of her knowledge or not. I gave her some useful pieces of information, however, and several excellent receipts, the value of which, she evidently could not appreciate, for she begged I would not trouble myself, as she lived in such a plain, quiet way, that she was sure she should never make use of them. 'No matter, my dear,' said I; 'it is what every respectable female ought to know;—and besides, though you are alone now, you will not be always so; you *have* been married, and probably—I might say almost certainly—will be again.' 'You are mistaken there Ma'am,' said she, almost haughtily; 'I am certain I never shall.'—But I told her *I* knew better."

"Some romantic young widow, I suppose," said I, "come there to end her days in solitude, and mourn in secret for the dear departed—but it won't last long."

"No, I think not," observed Rose; "for she didn't seem very disconsolate after all; and she's excessively pretty—handsome rather—you must see her Gilbert; you will call her a perfect beauty, though you could hardly pretend to discover a resemblance between her and Eliza Millward."

"Well, I can imagine many faces more beautiful than Eliza's, though not more charming. I allow she has small claims to perfection; but then, I maintain that, if she were more perfect, she would be less interesting."

"And so you prefer her faults to other people's perfections?"

"Just so—saving my mother's presence."

"Oh, my dear Gilbert, what nonsense you talk!—I know you don't mean it; it's quite out of the question," said my mother, getting up, and bustling out of the room, under pretence of household business, in order to escape the contradiction that was trembling on my tongue.

After that, Rose favoured me with further particulars respecting Mrs. Graham. Her appearance, manners, and dress, and the very furniture of the room she inhabited, were all set before me, with rather more clearness and precision than I cared to see them; but, as I was not a very attentive listener, I could not repeat the description if I would.

The next day was Saturday; and, on Sunday, everybody wondered whether or not the fair unknown would profit by the vicar's remonstrance, and come to church. I confess, I looked with some interest myself towards the old family pew, appertaining to Wildfell Hall, where the faded crimson cushions and lining had been unpressed and unrenewed so many years, and the grim escutcheons, with their lugubrious borders of rusty black cloth, frowned so sternly from the wall above.

And there I beheld a tall, lady-like figure, clad in black. Her face was towards me, and there was something in it, which, once seen, invited me to look again. Her hair was raven black, and disposed in long glossy ringlets, a style of coiffure, rather unusual in those days, but always graceful and becoming; her complexion was clear and pale; her eyes I could not see, for being bent upon her prayer-book they were concealed by their drooping lids and long black lashes, but the brows above were expressive and well defined, the forehead was lofty and intellectual, the nose, a perfect acquiline, and the features in general, unexceptionable—only there was a slight hollowness about the cheeks and eyes, and the lips, though finely formed, were a little too thin, a little too firmly compressed, and had something about them that betokened, I thought, no very soft or amiable temper; and I said in my heart—

"I would rather admire you from this distance, fair lady, than be the partner of your home."

Just then, she happened to raise her eyes, and they met mine, I did not choose to withdraw my gaze, and she turned again to her book, but with a momentary, indefinable expression of quiet scorn, that was inexpressibly provoking to me.

"She thinks me an impudent puppy," thought I. "Humph!—she shall change her mind before long, if I think it worth while."

But then, it flashed upon me that these were very improper thoughts for a place of worship, and that my behaviour, on the present occasion, was anything but what it ought to be. Previous, however, to directing my mind to the service, I glanced round the church to see if any one had been observing me;—but no,—all, who were not attending to their prayer-books, were attending to the strange lady,—my good mother and sister among the rest, and Mrs. Wilson and her daughter; and even Eliza Millward was slyly glancing from the corners of her eyes towards the object of general attraction. Then, she glanced at me, simpered a little, and blushed,—modestly looked at her prayer-book, and endeavoured to compose her features.

Here I was transgressing again; and this time I was made sensible of it by a sudden dig in the ribs, from the elbow of my pert brother. For the present, I could only resent the insult by pressing my foot upon his toes, deferring further vengeance till we got out of church.

Now, Halford, before I close this letter, I'll tell you who Eliza Millward was: she was the vicar's younger daughter, and a very engaging little creature, for whom I felt no small degree of partiality;—and she knew it, though I had never come to any direct explanation, and had no definite intention of so doing, for my mother, who maintained there was no one good enough for me, within twenty miles round, could not bear the thoughts of my marrying that insignificant, little thing, who, in addition to her numerous other disqualifications, had not twenty pounds to call her own. Eliza's figure was at once slight and plump, her face small, and nearly as round as my sister's,—complexion, something similar to hers, but more delicate and less decidedly blooming,—nose, *retroussé*,[1]—features, generally irregular;—and, altogether, she was rather charming than pretty. But her eyes—I must not forget those remarkable features, for therein her chief attraction lay—in outward aspect at least;—they were long and narrow in shape, the irids black, or very dark brown, the expression various, and ever changing, but always either preternaturally—I had almost said *diabolically*—wicked, or irresistibly bewitching—often both. Her voice was gentle and childish, her tread light and soft as that of a cat;—but her manners more frequently resembled those of a pretty, playful kitten, that is now pert and roguish, now timid and demure, according to its own sweet will.

Her sister, Mary, was several years older, several inches taller, and of a larger, coarser build—a plain, quiet, sensible girl, who had patiently nursed their mother, through her last long, tedious illness, and been the housekeeper, and family drudge, from thence to the present time. She was trusted and valued by her father, loved and courted by all dogs, cats, children, and poor people, and slighted and neglected by everybody else.

The Reverend Michael Millward, himself, was a tall, ponderous, elderly gentleman, who placed a shovel hat above his large, square, massive-featured face, carried a stout walking stick in his hand, and incased his still powerful limbs in knee breeches and gaiters,—or black silk stockings on state occasions. He was a man of fixed principles, strong prejudices, and regular habits,—intolerant of dissent in any shape, acting under a firm conviction that *his* opinions were always right, and whoever differed from them, must be, either most deplorably ignorant, or willfully blind.

In childhood, I had always been accustomed to regard him with a feeling of reverential awe—but lately, even now, surmounted, for, though he had a fatherly kindness for the well-behaved, he was a strict disciplinarian, and had often sternly reproved our juvenile failings and peccadillos; and moreover, in those days whenever he called upon our parents, we had to stand up before him, and say our catechism, or repeat "How doth the little busy bee,"[2] or some other hymn, or—worse than all—be questioned about his last test and the heads of the discourse, which we never could remember. Sometimes, the

---

1 Turned up, snub.

2 Isaac Watts (1674–1748), from "Against Idleness and Mischief," *Divine Songs for Children* (1715).

worthy gentleman would reprove my mother for being over indulgent to her sons, with a reference to old Eli, or David and Absalom,[1] which was particularly galling to her feelings; and, very highly as she respected him, and all his sayings, I once heard her exclaim, "I wish to goodness he had a son himself! He wouldn't be so ready with his advice to other people then;—he'd see what it is to have a couple of boys to keep in order."

He had a laudable care for his own bodily health—kept very early hours, regularly took a walk before breakfast, was vastly particular about warm and dry clothing, had never been known to preach a sermon without previously swallowing a raw egg—albeit he was gifted with good lungs and a powerful voice,—and was, generally, extremely particular about what he ate and drank, though by no means abstemious, and having a mode of dietary peculiar to himself,—being a great despiser of tea and such slops, and a patron of malt liquors, bacon and eggs, ham, hung beef,[2] and other strong meats, which agreed well enough with his digestive organs, and therefore were maintained by him to be good and wholesome for everybody, and confidently recommended to the most delicate convalescents or dyspeptics, who, if they failed to derive the promised benefit from his prescriptions, were told it was because they had not persevered, and if they complained of inconvenient results therefrom, were assured it was all fancy.

I will just touch upon two other persons whom I have mentioned, and then bring this long letter to a close. These are Mrs. Wilson and her daughter. The former was the widow of a substantial farmer, a narrow-minded, tattling old gossip, whose character is not worth describing. She had two sons, Robert, a rough countrified farmer, and Richard, a retiring, studious young man, who was studying the classics with the vicar's assistance, preparing for college, with a view to enter the church.

Their sister Jane was a young lady of some talents and more ambition. She had at her own desire, received a regular boarding-school education, superior to what any member of the family had obtained before. She had taken the polish well, acquired considerable elegance of manners, quite lost her provincial accent, and could boast of more accomplishments than the

---

1 Eli was a high priest, but as a father he failed to punish his two sons, Phineas and Hophni, for their sins. Although warned by God through Samuel that they would be punished for blaspheming, Eli still did not reprimand them. They were ultimately killed in battle, and Eli, upon hearing the news of their death, fell and died. Absalom is another example of a son with an overindulgent father. Absalom killed his stepbrother for violating his sister and then plotted against his father, David. Even though David knew of his son's plans, he was grief stricken when he learned of Absalom's death in a battle trying to overthrow him, and later had two monuments built in his honor.

2 Beef that is traditionally aged: it is hung for at least three weeks with no salt or additives of any sort.

vicar's daughters. She was considered a beauty besides; but never for a moment could she number me amongst her admirers. She was about six and twenty, rather tall and very slender, her hair was neither chestnut nor auburn, but a most decided, bright, light red, her complexion was remarkably fair and brilliant, her head small, neck long, chin well turned, but very short, lips thin and red, eyes clear hazel, quick and penetrating, but entirely destitute of poetry or feeling. She had, or might have had many suitors in her own rank of life, but scornfully repulsed or rejected them all; for none but a gentleman could please her refined taste, and none but a rich one could satisfy her soaring ambition. One gentleman there was, from whom she had lately received some rather pointed attentions, and upon whose heart, name, and fortune, it was whispered, she had serious designs. This was Mr. Lawrence, the young squire whose family had formerly occupied Wildfell Hall, but had deserted it, some fifteen years ago, for a more modern and commodious mansion in the neighbouring parish.

Now Halford, I bid you adieu for the present. This is the first installment of my debt. If the coin suits you, tell me so, and I'll send you the rest at my leisure: if you would rather remain my creditor than stuff your purse with such ungainly heavy pieces,—tell me still, and I'll pardon your bad taste, and willingly keep the treasure to myself.

Yours immutably,
Gilbert Markham.

CHAPTER II
AN INTERVIEW

I perceive, with joy, my most valued friend, that the cloud of your displeasure has passed away; the light of your countenance[1] blesses me once more, and you desire the continuation of my story: therefore, without more ado, you shall have it.

I think the day I last mentioned, was a certain Sunday, the latest in the October of 1827. On the following Tuesday I was out with my dog and gun, in pursuit of such game as I could find within the territory of Linden-Car; but finding none at all, I turned my arms against the hawks and carrion crows, whose depredations, as I suspected, had deprived me of better prey. To this end, I left the more frequented regions, the wooded valleys, the cornfields, and the meadow lands, and proceeded to mount the steep acclivity of Wildfell, the wildest and the loftiest eminence in our neighbourhood, where,

---

1 Markham is referring hyperbolically to Psalms 4:6: "There be many that say, Who shew us any good? Lord, lift thou up the light of thy countenance upon us."

as you ascend, the hedges, as well as the trees, become scanty and stunted, the former, at length, giving place to rough stone fences, partly greened over with ivy and moss, the latter to larches and Scotch fir-trees, or isolated black thorns. The fields, being rough and stony and wholly unfit for the plough, were mostly devoted to the pasturing of sheep and cattle; the soil was thin and poor: bits of grey rock here and there peeped out from the grassy hillocks; bilberry plants and heather—relics of more savage wildness,—grew under the walls; and in many of the enclosures, ragweeds and rushes usurped supremacy over the scanty herbage;—but these were not *my* property.

Near the top of this hill, about two miles from Linden-Car, stood Wildfell Hall, a superannuated mansion of the Elizabethan era, built of dark grey stone,—venerable and picturesque to look at, but, doubtless, cold and gloomy enough to inhabit, with its thick stone mullions and little latticed panes, its time-eaten air-holes, and its too lonely, too unsheltered situation,—only shielded from the war of wind and weather by a group of Scotch firs, themselves half blighted with storms, and looking as stern and gloomy as the Hall itself. Behind it lay a few desolate fields, and then, the brown, heath-clad summit of the hill; before it (enclosed by stone walls, and entered by an iron gate with large balls of grey granite—similar to those which decorated the roof and gables—surmounting the gateposts), was a garden,—once, stocked with such hardy plants and flowers as could best brook the soil and climate, and such trees and shrubs as could best endure the gardener's torturing shears, and most readily assume the shapes he chose to give them,—now, having been left so many years, untilled and untrimmed, abandoned to the weeds and the grass, to the frost and the wind, the rain and the drought, it presented a very singular appearance indeed. The close green walls of privet, that had bordered the principal walk, were two-thirds withered away, and the rest grown beyond all reasonable bounds; the old boxwood swan, that sat beside the scraper, had lost its neck and half its body; the castellated towers of laurel in the middle of the garden, the gigantic warrior that stood on one side of the gateway, and the lion that guarded the other were sprouted into such fantastic shapes as resembled nothing either in heaven or earth, or in the waters under the earth;[1] but, to my young imagination, they presented all of them a goblinish appearance, that harmonized well with the ghostly legions and dark traditions our old nurse had told us respecting the haunted hall and its departed occupants.

I had succeeded in killing a hawk and two crows when I came within sight of the mansion; and then, relinquishing further depredations, I sauntered on, to have a look at the old place, and see what changes had been

---

1 Exodus 20:4: " Thou shalt not make unto thee any graven image, or any likeness of any thing that is in heaven above, or that is in the earth beneath, or that is in the water under the earth."

wrought in it by its new inhabitant. I did not like to go quite to the front and stare in at the gate; but I paused beside the garden wall, and looked, and saw no change—except in one wing, where the broken windows and dilapidated roof had evidently been repaired, and where a thin wreath of smoke was curling up from the stack of chimneys.

While I thus stood, leaning on my gun, and looking up at the dark gables, sunk in an idle reverie, weaving a tissue of wayward fancies, in which old associations and the fair young hermit, now within those walls, bore a nearly equal part, I heard a slight rustling and scrambling just within the garden; and, glancing in the direction whence the sound proceeded, I beheld a tiny hand elevated above the wall: it clung to the topmost stone, and then another little hand was raised to take a firmer hold, and then appeared a small white forehead, surmounted with wreaths of light brown hair, with a pair of deep blue eyes beneath, and the upper portion of a diminutive ivory nose.

The eyes did not notice me, but sparkled with glee on beholding Sancho, my beautiful black and white setter, that was coursing about the field with its muzzle to the ground. The little creature raised its face and called aloud to the dog. The good-natured animal paused, looked up, and wagged his tail, but made no further advances. The child, (a little boy, apparently about five years old,) scrambled up to the top of the wall and called again and again; but finding this of no avail, apparently made up his mind, like Mahomet, to go to the mountain since the mountain would not come to him,[1] and attempted to get over; but a crabbed old cherry tree, that grew hard by, caught him by the frock[2] in one of its crooked scraggy arms that stretched over the wall. In attempting to disengage himself, his foot slipped, and down he tumbled—but not to the earth;—the tree still kept him suspended. There was a silent struggle, and then a piercing shriek;—but, in an instant, I had dropped my gun on the grass, and caught the little fellow in my arms.

I wiped his eyes with his frock, told him he was all right, and called Sancho to pacify him. He was just putting his little hand on the dog's neck and beginning to smile through his tears, when I heard, behind me, a click of the iron gate and a rustle of female garments, and lo! Mrs. Graham darted upon me,—her neck uncovered, her black locks streaming in the wind.

"Give me the child!"

She said in a voice scarce louder than a whisper, but with a tone of startling vehemence, and, seizing the boy, she snatched him from me, as if some

---

1   A proverb about determination, first used in Francis Bacon's (1561–1626) essay "Of Boldness" (1625): "If the Hill will not come to Mahomet, Mahomet will go to the hill" (*Concise Oxford Dictionary of Proverbs*, 3rd ed. [Oxford: Oxford UP, 1988], 188).

2   "The outer garment, for indoor wear, of women and children." Samuel Johnson (1709–84), English essayist and author, describes it as a "kind of gown for children" (*OED*).

dire contamination were in my touch, and then stood with one hand firmly clasping his, the other on his shoulder, fixing upon me her large, luminous, dark eyes—pale, breathless, quivering with agitation.

"I was not harming the child Madam," said I, scarce knowing whether to be most astonished or displeased, "he was tumbling off the wall there; and I was so fortunate as to catch him, while he hung suspended headlong from that tree, and prevent I know not what catastrophe."

"I beg your pardon sir," stammered she;—suddenly calming down,—the light of reason seeming to break upon her beclouded spirit, and a faint blush mantling on her cheek—"I did not know you;—and I thought"—

She stooped to kiss the child, and fondly clasped her arm round his neck.

"You thought I was going to kidnap your son, I suppose?"

She stroked his head with a half-embarrassed laugh, and replied,—

"I did not know he had attempted to climb the wall—I have the pleasure of addressing Mr. Markham, I believe?" she added somewhat abruptly.

I bowed, but ventured to ask how she knew me.

"Your sister called here, a few days ago, with Mrs. Markham."

"Is the resemblance so strong then?" I asked in some surprise, and not so greatly flattered at the idea as I ought to have been.

"There is a likeness about the eyes and complexion I think," replied she, somewhat dubiously surveying my face;—"and I think I saw you at church on Sunday."

I smiled.—There was something either in that smile or the recollections it awakened that was particularly displeasing to her, for she suddenly assumed again that proud, chilly look that had so unspeakably roused my corruption[1] at church—a look of repellent scorn, so easily assumed, and so entirely without the least distortion of a single feature that, while there, it seemed like the natural expression of the face, and was the more provoking to me, because I could not think it affected.

"Good morning, Mr. Markham," said she; and without another word or glance, she withdrew, with her child into the garden; and I returned home, angry and dissatisfied—I could scarcely tell you why—and therefore will not attempt it.

I only stayed to put away my gun and powder-horn, and give some requisite directions to one of the farming-men, and then repaired to the vicarage, to solace my spirit and soothe my ruffled temper with the company and conversation of Eliza Millward.

---

1   Corruption here refers to the flesh or the earthly body as distinct from the incorruptible, divine body or spirit of God; it also refers to Adam. See Romans 1:23, 1 Corinthians 15:42, and 1 Corinthians 15:50–54.

I found her, as usual, busy with some piece of soft embroidery, (the mania for Berlin wools[1] had not yet commenced), while her sister was seated at the chimney-corner, with the cat on her knee, mending a heap of stockings.

"Mary—Mary! put them away!" Eliza was hastily saying just as I entered the room.

"Not I, indeed!" was the phlegmatic reply; and my appearance prevented further discussion.

"You're *so* unfortunate, Mr. Markham!" observed the younger sister, with one of her arch, sidelong glances. "Papa's just gone out into the parish, and not likely to be back for an hour!"

"Never mind; I can manage to spend a few minutes with his daughters, if they'll allow me," said I, bringing a chair to the fire, and seating myself therein, without waiting to be asked.

"Well, if you'll be very good and amusing, we shan't object."

"Let your permission be unconditional, pray; for I came not to give pleasure, but to seek it," I answered.

However, I thought it but reasonable to make some slight exertion to render my company agreeable; and what little effort I made, was apparently pretty successful, for Miss Eliza was never in a better humour. We seemed, indeed, to be mutually pleased with each other, and managed to maintain between us a cheerful and animated, though not very profound conversation. It was little better than a tête-à-tête,[2] for Miss Millward never opened her lips, except occasionally to correct some random assertion or exaggerated expression of her sister's, and once to ask her to pick up the ball of cotton, that had rolled under the table. I did this myself, however, as in duty bound.

"Thank you, Mr. Markham," said she, as I presented it to her. "I would have picked it up myself; only I did not want to disturb the cat."

"Mary, dear, *that* won't excuse you in Mr. Markham's eyes," said Eliza; "he hates cats, I dare say, as cordially as he does old maids—like all other gentlemen—Don't you Mr. Markham?"

"I believe it is natural for our unamiable sex, to dislike the creatures," replied I; "for you ladies lavish so many caresses upon them."

"Bless them—little darlings!" cried she, in a sudden burst of enthusiasm, turning round and overwhelming her sister's pet with a shower of kisses.

"Don't Eliza!" said Miss Millward, somewhat gruffly as she impatiently pushed her away.

But it was time for me to be going: make what haste I would, I should still be too late for tea; and my mother was the soul of order and punctuality.

---

1   "A fine dyed wool used for knitting, tapestry, and the like" (*OED*).
2   French for "head to head"; thus, a private conversation.

My fair friend was evidently unwilling to bid me adieu. I tenderly squeezed her little hand at parting; and she repaid me with one of her softest smiles and most bewitching glances. I went home very happy, with a heart brimful of complacency for myself, and overflowing with love for Eliza.

CHAPTER III
A CONTROVERSY

TWO days after, Mrs. Graham called at Linden-Car, contrary to the expectation of Rose, who entertained an idea that the mysterious occupants of Wildfell Hall would wholly disregard the common observances of civilized life,—in which opinion she was supported by the Wilsons, who testified that neither their call nor the Millwards' had been returned as yet. Now however, the cause of that omission was explained, though not entirely to the satisfaction of Rose. Mrs. Graham had brought her child with her, and on my mother's expressing surprise that he could walk so far, she replied,—

"It is a long walk for him; but I must have either taken him with me, or relinquished the visit altogether: for I never leave him alone; and I think, Mrs. Markham, I must beg you to make my excuses to the Millwards and Mrs. Wilson, when you see them, as I fear I cannot do myself the pleasure of calling upon them till my little Arthur is able to accompany me."

"But you have a servant," said Rose; "could you not leave him with her?"

"She has her own occupations to attend to; and besides, she is too old to run after a child, and he is too mercurial to be tied to an elderly woman."

"But you left him to come to church."

"Yes, once; but I would not have left him for any other purpose; and I think, in future, I must contrive to bring him with me, or stay at home."

"Is he so mischievous?" asked my mother, considerably shocked.

"No," replied the lady, sadly smiling, as she stroked the wavy locks of her son, who was seated on a low stool at her feet, "but he is my only treasure; and I am his only friend, so we don't like to be separated."

"But my dear, I call that doting," said my plain-spoken parent. "You should try to suppress such foolish fondness, as well to save your son from ruin as yourself from ridicule."

"*Ruin*, Mrs. Markham?"

"Yes; it is spoiling the child. Even at *his* age, he ought not to be always tied to his mother's apron string; he should learn to be ashamed of it."

"Mrs. Markham, I beg you will not say such things in *his* presence, at least. I trust my son will *never* be ashamed to love his mother!" said Mrs. Graham, with a serious energy that startled the company.

My mother attempted to appease her by an explanation; but she seemed to think enough had been said on the subject, and abruptly turned the conversation.

"Just as I thought," said I to myself: "the lady's temper is none of the mildest, notwithstanding her sweet, pale face and lofty brow, where thought and suffering seem equally to have stamped their impress."

All this time, I was seated at a table on the other side of the room, apparently immersed in the perusal of a volume of the Farmer's Magazine,[1] which I happened to have been reading at the moment of our visitor's arrival and, not choosing to be over civil, I had merely bowed as she entered, and continued my occupation as before.

In a little while, however, I was sensible that some one was approaching me, with a light, but slow and hesitating tread. It was little Arthur, irresistibly attracted by my dog Sancho, that was lying at my feet. On looking up, I beheld him standing about two yards off, with his clear blue eyes wistfully gazing on the dog, transfixed to the spot, not by fear of the animal, but by a timid disinclination to approach its master. A little encouragement, however, induced him to come forward. The child, though shy, was not sullen. In a minute he was kneeling on the carpet, with his arms round Sancho's neck, and in a minute or two more, the little fellow was seated on my knee, surveying with eager interest the various specimens of horses, cattle, pigs, and model farms portrayed in the volume before me. I glanced at his mother now and then, to see how she relished the new-sprung intimacy; and I saw, by the unquiet aspect of her eye, that for some reason or other, she was uneasy at the child's position.

"Arthur," said she, at length, "come here. You are troublesome to Mr. Markham: he wishes to read."

"By no means, Mrs. Graham; pray let him stay. I am as much amused as he is," pleaded I. But still, with hand and eye, she silently called him to her side.

"No, mamma," said the child; "let me look at these pictures first; and then I'll come, and tell you all about them."

"We are going to have a small party on Monday, the fifth of November,"[2] said my mother; "and I hope you will not refuse to make one, Mrs. Graham. You can bring your little boy with you, you know—I dare say we shall be able to amuse him;—and then you can make your own apologies to the Millwards and Wilsons,—they will all be here I expect."

---

1 Gilbert is reading an old copy of the magazine here, as *The Farmer's Magazine ... Exclusively Devoted to Agriculture, and Rural Affairs* was published from 1800 to 1825 in Edinburgh.

2 November 5th is Guy Fawkes Day, a holiday celebrated in England to commemorate the failed attempt of Guy Fawkes (1570–1606) to blow up Parliament in 1605.

"Thank you, I never go to parties."

"Oh! but this will be quite a family concern—early hours, and nobody here but ourselves, and just the Millwards and Wilsons, most of whom you already know, and Mr. Lawrence, your landlord, whom you ought to make acquaintance with."

"I do know something of him—but you must excuse me this time; for the evenings, now, are dark and damp, and Arthur, I fear, is too delicate to risk exposure to their influence with impunity. We must defer the enjoyment of your hospitality, till the return of longer days and warmer nights."

Rose, now, at a hint from my mother, produced a decanter of wine, with accompaniments of glasses and cake, from the cupboard under the oak sideboard, and the refreshment was duly presented to the guests. They both partook of the cake, but obstinately refused the wine, in spite of their hostess's hospitable attempts to force it upon them. Arthur, especially shrank from the ruby nectar as if in terror and disgust, and was ready to cry when urged to take it.

"Never mind, Arthur," said his mamma, "Mrs. Markham thinks it will do you good, as you were tired with your walk; but she will not oblige you to take it;—I dare say you will do very well without. He detests the very sight of wine," she added, "and the smell of it most makes him sick. I have been accustomed to make him swallow a little wine or weak spirits-and-water, by way of medicine when he was sick, and, in fact, I have done what I could to make him hate them."

Everybody laughed, except the young widow and her son.

"Well, Mrs. Graham," said my mother, wiping the tears of merriment from her bright, blue eyes—"well, you surprise me! I really gave you credit for having more sense—The poor child will be the veriest milksop[1] that ever was sopped! Only think what a man you will make of him, if you persist in—"

"I think it a very excellent plan," interrupted Mrs. Graham with imperturbable gravity. "By that means I hope to save him from one degrading vice at least. I wish I could render the incentives to every other equally innoxious in his case."

"But by such means," said I, "you will never render him virtuous.—What is it that constitutes virtue, Mrs. Graham? Is it the circumstance of being able and willing to resist temptation; or that of having no temptations to resist?— Is he a strong man that overcomes great obstacles and performs surprising achievements, though by dint of great muscular exertion, and at the risk of some subsequent fatigue, or he that sits in his chair all day, with nothing to

---

1   "An effeminate spiritless young man or youth; one wanting in courage or manliness" (*OED*).

do more laborious than stirring the fire, and carrying his food to his mouth? If you would have your son to walk honourably through the world, you must not attempt to clear the stones from his path, but teach him to walk firmly over them—not insist upon leading him by the hand, but let him learn to go alone."

"I will lead him by the hand, Mr. Markham, till he has strength to go alone; and I will clear as many stones from his path as I can, and teach him to avoid the *rest*—or walk firmly over them, as you say;—for when I have done my utmost, in the way of clearance, there will still be plenty left to exercise all the agility, steadiness, and circumspection[1] he will ever have.—It is all very well to talk about noble resistance, and trials of virtue; but for fifty—or five hundred men that have yielded to temptation, show me one that has had virtue to resist. And why should I take it for granted that my son will be one in a thousand?—and not rather prepare for the worst, and suppose he will be like his—like the rest of mankind, unless I take care to prevent it?"

"You are very complimentary to us all," I observed.

"I know nothing about *you*—I speak of those I do know—and when I see the whole race of mankind, (with a few rare exceptions,) stumbling and blundering along the path of life, sinking into every pitfall, and breaking their shins over every impediment that lies in their way, shall I not use all the means in my power to ensure for him, a smoother and a safer passage?"[2]

"Yes, but the surest means will be, to endeavour to fortify him *against* temptation, not to remove it out of his way."

"I will do both, Mr. Markham. God knows he will have temptations enough to assail him, both from within and without, when I have done all I can to render vice as uninviting to him, as it is abominable in its own nature—myself, have had, indeed, but few incentives to what the world calls vice, but yet, I have experienced temptations and trials of another kind, that have required, on many occasions, more watchfulness and firmness to resist, than I have hitherto been able to muster against them. And this, I believe, is what most others would acknowledge, who are accustomed to reflection, and wishful to strive against their natural corruptions."

---

1 Helen echoes Ephesians 5:15: "See then that ye walk circumspectly, not as fools but as wise."

2 Helen is engaging in debates surrounding childrearing that range from political pieces such as Mary Wollstonecraft's (1759–97) *A Vindication of the Rights of Woman* (1792), which explores, among other issues, how boys and girls are raised differently regarding morality, to popular works stressing the importance of mothering to a child's moral development, as in John S.C. Abbott's (1805–77) *The Mother at Home; or the Principles of Maternal Duty Familiarly Illustrated* and Sarah Lewis's immensely popular *Woman's Mission* (1839). See Appendix C and E for samples of these and other relevant pieces.

"Yes," said my mother, but half apprehending her drift; "but you would not judge of a boy by yourself—and my dear Mrs. Graham, let me warn you in good time against the error—the fatal error, I may call it—of taking that boy's education upon yourself.—Because you are clever, in some things, and well informed, you may fancy yourself equal to the task; but indeed you are not; and, if you persist in the attempt, believe me, you will bitterly repent it when the mischief is done."

"I am to send him to school I suppose, to learn to despise his mother's authority and affection!" said the lady, with a rather bitter smile.

"Oh, no!—But if you would have a boy to despise his mother, let her keep him at home, and spend her life in petting him up, and slaving to indulge his follies and caprices."

"I perfectly agree with you Mrs. Markham; but nothing can be further from my principles and practice than such criminal weakness as that."

"Well, but you will treat him like a girl—you'll spoil his spirit, and make a mere Miss Nancy[1] of him—you will indeed, Mrs. Graham, whatever you may think.—But I'll get Mr. Millward to talk to you about it:—he'll tell you the consequences;—he'll set it before you as plain as the day;—and tell you what you ought to do, and all about it;—and, I don't doubt, he'll be able to convince you in a minute."

"No occasion to trouble the vicar," said Mrs. Graham, glancing at me—I suppose I was smiling at my mother's unbounded confidence in that worthy gentleman—"Mr. Markham here, thinks his powers of conviction at least equal to Mr. Millward's. If I hear not him, neither should I be convinced though one rose from the dead,[2] he would tell you.—Well Mr. Markham, you that maintain that a boy should not be shielded from evil, but sent out to battle against it, alone and unassisted—not taught to avoid the snares of life, but boldly to rush into them, or over them, as he may—to seek danger rather than shun it, and feed his virtue by temptation,—would you—"

"I beg your pardon, Mrs. Graham—but you get on too fast. I have not yet said that a boy should be taught to rush into the snares of life,—or even willfully to seek temptation for the sake of exercising his virtue by overcoming it;—I only say that it is better to arm and strengthen your hero, than

---

1   "An effeminate man." This term became "Nancy" or "Nancy-boy" at the turn of the twentieth century, and implies that the man in question is not just effeminate, but homosexual. John Ayto, *The Oxford Dictionary of Slang* (Oxford: Oxford University Press, 1998), 81.

2   Helen is using the brief mention of Lazarus, who rose from the dead, to underscore her refusal to change her mind on these issues. See Luke 16:31: "And [Jesus] said unto him, If they hear not Moses and the prophets, neither will they be persuaded, though one rose from the dead."

to disarm and enfeeble the foe;—and if you were to rear an oak sapling in a hothouse, tending it carefully night and day, and shielding it from every breath of wind, you could not expect it to become a hardy tree, like that which has grown up on the mountain-side, exposed to all the action of the elements, and not even sheltered from the shock of the tempest."

"Granted;—but would you use the same argument with regard to a girl?"

"Certainly not."

"No; you would have her to be tenderly and delicately nurtured, like a hot-house plant—taught to cling to others for direction and support, and guarded, as much as possible, from the very knowledge of evil. But will you be so good as to inform me, why you make this distinction? Is it that you think she *has* no virtue?"

"Assuredly not."

"Well, but you affirm that virtue is only elicited by temptation;—and you think that a woman cannot be too little exposed to temptation, or too little acquainted with vice, or any thing connected therewith.—It *must* be, either, that you think she is essentially so vicious, or so feeble-minded that she *cannot* withstand temptation,—and though she may be pure and innocent as long as she is kept in ignorance and restraint, yet, being destitute of *real* virtue, to teach her how to sin, is it at once to make her a sinner, and the greater her knowledge, the wider her liberty, the deeper will be her depravity,—whereas, in the nobler sex, there is a natural tendency to goodness, guarded by a superior fortitude, which, the more it is exercised by trials and dangers, is only the further developed—"

"Heaven forbid that I should think so!" I interrupted at last.

"Well then, it must be that you think they are *both* weak and prone to err, and the slightest error, the merest shadow of pollution will ruin the one, while the character of the other will be strengthened and embellished—his education properly finished by a little practical acquaintance with forbidden things. Such experience, to him, (to use a trite simile), will be like the storm to the oak, which, though it may scatter the leaves, and snap the smaller branches, serves but to rivet the roots, and to harden and condense the fibres of the tree. You would have us encourage our sons to prove all things by their own experience, while our daughters must not even profit by the experience of others. Now *I* would have both so to benefit by the experience of others, and the precepts of a higher authority, that they should know beforehand to refuse the evil and choose the good,[1] and require no experimental proofs to teach them the evil of transgression. I would not send a poor girl into the world, unarmed against her foes, and ignorant of the snares that beset her

---

1 Isaiah 7:15: "Butter and honey shall he eat, that he may know to refuse evil, and choose the good."

path:[1] nor would I watch and guard her, till, deprived of self-respect and self-reliance, she lost the power, or the will to watch and guard herself;—and as for my son—if I thought he would grow up to be what you call a man of the world—one that has '*seen life*,' and glories in his experience, even though he should so far profit by it, as to sober down, at length, into a useful and respected member of society—I would rather that he died to-morrow!—rather a thousand times!"[2] she earnestly repeated, pressing her darling to her side and kissing his forehead with intense affection. He had, already, left his new companion, and been standing for some time beside his mother's knee, looking up into her face, and listening in silent wonder to her incomprehensible discourse.

"Well! you ladies must always have the last word, I suppose," said I, observing her rise, and begin to take leave of my mother.

"You may have as many words as you please,—only I can't stay to hear them."

"No; that is the way: you hear just as much of an argument as you please; and the rest may be spoken to the wind."

"If you are anxious to say anything more on the subject," replied she, as she shook hands with Rose, "you must bring your sister to see me some fine day, and I'll listen, as patiently as you could wish, to whatever you please to say. I would rather be lectured by you than the vicar, because, I should have less remorse in telling you, at the end of the discourse, that I preserve my own opinion precisely the same as at the beginning—as would be the case, I am persuaded, with regard to either logician."

"Yes, of course," replied I, determined to be as provoking as herself; "for, when a lady does consent to listen to an argument against her own opinions, she is always predetermined to withstand it—to listen only with her bodily ears, keeping the mental organs resolutely closed against the strongest reasoning."

"Good morning, Mr. Markham," said my fair antagonist with a pitying smile; and deigning no further rejoinder, she slightly bowed, and was about to withdraw; but her son, with childish impertinence, arrested her by exclaiming,

"Mamma, you have not shaken hands with Mr. Markham!"

---

1 Note how Brontë repeats her character's phrasing in "Bell's" preface defending the morality of the novel on page 39.

2 Brontë's heroine is advancing a line of argument that follows Mary Wollstonecraft's, where Wollstonecraft asserts that an understanding of situations—not a learned ignorance of them—is a better way to preserve a person's virtue. (See Appendix C1.) She is also echoing Sarah Lewis's concerns about teaching boys to be good and instructing young women on how to make wise choices in marriage. (See Appendix C3 on women, and Appendix E4 on boys.)

She laughingly turned round, and held out her hand. I gave it a spiteful squeeze; for I was annoyed at the continual injustice she had done me from the very dawn of our acquaintance. Without knowing anything about my real disposition and principles, she was evidently prejudiced against me, and seemed bent upon showing me that her opinions respecting me, on every particular, fell far below those I entertained of myself. I was naturally touchy, or, it would not have vexed me so much. Perhaps, too, I was a little bit spoiled by my mother and sister, and some other ladies of my acquaintance;—and yet, I was by no means a fop—of that I am fully convinced, whether *you* are or not.

CHAPTER IV
THE PARTY

OUR party, on the fifth of November, passed off very well in spite of Mrs. Graham's refusal to grace it with her presence. Indeed, it is probable that, had she been there, there would have been less cordiality, freedom, and frolic amongst us than there was without her.

My mother, as usual, was cheerful and chatty, full of activity and good nature, and only faulty in being too anxious to make her guests happy, thereby forcing several of them to do what their soul abhorred,[1] in the way of eating or drinking, sitting opposite the blazing fire, or talking when they would be silent. Nevertheless, they bore it very well, being all in their holiday humours.

Mr. Millward was mighty in important dogmas and sententious jokes, pompous anecdotes and oracular discourses, dealt out for the edification of the whole assembly in general, and of the admiring Mrs. Markham, the polite Mr. Lawrence, the sedate Mary Millward, the quiet Richard Wilson, and the matter of fact Robert, in particular,—as being the most attentive listeners.

Mrs. Wilson was more brilliant than ever, with her budgets[2] of fresh news and old scandal, strung together with trivial questions and remarks, and oft repeated observations, uttered apparently for the sole purpose of denying a moment's rest to her inexhaustible organs of speech. She had brought her knitting with her, and it seemed as if her tongue had laid a wager with her fingers, to outdo them in swift and ceaseless motion.

Her daughter Jane was, of course, as graceful and elegant, as witty and seductive as she could possibly manage to be; for here were all the ladies to outshine, and all the gentlemen to charm,—and Mr. Lawrence, especially, to

---

1 Psalm 107:18: "Their soul abhorreth all manner of meat; and they draw near unto the gates of death."

2 "A bundle, a collection or stock" (*OED*).

capture and subdue. Her little arts to effect his subjugation were too subtle and impalpable to attract my observation; but I thought there was a certain *refined* affectation of superiority, and an ungenial self-consciousness about her, that negatived all her advantages, and after she was gone Rose interpreted to me her various looks, words, and actions with a mingled acuteness and asperity that made me wonder, equally, at the lady's artifice and my sister's penetration, and ask myself if she too had an eye to the squire—but never mind, Halford; she had not.

Richard Wilson, Jane's younger brother, sat in a corner, apparently good-tempered, but silent and shy, desirous to escape observation, but willing enough to listen and observe: and, although somewhat out of his element, he would have been happy enough in his own quiet way, if my mother could only have let him alone, but in her mistaken kindness, she would keep persecuting him with her attentions—pressing upon him all manner of viands, under the notion that he was too bashful to help himself, and obliging him to shout across the room his monosyllabic replies to the numerous questions and observations by which she vainly attempted to draw him into conversation.

Rose informed me that he never would have favoured us with his company, but for the importunities of his sister Jane, who was most anxious to show Mr. Lawrence that she had at least one brother more gentlemanly and refined than Robert. That worthy individual she had been equally solicitous to keep away; but he affirmed that he saw no reason why he should not enjoy a crack with Markham and the old lady, (my mother was not old really), and bonny Miss Rose and the parson, as well as the best;—and he was in the right of it too. So he talked common-place with my mother and Rose, and discussed parish affairs with the vicar, farming matters with me, and politics with us both.

Mary Millward was another mute,—not so much tormented with cruel kindness as Dick Wilson, because she had a certain short, decided way of answering and refusing, and was supposed to be rather sullen than diffident. However that might be, she certainly did not give much pleasure to the company;—nor did she appear to derive much from it. Eliza told me she had only come because her father insisted upon it, having taken it into his head that she devoted herself too exclusively to her household duties, to the neglect of such relaxations and innocent enjoyments as were proper to her age and sex. She seemed, to me, to be good-humoured enough on the whole. Once or twice she was provoked to laughter by the wit, or the merriment of some favoured individual amongst us; and then I observed she sought the eye of Richard Wilson, who sat over against her. As he studied with her father, she had some acquaintance with him, in spite of the retiring habits of both, and I suppose there was a kind of fellow-feeling established between them.

My Eliza was charming beyond description, coquettish without affectation, and evidently more desirous to engage my attention than that of all the room besides. Her delight in having me near her, seated or standing by her side, whispering in her ear, or pressing her hand in the dance, was plainly legible in her glowing face and heaving bosom, however belied by saucy words and gestures. But I had better hold my tongue: if I boast of these things now, I shall have to blush hereafter.

To proceed then, with the various individuals of our party; Rose was simple and natural as usual, and full of mirth and vivacity.

Fergus was impertinent and absurd; but his impertinence and folly served to make others laugh, if they did not raise himself in their estimation.

And finally, (for I omit myself), Mr. Lawrence was gentlemanly and inoffensive to all, and polite to the vicar and the ladies, especially his hostess and her daughter, and Miss Wilson—misguided man; he had not the taste to prefer Eliza Millward. Mr. Lawrence and I were on tolerably intimate terms. Essentially of reserved habits, and but seldom quitting the secluded place of his birth, where he had lived in solitary state since the death of his father, he had neither the opportunity nor the inclination for forming many acquaintances; and, of all he had ever known, I (judging by the results) was the companion most agreeable to his taste. I liked the man well enough, but he was too cold, and shy, and self-contained, to obtain my cordial sympathies. A spirit of candour and frankness, when wholly unaccompanied with coarseness, he admired in others, but he could not acquire it himself. His excessive reserve upon all his own concerns was, indeed, provoking and chilly enough; but I forgave it, from a conviction that it originated, less in pride and want of confidence in his friends, than in a certain morbid feeling of delicacy, and a peculiar diffidence, that he was sensible of, but wanted energy to overcome. His heart was like a sensitive plant, that opens for a moment in the sunshine, but curls up and shrinks into itself at the slightest touch of the finger, or the lightest breath of wind. And, upon the whole, our intimacy was rather a mutual predilection than a deep and solid friendship, such as has since arisen between myself and you, Halford, whom, in spite of your occasional crustiness, I can liken to nothing so well as an old coat, unimpeachable in texture, but easy and loose—that has conformed itself to the shape of the wearer, and which he may use as he pleases, without being bothered with the fear of spoiling it;—whereas Mr. Lawrence was like a new garment, all very neat and trim to look at, but so tight in the elbows that you would fear to split the seams by the unrestricted motion of your arms, and so smooth and fine in surface that you scruple to expose it to a single drop of rain.

Soon after the arrival of the guests, my mother mentioned Mrs. Graham, regretted she was not there to meet them, and explained to the Millwards and Wilsons, the reasons she had given for neglecting to return their calls, hoping they would excuse her, as she was sure she did not mean to be uncivil, and would be glad to see them at any time;—

"But she is a very singular lady, Mr. Lawrence," added she; "we don't know what to make of her—but I dare say you can tell us something about her; for she is your tenant, you know,—and she said she knew you a little."

All eyes were turned to Mr. Lawrence. I thought he looked unnecessarily confused at being so appealed to.

"I, Mrs. Markham!" said he, "you are mistaken—I don't—that is—have seen her certainly; but I am the last person you should apply to for information respecting Mrs. Graham."

He then immediately turned to Rose, and asked her to favour the company with a song, or a tune on the piano.

"No," said she; "you must ask Miss Wilson: she outshines us all in singing, and music too."

Miss Wilson demurred.

"*She'll* sing readily enough," said Fergus, "if you'll undertake to stand by her, Mr. Lawrence, and turn over the leaves for her."

"I shall be most happy to do so. Miss Wilson, will you allow me?"

She bridled her long neck and smiled, and suffered him to lead her to the instrument, where she played and sang, in her very best style, one piece after another; while he stood patiently by, leaning one hand on the back of her chair, and turning over the leaves of her book with the other. Perhaps, he was as much charmed with her performance as she was. It was all very fine in its way; but I cannot say that it moved me very deeply. There was plenty of skill and execution, but precious little feeling.

But we had not done with Mrs. Graham yet.

"I don't take wine Mrs. Markham," said Mr. Millward, upon the introduction of that beverage; "I'll take a little of your home-brewed ale. I always prefer your home-brewed to any thing else."

Flattered at this compliment, my mother rang the bell, and a china jug of our best ale was presently brought, and set before the worthy gentleman who so well knew how to appreciate its excellencies.

"Now THIS is the thing!" cried he, pouring out a glass of the same in a long stream, skillfully directed from the jug to the tumbler, so as to produce much foam without spilling a drop; and, having surveyed it for a moment opposite the candle, he took a deep draught, and then smacked his lips, drew a long breath, and refilled his glass, my mother looking on with the greatest satisfaction.

"There's nothing like this Mrs. Markham!" said he, "I always maintain that there's nothing to compare with your home-brewed ale."

"I'm sure I'm glad you like it, sir. I always look after the brewing myself, as well as the cheese and the butter—I like to have things well done, while we're about it."

"*Quite right* Mrs. Markham!"

"But then, Mr. Millward, you don't think it *wrong* to take a little wine now and then—or a little spirits either?" said my mother, as she handed a smoking tumbler of gin and water to Mrs. Wilson, who affirmed that wine sat heavy on her stomach, and whose son Robert was at that moment helping himself to a pretty stiff glass of the same.

"By no means!" replied the oracle with a Jove-like nod; "these things are all blessings and mercies, if we only knew how to make use of them."

"But Mrs. Graham doesn't think so. You shall just hear now, what she told us the other day—I *told* her I'd tell you."

And my mother favoured the company with a particular account of that lady's mistaken ideas and conduct regarding the matter in hand, concluding with, "Now don't you think it is wrong?"

"Wrong!" repeated the vicar, with more than common solemnity— "criminal, I should say—criminal!—Not only is it making a fool of the boy, but it is despising the gifts of Providence, and teaching him to trample them under his feet."[1]

He then entered more fully into the question, and explained at large the folly and impiety of such a proceeding.[2] My mother heard him with profoundest reverence; and even Mrs. Wilson vouchsafed to rest her tongue for a moment, and listen in silence, while she complacently sipped her gin and water. Mr. Lawrence sat with his elbow on the table, carelessly playing with his half-empty wine-glass, and covertly smiling to himself.

"But don't you think, Mr. Millward," suggested he, when at length that gentleman paused in his discourse, "that when a child may be naturally prone to intemperance—by the fault of its parents or ancestors, for instance—some precautions are advisable?" (Now it was generally believed that Mr. Lawrence's father had shortened his days by intemperance.)

"Some precautions, it may be; but temperance, sir, is one thing, and abstinence another."

"But I have heard that, with some persons, temperance—that is moderation—is almost impossible; and if abstinence be an evil, (which some have doubted) no one will deny that excess is a greater. Some parents have entirely prohibited their children from tasting intoxicating liquors; but a parent's authority cannot last for ever: children are naturally prone to hanker after forbidden things; and a child, in such a case, would be likely to have a strong curiosity to taste, and try the effect of what has been so lauded and

---

1   The Vicar alludes to Matthew 7:6: "Give not that which is holy unto the dogs, neither cast ye your pearls before swine, lest they trample under their feet, and turn again and rend you."

2   See Appendix F for other nineteenth-century arguments both for and against drinking alcohol.

enjoyed by others, so strictly forbidden to himself—which curiosity would generally be gratified on the first convenient opportunity; and the restraint once broken, serious consequences might ensue. I don't pretend to be a judge of such matters, but it seems to me, that this plan of Mrs. Graham's, as you describe it, Mrs. Markham, extraordinary as it may be, is not without its advantages; for here you see, the child is delivered at once from temptation; he has no secret curiosity, no hankering desire; he is as well acquainted with the tempting liquors as he ever wishes to be; and is thoroughly disgusted with them without having suffered from their effects."

"And is that right, sir? Have I not proven to you how wrong it is—how contrary to Scripture and to reason to teach a child to look with contempt and disgust upon the blessings of Providence, instead of to use them aright?"

"You may consider laudanum[1] a blessing of Providence, sir," replied Mr. Lawrence, smiling, "and yet, you will allow that most of us had better abstain from it, even in moderation; but," added he, "I would not desire you to follow out my simile too closely—in witness whereof I finish my glass."

"And take another I hope, Mr. Lawrence," said my mother, pushing the bottle towards him.

He politely declined, and pushing his chair a little away from the table, leant back towards me—I was seated a trifle behind, on the sofa beside Eliza Millward—and carelessly asked me if I knew Mrs. Graham.

"I have met her once or twice," I replied.

"What do you think of her?"

"I cannot say that I like her much. She is handsome—or rather I should say distinguished and interesting—in her appearance, but by no means amiable—a woman liable to take strong prejudices, I should fancy, and stick to them through thick and thin, twisting everything into conformity with her own preconceived opinions—too hard, too sharp, too bitter for my taste."

He made no reply, but looked down and bit his lip and shortly after rose and sauntered up to Miss Wilson, as much repelled by me, I fancy, as attracted by her. I scarcely noticed it at the time, but afterwards, I was led to recall this and other trifling facts, of a similar nature, to my remembrance, when—but I must not anticipate.

We wound up the evening with dancing—our worthy pastor thinking it no scandal to be present on the occasion, though one of the village musicians was engaged to direct our evolutions with his violin. But Mary Millward obstinately refused to join us; and so did Richard Wilson, though my mother earnestly entreated him to do so, and even offered to be his partner.

---

1 A painkiller whose chief ingredient was opium and known by the nineteenth century to be addictive. See, for example, Thomas De Quincey's (1785–1859) *Confessions of an English Opium Eater* (1822).

We managed very well without them, however. With a single set of quadrilles,[1] and several country dances, we carried it on to a pretty late hour; and at length, having called upon our musician to strike up a waltz, I was just about to whirl Eliza round in that delightful dance, accompanied by Lawrence and Jane Wilson, and Fergus and Rose, when Mr. Millward interposed with,—

"No, no, I don't allow that! Come it's time to be going now."

"Oh, no, papa!" pleaded Eliza.

"High time my girl—high time!—Moderation in all things remember! That's the plan—'Let your moderation be known unto all men!'"[2]

But in revenge, I followed Eliza into the dimly lighted passage, where under pretence of helping her on with her shawl, I fear I must plead guilty to snatching a kiss behind her father's back, while he was enveloping his throat and chin in the folds of a mighty comforter. But alas! in turning round, there was my mother close beside me. The consequence was, that no sooner were the guests departed, than I was doomed to a very serious remonstrance, which unpleasantly checked the galloping course of my spirits, and made a disagreeable close to the evening.

"My dear Gilbert," said she, "I wish you wouldn't do so! You know how deeply I have your advantage at heart, how I love you and prize you above everything else in the world, and how much I long to see you well settled in life—and how bitterly it would grieve me to see you married to that girl— or any other in the neighbourhood. What you *see* in her I don't know. It isn't only the want of money that I think about—nothing of the kind—but there's neither beauty, nor cleverness, nor goodness, nor anything else that's desirable. If you knew your own value as I do, you wouldn't dream of it. Do wait awhile and see! If you bind yourself to her, you'll repent it all your life-time when you look round you and see how many better there are. Take my word for it, you will."

"Well mother, do be quiet!—I hate to be lectured!—I'm not going to marry yet, I tell you; but—dear me! mayn't I enjoy myself at *all*?"

"Yes, my dear boy, but not in that way. Indeed you shouldn't do such things. You would be wronging the girl, if she were what she ought to be; but I assure you she is as artful a little hussy as anybody need wish to see; and you'll get entangled in her snares before you know where you are. And if you *do* marry her Gilbert, you'll break my heart—so there's an end of it."

"Well, don't cry about it mother," said I for the tears were gushing from her eyes, "there, let that kiss efface the one I gave Eliza; don't abuse her any more,

---

1 "A square dance, of French origin, usually performed by four couples and containing five sections or figures, each of which is a complete dance in itself" (*OED*).

2 Philippians 4:5.

and set your mind at rest; for I'll promise never to—that is, I'll promise to—to think twice before I take any important step you seriously disapprove of."

So saying, I lighted my candle, and went to bed, considerably quenched in spirit.[1]

CHAPTER V
THE STUDIO

IT was about the close of the month, that, yielding at length to the urgent importunities of Rose, I accompanied her in a visit to Wildfell Hall. To our surprise, we were ushered into a room where the first object that met the eye was a painter's easel, with a table beside it covered with rolls of canvass, bottles of oil and varnish, palette, brushes, paints, &c. Leaning against the wall were several sketches in various stages of progression, and a few finished paintings—mostly of landscapes and figures.[2]

"I must make you welcome to my studio," said Mrs. Graham; "there is no fire in the sitting room today, and it is rather too cold to show you into a place with an empty grate."

And disengaging a couple of chairs from the artistical lumber that usurped them, she bid us be seated, and resumed her place beside the easel—not facing it exactly, but now and then glancing at the picture upon it while she conversed, and giving it an occasional touch with her brush, as if she found it impossible to wean her attention entirely from her occupation to fix it upon her guests. It was a view of Wildfell Hall, as seen at early morning from the field below, rising in dark relief against a sky of clear silvery blue, with a few red streaks on the horizon, faithfully drawn and coloured, and very elegantly and artistically handled.

"I see your heart is in your work, Mrs. Graham," observed I: "I must beg you to go on with it; for if you suffer our presence to interrupt you, we shall be constrained to regard ourselves as unwelcome intruders."

"Oh, no!" replied she, throwing her brush on to the table, as if startled into politeness. "I am not so beset with visitors, but that I can readily spare a few minutes to the few that do favour me with their company."

"You have almost completed your painting," said I, approaching to observe it more closely, and surveying it with a greater degree of admi-

---

1 Brontë has Markham use a biblical allusion humorously here as Gilbert refers to the Bible's exhortation to "quench not the Spirit" (Thessalonians 5:19). Although the quotation refers to the Holy Spirit, Gilbert uses it to refer to his quite secular spirit.

2 For more information about the situation of professional women artists in the nineteenth century, see Appendix G.

ration and delight than I cared to express. "A few more touches in the foreground will finish it I should think.—But why have you called it Fernley Manor, Cumberland, instead of Wildfell Hall, —— shire?" I asked, alluding to the name she had traced in small characters at the bottom of the canvass.

But immediately I was sensible of having committed an act of impertinence in so doing; for she coloured and hesitated; but after a moment's pause, with a kind of desperate frankness, she replied,—

"Because I have friends—acquaintances at least—in the world, from whom I desire my present abode to be concealed; and as they might see the picture, and might possibly recognize the style in spite of the false initials I have put in the corner, I take the precaution to give a false name to the place also, in order to put them on a wrong scent, if they should attempt to trace me out by it."

"Then you don't intend to keep the picture?" said I, anxious to say anything to change the subject.

"No; I cannot afford to paint for my own amusement."

"Mamma sends all her pictures to London," said Arthur; "and somebody sells them for her there, and sends us the money."

In looking round upon the other pieces, I remarked a pretty sketch of Lindenhope from the top of the hill; another view of the old hall, basking in the sunny haze of a quiet summer afternoon; and a simple but striking little picture of a child brooding with looks of silent, but deep and sorrowful regret, over a handful of withered flowers, with glimpses of dark low hills and autumnal fields behind it, and a dull beclouded sky above.

"You see there is a sad dearth of subjects," observed the fair artist, "I took the old hall once on a moonlight night, and I suppose I must take it again on a snowy winter's day, and then again on a dark cloudy evening; for I really have nothing else to paint. I have been told that you have a fine view of the sea somewhere in the neighbourhood—Is it true?—and is it within walking distance?"

"Yes, if you don't object to walking four miles,—or nearly so—little short of eight miles there and back—and over a somewhat rough, fatiguing road."

"In what direction does it lie?"

I described the situation as well I could, and was entering upon an explanation of the various roads, lanes, and fields to be traversed in order to reach it, the goings straight on, and turnings to the right, and the left, when she checked me with,—

"Oh, stop!—don't tell me now: I shall forget every word of your directions before I require them. I shall not think about going till next spring; and then, perhaps, I may trouble you. At present we have the winter before us, and—"

She suddenly paused, with a suppressed exclamation started up from her seat, and saying, "Excuse me one moment," hurried from the room, and shut the door behind her.

Curious to see what had startled her so, I looked towards the window,—for her eyes had been carelessly fixed upon it the moment before—and just beheld the skirts of a man's coat vanishing behind a large holly bush that stood between the window and the porch.

"It's Mamma's friend," said Arthur.

Rose and I looked at each other.

"I don't know what to make of her, at all," whispered Rose.

The child looked at her in grave surprise. She straightway began to talk to him on indifferent matters, while I amused myself with looking at the pictures. There was one in an obscure corner that I had not before observed. It was a little child, seated on the grass with its lap full of flowers. The tiny features and large, blue eyes, smiling through a shock of light brown curls, shaken over the forehead as it bent above its treasure, bore sufficient resemblance to those of the young gentleman before me, to proclaim it a portrait of Arthur Graham in his early infancy.

In taking this up to bring it to the light, I discovered another behind it, with its face to the wall. I ventured to take that up too. It was the portrait of a gentleman in the full prime of youthful manhood—handsome enough, and not badly executed; but, if done by the same hand as the others, it was evidently some years before; for there was far more careful minuteness of detail, and less of that freshness of colouring and freedom of handling that delighted and surprised me in them. Nevertheless, I surveyed it with considerable interest. There was a certain individuality in the features and expression that stamped it, at once, a successful likeness. The bright, blue eyes regarded the spectator with a kind of lurking drollery—you almost expected to see them wink; the lips—a little too voluptuously full—seemed ready to break into a smile; the warmly tinted cheeks were embellished with a luxuriant growth of reddish whiskers; while the bright chestnut hair, clustering in abundant, wavy curls, trespassed too much upon the forehead, and seemed to intimate that the owner thereof was prouder of his beauty than his intellect—as perhaps, he had reason to be;—and yet he looked no fool.

I had not had the portrait in my hands two minutes before the fair artist returned.

"Only some one come about the pictures," said she, in apology for her abrupt departure: "I told him to wait."

"I fear it will be considered an act of impertinence," said I, "to presume to look at a picture that the artist has turned to the wall but may I ask"—

"It *is* an act of very great impertinence, sir; and therefore, I beg you will ask nothing about it, for your curiosity will not be gratified," replied she, attempting to cover the tartness of her rebuke with a smile;—but I could see, by her flushed cheek and kindling eye, that she was seriously annoyed.

"I was only going to ask if you had painted it yourself," said I, sulkily resigning the picture into her hands; for without a grain of ceremony, she took it from me; and quickly restoring it to the dark corner, with its face to the wall, placed the other against it as before, and then turned to me and laughed.

But I was in no humour for jesting. I carelessly turned to the window, and stood looking out upon the desolate garden, leaving her to talk to Rose for a minute or two; and then, telling my sister it was time to go, shook hands with the little gentleman, coolly bowed to the lady, and moved towards the door. But, having bid adieu to Rose, Mrs. Graham presented her hand to me, saying, with a soft voice, and by no means, a disagreeable smile,—

"Let not the sun go down upon your wrath,[1] Mr. Markham. I'm sorry I offended you by my abruptness."

When a lady condescends to apologize, there is no keeping one's anger of course; so we parted good friends for once; and *this* time, I squeezed her hand with a cordial, not a spiteful pressure.

CHAPTER VI
PROGRESSION

DURING the next four months, I did not enter Mrs. Graham's house, nor she mine; but still, the ladies continued to talk about her, and still, our acquaintance continued, though slowly, to advance. As for their talk, I paid but little attention to that (when it related to the fair hermit, I mean), and the only information, I derived from it, was that, one fine, frosty day, she had ventured to take her little boy as far as the vicarage, and that, unfortunately, nobody was at home but Miss Millward; nevertheless, she had sat a long time, and, by all accounts, they had found a good deal to say to each other, and parted with a mutual desire to meet again.—But Mary liked children, and fond mammas like those who can duly appreciate their treasures.

But sometimes, I saw her myself,—not only when she came to church, but when she was out on the hills with her son, whether taking a long, purpose-like walk, or—on specially fine days—leisurely rambling over the moor or the bleak pasture-lands, surrounding the old hall, herself with a book in her hand, her son gambolling about her; and, on any of these occasions, when I caught sight of her in my solitary walks or rides, or while following my agricultural pursuits, I generally contrived to meet or overtake her; for I rather liked to see Mrs. Graham, and to talk to her, and I decidedly

---

1 Ephesians 4:26: "Be ye angry, and sin not: let not the sun go down upon your wrath."

liked to talk to her little companion, whom, when once the ice of his shyness was fairly broken, I found to be a very amiable, intelligent, and entertaining little fellow; and we soon became excellent friends—how much to the gratification of his mamma, I cannot undertake to say. I suspected at first, that she was desirous of throwing cold water on this growing intimacy—to quench, as it were, the kindling flame of our friendship—but discovering, at length, in spite of her prejudice against me, that I was perfectly harmless, and even well-intentioned, and that, between myself and my dog, her son derived a great deal of pleasure from the acquaintance, that he would not otherwise have known, she ceased to object, and even welcomed my coming with a smile.

As for Arthur, he would shout his welcome from afar, and run to meet me fifty yards from his mother's side. If I happened to be on horseback, he was sure to get a canter or a gallop; or, if there was one of the draught horses within an available distance, he was treated to a steady ride upon that, which served his turn almost as well; but his mother would always follow and trudge beside him—not so much, I believe, to ensure his safe conduct, as to see that I instilled no objectionable notions into his infant mind; for she was ever on the watch, and never would allow him to be taken out of her sight. What pleased her best of all, was to see him romping and racing with Sancho, while I walked by her side—not, I fear, for love of my company (though I sometimes deluded myself with that idea), so much as for the delight she took in seeing her son thus happily engaged in the enjoyment of those active sports, so invigorating to his tender frame, yet so seldom exercised for want of playmates suited to his years; and, perhaps, her pleasure was sweetened, not a little, by the fact of my being with *her* instead of with *him*; and therefore,—incapable of doing him any injury directly or indirectly, designedly or otherwise—small thanks to her for that same.

But sometimes, I believe, she really had some little gratification in conversing with me; and one bright February morning, during twenty minutes' stroll along the moor, she laid aside her usual asperity and reserve, and fairly entered into conversation with me, discoursing with so much eloquence, and depth of thought and feeling, on a subject, happily coinciding with my own ideas, and looking so beautiful withal, that I went home enchanted; and on the way (morally) started to find myself thinking that, after all, it would, perhaps, be better to spend one's days with such a woman than with Eliza Millward;—and then, I (figuratively) blushed for my inconstancy.

On entering the parlour, I found Eliza there, with Rose and no one else. The surprise was not altogether so agreeable as it ought to have been. We chatted together a long time; but I found her rather frivolous, and even a little insipid, compared with the more mature and earnest Mrs. Graham.—Alas, for human constancy!

"However," thought I, "I ought not to marry Eliza since my mother so strongly objects to it, and I ought not to delude the girl with the idea that I intended to do so. Now, if this mood continue, I shall have less difficulty in emancipating my affections from her soft, yet unrelenting sway; and, though Mrs. Graham might be equally objectionable, I may be permitted, like the doctors, to cure a greater evil by a less; for I shall not fall seriously in love with the young widow, I think,—nor she with me—that's certain—but if I find a little pleasure in her society, I may surely be allowed to seek it; and if the star of her divinity be bright enough to dim the lustre of Eliza's, so much the better; but I scarcely can think it."

And thereafter, I seldom suffered a fine day to pass without paying a visit to Wildfell, about the time my new acquaintance usually left her hermitage; but so frequently was I balked in my expectations of another interview, so changeable was she in her times of coming forth, and in her places of resort, so transient were the occasional glimpses I was able to obtain, that I felt half inclined to think she took as much pains to avoid my company, as I to seek hers; but this was too disagreeable a supposition to be entertained a moment after it could, conveniently, be dismissed.

One calm, clear afternoon, however, in March, as I was superintending the rolling[1] of the meadow-land, and the repairing of a hedge in the valley, I saw Mrs. Graham down by the brook, with a sketch-book in her hand, absorbed in the exercise of her favourite art, while Arthur was putting on the time with constructing dams and breakwaters in the shallow, stony stream. I was rather in want of amusement, and so rare an opportunity was not to be neglected; so, leaving both meadow and hedge, I quickly repaired to the spot,—but not before Sancho, who, immediately upon perceiving his young friend, scoured at full gallop the intervening space, and pounced upon him with an impetuous mirth that precipitated the child almost into the middle of the beck; but, happily, the stones preserved him from any serious wetting, while their smoothness prevented his being too much hurt to laugh at the untoward event.

Mrs. Graham was studying the distinctive characters of the different varieties of trees in their winter nakedness, and copying, with a spirited, though delicate touch, their various ramifications. She did not talk much; but I stood and watched the progress of her pencil: it was a pleasure to behold it so dexterously guided by those fair and graceful fingers. But erelong their dexterity became impaired, they began to hesitate, to tremble slightly, and make false strokes, and, then, suddenly came to a pause, while their owner laughingly raised her face to mine, and told me that her sketch did not profit by my superintendence.

---

1 After seeds were planted some farmers would then roll the field, pressing the earth down over the freshly sown seeds.

"Then," said I, "I'll talk to Arthur, till you've done."

"I should like to have a ride, Mr. Markham, if Mamma will let me," said the child.

"What on, my boy?"

"I think there's a horse in that field," replied he, pointing to where the strong black mare was pulling the roller.

"No, no, Arthur; it's too far," objected his mother.

But I promised to bring him safe back, after a turn or two up and down the meadow; and when she looked at his eager face, she smiled and let him go. It was the first time she had even allowed me to take him so much as half a field's length from her side.

Enthroned upon his monstrous steed, and solemnly proceeding up and down the wide, steep field, he looked the very incarnation of quiet, gleeful satisfaction and delight. The rolling, however, was soon completed; but when I dismounted the gallant horseman, and restored him to his mother, she seemed rather displeased at my keeping him so long. She had shut up her sketch-book, and been, probably for some minutes, impatiently waiting his return.

It was now high time to go home, she said, and would have bid me good evening; but I was not going to leave her yet: I accompanied her half way up the hill. She became more sociable; and I was beginning to be very happy; but, on coming within sight of the grim old Hall, she stood still and turned towards me while she spoke, as if expecting I should go no further, that the conversation would end here, and I should now take leave and depart—as, indeed, it was time to do; for "the clear, cold eve" was fast "declining,"[1] the sun had set, and the gibbous moon was visibly brightening in the pale grey sky; but a feeling almost of compassion riveted me to the spot. It seemed hard to leave her to such a lonely, comfortless home. I looked up at it. Silent and grim it frowned before us. A faint, red light was gleaming from the lower windows of one wing; but all the other windows were in darkness, and many exhibited their black, cavernous gulfs, entirely destitute of glazing or frame work.

"Do you not find it a desolate place to live in?" said I, after a moment of silent contemplation.

"I do, sometimes," replied she. "On winter evenings, when Arthur is in bed, and I am sitting there alone, hearing the bleak wind moaning round me and howling through the ruinous old chambers, no books or occupations can repress the dismal thoughts and apprehensions that come crowding in—

---

1 From "Let Erin Remember the Days of Old" by Thomas Moore (1779–1852), Irish poet and lyricist. This song was first published in an edition of *Irish Melodies* (London: J. Powers, 1825?), which was published in ten parts between 1807 and 1835.

but it is folly to give way to such weakness I know.—If Rachel is satisfied with such a life, why should not I? —Indeed I cannot be too thankful for such an asylum, while it is left me."

The closing sentence was uttered in an under tone, as if spoken rather to herself than to me. She then bid me good evening and withdrew.

I had not proceeded many steps on my way homewards, when I perceived Mr. Lawrence, on his pretty grey pony, coming up the rugged lane that crossed over the hill top. I went a little out of my way to speak to him; for we had not met for some time.

"Was that Mrs. Graham you were speaking to just now?" said he, after the first few words of greeting had passed between us.

"Yes."

"Humph! I thought so." He looked contemplatively at his horse's mane, as if he had some serious cause of dissatisfaction with it, or something else.

"Well! what then?"

"Oh, nothing!" replied he. "Only, I thought you disliked her," he quietly added, curling his classic lip with a slightly sarcastic smile.

"Suppose I did; mayn't a man change his mind on further acquaintance?"

"Yes, of course," returned he, nicely reducing an entanglement in the pony's redundant, hoary mane. Then suddenly turning to me, and fixing his shy, hazel eyes upon me with a steady penetrating gaze, he added, "Then you *have* changed your mind?"

"I can't say that I have exactly. No; I think I hold the same opinion respecting her as before—but slightly ameliorated."

"Oh." He looked round for something else to talk about; and glancing up at the moon, made some remark upon the beauty of the evening, which I did not answer, as being irrelevant to the subject.

"Lawrence," said I, calmly looking him in the face, "are you in love with Mrs. Graham?"

Instead of his being deeply offended at this, as I more than half expected he would, the first start of surprise, at the audacious question, was followed by a tittering laugh, as if he was highly amused at the idea.

"*I* in love with her!" repeated he. "What makes you dream of such a thing?"

"From the interest you take in the progress of my acquaintance with the lady, and the changes of my opinion concerning her, I thought you might be jealous."

He laughed again. "Jealous! no—But I thought you were going to marry Eliza Millward."

"You thought wrong then; I am not going to marry either one or the other—that I know of."

"Then I think you'd better let them alone."

"Are you going to marry Jane Wilson?"

He coloured, and played with the mane again, but answered,—

"No, I think not."

"Then you had better let her alone."

She won't let me alone—he might have said; but he only looked silly and said nothing for the space of half a minute, and then, made another attempt to turn the conversation; and, this time, I let it pass; for he had borne enough: another word on the subject would have been like the last atom that breaks the camel's back.[1]

I was too late for tea; but my mother had kindly kept the tea-pot and muffin warm upon the hobs, and, though she scolded me a little, readily admitted my excuses; and when I complained of the flavour of the overdrawn tea, she poured the remainder into the slop basin, and bade Rose put some fresh into the pot, and reboil the kettle, which offices were performed with great commotion, and certain remarkable comments.

"Well!—if it had been *me* now, I should have had no tea at all—if it had been Fergus, even, he would have had to put up with such as there was, and been told to be thankful, for it was far too good for him; but *you*—we can't do too much for you.—It's always so—if there's anything particularly nice at table, Mamma winks and nods at me, to abstain from it, and if I don't attend to that, she whispers, 'Don't eat so much of that, Rose, Gilbert will like it for his supper'—*I'm* nothing at all—in the parlour, it's 'Come Rose, put away your things, and let's have the room nice and tidy against they come in; and keep up a good fire; Gilbert likes a cheerful fire.' In the kitchen—'Make that pie a large one, Rose, I dare say the boys'll be hungry;—and don't put so much pepper in, they'll not like it I'm sure'—or, 'Rose, don't put so many spices in the pudding, Gilbert likes it plain,'—or, 'Mind you put plenty of currants in the cake, Fergus likes plenty.' If I say, 'Well Mamma, *I* don't,' I'm told I ought not to think of myself—'You know Rose, in all household matters, we have only two things to consider, first, what's proper to be done, and secondly, what's most agreeable to the gentlemen of the house—any thing will do for the ladies.'"

"And very good doctrine too," said my mother. "Gilbert thinks so, I'm sure."

"Very convenient doctrine, for us at all events," said I; "but if you would really study my pleasure, Mother, you must consider your own comfort and convenience a little more than you do—as for Rose, I have no doubt she'll take care of herself; and whenever she does make a sacrifice or perform a remarkable act of devotedness, she'll take good care to let me know the extent of it. But for you, I might sink into the grossest condition of self-indulgence

---

1 A variation on the last straw that broke the camel's back.

and carelessness about the wants of others, from the mere habit of being constantly cared for myself, and having all my wants anticipated or immediately supplied, while left in total ignorance of what is done for me,—if Rose did not enlighten me now and then; and I should receive all your kindness as a matter of course, and never know how much I owe you."

"Ah! and you never *will* know, Gilbert, till you're married. Then, when you've got some trifling, self-conceited girl like Eliza Millward, careless of everything but her own immediate pleasure and advantage, or some misguided, obstinate woman like Mrs. Graham, ignorant of her principal duties, and clever only in what concerns her least to know—then, you'll find the difference."

"It will do me good Mother; I was not sent into the world merely to exercise the good capacities and good feelings of others—was I?—but to exert my own towards them; and when I marry, I shall expect to find more pleasure in making my wife happy and comfortable, than in being made so by her; I would rather give than receive."

"Oh! that's all nonsense, my dear—it's mere boy's talk that! You'll soon tire of petting and humouring your wife, be she ever so charming, and *then* comes the trial."

"Well, then, we must bear one another's burdens."[1]

"Then, you must fall each into your proper place. You'll do your business, and she, if she's worthy of you, will do hers; but it's your business to please yourself, and hers to please you. I'm sure your poor, dear father was as good a husband as ever lived, and after the first six months or so were over, I should as soon have expected him to fly, as to put himself out of his way to pleasure me. He always said I was a good wife, and did my duty; and he always did his—bless him!—he was steady and punctual, seldom found fault without a reason, always did justice to my good dinners, and hardly ever spoiled my cookery by delay—and that's as much as any woman can expect of any man."

Is it so Halford? Is that the extent of *your* domestic virtues; and does your happy wife exact no more?

CHAPTER VII
THE EXCURSION

NOT many days after this, on a mild sunny morning—rather soft under foot; for the last fall of snow was only just wasted away, leaving yet a thin ridge, here and there, lingering on the fresh, green grass beneath the hedges; but

---

1   A reference to Galatians 6:2: "Bear ye one another's burdens, and so fulfill the law of Christ."

beside them already, the young primroses were peeping from among their moist, dark foliage, and the lark above was singing of summer, and hope, and love, and every heavenly thing—I was out on the hill-side, enjoying these delights, and looking after the well-being of my young lambs and their mothers, when, on glancing round me, I beheld three persons ascending from the vale below. They were Eliza Millward, Fergus and Rose; so I crossed the field to meet them; and, being told they were going to Wildfell Hall, I declared myself willing to go with them, and offering my arm to Eliza, who readily accepted it in lieu of my brother's, told the latter he might go back, for I would accompany the ladies.

"I beg your pardon!" exclaimed he—"it's the ladies that are accompanying me, not I them. You had all had a peep at this wonderful stranger, but me, and I could endure my wretched ignorance no longer come what would, I must be satisfied; so I begged Rose to go with me to the Hall, and introduce me to her at once. She swore she would not, unless Miss Eliza would go too; so I ran to the vicarage and fetched her; and we've come hooked all the way, as fond as a pair of lovers—and now you've taken her from me; and you want to deprive me of my walk and my visit besides.—Go back to your fields and your cattle, you lubberly[1] fellow; you're not fit to associate with ladies and gentlemen, like us, that have nothing to do but to run snooking[2] about to our neighbours' houses, peeping into their private corners; and scenting out their secrets, and picking holes in their coats, when we don't find them ready made to our hands—you don't understand such refined sources of enjoyment."

"Can't you both go?" suggested Eliza, disregarding the latter half of the speech.

"Yes, both to be sure!" cried Rose; "the more the merrier—and I'm sure we shall want all the cheerfulness we can carry with us to that great, dark, gloomy room, with its narrow latticed windows, and its dismal old furniture—unless she shows us into her studio again."

So we went all in a body; and the meager old maidservant, that opened the door, ushered us into an apartment, such as Rose had described to me as the scene of her first introduction to Mrs. Graham, a tolerably spacious and lofty room, but obscurely lighted by the old-fashioned windows, the ceiling, panels and chimney-piece of grim black oak—the latter elaborately, but not very tastefully carved, with tables and chairs to match, an old bookcase on one side of the fireplace, stocked with a motley assemblage of books, and an elderly cabinet piano on the other.

---

1   Clumsy, stupid.

2   This is a variant of snoke which means "to snuff or smell," "to poke about with one's nose" (*OED*). Figuratively speaking, it means sneaking about.

The lady was seated in a stiff, high-backed arm chair, with a small, round table, containing a desk and a work basket, on one side of her, and her little boy on the other, who stood leaning his elbow on her knee, and reading to her, with wonderful fluency, from a small volume that lay in her lap; while she rested her hand on his shoulder, and abstractedly played with the long, wavy curls that fell on his ivory neck. They struck me as forming a pleasing contrast to all the surrounding objects; but of course their position was immediately changed on our entrance; I could only observe the picture during the few brief seconds that Rachel held the door for our admittance.

I do not think Mrs. Graham was particularly delighted to see us: there was something indescribably chilly in her quiet, calm civility; but I did not talk much to her. Seating myself near the window, a little back from the circle, I called Arthur to me, and he and I and Sancho amused ourselves very pleasantly together, while the two young ladies baited his mother with small talk, and Fergus sat opposite, with his legs crossed, and his hands in his breeches pockets, leaning back in his chair, and staring now up at the ceiling, now straight forward at his hostess, (in a manner that made me strongly inclined to kick him out of the room), now whistling *sotto voce*[1] to himself a snatch of a favourite air, now interrupting the conversation, or filling up a pause (as the case might be), with some most impertinent question or remark. At one time it was—

"It amazes me, Mrs. Graham, how you could choose such a dilapidated, rickety old place as this to live in. If you couldn't afford to occupy the whole house, and have it mended up, why couldn't you take a neat little cottage?"

"Perhaps, I was too proud, Mr. Fergus," replied she, smiling; "perhaps I took a particular fancy for this romantic, old-fashioned place—but indeed, it has many advantages over a cottage—in the first place, you see, the rooms are larger and more airy; in the second place, the unoccupied apartments, which I don't pay for, may serve as lumber-rooms, if I have anything to put in them; and they are very useful for my little boy to run about in on rainy days when he can't go out; and then, there is the garden for him to play in, and for me to work in. You see I have effected some little improvement already," continued she, turning to the window. "There is a bed of young vegetables in that corner, and here are some snowdrops and primroses already in bloom—and there, too, is a yellow crocus just opening in the sunshine."

"But then, how can you bear such a situation—your nearest neighbours two miles distant, and nobody looking in or passing by?—Rose would go stark mad in such a place. She can't put on life unless she sees half a dozen fresh gowns and bonnets a day—not to speak of the faces within; but you might sit watching at these windows all day long, and never see so much as an old woman carrying her eggs to market."

---

1 Quietly, privately. From the Italian *sotto* (under) and *voce* (voice).

"I am not sure the loneliness of the place was not one of its chief recommendations—I take no pleasure in watching people pass the windows; and I like to be quiet."

"Oh! as good as to say, you wish we would all of us mind our own business, and let you alone."

"No. I dislike an extensive acquaintance; but if I have a few friends, of course I am glad to see them occasionally. No one can be happy in eternal solitude. Therefore, Mr. Fergus, if you choose to enter my house as a friend, I will make you welcome; if not, I must confess, I would rather you kept away." She then turned and addressed some observation to Rose or Eliza.

"And, Mrs. Graham," said he again, five minutes after, "we were disputing, as we came along, a question that you can readily decide for us, as it mainly regarded yourself—and indeed, we often hold discussions about you; for some of us have nothing better to do than to talk about our neighbours' concerns, and we, the indigenous plants of the soil, have known each other so long, and talked each other over so often, that we are quite sick of that game; so that a stranger coming amongst us makes an invaluable addition to our exhausted sources of amusement. Well, the question, or questions you are requested to solve—"

"Hold your tongue, Fergus!" cried Rose, in a fever of apprehension and wrath.

"I won't I tell you. The questions you are requested to solve are these:— First, concerning your birth, extraction, and previous residence. Some will have it that you are a foreigner, and some an Englishwoman; some a native of the north country, and some of the south; some say—"

"Well, Mr. Fergus, I'll tell you. I'm an Englishwoman—and I don't see why any one should doubt it—and I was born in the country neither in the extreme north nor south of our happy isle; and in the country I have chiefly passed my life, and now, I hope, you are satisfied; for I am not disposed to answer any more questions at present."

"Except this.—"

"No, not one more!" laughed she, and instantly quitting her seat, she sought refuge at the window by which I was seated, and, in very desperation, to escape my brother's persecutions, endeavoured to draw me into conversation.

"Mr. Markham," said she, her rapid utterance and heightened colour too plainly evincing her disquietude; "have you forgotten the fine sea view we were speaking of some time ago? I think I must trouble you, now, to tell me the nearest way to it; for if this beautiful weather continues, I shall, perhaps, be able to walk there, and take my sketch, I have exhausted every other subject for painting; and I long to see it."

I was about to comply with her request; but Rose would not suffer me to proceed.

"Oh, don't tell her Gilbert!" cried she "she shall go with us. It's —— Bay you are thinking about I suppose, Mrs. Graham. It is a very long walk, too far for you, and out of the question for Arthur. But we were thinking about making a picnic to see it, some fine day; and, if you will wait till the settled fine weather comes, I'm sure we shall all be delighted to have you amongst us."

Poor Mrs. Graham looked dismayed, and attempted to make excuses, but Rose, either compassionating her lonely life, or anxious to cultivate her acquaintance, was determined to have her; and every objection was overruled. She was told it would only be a small party, and all friends, and that the best view of all was from —— Cliffs, full five miles distant.

"Just a nice walk for the gentlemen," continued Rose; "but the ladies will drive and walk by turns; for we shall have our pony-carriage, which will be plenty large enough to contain little Arthur and three ladies, together with your sketching apparatus, and our provisions."

So the proposal was finally acceded to; and, after some further discussion respecting the time and manner of the projected excursion, we rose, and took our leave.

But this was only March: a cold, wet April, and two weeks of May passed over before we could venture forth on our expedition with the reasonable hope of obtaining that pleasure we sought in pleasant prospects, cheerful society, fresh air, good cheer, and exercise, without the alloy of bad roads, cold winds, or threatening clouds. Then, on a glorious morning, we gathered our forces and set forth. The company consisted of Mrs. and Master[1] Graham, Mary and Eliza Millward, Jane and Richard Wilson, and Rose, Fergus, and Gilbert Markham.

Mr. Lawrence had been invited to join us, but, for some reason best known to himself, had refused to give us his company. I had solicited the favour myself. When I did so, he hesitated, and asked who were going. Upon my naming Miss Wilson among the rest, he seemed half inclined to go, but when I mentioned Mrs. Graham, thinking it might be a further inducement, it appeared to have a contrary effect, and he declined it altogether, and, to confess the truth, the decision was not displeasing to me, though I could scarcely tell you why.

It was about midday, when we reached the place of our destination. Mrs. Graham walked all the way to the cliffs; and little Arthur walked the greater part of it too; for he was now much more hardy and active, than when he first entered the neighbourhood, and he did not like being in the carriage with

---

1   While a man is referred to as Mister, a young boy is referred to as Master.

strangers, while all his four friends, Mamma, and Sancho, and Mr. Markham, and Miss Millward, were on foot, journeying far behind, or passing through distant fields and lanes.

I have a very pleasant recollection of that walk, along the hard, white, sunny road, shaded here and there with bright, green trees, and adorned with flowery banks and blossoming hedges of delicious fragrance; or through pleasant fields and lanes, all glorious in the sweet flowers, and brilliant verdure of delightful May. It was true, Eliza was not beside me; but she was with her friends in the pony-carriage, as happy, I trusted, as I was; and even when we pedestrians, having forsaken the highway for a short cut across the fields, beheld the little carriage far away, disappearing amid the green, embowering trees, I did not hate those trees for snatching the dear little bonnet and shawl from my sight, nor did I feel that all those intervening objects lay between my happiness and me; for, to confess the truth, I was too happy in the company of Mrs. Graham, to regret the absence of Eliza Millward.

The former, it is true, was most provokingly unsociable at first—seemingly bent upon talking to no one but Mary Millward and Arthur. She and Mary journeyed along together, generally with the child between them;— but where the road permitted, I always walked on the other side of her, Richard Wilson taking the other side of Miss Millward, and Fergus roving here and there according to his fancy; and after a while, she became more friendly, and at length, I succeeded in securing her attention, almost entirely to myself—and then I was happy indeed; for whenever she did condescend to converse, I liked to listen. Where her opinions and sentiments tallied with mine, it was her extreme good sense, her exquisite taste and feeling that delighted me; where they differed, it was still her uncompromising boldness in the avowal or defence of that difference—her earnestness and keenness that piqued my fancy: and even when she angered me by her unkind words or looks, and her uncharitable conclusions respecting me, it only made me the more dissatisfied with myself for having so unfavourably impressed her, and the more desirous to vindicate my character and disposition in her eyes, and if possible, to win her esteem.

At length our walk was ended. The increasing height and boldness of the hills had for some time intercepted the prospect; but, on gaining the summit of a steep acclivity, and looking downward, an opening lay before us—and the blue sea burst upon our sight!—deep violet blue—not deadly calm, but covered with glinting breakers—diminutive white specks twinkling on its bosom, and scarcely to be distinguished by the keenest vision, from the little sea-mews that sported above, their white wings glittering in the sunshine: only one or two vessels were visible; and those were far away.

I looked at my companion to see what she thought of this glorious scene. She said nothing: but she stood still, and fixed her eyes upon it with a gaze that assured me she was not disappointed. She had very fine eyes by the by—I don't know whether I've told you before, but they were full of soul, large, clear, and nearly black—not brown, but very dark grey. A cool, reviving breeze, blew from the sea—soft, pure, salubrious it waved her drooping ringlets, and imparted a livelier colour to her usually too pallid lip and cheek. She felt its exhilarating influence, and so did I—I felt it tingling through my frame, but dared not give way to it while she remained so quiet. There was an aspect of subdued exhilaration in her face, that kindled into almost a smile of exalted, glad intelligence as her eye met mine. Never had she looked so lovely: never had my heart so warmly cleaved to her as now. Had we been left two minutes longer, standing there alone, I cannot answer for the consequences. Happily for my discretion, perhaps for my enjoyment during the remainder of the day, we were speedily summoned to the repast—a very respectable collation, which Rose, assisted by Miss Wilson and Eliza, who, having shared her seat in the carriage, had arrived with her, a little before the rest, had set out upon an elevated platform overlooking the sea, and sheltered from the hot sun by a shelving rock and overhanging trees.

Mrs. Graham seated herself at a distance from me. Eliza was my nearest neighbour. She exerted herself to be agreeable, in her gentle, unobtrusive way, and was, no doubt, as fascinating and charming as ever, if I could only have felt it. But soon, my heart began to warm towards her once again; and we were all very merry and happy together—as far as I could see—throughout the protracted, social meal.

When that was over, Rose summoned Fergus to help her to gather up the fragments, and the knives, dishes, &c. and restore them to the baskets; and Mrs. Graham took her camp-stool and drawing materials; and having begged Miss Millward to take charge of her precious son, and strictly enjoined him not to wander from his new guardian's side, she left us and proceeded along the steep, stony hill, to a loftier, more precipitous eminence at some distance, whence a still finer prospect was to be had, where she preferred taking her sketch, though some of the ladies told her it was a frightful place, and advised her not to attempt it.

When she was gone, I felt as if there was to be no more fun—though it is difficult to say what she had contributed to the hilarity of the party. No jests, and little laughter had escaped her lips; but her smile had animated my mirth, a keen observation or a cheerful word from her had insensibly sharpened my wits, and thrown an interest over all that was done and said by the rest. Even my conversation with Eliza, had been enlivened by her presence, though I knew it not; and now that she was gone, Eliza's playful nonsense ceased to amuse me—nay, grew wearisome to my soul, and I grew weary of amusing her: I felt myself drawn by an irresistible attraction to that distant point where the fair artist sat and plied her solitary task—and not long did I attempt to resist it: while my little neighbour was exchanging a few words with Miss Wilson, I rose and cannily slipped away. A few rapid strides, and a little, active clambering, soon brought me to the place where she was seated—a narrow ledge of rock at the very verge of the cliff which descended with a steep, precipitous slant, quite down to the rocky shore.

She did not hear me coming: the falling of my shadow across her paper, gave her an electric start; and she looked hastily round—any other lady of my acquaintance would have screamed under such a sudden alarm.

"Oh! I didn't know it was you—Why did you startle me so?" said she, somewhat testily, "I hate anybody to come upon me so unexpectedly."

"Why, what did you take me for?" said I, "if I had known you were so nervous, I would have been more cautious; but—"

"Well, never mind. What did you come for? are they all coming?"

"No; this little ledge could scarcely contain them all."

"I'm glad, for I'm tired of talking."

"Well then, I won't talk. I'll only sit and watch your drawing."

"Oh, but you know I don't like that."

"Then I'll content myself with admiring this magnificent prospect."

She made no objection to this; and, for some time, sketched away in silence. But I could not help stealing a glance, now and then, from the splendid view at our feet to the elegant white hand that held the pencil, and the graceful neck and glossy raven curls that drooped over the paper.

"Now," thought I, "if I had but a pencil and a morsel of paper, I could make a lovelier sketch than hers, admitting I had the power to delineate faithfully what is before me."

But though this satisfaction was denied me, I was very well content to sit beside her there, and say nothing.

"Are you there still, Mr. Markham?" said she at length looking round upon me—for I was seated a little behind on a mossy projection of the cliff.—"Why don't you go and amuse yourself, with your friends?"

"Because I am tired of them, like you; and I shall have enough of them tomorrow—or at any time hence; but you, I may not have the pleasure of seeing again for I know not how long."

"What was Arthur doing when you came away?"

"He was with Miss Millward where you left him—all right, but hoping mamma would not be long away. You didn't entrust him to me, by the by," I grumbled, "though I had the honour of a much longer acquaintance; but Miss Millward has the art of conciliating and amusing children," I carelessly added, "if she is good for nothing else."

"Miss Millward has many estimable qualities, which such as you cannot be expected to perceive or appreciate. Will you tell Arthur that I shall come in a few minutes?"

"If that be the case, I will wait, with your permission, till those few minutes are past; and then I can assist you to descend this difficult path."

"Thank you—I always manage best, on such occasions, without assistance."

"But, at least, I can carry your stool and sketchbook."

She did not deny me this favour; but I was rather offended at her evident desire to be rid of me, and was beginning to repent of my pertinacity, when she somewhat appeased me by consulting my taste and judgment about some doubtful matter in her drawing. My opinion, happily, met her approbation, and the improvement I suggested was adopted without hesitation.

"I have often wished in vain," said she, "for another's judgment to appeal to when I could scarcely trust the direction of my own eye and head, they having been so long occupied with the contemplation of a single object, as to become almost incapable of forming a proper idea respecting it."

"That," replied I, "is only one of many evils to which a solitary life exposes us."

"True," said she; and again we relapsed into silence.

About two minutes after, however, she declared her sketch completed and closed the book.

On returning to the scene of our repast, we found all the company had deserted it, with the exception of three—Mary Millward, Richard Wilson, and Arthur Graham. The younger gentleman lay fast asleep with his head pillowed on the lady's lap; the other was seated beside her with a pocket edition of some classic author in his hand. He never went anywhere without such a companion wherewith to improve his leisure moments: all time seemed lost that was not devoted to study, or exacted, by his physical nature, for the bare support of life. Even now, he could not abandon himself to the enjoyment of that pure air and balmy sunshine—that splendid prospect, and those soothing sounds, the music of the waves and of the soft wind in the sheltering trees above him—not even with a lady by his side (though not a very charming one, I will allow)—he must pull out his book, and make the most of his time while digesting his temperate meal, and reposing his weary limbs, unused to so much exercise.

Perhaps, however, he spared a moment to exchange a word or a glance with his companion now and then—at any rate, she did not appear at all resentful of his conduct; for her homely features wore an expression of unusual cheerfulness and serenity, and she was studying his pale, thoughtful face with great complacency when we arrived.

The journey homeward was by no means so agreeable, to me, as the former part of the day; for now Mrs. Graham was in the carriage, and Eliza Millward was the companion of my walk. She had observed my preference for the young widow, and evidently felt herself neglected. She did not manifest her chagrin by keen reproaches, bitter sarcasms, or pouting sullen silence—any or all of these I could easily have endured, or lightly laughed away; but she showed it by a kind of gentle melancholy, a mild, reproachful sadness that cut me to the heart. I tried to cheer her up, and apparently succeeded in some degree, before the walk was over; but in the very act my conscience reproved me, knowing, as I did, that, sooner or later, the tie must be broken, and this was only nourishing false hopes, and putting off the evil day.

When the pony-carriage had approached as near Wildfell Hall as the road would permit—unless, indeed it proceeded up the long rough lane, which Mrs. Graham would not allow—the young widow and her son alighted, relinquishing the driver's seat to Rose; and I persuaded Eliza to take the latter's place. Having put her comfortably in, bid her take care of the evening air, and wished her a kind good-night, I felt considerably relieved, and hastened to offer my services to Mrs. Graham to carry her apparatus up the fields, but she had already hung her camp-stool on her arm and taken her sketchbook in her hand; and insisted upon bidding me adieu then and there, with the rest of the company. But this time, she declined my proffered aid in so kind and friendly a manner, that I almost forgave her.

CHAPTER VIII
THE PRESENT

SIX weeks had passed away. It was a splendid morning about the close of June. Most of the hay was cut, but the last week had been very unfavourable; and now that fine weather was come at last, being determined to make the most of it, I had gathered all hands together into the hayfield, and was working away myself, in the midst of them, in my shirt sleeves, with a light, shady straw hat on my head, catching up armfuls of moist, reeking grass, and shaking it out to the four winds of heaven, at the head of a goodly file of servants and hirelings—intending so to labour, from morning to night, with as much zeal and assiduity as I could look for from any of them, as well to prosper the work by my own exertion as to animate the workers by my example—when, lo! my resolutions were overthrown in a moment, by the simple fact of my brother's running up to me and putting into my hand a small parcel, just arrived from London, which I had been for some time expecting. I tore off the cover, and disclosed an elegant and portable edition of "Marmion."[1]

"I guess, I know who that's for," said Fergus, who stood looking on while I complacently examined the volume. "That's for Miss Eliza, now."

He pronounced this with a tone and look so prodigiously knowing, that I was glad to contradict him.

"You're wrong my lad," said I; and taking up my coat, I deposited the book in one of its pockets, and then put it on (i.e. the coat). "Now come

---

[1] Sir Walter Scott (1771–1832), *Marmion: A Tale of Flodden Field* (1808).

here you idle dog, and make yourself useful for once," I continued.—"Pull off your coat, and take my place in the field till I come back."

"Till you come back?—and where are you going, pray?"

"No matter—*where*—the *when* is all that concerns you;—and I shall be back by dinner, at least."

"Oh ho! and I'm to labour away till then, am I?—and to keep all these fellows hard at it besides—Well, well! I'll submit—for once in a way.—Come my lads, you must look sharp: *I'm* coming to help you now;—and woe be to that man, or woman either, that pauses for a moment amongst you—whether to stare about him, to scratch his head, or blow his nose—no pretext will serve—nothing but work, work, work in the sweat of your face,"—&c. &c.[1]

Leaving him thus haranguing the people, more to their amusement than edification, I returned to the house, and having made some alteration in my toilet, hastened away to Wildfell Hall, with the book in my pocket; for it was destined for the shelves of Mrs. Graham.

"What, then, had she and you got on so well together as to come to the giving and receiving of presents?"—Not precisely, old buck; this was my first experiment in that line; and I was very anxious to see the result of it.

We had met several times since the ——Bay excursion, and I had found she was not averse to my company, provided, I confined my conversation to the discussion of abstract matters, or topics of common interest;—the moment I touched upon the sentimental or the complimentary, or made the slightest approach to tenderness in word or look, I was not only punished by an immediate change in her manner at the time, but doomed to find her more cold and distant, if not entirely inaccessible, when next I sought her company. This circumstance did not greatly disconcert me however, because, I attributed it, not so much to any dislike of my person, as to some absolute resolution against a second marriage formed prior to the time of our acquaintance, whether from excess of affection for her late husband, or because she had had enough of him and the matrimonial state together. At first, indeed, she had seemed to take a pleasure in mortifying my vanity and crushing my presumption—relentlessly nipping off bud by bud as they ventured to appear; and then, I confess, I was deeply wounded, though, at the same time, stimulated to seek revenge;—but latterly, finding, beyond a doubt, that I was not that empty-headed coxcomb she had first supposed me, she had repulsed my modest advances in quite a different spirit. It was a kind of serious, almost sorrowful displeasure, which I soon learnt carefully to avoid awakening.

"Let me first establish my position as a friend," thought I,— "the patron and playfellow of her son, the sober, solid, plain-dealing friend of herself, and

---

1 A humorous reference to Genesis 3:19: "In the sweat of thy face shalt thou eat bread, till thou return unto the ground; for out of it wast thou taken: for dust thou art, and unto dust shalt thou return."

then, when I have made myself fairly necessary to her comfort and enjoyment in life (as I believe I can), we'll see what next may be effected."

So we talked about painting, poetry, and music, theology, geology, and philosophy: once or twice I lent her a book, and once she lent me one in return: I met her in her walks as often as I could; I came to her house as often as I dared. My first pretext for invading the sanctum, was to bring Arthur a little waddling puppy of which Sancho was the father, and which delighted the child beyond expression, and, consequently, could not fail to please his mamma. My second was to bring him a book, which, knowing his mother's particularity, I had carefully selected, and which I submitted for her approbation before presenting it to him. Then, I brought her some plants for her garden, in my sister's name—having previously persuaded Rose to send them. Each of these times I inquired after the picture she was painting from the sketch taken on the cliff, and was admitted into the studio, and asked my opinion or advice respecting its progress.

My last visit had been to return the book she had lent me; and then it was, that, in casually discussing the poetry of Sir Walter Scott, she had expressed a wish to see "Marmion," and I had conceived the presumptuous idea of making her a present of it, and, on my return home, instantly sent for the smart little volume I had this morning received. But an apology for invading the hermitage was still necessary; so I had furnished myself with a blue morocco[1] collar for Arthur's little dog; and that being given and received, with much more joy and gratitude, on the part of the receiver, than the worth of the gift, or the selfish motive of the giver deserved, I ventured to ask Mrs. Graham for one more look at the picture, if it was still there.

"Oh yes! come in," said she (for I had met them in the garden). "It is finished and framed, all ready for sending away; but give me your last opinion, and, if you can suggest any further improvement, it shall be—duly considered, at least."

The picture was strikingly beautiful: it was the very scene itself, transferred as if by magic to the canvass; but I expressed my approbation in guarded terms, and few words, for fear of displeasing her. She, however, attentively watched my looks, and her artist's pride was gratified, no doubt, to read my heart-felt admiration in my eyes. But, while I gazed, I thought upon the book, and wondered how it was to be presented. My heart failed me; but I determined not to be such a fool as to come away without having made the attempt. It was useless waiting for an opportunity, and useless trying to concoct a speech for the occasion. The more plainly and naturally the thing was done, the better, I thought; so I just looked out of the window to screw up my courage, and then pulled out the book, turned round, and put it into her hand, with this short explanation.

---

1   A type of leather made from goat skin.

"You were wishing to see 'Marmion,' Mrs. Graham; and here it is, if you will be so kind as to take it."

A momentary flush suffused her face—perhaps, a blush of sympathetic shame for such an awkward style of presentation: she gravely examined the volume on both sides; then silently turned over the leaves, knitting her brows the while, in serious cogitation; then closed the book, and, turning from it to me, quietly asked the price of it.—I felt the hot blood rush to my face.

"I'm sorry to offend you Mr. Markham," said she, "but unless I pay for the book, I cannot take it." And she laid it on the table.

"Why cannot you?"

"Because,"—she paused, and looked at the carpet.

"Why cannot you?" I repeated with a degree of irascibility that roused her to lift her eyes, and look me steadily in the face.

"Because, I don't like to put myself under obligations that I can never repay—I *am* obliged to you, already for your kindness to my son; but his grateful affection, and your own good feelings must reward you for that."

"Nonsense!" ejaculated I.

She turned her eyes on me again, with a look of quiet, grave surprise, that had the effect of a rebuke, whether intended for such or not.

"Then you won't take the book?" I asked, more mildly than I had yet spoken.

"I will gladly take it, if you will let me pay for it."

I told her the exact price, and the cost of the carriage besides, in as calm a tone as I could command—for in fact, I was ready to weep with disappointment and vexation.

She produced her purse, and coolly counted out the money, but hesitated to put it into my hand. Attentively regarding me, in a tone of soothing softness she observed,—

"You think yourself insulted Mr. Markham—I wish I could make you understand that—that I—"

"I do understand you, perfectly," I said. "You think that if you were to accept that trifle from me now, I should presume upon it hereafter; but you are mistaken:— if you will only oblige me by taking it, believe me, I shall build no hopes upon it, and consider this no precedent for future favours:—and it is nonsense to talk about putting yourself under obligations to *me* when you must know that in such a case the obligation is entirely on my side,—the favour on yours."

"Well then I'll take you at your word," she answered with a most angelic smile, returning the odious money to her purse—"but *remember!*"

"I will remember—what I have said;—but do not you punish my presumption by withdrawing your friendship entirely from me,—or expect me to atone for it by being *more* distant than before," said I, extending my hand to take leave, for I was too much excited to remain.

"Well then! let us be as we were," replied she, frankly placing her hand in mine; and while I held it there, I had much difficulty to refrain from pressing it to my lips;—but that would be suicidal madness: I had been bold enough already, and this premature offering had well-nigh given the death-blow to my hopes.

It was with an agitated burning heart and brain that I hurried homewards, regardless of that scorching noon-day sun—forgetful of everything but her I had just left—regretting nothing but her impenetrability, and my own precipitancy and want of tact—fearing nothing but her hateful resolution, and my inability to overcome it—hoping nothing—but halt,—I will not bore you with my conflicting hopes and fears—my serious cogitations and resolves.

CHAPTER IX
A SNAKE IN THE GRASS

THOUGH my affections might now be said to be fairly weaned from Eliza Millward, I did not yet entirely relinquish my visits to the vicarage, because I wanted, as it were, to let her down easy; without raising much sorrow, or incurring much resentment,—or making myself the talk of the parish; and besides, if I had wholly kept away, the vicar, who looked upon my visits as paid chiefly, if not entirely to himself, would have felt himself decidedly affronted by the neglect. But when I called there the day after my interview with Mrs. Graham, he happened to be from home—a circumstance by no means so agreeable to me now as it had been on former occasions. Miss Millward was there, it is true, but she, of course, would be little better than a nonentity. However, I resolved to make my visit a short one, and to talk to Eliza in a brotherly, friendly sort of way, such as our long acquaintance might warrant me in assuming, and which, I thought, could neither give offence nor serve to encourage false hopes.

It was never my custom to talk about Mrs. Graham either to her or any one else; but I had not been seated three minutes, before she brought that lady on to the carpet[1] herself, in a rather remarkable manner.

"Oh, Mr. Markham!" said she, with a shocked expression and voice subdued almost to a whisper—"what do you think of these shocking reports about Mrs. Graham?—can you encourage us to disbelieve them?"

---

1 Rosengarten and Smith explain that this expression is "used in the older sense of 'brought up for discussion'; from the obsolete use of 'carpet' for table cloth. Cf. French *mettre sur le tapis*, to bring forward" (*OTWH* 474).

"What reports?"

"Ah, now! *you* know!" she slyly smiled and shook her head.

"I know nothing about them—What in the world do you mean, Eliza?"

"Oh, don't ask *me*!—*I* can't explain it." She took up the cambric hand-kerchief which she had been beautifying with a deep lace border, and began to be very busy.

"What is it, Miss Millward? what does she mean?" said I, appealing to her sister, who seemed to be absorbed in the hemming of a large, coarse sheet.

"I don't know," replied she.—"Some idle slander, somebody has been inventing, I suppose. I never heard it till Eliza told me, the other day,—but if all the parish dinned[1] it in my ears, I shouldn't believe a word of it—I know Mrs. Graham too well!"

"Quite right Miss Millward!—and so do I—whatever it may be."

"Well!" observed Eliza, with a gentle sigh—"It's well to have such a comfortable assurance regarding the worth of those we love.—I only wish you may not find your confidence misplaced."

And she raised her face, and gave me such a look of sorrowful tenderness as might have melted my heart, but within those eyes there lurked a something that I did not like; and I wondered how I ever could have admired them: her sister's honest face and small grey optics appeared far more agreeable;—but I was out of temper with Eliza, at that moment, for her insinuations against Mrs. Graham—which were false, I was certain, whether she knew it or not.

I said nothing more on the subject, however, at the time, and but little on any other; for, finding I could not well recover my equanimity, I presently rose and took leave, excusing myself under the plea of business at the farm;—and to the farm I went—not troubling my mind one whit about the possible truth of these mysterious reports, but only wondering what they were, by whom originated, and on what foundations raised,—and how they could the most effectually be silenced or disproved.

A few days after this, we had another of our quiet little parties, to which the usual company of friends and neighbours had been invited, and Mrs. Graham among the number. She could not now absent herself under the plea of dark evenings or inclement weather, and, greatly to my relief, she came. Without her I should have found the whole affair an intolerable bore; but the moment of her arrival brought new life to the house; and though I must not neglect the other guests for her, or expect to engross much of her attention and conversation to myself alone, I anticipated an evening of no common enjoyment.

---

1 "Assailed or disturbed with din," a loud sound (*OED*).

Mr. Lawrence came too. He did not arrive till some time after the rest were assembled. I was curious to see how he would comport himself to Mrs. Graham. A slight bow was all that passed between them on his entrance; and having politely greeted the other members of the company; he seated himself quite aloof from the young widow, between my mother and Rose.

"Did you ever see such art!" whispered Eliza, who was my nearest neighbour. "Would you not say they were perfect strangers?"

"Almost;—but what then?"

"What then!—why you can't pretend to be ignorant?"

"Ignorant of *what*?" demanded I, so sharply that she started and replied—

"Oh, hush! Don't speak so loud."

"Well, tell me then," I answered in a lower tone; "what is it you mean? I hate enigmas."

"Well you know, I don't vouch for the truth of it—indeed, far from it—but haven't you heard—"

"I've heard *nothing*, except from you."

"You must be willfully deaf then; for any one will tell you that—but I shall only anger you by repeating it, I see; so I had better hold my tongue."

She closed her lips and folded her hands before her with an air of injured meekness.

"If you had wished not to anger me, you should have held your tongue from the beginning; or else spoken out plainly and honestly all you had to say."

She turned aside her face, pulled out her handkerchief, rose, and went to the window, where she stood for some time, evidently dissolved in tears. I was astounded, provoked, ashamed—not so much of my harshness as for her childish weakness. However, no one seemed to notice her, and shortly after, we were summoned to the tea-table; in those parts it was customary to sit to the table at tea-time, on all occasions, and make a meal of it; for we dined early. On taking my seat, I had Rose on one side of me, and an empty chair on the other.

"May I sit by you?" said a soft voice at my elbow.

"If you like," was the reply; and Eliza slipped into the vacant chair; then looking up in my face with a half sad, half playful smile, she whispered—

"You're so stern, Gilbert."

I handed down her tea with a slightly contemptuous smile, and said nothing, for I had nothing to say.

"What have I done to offend you?" said she, more plaintively. "I wish I knew."

"Come, take your tea Eliza, and don't be foolish," responded I, handing her the sugar and cream.

Just then, there arose a slight commotion on the other side of me, occasioned by Miss Wilson's coming to negotiate an exchange of seats with Rose.

"Will you be so good as to exchange places with me, Miss Markham?" said she, "for I don't like to sit by Mrs. Graham. If your mamma thinks proper to invite such persons to her house, she cannot object to her daughter's keeping company with them."

This latter clause was added in a sort of soliloquy when Rose was gone; but I was not polite enough to let it pass:

"Will you be so good as to tell me what you mean, Miss Wilson?" said I.

The question startled her a little, but not much.

"Why Mr. Markham," replied she coolly, having quickly recovered her self-possession, "it surprises me rather that Mrs. Markham should invite such a person as Mrs. Graham to her house; but, perhaps, she is not aware that the lady's character is considered scarcely respectable."

"She is not, nor am I; and therefore, you would oblige me by explaining your meaning a little further."

"This is scarcely the time or the place for such explanations; but I think you can hardly be so ignorant as you pretend: you must know her as well as I do."

"I think I do, perhaps a little better; and therefore, if you will inform me what you have heard, or imagined against her, I shall, perhaps, be able to set you right."

"Can you tell me, then, who was her husband; or if she ever had any?"

Indignation kept me silent. At such a time and place I could not trust myself to answer.

"Have you never observed," said Eliza, "what a striking likeness there is between that child of hers and—"

"And whom?" demanded Miss Wilson, with an air of cold, but keen severity.

Eliza was startled: the timidly spoken suggestion had been intended for my ear alone.

"Oh, I beg your pardon!" pleaded she, "I may be mistaken—perhaps I *was* mistaken." But she accompanied the words with a sly glance of derision directed to me from the corner of her disingenuous eye.

"There's no need to ask *my* pardon," replied her friend; "but I see no one here that at all resembles that child, except his mother; and when you hear ill-natured reports, Miss Eliza, I will thank you—that is, I think you will do well to refrain from repeating them. I presume the person you allude to is Mr. Lawrence; but I think I can assure you that your suspicions, in that respect, are utterly misplaced; and if he has any particular connection with the lady at all, (which no one has a right to assert), at least, he has (what cannot be said of some others) sufficient sense of propriety to withhold him from acknowledging anything more than a bowing acquaintance in the presence of respectable persons—he was evidently both surprised and annoyed to find her here."

"Go it!"[1] cried Fergus, who sat on the other side of Eliza, and was the only individual who shared that side of the table with us; "go it like bricks![2] mind you don't leave her one stone upon another."[3]

Miss Wilson drew herself up with a look of freezing scorn, but said nothing. Eliza would have replied, but I interrupted her by saying as calmly as I could, though in a tone which betrayed, no doubt, some little of what I felt within,—

"We have had enough of this subject: if we can only speak to slander our betters, let us hold our tongues."

"I think you'd better," observed Fergus; "and so does our good parson: he has been addressing the company in his richest vein all the while, and eyeing you, from time to time, with looks of stern distaste, while you sat there, irreverently whispering and muttering together; and once he paused in the middle of a story—or a sermon, I don't know which, and fixed his eyes upon you, Gilbert, as much as to say—'When Mr. Markham has done flirting with those two ladies I will proceed!'"

What more was said at the tea table I cannot tell; nor how I found patience to sit till the meal was over. I remember, however, that I swallowed with difficulty the remainder of the tea that was in my cup, and ate nothing; and that the first thing I did was to stare at Arthur Graham, who sat beside his mother on the opposite side of the table, and the second to stare at Mr. Lawrence, who sat below; and, first, it struck me that there *was* a likeness; but, on further contemplation, I concluded it was only in imagination. Both, it is true, had more delicate features and smaller bones than commonly fall to the lot of individuals of the rougher sex, and Lawrence's complexion was pale and clear, and Arthur's delicately fair; but Arthur's tiny, somewhat snubby nose could never become so long and straight as Mr. Lawrence's, and the outline of his face, though not full enough to be round, and too finely converging to the small, dimpled chin to be square, could never be drawn

---

1   "Go it!" is an expression that means "speak very strongly or frankly" and "Keep at it! Play, fight, etc. hard!" Eric Partridge, *The Routledge Dictionary of Historical Slang* (London: Routledge and Kegan Paul, 1970), 336.

2   "Like bricks" means "vigorously, energetically, thoroughly, very quickly, with a good will." Eric Partridge, *The Routledge Dictionary of Historical Slang* (London: Routledge and Kegan Paul, 1970), 92.

3   "One stone upon another" is a lighthearted quotation from the Bible. Fergus is referring to the prophecy regarding the destruction of the Temple in Jerusalem recounted using this phrase in Matthew 24:2, Mark 12:2, and Luke 19:44.

out to the long oval of the other's; while the child's hair was evidently of a lighter, warmer tint than the elder gentleman's had ever been, and his large, clear, blue eyes, though prematurely serious at times, were utterly dissimilar to the shy hazel eyes of Mr. Lawrence, whence the sensitive soul looked so distrustfully forth, as ever ready to retire within, from the offences of a too rude, too uncongenial world. Wretch that I was to harbour that detestable idea for a moment! Did I not know Mrs. Graham? Had I not seen her, conversed with her time after time? Was I not certain that she, in intellect, in purity and elevation of soul, was immeasurably superior to any of her detractors; that she was, in fact, the noblest, the most adorable, of her sex I had ever beheld, or even imagined to exist? Yes, and I would say with Mary Millward (sensible girl as she was) that if all the parish, aye, or all the world should din these horrible lies in my ears, I would not believe them; for I knew her better than they.

Meantime, my brain was on fire with indignation, and my heart seemed ready to burst from its prison with conflicting passions. I regarded my two fair neighbours with a feeling of abhorrence and loathing I scarcely endeavoured to conceal: I was rallied from several quarters for my abstraction and ungallant neglect of the ladies; but I cared little for that: all I cared about, besides that one grand subject of my thoughts, was to see the cups travel up to the tea-tray, and not come down again. I thought Mr. Millward never *would* cease telling us that he was no tea-drinker, and that it was highly injurious to keep loading the stomach with slops to the exclusion of more wholesome sustenance, and so give himself time to finish his fourth cup.

At length it was over; and I rose and left the table and the guests, without a word of apology—I could endure their company no longer. I rushed out to cool my brain in the balmy evening air, and to compose my mind, or indulge my passionate thoughts in the solitude of the garden.

To avoid being seen from the windows, I went down a quiet, little avenue, that skirted one side of the enclosure, at the bottom of which was a seat embowered in roses and honeysuckles. Here I sat down to think over the virtues and wrongs of the lady of Wildfell Hall; but I had not been so occupied two minutes, before voices and laughter, and glimpses of moving objects through the trees, informed me that the whole company had turned out to take an airing in the garden too. However, I nestled up in a corner of the bower, and hoped to retain possession of it, secure alike from observation and intrusion. But no—confound it—there was some one coming down the avenue! Why couldn't they enjoy the flowers and sunshine of the open garden, and leave that sunless nook to me, and the gnats and midges?

But peeping through my fragrant screen of interwoven branches to discover who the intruders were, (for a murmur of voices told me it was more than one), my vexation instantly subsided, and far other feelings agitated my still unquiet soul;[1] for there was Mrs. Graham, slowly moving down the walk with Arthur by her side, and no one else. Why were they alone? Had the poison of detracting tongues already spread through all; and had they all turned their backs upon her? I now recollected having seen Mrs. Wilson, in the early part of the evening, edging her chair close up to my mother, and bending forward, evidently in the delivery of some important, confidential intelligence; and from the incessant wagging of her head, the frequent distortions of her wrinkled physiognomy, and the winking and malicious twinkle of her little ugly eyes, I judged it was some spicy piece of scandal that engaged her powers; and from the cautious privacy of the communication, I supposed some person then present, was the luckless object of her calumnies; and from all these tokens, together with my mother's looks and gestures of mingled horror and incredulity, I now concluded, that object to have been Mrs. Graham. I did not emerge from my place of concealment, till she had nearly reached the bottom of the walk, lest my appearance should drive her away; and when I did step forward, she stood still and seemed inclined to turn back as it was.

"Oh, don't let us disturb you Mr. Markham!" said she. "We came here to seek retirement ourselves; not to intrude on your seclusion."

"I am no hermit, Mrs. Graham—though I own it looks rather like it, to absent myself in this uncourteous fashion from my guests."

"I feared you were unwell," said she with a look of real concern.

"I was rather, but it's over now. Do sit here a little, and rest, and tell me how you like this arbour," said I, and lifting Arthur by the shoulders, I planted him in the middle of the seat by way of securing his mamma, who, acknowledging it to be a tempting place of refuge, threw herself back in one corner, while I took possession of the other.

But that word refuge disturbed me. Had their unkindness then really driven her to seek for peace in solitude?

"Why have they left you alone?" I asked.

"It is I who have left them," was the smiling rejoinder. "I was wearied to death with small-talk—nothing wears me out like that. I cannot imagine how they *can* go on as they do."

I could not help smiling at the serious depth of her wonderment.

"Is it that they think it a *duty* to be continually talking," pursued she; "and so never pause to think, but fill up with aimless trifles and vain repetitions,[2] when subjects of real interest fail to present themselves?—or do they really take a pleasure in such discourse?"

---

1 See William Shakespeare (1564–1616), *The Merchant of Venice*: "For never shall you lie by Portia's side / With an unquiet soul" (II.ii.307–08).

2 Matthew 6:7: "But when ye pray, use no vain repetitions, as the heathen do: for they think that they shall be heard for their much speaking."

"Very likely they do," said I: "their shallow minds can hold no great ideas, and their light heads are carried away by trivialities, that would not move a better furnished skull;—and their only alternative to such discourse, is to plunge over head and ears into the slough of scandal—which is their chief delight."

"Not all of them surely?" cried the lady, astonished at the bitterness of my remark.

"No, certainly; I exonerate my sister from such degraded tastes—and my mother too, if you included *her* in your animadversions."

"I meant no animadversions against any one, and certainly intended no disrespectful allusions to your mother. I have known some sensible persons great adepts in that style of conversation, when circumstances impelled them to it; but it is a gift I cannot boast the possession of. I kept up my attention, on this occasion, as long as I could, but when my powers were exhausted, I stole away, to seek a few minutes repose in this quiet walk. I hate talking where there is no exchange of ideas or sentiments, and no good given or received."

"Well," said I, "if ever I trouble you with my loquacity, tell me so at once, and I promise not to be offended; for I possess the faculty of enjoying the company of those I——of my friends as well in silence as in conversation."

"I don't quite believe you; but if it were so, you would exactly suit me for a companion."

"I am all you wish, then, in other respects?"

"No, I don't mean that. How beautiful those little clusters of foliage look, where the sun comes through behind them!" said she, on purpose to change the subject.

And they did look beautiful, where at intervals the level rays of the sun penetrating the thickness of trees and shrubs on the opposite side of the path before us, relieved their dusky verdure by displaying patches of semitransparent leaves of resplendent golden green.

"I almost wish I were not a painter," observed my companion.

"Why so? one would think at such a time you would most exult in your privilege of being able to imitate the various brilliant and delightful touches of nature."

"No; for instead of delivering myself up to the full enjoyment of them as others do, I am always troubling my head about how I could produce the same effect upon canvass; and as that can never be done, it is mere vanity and vexation of spirit."[1]

"Perhaps you cannot do it to satisfy yourself, but you may and do succeed in delighting others with the result of your endeavours."

---

1 Ecclesiastes 1:14: "For I have seen all the works that are done under the sun; and, behold, all is vanity and vexation of spirit."

ANNE BRONTË

"Well, after all I should not complain: perhaps few people gain their liveli-hood with so much pleasure in their toil as I do. Here is some one coming."

She seemed vexed at the interruption.

"It is only Mr. Lawrence and Miss Wilson," said I, "coming to enjoy a quiet stroll. They will not disturb us."

I could not quite decipher the expression of her face; but I was satisfied there was no jealousy therein. What business had I to look for it?

"What sort of a person is Miss Wilson?" she asked.

"She is elegant and accomplished above the generality of her birth and station; and some say she is lady-like and agreeable."

"I thought her somewhat frigid, and rather supercilious in her manner today."

"Very likely she might be so to you. She has possibly taken a prejudice against you, for I think she regards you in the light of a rival."

"Me? Impossible Mr. Markham!" said she, evidently astonished and annoyed.

"Well, I know nothing about it," returned I, rather doggedly; for I thought her annoyance was chiefly against myself.

The pair had now approached within a few paces of us. Our arbour was set snugly back in a corner, before which, the avenue at its termination, turned off into the more airy walk along the bottom of the garden. As they approached this, I saw, by the aspect of Jane Wilson, that she was directing her companion's attention to us; and, as well by her cold, sarcastic smile, as by the few isolated words of her discourse that reached me, I knew full well that she was impressing him with the idea that we were strongly attached to each other. I noticed that he coloured up to the temples, gave us one furtive glance in passing, and walked on, looking grave, but seemingly offering no reply to her remarks.

It was true, then, that he *had* some designs upon Mrs. Graham; and, were they honourable, he would not be so anxious to conceal them. *She* was blameless, of course, but he was detestable beyond all count.

While these thoughts flashed through my mind, my companion abruptly rose, and calling her son, said they would now go in quest of the company, and departed up the avenue. Doubtless she had heard or guessed something of Miss Wilson's remarks, and therefore, it was natural enough she should choose to continue the tête-à-tête no longer, especially as at that moment my cheeks were burning with indignation against my former friend, the token of which she might mistake for a blush of stupid embarrassment. For this I owed Miss Wilson yet another grudge; and still the more I thought upon her conduct, the more I hated her.

It was late in the evening before I joined the company. I found Mrs. Gra-ham already equipped for departure, and taking leave of the rest, who were now returned to the house. I offered—nay, begged to accompany her home. Mr. Lawrence was standing by at the time, conversing with some one else. He did not look at us, but, on hearing my earnest request, he paused in the middle of a sentence to listen for her reply, and went on, with a look of quiet satisfaction the moment he found it was to be a denial.

A denial it was, decided, though not unkind. She could not be persuaded to think there was danger for herself or her child in traversing those lonely lanes and fields without attendance. It was daylight still, and she should meet no one; or if she did, the people were quiet and harmless she was well assured. In fact, she would not hear of any one's putting himself out of the way to accompany her, though Fergus vouchsafed to offer his services, in case they should be more acceptable than mine, and my mother begged she might send one of the farming-men to escort her.

When she was gone, the rest was all a blank, or worse. Lawrence attempted to draw me into conversation, but I snubbed him, and went to another part of the room. Shortly after, the party broke up, and he himself took leave. When he came to me, I was blind to his extended hand, and deaf to his good night till he repeated it a second time; and then, to get rid of him, I muttered an inarticulate reply accompanied by a sulky nod.

"What is the matter Markham?" whispered he.

I replied by a wrathful and contemptuous stare.

"Are you angry because Mrs. Graham would not let you go home with her?" he asked with a faint smile that nearly exasperated me beyond control.

But, swallowing down all fiercer answers, I merely demanded,—

"What business is it of yours?"

"Why, none," replied he, with provoking quietness; "only," and here he raised his eyes to my face, and spoke with unusual solemnity, "only let me tell you, Markham, that if you have any designs in that quarter they will certainly fail; and it grieves me to see you cherishing false hopes, and wasting your strength in useless efforts, for—"

"Hypocrite!" I exclaimed, and he held his breath, and looked very blank, turned white about the gills, and went away without another word.

I had wounded him to the quick; and I was glad of it.

CHAPTER X
A CONTRACT AND A QUARREL

WHEN all were gone, I learnt that the vile slander had indeed been circulated throughout the company, in the very presence of the victim. Rose, however, vowed she did not and would not believe it, and my mother made the same declaration, though not, I fear, with the same amount of real, unwavering incredulity. It seemed to dwell continually on her mind, and she kept irritating me from time to time by such expressions as—"Dear, dear, who would have thought it!—Well! I always thought there was something odd about her.—You see what it is for women to affect to be different to other people." And once it was,—

"I misdoubted that appearance of mystery from the very first—I *thought* there would no good come of it; but this is a sad, sad business to be sure!"

"Why mother, you said you didn't believe these tales," said Fergus.

"No more I do, my dear; but then, you know, there must be some foundation."

"The foundation is in the wickedness and falsehood of the world," said I, "and in the fact that Mr. Lawrence has been seen to go that way once or twice of an evening—and the village gossips say he goes to pay his addresses to the strange lady, and the scandal mongers have greedily seized the rumour, to make it the basis of their own infernal structure."

"Well, but Gilbert, there must be something in her *manner* to countenance such reports."

"Did *you* see anything in her manner?"

"No, certainly; but then you know, I always said there was something strange about her."

I believe it was on that very evening that I ventured on another invasion of Wildfell Hall. From the time of our party, which was upwards of a week ago, I had been making daily efforts to meet its mistress in her walks; and, always disappointed (she must have managed it so on purpose), had nightly kept revolving in my mind some pretext for another call. At length, I concluded that the separation could be endured no longer; (by this time, you will see I was pretty far gone) and, taking from the book case an old volume that I thought she might be interested in, though, from its unsightly and somewhat dilapidated condition, I had not yet ventured to offer it for her perusal, I hastened away,—but not without sundry misgivings as to how she would receive me, or how I could summon courage to present myself with so slight an excuse. But, perhaps, I might see her in the field or the garden, and then, there would be no great difficulty: it was the formal knocking at the door, with the prospect of being gravely ushered in, by Rachel, to the presence of a surprised, uncordial mistress, that so greatly disturbed me.

My wish, however, was not gratified. Mrs. Graham, herself, was not to be seen; but there was Arthur playing with his frolicsome little dog in the garden. I looked over the gate and called him to me. He wanted me to come in; but I told him I could not without his mother's leave.

"I'll go and ask her," said the child.

"No, no, Arthur, you mustn't do that, but if she's not engaged, just ask her to come here a minute: tell her I want to speak to her."

He ran to perform my bidding, and quickly returned with his mother. How lovely she looked with her dark ringlets streaming in the light summer breeze, her fair cheek slightly flushed, and her countenance radiant with smiles!—Dear Arthur! what did I not owe to you for this and every other happy meeting? Through him, I was at once delivered from all formality, and terror, and constraint. In love affairs, there is no mediator like a merry, simple-hearted child—ever ready to cement divided hearts, to span the un-friendly gulf of custom, to melt the ice of cold reserve, and overthrow the separating walls of dread formality and pride.

"Well, Mr. Markham, what is it?" said the young mother, accosting me with a pleasant smile.

"I want you to look at this book, and, if you please, to take it, and peruse it at your leisure. I make no apology for calling you out on such a lovely evening though it be for a matter of no greater importance."

"Tell him to come in, Mamma," said Arthur.

"Would you like to come in?" asked the lady.

"Yes; I should like to see your improvements in the garden."

"And how your sister's roots have prospered in my charge," added she, as she opened the gate.

And we sauntered through the garden, and talked of the flowers, the trees, and the book,—and then of other things. The evening was kind and genial, and so was my companion. By degrees, I waxed more warm and tender than, perhaps, I had ever been before; but still, I said nothing tangible, and she at-tempted no repulse; until, in passing a moss rose-tree that I had brought her some weeks since, in my sister's name, she plucked a beautiful half open bud and bade me give it to Rose.

"May I not keep it myself?" I asked.

"No; but here is another for you."

Instead of taking it quietly, I likewise took the hand that offered it, and looked into her face. She let me hold it for a moment, and I saw a flash of ecstatic brilliance in her eye, a glow of glad excitement on her face—I thought my hour of victory was come—but instantly, a painful recollection seemed to flash upon her; a cloud of anguish darkened her brow, a marble paleness blanched her cheek and lip; there seemed a moment of inward conflict,—and with a sudden effort, she withdrew her hand, and retreated a step or two back.

"Now Mr. Markham," said she, with a kind of desperate calmness, "I must tell you plainly, that I cannot do with this. I like your company, because I am alone here, and your conversation pleases me more than that of any other person; but if you cannot be content to regard me as a friend—a plain, cold, motherly, or sisterly friend, I must beg you to leave me now, and let me alone hereafter—in fact, we must be strangers for the future."

"I will, then—be your friend,—or brother, or anything you wish, if you will only let me continue to see you; but tell me why I cannot be anything more?"

There was a perplexed and thoughtful pause.

"Is it in consequence of some rash vow?"

"It is something of the kind," she answered—"some day I may tell you, but, at present you had better leave me; and never, Gilbert, put me to the painful necessity of repeating what I have just now said to you!"—she earnestly added, giving me her hand in serious kindness. How sweet, how musical my own name sounded in her mouth!

"I will not," I replied. "But you pardon *this* offence?"

"On condition that you never repeat it."

"And may I come to see you now and then?"

"Perhaps,—occasionally; provided you never abuse the privilege."

"I make no empty promises, but you shall see."

"The moment you do, our intimacy is at an end, that's all."

"And will you always call me Gilbert?—it sounds more sisterly, and it will serve to remind me of our contract."

She smiled, and once more bid me go,—and, at length, I judged it prudent to obey; and she re-entered the house, and I went down the hill. But as I went, the tramp of horses' hoofs fell on my ear, and broke the stillness of the dewy evening; and, looking towards the lane, I saw a solitary equestrian coming up. Inclining to dusk as it was, I knew him at a glance: it was Mr. Lawrence on his grey pony. I flew across the field—leaped the stone fence—and then walked down the lane to meet him. On seeing me, he suddenly drew in his little steed, and seemed inclined to turn back, but on second thought, apparently judged it better to continue his course as before. He accosted me with a slight bow, and, edging close to the wall, endeavoured to pass on—but I was not so minded: seizing his horse by the bridle, I exclaimed;—

"Now Lawrence, I will have this mystery explained! Tell me where you are going, and what you mean to do—at once, and distinctly!"

"Will you take your hand off the bridle?" said he, quietly—"you're hurting my pony's mouth."

"You and your pony be ——"

"What makes you so coarse and brutal, Markham? I'm quite ashamed of you."

"You answer my questions—before you leave this spot! I *will* know what you mean by this perfidious duplicity?"

"I shall answer *no* questions till you let go the bridle,—if you stand till morning."

"Now then," said I, unclosing my hand, but still standing before him.

"Ask me some other time, when you can speak like a gentleman," returned he, and he made an effort to pass me again; but I quickly re-captured the pony scarce less astonished than its master at such uncivil usage.

"Really Mr. Markham, this is *too* much!" said the latter. "Can I not go to see my tenant on matters of business, without being assaulted in this manner by—"

"This is no time for business sir!—I'll tell you, now, what I think of your conduct."

"You'd better defer your opinion to a more convenient season," interrupted he in a low tone—"here's the vicar."

And in truth, the vicar was just behind me, plodding homeward from some remote corner of his parish. I immediately released the squire; and he went on his way, saluting Mr. Millward as he passed.

"What, quarrelling Markham?" cried the latter, addressing himself to me,—"and about that young widow I doubt," he added, reproachfully shaking his head. "But let me tell you young man," (here he put his face into mine with an important, confidential air), "she's not worth it!" and he confirmed the assertion by a solemn nod.

"Mr. MILLWARD!" I exclaimed, in a tone of wrathful menace that made the reverend gentlemen look round—aghast—astounded at such unwonted insolence, and stare me in the face, with a look that plainly said: "What, this to me!" But I was too indignant to apologize, or to speak another word to him: I turned away, and hastened homewards, descending with rapid strides the steep, rough lane, and leaving him to follow as he pleased.

CHAPTER XI
THE VICAR AGAIN

YOU must suppose about three weeks passed over. Mrs. Graham and I were now established friends—or brother and sister as we rather chose to consider ourselves. She called me Gilbert, by my express desire, and I called her Helen, for I had seen that name written in her books. I seldom attempted to see her above twice a week; and still I made our meetings appear the result of accident as often as I could—for I found it necessary to be extremely careful—and, altogether, I behaved with such exceeding propriety that she never had occasion to reprove me once. Yet I could not but perceive that she was at times unhappy and dissatisfied with herself—or her position, and truly I myself was not quite contented with the latter: this assumption of brotherly nonchalance was very hard to sustain, and I often felt myself a most confounded hypocrite with it all; I saw too, or rather I felt, that, in spite of herself, "I was not indifferent to her,"[1] as the novel heroes modestly express it, and while I thankfully enjoyed my present good fortune, I could not fail to wish and hope for something better in future; but of course, I kept such dreams entirely to myself.

"Where are you going Gilbert?" said Rose, one evening, shortly after tea, when I had been busy with the farm all day.

"To take a walk," was the reply.

"Do you always brush your hat so carefully, and do your hair so nicely, and put on such smart new gloves when you take a walk?"

"Not always."

"You're going to Wildfell Hall, aren't you?"

"What makes you think so?"

"Because you look as if you were—but I wish you wouldn't go so often."

"Nonsense child! I don't go once in six weeks—what do you mean?"

"Well, but if I were you, I wouldn't have so much to do with Mrs. Graham."

"Why Rose, are you, too, giving in to the prevailing opinion?"

"No," returned she, hesitatingly—"but I've heard so much about her lately, both at the Wilsons and the vicarage;—and besides, mamma says, if she were a proper person, she would not be living there by herself—and don't you remember last winter, Gilbert, all that about the false name to the picture; and how she explained it—saying she had friends or acquaintances from whom she wished her present residence to be concealed, and that she was afraid of their tracing her out;—and then, how suddenly she started up and left the room when that person came—whom she took good care not to let us catch a glimpse of, and who Arthur, with such an air of mystery, told us was his mamma's friend?"

"Yes Rose, I remember it all; and I can forgive your uncharitable conclusions; for perhaps, if I did not know her myself, I should put all these things together, and believe the same as you do; but thank God, I do know her, and I should be unworthy the name of a man, if I could believe anything that was said against her, unless I heard it from her own lips.—I should as soon believe such things of you Rose."

"Oh, Gilbert!"

"Well, do you think I *could* believe anything of the kind,—whatever the Wilsons and Millwards dared to whisper?"

"I should hope *not* indeed!"

---

1   The "hero" to whom Gilbert refers is actually a heroine from another Brontë novel. Agnes Grey describes Rosalie Murray as "not so indifferent to him as she believes herself to be" (Anne Brontë, *Agnes Grey* [1847; London and Melbourne: J. M. Dent & Sons, 1985], 98).

"And why not?—Because I know you—well, and I know her just as well."

"Oh, no! you know nothing of her former life; and last year at this time, you did not know that such a person existed."

"No matter. There is such a thing as looking through a person's eyes into the heart, and learning more of the height, and breadth, and depth of another's soul in one hour, than it might take you a life time to discover, if he or she were not disposed to reveal it,—or if you had not the sense to understand it."

"Then you *are* going to see her this evening?"

"To be sure I am!"

"But what would mamma say, Gilbert?"

"Mamma needn't know."

"But she must know sometime, if you go on."

"Go on!—there's no going on in the matter—Mrs. Graham and I are two friends—and will be; and no man breathing shall hinder it,—or has a right to interfere between us."

"But if you knew how they talk, you would be more careful—for her sake as well as for your own. Jane Wilson thinks your visits to the old hall but another proof of her depravity—"

"Confound Jane Wilson!"

"And Eliza Millward is quite grieved about you."

"I hope she is."

"But I wouldn't if I were you."

"Wouldn't what?—How do they know that I go there?"

"There's nothing hid from them: they spy out everything."

"O, I never thought of this!—And so they dare to turn my friendship into food for further scandal against her!—That proves the falsehood of their other lies, at all events, if any proof were wanting.—Mind you contradict them Rose, whenever you can."

"But they don't speak openly to me about such things: it is only by hints and innuendoes, and by what I hear others say, that I know what they think."

"Well then, I won't go today, as it's getting latish. But oh, deuce take their cursed envenomed tongues!" I muttered in the bitterness of my soul.[1]

And just at that moment, the vicar entered the room: we had been too much absorbed in our conversation to observe his knock. After his customary, cheerful and fatherly greeting of Rose, who was rather a favourite with the old gentleman, he turned somewhat sternly to me:—

---

1   This is another instance of Gilbert quoting the Bible hyperbolically. See Job 7:11: "Therefore I will not refrain my mouth; I will speak in the anguish of my spirit; I will complain in the bitterness of my soul."

"Well sir!" said he, "you're quite a stranger. It is—let—me—see," he continued slowly, as he deposited his ponderous bulk in the arm chair that Rose officiously brought towards him, "it is just—six—weeks—by my reckoning, since you darkened—my—door!" He spoke it with emphasis, and struck his stick on the floor.

"Is it sir?" said I.

"Aye! It is so!" He added an affirmatory nod, and continued to gaze upon me with a kind of irate solemnity, holding his substantial stick between his knees, with his hands clasped upon its head.

"I have been busy," I said, for an apology was evidently demanded.

"Busy!" repeated he derisively.

"Yes; you know I've been getting in my hay; and now the harvest is beginning."

"Humph!"

Just then my mother came in, and created a diversion in my favour, by her loquacious and animated welcome of the reverend guest. She regretted deeply that he had not come a little earlier, in time for tea, but offered to have some immediately prepared, if he would do her the favour to partake of it.

"Not any for me, I thank you," replied he; "I shall be at home in a few minutes."

"Oh, but do stay and take a little! it will be ready in five minutes."

But he rejected the offer, with a majestic wave of the hand.

"I'll tell you what I'll take, Mrs. Markham," said he: "I'll take a glass of your excellent ale."

"With pleasure!" cried my mother, proceeding with alacrity to pull the bell and order the favoured beverage.

"I thought," continued he, "I'd just look in upon you as I passed, and taste your homebrewed ale. I've been to call on Mrs. Graham."

"Have you indeed?"

He nodded gravely, and added with awful emphasis—

"I thought it incumbent upon me to do so."

"Really!" ejaculated my mother.

"Why so, Mr. Millward?" asked I. He looked at me with some severity, and turning again to my mother, repeated—

"I thought it incumbent upon me!" and struck his stick on the floor again. My mother sat opposite, an awe-struck but admiring auditor.

"'Mrs. Graham,' said I," he continued shaking his head as he spoke, "'these are terrible reports!' 'What sir?' says she, affecting to be ignorant of my meaning. 'It is my—duty—as—your pastor,' said I, 'to tell you both everything that I myself see reprehensible in your conduct, and all I have reason to suspect, and what others tell me concerning you.'—So I told her!"

"You did sir?" cried I, starting from my seat, and striking my fist on the table. He merely glanced towards me, and continued—addressing his hostess;—

"It was a painful duty, Mrs. Markham—but I told her!"

"And how did she take it?" asked my mother.

"Hardened, I fear—hardened!" he replied, with a despondent shake of the head; "and at the same time, there was a strong display of unchastened, misdirected passions. She turned white in the face, and drew her breath through her teeth in a savage sort of way;—but she offered no extenuation or defence; and with a kind of shameless calmness—shocking indeed to witness, in one so young—as good as told me that my remonstrance was unavailing, and my pastoral advice quite thrown away upon her—nay, that my very *presence* was displeasing while I spoke such things. And I withdrew at length, too plainly seeing that nothing could be done—and sadly grieved to find her case so hopeless. But I am fully determined, Mrs. Markham, that *my* daughters—shall—not—consort with her. Do you adopt the same resolution with regard to yours!—As for your sons—as for *you*, young man," he continued, sternly turning to me.

"As for ME, sir,"—I began, but checked by some impediment in my utterance, and finding that my whole frame trembled with fury, I said no more—but took the wiser part of snatching up my hat and bolting from the room, slamming the door behind me, with a bang that shook the house to its foundations, and made my mother scream—and gave a momentary relief to my excited feelings.

The next minute saw me hurrying with rapid strides in the direction of Wildfell Hall—to what intent or purpose I could scarcely tell, but I must be moving somewhere, and no other goal would do—I must see her too, and speak to her—that was certain, but what to say or how to act, I had no definite idea. Such stormy thoughts—so many different resolutions crowded in upon me, that my mind was little better than a chaos of conflicting passions.

CHAPTER XII
A TÊTE-À-TÊTE AND A DISCOVERY

IN little more than twenty minutes, the journey was accomplished. I paused at the gate to wipe my streaming forehead, and recover my breath and some degree of composure. Already the rapid walking had somewhat mitigated my excitement; and with a firm and steady tread, I paced the garden walk. In passing the inhabited wing of the building, I caught a sight of Mrs. Graham, through the open window, slowly pacing up and down her lonely room.

She seemed agitated, and even dismayed at my arrival, as if she thought, I too was coming to accuse her. I had entered her presence intending to condole with her upon the wickedness of the world, and help her to abuse the vicar and his vile informants, but now I felt positively ashamed to mention the subject, and determined not to refer to it, unless she led the way.

"I am come at an unseasonable hour," said I, assuming a cheerfulness I did not feel, in order to reassure her; "but I won't stay many minutes."

She smiled upon me, faintly it is true, but most kindly—I had almost said thankfully, as her apprehensions were removed.

"How dismal you are, Helen! Why have you no fire?" I said, looking round on the gloomy apartment.

"It is summer yet," she replied.

"But *we always* have a fire in the evenings—if we can bear it;—and you, especially require one in this cold house and dreary room."

"You should have come a little sooner, and I would have had one lighted for you; but it is not worth while now—you won't stay many minutes you say, and Arthur is gone to bed."

"But I have a fancy for a fire, nevertheless. Will you order one, if I ring?"

"Why Gilbert, you don't look cold!" said she, smilingly regarding my face, which no doubt seemed warm enough.

"No," replied I, "but I want to see you comfortable before I go."

"Me comfortable!" repeated she, with a bitter laugh, as if there were something amusingly absurd in the idea. "It suits me better as it is," she added in a tone of mournful resignation.

But determined to have my own way I pulled the bell.

"There now, Helen!" I said, as the approaching steps of Rachel were heard in answer to the summons. There was nothing for it but to turn round and desire the maid to light the fire.

I owe Rachel a grudge to this day for the look she cast upon me ere she departed on her mission—the sour, suspicious, inquisitorial look that plainly demanded, "what are *you* here for, I wonder?" Her mistress did not fail to notice it, and a shade of uneasiness darkened her brow.

"You must not stay long Gilbert," said she, when the door was closed upon us.

"I'm not going to," said I, somewhat testily, though without a grain of anger in my heart against any one but the meddling old woman. "But Helen, I've something to say to you before I go."

"What is it?"

"No, not now—I don't know yet precisely what it is—or how to say it," replied I, with more truth than wisdom; and then, fearing lest she should turn me out of the house, I began talking about indifferent matters in order to gain time. Meanwhile Rachel came in to kindle the fire, which was soon effected by thrusting a red-hot poker between the bars of the grate, where the fuel was already disposed for ignition. She honoured me with another of her hard, inhospitable looks in departing, but, little moved thereby, I went on talking; and setting a chair for Mrs. Graham on one side of the hearth and one for myself on the other, I ventured to sit down, though half suspecting she would rather see me go.

In a little while we both relapsed into silence, and continued for several minutes gazing abstractedly into the fire—she intent upon her own sad thoughts, and I reflecting how delightful it would be to be seated thus beside her with no other presence to restrain our intercourse—not even that of Arthur, our mutual friend, without whom we had never met before—if only I could venture to speak my mind, and disburden my full heart of the feelings that had so long oppressed it, and which it now struggled to retain, with an effort that it seemed impossible to continue much longer,—and revolving the pros and cons for opening my heart to her there and then, and imploring a return of affection, the permission to regard her thenceforth as my own, and the right and the power to defend her from the calumnies of malicious tongues. On the one hand, I felt a new-born confidence in my powers of persuasion—a strong conviction that my own fervour of spirit would grant me eloquence—that my very determination—the absolute necessity for succeeding, that I felt must win me what I sought; while on the other, I feared to lose the ground I had already gained with so much toil and skill, and destroy all future hope by one rash effort, when time and patience might have won success. It was like setting my life upon the cast of a die; and yet, I was ready to resolve upon the attempt. At any rate I would entreat the explanation she had half promised to give me before: I would demand the reason of this hateful barrier, this mysterious impediment to my happiness and, as I trusted, to her own.

But while I considered in what manner I could best frame my request, my companion wakened from her reverie with a scarcely audible sigh, and looking towards the window where the blood-red harvest moon, just rising over one of the grim, fantastic evergreens, was shining in upon us, said,—

"Gilbert, it is getting late."

"I see," said I. "You want me to go, I suppose?"

"I think you ought. If my kind neighbours get to know of this visit—as no doubt they will—they will not turn it much to my advantage."

It was with what the Vicar would doubtless have called a savage sort of a smile that she said this.

"Let them turn it as they will," said I. "What are their thoughts to you or me, so long as we are satisfied with ourselves—and each other. Let them go to the deuce with their vile constructions, and their lying inventions!"

This outburst brought a flush of colour to her face.

"You have heard, then, what they say of me?"

"I heard some detestable falsehoods; but none but fools would credit them for a moment, Helen, so don't let them trouble you."

"I did not think Mr. Millward a fool, and he believes it all; but however little you may value the opinions of those about you—however little—you may esteem them as individuals, it is not pleasant to be looked upon as a liar and a hypocrite, to be thought to practice what you abhor, and to encourage the vices you would discountenance, to find your good intentions frustrated, and your hands crippled by your supposed unworthiness, and to bring disgrace on the principles you profess."

"True; and if I, by my thoughtlessness and selfish disregard to appearances, have at all assisted to expose you to these evils, let me entreat you not only to pardon me, but to enable me to make reparation; authorize me to clear your name from every imputation: give me the right to identify your honour with my own, and to defend your reputation as more precious than my life!"

"Are you hero enough to unite yourself to one whom you know to be suspected and despised by all around you, and identify your interests and your honour with hers? Think! it is a serious thing."

"I should be proud to do it Helen!—most happy—delighted beyond expression!—and if that be all the obstacle to our union, it is demolished, and you must—you shall be mine!"

And starting from my seat in a frenzy of ardour, I seized her hand and would have pressed it to my lips, but she as suddenly caught it away, exclaiming in the bitterness of intense affliction:—

"No, no, it is not all!"

"What is it then? You promised I should know some time, and—"

"You shall know some time—but not now—my head aches terribly," she said, pressing her hand to her forehead, "and I must have some repose—and surely, I have had misery enough today!" she added, almost wildly.

"But it could not harm you to tell it," I persisted: "it would ease your mind; and I should then know how to comfort you."

She shook her head despondingly. "If you knew all, you, too, would blame me—perhaps even more than I deserve—though I have cruelly wronged you," she added in a low murmur, as if she mused aloud.

"*You*, Helen? Impossible!"

"Yes, not willingly; for I did not know the strength and depth of your attachment—I thought—at least I endeavoured to think your regard for me was as cold and fraternal as you professed it to be."

"Or as yours?"

"Or as mine—ought to have been—of such a light and selfish, superficial nature that—"

"*There*, indeed, you wronged me."

"I know I did; and sometimes, I suspected it then; but I thought, upon the whole, there could be no great harm in leaving your fancies and your hopes to dream themselves to nothing—or flutter away to some more fitting object, while your friendly sympathies remained with me; but if I had known the depth of your regard, the generous disinterested affection you seem to feel—"

"*Seem*, Helen?"

"That you *do* feel, then, I would have acted differently."

"How? You *could* not have given me less encouragement, or treated me with greater severity than you did! And if you think you have wronged me by giving me your friendship, and occasionally admitting me to the enjoyment of your company and conversation, when all hopes of closer intimacy were vain—as indeed you always gave me to understand—if you think you have wronged me by this, you are mistaken; for such favours, in themselves alone, are not only delightful to my heart, but purifying, exalting, ennobling to my soul; and I would rather have your friendship than the love of any other woman in the world!"

Little comforted by this, she clasped her hands upon her knee, and glancing upward, seemed, in silent anguish, to implore divine assistance; then turning to me, she calmly said—

"Tomorrow, if you meet me on the moor about midday, I will tell you all you seek to know; and perhaps you will then see the necessity of discontinuing our intimacy—if, indeed, you do not willingly resign me as one no longer worthy of regard."

"I can safely answer no, to that: you cannot have such grave confessions to make—you must be trying my faith, Helen."

"No, no, no," she earnestly repeated—"I wish it were so! Thank Heaven;" she added, "I have no great crime to confess; but I have more than you will like to hear, or, perhaps, can readily excuse,—and more than I can tell you now; so let me entreat you to leave me!"

"I will; but answer me this one question first:—do you love me?"

"I will not answer it!"

"Then I will conclude you do; and so good night."

She turned from me to hide the emotion she could not quite control; but I took her hand and fervently kissed it.

"Gilbert, *do* leave me!" she cried, in a tone of such thrilling anguish that I felt it would be cruel to disobey.

But I gave one look back before I closed the door, and saw her leaning forward on the table, with her hands pressed against her eyes, sobbing convulsively; yet I withdrew in silence. I felt that to obtrude my consolations on her then would only serve to aggravate her sufferings.

To tell you all the questionings and conjectures—the fears, and hopes, and wild emotions that jostled and chased each other through my mind as I descended the hill, would almost fill a volume in itself. But before I was half way down a sentiment of strong sympathy for her I had left behind me had displaced all other feelings, and seemed imperatively to draw me back: I began to think, "Why am I hurrying so fast in this direction? Can I find comfort or consolation—peace, certainty, contentment, all—or anything that I want at home? and can I leave all perturbation, sorrow and anxiety behind me there?"

And I turned round to look at the old Hall. There was little besides the chimneys visible above my contracted horizon. I walked back to get a better view of it. When it rose in sight, I stood still a moment to look, and then continued moving towards the gloomy object of attraction. Something called me nearer—nearer still—and why not, pray? Might I not find more benefit in the contemplation of that venerable pile with the full moon in the cloudless heaven shining so calmly above it—with that warm yellow lustre peculiar to an August night—and the mistress of my soul within, than in returning to my home where all comparatively was light, and life, and cheerfulness, and therefore inimical to me in my present frame of mind,—and the more so that its inmates all were more or less imbued with that detestable belief the very *thought* of which made my blood boil in my veins—and how could I endure to hear it openly declared—or cautiously insinuated—which was worse?—I had had trouble enough already, with some babbling fiend that would keep whispering in my ear, "It may be true," till I had shouted aloud, "It is false! I defy you to make me suppose it!"

I could see the red fire-light dimly gleaming from her parlour window. I went up to the garden wall, and stood leaning over it, with my eyes fixed upon the lattice, wondering what she was doing, thinking, or suffering now, and wishing I could speak to her but one word, or even catch one glimpse of her, before I went.

I had not thus looked, and wished, and wondered long, before I vaulted over the barrier, unable to resist the temptation of taking one glance through the window, just to see if she were more composed than when we parted;—and if I found her still in deep distress, perhaps I might venture to attempt a word of comfort—to utter one of the many things I should have said before, instead of aggravating her sufferings by my stupid impetuosity. I looked. Her chair was vacant: so was the room. But at that moment some one opened the outer door, and a voice—*her* voice—said,—

"Come out—I want to see the moon, and breathe the evening air: they will do me good—if anything will."

Here, then, were she and Rachel coming to take a walk in the garden. I wished myself safe back over the wall. I stood, however, in the shadow of the tall holly bush, which, standing between the window and the porch, at present screened me from observation, but did not prevent me from seeing two figures come forth into the moonlight; Mrs. Graham followed by another—*not* Rachel, but a young man, slender and rather tall. Oh heavens, how my temples throbbed! Intense anxiety darkened my sight; but I thought—yes, and the voice confirmed it—it was Mr. Lawrence.

"You should not let it worry you so much, Helen," said he; "I will be more cautious in future; and in time—"

I did not hear the rest of the sentence; for he walked close beside her and spoke so gently that I could not catch the words. My heart was splitting with hatred; but I listened intently for her reply. I heard it plainly enough.

"But I must leave this place, Frederick," she said—"I never can be happy here,—nor anywhere else, indeed," she added, with a mirthless laugh,—"but I cannot rest here."

"But where could you find a better place?" replied he,—"so secluded— so near me, if you think anything of that."

"Yes," interrupted she, "it is all I could wish, if they could only have left me alone."

"But wherever you go, Helen, there will be the same sources of annoyance. I cannot consent to lose you: I must go with you, or come to you; and there are meddling fools elsewhere, as well as here."

While thus conversing, they had sauntered slowly past me, down the walk, and I heard no more of their discourse; but I saw him put his arm round her waist, while she lovingly rested her hand on his shoulder;—and then, a tremulous darkness obscured my sight, my heart sickened and my head burned like fire, I half rushed, half staggered from the spot where horror had kept me rooted, and leaped or tumbled over the wall—I hardly know which—but I know that, afterwards, like a passionate child, I dashed myself on the ground and lay there in a paroxysm of anger and despair—how long, I cannot undertake to say; but it must have been a considerable time; for when, having partially relieved myself by a torrent of tears, and looked up at the moon, shining so calmly and carelessly on, as little influenced by my misery as I was by its peaceful radiance, and earnestly prayed for death or forgetfulness, I had risen and journeyed homewards—little regarding the way, but carried instinctively by my feet to the door, I found it bolted against me, and every one in bed except my mother, who hastened to answer my impatient knocking, and received me with a shower of questions and rebukes.

"Oh, Gilbert, how *could* you do so? Where *have* you been? Do come in and take your supper—I've got it all ready, though you don't deserve it, for keeping me in such a fright, after the strange manner you left the house this evening. Mr. Millward was quite—Bless the boy! how ill he looks! Oh, gracious! what is the matter?"

"Nothing, nothing—give me a candle."

"But won't you take some supper?"

"No, I want to go to bed," said I, taking a candle and lighting it at the one she held in her hand.

"Oh, Gilbert, how you tremble!" exclaimed my anxious parent. "How white you look! Do tell me what it is? Has anything happened?"

"It's nothing!" cried I, ready to stamp with vexation because the candle would not light. Then, suppressing my irritation, I added, "I've been walking too fast, that's all. Good night," and marched off to bed, regardless of the "Walking too fast! where have you been?" that was called after me from below.

My mother followed me to the very door of my room with her questionings and advice concerning my health and my conduct; but I implored her to let me alone till morning; and she withdrew, and at length, I had the satisfaction to hear her close her own door. There was no sleep for me however, that night, as I thought; and instead of attempting to solicit it, I employed myself in rapidly pacing the chamber—having first removed my boots lest my mother should hear me. But the boards creaked, and she was watchful. I had not walked above a quarter of an hour before she was at the door again.

"Gilbert, why are you not in bed—you said you wanted to go?"

"Confound it! I'm going," said I.

"But why are you so long about it? you must have something on your mind—"

"For heaven's sake, let me alone, and get to bed yourself!"

"Can it be that Mrs. Graham that distresses you so?"

"No, no, I tell you—it's nothing!"

"I wish to goodness it mayn't!" murmured she with a sigh, as she returned to her own apartment, while I threw myself on the bed, feeling most undutifully disaffected towards her for having deprived me of what seemed the only shadow of a consolation that remained, and chained me to that wretched couch of thorns.

Never did I endure so long, so miserable a night as that. And yet, it was not wholly sleepless: towards morning my distracting thoughts began to lose all pretensions to coherency, and shape themselves into confused and feverish dreams, and, at length, there followed an interval of unconscious slumber. But then the dawn of bitter recollection that succeeded—the waking to find life a blank, and worse than a blank—teeming with torment and misery—not a mere barren wilderness, but full of thorns and briars—to find myself deceived, duped, hopeless, my affections trampled upon, my angel not an angel, and my friend a fiend incarnate—it was worse than if I had not slept at all.

It was a dull, gloomy morning, the weather had changed like my prospects, and the rain was pattering against the window. I rose nevertheless, and went out; not to look after the farm, though that would serve as my excuse, but to cool my brain, and regain, if possible, a sufficient degree of composure to meet the family at the morning meal without exciting inconvenient remarks. If I got a wetting, that, in conjunction with a pretended over-exertion before breakfast, might excuse my sudden loss of appetite; and if a cold ensued, the severer the better, it would help to account for the sullen moods and moping melancholy likely to cloud my brow for long enough.

CHAPTER XIII
A RETURN TO DUTY

"MY dear Gilbert! I wish you *would* try to be a little more amiable," said my mother, one morning after some display of unjustifiable ill humour on my part. "You say there is nothing the matter with you, and nothing has happened to grieve you, and yet, I never *saw* any one so altered as you within these last few days: you haven't a good word for any body—friends and strangers, equals and inferiors—it's all the same. I do wish you'd try to check it."

"Check what?"

"Why your strange temper. You don't know *how* it spoils you. I'm sure a finer disposition than yours, by nature, could not be, if you'd let it have fair play; so you've no excuse *that* way."

While she thus remonstrated, I took up a book, and laying it open on the table before me, pretended to be deeply absorbed in its perusal; for I was equally unable to justify myself, and unwilling to acknowledge my errors; and I wished to have nothing to say on the matter. But my excellent parent went on lecturing, and then came to coaxing, and began to stroke my hair; and I was getting to feel quite a good boy, but my mischievous brother who was idling about the room, revived my corruption by suddenly calling out:—

"Don't touch him mother! he'll bite! He's a very tiger in human form. I've given him up, for my part—fairly disowned him—cast him off, root and branch. It's as much as my life is worth to come within six yards of him. The other day he nearly fractured my skull for singing a pretty, inoffensive love song, on purpose to amuse him."

"Oh, Gilbert! how could you?" exclaimed my mother.

"I told you to hold your noise first, you know Fergus," said I.

"Yes, but when I assured you it was no trouble, and went on with the next verse, thinking you might like it better, you clutched me by the shoulder and dashed me away, right against the wall there, with such force, that I thought I had bitten my tongue in two, and expected to see the place plastered with my brains; and when I put my hand to my head and found my skull not broken, I thought it was a miracle and no mistake. But poor fellow!" added he, with a sentimental sigh—"his heart's broken—that's the truth of it—and his head's—"

"Will you be silent NOW?" cried I, starting up, and eyeing the fellow so fiercely that my mother, thinking I meant to inflict some grievous bodily injury, laid her hand on my arm, and besought me to let him alone, and he walked leisurely out, with his hands in his pockets, singing provokingly—"Shall I because a woman's fair,"[1] &c.

"I'm not going to defile my fingers with him," said I, in answer to the maternal intercession. "I wouldn't touch him with the tongs."

I now recollected that I had business with Robert Wilson, concerning the purchase of a certain field adjoining my farm—a business I had been putting off from day to day; for I had no interest in anything now; and besides, I was misanthropically inclined, and, moreover, had a particular objection to meeting Jane Wilson or her mother; for though I had too good reason, now, to credit their reports concerning Mrs. Graham, I did not like *them* a bit the better for it—or Eliza Millward either—and the thoughts of meeting them was the more repugnant to me, that I could not, now, defy their seeming calumnies and triumph in my own convictions as before. But today, I determined to make an effort to return to my duty. Though I found no pleasure in it, it would be less irksome than idleness—at all events it would be more profitable. If life promised no enjoyment within my vocation, at least it offered no allurements out of it; and henceforth, I would put my shoulder to the wheel and toil away, like any poor drudge of a cart-horse that was fairly broken in to its labour, and plod through life, not wholly useless if not agreeable, and uncomplaining if not contented with my lot.

Thus resolving, with a kind of sullen resignation, if such a term may be allowed, I wended my way to Ryecote Farm, scarcely expecting to find its owner within at this time of day, but hoping to learn in what part of the premises he was most likely to be found.

Absent he was, but expected home in a few minutes; and I was desired to step into the parlour and wait. Mrs. Wilson was busy in the kitchen, but the room was not empty; and I scarcely checked an involuntary recoil as I entered it; for there sat Miss Wilson chattering with Eliza Millward. However, I determined to be cool and civil. Eliza seemed to have made the same resolution on her part. We had not met since the evening of the tea party; but there was no visible emotion either of pleasure or pain, no attempt at pathos,

---

1   George Wither's (1588–1667) seventeenth-century poem, "Shall I, wasting in despair, / Die, because a woman's fair," a small portion of the much longer *Fair Virtue, The Mistress of Philarete*, which was first published in 1622.

no display of injured pride: she was cool in temper, civil in demeanour. There was even an ease and cheerfulness about her air and manner that I made no pretension to; but there was a depth of malice in her too expressive eye, that plainly told me I was not forgiven; for, though she no longer hoped to win me to herself, she still hated her rival, and evidently delighted to wreak her spite on me. On the other hand, Miss Wilson was as affable and courteous as heart could wish, and though I was in no very conversable humour myself, the two ladies between them managed to keep up a pretty continuous fire of small talk. But Eliza took advantage of the first convenient pause to ask if I had lately seen Mrs. Graham, in a tone of merely casual inquiry, but with a sidelong glance—intended to be playfully mischievous—really, brimful and running over with malice.

"Not lately," I replied, in a careless tone, but sternly repelling her odious glances with my eyes; for I was vexed to feel the colour mounting to my forehead, despite my strenuous efforts to appear unmoved.

"What! are you beginning to tire already? I thought so noble a creature would have power to attach you for a year at least!"

"I would rather not speak of her now."

"Ah! then you are convinced at last, of your mistake—you have at length discovered that your divinity is not quite the immaculate—"

"I desired you not to speak of her, Miss Eliza."

"Oh, I beg your pardon! I perceive Cupid's arrows have been too sharp for you: the wounds being more than skin-deep, are not yet healed and bleed afresh at every mention of the loved one's name."

"Say rather," interposed Miss Wilson, "that Mr. Markham feels that name is unworthy to be mentioned in the presence of right-minded females. I wonder Eliza, you should think of referring to that unfortunate person—you might know the mention of her would be anything but agreeable to any one here present."

How could this be borne? I rose and was about to clap my hat upon my head and burst away, in wrathful indignation, from the house; but recollecting—just in time to save my dignity—the folly of such a proceeding, and how it would only give my fair tormentors a merry laugh at my expense, for the sake of one I acknowledged in my own heart to be unworthy of the slightest sacrifice—though the ghost of my former reverence and love so hung about me still, that I could not bear to hear her name aspersed by others—I merely walked to the window, and having spent a few seconds in vengeably biting my lips, and sternly repressing the passionate heavings of my chest, I observed to Miss Wilson, that I could see nothing of her brother, and added that as my time was precious, it would perhaps be better to call again tomorrow, at some time when I should be sure to find him at home.

"Oh no!" said she, "if you wait a minute, he will be sure come; for he has business at L——" (that was our market town) "and will require a little refreshment before he goes."

I submitted accordingly, with the best grace I could; and happily, I had not long to wait. Mr. Wilson soon arrived, and indisposed for business as I was at that moment, and little as I cared for the field or its owner, I forced my attention to the matter in hand, with very creditable determination, and quickly concluded the bargain—perhaps more to the thrifty farmer's satisfaction, than he cared to acknowledge. Then, leaving him to the discussion of his substantial "refreshment," I gladly quitted the house, and went to look after my reapers.

Leaving them busy at work on the side of the valley, I ascended the hill, intending to visit a cornfield in the more elevated regions, and see when it would be ripe for the sickle. But I did *not* visit it that day; for, as I approached, I beheld at no great distance, Mrs. Graham and her son coming down in the opposite direction. They saw me; and Arthur, already, was running to meet me; but I immediately turned back and walked steadily homeward; for I had fully determined never to encounter his mother again; and regardless of the shrill voice in my ear, calling upon me to "wait a moment," I pursued the even tenor of my way; and he soon relinquished the pursuit as hopeless, or was called away by his mother. At all events, when I looked back, five minutes after, not a trace of either was to be seen.

This incident agitated and disturbed me most unaccountably—unless you would account for it by saying that Cupid's arrows not only had been too sharp for me, but they were barbed and deeply rooted, and I had not yet been able to wrench them from my heart. However that be, I was rendered doubly miserable for the remainder of the day.

CHAPTER XIV
AN ASSAULT

NEXT morning, I bethought me, I, too, had business at L——; so I mounted my horse and set forth on the expedition, soon after breakfast. It was a dull, drizzly day; but that was no matter: it was all the more suitable to my frame of mind. It was likely to be a lonely journey; for it was no market-day, and the road I traversed was little frequented at any other time; but that suited me all the better too.

As I trotted along, however, chewing the cud of—*bitter* fancies,[1] I heard another horse at no great distance behind me; but I never conjectured who

1 Shakespeare, *As You Like It*: "Chewing the food of sweet and bitter fancy" (IV.iii.102).

the rider might be—or troubled my head about him, till on slackening my pace to ascend a gentle acclivity—or rather suffering my horse to slacken its pace into a lazy walk; for, lost in my own reflections, I was letting it jog on as leisurely as it thought proper—I lost ground, and my fellow traveler overtook me. He accosted me by name; for it was no stranger—it was Mr. Lawrence! Instinctively the fingers of my whip-hand tingled, and grasped their charge with convulsive energy; but I restrained the impulse, and answering his salutation with a nod, attempted to push on; but he pushed on beside me and began to talk about the weather and the crops. I gave the briefest possible answers to his queries and observations, and fell back. He fell back too, and asked if my horse was lame. I replied, with a *look*—at which he placidly smiled.

I was as much astonished as exasperated at this singular pertinacity and imperturbable assurance on his part. I had thought the circumstances of our last meeting would have such an impression on his mind as to render him cold and distant ever after: instead of that he appeared, not only to have forgotten all former offences, but to be impenetrable to all present incivilities. Formerly, the slightest hint, or mere fancied coldness in tone or glance, had sufficed to repulse him: now, positive rudeness could not drive him away. Had he heard of my disappointment; and was he come to witness the result, and triumph in my despair? I grasped my whip with more determined energy than before—but still forbore to raise it, and rode on in silence, waiting for some more tangible cause of offence, before I opened the floodgates of my soul, and poured out the dammed up fury that was foaming and swelling within.

"Markham," said he, in his usual quiet tone, "why do you quarrel with your friends, because you have been disappointed in one quarter? You have found your hopes defeated; but how am *I* to blame for it? I warned you beforehand, you know, but you would not—"

He said no more; for, impelled by some fiend at my elbow, I had seized my whip by the small end, and—swift and sudden as a flash of lightning—brought the other down upon his head. It was not without a feeling of savage satisfaction that I beheld the instant, deadly pallor that overspread his face, and the few red drops that trickled down his forehead, while he reeled a moment in his saddle, and then fell backward to the ground. The pony, surprised to be so strangely relieved of its burden, started and capered, and kicked a little, and then made use of its freedom to go and crop the grass of the hedge bank; while its master lay as still and silent as a corpse. Had I killed him?—an icy hand seemed to grasp my heart and check its pulsation, as I bent over him, gazing with breathless intensity upon the ghastly, upturned face. But no; he moved his eyelids and uttered a slight groan. I breathed again—he was only stunned by the fall. It served him right—it would teach him better manners in future. Should I help him to his horse? No. For any other combination of offences I would; but his were too unpardonable. He might mount it himself, if he liked—in a while: already he was beginning to stir and look about him—and there it was for him, quietly browsing on the road-side.

So with a muttered execration, I left the fellow to his fate, and clapping spurs to my own horse, galloped away, excited by a combination of feelings it would not be easy to analyse; and perhaps, if I did so, the result would not be very creditable to my disposition; for I am not sure that a species of exultation in what I had done, was not one principal concomitant.

Shortly, however, the effervescence began to abate, and not many minutes elapsed before I had turned and gone back to look after the fate of my victim. It was no generous impulse—no kind relentings that led me to this—nor even the fear of what might be the consequences to myself, if I finished my assault upon the squire by leaving him thus neglected, and exposed to further injury; it was, simply, the voice of conscience; and I took great credit to myself for attending so promptly to its dictates—and judging the merit of the deed by the sacrifice it cost, I was not far wrong.

Mr. Lawrence and his pony had both altered their positions, in some degree. The pony had wandered eight or ten yards farther away; and he had managed, somehow, to remove himself from the middle of the road: I found him seated in a recumbent position on the bank,—looking very white and sickly still, and holding his cambric handkerchief (now more red than white) to his head. It must have been a powerful blow; but half the credit—or the blame of it (which you please) must be attributed to the whip, which was garnished with a massive horse's head of plated metal. The grass, being sodden with rain, afforded the young gentleman a rather inhospitable couch; his clothes were considerably bemired; and his hat was rolling in the mud, on the other side of the road. But his thoughts seemed chiefly bent upon his pony, on which he was wistfully gazing—half in helpless anxiety, and half in hopeless abandonment to his fate.

I dismounted however, and having fastened my own animal to the nearest tree, first picked up his hat, intending to clap it on his head; but either he considered his head unfit for a hat, or the hat, in its present condition, unfit for his head; for shrinking away the one, he took the other from my hand, and scornfully cast it aside.

"It's good enough for *you*," I muttered.

My next good office was to catch his pony and bring it to him, which was soon accomplished; for the beast was quiet enough in the main, and only winced and flirted a trifle, till I got a hold of the bridle,—but then, I must see him in the saddle.

"Here, you fellow—scoundrel—dog—give me your hand, and I'll help you to mount."

No; he turned from me in disgust. I attempted to take him by the arm. He shrank away as if there had been contamination in my touch.

"What, you won't? Well! you may sit there till doomsday, for what I care. But I suppose you don't want to lose all the blood in your body—I'll just condescend to bind that up for you."

"Let me alone, if you please."

"Humph! with all my heart. You may go to the d—l if you choose—and say I sent you."

But before I abandoned him to his fate, I flung his pony's bridle over a stake in the hedge, and threw him my handkerchief, as his own was now saturated with blood. He took it and cast it back to me, in abhorrence and contempt, with all the strength he could muster. It wanted but this to fill the measure of his offences. With execrations not loud but deep,[1] I left him to live or die as he could, well satisfied that I had done *my* duty in attempting to save him—but forgetting how I had erred in bringing him into such a condition, and how insultingly my after services had been offered—and sullenly prepared to meet the consequences if he should choose to say I had attempted to murder him,—which I thought not unlikely, as it seemed probable he was actuated by some such spiteful motives in so perseveringly refusing my assistance.

Having remounted my horse, I just looked back to see how he was getting on, before I rode away. He had risen from the ground, and grasping his pony's mane, was attempting to resume his seat in the saddle; but scarcely had he put his foot in the stirrup, when a sickness or dizziness seemed to overpower him: he leant forward a moment, with his head drooped on the animal's back, and then made one more effort, which proving ineffectual, he sank back on to the bank, where I left him, reposing his head on the oozy turf; and, to all appearance, as calmly reclining as if he had been taking his rest on the sofa at home.

I ought to have helped him in spite of himself—to have bound up the wound he was unable to stanch, and insisted upon getting him on to his horse and seeing him safe home; but, besides my bitter indignation against himself, there was the question what to say to his servants,—and what to my own family. Either I should have to acknowledge the deed, which would set me down as a madman, unless I acknowledged the motive too— and that seemed impossible,—or I must get up a lie, which seemed equally out of the question—especially as Mr. Lawrence would probably reveal the whole truth, and thereby bring me to tenfold disgrace,—unless I were villain enough, presuming on the absence of witnesses, to persist in my own version of the case, and make him out a still greater scoundrel than he was.

---

1   Shakespeare, *Macbeth*, "Curses, not loud but deep" (V.iii.27).

No; he had only received a cut above the temple, and perhaps, a few bruises from the fall, or the hoofs of his own pony: that could not kill him if he lay there half the day; and, if he could not help himself, surely some one would be coming by: it would be impossible that a whole day should pass and no one traverse the road but ourselves. As for what he might choose to say hereafter, I would take my chance about it: if he told lies, I would contradict him; if he told the truth, I would bear it as I best could. I was not *obliged* to enter into explanations, further than I thought proper. Perhaps, he might choose to be silent on the subject, for fear of raising enquiries as to the cause of the quarrel, and drawing the public attention to his connection with Mrs. Graham, which, whether for her sake or his own, he seemed so very desirous to conceal.

Thus reasoning, I trotted away to the town, where I duly transacted my business, and performed various little commissions for my mother and Rose, with very laudable exactitude, considering the different circumstances of the case. In returning home, I was troubled with sundry misgivings about the unfortunate Lawrence. The question, what if I should find him lying, still on the damp earth, fairly dying of cold and exhaustion—or already stark and chill?—thrust itself most unpleasantly upon my mind, and the appalling possibility pictured itself with painful vividness to my imagination as I approached the spot where I had left him. But no; thank Heaven, both man and horse were gone, and nothing was left to witness against me but two objects—unpleasant enough in themselves, to be sure, and presenting a very ugly, not to say murderous, appearance—in one place, the hat saturated with rain and coated with mud, indented and broken above the brim by that villainous whip-handle; in another, the crimson handkerchief, soaking in a deeply tinctured pool of water—for much rain had fallen in the interim.

Bad news fly fast: it was hardly four o'clock when I got home, but my mother gravely accosted me with—

"Oh, Gilbert!—*Such* an accident! Rose has been shopping in the village, and she's heard that Mr. Lawrence has been thrown from his horse and brought home dying!"

This shocked me a trifle, as you may suppose; but I was comforted to hear that he had frightfully fractured his skull and broken a leg; for, assured of the falsehood of this, I trusted the rest of the story was equally exaggerated; and when I heard my mother and sister so feelingly deploring his condition, I had considerable difficulty in preventing myself from telling them the real extent of the injuries, as far as I knew them.

"You must go and see him tomorrow," said my mother.

"Or today," suggested Rose: "there's plenty of time; and you can have the pony, your horse is tired. Won't you Gilbert—as soon as you've had something to eat?"

"No, no—How can we tell that it isn't all a false report? It's highly im——"

"Oh, I'm sure it isn't; for the village is all alive about it; and I saw two people that had seen others that had seen the man that found him. That sounds far fetched; but it isn't so, when you think of it."

"Well, but Lawrence is a good rider; it is not likely he would fall from his horse at all; and if he did, it is highly improbable he should break his bones in that way. It must be a gross exaggeration at least."

"No, but the horse kicked him—or something."

"What, his quiet little pony?"

"How do you know it was that?"

"He seldom rides any other."

"At any rate," said my mother, "you will call tomorrow. Whether it be true or false, exaggerated or otherwise we shall like to know how he is."

"Fergus may go."

"Why not you?"

"He has more time: I am busy just now."

"Oh! but Gilbert, how can you be so composed about it? You won't mind business, for an hour or two, in a case of this sort—when your friend is at the point of death!"

"He is *not*, I tell you!"

"For anything you know, he *may* be: you can't tell till you have seen him.—At all events, he must have met with some terrible accident, and you ought to see him: he'll take it very unkind of you if you don't."

"Confound it! I can't. He and I have not been on good terms, of late."

"O my *dear* boy! Surely, surely, you are not so unforgiving as to carry your little differences to such a length as—"

"Little differences, indeed!" I muttered.

"Well, but only remember the occasion! Think how—"

"Well, well, don't bother me now—I'll see about it," I replied.

And my seeing about it, was to send Fergus next morning, with my mother's compliments, to make the requisite enquiries: for, of course, my going was out of the question—or sending a message, either. He brought back intelligence that the young squire was laid up with the complicated evils of a broken head and certain contusions (occasioned by a fall—of which he did not trouble himself to relate the particulars—and the subsequent misconduct of his horse), and a severe cold, the consequence of lying on the wet ground in the rain; but there were no broken bones, and no immediate prospects of dissolution.

It was evident then, that, for Mrs. Graham's sake, it was not his intention to criminate me.

CHAPTER XV
AN ENCOUNTER AND ITS CONSEQUENCES

THAT day was rainy like its predecessor; but towards evening it began to clear up a little, and the next morning was fair and promising. I was out on the hill with the reapers. A light wind swept over the corn; and all nature laughed in the sunshine. The lark was rejoicing among the silvery floating clouds. The late rain had so sweetly freshened and cleared the air, and washed the sky, and left such glittering gems on branch and blade, that not even the farmers could have the heart to blame it. But no ray of sunshine could reach my heart, no breeze could freshen it; nothing could fill the void my faith, and hope, and joy in Helen Graham had left, or drive away the keen regrets, and bitter dregs of lingering love that still oppressed it.

While I stood, with folded arms, abstractedly gazing on the undulating swell of the corn not yet disturbed by the reapers, something gently pulled my skirts, and a small voice, no longer welcome to my ears, aroused me with the startling words:—

"Mr. Markham, mamma wants you."

"Wants *me*, Arthur?"

"Yes. Why do you look so queer?" said he, half laughing, half frightened at the unexpected aspect of my face in suddenly turning towards him—"and why have you kept so long away?—Come!—Won't you come?"

"I'm busy just now," I replied, scarce knowing what to answer.

He looked up in childish bewilderment; but before I could speak again, the lady herself was at my side.

"Gilbert, I *must* speak with you!" said she in a tone of suppressed vehemence.

I looked at her pale cheek and glittering eye,[1] but answered nothing.

"Only for a moment," pleaded she. "Just step aside into this other field," she glanced at the reapers, some of whom were directing looks of impertinent curiosity towards her—"I won't keep you a minute."

I accompanied her through the gap.

"Arthur, darling, run and gather those bluebells," said she, pointing to some that were gleaming, at some distance, under the hedge along which we walked. The child hesitated, as if unwilling to quit my side. "Go, love!" repeated she more urgently, and in a tone, which, though not unkind, demanded prompt obedience, and obtained it.

---

1 Gilbert's description of her "glittering eye" and Helen's desperate need to speak to him recalls the description of the insistent mariner in Samuel Taylor Coleridge's (1772–1834) *The Rime of the Ancient Mariner* (1798).

"Well, Mrs. Graham?" said I, calmly and coldly; for, though I saw she was miserable, and pitied her, I felt glad to have it in my power to torment her.

She fixed her eyes upon me with a look that pierced me to the heart;—and yet, it made me smile.

"I don't ask the reason of this change, Gilbert," said she with bitter calmness.—"I know it too well; but though I could see myself suspected and condemned by every one else, and bear it with calmness, I cannot endure it from you.—Why did you not come to hear my explanation on the day I appointed to give it?"

"Because, I happened, in the interim, to learn all you would have told me,—and a trifle more I imagine."

"Impossible, for I would have told you all!" cried she, passionately.—"But I won't now, for I see you are not worthy of it!"

And her pale lips quivered with agitation.

"Why not, may I ask?"

She repelled my mocking smile with a glance of scornful indignation.

"Because, you never understood me, or you would not soon have listened to my traducers—my confidence would be misplaced in you—you are not the man I thought you.—Go! I won't care *what* you think of me!"

She turned away, and I went; for I thought that would torment her as much as anything; and I believe I was right; for, looking back a minute after, I saw her turn half round, as if hoping or expecting to find me still beside her; and then she stood still, and cast one look behind. It was a look less expressive of anger than of bitter anguish and despair; but I immediately assumed an aspect of indifference, and affected to be gazing carelessly round me, and I suppose she went on; for after lingering awhile to see if she would come back or call, I ventured one more glance, and saw her a good way off, moving rapidly up the field with little Arthur running by her side and apparently talking as he went; but she kept her face averted from him, as if to hide some uncontrollable emotion. And I returned to my business.

But I soon began to regret my precipitancy in leaving her so soon. It was evident she loved me—probably, she was tired of Mr. Lawrence, and wished to exchange him for me; and if I had loved and reverenced her less to begin with, the preference might have gratified and amused me; but now, the contrast between her outward seeming and her inward mind, as I supposed,—between my former and my present opinion of her, was so harrowing—so distressing to my feelings, that it swallowed up every lighter consideration.

But still, I was curious to know what sort of an explanation she would have given me,—or would give now, if I pressed her for it—how much she would confess, and how she would endeavour to excuse herself. I longed to know what to despise, and what to admire in her, how much to pity, and how much to hate; and, what was more, I *would* know. I would see her once more, and fairly satisfy myself in what light to regard her, before we parted. Lost to me she was, for ever, of course; but still, I could not bear to think that we had parted, for the last time, with so much unkindness and misery on both sides. That last look of hers had sunk into my heart; I could not forget it.—But what a fool I was!—Had she not deceived me, injured me—blighted my happiness for life?—"Well I'll see her, however," was my concluding resolve,—"but not today: today and tonight, she may think upon her sins, and be as miserable as she will: tomorrow, I will see her once again, and know something more about her. The interview may be serviceable to her, or it may not.—At any rate, it will give a breath of excitement to the life she has doomed to stagnation, and may calm with certainty some agitating thoughts."

I did go on the morrow; but not till towards evening, after the business of the day was concluded, that is between six and seven; and the westering sun was gleaming redly on the old hall, and flaming in the latticed windows, as I reached it, imparting to the place a cheerfulness not its own. I need not dilate upon the feelings with which I approached the shrine of my former divinity—that spot teeming with a thousand delightful recollections and glorious dreams—all darkened now, by one disastrous truth.

Rachel admitted me into the parlour, and went to call her mistress, for she was not there; but there was her desk left open on the little round table beside the high-backed chair, with a book laid upon it. Her limited but choice collection of books was almost as familiar to me as my own; but this volume I had not seen before. I took it up. It was Sir Humphrey Davy's "Last days of a Philosopher,"[1] and on the first leaf was written,—"Frederick Lawrence." I closed the book, but kept it in my hand, and stood facing the door, with my back to the fireplace, calmly waiting her arrival; for I did not doubt she would come. And soon I heard her step in the hall. My heart was beginning to throb, but I checked it with an internal rebuke, and maintained my composure outwardly, at least. She entered, calm, pale, collected.

"To what am I indebted for this favour, Mr. Markham?" said she, with such severe but quiet dignity as almost disconcerted me; but I answered with a smile, and impudently enough:—

"Well, I am come to hear your explanation."

"I told you I would not give it," said she. "I said you were unworthy of my confidence."

"Oh, very well," replied I, moving to the door.

---

1   Gilbert's visit to Wildfell Hall occurs in August of 1828, yet Sir Humphrey Davy's (1778–1829) *Consolations in Travel, or The Last Days of a Philosopher* was not published until 1830. For a humorous, contemporary mention of Brontë's anachronism, see *The Literary World*'s note in their review of the novel (Appendix B4).

"Stay a moment," said she. "This is the last time I shall see you: don't go just yet."

I remained, awaiting her further commands.

"Tell me," resumed she, "on what grounds you believe these things against me; who told you; and what did they say?"

I paused a moment. She met my eye as unflinchingly as if her bosom had been steeled with conscious innocence. She was resolved to know the worst, and determined to dare it too. "I can crush that bold spirit," thought I. But while I secretly exulted in my power, I felt disposed to dally with my victim like a cat. Showing her the book that I still held in my hand, and pointing to the name on the fly leaf, but fixing my eye upon her face, I asked,—

"Do you know that gentleman?"

"Of course I do," replied she; and a sudden flush suffused her features— whether of shame or anger I could not tell: it rather resembled the latter. "What next sir?"

"How long is it since you saw him?"

"Who gave you the right to catechise me, on this or any other subject?"

"Oh, no one!—it's quite at your option whether to answer or not.— And now, let me ask—have you heard what has lately befallen this friend of yours?—because, if you have not—"

"I will not be insulted Mr. Markham!" cried she almost infuriated at my manner.—"So you had better leave the house at once, if you came only for that."

"I did not come to insult you: I came to hear your explanation."

"And I tell you I won't give it!" retorted she, pacing the room in a state of strong excitement, with her hands clasped tightly together, breathing short, and flashing fires of indignation from her eyes. "I will not condescend to explain myself to one that can make a jest of such horrible suspicions, and be so easily led to entertain them."

"I do not make a jest of them, Mrs. Graham," returned I, dropping at once, my tone of taunting sarcasm. "I heartily wish I could find them a jesting matter! And as to being easily led to suspect, God only knows what a blind, incredulous fool I have hitherto been, perseveringly shutting my eyes and stopping my ears against everything that threatened to shake my confidence in you, till proof itself confounded my infatuation!"

"What proof, sir?"

"Well, I'll tell, you. You remember that evening when I was here last?"

"I do."

"Even then, you dropped some hints that might have opened the eyes of a wiser man; but they had no such effect upon me: I went on trusting and believing, hoping against hope, and adoring where I could not comprehend.—It so happened, however, that after I had left you, I turned back—

drawn by pure depth of sympathy, and ardour of affection—not daring to intrude my presence openly upon you, but unable to resist the temptation of catching one glimpse through the window, just to see how you were; for I had left you apparently in great affliction, and I partly blamed my own want of forbearance and discretion as the cause of it. If I did wrong, love alone was my incentive, and the punishment was severe enough; for it was just as I had reached that tree, that you came out into the garden with your friend. Not choosing to show myself, under the circumstances, I stood still, in the shadow, till you had both passed by."

"And how much of our conversation did you hear?"

"I heard quite enough, Helen. And it was well for me that I did hear it; for nothing less could have cured my infatuation. I always said and thought, that I would never believe a word against you, unless I heard it from your own lips. All the hints and affirmations of others I treated as malignant, baseless slanders; your own self accusations I believed to be overstrained; and all that seemed unaccountable in your position, I trusted that you could count for if you chose."

Mrs. Graham had discontinued her walk. She leant against one end of the chimneypiece, opposite that near which I was standing, with her chin resting on her closed hand, her eyes—no longer burning with anger, but gleaming with restless excitement—sometimes glancing at me while I spoke, then coursing the opposite wall, or fixed upon the carpet.

"You should have come to me, after all," said she, "and heard what I had to say in my own justification. It was ungenerous and wrong to withdraw yourself so secretly and suddenly, immediately after such ardent protestations of attachment, without ever assigning a reason for the change. You should have told me all—no matter *how* bitterly—it would have been better than this silence."

"To what end should I have done so?—You could not have enlightened me farther, on the subject which alone concerned me; nor could you have made me discredit the evidence of my senses. I desired our intimacy to be discontinued at once, as you yourself had acknowledged would probably be the case if I knew all; but I did not wish to upbraid you,—though (as you also acknowledged) you had deeply wronged me.—Yes; you have done me an injury you can never repair—or any other either—you have blighted the freshness and promise of youth, and made my life a wilderness! I might live a hundred years, but I could never recover from the effects of this withering blow—and never forget it! Hereafter—You smile Mrs. Graham," said I, suddenly stopping short, checked in my passionate declamation by unutterable feelings to behold her actually *smiling* at the picture of the ruin she had wrought.

"Did I?" replied she, looking seriously up, "I was not aware of it. If I did, it was not for pleasure at the thoughts of the harm I had done you.—Heaven knows I have had torment enough at the bare possibility of that!—it was for joy to find that you had some depth of soul and feeling after all, and to hope that I had not been utterly mistaken in your worth. But smiles and tears are so alike with me; they are neither of them confined to any particular feelings: I often cry when I am happy, and smile when I am sad."

She looked at me again, and seemed to expect a reply; but I continued silent.

"Would you be *very* glad," resumed she, "to find that you were mistaken in your conclusions?"

"How can you ask it, Helen?"

"I don't say I can clear myself altogether," said she, speaking low and fast, while her heart beat visibly and her bosom heaved with excitement,—"but would you be glad to discover I was better than you think me?"

"Anything, that could, in the least degree, tend to restore my former opinion of you, to excuse the regard I still feel for you, and alleviate the pangs of unutterable regret that accompany it, would be only too gladly—too eagerly received!"

Her cheeks burned and her whole frame trembled, now, with excess of agitation. She did not speak, but flew to her desk, and snatching thence what seemed a thick album or manuscript volume, hastily tore away a few leaves from the end, and thrust the rest into my hand, saying, "You needn't read it all; but take it home with you,"—and hurried from the room. But when I had left the house, and was proceeding down the walk, she opened the window and called me back. It was only to say,—

"Bring it back when you have read it; and don't breathe a word of what it tells you to any living being—I trust to your honour."

Before I could answer, she had closed the casement and turned away. I saw her cast herself back in the old oak chair, and cover her face with her hands. Her feelings had been wrought to a pitch that rendered it necessary to seek relief in tears.

Panting with eagerness, and struggling to suppress my hopes, I hurried home, and rushed up stairs to my room,—having first provided myself with a candle, though it was scarcely twilight yet,—then, shut and bolted the door, determined to tolerate no interruption, and sitting down before the table, opened out my prize and delivered myself up to its perusal—first, hastily turning over the leaves and snatching a sentence here and there, and then, setting myself steadily to read it through.

I have it now before me; and though you could not of course, peruse it with half the interest that I did, I know you would not be satisfied with an abbreviation of its contents and you shall have the whole, save, perhaps, a few passages here and there of merely temporal interest to the writer, or such would serve to encumber the story rather than elucidate it. It begins somewhat abruptly, thus—but we will reserve its commencement for another chapter, and call it,—

CHAPTER XVI
THE WARNINGS OF EXPERIENCE

JUNE 1st, 1821.—We have just returned to Staningley—that is, we returned some days ago, and I am not yet settled, and feel as if I never should be. We left town sooner than was intended, in consequence of my uncle's indisposition—I wonder what would have been the result if we had stayed the full time. I am quite ashamed of my new-sprung distaste for country life. All my former occupations seem so tedious and dull, my former amusements so insipid and unprofitable. I cannot enjoy my music, because there is no one to hear it. I cannot enjoy my walks, because there is no one to meet. I cannot enjoy my books, because they have not power to arrest my attention: my head is so haunted with the recollections of the last few weeks that I cannot attend to them. My drawing suits me best, for I can draw and think at the same time; and if my productions cannot now be seen by any one but myself and those who do not care about them, they, possibly, may be, hereafter. But then, there is one face I am always trying to paint or to sketch, and always without success; and that vexes me. As for the owner of that face, I cannot get him out of my mind—and, indeed, I never try. I wonder whether he ever thinks of me; and I wonder whether I shall ever see him again. And then might follow a train of other wonderments—questions for time and fate to answer, concluding with:—supposing all the rest be answered in the affirmative, I wonder whether I shall ever repent it—as my aunt would tell me I should, if she knew what I was thinking about. How distinctly I remember our conversation that evening before our departure for town, when we were sitting together over the fire, my uncle having gone to bed with a slight attack of the gout.[1]

"Helen," said she, after a thoughtful silence, "do you ever think about marriage?"

"Yes aunt, often."

"And do you ever contemplate the possibility of being married yourself, or engaged, before the season is over?"

"Sometimes; but I don't think it at all likely that I *ever* shall."

"Why so?"

---

1 Gout is a disease that affects the joints, where a build-up of uric acid makes them painful. It can be caused by excessive drinking and eating rich foods, which overly taxes the kidneys and renders them unable to remove uric acid from the body.

"Because, I imagine there must be only a very, very few men in the world, that I should like to marry; and of those few, it is ten to one I may never be acquainted with one; or if I should, it is twenty to one, he may not happen to be single, or to take a fancy to me."

"That is no argument at all. It may be very true—and I hope *is* true, that there are very few men whom you would choose to marry, of yourself.—It is not, indeed, to be supposed that you would *wish* to marry *any* one, till you were asked: a girl's affections should never be won unsought. But when they *are* sought—when the citadel of the heart is fairly besieged, it is apt to surrender sooner than the owner is aware of, and often against her better judgment, and in opposition to all her preconceived ideas of what she could have loved, unless she be extremely careful and discreet. Now I want to warn you, Helen, of these things, and to exhort you to be watchful and circumspect from the very commencement of your career, and not to suffer your heart to be stolen from you by the first foolish or unprincipled person that covets the possession of it.—You know, my dear, you are only just eighteen; there is plenty of time before you, and neither your uncle nor I are in any hurry to get you off our hands; and, I may venture to say, there will be no lack of suitors; for you can boast a good family, a pretty considerable fortune and expectations, and, I may as well tell you likewise—for if I don't others will—that you have a fair share of beauty, besides—and I hope you may never have cause to regret it!—"

"I hope not, aunt; but why should you fear it?"

"Because, my dear, beauty is that quality which, next to money, is generally the most attractive to the worst kinds of men; and, therefore, it is likely to entail a great deal of trouble on the possessor."

"Have *you* been troubled in that way, aunt?"

"No, Helen," said she, with reproachful gravity, "but I know many that have; and some, through carelessness, have been the wretched victims of deceit; and some, through weakness, have fallen into snares and temptations[1] terrible to relate."

"Well, I shall be neither careless nor weak."

"Remember Peter, Helen! Don't boast, but *watch*.[2] Keep a guard over your eyes and ears as the inlets of your heart, and over your lips as the outlet, lest they betray you in a moment of unwariness. Receive, coldly and dispas-

---

1   A colloquial invocation of 2 Timothy 1:9: "But they that will be rich fall into temptation and a snare, and into many foolish and hurtful lusts, which drown men in destruction and perdition."

2   Helen's aunt is alluding to Matthew 26:41, where Jesus warns Peter in the Garden of Gethsemane to "Watch and pray, that ye enter not into temptation; the spirit indeed is willing, but the flesh is weak."

sionately, every attention, till you have ascertained and duly considered the worth of the aspirant; and let your affections be consequent upon approbation alone. First study; then approve; then love. Let your eyes be blind to all external attractions, your ears deaf to all the fascinations of flattery and light discourse.—These are nothing—and worse than nothing—snares and wiles of the tempter,[1] to lure the thoughtless to their own destruction. Principle is the first thing, after all; and next to that, good sense, respectability, and moderate wealth. If you should marry the handsomest, and most accomplished and superficially agreeable man in the world, you little know the misery that would overwhelm you, if, after all, you should find him to be a worthless reprobate, or even an impracticable fool."

"But what are all the poor fools and reprobates to do, aunt? If everybody followed your advice the world would soon come to an end."

"Never fear, my dear! the male fools[2] and reprobates will never want for partners while there are so many of the other sex to match them; but do *you* follow my advice. And this is no subject for jesting, Helen, I am sorry to see you treat the matter in that light way. Believe me, *matrimony is a serious thing*." And she spoke it *so* seriously that one might have fancied she had known it to her cost; but I asked no more impertinent questions, and merely answered,—

"I know it is; and I know there is truth and sense in what you say; but you need not fear me, for I, not only should think it *wrong* to marry a man that was deficient in sense or in principle, but I should never be *tempted* to do it; for I could not like him, if he were ever so handsome and ever so charming in other respects; I should hate him—despise him—pity him—anything but love him. My affections not only *ought* to be founded on approbation, but they will and must be so: for without approving I cannot love. It is needless to say I ought to be able to respect and honour the man I marry as *well* as love him, for I cannot love him without. So set your mind at rest."

"I hope it may be so," answered she.

"I *know* it is so," persisted I.

"You have not been tried yet, Helen: we can but hope," said she, in her cold, cautious way.

---

1   Helen's aunt is loosely referring to 1 Timothy 3:7: "Moreover, he must have a good report of them which are without; lest he fall into reproach and the snare of the devil." She is also alluding to Ephesians 6:11: "Put on the whole armour of God, that ye may be able to stand the wiles of the devil."

2   Helen's aunt could also be referring to nonbelievers as "fools," since in the King James Version of the Bible a fool is most often an unbeliever. See, for example, Psalm 53:1a: "The fool hath said in his heart, There is no God."

I was vexed at her incredulity; but I am not sure her doubts were entirely without sagacity; I fear I have found it much easier to remember her advice than to profit by it—indeed, I have sometimes been led to question the soundness of her doctrines on those subjects. Her counsels may be good, as far as they go—in the main points, at least;—but there are some things she has overlooked in her calculations. I wonder if *she* was ever in love.

I commenced my career—or my first campaign, as my uncle calls it—kindling with bright hopes and fancies—chiefly raised by this conversation—and full of confidence in my own discretion. At first, I was delighted with the novelty and excitement of our London life; but, soon, I began to weary of its mingled turbulence and constraint, and sigh for the freshness and freedom of home. My new acquaintances, both male and female, disappointed my expectations, and vexed and depressed me by turns; for I soon grew tired of studying their peculiarities, and laughing at their foibles—particularly as I was obliged to keep my criticisms to myself, for my aunt would not hear them—and they—the ladies especially—appeared so provokingly mindless, and heartless, and artificial. The gentlemen seemed better, but perhaps, it was because I knew them less, perhaps, because they flattered me; but I did not fall in love with any of them, and if their attentions pleased me one moment, they provoked me the next, because they put me out of humour with myself, by revealing my vanity and making me fear I was becoming like some of the ladies I so heartily despised.

There was one elderly gentleman that annoyed me very much; a rich old friend of my uncle's who, I believe, thought I could not do better than marry him; but, besides being old, he was ugly and disagreeable,—and wicked, I am sure, though my aunt scolded me for saying so; but she allowed he was no saint. And there was another, less hateful, but still *more* tiresome, because she favoured him, and was always thrusting him upon me, and sounding his praises in my ears, Mr. Boarham, by name, Bore'em as I prefer spelling it, for a terrible bore he was: I shudder still, at the remembrance of his voice, drone, drone, drone, in my ear, while he sat beside me, prosing away by the half-hour together, and beguiling himself with the notion that he was improving my mind by useful information, or, impressing his dogmas upon me, and reforming my errors of judgment, or perhaps, that he was talking down to my level, and amusing me with entertaining discourse. Yet he was a decent man enough, in the main, I dare say; and if he had kept his distance, I never would have hated him. As it was, it was almost impossible to help it; for he not only bothered me with the infliction of his own presence, but he kept me from the enjoyment of more agreeable society.

One night, however, at a ball, he had been more than usually tormenting, and my patience was quite exhausted.—It appeared as if the whole evening was fated to be insupportable: I had just had one dance with an empty-headed coxcomb, and then Mr. Boarham had come upon me, and seemed determined to cling to me for the rest of the night. He never danced himself, and there he sat, poking his head in my face, and impressing all beholders with the idea that he was a confirmed, acknowledged lover; my aunt looking complacently on, all the time, and wishing him God-speed. In vain I attempted to drive him away by giving a loose to my exasperated feelings, even to positive rudeness: nothing could convince him that his presence was disagreeable. Sullen silence was taken for rapt attention, and gave him greater room to talk; sharp answers were received as smart sallies of girlish vivacity, that only required an indulgent rebuke; and flat contradictions were but as oil to the flames, calling forth new strains of argument to support his dogmas, and bringing down upon me endless floods of reasoning to overwhelm me with conviction.

But there was one present who seemed to have a better appreciation of my frame of mind. A gentleman stood by, who had been watching our conference for some time, evidently much amused at my companion's remorseless pertinacity and my manifest annoyance, and laughing to himself at the asperity and uncompromising spirit of my replies. At length, however, he withdrew, and went to the lady of the house, apparently for the purpose of asking an introduction to me, for, shortly after, they both came up, and she introduced him as Mr. Huntingdon, the son of a late friend of my uncle's. He asked me to dance. I gladly consented, of course; and he was my companion during the remainder of my stay, which was not long, for my aunt, as usual, insisted upon an early departure.

I was sorry to go, for I had found my new acquaintance a very lively and entertaining companion. There was a certain, graceful ease and freedom about all he said and did, that gave a sense of repose and expansion to the mind, after so much constraint and formality as I had been doomed to suffer. There might be, it is true, a little too much careless boldness in his manner and address, but I was in so good a humour, and so grateful for my late deliverance from Mr. Boarham, that it did not anger me.

"Well, Helen, how do you like Mr. Boarham now?" said my aunt, as we took our seats in the carriage and drove away.

"Worse than ever," I replied.

She looked displeased but said no more on that subject.

"Who was the gentleman you danced with last," resumed she, after a pause—"that was so officious in helping you on with your shawl?"

"He was not officious at all, aunt: he never *attempted* to help me, till he saw Mr. Boarham coming to do so; and then he stepped laughingly forward and said, 'Come I'll preserve you from that infliction.'"

"Who was it, I ask?" said she, with frigid gravity.

"It was Mr. Huntingdon, the son of uncle's old friend."

"I have heard your uncle speak of young Mr. Huntingdon. I've heard him say, 'He's a fine lad, that young Huntingdon, but a bit wildish I fancy.' So I'd have you beware."

"What does 'a bit wildish' mean?" I enquired.

"It means destitute of principle, and prone to every vice that is common to youth."

"But I've heard uncle say he was a sad wild fellow himself, when he was young."

She sternly shook her head.

"He was jesting then, I suppose," said I, "and here he was speaking at random—at least, I cannot believe there is any harm in those laughing blue eyes."

"False reasoning, Helen!" said she with a sigh.

"Well, we ought to be charitable, you know, aunt—besides, I don't think it *is* false: I am an excellent physiognomist,[1] and I always judge of people's characters by their looks—not by whether they are handsome or ugly, but by the general cast of the countenance. For instance, I should know by your countenance that you were not of a cheerful, sanguine disposition; and I should know by Mr. Wilmot's[2] that he was a worthless old reprobate, and by Mr. Boarham's that he was not an agreeable companion, and by Mr. Huntingdon's that he was neither a fool nor a knave, though, possibly, neither a sage nor a saint—but that is no matter to me, as I am not likely to meet him again—unless as an occasional partner in the ballroom."

It was not so, however, for I met him again next morning. He came to call upon my uncle, apologizing for not having done so before, by saying he was only lately returned from the continent, and had not heard, till the previous night, of my uncle's arrival in town; and after that, I often met him; sometimes in public, sometimes at home; for he was very assiduous in paying his respects to his old friend, who did not, however, consider himself greatly obliged by the attention.

"I wonder what the deuce the lad means by coming so often," he would say,—"can *you* tell, Helen?—Hey? He wants none o' my company, nor I his—that's certain."

"I wish you'd tell him so, then," said my aunt.

---

1   Physiognomy was a popular nineteenth-century science, along with phrenology. Both purported to read people's characters by correlating certain facial features (physiognomy) or shapes of the skull (phrenology) with personality traits. Brontë could be pointing out how easy it is to *misread* faces, and also how flawed this "science" could be.

2   Wilmot, the "reprobate," could have gotten his name from John Wilmot (1647–80), second Earl of Rochester, a poet of the Restoration, known for the wit and sexual frankness of his works.

"Why, what for? If I don't want him, somebody does mayhap (winking at me). Besides, he's a pretty tidy fortune, Peggy, you know—not such a catch as Wilmot, but then Helen won't hear of that match; for, somehow, these old chaps don't go down with the girls—with *all* their money—and their experience to boot. I'll bet anything she'd rather have this young fellow without a penny, than Wilmot with his house full of gold—wouldn't you Nell?"

"Yes uncle; but that's not saying much for Mr. Huntingdon, for I'd rather be an old maid and a pauper, than Mrs. Wilmot."

"And Mrs. Huntingdon? What would you rather be than Mrs. Huntingdon? eh?"

"I'll tell you when I've considered the matter."

"Ah! It needs consideration then.—But come now—would you rather be an old maid—let alone the pauper?"

"I can't tell till I'm asked."

And I left the room immediately, to escape further examination. But five minutes after, in looking from my window, I beheld Mr. Boarham coming up to the door. I waited nearly half an hour in uncomfortable suspense, expecting every minute to be called, and vainly longing to hear him go. Then, footsteps were heard on the stairs, and my aunt entered the room with a solemn countenance, and closed the door behind her.

"Here is Mr. Boarham, Helen," said she. "He wishes to see you."

"Oh, aunt! Can't you tell him I'm indisposed?—I'm sure I am—to see *him*."

"Nonsense, my dear! this is no trifling matter. He is come on a very important errand—to ask your hand in marriage, of your uncle and me."

"I hope my uncle and you told him it was not in your power to give it. What right had he to ask *any* one before me?"

"Helen!"

"What did my uncle say?"

"He said he would not interfere in the matter; if you liked to accept Mr. Boarham's obliging offer, you—"

"Did he say obliging offer?"

"No; he said if you liked to take him you might; and if not, you might please yourself."

"He said right; and what did you say?"

"It is no matter what I said. What will *you* say?—that is the question. He is now waiting to ask you himself; but consider well before you go; and if you intend to refuse him, give me your reasons."

"I *shall* refuse him, of course, but you must tell me how, for I want to be civil and yet decided—and when I've got rid of him, I'll give you my reasons afterwards."

"But stay Helen; sit down a little, and compose yourself. Mr. Boarham is in no particular hurry, for he has little doubt of your acceptance; and I want to speak with you. Tell me, my dear, what are your objections to him? Do you deny that he is an upright, honourable man?"

"No."

"Do you deny that he is sensible, sober, respectable?"

"No; he may be all this, but—"

"*But* Helen! How many such men do you expect to meet with in the world? Upright, honourable, sensible, sober, respectable!—Is *this* such an every day character, that you should reject the possessor of such noble qualities, without a moment's hesitation?—Yes, *noble* I may call them; for, think of the full meaning of each, and how many inestimable virtues they include (and I might add many more to the list), and consider that all this is laid at your feet: it is in your power to secure this inestimable blessing for life—a worthy and excellent husband, who loves you tenderly, but not too fondly so as to blind him to your faults, and will be your guide throughout life's pilgrimage, and your partner in eternal bliss! Think how—"

"But I hate him, aunt," said I, interrupting this unusual flow of eloquence.

"Hate him, Helen! Is this a Christian spirit?—*you hate him?*—and he so good a man!"

"I don't hate him as a man, but as a husband. As a man, I love him so much, that I wish him a better wife than I—one as good as himself, or better—if you think that possible—provided, she could like him;—but I never could, and therefore—"

"But why not? What objection do you find?"

"Firstly, he is, at least, forty years old—considerably more I should think, and I am but eighteen; secondly, he is narrow-minded and bigoted in the extreme; thirdly, his tastes and feelings are wholly dissimilar to mine; fourthly, his looks, voice, and manner are particularly displeasing to me; and finally, I have an aversion to his whole person that I never can surmount."

"Then you ought to surmount it! And please to compare him for a moment with Mr. Huntingdon, and, good looks apart (which contribute nothing to the merit of the man, or to the happiness of married life, and which you have so often professed to hold in light esteem), tell me which is the better man."

"I have no doubt Mr. Huntingdon is a much better man than you think him,—but we are not talking about him, now, but about Mr. Boarham; and as I would rather grow, live and die in single blessedness[1] than be his wife, it

---

1   Helen is challenging her aunt by subverting Theseus's words from Shakespeare's *A Midsummer Night's Dream*, where he threatens his daughter, Hermia, with marrying Demetrius or being forced to enter a cloister where she would "Gro[w], liv[e], and di[e], in single blessedness" (I.i.78).

is but right that I should tell him so at once, and put him out of suspense—so let me go."

"But don't give him a flat denial; he has no idea of such a thing, and it would offend him greatly: say you have no thoughts of matrimony, at present—"

"But I *have* thoughts of it."

"Or that you desire a further acquaintance."

"But I don't desire a further acquaintance—quite the contrary."

And without waiting for further admonitions, I left the room, and went to seek Mr. Boarham. He was walking up and down the drawing room, humming snatches of tunes, and nibbling the end of his cane.

"My dear young lady," said he, bowing and smirking with great complacency. "I have your kind guardian's permission—"

"I know, sir," said I, wishing to shorten the scene as much as possible, "and I am greatly obliged for your preference, but must beg to decline the honour you wish to confer; for, I think, we were not made for each other—as you yourself would shortly discover if the experiment were tried."

My aunt was right: it was quite evident he had had little doubt of my acceptance, and no idea of a positive denial. He was amazed—astounded at such an answer, but too incredulous to be much offended; and after a little humming and hawing, he returned to the attack.

"I know, my dear, that there exists a considerable disparity between us in years, in temperament, and perhaps some other things, but let me assure you, I shall not be severe to mark the faults and foibles of a young and ardent nature such as yours, and while I acknowledge them to myself, and even rebuke them with all a father's care, believe me, no youthful lover could be more tenderly indulgent towards the object of his affections, than I to you; and, on the other hand, let me hope that my more experienced years and graver habits of reflection will be no disparagement in your eyes, as I shall endeavour to make them all conducive to your happiness. Come now! What do you say?—Let us have no young lady's affectations and caprices, but speak out at once!"

"I will, but only to repeat what I said before, that I am certain we were not made for each other."

"You really think so?"

"I do."

"But you don't know me—you wish for a further acquaintance—a longer time to—"

"No, I don't. I know you as well as I ever shall, and better than you know me, or you would never dream of uniting yourself to one so incongruous—so utterly unsuitable to you in every way."

"But my dear young lady, I don't look for perfection, I can excuse—"

"Thank you, Mr. Boarham, but I won't trespass upon your goodness. You may save your indulgence and consideration for some more worthy object, that won't tax them so heavily."

"But let me beg you to consult your aunt; that excellent lady, I am sure, will—"

"I have consulted her; and I know her wishes coincide with yours; but in such important matters, I take the liberty of judging for myself; and no persuasion can alter my inclinations, or induce me to believe that such a step would be conducive to my happiness, or yours—and I wonder that a man of your experience and discretion should think of choosing such a wife."

"Ah, well!" said he—"I have sometimes wondered at that myself, I have sometimes said to myself, 'Now Boarham, what is this you're after? Take care man—look before you leap! This is a sweet, bewitching creature, but remember, the brightest attractions to the lover, too often prove the husband's greatest torments!' I assure you my choice has not been made without much reasoning and reflection. The seeming imprudence of the match has cost me many an anxious thought by day, and many a sleepless hour by night; but at length, I satisfied myself, that it was not, in very deed, imprudent. I saw my sweet girl was not without her faults, but of these, her youth, I trusted, was not one, but rather an earnest[1] of virtues yet unblown—a strong ground of presumption that her little defects of temper, and errors of judgment, opinion, or manner were not irremediable, but might easily be removed or mitigated by the patient efforts of a watchful and judicious adviser, and where I failed to enlighten and control, I thought I might safely undertake to pardon, for the sake of her many excellencies. Therefore, my dearest girl, since *I* am satisfied, why should *you* object—on my account, at least."

"But to tell you the truth Mr. Boarham, it is on my own account I principally object; so let us—drop the subject," I would have said, "for it is worse than useless to pursue it any farther," but he pertinaciously interrupted me with—

"But why so? I would love you, cherish you, protect you, &c. &c."

I shall not trouble myself to put down all that passed between us. Suffice it to say, that I found him very troublesome, and very hard to convince that I really meant what I said, and really *was* so obstinate and blind to my own interests, that there was no shadow of a chance that either he or my aunt would ever be able to overcome my objections. Indeed, I am not sure that I succeeded after all, though wearied with his so pertinaciously returning to the same point and repeating the same arguments over and over again, forc-

---

1   Earnest in this context means "a foretaste, installment, pledge of anything afterwards to be received in greater abundance" (*OED*).

ing me to reiterate the same replies, I at length turned short and sharp upon him, and my last words were—

"I tell you plainly, that it cannot be. No consideration can induce me to marry against my inclinations. I respect you—at least, I would respect you, if you would behave like a sensible man—but I cannot love you, and never could—and the more you talk the farther you repel me; so pray don't say any more about it."

Whereupon, he wished me a good morning and withdrew, disconcerted and offended, no doubt; but surely it was not my fault.

CHAPTER XVII
FURTHER WARNINGS

THE next day, I accompanied my uncle and aunt to a dinner party at Mr. Wilmot's. He had two ladies staying with him, his niece Annabella, a fine dashing girl, or rather young woman, of some five and twenty, too great a flirt to be married, according to her own assertion, but greatly admired by the gentlemen, who universally pronounced her a splendid woman,—and her gentle cousin Milicent Hargrave, who had taken a violent fancy to me, mistaking me for something vastly better than I was. And I in return, was very fond of her—I should entirely exclude poor Milicent in my general animadversions against the ladies of my acquaintance. But it was not on her account, or her cousin's, that I have mentioned the party: it was for the sake of another of Mr. Wilmot's guests, to wit Mr. Huntingdon. I have good reason to remember his presence there, for this was the last time I saw him.

He did not sit near me at dinner; for it was his fate to hand in a capacious old dowager, and mine to be handed in by Mr. Grimsby, a friend of his, but a man I very greatly disliked: there was a sinister cast in his countenance, and a mixture of lurking ferocity and fulsome insincerity in his demeanour, that I could not away with. What a tiresome custom that is, by the by—one among the many sources of factitious annoyance of this ultra civilized life. If the gentlemen *must* lead the ladies into the dining-room, why cannot they take those they like best?

I am not sure, however, that Mr. Huntingdon would have taken me, if he *had* been at liberty to make his own selection. It is quite possible he might have chosen Miss Wilmot; for she seemed bent upon engrossing his attention to herself, and he seemed nothing loath to pay the homage she demanded. I thought so, at least, when I saw how they talked and laughed, and glanced across the table, to the neglect and evident umbrage of their respective neighbours—and afterwards, as the gentlemen joined us in the drawing-room, when she, immediately upon his entrance, loudly called upon him to be the arbiter of a dispute between herself and another lady, and he answered the summons with alacrity, and decided the question without a moment's hesitation in her favour—though, to my thinking, she was obviously in the wrong—and then stood chatting familiarly with her and a group of other ladies; while I sat with Milicent Hargrave, at the opposite end of the room, looking over the latter's drawings and aiding her with my critical observations and advice, at her particular desire. But in spite of my efforts to remain composed my attention wandered from the drawings to the merry group, and against my better judgment my wrath rose, and doubtless, my countenance lowered; for Milicent, observing that I must be tired of her daubs and scratches, begged I would join the company now, and defer the examination of the remainder to another opportunity. But while I was assuring her that I had no wish to join them, and was not tired, Mr. Huntingdon himself came up to the little round table at which we sat.

"Are these yours?" said he, carelessly taking up one of the drawings.

"No, they are Miss Hargrave's."

"Oh! well, let's have a look at them."

And, regardless of Miss Hargrave's protestations, that they were not worth looking at, he drew a chair to my side, and receiving the drawings, one by one from my hand, successively scanned them over, and threw them on the table, but said not a word about them, though he was talking all the time. I don't know what Milicent Hargrave thought of such conduct, but I found his conversation extremely interesting, though as I afterwards discovered, when I came to analyse it, it was chiefly confined to quizzing the different members of the company present; and albeit he made some clever remarks, and some excessively droll ones, I do not think the whole would appear anything very particular, if written here, without the adventitious aids of look, and tone, and gesture, and that ineffable but indefinite charm, which cast a halo over all he did and said, and which would have made it a delight to look in his face, and hear the music of his voice, if he had been talking positive nonsense—and which, moreover, made me feel so bitter at my aunt when she put a stop to this enjoyment, by coming composedly forward, under pretence of wishing to see the drawings, that she cared and knew nothing about, and while making believe to examine them, addressing herself to Mr. Huntingdon, with one of her coldest and most repellent aspects, and beginning a series of the most common place and formidably formal questions and observations, on purpose to wrest his attention from me—on purpose to vex me, as I thought: and having now looked through the portfolio, I left them to their tête-à-tête, and seated myself on a sofa, quite apart from the company—never thinking how strange such conduct would appear, but merely to indulge, at first, the vexation of the moment, and subsequently to enjoy my private thoughts.

But I was not left long alone, for Mr. Wilmot, of all men the least welcome, took advantage of my isolated position to come and plant himself beside me. I had flattered myself that I had so effectually repulsed his advances on all former occasions, that I had nothing more to apprehend from his unfortunate predilection; but it seems I was mistaken: so great was his confidence, either in his wealth or his remaining powers of attraction, and so firm his conviction of feminine weakness, that he thought himself warranted to return to the siege, which he did with renovated ardour, enkindled by the quantity of wine he had drunk—a circumstance that rendered him infinitely the more disgusting; but greatly as I abhorred him at that moment, I did not like to treat him with rudeness, as I was now his guest and had just been enjoying his hospitality; and I was no hand at a polite but determined rejection, nor would it have greatly availed me if I had; for he was too coarse-minded to take any repulse that was not as plain and positive as his own effrontery. The consequence was, that he waxed more fulsomely tender, and more repulsively warm, and I was driven to the very verge of desperation, and about to say, I know not what, when I felt my hand that hung over the arm of the sofa, suddenly taken by another and gently but fervently pressed. Instinctively, I guessed who it was, and on looking up, was less surprised than delighted, to see Mr. Huntingdon smiling upon me. It was like turning from some purgatorial fiend to an angel of light,[1] come to announce that the season of torment was past.

"Helen," said he, (he frequently called me Helen, and I never resented the freedom), "I want you to look at this picture: Mr. Wilmot will excuse you a moment, I'm sure."

I rose with alacrity. He drew my arm within his, and led me across the room to a splendid painting of Vandyke's[2] that I had noticed before, but not sufficiently examined. After a moment of silent contemplation, I was beginning to comment on its beauties and peculiarities, when, playfully pressing the hand he still retained within his arm, he interrupted me with—

"Never mind the picture, it was not for that I brought you here; it was to get you away from that scoundrelly old profligate yonder, who is looking as if he would like to challenge me for the affront."

"I am very much obliged to you," said I. "This is twice you have delivered me from such unpleasant companionship."

---

1   If Helen is unconsciously referring to 2 Corinthians 11:14–15 here, this foreshadows her rather grim future, as the biblical passage remarks on how "Satan himself is transformed into an angel of light."

2   Sir Anthony Vandyke (1599–1641) was a Flemish portrait painter who was a court painter to Charles I (1600–49).

"Don't be too thankful," he answered: "it is not all kindness to you; it is partly from a feeling of spite to your tormentors that makes me delighted to do the old fellows a bad turn, though I don't think I have any great reason to dread them as rivals—have I Helen?"

"You know I detest them both."

"And me?"

"I have no reason to detest *you*."

"But what are your sentiments towards me?—Helen—Speak!—How do you regard me?"

And again he pressed my hand; but I feared there was more of conscious power than tenderness in his demeanour, and I felt he had no right to extort a confession of attachment from me when he had made no correspondent avowal himself, and knew not what to answer. At last I said—

"How do *you* regard *me*?"

"Sweet angel, I adore you! I—"

"Helen, I want you a moment," said the distinct, low voice of my aunt, close beside us. And I left him, muttering maledictions against his evil angel.

"Well aunt, what is it? What do you want?" said I, following her to the embrasure of the window.

"I want you to join the company, when you are fit to be seen," returned she, severely regarding me; "but please to stay here a little till that shocking colour is somewhat abated, and your eyes have recovered something of their natural expression. I should be ashamed for any one to see you in your present state."

Of course, such a remark had no effect in reducing the "shocking colour;" on the contrary, I felt my face glow with redoubled fires kindled by a complication of emotions, of which indignant, swelling anger was the chief. I offered no reply, however, but pushed aside the curtain and looked into the night—or rather, into the lamp-lit square.

"Was Mr. Huntingdon proposing to you, Helen?" enquired my too watchful relative.

"No."

"What was he saying then? I heard something very like it."

"I don't know what he would have said, if you hadn't interrupted him."

"And would you have accepted him, Helen, if he had proposed?"

"Of course not—without consulting uncle and you."

"Oh! I'm glad, my dear, you have so much prudence left. Well now," she added, after a moment's pause, "you have made yourself conspicuous enough for one evening. The ladies are directing inquiring glances towards us at this moment I see. I shall join them. Do you come too, when you are sufficiently composed to appear as usual."

"I am so now."

"Speak gently then; and don't look so malicious," said my calm, but provoking aunt.

"We shall return home shortly, and then," she added with solemn significance, "I have much to say to you."

So I went home prepared for a formidable lecture. Little was said by either party in the carriage during our short transit homewards; but when I had entered my room and thrown myself into an easy chair to reflect on the events of the day, my aunt followed me thither, and having dismissed Rachel, who was carefully stowing away my ornaments, closed the door; and placing a chair beside me, or rather at right angles with mine, sat down. With due deference I offered her my more commodious seat. She declined it, and thus opened the conference:

"Do you remember, Helen, our conversation the night but one before we left Staningley?"

"Yes aunt."

"And do you remember how I warned you against letting your heart be stolen from you by those unworthy of its possession; and fixing your affections where approbation did not go before, and where reason and judgment withheld their sanction?"

"Yes, but *my* reason—"

"Pardon me—and do you remember assuring me that there was no occasion for uneasiness on your account; for you should never be *tempted* to marry a man who was deficient in sense or principle, however handsome or charming in other respects he might be, for you could not love him, you should hate—despise—pity—anything but love him—were not those your words?"

"Yes, but—"

"And did you not say that your affection *must* be founded on approbation; and that unless you could approve and honour and respect, you could not love?"

"Yes, but I do approve and honour, and respect—"

"How so, my dear? is Mr. Huntingdon a good man?"

"He is a much better man than you think him."

"That is nothing to the purpose. Is he a *good* man?"

"Yes—in some respects. He has a good disposition."

"Is he a man of *principle*?"

"Perhaps not, exactly; but it is only for want of thought: if he had some one to advise him, and remind him of what is right—"

"He would soon learn, you think—and you yourself would willingly undertake to be his teacher? But, my dear, he is, I believe, full ten years older than you—how is it that you are so before-hand in moral acquirements?"

"Thanks to you, aunt, I have been well brought up, and had good examples always before me, which he, most likely, has not;—and besides, he is of a sanguine[1] temperament, and a gay, thoughtless temper, and I am naturally inclined to reflection."

"Well, now you have made him out to be deficient in both sense and principle, by your own confession—"

"Then, my sense and my principle are at his service!"

"That sounds presumptuous, Helen! Do you think you have enough for both; and do you imagine your merry, thoughtless profligate would allow himself to be guided by a young girl like you?"

"No; I should not wish to guide him; but I think I might have influence sufficient to save him from some errors, and I should think my life well spent in the effort to preserve so noble a nature from destruction. He always listens attentively now, when I speak seriously to him, (and I often venture to reprove his random way of talking), and sometimes he says that if he had me always by his side he should never do or say a wicked thing, and that a little daily talk with me would make him quite a saint. It may be partly jest and partly flattery, but still—"

"But still you think it may be truth?"

"If I do think there is any mixture of truth in it, it is not from confidence in my own powers, but in *his* natural goodness.—And you have no right to call him a profligate, aunt; he is nothing of the kind."

"Who told you so, my dear? What was that story about his intrigue with a married lady—Lady who was it—Miss Wilmot herself was telling you the other day?"

"It was false—false!" I cried. "I don't believe a word of it."

"You think, then, that he is a virtuous, well-conducted young man?"

"I know nothing positive respecting his character. I only know that I have heard nothing definitive against it—nothing that could be proved, at least; and till people can prove their slanderous accusations, I will not believe them. And I know this, that if he has committed errors, they are only such as are common to youth, and such as nobody thinks anything about; for I see that

---

1   Using the word "sanguine" to describe temperament harks back to the theory of the four humors, a theory that ascribed physical and emotional characteristics to the balance—or, more often, imbalance—among the four humors (blood, black bile, yellow bile, and phlegm) present in the human body. To be sanguine signified an excess of blood, leading to a more passionate temperament and a cheerful disposition, frequently complemented by a ruddy complexion. Even though Victorians did not believe in this outdated scientific theory, which originated with the Greeks around 400 BC and was popular during the Middle Ages, it served as a shorthand method to describe personality.

everybody likes him, and all the mammas smile upon him, and their daughters—and Miss Wilmot herself are only too glad to attract his attention."

"Helen, the world *may* look upon such offences as venial; a few unprincipled mothers *may* be anxious to catch a young man of fortune without reference to his character; and thoughtless girls *may* be glad to win the smiles of so handsome a gentleman, without seeking to penetrate beyond the surface; but *you*, I trusted were better informed than to see with their eyes, and judge with their perverted judgment. I did not think *you* would call these venial errors!"

"Nor do I, aunt; but if I hate the sins I love the sinner,[1] and would do much for his salvation, even supposing your suspicions to be mainly true—which I do not and will not believe."

"Well my dear, ask your uncle what sort of company he keeps, and if he is not banded with a set of loose, profligate young men, whom he calls his friends—his jolly companions, and whose chief delight is to wallow in vice, and vie with each other who can run fastest and farthest down the headlong road,[2] to the place prepared for the devil and his angels."[3]

"Then, I will save him from them."

"Oh, Helen, Helen! you little know the misery of uniting your fortunes to such a man!"

"I have such confidence in him, aunt, notwithstanding all you say, that I would willingly risk my happiness for the chance of securing his. I will leave better men to those who only consider their own advantage. If he has done amiss, I shall consider my life well spent in saving him from the consequences of his early errors, and striving to recall him to the path of virtue[4]—God grant me success!"

---

1 A version of "With love for mankind and hatred of sins, often quoted 'love the sinner but hate the sin,' St. Augustine of Hippo (354–430): letter 211; J.P. Migne (ed.) *Patrologiae Latinae* (1845)," *The Oxford Dictionary of Phrase, Saying, and Quotation*, ed. Elizabeth Knowles (Oxford: Oxford University Press, 1997), 191. See Appendix F4 for Thomas Buchanan Read's (1822–72) poem "What a Word May Do," a later nineteenth-century, popular iteration of this phrase and sentiment.

2 Stevie Davies points out that this phrase alludes to a portion of Matthew 7:13: "for wide is the gate and broad is the way that leadeth to destruction" (*PTWH* 506).

3 Matthew 25:41: "Then he shall say also unto them on the left hand, Depart from me, ye cursed, into everlasting fire, prepared for the devil and his angels."

4 Rosengarten and Smith explain how Helen's words reiterate those of Samuel Richardson's (1689–1761), novel, *Clarissa* (1748) here. Clarissa Harlowe "contemplates the 'secret pleasure' it would be to save the aristocratic rake Lovelace, if only she were 'able to reclaim such a man to the path of virtue and honour' (*Clarissa*, ed. Ross [1985], 183)" (*OTWH* 476). Stevie Davies gives a strong reading of how Brontë's novel revises *Clarissa* in her introduction to the Penguin edition of the novel (see *PTWH* xii–xiii).

Here the conversation ended, for at this juncture, my uncle's voice was heard, from his chamber, loudly calling upon my aunt to come to bed. He was in a bad humour that night; for his gout was worse. It had been gradually increasing upon him ever since we came to town; and my aunt took advantage of the circumstance, next morning, to persuade him to return to the country immediately without waiting for the close of the season. His physician supported and enforced her arguments; and contrary to her usual habits, she so hurried the preparations for removal (as much for my sake as my uncle's, I think), that in a very few days we departed; and I saw no more of Mr. Huntingdon. My aunt flatters herself I shall soon forget him—perhaps, she thinks I have forgotten him, already, for I never mention his name; and she may continue to think so, till we meet again,—if ever that should be. I wonder if it will.

CHAPTER XVIII
THE MINIATURE

AUGUST 25th.—I am now quite settled down to my usual routine of steady occupations and quiet amusements—tolerably contented and cheerful, but still looking forward to spring with the hope of returning to town, not for its gaieties and dissipations, but for the chance of meeting Mr. Huntingdon once again; for still, he is always in my thoughts and in my dreams. In all my employments, whatever I do, or see, or hear, has an ultimate reference to him; whatever skill or knowledge I acquire is some day to be turned to his advantage or amusement; whatever new beauties in nature or art I discover, are to be depicted to meet his eye, or stored in my memory to be told him at some future period. This, at least, is the hope that I cherish, the fancy that lights me on my lonely way. It may be only an ignis fatuus,[1] after all, but it can do no harm to follow it with my eyes and rejoice in its lustre, as long as it does not lure me from the path I ought to keep; and I think it will not, for I have thought deeply on my aunt's advice, and I see clearly, now, the folly of throwing myself away on one that is unworthy of all the love I have to give, and incapable of responding to the best and deepest feelings of my inmost heart—so clearly that even if I should see him again, and if he should remember me and love me still (which, alas! is too little probable, consider-

---

1 "A phosphorescent light seen hovering or flitting over marshy ground, and supposed to be due to the spontaneous combustion of an inflammable gas ... derived from decaying organic matter. ... When approached the ignis fatuus appeared to recede and finally to vanish, sometimes reappearing in another direction. This led to the notion that it was the work of a mischievous sprite, intentionally leading benighted travellers astray" (*OED*).

ing how he is situated, and by whom surrounded), and if he should ask me to marry him,—I am determined not to consent until I know for certain whether my aunt's opinion of him or mine is nearest the truth; for if mine is altogether wrong, it is not he that I love; it is a creature of my own imagination. But I think it is not wrong—no, no—there is a secret something—an inward instinct that assures me I am right. There *is* essential goodness in him;—and what delight to unfold it! If he has wandered, what bliss to recall him! If he is now exposed to the baneful influence of corrupting and wicked companions, what glory to deliver him from them!—Oh! if I could but believe that Heaven has designed me for this!

★　★　★　★　★

Today is the first of September; but my uncle has ordered the gamekeeper to spare the partridges[1] till the gentlemen come. "What gentlemen?" I asked when I heard it—a small party he had invited to shoot. His friend Mr. Wilmot was one, and my aunt's friend Mr. Boarham another. This struck me as terrible news, at the moment, but all regret and apprehension vanished like a dream when I heard that Mr. Huntingdon was actually to be a third! My aunt is greatly against his coming, of course: she earnestly endeavoured to dissuade my uncle from asking him; but he, laughing at her objections, told her it was no use talking for the mischief was already done: he had invited Huntingdon and his friend Lord Lowborough before we left London, and nothing now remained but to fix the day for their coming. So he is safe, and I am sure of seeing him. I cannot express my joy—I find it very difficult to conceal it from my aunt; but I don't wish to trouble her with my feelings till I know whether I ought to indulge them or not. If I find it my absolute duty to suppress them, they shall trouble no one but myself; and if I can really feel myself justified in indulging this attachment, I can dare anything, even the anger and grief of my best friend, for its object—surely, I shall soon know. But they are not coming till about the middle of the month.

We are to have two lady visitors also: Mr. Wilmot is to bring his niece and her cousin Milicent. I suppose, my aunt thinks the latter will benefit me by her society and the salutary example, of her gentle deportment, and lowly and tractable spirit;[2] and the former, I suspect she intends as a species of counter-attraction to win Mr. Huntingdon's attention from me. I don't

---

1　After the Game Reform Act of 1831, it was illegal to shoot partridges from 1 February until 1 September.

2　Here Helen's aunt is echoing some of Peter's exhortations to women on being a good wife. See, for example, 1 Peter 3:1-6, especially verse 4, where a good wife is described as having "a meek and quiet spirit, which is in the sight of God of great price."

thank her for this; but I shall be glad of Milicent's company: she is a sweet, good girl, and I wish I were like her—*more* like her, at least, than I am.

★ ★ ★ ★ ★

19th. They are come. They came the day before yesterday. The gentlemen are all gone out to shoot, and the ladies are with my aunt, at work,[1] in the drawing-room. I have retired to the library, for I am very unhappy, and I want to be alone. Books cannot divert me; so having opened my desk, I will try what may be done by detailing the cause of my uneasiness. This paper will serve instead of a confidential friend into whose ear I might pour forth the overflowings of my heart. It will not sympathize with my distresses, but then, it will not laugh at them, and, if I keep it close, it cannot tell again; so it is perhaps, the best friend I could have for the purpose.

First, let me speak of his arrival—how I sat at my window and watched for nearly two hours, before his carriage entered the park gates—for they all came before him,—and how deeply I was disappointed at every arrival, because it was not his. First came Mr. Wilmot and the ladies. When Milicent had got into her room, I quitted my post a few minutes, to look in upon her and have a little private conversation, for she was now my intimate friend, several long epistles having passed between us since our parting. On returning to my window, I beheld another carriage at the door. Was it his? No; it was Mr. Boarham's plain, dark chariot;[2] and there stood he upon the steps, carefully superintending the dislodging of his various boxes and packages. What a collection! one would have thought he projected a visit of six months at least. A considerable time after, came Lord Lowborough in his barouche.[3] Is he one of the profligate friends, I wonder? I should think not; for no one could call *him* a jolly companion, I'm sure,—and besides, he appears too sober and gentlemanly in his demeanour, to merit such suspicions. He is a tall, thin, gloomy looking man, apparently between thirty and forty, and of a somewhat sickly, careworn aspect.

At last, Mr. Huntingdon's light phaeton[4] came bowling merrily up the lawn. I had but a transient glimpse of him, for the moment it stopped, he

---

1 "Work" means sewing, embroidery, or other types of needlework.

2 "A light four-wheeled carriage with only back seats" (*OED*).

3 "A four wheeled carriage with a half-head behind, which can be raised or let down at pleasure, having a seat in front for the driver and seats inside for two couples to sit facing each other" (*OED*).

4 "A species of four-wheeled open carriage, of light construction; usually drawn by a pair of horses, and with one or (now generally) two seats facing forward" (*OED*). Huntingdon's carriage is the most trendy of the three carriages Helen has described.

sprang out over the side on to the portico[1] steps, and disappeared into the house.

I now submitted to be dressed for dinner—a duty which Rachel had been urging upon me for the last twenty minutes; and when that important business was completed, I repaired to the drawing-room where I found Mr. and Miss Wilmot, and Milicent Hargrave already assembled. Shortly after, Lord Lowborough entered, and then Mr. Boarham, who seemed quite willing to forget and forgive my former conduct, and to hope that a little conciliation and steady perseverance on his part might yet succeed in bringing me to reason. While I stood at the window, conversing with Milicent, he came up to me, and was beginning to talk in nearly his usual strain, when Mr. Huntingdon entered the room.

"How will he greet me, I wonder?" said my bounding heart; and instead of advancing to meet him, I turned to the window to hide or subdue my emotion. But having saluted his host and hostess, and the rest of the company, he came to me, ardently squeezed my hand, and murmured he was glad to see me once again. At that moment dinner was announced, my aunt desired him to take Miss Hargrave into the dining-room; and odious Mr. Wilmot, with unspeakable grimaces, offered his arm to me; and I was condemned to sit between himself and Mr. Boarham. But afterwards, when we were all again assembled in the drawing-room, I was indemnified for so much suffering by a few delightful minutes of conversation with Mr. Huntingdon.

In the course of the evening, Miss Wilmot was called upon to sing and play for the amusement of the company, and I to exhibit my drawings, and, though he likes music, and she is an accomplished musician, I think I am right in affirming that he paid more attention to my drawings than to her music.

So far, so good;—but, hearing him pronounce, *sotto voce*,[2] but with peculiar emphasis concerning one of the pieces, "This is better than all!"—I looked up, curious to see which it was, and, to my horror, beheld him complacently gazing at the *back* of the picture—it was his own face that I had sketched there and forgotten to rub out! To make matters worse in the agony of the moment, I attempted to snatch it from his hand;—but he prevented me, and exclaiming, "No—by George, I'll keep it!" placed it against his waistcoat, and buttoned his coat upon it with a delighted chuckle.

Then, drawing a candle close to his elbow, he gathered all the drawings to himself, as well what he had seen as the others, and muttering, "I must look at *both* sides now," he eagerly commenced an examination which I watched, at first, with tolerable composure, in the confidence that his vanity

---

1 Porch.
2 Quietly, under his breath.

would not be gratified by any further discoveries; for, though I must plead guilty to having disfigured the backs of several with abortive attempts to delineate that too fascinating physiognomy, I was sure that, with that one unfortunate exception, I had carefully obliterated all such witnesses of my infatuation. But the pencil frequently leaves an impression upon cardboard that no amount of rubbing can efface. Such, it seems, was the case with most of these; and I confess I trembled when I saw him holding them so close to the candle, and poring so intently over the seeming blanks; but still, I trusted he would not be able to make out these dim traces to his own satisfaction. I was mistaken however—having ended his scrutiny, he quietly remarked,—

"I perceive, the backs of young ladies' drawings, like the postscripts of their letters, are the most important and interesting part of the concern."[1]

Then, leaning back in his chair, he reflected a few minutes in silence, complacently smiling to himself, and, while I was concocting some cutting speech wherewith to check his gratification, he rose, and passing over to where Annabella Wilmot sat vehemently coquetting with Lord Lowborough, seated himself on the sofa beside her, and attached himself to her for the rest of the evening.

"So then!" thought I—"he despises me, because he knows I love him."

And the reflection made me so miserable I knew not what to do. Milicent came and began to admire my drawings and make remarks upon them; but I could not talk to her—I could talk to no one; and upon the introduction of tea, I took advantage of the open door and the slight diversion caused by its entrance, to slip out—for I was sure I could not take any—and take refuge in the library. My aunt sent Thomas in quest of me, to ask if I were not coming to tea; but I bade him say I should not take any tonight; and happily she was too much occupied with her guests to make any further enquires at the time.

As most of the company had travelled far that day, they retired early to rest; and having heard them all, as I thought, go up stairs, I ventured out, to get my candlestick from the drawing-room side-board. But Mr. Huntingdon had lingered behind the rest: he was just at the foot of the stairs when I opened the door; and hearing my step in the hall—though I could hardly hear it myself—he instantly turned back.

"Helen, is that you?" said he, "why did you run away from us?"

---

1 In the *Spectator* 79 (31 May 1711), Richard Steele (1672-1729) wrote, "A Woman seldom writes her Mind but in her Postscript." Brontë also has Agnes Grey describe a conversation she has with Rosalie Murray thusly: "I had enquires to make, and, like the substances of a lady's postscript, the most important must come last" (*Agnes Grey*, [London and Melbourne: Dent, 1987], 146-47).

"Good night, Mr. Huntingdon," said I, coldly, not choosing to answer the question. And I turned away to enter the drawing-room.

"But you'll shake hands, won't you?" said he, placing himself in the doorway before me. And he seized my hand, and held it much against my will.

"Let me go, Mr. Huntingdon!" said I—"I want to get a candle."

"The candle will keep," returned he.

I made a desperate effort to free my hand from his grasp.

"Why are you in such a hurry to leave me, Helen?" he said, with a smile of the most provoking self-sufficiency—"you don't hate me, you *know*."

"Yes, I do—at this moment."

"Not you! It is Annabella Wilmot you hate, not me."

"I have nothing to do with Annabella Wilmot," said I, burning with indignation.

"But *I* have, you know," returned he, with peculiar emphasis.

"That is nothing to me sir!" I retorted.

"*Is* it nothing to you, Helen?—Will you swear it?—Will you?"

"No, I won't, Mr. Huntingdon! and I *will* go!" cried I, not knowing whether to laugh or to cry, or to break out into a tempest of fury.

"Go then, you vixen!" he said; but the instant he released my hand, be had the audacity to put his arm round my neck and kiss me.

Trembling with anger and agitation—and I don't know what besides, I broke away, and got my candle and rushed up stairs to my room. He would not have done so but for that hateful picture! And there he had it still in his possession, an eternal monument to his pride and my humiliation!

It was but little sleep I got that night; and in the morning I rose perplexed and troubled with the thoughts of meeting him at breakfast. I knew not how it was to be done; an assumption of dignified, cold indifference would hardly do after what he knew of my devotion—to his face, at least. Yet something must be done to check his presumption—I would not submit to be tyrannized over by those bright, laughing eyes. And accordingly, I received his cheerful morning salutation as calmly and coldly as my aunt could have wished, and defeated with brief answers his one or two attempts to draw me into conversation; while I comported myself with unusual cheerfulness and complaisance towards every other member of the party, especially Annabella Wilmot, and even her uncle and Mr. Boarham were treated with an extra amount of civility on the occasion, not from any motives of coquetry, but just to show him that my particular coolness and reserve arose from no general ill-humour or depression of spirits.

He was not, however, to be repelled by such acting as this. He did not talk much to me, but when he did speak, it was with a degree of freedom and openness—and *kindliness* too—that plainly seemed to intimate he knew his words were music to my ears; and when his looks met mine, it was with a smile—presumptuous it might be—but oh, so sweet, so bright, so genial, that I could not possibly retain my anger; every vestige of displeasure soon melted away beneath it, like morning clouds before the summer sun.

Soon after breakfast all the gentlemen save one, with boyish eagerness, set out on their expedition against the hapless partridges; my uncle and Mr. Wilmot on their shooting ponies, Mr. Huntingdon and Lord Lowborough on their legs; the one exception being Mr. Boarham, who, in consideration of the rain that had fallen during the night, thought it prudent to remain behind a little, and join them in a while, when the sun had dried the grass. And he favoured us all with a long and minute disquisition upon the evils and dangers attendant upon damp feet, delivered with the most imperturbable gravity, amid the jeers and laughter of Mr. Huntingdon and my uncle, who, leaving the prudent sportsman to entertain the ladies with his medical discussions, sallied forth with their guns, bending their steps to the stables first, to have a look at the horses, and let out the dogs.

Not desirous of sharing Mr. Boarham's company for the whole of the morning, I betook myself to the library; and there brought forth my easel, and began to paint. The easel and the painting apparatus would serve as an excuse for abandoning the drawing-room, if my aunt should come to complain of the desertion; and besides, I wanted to finish the picture. It was one I had taken great pains with, and I intended it to be my masterpiece, though it was somewhat presumptuous in the design. By the bright azure of the sky, and by the warm and brilliant lights, and deep, long shadows, I had endeavoured to convey the idea of a sunny morning. I had ventured to give more of the bright verdure of spring or early summer to the grass and foliage, than is commonly attempted in painting. The scene represented was an open glade in a wood. A group of dark Scotch firs was introduced in the middle distance to relieve the prevailing freshness of the rest; but in the foreground, were part of the gnarled trunk and of the spreading boughs of a large forest tree, whose foliage was of a brilliant golden green—not golden from autumnal mellowness, but from the sunshine, and the very immaturity of the scarce expanded leaves. Upon this bough, that stood out in bold relief against the sombre firs, were seated an amorous pair of turtle doves, whose soft sad coloured plumage afforded a contrast of another nature; and beneath it, a young girl was kneeling on the daisy-spangled turf, with head thrown back and masses of fair hair falling on her shoulders, her hands clasped, lips parted, and eyes intently gazing upward in pleased, yet earnest contemplation of those feathered lovers—too deeply absorbed in each other to notice her.

I had scarcely settled to my work—which, however, wanted but a few touches to the finishing—when the sportsmen passed the window on their return from the stables. It was partly open, and Mr. Huntingdon must have seen me as he went by, for in half a minute he came back, and setting his gun against the wall, threw up the sash, and sprang in, and set himself before my picture.

"Very pretty, i'faith!" said he, after attentively regarding it for a few seconds—"and a very fitting study for a young lady.—Spring just opening into summer—morning just approaching noon—girlhood just ripening into womanhood—and hope just verging on fruition. She's a sweet creature! but why didn't you make her black hair?"

"I thought light hair would suit her better. You see I have made her blue-eyed, and plump, and fair and rosy."

"Upon my word—a very Hebe![1] I should fall in love with her, if I hadn't the artist before me. Sweet innocent! She's thinking there will come a time when she will be wooed and won like that pretty hen-dove, by as fond and fervent a lover; and she's thinking how pleasant it will be, and how tender and faithful he will find her."

"And perhaps," suggested I, "how tender and faithful she shall find him."

"Perhaps—for there is no limit to the wild extravagance of hope's imaginings, at such an age."

"Do you call *that*, then, one of her wild, extravagant delusions?"

"No; my heart tells me it is not. I might have thought so once, but now, I say, give me the girl I love, and I will swear eternal constancy to her and her alone, through summer and winter, through youth and age, and life and death! if age and death *must* come."

He spoke this in such serious earnest that my heart bounded with delight; but the minute after he changed his tone, and asked, with a significant smile, if I had "any more portraits."

"No," replied I, reddening with confusion and wrath. But my portfolio was on the table; he took it up, and coolly sat down to examine its contents.

"Mr. Huntingdon, those are my unfinished sketches," cried I, "and I never let any one see them."

And I placed my hand on the portfolio to wrest it from him; but he maintained his hold, assuring me that he "liked unfinished sketches of all things."

"But I hate them to be seen," returned I. "I can't let you have it, indeed!"

"Let me have its bowels then," said he; and just as I wrenched the portfolio from his hand, he deftly abstracted the greater part of its contents, and after turning them over a moment, he cried out,—

---

1 Hebe was the daughter of Zeus and Hera. She was the cup-bearer to the gods, serving them the ambrosia that keeps them immortal. Her position as cup-bearer was later taken by Ganymede. The *OED* points out that because of her position as cup-bearer and her affiliation with youth, "Hebe" can be figuratively applied to "a waitress [or] barmaid … [or] a woman in her early youth."

"Bless my stars, here's another!" and slipped a small oval of ivory paper[1] into his waistcoat pocket—a complete miniature portrait, that I had sketched with such tolerable success, as to be induced to colour it with great pains and care. But I was determined he should not keep it.

"Mr. Huntingdon," cried I, "I *insist* upon having that back! It is mine, and you have no *right* to take it. Give it me, directly—I'll never forgive you, if you don't!"

But the more vehemently I insisted, the more he aggravated my distress by his insulting gleeful laugh. At length however, he restored it to me, saying—

"Well, well, since you value it so much, I'll not deprive you of it."

To show him how I valued it, I tore it in two, and threw it into the fire. He was not prepared for this. His merriment suddenly ceasing, he stared in mute amazement at the consuming treasure; and then, with a careless "Humph! I'll go and shoot now," he turned on his heel, and vacated the apartment by the window as he came, and setting on his hat with an air, took up his gun and walked away, whistling as he went—and leaving me not too much agitated to finish my picture; for I was glad, at the moment, that I had vexed him.

When I returned to the drawing-room, I found Mr. Boarham had ventured to follow his comrades to the field; and shortly after lunch, to which they did not think of returning, I volunteered to accompany the ladies in a walk, and show Annabella and Milicent the beauties of the country. We took a long ramble and reentered the park just as the sportsmen were returning from their expedition. Toil-spent and travel-stained, the main body of them crossed over the grass to avoid us; but Mr. Huntingdon, all spattered and splashed as he was, and stained with the blood of his prey—to the no small offence of my aunt's strict sense of propriety—came out of his way to meet us, with cheerful smiles and words for all but me, and placing himself between Annabella Wilmot, and myself, walked up the road and began to relate the various exploits and disasters of the day, in a manner that would have convulsed me with laughter, if I had been on good terms with him; but he addressed himself entirely to Annabella, and I, of course, left all the laughter and all the badinage to her, and affecting the utmost indifference to whatever passed between them, walked along a few paces apart, and looking every way but theirs; while my aunt and Milicent went before, linked arm in arm, and gravely discoursing together. At length, Mr. Huntingdon turned to me, and addressing me in a confidential whisper, said—

"Helen, why did you burn my picture?"

"Because, I wished to destroy it," I answered, with an asperity it is useless now to lament.

---

1 "A thick paper or thin cardboard with a finely prepared polished surface, used by artists" (*OED*).

"Oh, very good!" was the reply, "if *you* don't value me, I must turn to somebody that will."

I thought it was partly in jest—a half playful mixture of mock resignation and pretended indifference; but immediately he resumed his place beside Miss Wilmot, and from that hour to this—during all that evening, and all the next day, and the next, and the next, and all this morning (the 22nd,) he has never given me one kind word or one pleasant look—never spoken to me, but from pure necessity—never glanced towards me, but with a cold, unfriendly look I thought him quite incapable of assuming.

My aunt observes the change, and though she has not enquired the cause or made any remark to me on the subject, I see it gives her pleasure. Miss Wilmot observes it too, and triumphantly ascribes it to her own superior charms and blandishments; but I am truly miserable—more so than I like to acknowledge to myself. Pride refuses to aid me. It has brought me into the scrape, and will not help me out of it.

He meant no harm—it was only his joyous, playful spirit; and I, by my acrimonious resentment—so serious, so disproportioned to the offence—have so wounded his feelings—so deeply offended him, that I fear he will never forgive me—and all for a mere jest! He thinks I dislike him,—and he must continue to think so. I must lose him forever; and Annabella may win him, and triumph as she will.

But it is not my loss, nor her triumph that I deplore so greatly as the wreck of my fond hopes for his advantage, and her unworthiness of his affection, and the injury he will do himself by trusting his happiness to her. *She* does not love him: she thinks only of herself. She cannot appreciate the good that is in him: she will neither see it, nor value it, nor cherish it. She will neither deplore his faults nor attempt their amendment, but rather aggravate them by her own. And I doubt whether she will not deceive him after all: I see she is playing double between him and Lord Lowborough, and while she amuses herself with the lively Huntingdon, she tries her utmost to enslave his moody friend; and should she succeed in bringing both to her feet, the fascinating commoner will have but little chance against the lordly peer. If he observes her artful by-play, it gives him no uneasiness, but rather adds new zest to his diversion by opposing a stimulating check to his otherwise too easy conquest.

Messrs. Wilmot and Boarham, have severally taken occasion by his neglect of me to renew their advances; and if I were like Annabella and some others, I should take advantage of their perseverance to endeavour to pique him into a revival of affection; but, justice and honesty apart, I could not *bear* to do it; I am annoyed enough by their present persecutions without encouraging them farther;—and even if I did, it would have precious little effect upon him. He sees me suffering under the condescending attentions and prosaic discourses of the one, and the repulsive obtrusions of the other, without so much as a shadow of commiseration for me, or resentment against my tormentors. He never could have loved me, or he would not have resigned me so willingly, and he would not go on talking to everybody else so cheerfully as he does—laughing and jesting with Lord Lowborough and my uncle, teasing Milicent Hargrave, and flirting with Annabella Wilmot—as if nothing were on his mind. Oh, why can't I hate him?[1] I must be infatuated, or I should, *scorn* to regret him as I do! But I must rally all the powers I have remaining, and try to tear him from my heart. There goes the dinner bell—and here comes my aunt to scold me for sitting here at my desk all day, instead of staying with the company—I wish the company were—gone.

CHAPTER XIX
AN INCIDENT

TWENTY-SECOND. Night—What have I done? and what will be the end of it? I cannot calmly reflect upon it; I cannot sleep. I must have recourse to my diary again; I will commit it to paper tonight, and see what I shall think of it tomorrow.

I went down to dinner resolving to be cheerful and well-conducted, and kept my resolution very creditably, considering how my head ached, and how internally wretched I felt.—I don't know what is come over me of late; my very energies both mental and physical must be strangely impaired, or I should not have acted so weakly in many respects, as I have done;—but I have not been well this last day or two: I suppose it is with sleeping and eating so little, and thinking so much, and being so continually out of humour. But to return: I was exerting myself to sing and play for the amusement, and at the request of my aunt and Milicent, before the gentlemen came into the drawing-room (Miss Wilmot never likes to waste her musical efforts on ladies' ears alone): Milicent had asked for a little Scotch song, and I was just in the middle of it when they entered. The first thing Mr. Huntingdon did, was to walk up to Annabella:—

"Now, Miss Wilmot, won't *you* give us some music tonight?" said he. "Do now! I know you will, when I tell you that I have been hungering and thirsting all day, for the sound of your voice. Come! the piano's vacant."

---

1 Rosengarten and Smith, and Davies point out that this phrase recalls Samuel Richardson's *Pamela* (1740), when she says, "What is the matter, that, with all his ill usage of me, I cannot hate him" (*Pamela*, ed. P. Sabor [London: Penguin, 1980], 218, quoted in *OTWH* 477 and *PTWH* 508).

It was; for I had quitted it immediately upon hearing his petition. Had I been endowed with a proper degree of self-possession, I should have turned to the lady myself, and cheerfully joined my entreaties to his; whereby I should have disappointed his expectations, if the affront had been purposely given, or made him sensible of the wrong, if it had only arisen from thoughtlessness; but I felt it too deeply to do anything but rise from the music-stool, and throw myself back on the sofa, suppressing with difficulty the audible expression of the bitterness I felt within. I knew Annabella's musical talents were superior to mine, but that was no reason why I should be treated as a perfect nonentity. The time and the manner of his asking her appeared like a gratuitous insult to me; and I could have wept with pure vexation.

Meantime, she exultantly seated herself at the piano, and favoured him with two of his favourite songs, in such superior style that even I soon lost my anger in admiration, and listened with a sort of gloomy pleasure to the skilful modulations of her full-toned and powerful voice, so judiciously aided by her rounded and spirited touch; and while my ears drank in the sound, my eyes rested on the face of her principal auditor, and derived an equal or superior delight from the contemplation of his speaking countenance, as he stood beside her—that eye and brow lighted up with keen enthusiasm, and that sweet smile passing and appearing like gleams of sunshine on an April day. No wonder he should hunger and thirst to hear her sing. I now forgave him, from my heart, his reckless slight of me, and I felt ashamed at my pettish resentment of such a trifle—ashamed too of those bitter envious pangs that gnawed my inmost heart, in spite of all this admiration and delight.

"There now!" said she, playfully running her fingers over the keys, when she had concluded the second song. "What shall I give you next?"

But in saying this, she looked back at Lord Lowborough, who was standing a little behind leaning against the back of a chair—an attentive listener, too, experiencing, to judge by his countenance, much the same feelings of mingled pleasure and sadness as I did. But the look she gave him, plainly said, "Do you choose for me now: I have done enough for him, and will gladly exert myself to gratify you;" and thus encouraged, his lordship came forward, and turning over the music, presently set before her a little song that I had noticed before, and read more than once, with an interest arising from the circumstance of my connecting it in my mind with the reigning tyrant of my thoughts. And now with my nerves already excited and half unstrung, I could not hear those words so sweetly warbled forth, without some symptoms of emotion I was not able to suppress. Tears rose unbidden to my eyes, and I buried my face in the sofa-pillow that they might flow unseen while I listened. The air was simple, sweet, and sad, it is still running in my head,—and so are the words:—

"Farewell to thee![1] but not farewell
To all my fondest thoughts of thee:
Within my heart they still shall dwell;
And they shall cheer and comfort me.

O, beautiful, and full of grace!
If thou hadst never met mine eye,
I had not dreamed a living face
Could fancied charms so far outvie.

If I may ne'er behold again
That form and face, so dear to me,
Nor hear thy voice, still would I fain
Preserve, for aye, their memory.

That voice, the magic of whose tone
Can wake an echo in my breast,
Creating feelings that, alone,
Can make my tranced spirit blest.

That laughing eye, whose sunny beam
My memory would not cherish less;—
And oh, that smile whose joyous gleam
No mortal language[2] can express.

Adieu! but let me cherish, still,
The hope with which I cannot part.
Contempt may wound, and coldness chill,
But still it lingers in my heart.

And who can tell but Heaven, at last,
May answer all my thousand prayers,
And bid the future pay the past
With joy for anguish, smile for tears?"

When it ceased, I longed for nothing so much as to be out of the room.
The sofa was not far from the door, but I did not dare to raise my head, for I

---

1   This poem was written by Anne Brontë. See Edward Chitham, *The Poems of Anne
   Brontë. A New Text and Commentary* (London: Macmillan, 1979), 171–72.
2   "Languish" is the word found in the Newby edition of the novel, but clearly the sense
   of the line makes "language" the correct word.

knew Mr. Huntingdon was standing near me, and I knew by the sound of his voice, as he spoke in answer to some remark of Lord Lowborough's, that his face was turned towards me. Perhaps, a half suppressed sob had caught his ear, and caused him to look round—Heaven forbid! But, with a violent effort, I checked all further signs of weakness, dried my tears, and, when I thought he had turned away again, rose, and instantly left the apartment, taking refuge in my favourite resort, the library.

There was no light there but the faint red glow of the neglected fire;—but I did not want a light; I only wanted to indulge my thoughts, unnoticed and undisturbed; and sitting down on a low stool before the easy chair, I sunk my head upon its cushioned seat, and thought, and thought, until the tears gushed out again, and I wept like any child. Presently, however, the door was gently opened and some one entered the room. I trusted it was only a servant, and did not stir. The door was closed again—but I was not alone: a hand gently touched my shoulder, and a voice said, softly—

"Helen, what is the matter?"

I could not answer at the moment.

"You must and shall tell me," was added more vehemently, and the speaker threw himself on his knees, beside me on the rug, and forcibly possessed himself of my hand; but I hastily caught it away, and replied—

"It is nothing to you, Mr. Huntingdon."

"Are you sure it is nothing to me?" he returned, "can you swear that you were not thinking of me while you wept?"

This was unendurable. I made an effort to rise, but he was kneeling on my dress.

"Tell me," continued he—"I want to know,—because, if you were, I have something to say to you,—and if not, I'll go."

"Go then!" I cried; but, fearing he would obey too well, and never come again, I hastily added—"Or say what you have to say, and have done with it!"

"But which?" said he—"for I shall only say it if you really were thinking of me. So tell me, Helen."

"You're excessively impertinent, Mr. Huntingdon!"

"Not at all—too pertinent, you mean—so you won't tell me?—Well, I'll spare your woman's pride, and, construing your silence into 'Yes,' I'll take it for granted that I *was* the subject of your thoughts, and the cause of your affliction—"

"Indeed, sir—"

"If you deny it, I won't tell you my secret," threatened he; and I did not interrupt him again—or even attempt to repulse him, though he had taken my hand once more, and half embraced me with his other arm—I was scarcely conscious of it, at the time.

"It is this," resumed he: "that Annabella Wilmot, in comparison with you, is like a flaunting peony compared with a sweet, wild rosebud gemmed with dew—and I love you to distraction!—Now, tell me if that intelligence gives you any pleasure.—Silence again? That means yes.—Then let me add, that I cannot live without you, and if you answer, No, to this last question, you will drive me mad.—Will you bestow yourself upon me?—you will!" he cried, nearly squeezing me to death in his arms.

"No, no!" I exclaimed, struggling to free myself from him—"you must ask my uncle and aunt."

"They won't refuse me, if you don't."

"I'm not so sure of that—my aunt dislikes you."

"But *you* don't, Helen—say you love me, and I'll go."

"I wish you *would* go!" I replied.

"I will, this instant,—if you'll only say you love me."

"You know I do," I answered. And again he caught me in his arms, and smothered me with kisses.

At that moment, my aunt opened wide the door, and stood before us, candle in hand, in shocked and horrified amazement, gazing alternately at Mr. Huntingdon and me—for we had both started up, and now stood wide enough asunder. But *his* confusion was only for a moment. Rallying in an instant, with the most enviable assurance, he began—

"I beg ten thousand pardons, Mrs. Maxwell! Don't be too severe upon me. I've been asking your sweet niece to take me for better, for worse; and she, like a good girl, informs me she cannot think of it without her uncle's and aunt's consent. So let me implore you not to condemn me to eternal wretchedness: if *you* favour my cause, I am safe; for Mr. Maxwell, I am certain, can refuse you nothing."

"We will talk of this tomorrow, sir," said my aunt, coldly. "It is a subject that demands mature and serious deliberation. At present, you had better return to the drawing-room."

"But meantime," pleaded he, "let me commend my cause to your most indulgent—"

"No indulgence for you, Mr. Huntingdon, must come between me and the consideration of my niece's happiness."

"Ah, true! I know she is an angel, and I am a presumptuous dog to dream of possessing such a treasure; but, nevertheless, I would sooner die than relinquish her in favour of the best man that ever went to heaven—and as for her happiness, I would sacrifice my body and soul—"

"Body and *soul* Mr. Huntingdon—sacrifice your *soul*?"

"Well, I would lay down life—"

"You would not be required to lay it down."

"I would spend it, then—devote my life—and all its powers to the promotion and preservation—"

"Another time, sir, we will talk of this—and I should have felt disposed to judge more favourably of your pretensions, if you too had chosen another time and place, and—let me add—another *manner* for your declaration."

"Why, you see, Mrs. Maxwell," he began—

"Pardon me, sir," said she, with dignity—"The company are enquiring for you in the other room." And she turned to me.

"Then *you* must plead for me, Helen," said he, and at length withdrew.

"You had better retire to your room, Helen," said my aunt, gravely. "I will discuss this matter with you, too, tomorrow."

"Don't be angry, aunt," said I.

"My dear, I am not angry," she replied: "I am *surprised*. If it is true that you told him you could not accept his offer without our consent—"

"It *is* true," interrupted I.

"Then how could you permit—"

"I couldn't help it, aunt," I cried bursting into tears. They were not altogether the tears of sorrow, or of fear for her displeasure, but rather the outbreak of the general tumultuous excitement of my feeling. But my good aunt was touched at my agitation. In a softer tone, she repeated her recommendation to retire, and gently kissing my forehead, bade me goodnight, and put her candle in my hand; and I went;—but my brain worked so, I could not think of sleeping. I feel calmer now, that I have written all this; and I will go to bed, and try to win tired nature's sweet restorer.[1]

CHAPTER XX
PERSISTENCE

SEPTEMBER 24th.—In the morning I rose, light and cheerful, nay, intensely happy. The hovering cloud cast over me by my aunt's views, and by the fear of not obtaining her consent, was lost in the bright effulgence of my own hopes, and the too delightful consciousness of requited love. It was a splendid morning; and I went out to enjoy it, in a quiet ramble in company with my own blissful thoughts. The dew was on the grass, and ten thousand gossamers were waving in the breeze; the happy red-breast was pouring out its little soul in song, and my heart overflowed with silent hymns of gratitude and praise to Heaven.[2]

---

1 Edward Young's (1683–1765) *The Complaint, or Night Thoughts on Life, Death and Immortality* (1742) opens with "Tir'd Nature's sweet Restorer, balmy *Sleep!*" *Night Thoughts* was a very popular and influential eighteenth-century poem; the Brontës owned a copy of it.

2 This Romantic description of the morning loosely evokes William Wordsworth's (1770–1850) "I Wandered Lonely as a Cloud" (1804), his "daffodil" poem, and the opening of "Resolution and Independence" (1807).

But I had not wandered far before my solitude was interrupted by the only person that could have disturbed my musings, at that moment, without being looked upon as an unwelcome intruder: Mr. Huntingdon came suddenly upon me. So unexpected was the apparition, that I might have thought it the creation of an over-excited imagination, had the sense of sight alone borne witness to his presence; but immediately I felt his strong arm round my waist and his warm kiss on my cheek, while his keen and gleeful salutation, "My own Helen!" was ringing in my ear.

"Not[1] yours yet," said I, hastily swerving aside from this too presumptuous greeting—"remember my guardians. You will not easily attain my aunt's consent. Don't you see she is prejudiced against you?"

"I do, dearest; and you must tell me why, that I may best know how to combat her objections. I suppose she thinks I am a prodigal," pursued he, observing that I was unwilling to reply, "and concludes that I shall have but little worldly goods wherewith to endow my better half? If so, you must tell her that my property is mostly entailed,[2] and I cannot get rid of it. There may be a few mortgages on the rest—a few trifling debts and encumbrances here and there, but nothing to speak of; and though I acknowledge I am not so rich as I might be—or have been—still, I think, we could manage pretty comfortably on what's left. My father, you know, was something of a miser, and in his latter days especially, saw no pleasure in life but to amass riches; and so it is no wonder that his son should make it his chief delight to spend them, which was accordingly the case, until my acquaintance with you, dear Helen, taught me other views and nobler aims. And the very idea of having you to care for under my roof, would force me to moderate my expenses and live like a Christian—not to speak of all the prudence and virtue you would instill into my mind by your wise counsels and sweet, attractive goodness."

"But it is not that," said I, "it is not money my aunt thinks about. She knows better than to value worldly wealth above its price."

"What is it then?"

"She wishes me to—to marry none but a really good man."

"What, a man of 'decided piety?'[3]—ahem!—Well, come, I'll manage that too! It's Sunday today, isn't it? I'll go to church morning, afternoon, and evening, and comport myself in such a godly sort that she shall regard me

---

1   The Newby edition reads "nor," but it's clear from the conversation that the correct word is "not."

2   "The settlement of the succession of a landed estate, so that it cannot be bequeathed at pleasure by any one possessor" (*OED*).

3   Virgil, *The Aeneid*, I.151, "*vir pietate gravis.*" This is translated as a man confirmed in piety or full of piety.

with admiration and sisterly love, as a brand plucked from the burning.[1] I'll come home sighing like a furnace, and full of the savour and unction of dear Mr. Blatant's discourse—"

"Mr. Leighton," said I, dryly.

"Is Mr. Leighton a 'sweet preacher,' Helen—a 'dear, delightful, heavenly-minded man?'"[2]

"He is a *good* man, Mr. Huntingdon. I wish I could say half as much for you."

"Oh, I forgot, you are a saint, too. I crave your pardon, dearest—but don't call me Mr. Huntingdon, my name is Arthur."

"I'll call you nothing—for I'll have nothing at all to do with you, if you talk in that way any more. If you really mean to deceive my aunt as you say, you are very wicked; and if not, you are very wrong to jest on such a subject."

"I stand corrected," said he, concluding his laugh with a sorrowful sigh. "Now," resumed he, after a momentary pause, "let us talk about something else. And come nearer to me, Helen, and take my arm; and then I'll let you alone. I can't be quiet while I see you walking there."

I complied; but said we must soon return to the house.

"No one will be down to breakfast yet, for long enough," he answered. "You spoke of your guardians just now, Helen, but is not your father still living?"

"Yes, but I always look upon my uncle and aunt as my guardians, for they are so, in deed, though not in name. My father has entirely given me up to their care. I have never seen him, since dear mamma died when I was a very little girl, and my aunt, at her request, offered to take charge of me, and took me away to Staningley, where I have remained ever since; and I don't think he would object to anything for me, that she thought proper to sanction."

"But would he sanction anything to which she thought proper to object?"

"No, I don't think he cares enough about me."

---

1   Although this phrase is meant to invoke portions of Zechariah 3:2 ("a brand plucked out of the fire") and Amos 4:11 ("a firebrand plucked out of the burning"), this phrase has long been associated with Dissent and Methodism in particular. John Wesley used it to describe himself literally, since he escaped a fire at Epworth Rectory when young, as well as the more conventional, figurative usage of one saved from damnation by religion. Charlotte Brontë also uses this phrase in *Jane Eyre* when St John Rivers tries to convince Jane to marry him and become a missionary's wife: "He asked, he urged, he claimed the boon of a brand snatched from the burning" (*Jane Eyre*, ed. Richard Nemesvari [Peterborough, ON: Broadview Press, 1999], 517).

2   Although these words cannot be attributed to any one source, given the way Huntingdon is joking about religious matters, they are probably quotations from or about a nineteenth-century Dissenting minister that Victorian readers would have recognized.

"He is very much to blame—but he doesn't know what an angel he has for his daughter—which is all the better for me, as, if he did, he would not be willing to part with such a treasure."

"And Mr. Huntingdon," said I. "I suppose you *know* I am not an heiress?"

He protested he had never given it a thought, and begged I would not disturb his present enjoyment by the mention of such uninteresting subjects. I was glad of this proof of disinterested affection; for Annabella Wilmot is the probable heiress to all her uncle's wealth, in addition to her late father's property, which she has already in possession.

I now insisted upon retracing our steps to the house; but we walked slowly, and went on talking as we proceeded. I need not repeat all we said: let me rather refer to what passed between my aunt and me, after breakfast, when Mr. Huntingdon called my uncle aside, no doubt to make his proposals, and she beckoned me into another room, where she once more commenced a solemn remonstrance which, however, entirely failed to convince me that her view of the case was preferable to my own.

"You judge him uncharitably, aunt, I know," said I. "His very friends are not half so bad as you represent them. There is Walter Hargrave, Milicent's brother, for one: he is but a little lower than the angels,[1] if half she says of him is true. She is continually talking to me about him, and lauding his many virtues to the skies."

"You will form a very inadequate estimate of a man's character," replied she, "if you judge by what a fond sister says of him. The worst of them generally know how to hide their misdeeds from their sister's eyes, and their mother's too."

"And there is Lord Lowborough," continued I, "quite a decent man."

"Who told you so? Lord Lowborough is a *desperate* man. He has dissipated his fortune in gambling and other things, and is now seeking an heiress to retrieve it. I told Miss Wilmot so; but you're all alike: she haughtily answered she was very much obliged to me, but she believed *she* knew when a man was seeking her for her fortune, and when for herself; she flattered herself she had had experience enough in those matters, to be justified in trusting to her own judgment—and as for his lordship's lack of fortune, she cared nothing about that, as she hoped her own would suffice for both; and as for his wildness, she supposed he was no worse than others—besides he was reformed now.—Yes, they can all play the hypocrite when they want to take in a fond, misguided woman!"

---

1 Psalm 8:5: "For thou has made him a little lower than the angels, and hast crowned him with glory and honour"; and Hebrews 2:9: "But we see that Jesus, who was made a little lower than the angels for the suffering of death, crowned with glory and honour; that he by the grace of God should taste death for every man."

"Well, I think he's about as good as she is," said I. "But when Mr. Hunting-don is married, he won't have many opportunities of consorting with his bachelor friends;—and the worse they are, the more I long to deliver him from them."

"To be sure, my dear; and the worse *he* is, I suppose, the more you long to deliver him from himself."

"Yes, provided he is not incorrigible—that is, the more I long to deliver him from his faults—to give him an opportunity of shaking off the adventi-tious evil got from contact with others worse than himself, and shining out in the unclouded light of his own genuine goodness—to do my utmost to help his better self against his worse, and make him what he would have been if he had not, from the beginning, had a bad, selfish, miserly father, who to gratify his own sordid passions, restricted him in the most innocent enjoyments of childhood and youth, and so disgusted him with every kind of restraint;—and a foolish mother who indulged him to the top of his bent,[1] deceiving her husband for him, and doing her utmost to encourage those germs of folly and vice it was her duty to suppress,—and then, such a set of companions as you represent his friends to be—"

"Poor man!" said she, sarcastically, "his kind have greatly wronged him!"

"They have!" cried I—"and they shall wrong him no more—his wife shall undo what his mother did!"

"Well!" said she, after a short pause. "I must say, Helen, I thought bet-ter of your judgment than this—and your taste too. How you can love such a man I cannot tell, or what pleasure you can find in his company; for 'What fellowship hath light with darkness; or he that believeth with an infidel?'"[2]

"He is not an infidel;—and I am not light, and he is not darkness, his worst and only vice is thoughtlessness."

"And thoughtlessness," pursued my aunt, "may lead to every crime, and will but poorly excuse our errors in the sight of God. Mr. Huntingdon, I sup-pose, is not without the common faculties of men: he is not so light-headed as to be irresponsible: his maker has endowed him with reason and con-science as well as the rest of us; the scriptures are open to him as well as to others;—and 'If he hear not them, neither will he hear though one rose from

---

1   Shakespeare, *Hamlet* III.ii.377: "They fool me to the top of my bent."

2   This is a combination of two sentences from 2 Corinthians 6:14–15: "Be ye not equally yoked together with unbelievers; for what fellowship hath righteous with unrighteous and what communion hath light with darkness? And what concord hath Christ with Belial [Satan]? Or what part hath he that believeth with an infidel?" This idea of being "unequally yoked" with someone was not an unusual topic of contemplation. See, for example, Anonymous, "On Being Unequally Yoked," *The Methodist Magazine* Vol. 34 (Oct. 1811): 776–79.

the dead.'[1] And, remember, Helen," continued she solemnly, "'The wicked shall be turned into hell, and they that *forget* God!'[2] And suppose, even, that he should continue to love you, and you him, and that you should pass through life together with tolerable comfort,—how will it be in the end, when you see yourselves parted for ever; you, perhaps, taken into eternal bliss, and he cast into the lake that burneth with unquenchable fire[3]—there for ever to—"

"Not for ever,"[4] I exclaimed, "'only till he has paid the uttermost farthing;'[5] for 'If any man's work abide not the fire, he shall suffer loss, yet himself shall be saved, but so as by fire,'[6] and he that 'is able to subdue all things to himself, will have all men to be saved,'[7] and 'will in the fullness of time, gather together in one all things in Christ Jesus, who tasted death for every man, and in whom God will reconcile all things to himself, whether they be things in earth or things in heaven.'"[8]

"Oh, Helen! where did you learn all this?"

---

1   Helen later uses this same passage about Lazarus from Luke 16:31 when she is at the Markhams' home discussing child-rearing practices (59).

2   Psalm 9:17, although Helen's aunt substitutes "they" for "all the nations."

3   Helen's aunt is referring to Revelation 20:10 ("And the devil that deceived them was cast into the lake of fire and brimstone, where the beast and the false prophet are, and shall be tormented day and night forever and ever.") and Revelation 21:8 ("But the fearful, and unbelieving, and the abominable, and murderers, and whoremongers and sorcerers, and idolaters, and all liars, shall have their part in the lake which burneth with fire and brimstone: which is the second death.").

4   Here it becomes clear that Helen believes in the doctrine of universal salvation. See Brontë's letter to the Reverend David Thom for her explanation of how "in my late novel … I have given as many hints in support of the doctrine as I could venture to introduce into a work of that description" (Appendix A1).

5   A slightly revised portion of Matthew 5:26. The original phrase is "till thou has paid the uttermost farthing."

6   A version of 1 Corinthians 3:15: "If any man's work shall be burned, he shall suffer loss but he himself shall be saved; yet so as by fire."

7   A combination of Philippians 3:21: "[Christ] shall change our vile body, that it may be fashioned like unto his glorious body, according to the working whereby he is able even to subdue all things unto himself" and 1 Timothy 2:4: "[Christ] will have all men to be saved, and to come unto the knowledge of the truth."

8   A conflation of Ephesians 1:10 ("That in the dispensation of the fullness of times he might gather together in one all things in Christ, both which are in heaven, and which are on earth…"); Hebrews 2:9 ("But we see in Jesus who was made a little lower than the angels for the suffering of death, crowned with glory and honour; that he by the grace of God should taste death for every man"); and Colossians 1:20 ("And, having made peace through the blood of his cross, by him to reconcile all things unto himself; by him, I say, whether they be things in earth, or things in heaven").

"In the Bible, aunt. I have searched it through, and found nearly thirty passages, all tending to support the same theory."

"And is *that* the use you make of your Bible? And did you find no passages tending to prove the danger and the falsity of such a belief?"

"No: I found, indeed some passages that taken by themselves, might seem to contradict that opinion; but they will all bear a different construction to that which is commonly given, and in most the only difficulty is in the word which we translate 'everlasting' or 'eternal:'[1] I don't know the Greek, but I believe it strictly means for ages, and might signify either endless or long-enduring. And as for the danger of the belief, I would not publish it abroad, if I thought any poor wretch would be likely to presume upon it to his own destruction, but it is a glorious thought to cherish in one's own heart, and I would not part with it for all the world can give!"

Here our conference ended, for it was now high time to prepare for church. Every one attended the morning service, except my uncle, who hardly ever goes, and Mr. Wilmot, who stayed at home with him to enjoy a quiet game of cribbage. In the afternoon Miss Wilmot and Lord Lowborough likewise excused themselves from attending; but Mr. Huntingdon vouchsafed to accompany us again. Whether it was to ingratiate himself with my aunt I cannot tell, but, if so, he certainly should have behaved better. I must confess, I did not like his conduct during service at all. Holding his prayer book upside down, or open at any place but the right, he did nothing but stare about him, unless he happened to catch my aunt's eye or mine, and then he would drop his own on his book, with a puritanical air of mock solemnity that would have been ludicrous, if it had not been too provoking. Once, during the sermon, after attentively regarding Mr. Leighton for a few minutes, he suddenly produced his gold pencil case and snatched up a Bible. Perceiving that I observed the movement, he whispered he was going to make a note of the sermon; but instead of that—as I sat next him I could not help seeing that he was making a caricature of the preacher, giving to the respectable, pious, elderly gentleman, the air and aspect of a most absurd old hypocrite. And yet, upon his return, he talked to my aunt about the sermon with a degree of modest, serious discrimination that tempted me to believe he had really attended and profited by the discourse.

Just before dinner my uncle called me into the library for the discussion of a very important matter, which was dismissed in few words.

"Now Nell," said he, "this young Huntingdon has been asking for you: what must I say about it? Your aunt would answer 'No'—but what say you?"

"I say yes, uncle," replied I, without a moment's hesitation; for I had thoroughly made up my mind on the subject.

---

1 The Greek is *aionios*, which is also the root for the word "aeon."

"Very good!" cried he. "Now that's a good honest answer—wonderful for a girl!—Well, I'll write to your father tomorrow. He's sure to give his consent; so you may look on the matter as settled. You'd have done a deal better if you'd taken Wilmot, I can tell you; but that you won't believe. At your time of life, it's love that rules the roast:[1] at mine, it's solid, serviceable gold. I suppose now, you'd never dream of looking into the state of your husband's finances, or troubling your head about settlements, or anything of that sort?"

"I don't think I should."

"Well, be thankful, then, that you've wiser heads to think for you. I haven't had time, yet, to examine thoroughly into this young rascal's affairs, but I see that a great part of his father's fine property has been squandered away;—but still, I think there's a pretty fair share of it left, and a little careful nursing may make a handsome thing of it yet; and then we must persuade your father to give you a decent fortune, as he has only one besides yourself to care for;—and, if you behave well, who knows but what I may be induced to remember you in my will?" continued he, putting his finger to his nose, with a knowing wink.

"Thanks uncle, for that and all your kindness," replied I.

"Well, and I questioned this young spark on the matter of settlements," continued he; "and he seemed disposed to be generous enough on that point—"

"I knew he would!" said I. "But pray don't trouble your head—or his, or mine about that; for all I have will be his, and all he has will be mine; and what more could either of us require?" And I was about to make my exit, but he called me back.

"Stop, stop!" cried he—"we haven't mentioned the time yet. When must it be? Your aunt would put it off till the Lord knows when, but he is anxious to be bound as soon as may be: he won't hear of waiting beyond next month; and you, I guess, will be of the same mind, so—"

"Not at all, uncle; on the contrary, I should like to wait till after Christmas, at least."

"Oh! pooh, pooh! never tell me that tale—I know better," cried he; and he persisted in his incredulity. Nevertheless, it is quite true. I am in no hurry at all. How can I be, when I think of the momentous change that awaits me, and of all I have to leave? It is happiness enough, to know that we *are* to be united; and that he really loves me, and I may love *him* as devotedly, and think of him as often as I please. However, I insisted upon consulting my aunt about the *time* of the wedding, for I determined her counsels should not be utterly disregarded; and no conclusions on that particular are come to yet.

---

1 From the sixteenth through the nineteenth centuries, this form of the expression "rules the roost" was common (*OED*).

CHAPTER XXI
OPINIONS

OCTOBER 1st—All is settled now. My father has given his consent, and the time is fixed for Christmas, by a sort of compromise between the respective advocates for hurry and delay. Milicent Hargrave is to be one bridesmaid, and Annabella Wilmot the other—not that I am particularly fond of the latter, but she is an intimate of the family, and I have not another friend.

When I told Milicent of my engagement, she rather provoked me by her manner of taking it. After staring a moment in mute surprise, she said—

"Well Helen, I suppose I ought to congratulate you—and I *am* glad to see you so happy; but I did not think you would take him; and I can't help feeling surprised that you should like him so much."

"Why so?"

"Because you are so superior to him in every way, and there's something so bold—and reckless about him—so, I don't know how—but I always feel a wish to get out of his way, when I see him approach."

"You are timid, Milicent, but that's no fault of his."

"And then his look," continued she. "People say he's handsome, and of course he is, but *I* don't *like* that kind of beauty; and I wonder that you should."

"Why so, pray?"

"Well, you know, I think there's nothing noble or lofty in his appearance."[1]

"In fact, you wonder that I can like any one so unlike the stilted heroes of romance? Well! give me my flesh and blood lover, and I'll leave all the Sir Herberts and Valentines[2] to you—if you can find them."

"I don't want them," said she. "I'll be satisfied with flesh and blood too—only the spirit must shine through and predominate. But don't you think Mr. Huntingdon's face is too red?"[3]

---

1 Possibly a reference to physiognomy and/or phrenology. These were nineteenth-century "sciences" that read the size and shape of facial attributes along with skull size and shape for meaning, determining a person's character and potential based upon the shape of his or her head. Thus someone could "look" noble or depraved.

2 Helen is rejecting the highly civilized men of courtly romance and refers to *Valentine and Orson*, the French romance first published in 1489 about twin brothers abandoned in the woods during their infancy. Valentine was raised in court, while Orson was raised in the woods, a feral child. This story has a long history in England too, as the first known English version was printed in 1550 (*The Historye of the two Valyannte Brethren: Valentyne and Orson* by Henry Watson). She could also be referring to the play by Thomas J. Dibdin (1771–1814), *Valentine and Orson: Or, the Wildman of the Woods* (London: Barker and Son [etc.], 1804).

3 An overly red face can be a sign of excessive alcohol consumption.

"No!" cried I, indignantly. "It is not red at all. There is just a pleasant glow—a healthy freshness in his complexion, the warm, pinky tint of the whole harmonizing with the deeper colour of the cheeks, exactly as it ought to do. I hate a man to be red and white, like a painted doll—or all sickly white, or smoky black, or cadaverous yellow!"[1]

"Well, tastes differ—but *I* like pale or dark," replied she. "But, to tell you the truth Helen, I had been deluding myself with the hope that you would one day be my sister. I expected Walter would be introduced to you next season; and I thought you would like him, and was certain he would like you; and I flattered myself I should thus have the felicity of seeing the two persons I like best in the world—except mamma—united in one. He mayn't be exactly what you would call handsome, but he's far more distinguished-looking, and nicer and better than Mr. Huntingdon;—and I'm sure you would say so, if you knew him."

"Impossible, Milicent! You think so, because you're his sister; and, on that account, I'll forgive you; but nobody else should so disparage Arthur Huntingdon to me, with impunity."

Miss Wilmot expressed her feelings on the subject, almost as openly.

"And so, Helen," said she, coming up to me with a smile of no amiable import, "you are to be Mrs. Huntingdon, I suppose?"

"Yes," replied I. "Don't you envy me?"

"Oh, *dear*, no!" she exclaimed, "I shall probably be Lady Lowborough some day, and then you know, dear, I shall be in a capacity to enquire, 'Don't you envy *me*?'"

"Henceforth, I shall envy no one," returned I.

"Indeed! Are you so happy then?" said she thoughtfully; and something very like a cloud of disappointment shadowed her face. "And does he love you—I mean, does he idolize you as much as you do him?" she added, fixing her eyes upon me with ill-disguised anxiety for the reply.

"I don't want to be idolized," I answered, "but I am well assured that he *loves* me more than anybody else in the world—as I do him."

"Exactly," said she with a nod. "I wish—" she paused.

"What do you wish?" asked I, annoyed at the vindictive expression of her countenance.

"I wish," returned she, with a short laugh, "that all the attractive points and desirable qualifications of the two gentlemen were united in one—that Lord Lowborough had Huntingdon's handsome face and good temper, and all his wit, and mirth and charm, or else that Huntingdon had Lowborough's

---

1 Possibly another reference to humoral theory, as the complexion colors she describes correlate to the bodily fluids so central to those ideas: blood, phlegm, black bile, and yellow bile. (See n. 1, page 146 for more information.)

pedigree, and title, and delightful old family seat, and I had him; and you might have the other and welcome."

"Thank you, dear Annabella, I am better satisfied with things as they are, for my own part; and for you, I wish you were as well content with your intended, as I am with mine," said I; and it was true enough; for, though vexed at first at her unamiable spirit, her frankness touched me, and the contrast between our situations was such, that I could well afford to pity her and wish her well.

Mr. Huntingdon's acquaintances appear to be no better pleased with our approaching union than mine. This morning's post brought him letters from several of his friends, during the perusal of which, at the breakfast-table, he excited the attention of the company, by the singular variety of his grimaces. But he crushed them all into his pocket, with a private laugh, and said nothing till the meal was concluded. Then, while the company were hanging over the fire or loitering through the room, previous to settling to their various morning's avocations, he came and leant over the back of my chair, with his face in contact with my curls, and commencing with a quiet little kiss, poured forth the following complaints into my ear—

"Helen, you witch, do you know that you've entailed upon me the curses of all my friends? I wrote to them the other day, to tell them of my happy prospects, and now, instead of a bundle of congratulations, I've got a pocket-full of bitter execrations and reproaches. There's not one kind wish for me, or one good word for you among them all. They say there'll be no more fun now, no more merry days and glorious nights—and all my fault—I am the first to break up the jovial band, and others in pure despair, will follow my example. I was the very life and prop of the community, they do me the honour to say, and I have shamefully betrayed my trust—"

"You may join them again, if you like," said I, somewhat piqued at the sorrowful tone of his discourse. "I should be sorry to stand between any man—or body of men and so much happiness; and perhaps I can manage to do without you, as well as your poor deserted friends."

"Bless you! no," murmured he. "It's 'all for love or the world well lost,'[1] with me. Let them go to—where they belong, to speak politely. But if you saw how they abuse me, Helen, you would love me all the more, for having ventured so much for your sake."

He pulled out his crumpled letters. I thought he was going to show them to me, and told him I did not wish to see them.

"I'm not going to show them to you, love," said he. "They're hardly fit for a lady's eyes—the most part of them. But look here. This is Grimsby's scrawl—only three lines, the sulky dog! He doesn't say much, to be sure, but

---

1   Title of a play by John Dryden (1631–1700), published in 1678.

his very silence implies more than all the others' words, and the less he says, the more he thinks—G—d d—n him!—I beg your pardon, dearest—and this is Hargrave's missive. He is particularly grieved at me, because, forsooth, he had fallen in love with you from his sister's reports, and meant to have married you himself, as soon as he had sown his wild oats."

"I'm vastly obliged to him," observed I.

"And so am I," said he. "And look at this. This is Hattersley's—every page stuffed full of railing accusations, bitter curses, and lamentable complaints, ending up with swearing that he'll get married himself in revenge: he'll throw himself away on the first old maid that chooses to set her cap at him,—as if I cared what he did with himself."

"Well," said I, "if you do give up your intimacy with these men, I don't think you will have much cause to regret the loss of their society; for it's my belief they never did you much good."

"Maybe not; but we'd a merry time of it, too, though mingled with sorrow and pain, as Lowborough knows to his cost—ha, ha!" And while he was laughing at the recollection of Lowborough's troubles, my uncle came and clapped him on the shoulder.

"Come my lad!" said he. "Are you too busy making love to my niece, to make war with the pheasants?—First of October remember![1]—Sun shines out—rain ceased—even Boarham's not afraid to venture in his waterproof boots; and Wilmot and I are going to beat you all. I declare, we old 'uns are the keenest sportsmen of the lot!"

"I'll show you what I can do today, however," said my companion. "I'll murder your birds by wholesale, just for keeping me away from better company than either you or them."

And so saying he departed; and I saw no more of him till dinner. It seemed a weary time: I wonder what I shall do without him.

It is very true that the three elder gentlemen have proved themselves much keener sportsmen than the two younger ones; for both Lord Lowborough and Arthur Huntingdon have of late, almost daily neglected the shooting excursions to accompany us in our various rides and rambles. But these merry times are fast drawing to a close. In less than a fortnight the party breaks up, much to my sorrow, for every day I enjoy it more and more—now that Messrs. Boarham and Wilmot have ceased to tease me, and my aunt has ceased to lecture me, and I have ceased to be jealous of Annabella—and even to dislike her—and now that Mr. Huntingdon is become *my* Arthur, and I may enjoy his society without restraint.—What *shall* I do without him, I repeat?

---

1   The Game Reform Act of 1831 would eventually make it illegal to shoot pheasants from 1 February to 1 October.

CHAPTER XXII
TRAITS OF FRIENDSHIP

OCTOBER 5th.—My cup of sweets is not unmingled: it is dashed with a bitterness that I cannot hide from myself, disguise it as I will. I may try to persuade myself that the sweetness overpowers it; I may call it a pleasant aromatic flavour; but, say what I will, it is still there, and I cannot but taste it. I cannot shut my eyes to Arthur's faults; and the more I love him the more they trouble me. His very heart, that I trusted so, is, I fear, less warm and generous than I thought it. At least, he gave me a specimen of his character today, that seemed to merit a harder name than thoughtlessness. He and Lord Lowborough were accompanying Annabella and me in a long, delightful ride; he was riding by my side, as usual, and Annabella and Lord Lowborough were a little before us, the latter bending towards his companion as if in tender and confidential discourse.

"Those two will get the start of us, Helen, if we don't look sharp," observed Huntingdon. "They'll make a match of it, as sure as can be. That Lowborough's fairly besotted. But he'll find himself in a fix when he's got her, I doubt."

"And she'll find herself in a fix when she's got him," said I, "if what I have heard of him is true."

"Not a bit of it. She knows what she's about; but he, poor fool, deludes himself with the notion that she'll make him a good wife, and because she has amused[1] him with some rodomontade[2] about despising rank and wealth in matters of love and marriage, he flatters himself that she's devotedly attached to him; that she will not refuse him for his poverty, and does not court him for his rank, but loves him for himself alone."

"But is not he courting her for her fortune?"

"No, not he. That was the first attraction, certainly; but now, he has quite lost sight of it: it never enters his calculations, except merely as an essential without which, for the lady's own sake, he could not think of marrying her. No; he's fairly in love. He thought he never could be again, but he's in for it once more. He was to have been married before, some two or three years ago; but he lost his bride by losing his fortune. He got into a bad way among us in London: he had an unfortunate taste for gambling; and surely the fellow was born under an unlucky star, for he always lost thrice where he gained once. That's a mode of self-torment I never was much addicted to, when I spend my money I like to enjoy the full value of it: I see no fun in wasting it

---

1 Beguiled or deceived, the archaic meaning of amused.
2 Vain and empty boasting.

on thieves and blacklegs;[1] and as for *gaining* money, hitherto I have always had sufficient; it's time enough to be clutching for more, I think, when you begin to see the end of what you have. But I have sometimes frequented the gam-ing-houses just to watch the on-goings of those mad votaries of chance—a very interesting study, I assure you, Helen, and sometimes very diverting: I've had many a laugh at the boobies and bedlamites.[2] Lowborough was quite infatuated—not willingly, but of necessity,—he was always resolving to give it up, and always breaking his resolutions. Every venture was the 'just once more:' if he gained a little, he hoped to gain a little more next time, and if he lost, it would not do to leave off at that juncture; he must go on till he had retrieved that last misfortune, at least: bad luck could not last for ever; and every lucky hit was looked upon as the dawn of better times, till experience proved the contrary. At length he grew desperate, and we were daily on the look out for a case of felo-de-se[3]—no great matter, some of us whispered, as his existence had ceased to be an acquisition to our club. At last, however, he came to a check. He made a large stake which he determined should be the last, whether he lost or won. He had often so determined before, to be sure, and as often broken his determination; and so it was this time. He lost; and while his antagonist smilingly swept away the stakes, he, turning chalky white, drew back in silence and wiped his forehead. I was present at the time; and while he stood with folded arms and eyes fixed on the ground, I knew well enough what was passing in his mind.

"'Is it to be the last, Lowborough?' said I, stepping up to him.

"'The last but ONE,' he answered, with a grim smile; and then, rushing back to the table, he struck his hand upon it, and raising his voice high above all the confusion of jingling coins and muttered oaths and curses in the room, he swore a deep and solemn oath that, come what would, THIS trial *should* be the last, and imprecated unspeakable curses on his head, if ever he should shuffle a card or rattle a dice-box again. He then doubled his former stake, and challenged any one present to play against him. Grimsby instantly pre-sented himself. Lowborough glared fiercely at him, for Grimsby was almost as celebrated for his luck as *he* was for his ill-fortune. However, they fell to work. But Grimsby had much skill and little scruple, and whether he took advantage of the other's trembling, blinded eagerness to deal unfairly by him, I cannot undertake to say; but Lowborough lost again, and fell dead sick.

"'You'd better try once more,' said Grimsby, leaning across the table. And then he winked at me.

"'I've nothing to try with,' said the poor devil, with a ghastly smile.

---

1   "Swindlers at gambling" (*OED*).
2   Lunatics; Bedlam was a famous insane asylum.
3   Suicide.

"'Oh, Huntingdon will lend you what you want,' said the other.

"'No; you heard my oath,' answered Lowborough, turning away in quiet despair. And I took him by the arm and led him out.

"'Is it to be the last, Lowborough?' I asked, when I got him into the street.

"'The last,' he answered, somewhat against my expectation. And I took him home—that is, to our club—for he was as submissive as a child, and plied him with brandy and water till he began to look rather brighter—rather more alive, at least.

"'Huntingdon, I'm ruined!' said he, taking the third glass from my hand—he had drunk the other in dead silence.

"'Not you!' said I. 'You'll find a man can live without his money as merrily as a tortoise without its head, or a wasp without its body.'

"'But I'm in debt,' said he—'deep in debt! And I can never, *never* get out of it!'

"'Well, what of that? many a better man than you, has lived and died in debt, and they can't put you in prison, you know, because you're a peer.'[1] And I handed him his fourth tumbler.

"'But I hate to be in debt!' he shouted. 'I wasn't born for it, and I cannot *bear* it!'

"'What can't be cured must be endured,' said I, beginning to mix the fifth.

"'And then, I've lost my Caroline.' And he began to snivel then, for the brandy had softened his heart.

"'No matter,' I answered, 'there are more Carolines in the world than one.'

"'There's only one for me,' he replied, with a dolorous sigh. 'And if there were fifty more, who's to get them, I wonder, without money?'

"'Oh, somebody will take you for your title; and then you've your family estate yet; that's entailed,[2] you know.'

"'I wish to God I could sell it to pay my debts,' he muttered.

"'And then,' said Grimsby, who had just come in, 'you can *try again*, you know. I *would* have one more chance if I were you. I'd never stop here.'

"'I *won't*, I tell you!' shouted he. And he started up and left the room—walking rather unsteadily, for the liquor had got into his head. He was not so much used to it then, but after that, he took to it kindly to solace his cares.

"He kept his oath about gambling (not a little to the surprise of us all), though Grimsby did his utmost to tempt him to break it; but now he had got hold of another habit that bothered him nearly as much, for he soon discovered that the demon of drink was as black as the demon of play, and nearly as hard to get rid of—especially as his kind friends did all they could to second the promptings of his own insatiable cravings.'"

---

1 Although peers could not be arrested for debt, their property could be taken away.

2 "The settlement of the succession of a landed estate, so that it cannot be bequeathed at pleasure by any one possessor" (*OED*).

"Then, they were demons themselves," cried I, unable to contain my indignation. "And you, Mr. Huntingdon, it seems, were the first to tempt him."

"Well, what could we do?" replied he, deprecatingly— "We meant it in kindness—we couldn't bear to see the poor fellow so miserable:—and besides, he was such a damper upon us, sitting there, silent and glum, when he was under the threefold influence of the loss of his sweetheart, the loss of his fortune, and the reaction of the last night's debauch; whereas, when he had something in him, if he was not merry himself, he was an unfailing source of merriment to us. Even Grimsby could chuckle over his odd sayings: they delighted him far more than my merry jests or Hattersley's riotous mirth. But one evening, when we were sitting over our wine, after one of our club dinners, and had all been hearty together,—Lowborough giving us mad toasts, and hearing our wild songs and bearing a hand in the applause, if he did not help us to sing them himself,—he suddenly relapsed into silence, sinking his head on his hand, and never lifting his glass to his lips;—but this was nothing new; so we let him alone, and went on with our jollification, till, suddenly raising his head, he interrupted us in the middle of a roar of laughter, by exclaiming,—

"'Gentlemen, where is all this to end?—Will you just tell me *that* now?—Where is it all to end?'

"'In hell fire,'[1] growled Grimsby.

"'You've hit it—I thought so!' cried he. 'Well then, I'll tell you what'—he rose.

"'A speech, a speech!' shouted we. 'Hear, hear! Lowborough's going to give us a speech!'

"He waited calmly till the thunders of applause and jingling of glasses had ceased, and then proceeded,—

"'It's only this, gentlemen,—that I think we'd better go no farther. We'd better stop while we can.'

"'Just so!' cried Hattersley—

> "Stop poor sinner, stop and think
> Before you farther go,
> No longer sport upon the brink
> Of everlasting woe."[2]

---

1   Rosengarten and Smith, and Davies, suggest that Grimsby's reference to hell fire and the other phrases he uses, such as "our orgies" and "devil's den," signal the notorious Hell Fire Club founded by Sir Francis Dashwood (1708–81) at Medmenham Abbey. This infamous group's activities are described in *Chrysal: or the Adventures of a Guinea* (1760–65) by Charles Johnstone (1719?–1800?) (*OTWH* 478 and *PTWH* 511–12).

2   This is most likely written by Anne Brontë and is possibly a parody of a Methodist hymn. *The Methodist Magazine*, a publication the Brontës probably read, published

"'Exactly!' replied his lordship, with the utmost gravity. 'And if *you* choose to visit the bottomless pit,[1] I won't go with you—we must part company, for I swear I'll not move another step towards it!—What's this?' he said, taking up his glass of wine.

"'Taste it,' suggested I.

"'This is hell broth!' he exclaimed. 'I renounce it for ever!' And he threw it out into the middle of the table.

"'Fill again!' said I, handing him the bottle—'and let us drink, to your renunciation.'

"'It's rank poison,' said he, grasping the bottle by the neck, 'and I forswear it! I've given up gambling, and I'll give up this too.' He was on the point of deliberately pouring the whole contents of the bottle on to the table, but Hargrave wrested it from him. 'On you be the curse, then!' said he. And backing from the room, he shouted, 'Farewell, ye tempters!' and vanished amid shouts of laughter and applause.

"We expected him back among us the next day; but to our surprise, the place remained vacant: we saw nothing of him for a whole week; and we really began to think he was going to keep his word. At last, one evening, when we were most of us assembled together again, he entered, silent and grim as a ghost, and would have quietly slipped into his usual seat at my elbow, but we all rose to welcome him, and several voices were raised to ask what he would have, and several hands were busy with bottle and glass to serve him; but I knew a smoking tumbler of brandy and water would comfort him best, and had nearly prepared it, when he peevishly pushed it away, saying,

"'Do let me alone, Huntingdon! Do be quiet, all of you! I'm not come to join you: I'm only come to be with you awhile, because I can't bear my own thoughts.' And he folded his arms and leant back in his chair; so we let him be. But I left the glass by him; and after a while, Grimsby directed my attention towards it, by a significant wink; and, on turning my head, I saw it was drained to the bottom. He made me a sign to replenish, and quietly pushed up the bottle. I willingly complied; but Lowborough detected the pantomime, and, nettled at the intelligent grins that were passing between us, snatched the glass from my hand, dashed the contents of it in Grimsby's face, threw the empty tumbler at me, and then bolted from the room."

"I hope he broke your head," said I.

---

hymns by Charles and John Wesley in every issue. Charlotte Brontë also parodied Methodist hymns in her fiction. (See, for example, *Shirley* [1849], ed. Andrew and Judith Hook [Harmondsworth, England: Penguin, 1985] 163–65).

1   "Bottomless pit" is used repeatedly to describe hell in Revelation. See Revelation 9:1–2, 11:7, 17:8, and 20:1–3.

"No, love," replied he, laughing immoderately at the recollection of the whole affair, "he would have done so,—and perhaps spoilt my face, too, but providentially, this forest of curls," (taking off his hat and showing his luxuriant chestnut locks) "saved my skull, and prevented the glass from breaking till it reached the table."

"After that," he continued, "Lowborough kept aloof from us a week or two longer. I used to meet him occasionally in the town; and then, as I was too good natured to resent his unmannerly conduct, and he bore no malice against me,—he was never unwilling to talk to me; on the contrary, he would cling to me and follow me anywhere,—but to the club, and the gaming-houses, and such like dangerous places of resort—he was so weary of his own moping, melancholy mind. At last, I got him to come in with me to the club, on condition that I would not tempt him to drink; and for some time, he continued to look in upon us pretty regularly of an evening,—still abstaining, with wonderful perseverance, from the 'rank poison' he had so bravely forsworn. But some of our members protested against this conduct. They did not like to have him sitting there like a skeleton at a feast,[1] instead of contributing his quota to the general amusement, casting a cloud over all, and watching, with greedy eyes, every drop they carried to their lips, they vowed it was not fair; and some of them maintained that he should either be compelled to do as others did or expelled from the society, and swore that, next time he showed himself, they would tell him as much, and, if he did not take the warning, proceed to active measures. However, I befriended him on this occasion, and recommended them to let him be for a while, intimating that, with a little patience on our parts, he would soon come round again—But, to be sure, it *was* rather provoking; for though he refused to drink like an honest Christian, it was well known to me, that he kept a private bottle of laudanum[2] about him, which he was continually soaking at—or rather, holding off and on with, abstaining one day and exceeding the next, just like the spirits.

"One night, however, during one of our orgies—one of our high festivals, I mean—he glided in, like the ghost in Macbeth,[3] and seated himself, as usual, a little back from the table, in the chair we always placed for 'the spectre,'[4] whether it chose to fill it or not. I saw by his face that he was suffering

---

1 A proverb about something spoiling one's pleasure that dates back to 1651. See the *Oxford Dictionary of English Proverbs*, compiled by William George Smith (London: Oxford UP, 1948), 564.

2 Laudanum is a tincture of opium that was widely used at this time as a painkiller; it was known to be addictive. See also n. 1, page 67.

3 See *Macbeth* III.iv.

4 Charles Andrews, *The Spectre* (1789).

from the effects of an overdose of his insidious comforter; but nobody spoke to him, and he spoke to nobody. A few sidelong glances, and a whispered observation that 'the ghost was come,' was all the notice he drew by his appearance, and we went on with our merry carousals as before, till he startled us all by suddenly drawing in his chair and leaning forward with his elbows on the table, and exclaiming with portentous solemnity,—

"'Well! it puzzles me what you can find to be so merry about. What *you* see in life I don't know—*I* see only the blackness of darkness[1] and a fearful looking for of judgment and fiery indignation!'[2]

"All the company simultaneously pushed up their glasses to him, and I set them before him in a semicircle, and, tenderly patting him on the back, bid him drink and he would soon see as bright a prospect as any of us; but he pushed them back, muttering,—

"'Take them away! I won't taste it, I tell you—I won't—I won't!' So I handed them down again to the owners; but I saw that he followed them with a glare of hungry regret as they departed. Then, he clasped his hands before his eyes to shut out the sight, and two minutes after, lifted his head again, and said, in a hoarse but vehement whisper,—

"'And yet I must! Huntingdon, get me a glass!'

"'Take the bottle, man!' said I, thrusting the brandy-bottle into his hand—but stop. I'm telling too much," muttered the narrator, startled at the look I turned upon him. "But no matter," he recklessly added, and thus continued his relation:—"In his desperate eagerness, he seized the bottle and sucked away, till he suddenly dropped from his chair, disappearing under the table amid a tempest of applause. The consequence of this imprudence was something like an apoplectic fit, followed by a rather severe brain fever—"

"And what did you think of *yourself* sir?" said I, quickly.

"Of course, I was very penitent," he replied. "I went to see him once or twice—nay, twice or thrice—or, by'r lady,[3] some four times,—and when he got better, I tenderly brought him back to the fold."[4]

---

1 Jude 13: "Raging waves of the sea, foaming out their own shame; wandering stars, to whom is reserved the blackness of darkness for ever."

2 Hebrews 10:26–27: "But if we sin willfully after that we have received the knowledge of the truth, there remaineth no more sacrifice for sins, [b]ut a certain fearful looking for of judgment and fiery indignation, which shall devour the adversaries."

3 "By our lady" is an oath, a rude invocation of the Virgin Mary. Shakespeare uses "by'r lady" in a number of plays. See, for example, *Romeo and Juliet* I.v.33; *Much Ado about Nothing* III.iv.77, and *1 Henry IV* II.iv.50 and 467.

4 Here Huntingdon may be joking about the parable of the lost sheep, only rather than shepherding someone into the fold for good, he's bringing Lowborough back into the fold of debauched behavior. See, for example, the parable of the lost sheep recounted in Luke 15:3–7 and Jesus' sermon on the Good Shepherd in John 10.

"What do you mean?"

"I mean, I restored him to the bosom of the club, and compassionating the feebleness of his health and extreme lowness of his spirits, I recommended him to 'take a little wine for his stomach's sake,'[1] and, when he was sufficiently reestablished, to embrace the media-via,[2] ni-jamais-ni-toujours[3] plan—not to kill himself like a fool, and not to abstain like a ninny—in a word, to enjoy himself like a rational creature, and do as I did;—for don't think, Helen, that I'm a tippler; I'm nothing at all of the kind, and never was, and never shall be. I value my comfort far too much. I see that a man cannot give himself up to drinking without being miserable one half his days and mad the other;—besides, I like to enjoy my life at all sides and ends, which cannot be done by one that suffers himself to be the slave of a single propensity—and moreover, drinking spoils one's good looks," he concluded, with a most conceited smile that ought to have provoked me more than it did.

"And did Lord Lowborough profit by your advice?" I asked.

"Why, yes, in a manner. For a while, he managed very well; indeed, he was a model of moderation and prudence—something too much so for the tastes of our wild community;—but, somehow, Lowborough had not the gift of moderation: if he stumbled a little to one side, he must go down before he could right himself: if he overshot the mark one night, the effects of it rendered him so miserable the next day that he must repeat the offence to mend it; and so on from day to day, till his clamorous conscience brought him to a stand.—And then, in his sober moments, he so bothered his friends with his remorse, and his terrors and woes, that they were obliged, in self-defense, to get him to drown his sorrows in wine, or any more potent beverage that came to hand; and when his first scruples of conscience were overcome, he would need no more persuading, he would often grow desperate, and be as great a blackguard[4] as any of them could desire—but only to lament his own unutterable wickedness and degradation the more when the fit was over.

"At last, one day when he and I were alone together, after pondering awhile in one of his gloomy, abstracted moods, with his arms folded and his head sunk on his breast,—he suddenly woke up, and vehemently grasping my arm, said,—

"'Huntingdon, this won't do! I'm resolved to have done with it.'

"'What, are you going to shoot yourself?' said I.

---

1 1 Timothy 5:23: "Drink no longer water, but use a little wine for thy stomach's sake and thine often infirmities."

2 Latin for "middle road or way."

3 French for "neither never nor always."

4 "One of the idle criminal class: a 'rough'; hence, a low worthless character addicted to or ready for crime; an open scoundrel (a term of the utmost opprobrium)" (*OED*).

"'No; I'm going to reform.'

"'Oh, *that's* nothing new! You've been going to reform these twelve months and more.'

"'Yes, but you wouldn't let me; and I was such a fool I couldn't live without you. But now I see what it is that keeps me back, and what's wanted to save me; and I'd compass sea and land to get it—only I'm afraid there's no chance.' And he sighed as if his heart would break.

"'What is it Lowborough?' said I, thinking he was fairly cracked at last.

"'A wife,' he answered; 'for I can't live alone, because my own mind distracts me, and I can't live with you, because you take the devil's part against me.'

"'Who—I?'

"'Yes—all of you do,—and you more than any of them, you know. But if I could get a wife, with fortune enough to pay off my debts and set me straight in the world—'

"'To be sure,' said I.

"'And sweetness and goodness enough,' he continued, 'to make home tolerable, and to reconcile me to myself,—I think I should do, yet. I shall never be in love again that's certain; but perhaps that would be no great matter, it would enable me to choose with my eyes open,—and I should make a good husband in spite of it; but could any one be in love with *me*?—that's the question.—With *your* good looks and powers of fascination,' (he was pleased to say) 'I might hope; but as it is, Huntingdon, do you think *any* body would take me—ruined and wretched as I am?'

"'Yes, certainly.'

"'Who?'

"'Why, any neglected old maid, fast sinking in despair, would be delighted to—'

"'No, no,' said he—'it must be somebody that I can love.'

"'Why, you just said you never could be in love again?'

"'Well, love is not the word,—but somebody that I can like.—I'll search all England through, at all events!' he cried, with a sudden burst of hope, or desperation. 'Succeed or fail, it will be better than rushing headlong to destruction at that d——d club: so farewell to it and you. Whenever I meet you on honest ground or under a Christian roof, I shall be glad to see you; but never more shall you entice me to that *devil's den*!'

"This was shameful language, but I shook hands with him, and we parted. He kept his word; and from that time forward, he has been a pattern of propriety, as far as I can tell; but, till lately, I have not had very much to do with him. He occasionally sought my company but as frequently shrunk from it, fearing lest I should wile him back to destruction, and I found his not very entertaining, especially, as he sometimes attempted to awaken my conscience and draw me from the perdition he considered himself to have escaped; but when I did happen to meet him, I seldom failed to ask after the progress of his matrimonial efforts and researches, and, in general he could give me but a poor account. The mothers were repelled by his empty coffers and his reputation for gambling, and the daughters by his cloudy brow and melancholy temper,—besides, he didn't understand them; he wanted the spirit and assurance to carry his point.

"I left him at it when I went to the continent; and on my return, at the year's end, I found him still a disconsolate bachelor—though, certainly, looking somewhat less like an unblessed exile from the tomb than before. The young ladies had ceased to be afraid of him, and were beginning to think him quite interesting; but the mammas were still unrelenting. It was about this time, Helen, that my good angel brought me into conjunction with you; and then I had eyes and ears for nobody else. But meantime, Lowborough became acquainted with our charming friend, Miss Wilmot— through the intervention of *his* good angel, no doubt he would tell you, though he did not dare to fix his hopes on one so courted and admired, till after they were brought into closer contact here at Staningley, and she, in the absence of her other admirers, indubitably courted his notice and held out every encouragement to his timid advances. Then indeed, he began to hope for a dawn of brighter days; and if for a while, I darkened his prospects by standing between him and his sun—and so, nearly plunged him again into the abyss of despair—it only intensified his ardour and strengthened his hopes when I chose to abandon the field in the pursuit of a brighter treasure. In a word, as I told you, he is fairly besotted. At first, he could dimly perceive her faults, and they gave him considerable uneasiness; but now his passion and her art together, have blinded him to everything but her perfections and his amazing good fortune. Last night, he came to me brimful of his new-found felicity:

"'Huntingdon, I am not a castaway!'[1] said he, seizing my hand and squeezing it like a vice. 'There is happiness in store for me, yet—even in this life— she loves me!'

"'Indeed!' said I. 'Has she told you so?'

"'No, but I can no longer doubt it. Do you not see how pointedly kind and affectionate she is? And she knows the utmost extent of my poverty, and cares nothing about it! She knows all the folly and all the wickedness of my former life, and is not afraid to trust me—and my rank and title are no allurements to her; for them, she utterly disregards. She is the most generous,

---

1 William Cowper's (1731–1800) poem "The Castaway" (composed in 1799 and published in 1803) was well known to Anne Brontë; she even wrote a rebuttal, "To Cowper" (1836), published in *Poems by Currer, Ellis and Acton Bell* (see Appendix A2).

high-minded being that can be conceived of. She will save me, body and soul, from destruction. Already, she has ennobled me in my own estimation, and made me three times better, wiser, greater than I was. Oh! if I had but known her before, how much degradation and misery I should have been spared! But what have I done to deserve so magnificent a creature?'

"And the cream of the jest," continued Mr. Huntingdon, laughing, "is that the artful minx loves nothing about him, but his title and pedigree, and 'that delightful old family seat.'"

"How do you know?" said I.

"She told me so herself; she said, 'as for the man himself, I thoroughly despise him; but then, I suppose, it is time to be making my choice, and if I waited for some one capable of eliciting my esteem and affection, I should have to pass my life in single blessedness, for I detest you all!' Ha, ha! I suspect she was wrong there;—but however, it is evident she has no love for *him*, poor fellow."

"Then you ought to tell him so."

"What, and spoil all her plans and prospects, poor girl? No, no: that would be a breach of confidence, wouldn't it Helen? Ha, ha! Besides, it would break his heart." And he laughed again.

"Well, Mr. Huntingdon, I don't know what you see so amazingly diverting in the matter; *I* see nothing to laugh at."

"I'm laughing at *you*, just now love," said he, redoubling his cachinnations.[1]

And leaving him to enjoy his merriment alone, I touched Ruby with the whip, and cantered on to rejoin our companions; for we had been walking our horses all this time, and were consequently a long way behind. Arthur was soon at my side again; but not disposed to talk to him, I broke into a gallop. He did the same; and we did not slacken our pace till we came up with Miss Wilmot and Lord Lowborough, which was within half a mile of the park gates. I avoided all further conversation with him, till we came to the end of our ride, when I meant to jump off my horse and vanish into the house, before he could offer his assistance; but while I was disengaging my habit[2] from the crutch,[3] he lifted me off, and held me by both hands, asserting that he would not let me go till I had forgiven him.

"I have nothing to forgive," said I. "You have not injured *me*."

"No, darling—God forbid that I should!—but you are angry, because it was to me that Annabella confessed her lack of esteem for her lover."

---

1   "Loud or immoderate laughter" (*OED*).

2   Dress, garments.

3   Rosengarten and Smith explain that this is a forked leg rest on a side saddle (*OTWH* 479).

"No, Arthur, it is not *that* that displeases me: it is the whole system of your conduct towards your friend; and if you wish me to forget it, go, now, and tell him what sort of a woman it is, that he adores so madly, and on whom he has hung his hopes of future happiness."

"I tell you, Helen, it would break his heart—it would be the death of him,—besides being a scandalous trick to poor Annabella. There is no help for him now; he is past praying for. Besides, she may keep up the deception to the end of the chapter; and then he will be just as happy in the illusion as if it were reality; or perhaps, he will only discover his mistake when he has ceased to love her;—and if not, it is much better that the truth should dawn gradually upon him. So now, my angel, I hope I have made out a clear case, and fully convinced you that I cannot make the atonement you require. What other requisition have you to make? Speak, and I will gladly obey."

"I have none but this," said I, as gravely as before; "that, in future, you will never make a jest of the sufferings of others, and always use your influence with your friends for their own advantage against their evil propensities, instead of seconding their evil propensities against themselves."

"I will do my utmost," said he, "to remember and perform the injunctions of my angel monitress,"[1] and after kissing both my gloved hands, he let me go.

When I entered my room, I was surprised to see Annabella Wilmot standing before my toilet-table, composedly surveying her features in the glass, with one hand flirting[2] her goldmounted whip, and the other holding up her long habit.

"She certainly *is* a magnificent creature!" thought I, as I beheld that tall, finely developed figure, and the reflection of the handsome face in the mirror before me, with the glossy dark hair, slightly and not ungracefully disordered by the breezy ride, the rich brown complexion glowing with exercise, and the black eyes sparkling with unwonted brilliance. On perceiving me, she turned round exclaiming, with a laugh that savoured more of malice than of mirth,—

"Why Helen! what *have* you been doing so long?—I came to tell you my good fortune," she continued, regardless of Rachel's presence. "Lord Lowborough has proposed, and I have been graciously pleased to accept him. Don't you envy me, dear?"

"No, love," said I—"or him either," I mentally added. "And do you like him Annabella?"

"Like him! yes, to be sure—over head and ears in love!"

"Well, I hope you'll make him a good wife."

"Thank you, my dear! And what besides do you hope?"

---

1 A female monitor.

2 "To give a brisk sudden motion to; to flick" (*OED*).

"I hope you will both love each other, and both be happy."

"Thanks;—and I hope you will make a *very* good wife to Mr. Huntingdon!" said she, with a queenly bow, and retired.

"Oh, Miss! how could you say so to her?" cried Rachel.

"Say what?" replied I.

"Why, that you hoped she would make him a good wife—I never heard such a thing!"

"Because, I do hope it—or rather, I wish it—she's almost past hope."

"Well!" said she, "I'm sure I hope he'll make *her* a good husband. They tell queer things about him down stairs. They were saying—"

"I know Rachel—I've heard all about him; but he's reformed now. And they have no business to tell tales about their masters."

"No mum—or else, they *have* said some things about Mr. Huntingdon too."

"I won't hear them, Rachel; they tell lies."

"Yes mum," said she, quietly, as she went on arranging my hair.

"Do *you* believe them, Rachel?" I asked, after a short pause.

"No, Miss, not all. You know when a lot of servants gets together, they like to talk about their betters; and some, for a bit of swagger, likes to make it appear as though they knew more than they do, and to throw out hints and things, just to astonish the others. But I think, if I was you, Miss Helen, I'd look *very* well before I leaped. I do believe a young lady can't be too careful who she marries."

"Of course not," said I—"but be quick, will you, Rachel? I want to be dressed."

And indeed, I was anxious to be rid of the good woman, for I was in such a melancholy frame I could hardly keep the tears out of my eyes while she dressed me. It was not for Lord Lowborough—it was not for Annabella—it was not for myself—it was for Arthur Huntingdon that they rose.

$$\ast \quad \ast \quad \ast \quad \ast \quad \ast$$

13th. They are gone—and he is gone. We are to be parted for more than two months—above ten weeks! a long, long time to live and not to see him. But he has promised to write often, and made me promise to write still oftener, because he will be busy settling his affairs, and I shall have nothing better to do. Well, I think I shall always have plenty to say.—But O! for the time when we shall be always together, and can exchange our thoughts without the intervention of these cold go-betweens, pen, ink, and paper!

$$\ast \quad \ast \quad \ast \quad \ast \quad \ast$$

22nd. I have had several letters from Arthur, already. They are not long, but passing sweet, and just like himself—full of ardent affection, and playful, lively humour; but—there is always a *but* in this imperfect world—I do wish he would *sometimes* be serious. I cannot get him to write or speak in real, solid earnest. I don't much mind it *now*; but if it be always so, what shall I do with the serious part of myself?

CHAPTER XXIII
FIRST WEEKS OF MATRIMONY

FEB. 18th, 1822. Early this morning, Arthur mounted his hunter and set off in high glee to meet the —— hounds. He will be away all day; and so I will amuse myself with my neglected diary—if I can give that name to such an irregular composition. It is exactly four months since I opened it last.

I am married now, and settled down as Mrs. Huntingdon of Grassdale Manor. I have had eight weeks experience of matrimony. And do I regret the step I have taken?—No—though I must confess, in my secret heart, that Arthur is not what I thought him at first, and if I had known him in the beginning, as thoroughly as I do now, I probably never should have loved him, and if I had loved him first, and then made the discovery, I fear I should have thought it my duty not to have married him. To be sure, I might have known him, for every one was willing enough to tell me about him, and he himself was no accomplished hypocrite, but I was willfully blind, and now, instead of regretting that I did not discern his full character before I was indissolubly bound to him, I am *glad*; for it has saved me a great deal of battling with my conscience, and a great deal of consequent trouble and pain; and, whatever I *ought* to have done, my duty, now, is plainly to love him and to cleave[1] to him; and this just tallies with my inclination.

He is very fond of me—almost *too* fond. I could do with less caressing and more rationality: I should like to be less of a pet and more of a friend, if I might choose—but I won't complain of that: I am only afraid his affection loses in depth where it gains in ardour. I sometimes liken it to a fire of dry twigs and branches compared with one of solid coal,—very bright and hot, but if it should burn itself out and leave nothing but ashes behind, what shall I do? But it won't—it *shan't*, I am determined—and surely I have power to keep it alive. So let me dismiss *that* thought at once. But Arthur is selfish—I am constrained to acknowledge that; and, indeed, the admission gives me

---

1   Helen may be using the verb "cleave" here to invoke Genesis 2:24: "Therefore shall a man leave his father and mother, and shall cleave unto his wife: and they shall be one flesh."

less pain than might be expected; for, since *I* love him so much, I can easily forgive him for loving himself: he likes to be pleased, and it is my delight to please him,—and when I regret this tendency of his, it is for his own sake, not for mine.

The first instance he gave was on the occasion of our bridal tour. He wanted to hurry it over, for all the continental scenes were already familiar to him: many had lost their interest in his eyes, and others had never had anything to lose. The consequence was, that, after a flying transit through part of France and part of Italy, I came back nearly as ignorant as I went, having made no acquaintance with persons and manners, and very little with things,—my head swarming with a motley confusion of objects and scenes—some, it is true, leaving a deeper and more pleasing impression than others, but these embittered by the recollection that my emotions had not been shared by my companion, but that, on the contrary, when I had expressed a particular interest in anything that I saw or desired to see, it had been displeasing to him in as much as it proved that I could take delight in anything disconnected with himself.

As for Paris, we only just touched at that, and he would not give me time to see one tenth of the beauties and interesting objects of Rome. He wanted to get me home, he said, to have me all to himself, and to see me safely installed as the mistress of Grassdale Manor, just as single-minded, as naive, and piquante as I was; and, as if I had been some frail butterfly, he expressed himself fearful of rubbing the silver off my wings by bringing me into contact with society, especially that of Paris and Rome; and, moreover, he did not scruple to tell me that there were ladies in both places that would tear his eyes out if they happened to meet him with me.

Of course I was vexed at all this; but, still, it was less the disappointment to myself that annoyed me, than the disappointment *in him*, and the trouble I was at to frame excuses to my friends for having seen and observed so little, without imputing one particle of blame to my companion. But when we got home—to my new, delightful home—I was so happy and he was so kind that I freely forgave him all;—and I was beginning to think my lot *too* happy, and my husband actually too good for me, if not too good for this world, when, on the second Sunday after our arrival, he shocked and horrified me by another instance of his unreasonable exaction. We were walking home from the morning service—for it was a fine frosty day, and, as we are so near the church, I had requested the carriage should not be used:—

"Helen," said he, with unusual gravity, "I am not quite satisfied with you."

I desired to know what was wrong.

"But will you promise to reform, if I tell you?"

"Yes, if I can—and without offending a higher authority."

"Ah! there it is, you see—you don't love me with all your heart."[1]

"I don't understand you, Arthur (at least, I hope I don't): pray tell me what I have done or said amiss?"

"It is nothing you have done or said; it is something that you *are*: you are too religious. Now I like a woman to be religious, and I think your piety one of your greatest charms, but then, like all other good things, it may be carried too far. To my thinking, a woman's religion ought not to lessen her devotion to her earthly lord. She should have enough to purify and etherial-ize her soul, but not enough to refine away her heart, and raise her above all human sympathies."

"And am *I* above all human sympathies?" said I.

"No, darling; but you are making more progress towards that saintly con-dition than I like; for, all these two hours, I have been thinking of you and wanting to catch your eye, and you were so absorbed in your devotions that you had not even a glance to spare for me—I declare, it is enough to make one jealous of one's Maker—which is very wrong, you know; so don't excite such wicked passions again, for my soul's sake."

"I will give my whole heart and soul to my Maker[2] if I can," I answered, "and not one atom more of it to you than he allows. What are *you*, sir, that you should set yourself up as a god, and presume to dispute possession of my heart with Him to whom I owe all I have and all I am, every blessing I ever did or ever can enjoy—and yourself among the rest—if you *are* a blessing, which I am half inclined to doubt."

"Don't be so hard upon me, Helen; and don't pinch my arm so, you're squeezing your fingers into the bone."

"Arthur," continued I, relaxing my hold of his arm, "you don't love me half as much as I do you; and yet, if you loved me far less than you do, I would not complain, provided you loved your Maker more. I should *rejoice* to see you at any time, so deeply absorbed in your devotions that you had not a single thought to spare for me. But, indeed, I should lose nothing by the change, for the more you loved your God the more deep and pure and true would be your love to me."

---

1 Here Arthur is playfully invoking scripture in a way that would alert Victorian readers to his sinful nature, as he has co-opted Biblical language used to express people's love of God to describe Helen's love of him. See Matthew 22:37: "And Jesus said unto him, Thou shalt love the Lord thy God with all thy heart, and with all thy soul, and with all thy mind."

2 Helen is loosely invoking Mark 12:30: "And thou shalt love the Lord thy God with all thy heart, and with all thy soul, and with all thy mind, and with all thy strength: this is the first commandment."

At this he only laughed, and kissed my hand, calling me a sweet enthusiast.[1] Then taking off his hat, he added—

"But look here, Helen—what can a man do with such a head as this?"

The head looked right enough, but when he placed my hand on the top of it, it sunk in a bed of curls, rather alarmingly low, especially in the middle.

"You see I was not made to be a saint," said he, laughing. "If God meant me to be religious, why didn't he give me a proper organ of veneration?"[2]

"You are like the servant," I replied, "who instead of employing his one talent in his master's service, restored it to him unimproved, alleging, as an excuse, that he knew him 'to be a hard man, reaping where he had not sown and gathering where he had not strawed.'[3] Of him, to whom less is given, less will be required; but our utmost exertions are required of us all.[4] You are not without the capacity of veneration, and faith and hope, and conscience and reason, and every other requisite to a Christian's character, if you choose to employ them; but all our talents increase in the using, and every faculty, both good and bad, strengthens by exercise; therefore, if you choose to use the bad—or those which tend to evil till they become your masters and neglect the good till they dwindle away, you have only yourself to blame. But you *have* talents, Arthur—natural endowments, both of heart and mind, and temper such as many a better Christian would be glad to possess—if you would only employ them in God's service. I should never expect to see you a devotee, but it is quite possible to be a good Christian without ceasing to be a happy, merry-hearted man."

"You speak like an oracle, Helen, and all you say is indisputably true; but listen here: I am hungry, and I see before me a good substantial dinner; I am told that, if I abstain from this today, I shall have a sumptuous feast tomorrow, consisting of all manner of dainties and delicacies. Now in the first place, I should be loath to wait till tomorrow, when I have the means of appeasing

---

1 Although the definition of "enthusiast" means "one who is (really or seemingly) possessed by a god" (*OED*), in the nineteenth century to call someone an "enthusiast" would be an insult allying that person with Dissenting faiths, but also with religious frenzy or passion. Helen's comments here are hardly the remarks of an enthusiast; thus Arthur's joking would again alert Victorian readers to his propensity for depravity.

2 In the nineteenth-century "science" of phrenology, which equated the lumps and bumps of one's skull with meaning about one's personality, the area of the skull Helen and Arthur are discussing showed one's capacity for worship (veneration). Unsurprisingly, Arthur's is not very well developed.

3 Matthew 25:24, the parable of the five talents. "Strawed" means strewn or scattered; here the master is rebuking his servant for not putting his money or skills to good use.

4 Helen is inverting a biblical passage to convey the same meaning to Arthur. See Luke 12:48: "For unto whomsoever much is given, of him shall be much required: and to whom men have committed much, of him they will ask the more."

my hunger already before me; in the second place, the solid viands of today are more to my taste than the dainties that are promised me; in the third place, I don't *see* tomorrow's banquet, and how can I tell that it is not all a fable, got up by the greasy-faced fellow that is advising me to abstain, in order that he may have all the good victuals to himself? in the fourth place, this table must be spread for somebody, and, as Solomon says, 'Who can eat, or who else can hasten hereunto more than I?'[1] and finally, with your leave, I'll sit down and satisfy my cravings of today, and leave tomorrow to shift for itself—who knows but what I may secure both this and that?"

"But you are not required to abstain from the substantial dinner of today; you are only advised to partake of these coarser viands in such moderation as not to incapacitate you from enjoying the choicer banquet of tomorrow. If, regardless of that counsel, you choose to make a beast of yourself now, and over-eat and over-drink yourself till you turn the good victuals into poison, who is to blame if, hereafter, while you are suffering the torments of yesterday's gluttony and drunkenness, you see more temperate men sitting down to enjoy themselves at that splendid entertainment which you are unable to taste?"

"Most true my patron saint; but again, our friend Solomon says,—'There is nothing better for a man than to eat and to drink, and to be merry.'"[2]

"And again," returned I, "he says, 'Rejoice, O young man, in thy youth, and walk in the ways of thine heart and in the sight of thine eyes; but know thou that, for all these things, God will bring thee into judgment.'"[3]

"Well but, Helen, I'm sure I've been very good these last few weeks. What have you seen amiss in me; and what would you have me to do?"

"Nothing—more than you do, Arthur: your actions are all right, so far; but I would have your thoughts changed; I would have you to fortify yourself against temptation, and not to call evil good, and good, evil; I should wish you to think more deeply, to look farther, and aim higher than you do."

We now stood before our own door, and I said no more; but, with an ardent and tearful embrace, I left him, and went into the house, and upstairs to take off my bonnet and mantle. I wished to say nothing more on that subject at the time, lest I should disgust him with both it and me.[4]

---

1 Ecclesiastes 2:25.

2 A version of Ecclesiastes 8:15; the relevant passage reads "because a man hath no better thing under the sun, than to eat and to drink, and to be merry."

3 Ecclesiastes 11:9. Note as well the passage that follows what Helen is quoting: "Therefore remove sorrow from thy heart, and put away evil from thy flesh: for childhood and youth are vanity" (Ecclesiastes 11:10).

4 Here Helen is adhering to the biblical recommendations for good wifely behavior to bring errant husbands back into the fold of good, Christian men. See especially 1 Peter

CHAPTER XXIV
FIRST QUARREL

MARCH 25th.—Arthur is getting tired—not of me I trust, but of the idle, quiet life he leads—and no wonder, for he has so few sources of amusement; he never reads anything but newspapers and sporting magazines; and when he sees me occupied with a book, he won't let me rest till I close it. In fine weather he generally manages to get through the time pretty well; but on rainy days, of which we have had a good many of late, it is quite painful to witness his ennui. I do all I can to amuse him, but it is impossible to get him to feel interested in what I most like to talk about; while, on the other hand, he likes to talk about things that cannot interest me—or even that annoy me—and these please him the most of all; for his favourite amusement is to sit or loll beside me on the sofa and tell me stories of his former amours, always turning upon the ruin of some confiding girl or the cozening of some unsuspecting husband; and when I express my horror and indignation, he lays it all to the charge of jealousy, and laughs till the tears run down his cheeks. I used to fly into passions or melt into tears at first, but seeing that his delight increased in proportion to my anger and agitation, I have since endeavoured to suppress my feelings and receive his revelations in the silence of calm contempt; but still, he reads the inward struggle in my face, and misconstrues my bitterness of soul for his unworthiness into the pangs of wounded jealousy; and when he has sufficiently diverted himself with that, or fears my displeasure will become too serious for his comfort, he tries to kiss and soothe me into smiles again—never were his caresses so little welcome as then! This is *double* selfishness, displayed to me and to the victims of his former love. There are times when, with a momentary pang—a flash of wild dismay, I ask myself, "Helen, what have you done?" But I rebuke the inward questioner, and repel the obtrusive thoughts that crowd upon me; for, were he ten times as sensual and impenetrable to good and lofty thoughts, I well know I have no right to complain. And I don't and won't complain. I do and will love him still; and I do not and will not regret that I have linked my fate with his.[1]

3:1: "Likewise, ye wives, be in subjection to your own husbands; that, if any obey not the word, they also may without the word be won by the conversation of the wives."

1   See n. 2, page 167 for some of the religious reflections on marrying someone not your spiritual equal, and 1 Peter 3:1–9 for a biblical description of one's wifely duties. Lastly, see the extract from Hannah More's immensely popular *Coelebs in Search of a Wife* (1808) in Appendix D1 for an example of the type of story against which Brontë was writing.

April 4th.—We have had a downright quarrel. The particulars are as fol-lows:—Arthur had told me, at different intervals, the whole story of his intrigue with Lady F——, which I would not believe before. It was some consolation, however, to find that, in this instance, the lady had been more to blame than he; for he was very young at the time, and she had decidedly made the first advances, if what he said was true. I hated her for it, for it seemed as if she had chiefly contributed to his corruption, and when he was beginning to talk about her the other day, I begged he would not mention her, for I detested the very sound of her name.

"Not because you loved her, Arthur, mind, but because she injured you, and deceived her husband, and was altogether a very abominable woman, whom you ought to be ashamed to mention."[1]

But he defended her by saying that she had a doting old husband, whom it was impossible to love.

"Then why did she marry him?" said I.

"For his money," was the reply.

"Then that was another crime, and her solemn promise to love and hon-our him was another, that only increased the enormity of the last."

"You are too severe upon the poor lady," laughed he. "But never mind, Helen, I don't care for her now; and I never loved any of them half as much as I do you; so you needn't fear to be forsaken like them."

"If you had told me these things before, Arthur, I never should have given you the chance."

"*Wouldn't* you, my darling!"

"Most certainly not!"

He laughed incredulously.

"I wish I could convince you of it now!" cried I, starting up from beside him; and for the first time in my life, and I hope the last, I wished I had not married him.

"Helen," said he, more gravely, "do you know that if I believed you now, I should be very angry?—but thank Heaven I don't. Though you stand there with your white face and flashing eyes, looking at me like a very tigress, I know the heart within you, perhaps a trifle better than you know it yourself."

Without another word, I left the room, and locked myself up in my own chamber. In about half an hour, he came to the door; and first he tried the handle, then he knocked.

"Won't you let me in, Helen?" said he.

---

1 This story about Lady F— could be a reference to Branwell's affair with Mrs. Robin-son while Anne was governess at Thorpe Greene. See Charlotte Brontë's writings on how Anne was affected by witnessing this in Appendix A4.

"No; you have displeased me," I replied, "and I don't want to see your face or hear your voice again till the morning."

He paused a moment, as if dumbfounded[1] or uncertain how to answer such a speech, and then turned and walked away. This was only an hour after dinner: I knew he would find it very dull to sit alone all the evening; and this considerably softened my resentment, though it did not make me relent. I was determined to show him that my heart was not his slave, and I could live without him if I chose; and I sat down and wrote a long letter to my aunt—of course telling her nothing of all this. Soon after ten o'clock, I heard him come up again; but he passed my door and went straight to his own dressing-room, where he shut himself in for the night.

I was rather anxious to see how he would meet me in the morning, and not a little disappointed to behold him enter the breakfast-room with a careless smile.

"Are you cross still, Helen?" said he, approaching as if to salute me. I coldly turned to the table, and began to pour out the coffee, observing that he was rather late.

He uttered a low whistle and sauntered away to the window, where he stood for some minutes looking out upon the pleasing prospect of sullen, grey clouds, streaming rain, soaking lawn, and dripping, leafless trees—and muttering execrations on the weather, and then sat down to breakfast. While taking his coffee, he muttered it was "d—d cold."

"You should not have left it so long," said I.

He made no answer, and the meal was concluded in silence. It was a relief to both when the letter-bag was brought in. It contained, upon examination, a newspaper and one or two letters for him, and a couple of letters for me, which he tossed across the table without a remark. One was from my brother, the other from Milicent Hargrave, who is now in London with her mother. His, I think, were business letters, and apparently not much to his mind, for he crushed them into his pocket with some muttered expletives, that I should have reproved him for at any other time. The paper, he set before him, and pretended to be deeply absorbed in its contents during the remainder of breakfast, and a considerable time after.

The reading and answering of my letters, and the direction of household concerns afforded me ample employment for the morning; after lunch, I got my drawing, and from dinner till bed time, I read. Meanwhile, poor Arthur was sadly at a loss for something to amuse him or to occupy his time. He wanted to appear as busy and as unconcerned as I did: had the weather at all permitted, he would doubtless have ordered his horse and set off to some distant region—no matter where—immediately after

---

1 Variant of "dumbfound" or "dumbfounded" (*OED*).

breakfast, and not returned till night; had there been a lady anywhere within reach, of any age between fifteen and forty-five, he would have sought revenge and found employment in getting up—or trying to get up a desperate flirtation with her; but being, to my private satisfaction, entirely cut off from both these sources of diversion, his sufferings were truly deplorable. When he had done yawning over his paper and scribbling short answers to his shorter letters, he spent the remainder of the morning and the whole of the afternoon in fidgeting about from room to room, watching the clouds, cursing the rain, alternately petting, and teasing, and abusing his dogs, sometimes lounging on the sofa with a book that he could not force himself to read, and very often fixedly gazing at me, when he thought I did not perceive it, with the vain hope of detecting some traces of tears, or some tokens of remorseful anguish in my face. But I managed to preserve an undisturbed, though grave serenity throughout the day. I was not really angry: I felt for him all the time, and longed to be reconciled; but I determined he should make the first advances, or at least show some signs of an humble and contrite spirit, first; for, if I began, it would only minister to his self-conceit, increase his arrogance, and quite destroy the lesson I wanted to give him.

He made a long stay in the dining-room after dinner, and, I fear, took an unusual quantity of wine, but not enough to loosen his tongue; for when he came in and found me quietly occupied with my book, too busy to lift my head on his entrance, he merely murmured an expression of suppressed disapprobation, and, shutting the door with a bang, went and stretched himself at full length on the sofa, and composed himself to sleep. But his favourite cocker, Dash, that had been lying at my feet, took the liberty of jumping upon him and beginning to lick his face. He struck it off with a smart blow; and the poor dog squeaked, and ran cowering back to me. When he woke up, about half an hour after, he called it to him again; but Dash only looked sheepish and wagged the tip of his tail. He called again, more sharply, but Dash only clung the closer to me, and licked my hand as if imploring protection. Enraged at this, his master snatched up a heavy book and hurled it at his head. The poor dog set up a piteous outcry and ran to the door. I let him out, and then quietly took up the book.

"Give that book to me," said Arthur, in no very courteous tone. I gave it to him.

"Why did you let the dog out?" he asked. "You knew I wanted him."

"By what token?" I replied; "by your throwing the book at him? but perhaps, it was intended for me?"

"No—but I see you've got a taste of it," said he, looking at my hand, that had also been struck, and was rather severely grazed.

I returned to my reading; and he endeavoured to occupy himself in the same manner; but, in a little while, after several portentous yawns, he pronounced *his* book to be "cursed trash," and threw it on to the table. Then followed eight or ten minutes of silence, during the greater part of which, I believe, he was staring at me. At last his patience was tired out.

"What *is* that book, Helen?" he exclaimed.

I told him.

"Is it interesting?"

"Yes, very."

"Humph!"

I went on reading—or pretending to read, at least—I cannot say there was much communication between my eyes and my brain; for, while the former ran over the pages, the latter was earnestly wondering when Arthur would speak next, and what he would say, and what I should answer. But he did not speak again till I rose to make the tea, and then it was only to say he should not take any. He continued lounging on the sofa, and alternately closing his eyes and looking at his watch and at me, till bed-time, when I rose, and took my candle and retired.

"Helen!" cried he, the moment I had left the room. I turned back, and stood awaiting his commands.

"What do you want, Arthur?" I said at length.

"Nothing," replied he. "Go!"

I went, but hearing him mutter something as I was closing the door, I turned again. It sounded very like "confounded slut," but I was quite willing it should be something else.

"Were you speaking Arthur?" I asked.

"No," was the answer; and I shut the door and departed. I saw nothing more of him till the following morning at breakfast, when he came down a full hour after the usual time.

"You're very late," was my morning's salutation.

"You needn't have waited for me," was his; and he walked up to the window again. It was just such weather as yesterday.

"Oh, this confounded rain!" he muttered. But after studiously regarding it for a minute or two, a bright idea seemed to strike him, for he suddenly exclaimed, "But I know what I'll do!" and then returned and took his seat at the table. The letter-bag was already there, waiting to be opened. He unlocked it and examined the contents, but said nothing about them.

"Is there anything for me?" I asked.

"No."

He opened the newspaper and began to read.

"You'd better take your coffee," suggested I; "it will be cold again."

"You may go," said he, "if you've done. I don't want you."

I rose, and withdrew to the next room, wondering if we were to have another such miserable day as yesterday, and wishing intensely for an end of these mutually inflicted torments. Shortly after, I heard him ring the bell and give some orders about his wardrobe that sounded as if he meditated a long journey. He then sent for the coachman, and I heard something about the carriage and the horses, and London, and seven o'clock tomorrow morning, that startled and disturbed me not a little.

"I must not let him go to London, whatever comes of it," said I to myself: "he will run into all kinds of mischief, and I shall be the cause of it. But the question is, how am I to alter his purpose?—Well, I will wait awhile, and see if he mentions it."

I waited most anxiously, from hour to hour; but not a word was spoken, on that or any other subject, to me. He whistled, and talked to his dogs, and wandered from room to room, much the same as on the previous day. At last I began to think I must introduce the subject myself, and was pondering how to bring it about, when John unwittingly came to my relief with the following message from the coachman.

"Please sir, Richard says one of the horses has got a very bad cold, and he thinks, sir, if you could make it convenient to go the day after tomorrow, instead of tomorrow, he could physic it today so as—"

"Confound his impudence!" interjected the master.

"Please sir, he says it would be a deal better if you could," persisted John, "for he hopes there'll be a change in the weather shortly, and he says it's not *likely*, when a horse is so bad with a cold, and physicked and all—"

"Devil take the horse!" cried the gentleman—"Well, tell him I'll think about it," he added, after a moment's reflection. He cast a searching glance at me, as the servant withdrew, expecting to see some token of deep astonishment and alarm; but, being previously prepared, I preserved an aspect of stoical indifference. His countenance fell as he met my steady gaze, and he turned away in very obvious disappointment, and walked up to the fireplace, where he stood in an attitude of undisguised dejection, leaning against the chimney-piece with his forehead sunk upon his arm.

"Where do you want to go, Arthur?" said I.

"To London," replied he, gravely.

"What for?" I asked.

"Because I cannot be happy here."

"Why not?"

"Because my wife doesn't love me."

"She would love you with all her heart, if you deserved it."

"What must I do to deserve it?"

This seemed humble and earnest enough; and I was so much affected, between sorrow and joy, that I was obliged to pause a few seconds before I could steady my voice to reply.

"If she gives you her heart," said I, "you must take it thankfully, and use it well, and not pull it in pieces, and laugh in her face, because she cannot snatch it away."

He now turned round and stood facing me, with his back to the fire.

"Come then, Helen, are you going to be a good girl?" said he.

This sounded rather too arrogant, and the smile that accompanied it did not please me. I therefore hesitated to reply. Perhaps, my former answer had implied too much: he had heard my voice falter, and might have seen me brush away a tear.

"Are you going to forgive me, Helen?" he resumed, more humbly.

"Are *you* penitent!" I replied, stepping up to him and smiling in his face.

"Heart-broken!" he answered, with a rueful countenance—yet with a merry smile just lurking within his eyes and about the corners of his mouth; but this could not repulse me, and I flew into his arms. He fervently embraced me and though I shed a torrent of tears, I think I never was happier in my life than at that moment.

"Then you won't go to London, Arthur?" I said, when the first transport of tears and kisses had subsided.

"No, love,—unless you will go with me."

"I will, gladly," I answered, "if you think the change will amuse you, and if you will put off the journey till next week."

He readily consented, but said there was no need of much preparation, as he should not be for staying long, for he did not wish me to be Londonized, and to lose my country freshness and originality by too much intercourse with the ladies of the world. I thought this folly; but I did not wish to contradict him now: I merely said that I was of very domestic habits, as he well knew, and had no particular wish to mingle with the world.

So we are to go to London on Monday, the day after tomorrow. It is now four days since the termination of our quarrel, and I'm sure it has done us both good: it has made me like Arthur a great deal better and made him behave a great deal better to me. He has never once attempted to annoy me, since, by the most distant allusion to Lady F—— or any of those disagreeable reminiscences of his former life—I wish I could blot them from my memory, or else get him to regard such matters in the same light as I do. Well! it is something, however, to have made him see that they are not fit subjects for a conjugal jest. He may see farther sometime—I will put no limits to my hopes; and, in spite of my aunt's forebodings and my own unspoken fears, I trust we shall be happy yet.

CHAPTER XXV
FIRST ABSENCE

ON the eighth of April, we went to London; on the eighth of May I returned, in obedience to Arthur's wish: very much against my own, because I left him behind. If he had come with me, I should have been very glad to get home again, for he led me such a round of restless dissipation, while there, that, in that short space of time, I was quite tired out. He seemed bent upon displaying me to his friends and acquaintances in particular, and the public in general, on every possible occasion and to the greatest possible advantage. It was something to feel that he considered me a worthy object of pride; but I paid dear for the gratification, for in the first place, to please him, I had to violate my cherished predilections—my almost rooted principles in favour of a plain, dark, sober style of dress; I must sparkle in costly jewels and deck myself out like a painted butterfly, just as I had, long since, determined I would never do—and this was no trifling sacrifice;—in the second place, I was continually straining to satisfy his sanguine expectations and do honour to his choice, by my general conduct and deportment, and fearing to disappoint him by some awkward misdemeanour, or some trait of inexperienced ignorance about the customs of society, especially when I acted the part of hostess, which I was not unfrequently called upon to do; and in the third place, as I intimated before, I was wearied of the throng and bustle, the restless hurry and ceaseless change of a life so alien to all my previous habits. At last, he suddenly discovered that the London air did not agree with me, and I was languishing for my country home and must immediately return to Grassdale.

I laughingly assured him that the case was not so urgent as he appeared to think it, but I was quite willing to go home if he was. He replied that he should be obliged to remain a week or two longer, as he had business that required his presence.

"Then I will stay with you," said I.

"But I can't do with you, Helen," was his answer: "as long as you stay, I shall attend to you and neglect my business."

"But I won't let you," I returned: "now that I know you have business to attend to, I shall insist upon your attending to it, and letting me alone—and, to tell you the truth, I shall be glad of a little rest. I can take my rides and walks in the park as usual; and your business cannot occupy all your time; I shall see you at mealtimes and in the evenings, at least, and that will be better than being leagues away and never seeing you at all."

"But my love, I cannot let you stay. How can I settle my affairs when I know that you are here, neglected—"

"I shall not feel myself neglected: while you are doing your duty, Arthur, I shall never complain of neglect. If you had told me, before, that you had anything to do, it would have been half done before this; and now you must make up for lost time by redoubled exertions. Tell me what it is; and I will be your taskmaster, instead of being a hindrance."

"No, no," persisted the impracticable creature; "you *must* go home, Helen; I must have the satisfaction of knowing that you are safe and well, though far away. Don't I see that you are looking quite rakish?—Your bright eyes are faded, and that tender, delicate bloom has quite deserted your cheek."

"That is only with too much gaiety and fatigue."

"It is not, I tell you; it is the London air: you are pining for the fresh breezes of your country home—and you shall feel them, before you are two days older. And remember your situation, dearest Helen; on your health, you know, depends the health, if not the life of our future hope."

"Then you really wish to get rid of me?"

"Positively, I do; and I will take you down myself to Grassdale, and then return. I shall not be absent above a week—or fortnight at most."

"But if I must go, I will go alone: if you must stay, it is needless to waste your time in the journey there and back."

But he did not like the idea of sending me alone.

"Why, what helpless creature do you take me for," I replied, "that you cannot trust me to go a hundred miles in our own carriage with our own footman and maid to attend me? If you come with me I shall assuredly keep you. But tell me, Arthur, what *is* this tiresome business; and why did you never mention it before?"

"It is only a little business with my lawyer," said he; and he told me something about a piece of property he wanted to sell in order to pay off a part of the encumbrances on his estate; but either the account was a little confused or I was rather dull of comprehension, for I could not clearly understand how that should keep him in town a fortnight after me. Still less can I now comprehend how it should keep him a month—for it is nearly that time since I left him, and no signs of his return as yet. In every letter he promises to be with me in a few days, and every time deceives me—or deceives himself. His excuses are vague and insufficient. I cannot doubt that he is got among his former companions again—oh, why did I leave him? I wish—I do intensely wish he would return!

June 29th.—No Arthur yet; and for many days I have been looking and longing in vain for a letter. His letters, when they come, are kind—if fair words and endearing epithets can give them a claim to the title—but very short, and full of trivial excuses and promises that I cannot trust; and yet how anxiously I look forward to them! how eagerly I open and devour one of those little, hastily scribbled returns for the three or four long letters, hitherto unanswered, he has had from me!

Oh, it is cruel to leave me so long alone! He knows I have no one but Rachel to speak to, for we have no neighbours here, except the Hargraves, whose residence I can dimly descry from these upper windows embosomed among those low, woody hills beyond the Dale. I was glad when I learnt that Milicent was so near us; and her company would be a soothing solace to me now, but she is still in town with her mother: there is no one at the grove but little Esther and her French governess, for Walter is always away. I saw that paragon of manly perfections in London: he seemed scarcely to merit the eulogiums of his mother and sister, though he certainly appeared more conversable and agreeable than Lord Lowborough, more candid and high-minded than Mr. Grimsby, and more polished and gentlemanly than Mr. Hattersley, Arthur's only other friend whom he judged fit to introduce to me.—O Arthur, why won't you come! why won't you write to me at least! You talked about my health—how can you expect me to gather bloom and vigour here; pining in solitude and restless anxiety from day to day?—It would serve you right to come back and find my good looks entirely wasted away. I would beg my uncle and aunt, or my brother to come and see me, but I do not like to complain of my loneliness to them,—and indeed, loneliness is the least of my sufferings; but what is he doing—what is it that keeps him away? It is this ever-recurring question and the horrible suggestions it raises that distract me.

July 3rd.—My last bitter letter has wrung from him an answer at last,—and a rather longer one than usual; but still, I don't know what to make of it. He playfully abuses me for the gall and vinegar[1] of my latest effusion, tells me I can have no conception of the multitudinous engagements that keep him away, but avers that, in spite of them all, he will assuredly be with me before the close of next week; though it is impossible for a man, so circumstanced as he is, to fix the precise day of his return: meantime, he exhorts me to the exercise of patience, "that first of woman's virtues," and desires me to remember the saying, "Absence makes the heart grow fonder," and comfort myself with the assurance that the longer he stays away, the better he shall love me when he returns; and till he does return, he begs I will continue to write to him constantly, for, though he is sometimes too idle and often too busy to answer my letters as they come, he likes to receive them daily, and if I fulfill my threat of punishing his seeming neglect by ceasing to write, he shall be so angry that he will do his utmost to forget me. He adds this piece of intelligence respecting poor Milicent Hargrave:—

"Your little friend Milicent is likely, before long, to follow your example, and take upon her the yoke of matrimony in conjunction with a friend of

---

1 See Matthew 27:34: "They gave him vinegar to drink mingled with gall; and when he had tasted thereof, he would not drink."

mine. Hattersley, you know, has not yet fulfilled his direful threat of throwing his precious person away on the first old maid that chose to evince a tenderness for him; but he still preserves a resolute determination to see himself a married man before the year is out: 'Only,' said he to me, 'I must have somebody that will let me have my own way in everything—not like *your* wife, Huntingdon, she is a charming creature, but she looks as if she had a will of her own, and could play the vixen upon occasion,' (I thought 'you're right there, man,' but I didn't say so). 'I must have some good, quiet soul that will let me just do what I like and go where I like, keep at home or stay away, without a word of reproach or complaint; for I can't do with being bothered.' 'Well,' said I. 'I know somebody that will suit you to a tee, if you don't care for money, and that's Hargrave's sister, Milicent.' He desired to be introduced to her forthwith, for he said he had plenty of the needful himself—or should have, when his old governor[1] chose to quit the stage. So you see, Helen, I have managed pretty well, both for your friend and mine."

Poor Milicent! But I cannot imagine she will ever be led to accept such a suitor—one so repugnant to all her ideas of a man to be honoured and loved.

5th.—Alas! I was mistaken. I have got a long letter from her this morning, telling me she is already engaged, and expects to be married before the close of the month.

"I hardly know what to say about it," she writes, "or what to think. To tell you the truth, Helen, I don't like the thoughts of it at all. If I *am* to be Mr. Hattersley's wife, I must try to love him; and I do try with all my might; but I have made very little progress yet; and the worst symptom of the case is, that the further he is from me the better I like him: he frightens me with his abrupt manners and strange hectoring ways, and I dread the thoughts of marrying him. 'Then why have you accepted him,' you will ask; and I didn't know I had accepted him; but mamma tells me I have, and he seems to think so too. I certainly didn't mean to do so; but I did not like to give him a flat refusal for fear mamma should be grieved and angry, (for I knew she wished me to marry him,) and I wanted to talk to her first about it, so I gave him what *I* thought was an evasive, half negative answer; but she says it was as good as an acceptance, and he would think me very capricious if I were to attempt to draw back—and indeed, I was so confused and frightened at the moment, I can hardly tell what I said. And next time I saw him, he accosted me in all confidence as his affianced bride, and immediately began to settle matters with mamma. I had not courage to contradict them then, and how can I do it now? I cannot: they would think me mad. Besides, mamma is so delighted with the idea of the match; she thinks she has managed so well for me; and I cannot bear to disappoint her. I do object sometimes, and tell her

---

1 Colloquial expression for father.

what I feel, but you don't know *how* she talks. Mr. Hattersley, you know, is the son of a rich banker, and as Esther and I have no fortunes and Walter very little, our dear mamma is very anxious to see us all well married, that is, united to rich partners—it is not *my* idea of being well married, but she means it all for the best. She says when I am safe off her hands it will be such a relief to her mind; and she assures me it will be a good thing for the family as well as for me. Even Walter is pleased at the prospect, and when I confessed my reluctance to him, he said it was all childish nonsense. Do *you* think it nonsense, Helen? I should not care if I could see any prospect of being able to love and admire him, but I can't. There is nothing about him to hang one's esteem and affection upon: he is so diametrically opposite to what I imagined my husband should be. Do write to me, and say all you can to encourage me. Don't attempt to dissuade me, for my fate is fixed: preparations for the important event are already going on around me; and don't say a word against Mr. Hattersley, for I want to think well of him; and though I have spoken against him myself, it is for the last time: hereafter, I shall never permit myself to utter a word in his dispraise, however he may seem to deserve it; and whoever ventures to speak slightingly of the man I have promised to love, to honour, and obey, must expect my serious displeasure. After all, I think he is quite as good as Mr. Huntingdon, if not better; and yet, you love *him*, and seem to be happy and contented; and perhaps I may manage as well. You must tell me, if you can, that Mr. Hattersley is better than he seems—that he is upright, honourable, and open-hearted—in fact, a perfect diamond in the rough. He may be all this, but I don't know him—I know only the exterior and what I trust is the worst part of him."

She concludes with "Good bye, dear Helen, I am waiting anxiously for your advice—but mind you let it be all on the right side."

Alas! poor Milicent, what encouragement can I give you?—or what advice—except that it is better to make a bold stand now, though at the expense of disappointing and angering both mother and brother, and lover, than to devote your whole life, hereafter, to misery and vain regret?

Saturday, 13th. The week is over, and he is not come. All the sweet summer is passing away without one breath of pleasure to me or benefit to him. And I had all along been looking forward to this season with the fond, delusive hope that we should enjoy it so sweetly together; and that, with God's help and my exertions, it would be the means of elevating his mind, and refining his taste to a due appreciation of the salutary and pure delights of nature, and peace, and holy love. But now,—at evening, when I see the round, red sun sink quietly down behind those woody hills, leaving them sleeping in a warm, red, golden haze, I only think another lovely day is lost to him and me;—and at morning, when roused by the flutter and chirp of the sparrows, and the gleeful twitter of the swallows—all intent upon feeding their young, and full of life and joy in their own little frames—I open the window to inhale the balmy, soul-reviving air, and look out upon the lovely landscape, laughing in dew and sunshine,—I too often shame that glorious scene with tears of thankless misery, because *he* cannot feel its freshening influence;—and when I wander in the ancient woods, and meet the little wild-flowers smiling in my path, or sit in the shadow of our noble ash-trees by the water-side, with their branches gently swaying in the light summer breeze that murmurs through their feathery foliage—my ears full of that low music mingled with the dreamy hum of insects, my eyes abstractedly gazing on the glassy surface of the little lake before me, with the trees that crowd about its bank, some gracefully bending to kiss its waters, some rearing their stately heads high above, but stretching their wide arms over its margin, all faithfully mirrored far, far down in its glassy depth— though sometimes the images are partially broken by the sport of aquatic insects, and sometimes, for a moment, the whole is shivered into trembling fragments by a transient breeze that swept the surface too roughly,—still I have no pleasure; for the greater the happiness that nature sets before me, the more I lament that *he* is not here to taste it: the greater the bliss we might enjoy together, the more I feel our present wretchedness apart (yes, ours; he must be wretched, though he may not know it); and the more my senses are pleased, the more my heart is oppressed; for he keeps it with him confined amid the dust and smoke of London,—perhaps, shut up within the walls of his own abominable club.

But most of all, at night, when I enter my lonely chamber, and look out upon the summer moon, 'sweet regent of the sky,'[1] floating above me in the 'black blue vault of heaven,'[2] shedding a flood of silver radiance over park, and wood, and water, so pure, so peaceful, so divine,—and think Where is he now?—what is he doing at this moment?—wholly unconscious of this heavenly scene,—perhaps, revelling with his boon companions, perhaps—God help me, it is too—*too* much!

23rd. Thank heaven, he is come at last! But how altered!—flushed and feverish, listless and languid, his beauty strangely diminished, his vigour and

---

1   From William Mickle's (1735–88) poem "Cumnor Hall." This ballad, originally published in 1784, inspired Sir Walter Scott (1771–1832) to write his novel *Kenilworth* (1821). Significantly for Helen here, the speaker of the poem is Amy Robsart, a woman forsaken by her husband, Lord Robert Dudley, earl of Leicester, for Elizabeth I. In the ballad she laments the fact that "thy love/ that thou so oft has sworn to me / to leave me in this lonely grove [Cumnor Hall],/ immurr'd in shameful privitie" (9–12). Helen Huntingdon may well suspect her husband is having an affair, given her use of Mickle's ballad to describe the moon.

2   William Wordsworth's "A Night-Piece" (1815).

vivacity quite departed. I have not upbraided him by word or look; I have not even asked him what he has been doing. I have not the heart to do it, for I think he is ashamed of himself—he must be so indeed,—and such enquiries could not fail to be painful to both. My forbearance pleases him—touches him even, I am inclined to think. He says he is glad to be home again, and God knows how glad I am to get him back, even as he is. He lies on the sofa nearly all day long; and I play and sing to him for hours together. I write his letters for him, and get him everything he wants; and sometimes I read to him, and sometimes I talk, and sometimes only sit by him and soothe him with silent caresses. I know he does not deserve it; and I fear I am spoiling him; but this once, I will forgive him, freely and entirely—I will shame him into virtue if I can, and I will never let him leave me again.

He is pleased with my attentions—it may be, grateful for them. He likes to have me near him; and though he is peevish and testy with his servants and his dogs, he is gentle and kind to me. What he would be, if I did not so watchfully anticipate his wants, and so carefully avoid, or immediately desist from doing anything that has a tendency to irritate or disturb him, with however little reason, I cannot tell. How intensely I wish he were worthy of all this care! Last night as I sat beside him, with his head in my lap, passing my fingers through his beautiful curls, this thought made my eyes overflow with sorrowful tears—as it often does,—but this time, a tear fell on his face and made him look up. He smiled, but not insultingly.

"Dear Helen!" he said—"why do you cry? you know that I love you" (and he pressed my hand to his feverish lips), "and what more could you desire?"

"Only, Arthur, that you would love *yourself*, as truly and as faithfully as you are loved by me."

"That would be hard indeed!" he replied, tenderly squeezing my hand.

I don't know whether he fully understood my meaning, but he smiled—thoughtfully and even sadly—a most unusual thing with him;—and then he closed his eyes and fell asleep, looking as careless and sinless as a child. As I watched that placid slumber, my heart swelled fuller than ever, and my tears flowed unrestrained.

August 24. Arthur is himself again, as lusty and reckless, as light of heart and head as ever, and as restless and hard to amuse as a spoilt child,—and almost as full of mischief too, especially when wet weather keeps him within doors. I wish he had something to do, some useful trade, or profession, or employment—anything to occupy his head or his hands for a few hours a day, and give him something besides his own pleasure to think about. If he would play the country gentleman, and attend to the farm—but that he knows nothing about, and won't give his mind to consider,—or if he would take up with some literary study, or learn to draw or to play—as he is so fond of music, I often try to persuade him to learn the piano, but he is far too idle for such an undertaking: he has no more idea of exerting himself to overcome obstacles than he has of restraining his natural appetites; and these two things are the ruin of him. I lay them both to the charge of his harsh yet careless father and his madly indulgent mother. If ever I am a mother I will zealously strive against this *crime* of over indulgence—I can hardly give it a milder name when I think of the evils it brings.

Happily, it will soon be the shooting season,[1] and then, if the weather permit, he will find occupation enough in the pursuit and destruction of the partridges and pheasants: we have no grouse, or he might have been similarly occupied at this moment, instead of lying under the acacia tree pulling poor Dash's ears. But he says it is dull work shooting alone; he must have a friend or two to help him.

"Let them be tolerably decent then, Arthur," said I.—The word "friend," in his mouth makes me shudder: I know it was some of his "friends" that induced him to stay behind me in London, and kept him away so long—indeed, from what he has unguardedly told me, or hinted from time to time, I cannot doubt that he frequently showed them my letters, to let them see how fondly his wife watched over his interests and how keenly she regretted his absence; and that they induced him to remain week after week, and to plunge into all manner of excesses to avoid being laughed at for a wife-ridden fool, and, perhaps, to show how far he could venture to go without danger of shaking the fond creature's devoted attachment. It is a hateful idea, but I cannot believe it is a false one.

"Well," replied he, "I thought of Lord Lowborough for one; but there is no possibility of getting him without his better half, our mutual friend Annabella; so we must ask them both. You're not afraid of her, are you Helen?" he asked, with a mischievous twinkle in his eyes.

"Of course not," I answered: "why should I?—And who besides?"

"Hargrave for one—he will be glad to come, though his own place is so near, for he has little enough land of his own to shoot over, and we can extend our depredations into it, if we like;—and he is thoroughly respectable, you know, Helen, quite a lady's man:—and I think, Grimsby for another: he's a decent, quiet fellow enough—you'll not object to Grimsby?"

"I hate him; but however, if you wish it, I'll try to endure his presence for a while."

"All a prejudice Helen—a mere woman's antipathy."

"No; I have solid grounds for my dislike. And is that all?"

---

1 "Shooting season" varied according to species. It was illegal to shoot partridges from 1 February to 1 September, pheasants from 1 February to 1 October, and grouse from 10 December to 12 August.

"Why, yes, I think so. Hattersley will be too busy billing and cooing with his bride to have much time to spare for guns and dogs, at present," he replied.—And that reminds me that I have had several letters from Milicent since her marriage, and that she either is or pretends to be quite reconciled to her lot. She professes to have discovered numberless virtues and perfections in her husband, some of which, I fear, less partial eyes would fail to distinguish, though they sought them carefully with tears;[1] and now that she is accustomed to his loud voice and abrupt, uncourteous manners, she affirms she finds no difficulty in loving him as a wife should do, and begs I will burn that letter wherein she spoke so unadvisedly against him. So that I trust she may yet be happy; but if she is, it will be entirely the reward of her own goodness of heart; for had she chosen to consider herself the victim of fate, or of her mother's worldly wisdom, she might have been thoroughly miserable; and, if, for duty's sake, she had not made every effort to love her husband, she would doubtless have hated him to the end of her days.

CHAPTER XXVI
THE GUESTS

SEPT. 23rd. Our guests arrived about three weeks ago. Lord and Lady Lowborough have now been married above eight months; and I will do the lady the credit to say that her husband is quite an altered man: his looks, his spirits, and his temper are all perceptibly changed for the better since I last saw him. But there is room for improvement still. He is not always cheerful nor always contented, and she often complains of his ill-humour, which, however, of all persons, *she* ought to be the last to accuse him of, as he never displays it against her, except for such conduct as would provoke a saint. He adores her still, and would go to the world's end to please her. She knows her power, and she uses it too; but well knowing that to wheedle and coax is safer than to command, she judiciously tempers her despotism with flattery and blandishments enough to make him deem himself a favoured and a happy man.[2] And yet, at times, a som-

---

1 Hebrews 12:17: "For you know how that afterward, when he would have inherited the blessing, he was rejected; for he found no place of repentance, though he sought it carefully with tears." Milicent's search for Hattersley's virtues is described using the expression associated with Esau's search for a loophole to try to retrieve his birthright. The history behind Esau's rejection of his birthright is told in Genesis 25:21–34 and Genesis 27:1–46.

2 Mary Wollstonecraft argues that behavior like Lady Lowborough's is common in a society that does not treat its men and women equally. She believes that the "artificial weakness" produced by patriarchy "produces a propensity to tyrannize, and gives birth to cunning" (Appendix C1).

bre shadow over-clouds his brow even in her presence, but evidently the result of despondency rather than of ill-humour, and generally occasioned by some display of her ill-regulated temper or misguided mind—some wanton trampling upon his most cherished opinions—some reckless disregard of principle that makes him bitterly regret that she is not as good as she is charming and beloved. I pity him from my heart, for I know the misery of such regrets.

But she has another way of tormenting him, in which I am a fellow sufferer—or might be, if I chose to regard myself as such. This is by openly but not too glaringly coquetting with Mr. Huntingdon, who is quite willing to be her partner in the game; but I don't care for it, because with him, I know there is nothing but personal vanity and a mischievous desire to excite my jealousy, and perhaps to torment his friend; and she, no doubt, is actuated by much the same motives; only there is more of malice and less of playfulness in *her* manoeuvres. It is obviously, therefore, my interest to disappoint them both, as far as I am concerned, by preserving a cheerful, undisturbed serenity throughout; and accordingly I endeavour to show the fullest confidence in my husband and the greatest indifference to the arts of my attractive guest. I have never reproached the former but once, and that was for laughing at Lord Lowborough's depressed and anxious countenance one evening, when they had both been particularly provoking; and then, indeed, I said a good deal on the subject, and rebuked him sternly enough; but he only laughed, and said—

"You can feel for him, Helen—can't you?"

"I can feel for any[1] one that is unjustly treated," I replied, "and I can feel for those that injure them too."

"Why Helen, you are as jealous as he is!" cried he, laughing still more; and I found it impossible to convince him of his mistake. So from that time I have carefully refrained from any notice of the subject whatever, and left Lord Lowborough to take care of himself. He either has not[2] the sense or the power to follow my example, though he does try to conceal his uneasiness as well as he can; but still, it will appear in his face, and his ill-humour will peep out at intervals, though not in the expression of open resentment—they never go far enough for that. But I confess I do feel jealous at times—most painfully, bitterly so—when she sings and plays to him, and he hangs over the instrument and dwells upon her voice with no affected interest; for then, I know he is really delighted, and I have no power to awaken similar fervour. I can amuse and please him with my simple songs, but not delight him thus.

I might retaliate if I chose, for Mr. Hargrave is disposed to be very polite and attentive to me as his hostess—especially so when Arthur is the most

---

1   Brontë has crossed out "any" and written in "every" in the AOC of *Tenant*.
2   In the AOC Brontë has crossed out "has not" and has written "lacks" in the margin instead.

neglectful, whether in mistaken compassion for me, or ambitious to show off his own good breeding by comparison with his friend's remissness, I cannot tell; but in either case, his civilities are highly distasteful to me. If Arthur is a little careless, of course it is unpleasant to have the fault exaggerated by contrast; and to be pitied as a neglected wife when I am not such, is an insult I can ill endure. But for hospitality's sake, I endeavour to suppress my impulse of scarcely reasonable resentment, and behave with decent civility to our guest, who, to give him his due, is by no means a disagreeable companion: he has good conversational powers and considerable information and taste, and talks about things that Arthur never could be brought to discuss, or to feel any interest in. But Arthur dislikes me to talk to him, and is visibly annoyed by his commonest acts of politeness; not that my husband has any unworthy suspicions of me—or of his friend either, as I believe—but he dislikes me to have any pleasure but in himself, any shadow of homage or kindness but such as he chooses to vouchsafe: he knows he is my sun, but when he chooses to withhold his light, he would have my sky to be all darkness; he cannot bear that I should have a moon to mitigate the deprivation. This is unjust; and I am sometimes tempted to tease him accordingly; but I won't yield to the temptation: if he should carry his trifling with my feelings too far, I shall find some other means of checking him.

28th.—Yesterday we all went to the Grove, Mr. Hargrave's much neglected home. His mother frequently asks us over that she may have the pleasure of her dear Walter's company; and this time she had invited us to a dinner party, and got together as many of the country gentry as were within reach to meet us. The entertainment was very well got up; but I could not help thinking about the cost of it all the time. I don't like Mrs. Hargrave; she is a hard, pretentious, worldly-minded woman. She has money enough to live very comfortably, if she only knew how to use it judiciously, and had taught her son to do the same; but she is ever straining to keep up appearances, with that despicable pride that shuns the semblance of poverty as of a shameful crime. She grinds her dependants, pinches her servants, and deprives even her daughters and herself of the real comforts of life, because she will not consent to yield the palm in outward show to those who have three times her wealth, and, above all, because she is determined her cherished son shall be enabled to "hold up his head with the highest gentleman in the land." This same son, I imagine, is a man of expensive habits—no reckless spendthrift, and no abandoned sensualist, but one who likes to have "everything handsome about him,"[1] and to go to a certain length in youthful indulgenc-

---

1   Helen quotes Shakespeare's *Much Ado About Nothing* to underscore her point. Although Dogberry may have "everything handsome about him" (IV.ii.76–77), he is still a foolish "ass" (IV.ii.78).

es—not so much to gratify his own tastes as to maintain his reputation as a man of fashion in the world, and a respectable fellow among his own lawless companions; while he is too selfish to consider how many comforts might be obtained for his fond mother and sisters with the money he thus wastes upon himself: as long as they can contrive to make a respectable appearance once a year when they come to town, he gives himself little concern about their private stintings and struggles at home. This is a harsh judgment to form of "dear, noble-minded, generous-hearted Walter," but I fear it is too just.

Mrs. Hargrave's anxiety to make good matches for her daughters is partly the cause and partly the result of these errors: by making a figure in the world and showing them off to advantage, she hopes to obtain better chances for them; and by thus living beyond her legitimate means and lavishing so much on their brother, she renders them portionless, and makes them burdens on her hands. Poor Milicent, I fear, has already fallen a sacrifice to the manoeuvrings of this mistaken mother, who congratulates herself on having so satisfactorily discharged her maternal duty, and hopes to do as well for Esther. But Esther is a child as yet—a little merry romp of fourteen: as honest-hearted, and as guileless and simple as her sister, but with a fearless spirit of her own, that I fancy, her mother will find some difficulty in bending to her purposes.

CHAPTER XXVII
A MISDEMEANOUR

OCTOBER 9th.—While the gentlemen are ranging the woods and Lady Lowborough is busy writing her letters, I will return to my chronicle for the purpose of recording sayings and doings, the last of the kind I hope I shall ever have cause to describe. It was on the night of the 4th, a little after tea, that Annabella had been singing and playing, with Arthur as usual at her side: she had ended her song, but still she sat at the instrument; and he stood leaning on the back of her chair, conversing in scarcely audible tones, with his face in very close proximity with hers. I looked at Lord Lowborough. He was at the other end of the room, talking with Messrs. Hargrave and Grimsby; but I saw him dart towards his lady and his host, a quick, impatient glance, expressive of intense disquietude, at which Grimsby smiled. Determined to interrupt the tête-à-tête, I rose, and selecting a piece of music from the music-stand, stepped up to the piano, intending to ask the lady to play it; but I stood transfixed and speechless on seeing her seated there, listening with what seemed an exultant smile on her flushed face, to his soft murmurings, with her hand quietly surrendered to his clasp. The blood rushed first to my heart and then to my head—for there was more than this; almost at the moment of my approach, he cast a hurried glance over his shoulder towards the other occupants of the room, and then ardently pressed the unresisting hand to his lips. On raising his eyes he beheld me and dropped them again, confounded and dismayed. She saw me too, and confronted me with a look of hard defiance. I laid the music on the piano, and retired. I felt ill; but I did not leave the room: happily, it was getting late and could not be long before the company dispersed. I went to the fire and leant my head against the chimney-piece. In a minute or two, some one asked me if I felt unwell. I did not answer—indeed, at the time I knew not what was said—but I mechanically looked up, and saw Mr. Hargrave standing beside me on the rug.

"Shall I get you a glass of wine?" said he.

"No, thank you," I replied; and turning from him, I looked round. Lady Lowborough was beside her husband, bending over him as he sat, with her hand on his shoulder, softly talking and smiling in his face; and Arthur was at the table turning over a book of engravings. I seated myself in the nearest chair; and Mr. Hargrave, finding his services were not desired, judiciously withdrew. Shortly after, the company broke up, and as the guests were retiring to their rooms, Arthur approached me, smiling with the utmost assurance.

"Are you *very* angry, Helen?" murmured he.

"This is no jest, Arthur," said I seriously, but as calmly as I could—"unless you think it a jest to lose my affection for ever."

"What! so bitter?" he exclaimed, laughingly clasping my hand between both his; but I snatched it away, in indignation—almost in disgust, for he was obviously affected with wine.

"Then I must go down on my knees," said he; and kneeling before me with clasped hands uplifted in mock humiliation, he continued imploringly—"Forgive me, Helen!—dear Helen forgive me, and I'll *never* do it again!" and burying his face in his handkerchief, he affected to sob aloud.

Leaving him thus employed, I took my candle, and slipping quietly from the room, hastened up stairs as fast as I could. But he soon discovered that I had left him, and rushing up after me, caught me in his arms, just as I had entered the chamber, and was about to shut the door in his face.

"No, no, by heaven, you shan't escape me so!" he cried. Then, alarmed at my agitation, he begged me not to put myself in such a passion, telling me I was white in the face, and should kill myself if I did so.

"Let me go then," I murmured; and immediately he released me—and it was well he did, for I was really in a passion. I sunk into the easy-chair and endeavoured to compose myself, for I wanted to speak to him calmly. He stood beside me, but did not venture to touch me or to speak, for a few seconds; then approaching a little nearer, he dropped on one knee—not in mock humility, but to bring himself nearer my level, and leaning his hand on the arm of the chair, he began in a low voice—

"It is all nonsense, Helen—a jest, a mere nothing—not worth a thought. Will you *never* learn?" he continued more boldly, "that you have nothing to fear from me? that I love you wholly and entirely?—or if," he added with a lurking smile, "I ever give a thought to another you may well spare it, for those fancies are here and gone like a flash of lightning, while my love for you burns on steadily, and for ever like the sun. You little exorbitant tyrant, will not *that*—"

"Be quiet a moment, will you Arthur," said I, "and listen to me—and don't think I'm in a jealous fury: I am perfectly calm. Feel my hand." And I gravely extended it towards him—but closed it upon his with an energy that seemed to disprove the assertion, and made him smile. "You needn't smile, sir," said I, still tightening my grasp, and looking steadfastly on him till he almost quailed before me. "You may think it all very fine, Mr. Huntingdon, to amuse yourself with rousing my jealousy; but take care you don't rouse my hate instead. And when you have once extinguished my love, you will find it no easy matter to kindle it again."

"Well Helen, I won't repeat the offence. But I meant nothing by it, I assure you. I had taken too much wine, and I was scarcely myself, at the time."

"You often take too much;—and that is another practice I detest." He looked up astonished at my warmth. "Yes," I continued. "I never mentioned it before, because I was ashamed to do so; but now I'll tell you that it distresses me, and may disgust me, if you go on and suffer the habit to grow upon you, as it will, if you don't check it in time. But the whole system of your conduct to Lady Lowborough, is not referable to wine; and this night you knew perfectly well what you were doing."

"Well, I'm sorry for it," replied he, with more of sulkiness than contrition: "what more would you have?"

"You are sorry that I saw you, no doubt," I answered coldly.

"If you had not seen me," he muttered, fixing his eyes on the carpet, "it would have done no harm."

My heart felt ready to burst; but I resolutely swallowed back my emotion, and answered calmly, "You think not?"

"No," replied he, boldly. "After all, what have I done? It's nothing—except as you choose to make it a subject of accusation and distress."

"What would Lord Lowborough, your *friend* think, if he knew all? or what would you yourself think, if he or any other had acted the same part to me, throughout, as you have to Annabella?"

"I would blow his brains out."

"Well then, Arthur, how can you call it nothing—an offence for which you would think yourself justified in blowing another man's brains out? Is it nothing to trifle with your friend's feelings and mine—to endeavour to steal a woman's affections from her husband—what he values more than his gold, and therefore what it is more dishonest to take? Are the marriage vows a jest; and is it nothing to make it your sport to break them, and to tempt another to do the same? Can I love a man that does such things, and coolly maintains it is nothing?"

"You are breaking your marriage vows yourself," said he, indignantly rising and pacing to and fro. "You promised to honour and obey me, and now you attempt to hector over me, and threaten and accuse me and call me worse than a highwayman. If it were not for your situation Helen, I would not submit to it so tamely. I won't be dictated to by a woman, though she be my wife."

"What will you do then? Will you go on till I hate you; and then accuse me of breaking my vows?"

He was silent a moment, and then replied,

"You never will hate me." Returning and resuming his former position at my feet, he repeated more vehemently—"You cannot hate me, as long as I love you."

"But how can I believe that you love me, if you continue to act in this way? Just imagine yourself in my place: would *you* think I loved *you*, if *I* did so? Would you believe my protestations, and honour and trust me under such circumstances?"

"The cases are different," he replied. "It is a woman's nature to be constant—to love one and one only, blindly, tenderly, and for ever—bless them, dear creatures! and you above them all—but you must have some commiseration for us, Helen; you must give us a little more license, for as Shakespeare has it—

'However we do praise ourselves,
Our fancies are more giddy and unfirm,
More longing, wavering, sooner lost and won
Than women's are.'"[1]

"Do you mean by that, that your fancies are lost to me, and won by Lady Lowborough?"

"No; Heaven is my witness that I think her mere dust and ashes in comparison with you,—and shall continue to think so, unless you drive me from you by too much severity. She is a daughter of earth; you are an angel of heaven; only be not too austere in your divinity, and remember that I am a poor, fallible mortal. Come now, Helen; won't you forgive me?" he said, gently taking my hand, and looking up with an innocent smile.

"If I do, you will repeat the offence."

"I swear by—"

---

1 Shakespeare, *Twelfth Night* II.iv.31-35.

"Don't swear; I'll believe your word as well as your oath. I wish I could have confidence in either."

"Try me then, Helen: only trust and pardon me this once, and you shall see! Come, I am in hell's torments till you speak the word."

I did not speak it, but I put my hand on his shoulder and kissed his forehead, and then burst into tears. He embraced me tenderly; and we have been good friends ever since. He has been decently temperate at table, and well-conducted towards Lady Lowborough. The first day, he held himself aloof from her, as far as he could without any flagrant breach of hospitality: since that, he has been friendly and civil but nothing more—in my presence, at least, nor, I think, at any other time; for she seems haughty and displeased, and Lord Lowborough is manifestly more cheerful, and more cordial towards his host than before. But I shall be glad when they are gone, for I have so little love for Annabella that it is quite a task to be civil to her, and as she is the only woman here besides myself, we are necessarily thrown so much together. Next time Mrs. Hargrave calls, I shall hail her advent as quite a relief. I have a good mind to ask Arthur's leave to invite the old lady to stay with us till our guests depart. I think I will. She will take it as a kind attention, and, though I have little relish for her society, she will be truly welcome as a third to stand between Lady Lowborough and me.

The first time the latter and I were alone together, after that unhappy evening, was an hour or two after breakfast on the following day, when the gentlemen were gone out after the usual time spent in the writing of letters, the reading of newspapers, and desultory conversation. We sat silent for two or three minutes. She was busy with her work and I was running over the columns of a paper from which I had extracted all the pith some twenty minutes before. It was a moment of painful embarrassment to me, and I thought it must be infinitely more so to her; but it seems I was mistaken. She was the first to speak; and, smiling with the coolest assurance, she began,—

"Your husband was merry last night, Helen: is he often so?"

My blood boiled in my face; but it was better she should seem to attribute his conduct to this than to anything else.

"No," replied I, "and never will be so again I trust."

"You gave him a curtain lecture,[1] did you?"

"No; but I told him I disliked such conduct, and he promised me not to repeat it."

"I *thought* he looked rather subdued this morning," she continued; "and you, Helen; you've been weeping I see—that's our grand resource,[2] you

---

1   "'A reproof given by a wife to her husband in bed,' Johnson" (*OED*).
2   Lady Lowborough is again exhibiting the behavior Wollstonecraft believes is a product of the patriarchy (see n. 2, page 208, as well as Appendix C1).

know—but doesn't it make your eyes smart?—and do you always find it to answer?"

"I never cry for effect; nor can I conceive how any one can."

"Well, I don't know: I never had occasion to try it;—but I think if Lowborough were to commit such improprieties, I'd make *him* cry. I don't wonder at your being angry, for I'm sure I'd give my husband a lesson he would not soon forget for a lighter offence than that. But then he never *will* do anything of the kind; for I keep him in too good order for that."

"Are you sure you don't arrogate too much of the credit to yourself? Lord Lowborough was quite as remarkable for his abstemiousness for some time before you married him, as he is now, I have heard."

"Oh, about the *wine* you mean—yes, he's safe enough for that. And as to looking askance to[1] another woman—he's safe enough for that too, while I live, for he worships the very ground I tread on."

"Indeed! and are you sure you deserve it?"

"Why, as to that, I can't say: you know we're all fallible creatures, Helen; we none of us deserve to be worshipped. But are *you* sure your darling Huntingdon deserves all the love you give to *him*?"

I knew not what to answer to this. I was burning with anger; but I suppressed all outward manifestations of it, and only bit my lip and pretended to arrange my work.

"At any rate," resumed she, pursuing her advantage, "you can console yourself with the assurance that *you* are worthy of all the love he gives to you."

"You flatter me," said I; "but at least, I can try to be worthy of it." And then I turned the conversation.

CHAPTER XXVIII
PARENTAL FEELINGS

DECEMBER 25th.—Last Christmas I was a bride, with a heart overflowing with present bliss, and full of ardent hopes for the future—though not unmingled with foreboding fears. Now I am a wife: my bliss is sobered, but not destroyed; my hopes diminished, but not departed; my fears increased, but not yet thoroughly confirmed;—and, thank Heaven, I am a mother too. God has sent me a soul to educate for heaven,[2] and given me a new and

---

1   Brontë has written "at" in the margin of her copy of the novel, crossing out the published "to."

2   Helen's focus on the significance of her child's afterlife is in keeping with nineteenth-century ideas about childrearing. The idea of educating a soul for heaven is found, in

calmer bliss, and stronger hopes to comfort me. But where hope rises fear *must* lurk behind, and when I clasp my little darling to my breast, or hang over his slumbers with unutterable delight, and a world of hope within my heart, one of two thoughts is ever at hand to check my swelling bliss; the one: He may be taken from me; the other: He may live to curse his own existence. In the first, I have this consolation: that the bud, though plucked, would not be withered, only transplanted to a fitter soil to ripen and blow beneath a brighter sun; and though I might not cherish and watch my child's unfolding intellect, he would be snatched away from all the suffering and sins of earth; and my understanding tells me this would be no great evil; but my heart shrinks from the contemplation of such a possibility, and whispers I could not bear to see him die, and relinquish to the cold and cruel grave this cherished form, now warm with tender life, flesh of my flesh[1] and shrine of that pure spark which it should be my life's sweet labour to keep unsullied from the world,—and ardently implores that heaven would spare him still, to be my comfort and my joy, and me to be his shield, instructor, friend—to guide him along the perilous path of youth, and train him to be God's serv- ant while on earth, a blessed and honoured saint in heaven. But in the other case, if he should live to disappoint my hopes, and frustrate all my efforts—to be a slave of sin, the victim of vice and misery, a curse to others and him- self—Eternal Father, if Thou beholdest such a life before him, tear him from me now in spite of all my anguish, and take him from my bosom to thine own, while he is yet a guileless, unpolluted lamb!

My little Arthur! there you lie in sweet, unconscious slumber, the tiny epitome of your father, but stainless yet as that pure snow, new fallen from heaven—God shield thee from his errors! How will I watch and toil to guard thee from them! He wakes; his tiny arms are stretched towards me; his eyes unclose; they meet my gaze, but will not answer it. Little angel! you do not know me; you cannot think of me or love me yet; and yet how fervently my heart is knit to yours; how grateful I am for all the joy you give me! Would that your father could share it with me—that he could feel my love, my hope, and take an equal part in my resolves and projects for the future—nay, if he could but sympathize in half my views, and share one half my feelings, it would be indeed a blessing to both himself and me: it would elevate and purify his mind, and bind him closer to his home and me.

---

part, in Proverbs 22:6: "Train up a child in the way he should go: and when he is old he will not depart from it." For popular Victorian examples of this understanding, see Ap- pendix E, especially S.C. Abbott's *The Mother at Home* (1833), or Sarah Lewis's *Woman's Mission* (1839).

1 Genesis 2:23: "And Adam said, This is now bone of my bones, and flesh of my flesh: she shall be called Woman, because she was taken out of Man."

Perhaps, he will feel awakening interest and affection for his child as it grows older. At present, he is pleased with the acquisition, and hopes it will become a fine boy and a worthy heir; and that is nearly all I can say. At first, it was a thing to wonder and laugh at, not to touch: now, it is an object almost of indifference, except when his impatience is roused by its "utter helplessness" and "imperturbable stupidity" (as he calls it), or my too close attention to its wants. He frequently comes and sits beside me while I am busied with my maternal cares. I hoped at first it was for the pleasure of contemplating our priceless treasure; but I soon found it was only to enjoy my company, or escape the pains of solitude. He is kindly welcome of course, but the best compliment to a mother is to appreciate her little one. He shocked me very much on one occasion: it was about a fortnight after the birth of our son, and he was with me in the nursery. We had neither of us spoken for some time: I was lost in the contemplation of my nursling, and I thought he was similarly occupied—as far, at least, as I thought about him at all. But suddenly he startled me from my reverie by impatiently exclaiming,—

"Helen, I shall positively hate that little wretch, if you worship it so madly! You are absolutely infatuated about it."

I looked up in astonishment, to see if he could be in earnest.

"You have not a thought to spare for anything else," he continued in the same strain: "I may go or come, be present or absent, cheerful or sad; it's all the same to you. As long as you have that ugly little creature to dote upon, you care not a farthing what becomes of me."

"It is false, Arthur; when you enter the room, it always doubles my happiness; when you are near me, the sense of your presence delights me, though I don't look at you; and when I think about our child, I please myself with the idea that you share my thoughts and feelings, though I don't speak them."

"How the devil can I waste my thoughts and feelings on a little worthless idiot like that?"

"It is your own son Arthur,—or, if that consideration has no weight with you, it is mine; and you ought to respect my feelings."

"Well, don't be cross; it was only a slip of the tongue," pleaded he. "The little fellow is well enough, only I can't worship him as you do."

"You shall nurse him for me, as a punishment," said I, rising to put my baby in its father's arms.

"No, don't, Helen—don't!" cried he, in real disquietude.

"I will: you'll love him better, when you feel the little creature in your arms."

I deposited the precious burden in his hands, and retreated to the other side of the room, laughing at the ludicrous, half embarrassed air with which he sat, holding it at arm's length, and looking upon it as if it were some curious being of quite a different species to himself.

"Come, take it, Helen; take it," he cried at length. "I shall drop it, if you don't."

Compassionating his distress—or rather the child's unsafe position—I relieved him of the charge.

"Kiss it, Arthur; do—you've never kissed it yet!" said I, kneeling and presenting it before him.

"I would rather kiss its mother," replied he, embracing me. "There now; won't that do as well?"

I resumed my seat in the easy chair, and gave my little one a shower of gentle kisses to make up for its other parent's refusal.

"There goes!" cried the jealous father. "That's more, in one minute, lavished on that little senseless, thankless oyster, than you have given me these three weeks past."

"Come here then, you insatiable monopolist, and you shall have as many as you like, incorrigible and undeserving as you are.—There now, won't that suffice? I have a good mind never to give you another till you have learnt to love my baby as a father should."

"I like the little devil—"

"Arthur!"

"Well, the little angel—well enough," and he pinched its delicate little nose to prove his affection, "only I can't *love* it—what is there to love? It can't love me—or you either; it can't understand a single word you say to it, or feel one spark of gratitude for all your kindness. Wait till it can show some little affection for me, and then I'll see about loving it. At present it is nothing more than a little selfish, senseless, sensualist, and if *you* see anything adorable in it, it's all very well—I only wonder how you can."

"If you were less selfish yourself, Arthur, you would not regard it in that light."

"Possibly not, love; but so it is: there's no help for it."

CHAPTER XXIX
THE NEIGHBOUR

DEC. 25th, 1823. Another year is gone. My little Arthur lives and thrives. He is healthy but not robust, full of gentle playfulness and vivacity, already affectionate and susceptible of passions and emotions it will be long ere he can find words to express. He has won his father's heart at last; and now my constant terror is, lest he should be ruined by that father's thoughtless indulgence. But I must beware of my own weakness too, for I never knew till now how strong are a parent's temptations to spoil an only child.

I have need of consolation in my son, for (to this silent paper I may confess it) I have but little in my husband. I love him still; and he loves me, in his own way—but oh, how different from the love I could have given, and once had hoped to receive! how little real sympathy there exists between us; how many of my thoughts and feelings are gloomily cloistered within my own mind; how much of my higher and better self is indeed unmarried—doomed either to harden and sour in the sunless shade of solitude, or to quite degenerate and fall away for lack of nutriment in this unwholesome soil![1]—But, I repeat, I have no right to complain: only let me state the truth—some of the truth at least,—and see hereafter, if any darker truths will blot these pages. We have now been full two years united—the "romance" of our attachment must be worn away. Surely I have now got down to the lowest gradation in Arthur's affection, and discovered all the evils of his nature: if there be any further change, it must be for the better, as we become still more accustomed to each other: surely we shall find no lower depth than this. And, if so, I can bear it well—as well, at least, as I have borne it hitherto.

Arthur is not what is commonly called a *bad* man: he has many good qualities; but he is a man without self-restraint or lofty aspirations—a lover of pleasure, given up to animal enjoyments: he is not a bad husband, but his notions of matrimonial duties and comforts are not my notions. Judging from appearances, his idea of a wife, is a thing to love one devotedly and to stay at home—to wait upon her husband, and amuse him and minister to his comfort in every possible way, while he chooses to stay with her; and, when he is absent, to attend to his interests, domestic or otherwise, and patiently wait his return; no matter how he may be occupied in the meantime.

Early in spring, he announced his intention of going to London: his affairs there demanded his attendance, he said, and he could refuse it no longer. He expressed his regret at having to leave me, but hoped I would amuse myself with the baby till he returned.

"But why leave me?" I said. "I can go with you: I can be ready at any time."

"You would not take that child to town?"

"Yes—why not?"

The thing was absurd: the air of the town would be certain to disagree with him, and with me as a nurse: the late hours and London habits would not suit me under such circumstances; and altogether he assured me that it would be excessively troublesome, injurious, and unsafe. I overruled his objections as well as I could, for I trembled at the thoughts of his going alone, and would sacrifice almost anything for myself, much even for my child, to

---

1 Helen clearly articulates the grave spiritual problem of being married to someone who was not an equal in faith and practice here. See n. 2, page 167 and n. 1, page 193 for more discussion of this issue.

prevent it; but at length he told me, plainly, and somewhat testily, that he could not do with me: he was worn out with the baby's restless nights, and must have some repose. I proposed separate apartments; but it would not do.

"The truth is, Arthur," I said at last, "you are weary of my company, and determined not to have me with you. You might as well have said so at once."

He denied it; but I immediately left the room, and flew to the nursery to hide my feelings, if I could not soothe them, there.

I was too much hurt to express any further dissatisfaction with his plans, or at all to refer to the subject again, except for the necessary arrangements concerning his departure and the conduct of affairs during his absence,—till the day before he went, when I earnestly exhorted him to take care of himself and keep out of the way of temptation. He laughed at my anxiety, but assured me there was no cause for it, and promised to attend to my advice.

"I suppose it is no use asking you to fix a day for your return?" said I.

"Why, no: I hardly can, under the circumstances; but be assured, love, I shall not be long away."

"I don't wish to keep you a prisoner at home," I replied: "I should not grumble at your staying whole months away—if you can be happy so long without me—provided, I knew you were safe; but I don't like the idea of your being there, among your friends, as you call them."

"Pooh, pooh, you silly girl! Do you think I can't take care of myself?"

"You didn't last time.—But THIS time, Arthur," I added, earnestly, "show me that you can, and teach me that I need not fear to trust you!"

He promised fair, but in such a manner as we seek to soothe a child. And did he keep his promise? No;—and, henceforth, *I can never trust his word*. Bitter, bitter confession! Tears blind me while I write. It was early in March that he went, and he did not return till July. This time, he did not trouble himself to make excuses as before, and his letters were less frequent, and shorter and less affectionate, especially after the first few weeks: they came slower and slower, and more terse and careless every time. But still, when *I* omitted writing he complained of my neglect. When I wrote sternly and coldly, as I confess I frequently did at the last, he blamed my harshness, and said it was enough to scare him from his home: when I tried mild persuasion, he was a little more gentle in his replies, and promised to return; but I had learnt, at last, to disregard his promises.

Those were four miserable months, alternating between intense anxiety, despair, and indignation; pity for him, and pity for myself. And yet, through all, I was not wholly comfortless; I had my darling, sinless,[1] inoffensive little

---

1   Helen's description of her son as "sinless" positions her as a Christian who believes in the inherent virtue of children, not their sinfulness. She would not support the adage "spare the rod and spoil the child." See Appendices E1, E5, and E6 for examples of both perspectives on the nature of children.

one to console me, but even this consolation was embittered by the constantly recurring thought, "How shall I teach him, hereafter, to respect his father, and yet to avoid his example?"

But I remembered that I had brought all these afflictions, in a manner willfully, upon myself; and I determined to bear them without a murmur. At the same time I resolved not to give myself *up* to misery for the transgressions of another, and endeavoured to divert myself as much as I could; and besides the companionship of my child and my dear, faithful Rachel, who evidently guessed my sorrows and felt for them, though she was too discreet to allude to them,—I had my books and pencil, my domestic affairs, and the welfare and comfort of Arthur's poor tenants and labourers to attend to; and I sometimes sought and obtained amusement in the company of my young friend Esther Hargrave: occasionally, I rode over to see her, and once or twice I had her to spend the day with me at the manor. Mrs. Hargrave did not visit London that season: having no daughter to marry, she thought it as well to stay at home and economise; and, for a wonder, Walter came down to join her in the beginning of June and stayed till near the close of August.

The first time I saw him was on a sweet, warm evening, when I was sauntering in the park with little Arthur and Rachel, who is head-nurse and lady's-maid in one—for, with my secluded life and tolerably active habits, I require but little attendance, and as she had nursed me and coveted to nurse my child, and was moreover so very trustworthy, I preferred committing the important charge to her, with a young nursery-maid under her directions, to engaging any one else:—besides it saves money; and since I have made acquaintance with Arthur's affairs, I have learnt to regard that as no trifling recommendation; for, by my own desire, nearly the whole of the income of my fortune is devoted, for years to come, to the paying off of his debts, and the money he contrives to squander away in London is incomprehensible.— But to return to Mr. Hargrave:—I was standing with Rachel beside the water, amusing the laughing baby in her arms, with a twig of willow laden with golden catkins, when greatly to my surprise, he entered the park, mounted on his costly black hunter, and crossed over the grass to meet me. He saluted me with a very fine compliment, delicately worded, and modestly delivered withal, which, he had doubtless concocted as he rode along. He told me he had brought a message from his mother, who, as he was riding that way, had desired him to call at the manor and beg the pleasure of my company to a friendly, family dinner tomorrow.

"There is no one to meet but ourselves," said he; "but Esther is very anxious to see you; and my mother fears you will feel solitary in this great house so much alone, and wishes she could persuade you to give her the pleasure of your company more frequently, and make yourself at home in our more humble dwelling, till Mr. Huntingdon's return shall render this a little more conducive to your comfort."

"She is very kind," I answered, "but I am not alone, you see;—and those, whose time is fully occupied, seldom complain of solitude."

"Will you not come tomorrow, then? She will be sadly disappointed if you refuse."

I did not relish being thus compassionated for my loneliness; but however, I promised to come.

"What a sweet evening this is!" observed he, looking round upon the sunny park, with its imposing swell and slope, its placid water, and majestic clumps of trees. "And what a paradise you live in!"

"It is a lovely evening," answered I; and I sighed to think how little I had felt its loveliness, and how little of a paradise sweet Grassdale was to me— how still less to the voluntary exile from its scenes. Whether Mr. Hargrave divined my thoughts, I cannot tell, but, with a half-hesitating, sympathizing seriousness of tone and manner, he asked if I had lately heard from Mr. Huntingdon.

"Not lately." I replied.

"I thought not," he muttered, as if to himself, looking thoughtfully on the ground.

"Are you not lately returned from London?" I asked.

"Only yesterday."

"And did you see him there?"

"Yes—I saw him."

"Was he well?"

"Yes—that is," said he, with increasing hesitation and an appearance of suppressed indignation, "he was as well as—as he deserved to be, but under circumstances I should have deemed incredible for a man so favoured as he is." He here looked up and pointed the sentence with a serious bow to me. I suppose my face was crimson.

"Pardon me, Mrs. Huntingdon," he continued, "but I cannot suppress my indignation when I behold such infatuated blindness and perversion of taste;—but, perhaps you are not aware—" He paused.

"I am aware of nothing sir—except that he delays his coming longer than I expected; and if at present, he prefers the society of his friends to that of his wife, and the dissipations of the town to the quiet of country life, I suppose I have those friends to thank for it. *Their* tastes and occupations are similar to his, and I don't see why his conduct should awaken either their indignation or surprise."

"You wrong me cruelly," answered he: "I have shared but little of Mr. Huntingdon's society, for the last few weeks; and as for his tastes and oc-cupations, they are quite beyond me—lonely wanderer as I am. Where I have but sipped and tasted, he drains the cup to the dregs; and if ever for a moment I have sought to drown the voice of reflection in madness and folly, or if I have wasted too much of my time and talents among reckless and dissipated companions, God knows I would gladly renounce them entirely and for ever, if I had but *half* the blessings that man so thanklessly casts behind his back—but *half* the inducements to virtue and domestic orderly habits that he despises—but *such* a home, and *such* a partner to share it!—It is infamous!" he muttered between his teeth. "And don't think, Mrs. Huntingdon," he added aloud, "that I could be guilty of inciting him to persevere in his present pursuits: on the contrary, I have remonstrated with him again and again; I have frequently expressed my surprise at his conduct and reminded him of his duties and his privileges—but to no purpose; he only—"

"Enough, Mr. Hargrave; you ought to be aware that whatever my husband's faults may be, it can only aggravate the evil for me to hear them from a stranger's lips."

"*Am* I then a stranger?" said he in a sorrowful tone. "I am your nearest neighbour, your son's god-father, and your husband's friend: may I not be yours also?"

"Intimate acquaintance must precede real friendship: I know but little of you, Mr. Hargrave, except from report."

"Have you then forgotten the six or seven weeks I spent under your roof last autumn? *I* have not forgotten them. And I know enough of *you*, Mrs. Huntingdon, to think that your husband is the most enviable man in the world, and I should be the next if you would deem me worthy of your friendship."

"If you knew more of me, you would not think it—or if you did, you would not say it, and expect me to be flattered by the compliment."

I stepped backward as I spoke. He saw that I wished the conversation to end; and immediately taking the hint, he gravely bowed, wished me good evening, and turned his horse towards the road. He appeared grieved and hurt at my unkind reception of his sympathizing overtures. I was not sure that I had done right in speaking so harshly to him; but at the time, I had felt irritated—almost insulted by his conduct; it seemed as if he was presuming upon the absence and neglect of my husband, and insinuating even more than the truth against him.

Rachel had moved on, during our conversation, to some yards distance. He rode up to her, and asked to see the child. He took it carefully into his arms, looked upon it with an almost paternal smile, and I heard him say, as I approached—

"And this too, he has forsaken!"

He then tenderly kissed it, and restored it to the gratified nurse.

"Are you fond of children, Mr. Hargrave?" said I, a little softened towards him.

"Not in general," he replied; "but that is such a *sweet* child—and so like its mother," he added in a lower tone.

"You are mistaken there; it is its father it resembles."

"Am I not right, nurse?" said he, appealing to Rachel.

"I think, sir, there's a bit of both," she replied.

He departed; and Rachel pronounced him a very nice gentleman. I had still my doubts on the subject.

When I met him on the morrow, under his own roof, he did not offend me with any more of his virtuous indignation against Arthur or unwelcome sympathy for me; and, indeed, when his mother began, in guarded terms, to intimate her sorrow and surprise at my husband's conduct, he, perceiving my annoyance, instantly came to the rescue, and delicately turned the conversation, at the same time warning her, by a sidelong glance, not to recur to the subject again. He seemed bent upon doing the honours of his house in the most unexceptionable manner, and exerting all his powers for the entertainment of his guest, and the display of his own qualifications as a host, a gentleman, and a companion; and actually succeeded in making himself very agreeable—only that he was too polite.—And yet, Mr. Hargrave, I don't much like you; there is a certain want of openness about you that does not take my fancy, and a lurking selfishness, at the bottom of all your fine qualities, that I do not intend to lose sight of. No; for, instead of combating my slight prejudice against you as uncharitable, I mean to cherish it, until I am convinced that I have no reason to distrust this kind, insinuating friendship you are so anxious to push upon me.

In the course of the following six weeks, I met him several times, but always, save once, in company with his mother or his sister, or both. When I called on them, he always happened to be at home, and when they called on me, it was always he that drove them over in the phaeton.[1] His mother, evidently, was quite delighted with his dutiful attentions and newly acquired domestic habits.

The time that I met him alone was on a bright but not oppressively hot day in the beginning of July: I had taken little Arthur into the wood that skirts the park, and there seated him on the moss-cushioned roots of an old oak; and, having gathered a handful of bluebells and wild roses, I was kneeling before him, and presenting them, one by one, to the grasp of his tiny fingers; enjoying the heavenly beauty of the flowers, through the medium of his smiling eyes; forgetting, for the moment, all my cares, laughing at his gleeful

---

1   "A species of four-wheeled open carriage, of light construction; usually drawn by a pair of horses, and with one or (now generally) two seats facing forward" (*OED*).

laughter, and delighting myself with his delight,—when a shadow suddenly eclipsed the little space of sunshine on the grass before us; and, looking up, I beheld Walter Hargrave standing and gazing upon us.

"Excuse me, Mrs. Huntingdon," said he, "but I was spell-bound; I had neither the power to come forward and interrupt you, nor to withdraw from the contemplation of such a scene.—How vigorous my little godson grows! and how merry he is this morning." He approached the child and stooped to take his hand; but, on seeing that his caresses were likely to produce tears and lamentations instead of a reciprocation of friendly demonstrations, he prudently drew back.

"What a pleasure and comfort that little creature must be to you. Mrs. Huntingdon!" he observed with a touch of sadness in his intonation, as he admiringly contemplated the infant.

"It is," replied I; and then I asked after his mother and sister.

He politely answered my enquiries, and then returned again to the subject I wished to avoid; though with a degree of timidity that witnessed his fear to offend.

"You have not heard from Huntingdon lately?" he said.

"Not this week," I replied.—Not these three weeks, I might have said.

"I had a letter from him this morning. I wish it were such a one as I could show to his lady." He half drew from his waistcoat pocket a letter with Arthur's still beloved hand on the address, scowled at it, and put it back again, adding—"But he tells me he is about to return next week."

"He tells *me* so every time he writes."

"Indeed!—Well, it is like him.—But to *me* he always avowed it his intention to stay till the present month."

It struck me like a blow, this proof of premeditated transgression and systematic disregard of truth.

"It is only of a piece with the rest of his conduct," observed Mr. Hargrave, thoughtfully regarding me, and reading, I suppose, my feelings in my face.

"Then he is really coming next week?" said I, after a pause.

"You may rely upon it—if the assurance can give you any pleasure.— And is it *possible*, Mrs. Huntingdon, that you can rejoice at his return?" he exclaimed, attentively perusing my features again.

"Of course, Mr. Hargrave; is he not my husband?"

"Oh, Huntingdon, you know not *what* you slight!" he passionately murmured.

I took up my baby and, wishing him good morning, departed, to indulge my thoughts unscrutinized, within the sanctum of my home.

And *was* I glad?—Yes, delighted;—though I was angered by Arthur's conduct, and though I felt that he had wronged me, and was determined he should feel it too.

CHAPTER XXX
DOMESTIC SCENES

ON the following morning, I received a few lines from him myself, confirming Hargrave's intimations respecting his approaching return. And he did come next week, but in a condition of body and mind even worse than before. I did not however intend to pass over his derelictions this time without a remark;—I found it would not do. But the first day, he was weary with his journey, and I was glad to get him back: I would not upbraid him then; I would wait till tomorrow. Next morning, he was weary still: I would wait a little longer. But at dinner, when, after breakfasting at twelve o'clock on a bottle of soda-water and a cup of strong coffee, and lunching at two on another bottle of soda-water mingled with brandy, he was finding fault with everything on the table and declaring we must change our cook—I thought the time was come.

"It is the same cook as we had before you went, Arthur," said I. "You were generally pretty well satisfied with her then."

"You must have been letting her get into slovenly habits then, while I was away. It is enough to poison one—eating such a disgusting mess!" And he pettishly pushed away his plate, and leant back despairingly in his chair.

"I think it is you that are changed, not she," said I, but with the utmost gentleness, for I did not wish to irritate him.

"It may be so," he replied carelessly, as he seized a tumbler of wine and water, adding, when he had tossed it off—"for I have an infernal fire in my veins, that all the waters of the ocean cannot quench!"

"What kindled it?" I was about to ask, but at that moment the butler entered and began to take away the things.

"Be quick Benson—do have done with that infernal clatter!" cried his master.—"And *don't* bring the cheese!—unless you want to make me sick outright."

Benson, in some surprise, removed the cheese, and did his best to effect a quiet and speedy clearance of the rest, but, unfortunately, there was a rumple in the carpet, caused by the hasty pushing back of his master's chair, at which he tripped and stumbled, causing a rather alarming concussion with the trayful of crockery in his hands, but no positive damage, save the fall and breaking of a sauce-tureen;—but, to my unspeakable shame and dismay, Arthur turned furiously around[1] upon him, and swore at him with savage coarseness. The poor man turned pale, and visibly trembled as he stooped to pick up the fragments.

---

[1] Brontë has changed this in the AOC from "around" to the more colloquial "round."

"He couldn't help it, Arthur," said I; "the carpet caught his foot—and there's no great harm done. Never mind the pieces now, Benson, you can clear them away afterwards."

Glad to be released, Benson expeditiously set out the dessert and withdrew.

"What *could* you mean, Helen, by taking the servant's part against me," said Arthur, as soon as the door was closed, "when you knew I was distracted?"

"I did not know you were distracted, Arthur, and the poor man was quite frightened and hurt at your sudden explosion."

"Poor man indeed! and do you think I could stop to consider the feelings of an insensate brute like that, when my own nerves were racked and torn to pieces by his confounded blunders?"

"I never heard you complain of your nerves before."

"And why shouldn't I have nerves as well as you?"

"Oh, I don't dispute your claim to their possession, but *I* never complain of mine."

"No—how should you, when you never do anything to try them?"

"Then why do you try yours, Arthur?"

"Do you think I have nothing to do but to stay at home and take care of myself like a woman?"

"Is it impossible then, to take care of yourself like a man when you go abroad? You told me that you could—and would too; and you promised—"

"Come, come, Helen, don't begin with that nonsense now; I can't bear it."

"Can't bear what?—to be reminded of the promises you have broken?"

"Helen, you are cruel. If you knew how my heart throbbed, and how every nerve thrilled through me while you spoke, you would spare me. You can pity a dolt of a servant for breaking a dish; but you have no compassion for *me*, when my head is split in two and all on fire with this consuming fever."

He leant his head on his hand, and sighed. I went to him and put my hand on his forehead. It was burning indeed.

"Then come with me into the drawing-room, Arthur; and don't take any more wine; you have taken several glasses since dinner, and eaten next to nothing all the day. How can *that* make you better?"

With some coaxing and persuasion, I got him to leave the table. When the baby was brought I tried to amuse him with that; but poor little Arthur was cutting his teeth, and his father could not bear his complaints; sentence of immediate banishment was passed upon him on the first indication of fretfulness; and, because, in the course of the evening, I went to share his exile for a little while, I was reproached, on my return, for preferring my child to my husband. I found the latter reclining on the sofa just as I had left him.

"Well!" exclaimed the injured man, in a tone of pseudo-resignation. "I thought I wouldn't send for you; I thought I'd just see—how long it would please you to leave me alone."

"I have not been *very* long, have I, Arthur? I have not been an hour, I'm sure."

"Oh, of course, an hour is nothing to you, so pleasantly employed; but to *me*—"

"It has not been pleasantly employed," interrupted I. "I have been nursing our poor little baby, who is very far from well, and I could not leave him till I got him to sleep."

"Oh to be sure, you're overflowing with kindness and pity for everything but me."

"And why should I pity *you?* what is the matter with you?"

"Well! that passes everything! After all the wear and tear that I've had, when I come home sick and weary, longing for comfort, and expecting to find attention and kindness, at least, from my wife,—she calmly asks what is the matter with me!"

"There is *nothing* the matter with you," returned I, "except what you have willfully brought upon yourself against my earnest exhortation and entreaty."

"Now, Helen," said he, emphatically, half rising from his recumbent posture, "if you bother me with another word, I'll ring the bell and order six bottles of wine—and, by Heaven, I'll drink them dry before I stir from this place!"

I said no more but sat down before the table and drew a book towards me.

"Do let me have quietness at least!" continued he, "if you deny me every other comfort," and sinking back into his former position, with an impatient expiration between a sigh and a groan, he languidly closed his eyes as if to sleep.

What the book was, that lay open on the table before me, I cannot tell, for I never looked at it. With an elbow on each side of it, and my hands clasped before my eyes, I delivered myself up to silent weeping. But Arthur was not asleep: at the first slight sob, he raised his head and looked round, impatiently exclaiming—

"What are you crying for, Helen? What the deuce is the matter *now?*"

"I'm crying for you Arthur," I replied, speedily drying my tears; and starting up, I threw myself on my knees before him, and, clasping his nerveless hand between my own, continued: "Don't you know that you are a part of myself? And do you think you can injure and degrade yourself, and I not feel it?"

"*Degrade* myself, Helen?"

"Yes, degrade! What have you been doing all this time?"

"You'd better not ask," said he with a faint smile.

"And you had better not tell—but you cannot deny that you *have* degraded yourself miserably. You have shamefully wronged yourself, body and soul—and me too; and I can't endure it quietly—and I won't!"

"Well, don't squeeze my hand so frantically and don't agitate me so, for Heaven's sake! Oh, Hattersley! you were right; this woman will be the death of me, with her keen feelings and her interesting force of character.—There, there, do spare me a little."

"Arthur, you *must* repent!" cried I, in a frenzy of desperation, throwing my arms around him and burying my face in his bosom. "You *shall* say you are sorry for what you have done!"

"Well, well, I am."

"You are not! You'll do it again."

"I shall never live to do it again, if you treat me so savagely," replied he, pushing me from him. "You've nearly squeezed the breath out of my body." He pressed his hand to his heart, and looked really agitated and ill.

"Now get me a glass of wine," said he, "to remedy what you've done, you she tiger! I'm almost ready to faint."

I flew to get the required remedy. It seemed to revive him considerably.

"What a shame it is," said I, as I took the empty glass from his hand, "for a strong young man like you to reduce yourself to such a state!"

"If you knew all, my girl, you'd say rather, 'What a wonder it is you can bear it so well as you do!' I've lived more in these four months, Helen, than you have in the whole course of your existence, or will to the end of your days, if they numbered a hundred years;—so I must expect to pay for it in some shape."

"You will have to pay a higher price than you anticipate, if you don't take care—there will be the total loss of your own health, and of my affection too—if *that* is of any value to you."

"What, you're at that game of threatening me with the loss of your affection again, are you? I think it couldn't have been very genuine stuff to begin with, if it's so easily demolished. If you don't mind, my pretty tyrant, you'll make me regret my choice in good earnest, and envy my friend Hattersley, his meek little wife—she's quite a pattern to her sex, Helen: he had her with him in London all the season, and she was no trouble at all. He might amuse himself just as he pleased, in regular bachelor style, and she never complained of neglect; he might come home at any hour of the night or morning, or not come home at all; be sullen sober, or glorious[1] drunk; and play the fool or the madman[2] to his own heart's desire without any fear or botheration. She never gives him a word of reproach or complaint, do what he will. He

---

1 In the AOC, Brontë has added an "ly" to "glorious," underlined the following "own," and placed a question mark beside it in the margin.

2 See Shakespeare's *Twelfth Night*. When Olivia asks Feste what a drunk man is like, he responds, "Like a drowned man, a fool, and a madman: one draught above heat makes him a fool, the second mads him, and a third drowns him" (I.v.125–26).

says there's not such a jewel in all England, and swears he wouldn't take a kingdom for her."

"But he makes her life a curse to her."

"Not he! She has no will but his, and is always contented and happy as long as he is enjoying himself."

"In that case, she is as great a fool as he is; but it is not so. I have several letters from her, expressing the greatest anxiety about his proceedings, and complaining that you incite him to commit those extravagances—one especially, in which she implores me to use my influence with you to get you away from London, and affirms that her husband never did such things before you came, and would certainly discontinue them as soon as you departed and left him to the guidance of his own good sense."

"The detestable little traitor! Give me the letter, and he shall see it as sure as I'm a living man."

"No, he shall not see it without her consent; but if he did, there is nothing there to anger him—nor in any of the others. She never speaks a word against him; it is only anxiety *for* him that she expresses. She only alludes to his conduct in the most delicate terms, and makes every excuse for him that she can possibly think of—and as for her own misery, I rather *feel* it than *see* it expressed in her letters."

"But she abuses *me*; and no doubt you helped her."

"No; I told her she over-rated my influence with you, that I would gladly draw you away from the temptations of the town if I could, but had little hopes of success, and that I thought she was wrong in supposing that you enticed Mr. Hattersley or any one else into error. I had, myself, held the *contrary* opinion at one time, but I now believed that you mutually corrupted each other; and, perhaps, if she used a little gentle, but serious remonstrance with her husband, it might be of some service, as though he was more rough hewn than mine, I believed he was of a less impenetrable material."

"And so *that* is the way you go on—heartening each other up to mutiny, and abusing each other's partners, and throwing out implications[1] against your own, to the mutual gratification of both!"

"According to your own account," said I, "my evil counsel has had but little effect upon *her*. And as to abuse and aspersions, we are both of us far too deeply ashamed of the errors and vices of our other halves, to make them the common subject of our correspondence. Friends as we are, we would willingly keep your failings to ourselves—even *from* ourselves if we could, unless by knowing them we could deliver you from them."

---

1   In the AOC, Brontë has underlined "implications" and written "insinuations" in the margin, crossed that out, and then written "innuendos." See Talley's "The Case for Anne Brontë's Marginalia in the Author's Own Copy of *The Tenant of Wildfell Hall*" (*Brontë Studies* 32 [July 2007]: 132–37) for information on the implications of these changes.

"Well, well! don't worry me about them: you'll never effect any good by that. Have patience with me, and bear with my languor and crossness a little while, till I get this cursed low fever out of my veins, and then you'll find me cheerful and kind as ever. Why can't you be gentle and good as you were last time?—I'm sure I was very grateful for it."

"And what good did your gratitude do? I deluded myself with the idea that you were ashamed of your transgressions, and hoped you would never repeat them again; but now, you have left me nothing to hope!"

"My case is quite desperate, is it? A very blessed consideration, if it will only secure me from the pain and worry of my dear, anxious wife's efforts to convert me, and her from the toil and trouble of such exertions, and her sweet face and silver accents from the ruinous effects of the same.[1] A burst of passion is a fine, rousing thing upon occasion, Helen, and a flood of tears is marvellously affecting, but, when indulged too often, they are both deuced plaguy things for spoiling one's beauty and tiring out one's friends."

Thenceforth, I restrained my tears and passions as much as I could. I spared him my exhortations and fruitless efforts at conversion too, for I saw it was all in vain: God might awaken that heart supine and stupified with self-indulgence, and remove the film of sensual darkness from his eyes, but I could not. His injustice and ill-humour towards his inferiors, who could not defend themselves, I still resented and withstood; but when I alone was their object, as was frequently the case, I endured it with calm forbearance, except at times when my temper, worn out by repeated annoyances, or stung to distraction by some new instance of irrationality, gave way in spite of myself, and exposed me to the imputations of fierceness, cruelty, and impatience. I attended carefully to his wants and amusements, but not, I own, with the same devoted fondness as before, because, I could not feel it: besides, I had now another claimant on my time and care—my ailing infant, for whose sake I frequently braved and suffered the reproaches and complaints of his unreasonably exacting father.

But Arthur is not naturally a peevish or irritable man—so far from it that there was something almost ludicrous in the incongruity of this adventitious fretfulness and nervous irritability, rather calculated to excite laughter than anger, if it were not for the intensely painful considerations attendant upon those symptoms of a disordered frame,—and his temper gradually improved as his bodily health was restored which was much sooner than would have been the case, but for my strenuous exertions; for there was still one thing about him that I did not give up in despair, and one effort for his preser-

---

1 Brontë's realism here is working directly against more popular fictions about wives' abilities to reform or convert their husbands. See, for example, More's *Coelebs* (Appendix D1) and Thomas Buchanan Read's "What a Word May Do" (Appendix F4).

vation that I would not remit. His appetite for the stimulus of wine had increased upon him, as I had too well foreseen. It was now something more to him than an accessory to social enjoyment: it was an important source of enjoyment in itself. In this time of weakness and depression he would have made it his medicine and support, his comforter, his recreation, and his friend,—and thereby sunk deeper and deeper—and bound himself down for ever in the bathos whereinto he had fallen. But I determined this should never be, as long as I had any influence left; and though I could not prevent him from taking more than was good for him, still, by incessant perseverance, by kindness, and firmness, and vigilance, by coaxing, and daring, and determination,—I succeeded in preserving him from absolute bondage to that detestable propensity, so insidious in its advances, so inexorable in its tyranny, so disastrous in its effects.

And here, I must not forget that I am not a little indebted to his friend Mr. Hargrave. About that time he frequently called at Grassdale, and often dined with us, on which occasions, I fear, Arthur would willingly have cast prudence and decorum to the winds and made "a night of it," as often as his friend would have consented to join him in that exalted pastime; and if the latter had chosen to comply, he might in a night or two, have ruined the labour of weeks, and overthrown with a touch, the frail bulwark it had cost me such trouble and toil to construct. I was so fearful of this at first, that I humbled myself to intimate to him in private, my apprehensions of Arthur's proneness to these excesses and to express a hope that he would not encourage it. He was pleased with this mark of confidence, and certainly did not betray it. On that and every subsequent occasion, his presence served rather as a check upon his host, than an incitement to further acts of intemperance; and he always succeeded in bringing him from the dining room in good time and in tolerably good condition; for if Arthur disregarded such intimations, as "Well, I must not detain you from your lady," or "We must not forget that Mrs. Huntingdon is alone," he would insist upon leaving the table himself, to join me, and his host, however unwillingly, was obliged to follow.

Hence, I learnt to welcome Mr. Hargrave, as a real friend to the family, a harmless companion for Arthur, to cheer his spirits and preserve him from the tedium of absolute idleness and a total isolation from all society but mine, and a useful ally to me. I could not but feel grateful to him under such circumstances; and I did not scruple to acknowledge my obligation on the first convenient opportunity; yet, as I did so, my heart whispered all was not right, and brought a glow to my face, which he heightened by his steady, serious gaze, while, by his manner of receiving those acknowledgements, he more than doubled my misgivings. His high delight at being able to serve me, was chastened by sympathy for me and commiseration for himself—about I know not what, for I would not stay to inquire or suffer him to unburden his sorrows to me. His sighs and intimations of suppressed affliction seemed to come from a full heart; but either he must contrive to retain them within it, or breathe them forth in other ears than mine: there was enough of confidence between us already. It seemed wrong that there should exist a secret understanding between my husband's friend and me, unknown to him, of which he was the object. But my after thought was, "If it is wrong, surely Arthur's is the fault, not mine."

And indeed, I know not whether at the time, it was not for *him* rather than myself that I blushed; for, since he and I are one, I so identify myself with him, that I feel his degradation, his failings, and transgressions as my own; I blush for him, I fear for him; I repent for him, weep, pray, and feel for him as for myself; but I cannot act for him; and hence, I must be and I am debased, contaminated by the union, both in my own eyes, and in the actual truth.[1] I am so determined to love him—so intensely anxious to excuse his errors, that I am continually dwelling upon them, and labouring to extenuate the loosest of his principles and the worst of his practices, till I am familiarized with vice and almost a partaker in his sins. Things that formerly shocked and disgusted me, now seem only natural. I know them to be wrong, because reason and God's word declare them to be so; but I am gradually losing that instinctive horror and repulsion which was given me by nature, or instilled into me by the precepts and example of my aunt. Perhaps, then, I was too severe in my judgments, for I abhorred the sinner as well as the sin; now, I flatter myself I am more charitable and considerate; but am I not becoming more indifferent and insensate too? Fool that I was to dream that I had strength and purity enough to save myself and him! Such vain presumption would be rightly served, if I should perish with him in the gulf from which I sought to save him! Yet, God preserve me from it!—and him too. Yes, poor Arthur, I will still hope and pray for you; and though I write as if you were some abandoned wretch, past hope and past reprieve, it is only my anxious fears—my strong desires that make me do so; one who loved you less would be less bitter—less dissatisfied.

His conduct has of late, been what the world calls irreproachable; but then I know his heart is still unchanged;—and I know that spring is approaching, and deeply dread the consequences.

As he began to recover the tone and vigour of his exhausted frame, and with it something of his former impatience of retirement and repose, I suggested a short residence by the seaside, for his recreation and further restoration, and for the benefit of our little one as well. But no; watering-places

---

1 Under the system of coverture, Helen and Arthur would have been regarded legally as one body. Helen could also be referring to Genesis 2:24, which describes a married man and woman as "one flesh."

were so intolerably dull—besides, he had been invited by one of his friends to spend a month or two in Scotland for the better recreation of grouse-shooting and deer-stalking, and had promised to go.

"Then you will leave me again, Arthur?" said I.

"Yes, dearest, but only to love you the better when I come back, and make up for all past offences and short-comings; and you needn't fear me this time; there are no temptations on the mountains. And during my absence you may pay a visit to Staningley, if you like: your uncle and aunt have long been wanting us to go there, you know; but somehow, there's such a repulsion between the good lady and me, that I never could bring myself up to the scratch."

I was perfectly willing to avail myself of this permission, though not a little apprehensive of my aunt's questions and comments concerning my matrimonial experience, regarding which I had been very reserved in my letters, for I had not much that was pleasant to communicate.

About the third week in August, Arthur set out for Scotland, and Mr. Hargrave accompanied him thither, to my private satisfaction. Shortly after, I, with little Arthur and Rachel, went to Staningley, my dear old home, which, as well as my dear old friends its inhabitants, I saw again with mingled feelings of pleasure and pain so intimately blended that I could scarcely distinguish the one from the other, or tell to which to attribute the various tears, and smiles, and sighs awakened by those old familiar scenes, and tones, and faces. Not quite two years had passed since I had seen and heard them last; but it seemed a far, far longer time; and well it might, for how immeasurably changed was I! how many things had I not seen, and felt, and learnt since then! My uncle too appeared perceptibly more aged and infirm, my aunt more sad and grave. I believe she thought I had repented of my rashness; though she did not openly express her conviction, or triumphantly remind me of her slighted counsels, as I had partly feared she would; but she observed me narrowly—more narrowly than I liked to be observed—and seemed to mistrust my cheerfulness and unduly mark each little indication of sadness or serious thought, to notice all my casual observations, and silently draw her own inferences from them; while, by a system of quiet cross-questioning renewed from time to time, she drew from me many things I should not otherwise have told her, and laying this and that together, obtained, I fear, a pretty clear conception of my husband's faults and my afflictions, though not of my remaining sources of comfort and hope, for though I endeavoured to impress her strongly with the notion of Arthur's redeeming qualities, of our mutual affection, and the many causes I had for thankfulness and self-congratulation, she received all such intimations coldly and calmly as if mentally making her own deductions—which deductions, I am persuaded, were generally far beyond the truth; though I certainly did exaggerate a little in attempting to picture the bright side of my position. Was it pride that made me so extremely anxious to appear satisfied with my lot,—or merely a just determination to bear my self-imposed burden alone, and preserve my best friend from the slightest participation in those sorrows from which she had striven so hard to save me? It might have been something of each, but I am sure the latter motive was predominant.

I did not much prolong my visit, for, not only did I feel my aunt's relentless watchfulness and incredulity to be a restraint upon me, and a silent reproach that oppressed me more than she could well imagine, but I was sensible that my little Arthur was an annoyance to his uncle, though the latter wished him well, and no great amusement to his aunt, though an object of her earnest affection and anxious solicitude.

Dear aunt! have you so tenderly reared me from infancy, so carefully guided and instructed me in childhood and youth; and could I give you no return but this—to disappoint your hopes, oppose your wishes, scorn your warnings and advice, and darken your latter years with anxious fears and sorrow for the sufferings you cannot relieve?—It almost broke my heart to think of it; and again and again I endeavoured to convince her that I was happy and contented with my lot; but her last words, as she embraced me and kissed the child in my arms, before I entered the carriage, were,—

"Take care of your son, Helen, and there may be happy days in store for you, yet. How great a comfort and treasure he is to you now I can well imagine; but if you spoil him to gratify your present feelings, it will be too late to repent it when your heart is broken."

Arthur did not come home till several weeks after my return to Grassdale; but I did not feel so anxious about him now: to think of him engaged in active sports among the wild hills of Scotland, was very different from knowing him to be immersed amid the corruptions and temptations of London. His letters, now, though neither long nor lover-like, were more regular than ever they had been before; and when he did return, to my great joy instead of being worse than when he went, he was more cheerful and vigorous, and better in every respect. Since that time, I have had little cause to complain. He still has an unfortunate predilection for the pleasures of the table, against which I have to struggle and watch; but he has begun to notice his boy, and that is an increasing source of amusement to him within doors; while his fox-hunting and coursing are a sufficient occupation for him without, when the ground is not hardened by frost; so that he is not wholly dependant on me for entertainment. But it is now January: spring is approaching; and, I repeat, I dread the consequences of its arrival. That sweet season, I once so joyously welcomed as the time of hope and gladness, awakens, now, far other anticipations by its return.

CHAPTER XXXI
SOCIAL VIRTUES

MARCH 20th, 1824. The dreaded time is come, and Arthur is gone, as I expected. This time he announced it his intention to make but a short stay in London, and pass over to the continent, where he should probably stay a few weeks; but I shall not expect him till after the lapse of many weeks: I now know that, with him, days signify weeks, and weeks months.

I was to have accompanied him, but, a little before the time arranged for our departure, he allowed—and even urged me, with an appearance of wonderful self-sacrifice, to go and see my unfortunate father, who is very ill, and my brother, who is very unhappy in consequence of both the illness and its cause, and whom I had not seen since the day our child was christened, when he stood sponsor along with Mr. Hargrave and my aunt. Not willing to impose upon my husband's good-nature in thus allowing me to leave him, I made but a very short stay; but when I returned to Grassdale—he was gone.

He left a note to explain his so hasty departure, pretending that some sudden emergency had demanded his immediate presence in London, and rendered it impossible to await my return; adding that I had better not trouble myself to follow him, as he intended to make such a short stay, that it would hardly be worth while; and as, of course, he could travel alone at less than half the expense than if I accompanied him, it would perhaps be better to defer the excursion to another year, when he should have got our affairs into a rather more settled state, as he was now endeavouring to do.

Was it really so?—or was the whole a contrivance to ensure his going forth upon his pleasure-seeking excursion, without my presence to restrain him? It is painful to doubt the sincerity of those we love, but after so many proofs of falsity and utter disregard to principle how can I believe so improbable a story?

I have this one source of consolation left:—he had told me some time previously, that if ever he went to London or Paris again, he should observe more moderation in his indulgences than before, lest he should destroy his capacity for enjoyment altogether: he had no ambition to live to a prodigious old age, but he should like to have his share of life, and above all, to relish its pleasures to the last—to which end, he found it necessary to economize, for already, he feared, he was not so handsome a fellow as he had been, and young as he was, he had lately detected some grey hairs among his beloved chestnut locks; he suspected he was getting a trifle fatter too, than was quite desirable—but that was with good living and idleness; and for the rest, he trusted he was as strong and hearty as ever: only there was no saying what *another* such a season of unlimited madness and devilment, as the last, might not do towards bringing him down. Yes; he said this to *me*—with unblushing effrontery, and that same blithe, roguish twinkle of the eyes I once so loved to see, and that low, joyous laugh it used to warm my heart to hear.

Well! such considerations will doubtless have more weight with him than any that I could urge. We shall see what *they* can do towards his preservation, since no better hope remains.

July 30th.—He returned about three weeks ago, rather better in health, certainly, than before, but still worse in temper. And yet, perhaps, I am wrong: it is *I* that am less patient and forbearing. I am tired out with his injustice, his selfishness and hopeless *depravity*—I wish a milder word would do—; I am no angel and my corruption rises against it. My poor father died last week: Arthur was vexed to hear of it, because he saw that I was shocked and grieved, and he feared the circumstance would mar his comfort. When I spoke of ordering my mourning, he exclaimed—

"Oh, I hate black! But however, I suppose you must wear it awhile, for form's sake; but I hope, Helen, you won't think it your bounden duty to compose your face and manners into conformity with your funereal garb. Why should you sigh and groan, and I be made uncomfortable because an old gentleman in ——shire, a perfect stranger to us both, has thought proper to drink himself to death?—There now, I declare you're crying! Well, it must be affectation."

He would not hear of my attending the funeral, or going for a day or two, to cheer poor Frederick's solitude. It was quite unnecessary, he said, and I was unreasonable to wish it. What was my father to me? I had never seen him, but once since I was a baby, and I well knew he had never cared a stiver[1] about me;—and my brother too, was little better than a stranger. "Besides, dear Helen," said he, embracing me with flattering fondness, "I cannot spare you for a single day."

"Then how have you managed without me, these *many* days?" said I.

"Ah! then I was knocking about the world, now I am at home; and home without you, my household deity, would be intolerable."

"Yes, as long as I am necessary to your comfort; but you did not say so before, when you urged me to leave you, in order that you might get away from your home without me," retorted I; but before the words were well out of my mouth, I regretted having uttered them. It seemed so heavy a charge: if false, too gross an insult; if true, too humiliating a fact to be thus openly cast in his teeth. But I might have spared myself that momentary pang of self-reproach. The accusation awoke neither shame nor indignation in him: he attempted neither denial nor excuse, but only answered with a long, low, chuckling laugh as if he viewed the whole transaction as a clever, merry jest from beginning to end. Surely that man will make me dislike him at last!

---

1 "Used (like *penny*) as a type of a coin of small value, or of a small amount of money" (*OED*).

"Sine as ye brew, my maiden fair,
Keep mind that ye maun drink the yill."[1]

Yes; and I *will* drink it to the very dregs: and none but myself shall know how bitter I find it!

August 20th.—We are shaken down again to about our usual position. Arthur has returned to nearly his former condition and habits; and I have found it my wisest plan to shut my eyes against the past and future, as far as *he* at least is concerned, and live only for the present; to love him when I can; to smile (if possible) when he smiles, be cheerful when he is cheerful, and pleased when he is agreeable; and when he is not, to try to make him so—and if that won't answer, to bear with him, to excuse him, and forgive him, as well as I can, and restrain my own evil passions from aggravating his; and yet, while I thus yield and minister to his more harmless propensities to self-indulgence, to do all in my power to save him from the worse.

But we shall not be long alone together. I shall shortly be called upon to entertain the same select body of friends as we had the autumn before last, with the addition of Mr. Hattersley and, at my special request, his wife and child. I long to see Milicent—and her little girl too. The latter is now above a year old; she will be a charming playmate for my little Arthur.

September 30th.—Our guests have been here a week or two; but I have had no leisure to pass any comments upon them till now. I cannot get over my dislike to Lady Lowborough. It is not founded on mere personal pique; it is the woman herself that I dislike, because I so thoroughly disapprove of her. I always avoid her company as much as I can without violating the laws of hospitality; but when we do speak or converse together, it is with the utmost civility—even apparent cordiality on her part; but preserve me from such cordiality! It is like handling briar-roses and may-blossoms—bright enough to the eye, and outwardly soft to the touch, but you know there are thorns beneath, and every now and then you feel them too; and perhaps resent the injury by crushing them in till you have destroyed their power, though somewhat to the detriment of your own finger.

Of late, however, I have seen nothing in her conduct towards Arthur to anger or alarm me. During the first few days I thought she seemed very

---

1   A bitter invocation of Robert Burns's (1759–96) "Country Lassie" (1792), where an older woman advises a younger woman to marry a man who could provide for her better than the one she prefers. When the girl tells the woman that she will not change her mind, the older woman reminds her that she will have to live with that choice, figuratively describing to her how she must ("maun") drink the ale ("yill") she has brewed. Burns is poetically reworking a proverb all about consequences: "As they brew, so let them bake (drink)." See the *Oxford Dictionary of English Proverbs*, compiled by William George Smith (London: Oxford UP, 1948), 64.

solicitous to win his admiration. Her efforts were not unnoticed by him: I frequently saw him smiling to himself at her artful manoeuvres: but, to his praise be it spoken, her shafts fell powerless by his side. Her most bewitching smiles, her haughtiest frowns were ever received with the same immutable, careless good-humour; till, finding he was indeed impenetrable, she suddenly remitted her efforts, and became, to all appearance, as perfectly indifferent as himself. Nor have I since witnessed any symptom of pique on his part, or renewed attempts at conquest upon hers.

This is as it should be; but Arthur never will let me be satisfied with him. I have never, for a single hour since I married him, known what it is to realize that sweet idea, "In quietness and confidence shall be your rest."[1] Those two detestable men Grimsby and Hattersley have destroyed all my labour against his love of wine. They encourage him daily to overstep the bounds of moderation, and, not unfrequently, to disgrace himself by positive excess. I shall not soon forget the second night after their arrival. Just as I had retired from the dining-room, with the ladies, before the door was closed upon us, Arthur exclaimed—"Now then, my lads, what say you to a regular jollification?"

Milicent glanced at me with a half reproachful look, as if *I* could hinder it; but her countenance changed when she heard Hattersley's voice shouting through door and wall.

"*I'm* your man! Send for more wine: here isn't *half* enough!"

We had scarcely entered the drawing-room before we were joined by Lord Lowborough.

"What *can* induce you to come so soon?" exclaimed his lady, with a most ungracious air of dissatisfaction.

"You know I never drink, Annabella," replied he, seriously.

"Well, but you might stay with them a little: it looks so silly to be always dangling after the women—I wonder you can!"

He reproached her with a look of mingled bitterness and surprise, and sinking into a chair, suppressed a heavy sigh, bit his pale lips, and fixed his eyes upon the floor.

"You did right to leave them, Lord Lowborough," said I. "I trust you will always continue to honour us so early with your company. And if Annabella knew the value of true wisdom, and the misery of folly and—and intemperance, she would not talk such nonsense—even in jest."

He raised his eyes while I spoke, and gravely turned them upon me with a half surprised, half abstracted look, and then bent them on his wife.

"At least," said she, "I know the value of a warm heart and a bold, manly spirit!"

---

1   Isaiah 30:15.

And she pointed her words with a glance of triumph at me, which seemed to say, "And that is more than *you* do," and a look of scorn at her husband, that entered into his soul. I was intensely exasperated; but it was not for me to reprove her, or, as it seemed, to express my sympathy with her husband without insulting his feelings. All I could do, to obey my inward impulse, was to hand him a cup of coffee, bringing it to him myself, and before I served either of the ladies, by way of balancing her contempt by my exceeding deference. He took it mechanically from my hand, with a slight inclination, and, next minute, rose and placed it untasted on the table, looking, not at it, but at her.

"Well, Annabella," said he, in a deep and hollow tone, "since my presence is disagreeable to you, I will relieve you of it."

"Are you going back to them, then?" said she, carelessly.

"No," exclaimed he, with harsh and startling emphasis; "I will NOT go back to them! And I will never stay with them one moment longer than I think right, for you or any other tempter! But you needn't mind that— I shall never trouble you again, by intruding my company upon you so unseasonably."

He left the room, I heard the hall door open and shut, and immediately after, on putting aside the curtain, I saw him pacing down the park, in the comfortless gloom of the damp, cloudy twilight.

Such scenes as this are always disagreeable to witness. Our little party was completely silenced for a moment. Milicent played with her teaspoon, and looked confounded and uncomfortable. If Annabella felt any shame or uneasiness, she attempted to hide it by a short, reckless laugh, and calmly betook herself to her coffee.

"It would serve you right, Annabella," said I at length, "if Lord Lowborough were to return to his old habits, which had so nearly effected his ruin, and which it cost him such an effort to break. You would then see cause to repent such conduct as this."

"Not at all, my dear! I should not mind if his Lordship were to see fit to intoxicate himself every day: I should only the sooner be rid of him."

"Oh, Annabella!" cried Milicent. "How *can* you say such wicked things! It would indeed be a just punishment, as far as you are concerned, if providence should take you at your word, and make you feel what others feel that—" She paused as a sudden burst of loud talking and laughter reached us from the dining room, in which the voice of Hattersley was pre-eminently conspicuous, even to my unpractised ear.

"What *you* feel at this moment, I suppose?" said Lady Lowborough, with a malicious smile, fixing her eyes upon her cousin's distressed countenance.

The latter offered no reply, but averted her face and brushed away a tear. At that moment the door opened and admitted Mr. Hargrave; just a little flushed, his dark eyes sparkling with unwonted vivacity.

"Oh, I'm glad you're come, Walter!" cried his sister—"But I wish you could have got Ralph to come too."

"Utterly impossible, dear Milicent," replied he, gaily. "I had much ado to get away myself. Ralph attempted to keep me by violence; Huntingdon threatened me with the eternal loss of his friendship; and Grimsby, worse than all, endeavoured to make me ashamed of my virtue, by such galling sarcasms and innuendos as he knew would wound me the most. So you see, ladies, you ought to make me welcome when I have braved and suffered so much for the favour of your sweet society. He smilingly turned to me and bowed as he finished the sentence.

"Isn't he *handsome* now Helen?" whispered Milicent, her sisterly pride overcoming, for the moment, all other considerations.

"He would be," I returned, "if that brilliance of eye, and lip, and cheek were natural to him; but look again, a few hours hence."

Here the gentleman took a seat near me at the table, and petitioned for a cup of coffee.

"I consider this an apt illustration of Heaven taken by storm," said he, as I handed one to him. "I am in paradise now; but I have fought my way through flood and fire to win it. Ralph Hattersley's last resource was to set his back against the door, and swear I should find no passage but through his body (a pretty substantial one too). Happily, however, that was not the only door, and I effected my escape by the side entrance, through the butler's pantry, to the infinite amazement of Benson, who was cleaning the plate."

Mr. Hargrave laughed, and so did his cousin; but his sister and I remained silent and grave.

"Pardon my levity, Mrs. Huntingdon," murmured he, more seriously, as he raised his eyes to my face. "You are not used to these things: you suffer them to affect your delicate mind too sensibly. But I thought of you in the midst of those lawless roisterers; and I endeavoured to persuade Mr. Huntingdon to think of you too; but to no purpose: I fear he is fully determined to enjoy himself this night; and it will be no use keeping the coffee waiting for him or his companions: it will be much if they join us at tea. Meantime, I earnestly wish I could banish the thoughts of them from your mind—and my own too, for I hate to think of them—yes—even of my dear friend Huntingdon, when I consider the power he possesses over the happiness of one so immeasurably superior to himself, and the use he makes of it—I positively *detest* the man!"

"You had better not say so to me, then," said I; "for, bad as he is, he is part of myself,[1] and you cannot abuse him without offending me."

---

1   A reference to Genesis 2:24: "therefore shall a man leave his father and his mother, and shall cleave unto his wife: and they shall be as one flesh."

"Pardon me, then, for I would sooner die than offend you.—But let us say no more of him for the present if you please."

He then entirely changed the subject of discourse, and exerting all his powers to entertain our little circle, conversed on different topics with more than his usual brilliance and fluency, addressing himself, sometimes, exclusively to me, sometimes to the whole trio of ladies. Annabella cheerfully bore her part in the conversation; but I was sick at heart,—especially when loud bursts of laughter and incoherent songs, pealing through the triple doors of hall and ante-room, startled my ear and pierced my aching temples;—and Milicent partly shared my feelings; so that, to us, the evening appeared a very long one, in spite of Hargrave's apparently good-natured exertions to give it a contrary effect.

At last, they came; but not till after ten, when tea, which had been delayed for more than half an hour, was nearly over. Much as I had longed for their coming, my heart failed me at the riotous uproar of their approach; and Milicent turned pale and almost started from her seat as Mr. Hattersley burst into the room with a clamorous volley of oaths in his mouth, which Hargrave endeavoured to check by entreating him to remember the ladies.

"Ah! you do well to remind me of the ladies, you dastardly deserter," cried he, shaking his formidable fist at his brother-in-law; "if it were not for them, you well know, I'd demolish you in the twinkling of an eye, and give your body to the fowls of heaven and the lilies of the field!"[1] Then, planting a chair by Lady Lowborough's side, he stationed himself in it, and began to talk to her, with a mixture of absurdity and rascally impudence that seemed rather to amuse than to offend her; though she affected to resent his insolence, and to keep him at bay with sallies of smart and spirited repartee.

Meantime, Mr. Grimsby seated himself by me, in the chair vacated by Hargrave as they entered, and gravely stated that he would thank me for a cup of tea: and Arthur placed himself beside poor Milicent, confidentially pushing his head into her face, and drawing in closer to her as she shrunk away from him. He was not so noisy as Hattersley, but his face was exceedingly flushed, he laughed incessantly, and while I blushed for all I saw and heard of him, I was glad that he chose to talk to his companion in so low a tone that no one could hear what he said but herself. It must have been intolerable nonsense at best, for she looked excessively annoyed, and first went red in the face, then indignantly pushed back her chair, and finally took refuge behind me on the sofa. Arthur's sole intention seemed to have been to produce some such disagreeable effects: he laughed immoderately on finding

---

1 Hattersley is conflating portions of Matthew 6:26 and 6:28 to threaten Hargrave. He is using Jesus' words about how God cares for "the fowls of the air" (6:26) and "the lilies of the field" (6:28) to insult someone—a clear sign to Victorian readers of his perfidy.

he had driven her away—drawing in his chair to the table, he leant his folded arms upon it, and delivered himself up to a paroxysm of weak, low, foolish laughter. When he was tired of this exercise he lifted his head and called aloud to Hattersley, and there ensued a clamorous contest between them about I know not what.

"What fools they are!" drawled Mr. Grimsby, who had been talking away, at my elbow, with sententious gravity all the time; but I had been too much absorbed in contemplating the deplorable state of the other two—especially Arthur—to attend to him.

"Did you ever hear such nonsense as they talk, Mrs. Huntingdon?" he continued, "I'm quite ashamed of them for my part: they can't take so much as a bottle between them without its getting into their heads—"

"You are pouring the cream into your saucer, Mr. Grimsby."

"Ah! yes, I see, but we're almost in darkness here. Hargrave, snuff those candles, will you?"

"They're wax; they don't require snuffing,"[1] said I.

"'The light of the body is the eye,'" observed Hargrave, with a sarcastic smile. "'If thine eye be *single* thy whole body shall be full of light.'"[2]

Grimsby repulsed him with a solemn wave of the hand, and then, turning to me, continued, with the same drawling tones, and strange uncertainty of utterance and heavy gravity of aspect as before, "But as I was saying, Mrs. Huntingdon,—they have no head at all: they can't take half a bottle without being affected some way; whereas I—well, I've taken three times as much as they have tonight, and you see I'm perfectly steady. Now that may strike you as very singular, but I think I can explain it:—you see *their* brains—I mention no names, but you'll understand to whom I allude—*their* brains are light to begin with, and the fumes of the fermented liquor render them lighter still, and produce an entire light-headedness, or giddiness, resulting in intoxication; whereas *my* brains being composed of more solid materials will absorb a considerable quantity of this alcoholic vapour without the production of any sensible result—"

"I think you will find a sensible result produced on that tea," interrupted Mr. Hargrave, "by the quantity of sugar you have put into it. Instead of your usual complement of one lump you have put in six."

---

1   Rosengarten and Smith point out that "unlike the wicks of cheap tallow candles made of animal fat, those of wax candles rarely needed trimming ('snuffing'), especially after the development of the plaited wick in 1825" (*OTWH* 481). Either Brontë has unintentionally introduced an anachronism into the text—since the action here occurs in 1823—or Helen is referring to them as good wax candles regardless of their wicks.

2   Hargrave is sarcastically quoting Matthew 6:22 and Luke 11:34. The version in Luke contains the information of Matthew 6:23 as well: "The light of the body is the eye: therefore when thine eye is single, thy whole body also is full of light; but when thine eye is evil, thy body also is full of darkness."

"Have I so?" replied the philosopher, diving with his spoon into the cup and bringing up several half-dissolved pieces in confirmation of the assertion. "Um! I perceive. Thus, Madam, you see the evil of absence of mind—of thinking too much while engaged in the common concerns of life. Now if I had had my wits about me, like ordinary men, instead of within me like a philosopher, I should not have spoiled this cup of tea, and been constrained to trouble you for another.—With your permission, I'll turn this into the slop-basin."

"That is the sugar basin, Mr. Grimsby. Now you have spoiled the sugar too; and I'll thank you to ring for some more—for here is Lord Lowborough, at last; and I hope his lordship will condescend to sit down with us, such as we are, and allow me to give him some tea."

His lordship gravely bowed in answer to my appeal, but said nothing. Meantime, Hargrave volunteered to ring for the sugar, while Grimsby lamented his mistake, and attempted to prove that it was owing to the shadow of the urn and the badness of the lights.

Lord Lowborough had entered a minute or two before, unobserved by any one but me, and been standing before the door, grimly surveying the company. He now stepped up to Annabella, who sat with her back towards him, with Hattersley still beside her, though not now attending to her, being occupied in vociferously abusing and bullying his host.

"Well, Annabella," said her husband, as he leant over the back of her chair, "which of these three 'bold, manly spirits' would you have me to resemble?"

"By heaven and earth, you shall resemble us all!" cried Hattersley, starting up and rudely seizing him by the arm. "Hallo Huntingdon!" he shouted— "*I've* got him! Come, man, and help me! And d—n me body and soul if I don't make him blind drunk before I let him go! He shall make up for all past delinquencies as sure as I'm a living soul!"

There followed a disgraceful contest; Lord Lowborough, in desperate earnest, and pale with anger, silently struggling to release himself from the powerful madman that was striving to drag him from the room. I attempted to urge Arthur to interfere in behalf of his outraged guest, but he could do nothing but laugh.

"Huntingdon, you fool, come and help me, can't you!" cried Hattersley, himself somewhat weakened by his excesses.

"I'm wishing you God-speed, Hattersley," cried Arthur, "and aiding you with my prayers: I can't do anything else if my life depended on it! I'm quite used up. Oh, ho!" and leaning back in his seat, he clapped his hands on his sides and groaned aloud.

"Annabella, give me a candle!" said Lowborough whose antagonist had now got him round the waist and was endeavouring to root him from the door-post to which he madly clung with all the energy of desperation.

"*I* shall take no part in your rude sports!" replied the lady, coldly drawing back, "I wonder you can expect it."

But I snatched up a candle and brought it to him. He took it and held the flame to Hattersley's hands till, roaring like a wild beast, the latter unclasped them and let him go. He vanished, I suppose to his own apartment, for nothing more was seen of him till the morning. Swearing and cursing like a maniac, Hattersley threw himself on to the ottoman beside the window. The door being now free, Milicent attempted to make her escape from the scene of her husband's disgrace; but he called her back, and insisted upon her coming to him.

"What do you want Ralph?" murmured she, reluctantly approaching him.

"I want to know what's the matter with you," said he, pulling her on to his knee like a child. "What are you crying for Milicent?—Tell me!"

"I'm not crying."

"You are," persisted he, rudely pulling her hands from her face. "How dare you tell such a lie?"

"I'm not crying now," pleaded she.

"But you have been—and just this minute too; and I *will* know what for. Come now, you *shall* tell me!"

"Do let me alone Ralph! remember we are not at home."

"No matter: you *shall* answer my question!" exclaimed her tormentor; and he attempted to extort the confession by shaking her and remorselessly crushing her slight arms in the grip of his powerful fingers.

"Don't let him treat your sister in that way," said I to Mr. Hargrave.

"Come now, Hattersley, I can't allow that," said that gentleman, stepping up to the ill-assorted couple. "You let my sister alone, if you please." And he made an effort to unclasp the ruffian's fingers from her arm, but was suddenly driven backward and nearly laid upon the floor by a violent blow in the chest accompanied with the admonition,

"Take that for your insolence!—and learn not to interfere between me and mine again."

"If you were not beastly drunk, I'd have satisfaction for that!" gasped Hargrave, white and breathless as much from passion as from the immediate effects of the blow.

"Go to the devil!" responded his brother-in-law. "Now Milicent, tell me what you were crying for."

"I'll tell you some other time," murmured she, "when we are alone."

"Tell me now!" said he with another shake and a squeeze that made her draw in her breath and bite her lip to suppress a cry of pain.

"*I'll* tell you, Mr. Hattersley," said I. "She was crying from pure shame and humiliation for you; because she could not bear to see you conduct yourself so disgracefully."

"Confound you, Madam!" muttered he, with a stare of stupid amazement at my 'impudence,' "It was *not* that—was it Milicent?"

She was silent.

"Come, speak up child!"

"I can't tell now," sobbed she.

"But you can say 'yes' or 'no' as well as 'I can't tell'—Come!"

"Yes," she whispered, hanging her head and blushing at the awful acknowledgement.

"Curse you for an impertinent huzzy then!" cried he, throwing her from him with such violence that she fell on her side; but she was up again before either I or her brother could come to her assistance, and made the best of her way out of the room and, I suppose, up stairs, with out loss of time.

The next object of assault was Arthur, who sat opposite, and had no doubt richly enjoyed the whole scene.

"Now Huntingdon," exclaimed his irascible friend, "I WILL NOT have you sitting there and laughing like an idiot!"

"Oh, Hattersley!" cried he, wiping his swimming eyes—"you'll be the death of me."

"Yes I will, but not as you suppose: I'll have the heart out of your body, man, if you irritate me with any more of that imbecile laughter!—What! are you at it yet?—There! see if that'll settle you!" cried Hattersley, snatching up a footstool and hurling it at the head of his host; but he missed his aim and the latter still sat collapsed and quaking with feeble laughter, with the tears running down his face; a deplorable spectacle indeed.

Hattersley tried cursing and swearing, but it would not do; he then took a number of books from the table beside him and threw them, one by one, at the object of his wrath, but Arthur only laughed the more; and, finally, Hattersley rushed upon him in a frenzy, and, seizing him by the shoulders, gave him a violent shaking, under which he laughed and shrieked alarmingly. But I saw no more: I thought I had witnessed enough of my husband's degradation; and, leaving Annabella and the rest to follow when they pleased, I withdrew—but not to bed. Dismissing Rachel to her rest, I walked up and down my room, in an agony of misery, for what had been done, and suspense, not knowing what might further happen or how or when that unhappy creature would come up to bed.

At last he came, slowly and stumblingly, ascending the stairs, supported by Grimsby and Hattersley, who neither of them walked quite steadily themselves, but were both laughing and joking at him, and making noise enough for all the servants to hear. He himself was no longer laughing now, but sick and stupid—I will write no more about *that*.

Such disgraceful scenes (or nearly such) have been repeated more than once. I don't say much to Arthur about it, for if I did, it would do more harm than good; but I let him know that I intensely dislike such exhibitions; and each time he has promised they should never again be repeated; but I fear he is losing the little self-command and self-respect he once possessed: formerly, he would have been ashamed to act thus—at least, before any other witnesses than his boon companions, or such as they. His friend, Hargrave, with a prudence and self-government that I envy for *him*, never disgraces himself by taking more than sufficient to render him a little 'elevated,' and is always the first to leave the table, after Lord Lowborough, who, wiser still, perseveres in vacating the dining-room immediately after us; but never once, since Annabella offended him so deeply, has he entered the drawing-room before the rest; always spending the interim in the library, which I take care to have lighted for his accommodation—or, on fine moonlight nights, in roaming about the grounds. But I think she regrets her misconduct, for she has never repeated it since, and of late she has comported herself with wonderful propriety towards him, treating him with more uniform kindness and consideration than ever I have observed her to do before. I date the time of this improvement from the period when she ceased to hope and strive for Arthur's admiration.

CHAPTER XXXII
COMPARISONS: INFORMATION REJECTED

OCTOBER 5th.—Esther Hargrave is getting a fine girl. She is not out of the school-room yet, but her mother frequently brings her over to call in the mornings when the gentlemen are out, and sometimes she spends an hour or two in company with her sister, and me, and the children; and when we go to the Grove, I always contrive to see her, and talk more to her than to any one else, for I am very much attached to my little friend, and so is she to me. I wonder what she can see to like in me though, for I am no longer the happy, lively girl I used to be; but she has no other society—save that of her uncongenial mother, and her governess (as artificial and conventional a person as that prudent mother could procure to rectify the pupil's natural qualities), and, now and then, her subdued, quiet sister. I often wonder what will be *her* lot in life—and so does she; but *her* speculations on the future are full of buoyant hope—so were mine once. I shudder to think of her being awakened like me to a sense of their delusive vanity. It seems as if I should feel her disappointment even more deeply than my own: I feel, almost, as if I were born for such a fate, but *she* is so joyous and fresh, so light of heart and free of spirit, and so guileless and unsuspecting too—Oh, it would be cruel to make her feel as I feel now, and know what I have known!

Her sister trembles for her too. Yesterday morning, one of October's brightest loveliest days, Milicent and I were in the garden enjoying a brief half hour together with our children, while Annabella was lying on the drawing-room sofa, deep in the last new novel. We had been romping with the little creatures, almost as merry and wild as themselves, and now paused in the shade of the tall copper beech, to recover breath and rectify our hair, disordered by the rough play and the frolicsome breeze—while they toddled together along the broad, sunny walk; my Arthur supporting the feebler steps of her little Helen, and sagaciously pointing out to her the brightest beauties of the border as they passed, with semi-articulate prattle that did as well for her as any other mode of discourse. From laughing at the pretty sight, we began to talk of the children's future life; and that made us thoughtful. We both relapsed into silent musing as we slowly proceeded up the walk; and I suppose Milicent by a train of associations was led to think of her sister.

"Helen," said she, "you often see Esther, don't you?"

"Not very often."

"But you have more frequent opportunities of meeting her than I have: and she loves you I know, and reverences you too: there is nobody's opinion she thinks so much of; and she says you have more sense than mamma."

"That is because she is self-willed, and my opinions more generally coincide with her own than your mamma's. But what then, Milicent?"

"Well, since you have so much influence with her, I wish you would seriously impress it upon her, never, on any account, or for any body's persuasion, to marry for the sake of money, or rank, or establishment, or any earthly thing, but true affection and well-grounded esteem."

"There is no necessity for that," said I: "for we have had some discourse on that subject already, and I assure you her ideas of love and matrimony are as romantic as any one could desire."

"But romantic notions will not do: I want her to have true notions."

"Very right, but in my judgment, what the world stigmatizes as romantic, is often more nearly allied to the truth than is commonly supposed; for, if the generous ideas of youth are too often overclouded by the sordid views of after-life, that scarcely proves them to be false."

"Well, but if you think her ideas are what they ought to be, strengthen them, will you? and confirm them, as far as you can; for I had romantic notions once, and—I don't mean to say that I regret my lot, for I am quite sure I don't—but—"

"I understand you," said I; "you are contented for yourself, but you would not have your sister to suffer the same as you."

"No—or worse. She might have far worse to suffer than I—for I *am* really contented, Helen, though you mayn't think it: I speak the solemn truth in saying that I would not exchange my husband for any man on earth, if I might do it by the plucking of this leaf."

"Well, I believe you: now that you have him, you would not exchange *him* for another; but then you would gladly exchange some of his qualities for those of better men."

"Yes; just as I would gladly exchange some of my own qualities for those of better women; for neither he nor I are perfect, and I desire his improvement as earnestly as my own. And he will improve—don't you think so Helen?—he's only six and twenty yet."

"He may," I answered.

"He will—he WILL!" repeated she.

"Excuse the faintness of my acquiescence, Milicent; I would not discourage your hopes for the world, but mine have been so often disappointed, that I am become as cold and doubtful in my expectations as the flattest of octogenarians."

"And yet you do hope, still—even for Mr. Huntingdon?"

"I do, I confess—'even' for *him*; for it seems as if life and hope must cease together. And is he so *much* worse, Milicent, than Mr. Hattersley?"

"Well, to give you my candid opinion, I think there is no comparison between them. But you mustn't be offended, Helen, for you know I always speak my mind; and you may speak yours too; I shan't care."

"I am not offended, love; and *my* opinion is that if there *be* a comparison made between the two, the difference, for the most part, is certainly in Hattersley's favour."

Milicent's own heart told her how much it cost me to make this acknowledgment; and, with a childlike impulse, she expressed her sympathy by suddenly kissing my cheek, without a word of reply, and then turning quickly away caught up her baby, and hid her face in its frock. How odd it is that we so often weep for each other's distresses, when we shed not a tear for our own! Her heart had been full enough of her own sorrows, but it overflowed at the idea of mine;—and I too, shed tears at the sight of her sympathetic emotion, though I had not wept for myself for many a week.

But Milicent's satisfaction in her choice is not entirely feigned: she really loves her husband; and it is too true that he loses nothing by comparison with mine. Either he is less unbridled in his excesses, or owing to his stronger, hardier frame, they produce a much less deleterious effect upon him; for he never reduces himself to a state in any degree bordering on imbecility, and with him the worst effect of a night's debauch is a slight increase of irascibility, or it may be a season of sullen ferocity on the following morning: there is nothing of that lost, depressing appearance—that peevish, ignoble fretfulness, that wears one out with very shame for the transgressor. But then, it was not formerly so with Arthur: he can bear less now than he could at Hattersley's age; and if the latter does not reform, his powers of endurance may be equally impaired when he has tried them as long. He has five years the advantage of his friend, and his vices have not mastered him yet: he has not folded them to him and made them a part of himself. They seem to sit loose upon him, like a cloak[1] that he could throw aside at any moment if he would—but how long will that option be left him?—Though a creature of passion and sense, regardless of the duties and the higher privileges of intelligent beings, he is no voluptuary: he prefers the more active and invigorating animal enjoyments, to those of a more relaxing, enervating kind. He does not make a *science* of the gratification of his appetites either in the pleasures of the table or anything else; he eats heartily what is set before him, without demeaning himself by any of that abandonment to the palate and the eye—that unbecoming particularity in approval or disapproval which it is so hateful to witness in those we would esteem. Arthur, I fear, would give himself up to luxury as the chief good, and might ultimately plunge into the grossest excesses, but for the fear of irremediably blunting his appetites, and destroying his powers of further enjoyment. For Hattersley, graceless ruffian as he is, I believe there is more reasonable ground of hope; and—far be it from me to blame poor Milicent for his delinquencies—but I do think that if she had the courage or the will to speak her mind about them, and maintain her point unflinchingly, there would be more chance of his reclamation, and he would be likely to treat her better, and love her more, in the end. I am partly led to think so by what he said to me himself, not many days ago—I purpose to give her a little advice on the subject some time; but still, I hesitate from the consciousness that her ideas and disposition are both against it, and if my counsels failed to do good, they would do harm by making her more unhappy.

It was one rainy day last week: most of the company were killing time in the billiard-room, but Milicent and I were with little Arthur and Helen in the library, and between our books, our children, and each other, we expected to make out a very agreeable morning. We had not been thus secluded above two hours, however, when Mr. Hattersley came in attracted, I suppose, by the voice of his child as he was crossing the hall, for he is prodigiously fond of her, and she of him.

He was redolent of the stables, where he had been regaling himself with the company of his fellow-creatures, the horses, ever since breakfast. But that was no matter to my little namesake: as soon as the colossal person of her father darkened the door, she uttered a shrill scream of delight, and, quitting her mother's side, ran crowing towards him—balancing her course with outstretched arms,—and, embracing his knee, threw back her head and laughed in his face. He might well look smilingly down upon those small, fair features

---

1   See *Macbeth* V.ii.20–2: "Now does he feel his title hang loose upon him, like a giant's robe upon a dwarfish thief."

radiant with innocent mirth, those clear, blue, shining eyes, and that soft flaxen hair cast back upon the little ivory neck and shoulders. Did he not think how unworthy he was of such a possession? I fear no such idea crossed his mind. He caught her up, and there followed some minutes of very rough play, during which it is difficult to say whether the father or the daughter laughed and shouted the loudest. At length, however, the boisterous pastime terminated—suddenly, as might be expected: the little one was hurt and began to cry; and its ungentle playfellow tossed it into its mother's lap, bidding her "make all straight." As happy to return to that gentle comforter as it had been to leave her, the child nestled in her arms and hushed its cries in a moment; and, sinking its little weary head on her bosom, soon dropped asleep.

Meantime, Mr. Hattersley strode up to the fire, and, interposing his height and breadth between us and it, stood, with arms akimbo, expanding his chest, and gazing round him as if the house and all its appurtenances and contents were his own undisputed possessions.

"Deuced bad weather this!" he began. "There'll be no shooting today, I guess."

Then, suddenly lifting up his voice, he regaled us with a few bars of a rollicking song, which abruptly ceasing, he finished the tune with a whistle, and then continued,—"I say Mrs. Huntingdon, what a fine stud your husband has! —not large but good.—I've been looking at them a bit this morning; and upon my word, Black Bess, and Grey Tom, and that young Nimrod[1] are the finest animals I've seen for many a day!" Then followed a particular discussion of their various merits, succeeded by a sketch of the great things *he* intended to do in the horse-jockey line when his old governor thought proper to quit the stage.—"Not that I wish him to close his accounts," added he; "the old Trojan is welcome to keep his books open as long as he pleases for me."

"I hope so, *indeed*, Mr. Hattersley!"

"Oh yes! It's only my way of talking. The event must come, sometime, and so I look to the bright side of it—that's the right plan, isn't it, Mrs. H.?— What are you two doing here, by the by—where's Lady Lowborough?"

"In the billiard room."

"What a splendid creature she *is*!" continued he, fixing his eyes on his wife, who changed colour, and looked more and more disconcerted as he proceeded. "What a noble figure she has! and what magnificent black eyes; and what a fine spirit of her own;—and what a tongue of her own, too, when she likes to use it—I perfectly adore her!—But never mind, Milicent:

---

1 The name of a "mighty hunter" from Genesis 10:9; Rosengarten and Smith point out that Nimrod was the pseudonym used by Charles Apperley (1779–1843), a sports and hunting writer, and that "'Black Bess' was the mare said to have carried the highwayman Dick Turpin [1705–39] from London to York" (*OTWH* 481).

I wouldn't have her for my wife—not if she'd a kingdom for her dowry! I'm better satisfied with the one I have.—Now *then*! what do you look so sulky for? Don't you believe me?"

"Yes, I believe you," murmured she, in a tone of half sad, half sullen resignation, as she turned away to stroke the hair of her sleeping infant, that she had laid on the sofa beside her.

"Well *then*, what makes you so cross? Come here Milly, and tell me why you can't be satisfied with my assurance."

She went, and, putting her little hand within his arm, looked up in his face, and said softly,—

"What does it amount to Ralph? Only to this, that though you admire Annabella so much, and for qualities that I don't possess, you would still rather have me than her for your wife which merely proves that you don't think it necessary to love your wife: you are satisfied if she can keep your house and take care of your child. But I'm not cross; I'm only sorry; for," added she in a low, tremulous accent, withdrawing her hand from his arm, and bending her looks on the rug, "if you don't love me, you don't, and it can't be helped."

"Very true: but who told you I didn't? Did I say I loved Annabella?"

"You said you adored her."

"True, but adoration isn't love. I adore Annabella, but I don't love her; and I love thee Milicent, but I don't adore thee." In proof of his affection, he clutched a handful of her light brown ringlets and appeared to twist them unmercifully.

"Do you really, Ralph?" murmured she with a faint smile beaming through her tears, just putting up her hand to his, in token that he pulled *rather* too hard.

"To be sure I do," responded he: "only you bother me rather, sometimes."

"*I* bother you!" cried she in very natural surprise.

"Yes, *you*—but only by your exceeding goodness—when a boy has been cramming raisins and sugar-plums all day, he longs for a squeeze of sour orange by way of a change. And did you never, Milly, observe the sands on the sea-shore; how nice and smooth they look, and how soft and easy they feel to the foot? But if you plod along, for half an hour, over this soft, easy carpet—giving way at every step, yielding the more the harder you press,— you'll find it rather wearisome work, and be glad enough to come to a bit of good, firm rock, that won't budge an inch whether you stand, walk, or stamp upon it; and, though it be hard as the nether millstone,[1] you'll find it the easier footing after all."

---

1 A brief reference to Job 41:24: "His heart is as firm as a stone; yea, as hard as a piece of the nether millstone."

"I know what you mean, Ralph," said she, nervously playing with her watch-guard and tracing the figure on the rug with the point of her tiny foot, "I know what you mean, but I thought you always liked to be yielded to; and I can't alter now."

"I do like it," replied he, bringing her to him by another tug at her hair. "You mustn't mind my talk Milly. A man must have something to grumble about; and if he can't complain that his wife harries him to death with her perversity and ill-humour, he must complain that she wears him out with her kindness and gentleness."

"But why complain at all, unless, because you are tired and dissatisfied?"

"To excuse my own failings, to be sure. Do you think I'll bear all the burden of my sins on my own shoulders, as long as there's another ready to help me, with none of her own to carry?"

"There is no such one on earth," said she seriously; and then, taking his hand from her head, she kissed it with an air of genuine devotion, and tripped away to the door.

"What now?" said he. "Where are you going?"

"To tidy my hair," she answered, smiling through her disordered locks: "you've made it all come down."

"Off with you then!—An excellent little woman," he remarked when she was gone, "but a thought too soft—she almost melts in one's hands. I positively think I ill-use her sometimes, when I've taken too much—but I can't help it, for she never complains, either at the time or after. I suppose she doesn't mind it."

"I can enlighten you on that subject, Mr. Hattersley," said I: "she *does* mind it; and some other things she minds still more, which, yet, you may never hear her complain of."

"How do you know?—does she complain to you?" demanded he, with a sudden spark of fury ready to burst into a flame if I should answer 'Yes.'

"No," I replied; "but I have known her longer and studied her more closely than you have done.—And I can tell you, Mr. Hattersley, that Milicent loves you more than you deserve, and that you have it in your power to make her very happy, instead of which you are her evil genius, and, I will venture to say, there is not a single day passes in which you do not inflict upon her some pang that you might spare her if you would."

"Well—it's not *my* fault," said he, gazing carelessly up at the ceiling and plunging his hands into his pockets: "if my ongoings don't suit her, she should tell me so."

"Is she not exactly the wife you wanted? Did you not tell Mr. Hunting-don you must have one that would submit to anything without a murmur, and never blame you, whatever you did?"

"True, but we shouldn't always have what we want: it spoils the best of us, doesn't it? How can I help playing the deuce when I see it's all one to her whether I behave like a Christian or like a scoundrel such as nature made me?—and how can I help teasing her when she's so invitingly meek and mim[1]—when she lies down like a spaniel at my feet and never so much as squeaks to tell me that's enough?"

"If you are a tyrant by nature, the temptation is strong, I allow; but no generous mind delights to oppress the weak, but rather to cherish and protect."

"I *don't* oppress her; but it's so confounded flat[2] to be always cherishing and protecting;—and then how can I tell that I *am* oppressing her when she 'melts away and makes no sign?'[3] I sometimes think she has no feeling at all; and then I go on till she cries—and that satisfies me."

"Then you *do* delight to oppress her."

"I don't, I tell you!—only when I'm in a bad humour—or a particularly good one, and want to afflict for the pleasure of comforting; or when she looks flat and wants shaking up a bit. And sometimes, she provokes me by crying for nothing, and won't tell me what it's for; and then, I allow, it enrages me past bearing—especially, when I'm not my own man."

"As is no doubt generally the case on such occasions," said I. "But in future, Mr. Hattersley, when you see her looking flat or crying for 'nothing' (as you call it), ascribe it all to yourself: be assured it is something you have done amiss, or your general misconduct that distresses her."

"I don't believe it. If it were, she should tell me so: I don't like that way of moping and fretting in silence, and saying nothing—it's not honest. How can she expect me to mend my ways at that rate?"

"Perhaps she gives you credit for having more sense than you possess, and deludes herself with the hope that you will one day see your own errors and repair them, if left to your own reflection."

"None of your sneers, Mrs. Huntingdon! I *have* the sense to see that I'm not always quite correct—but sometimes I think that's no great matter, as long as I injure nobody but myself—"

"It *is* a great matter," interrupted I, "both to yourself (as you will hereafter find to your cost) and to all connected with you—most especially your wife—but indeed, it is nonsense to talk about injuring no one but yourself; it is impossible to injure yourself—especially by such acts as we allude to—without injuring hundreds, if not thousands, besides, in a greater or less degree, either by the evil you do or the good you leave undone."

---

1   "Affectedly modest, demure, primly silent or quiet" (*OED*).
2   Dull or boring.
3   See Shakespeare's *2 Henry VI*: "He dies and makes no sign" (III.iii.29).

"And as I was saying," continued he—"or would have said if you hadn't taken me up so short—I sometimes think I should do better if I were joined to one that would always remind me when I was wrong, and give me a motive for doing good and eschewing evil by decidedly showing her approval of the one, and disapproval of the other."

"If you had no higher motive than the approval of your fellow mortal, it would do you little good."

"Well, but if I had a mate that would not always be yielding, and always equally kind, but that would have the spirit to stand at bay now and then, and honestly tell me her mind at all times—such a one as yourself for instance—now if I went on with you as I do with her when I'm in London, you'd make the house too hot to hold me at times, I'll be sworn."

"You mistake me: I'm no termagant."[1]

"Well, all the better for that, for I can't stand contradiction—in a general way—and I'm as fond of my own will as another: only I think too much of it doesn't answer for any man."

"Well, I would never contradict you without a cause, but certainly I would always let you know what I thought of your conduct; and if you oppressed me, in body, mind, or estate, you should at least have no reason to suppose 'I didn't mind it.'"

"I know that my lady; and I think if my little wife were to follow the same plan it would be better for us both."

"I'll tell her."

"No, no, let her be; there's much to be said on both sides—and, now I think upon it, Huntingdon often regrets that you are not more like her—scoundrelly dog that he is—and you see, after all, you can't reform *him*: he's *ten* times worse than I.—He's afraid of you, to be sure—that is, he's always on his best behaviour in your presence—but—"

"I wonder what his worst behaviour is like, then?" I could not forbear observing.

"Why, to tell you the truth, it's very bad indeed—isn't it, Hargrave?" said he, addressing that gentleman, who had entered the room unperceived by me, for I was now standing near the fire with my back to the door. "Isn't Huntingdon," he continued, "as great a reprobate as ever was d—d?"

"His lady will not hear him censured with impunity," replied Mr. Hargrave, coming forward, "but I must say, I thank God I am not such another."

"Perhaps it would become you better," said I, "to look at what you are, and say, 'God be merciful to me a sinner.'"[2]

---

1 An overbearing woman prone to quarreling; a shrew.

2 Luke 18:13.

"You are severe," returned he, bowing slightly and drawing himself up with a proud yet injured air. Hattersley laughed, and clapped him on the shoulder. Moving from under his hand with a gesture of insulted dignity, Mr. Hargrave took himself away to the other end of the rug.

"Isn't it a shame, Mrs. Huntingdon?" cried his brother-in-law—"I struck Walter Hargrave when I was drunk, the second night after we came, and he's turned a cold shoulder on me ever since; though I asked his pardon the very morning after it was done!"

"Your manner of asking it," returned the other, "and the clearness with which you remembered the whole transaction, showed you were not too drunk to be fully conscious of what you were about, and quite responsible for the deed."

"You wanted to interfere between me and my wife," grumbled Hattersley, "and that is enough to provoke any man."

"You justify it then?" said his opponent, darting upon him a most vindictive glance.

"No, I tell you I wouldn't have done it if I hadn't been under excitement; and if you choose to bear malice for it, after all the handsome things I've said—do so and be damned!"

"I *would* refrain from such language in a *lady's* presence, at least," said Mr. Hargrave, hiding his anger under a mask of disgust.

"What have I said?" returned Hattersley, "Nothing but Heaven's truth— he will be damned, won't he, Mrs. Huntingdon, if he doesn't forgive his brother's trespasses?"[1]

"You ought to forgive him, Mr. Hargrave, since he asks you," said I.

"Do you say so? Then I will!" And, smiling almost frankly, he stepped forward and offered his hand. It was immediately clasped in that of his relative, and the reconciliation was apparently cordial on both sides.

"The affront," continued Hargrave, turning to me, "owed half its bitterness to the fact of its being offered in your presence; and since you bid me forgive it, I will—and forget it too."

"I guess the best return I can make, will be to take myself off," muttered Hattersley, with a broad grin. His companion smiled; and he left the room. This put me on my guard. Mr. Hargrave turned seriously to me, and earnestly began—

"Dear Mrs. Huntingdon, how I have longed for, yet dreaded this hour! Do not be alarmed," he added, for my face was crimson with anger; "I am not about to offend you with any useless entreaties or complaints. I am not going to presume to trouble you with the mention of my own feelings or

---

1   Matthew 6:14–15 and Luke 17:3–4 discuss forgiving one's brother's trespasses and God's forgiveness of one's own.

your perfections, but I have something to reveal to you which you ought to know, and which, yet, it pains me inexpressibly—"

"Then don't trouble yourself to reveal it!"

"But it is of importance—"

"If so, I shall hear it soon enough—especially if it is bad news, as you seem to consider it. At present, I am going to take the children to the nursery."

"But can't you ring, and send them?"

"No; I want the exercise of a run to the top of the house.—Come Arthur."

"But you will return?"

"Not yet; don't wait."

"Then, when may I see you again?"

"At lunch," said I, departing with little Helen in one arm, and leading Arthur by the hand.

He turned away, muttering some sentence of impatient censure or complaint, in which "heartless" was the only distinguishable word.

"What nonsense is this Mr. Hargrave?" said I, pausing in the doorway. "What do you mean?"

"Oh, nothing—I did not intend you should hear my soliloquy. But the fact is, Mrs. Huntingdon, I have a disclosure to make—painful for me to offer as for you to hear—and I want you to give me a few minutes of your attention in private, at any time and place you like to appoint. It is from no selfish motive that I ask it, and not for any cause that could alarm your super-human purity; therefore, you need not kill me with that look of cold and pitiless disdain. I know too well the feelings with which the bearers of bad tidings are commonly regarded, not to—"

"What *is* this wonderful piece of intelligence?" said I, impatiently interrupting him. "If it is anything of real importance, speak it in three words before I go."

"In three words I cannot. Send those children away, and stay with me."

"No; keep your bad tidings to yourself. I know it is something I don't want to hear, and something you would displease me by telling."

"You have divined too truly I fear; but still since I know it, I feel it my duty to disclose it to you."

"Oh, spare us both the infliction—and I will exonerate you from the duty. You have offered to tell; I have refused to hear: my ignorance will not be charged on you."

"Be it so—you shall not hear it from me. But if the blow fall too suddenly upon you when it comes, remember—I wished to soften it!"

I left him. I was determined his words should not alarm me. What could *he* of all men, have to reveal that was of importance for *me* to hear? It was, no doubt some exaggerated tale about my unfortunate husband, that he wished to make the most of to serve his own bad purposes.

6th. He has not alluded to this momentous mystery since; and I have seen no reason to repent of my unwillingness to hear it. The threatened blow has not been struck yet; and I do not greatly fear it. At present I am pleased with Arthur: he has not positively disgraced himself for upwards of a fortnight, and all this last week, has been so very moderate in his indulgence at table, that I can perceive a marked difference in his general temper and appearance. Dare I hope this will continue?

CHAPTER XXXIII
TWO EVENINGS

SEVENTH. Yes, I *will* hope! Tonight, I heard Grimsby and Hattersley grumbling together, about the inhospitality of their host. They did not know I was near, for I happened to be standing behind the curtain, in the bow of the window, watching the moon rising over the clump of tall, dark elm-trees below the lawn and wondering why Arthur was so sentimental as to stand without, leaning against the outer pillar of the portico, apparently watching it too.

"So, I suppose we've seen the last of our merry carousals in this house," said Mr. Hattersley, "I *thought* his good-fellowship wouldn't last long.—But," added he, laughing, "I didn't expect it would meet its end this way. I rather thought our pretty hostess would be setting up her porcupine quills, and threatening to turn us out of the house, if we didn't mind our manners."

"You didn't foresee *this*, then?" answered Grimsby with a guttural chuckle. "But he'll change again when he's sick of her. If we come here a year or two hence, we shall have all our own way, you'll see."

"I don't know," replied the other: "she's not the style of woman you soon tire of—but be that as it may, it's devilish provoking now, that we can't be jolly, because he chooses to be on his good behaviour."

"It's all these cursed women!" muttered Grimsby. "They're the very bane of the world! They bring trouble and discomfort wherever they come, with their false, fair faces and their d—d deceitful tongues."

At this juncture, I issued from my retreat, and smiling on Mr. Grimsby as I passed, left the room and went out in search of Arthur. Having seen him bend his course towards the shrubbery, I followed him thither, and found him just entering the shadowy walk. I was so light of heart, so overflowing with affection, that I sprang upon him and clasped him in my arms. This startling conduct had a singular effect upon him: first, he murmured, "Bless you darling!" and returned my close embrace with a fervour like old times, and *then* he started, and in a tone of absolute terror, exclaimed—

"Helen!—What the devil is this!" and I saw, by the faint light gleaming through the overshadowing tree, that he was positively pale with the shock.

How strange that the instinctive impulse of affection should come first, and then the shock of the surprise! It shows, at least that the affection is genuine: he is not sick of me yet.

"I startled you, Arthur," said I, laughing in my glee. "How nervous you are!"

"What the deuce did you do it for?" cried he, quite testily, extricating himself from my arms, and wiping his forehead with his handkerchief. "Go back, Helen—go back directly! You'll get your death of cold!"

"I won't—till I've told you what I came for. They are blaming you, Arthur, for your temperance and sobriety, and I'm come to thank you for it. They say it is all 'these cursed women,' and that we are the bane of the world; but don't let them laugh, or grumble you out of your good resolutions, or your affection for me."

He laughed. I squeezed him in my arms again, and cried in tearful earnest—

"Do—do persevere!—and I'll love you better than ever I did before!"

"Well, well, I will!" said he, hastily kissing me. "There now, go.—You mad creature, how *could* you come out in your light evening dress, this chill autumn night?"

"It is a glorious night," said I.

"It is a night that will give you your death, in another minute. Run away, do!"

"Do you see my death among those trees, Arthur?" said I, for he was gazing intently at the shrubs, as if he saw it coming, and I was reluctant to leave him, in my new-found happiness and revival of hope and love. But he grew angry at my delay, so I kissed him and ran back to the house.

I was in such a good humour that night: Milicent told me I was the life of the party, and whispered she had never seen me so brilliant. Certainly, I talked enough for twenty, and smiled upon them all. Grimsby, Hattersley, Hargrave, Lady Lowborough—all shared my sisterly kindness. Grimsby stared and wondered; Hattersley laughed and jested, (in spite of the little wine he had been suffered to imbibe), but still, behaved as well as he knew how; Hargrave and Annabella, from different motives and in different ways emulated me, and doubtless both surpassed me, the former in his discursive versatility and eloquence, the latter in boldness and animation at least. Milicent, delighted to see her husband, her brother and her over-estimated friend acquitting themselves so well, was lively and gay too, in her quiet way. Even Lord Lowborough caught the general contagion: his dark, greenish eyes were lighted up beneath their moody brows; his sombre countenance was beautified by smiles; all traces of gloom, and proud or cold reserve had vanished for the time; and he astonished us all, not only by his general cheerfulness and animation, but by the positive flashes of true force and brilliance he emitted from time to time. Arthur did not talk much, but he laughed, and listened to the rest, and was in perfect good-humour, though not excited by wine. So that, altogether we made a very merry, innocent and entertaining party.

9th. Yesterday, when Rachel came to dress me for dinner, I saw that she had been crying.

I wanted to know the cause of it, but she seemed reluctant to tell. Was she unwell? No. Had she heard bad news from her friends? No. Had any of the servants vexed her?

"Oh, no Ma'am!" she answered.—"It's not for myself."

"What then, Rachel? Have you been reading novels?"

"Bless you, no!" said she with a sorrowful shake of the head; and then she sighed and continued, "But to tell you the truth, Ma'am, I don't like master's ways of going on."

"What do you mean Rachel?—He's going on very properly—at present."

"Well ma'am, if you think so, it's right."

And she went on dressing my hair, in a hurried way, quite unlike her usual calm, collected manner,—murmuring, half to herself, she was sure it was beautiful hair, she "could like to see 'em match it." When it was done, she fondly stroked it and gently patted my head.

"Is that affectionate ebullition intended for my hair, or myself, nurse?" said I, laughingly turning round upon her;—but a tear was even now in her eye.

"What *do* you mean, Rachel?" I exclaimed.

"Well, ma'am, I don't know,—but if—"

"If what?"

"Well, if I was you, I wouldn't have that Lady Lowborough in the house another minute—not another *minute* I wouldn't!"

I was thunderstruck; but before I could recover from the shock sufficiently to demand an explanation, Milicent entered my room—as she frequently does, when she is dressed before me; and she stayed with me till it was time to go down. She must have found me a very unsociable companion this time, for Rachel's last words rung in my ears. But still, I hoped—I trusted they had no foundation but in some idle rumour of the servants from what they had seen in Lady Lowborough's manner last month; or, perhaps, from something that had passed between their master and her during her former visit. At dinner, I narrowly observed both her and Arthur, and saw nothing extraordinary in the conduct of either—nothing calculated to excite suspicion, except in distrustful minds—which mine was not, and therefore I would not suspect.

Almost immediately after dinner, Annabella went out with her husband to share his moonlight ramble, for it was a splendid evening like the last. Mr. Hargrave entered the drawing-room a little before the others, and challenged me to a game of chess. He did it without any of that sad, but proud humility he usually assumes in addressing me, unless he is excited with wine. I looked at his face to see if that was the case now. His eye met mine keenly, but steadily: there was something about him I did not understand, but he seemed sober enough. Not choosing to engage with him, I referred him to Milicent.

"She plays badly," said he: "I want to match my skill with yours. Come now!—you can't pretend you are reluctant to lay down your work—I know you never take it up except to pass an idle hour, when there is nothing better you can do."

"But chess players are so unsociable," I objected; "they are no company for any but themselves."

"There is no one here—but Milicent, and she—"

"Oh, I shall be delighted to watch you!" cried our mutual friend—"Two *such* players—it will be quite a treat! I wonder which will conquer."

I consented.

"Now Mrs. Huntingdon," said Hargrave, as he arranged the men on the board, speaking distinctly, and with a peculiar emphasis as if he had a double meaning to all his words, "you are a good player,—but I am a better: we shall have a long game, and you will give me some trouble; but I can be as patient as you, and, in the end, I shall certainly win." He fixed his eyes upon me with a glance I did not like—keen, crafty, bold, and almost impudent; already half triumphant in his anticipated success.

"I hope not, Mr. Hargrave!" returned I, with a vehemence that must have startled Milicent at least; but *he* only smiled and murmured,

"Time will show."

We set to work; he, sufficiently interested in the game, but calm and fearless in the consciousness of superior skill; I, intensely eager to disappoint his expectations, for I considered this the type of a more serious contest—as I imagined he did—and I felt an almost superstitious dread of being beaten: at all events, I could ill endure that present success should add one tittle to his conscious power (his insolent self-confidence, I ought to say), or encourage, for a moment, his dream of future conquest. His play was cautious and deep, but I struggled hard against him. For some time the combat was doubtful, at length, to my joy, the victory seemed inclining to my side: I had taken several of his best pieces, and manifestly baffled his projects. He put his hand to his brow and paused, in evident perplexity. I rejoiced in my advantage, but dared not glory in it yet. At length, he lifted his head, and, quietly making his move, looked at me and said, calmly,—

"Now you think you will win, don't you."

"I hope so," replied I, taking his pawn, that he had pushed into the way of my bishop with so careless an air that I thought it was an oversight, but was not generous enough, under the circumstances, to direct his attention to it, and too heedless, at the moment, to foresee the after consequences of my move.

"It is those bishops that trouble me," said he; "but the bold knight can overleap the reverend gentleman," taking my last bishop with his knight;— "and now, those sacred persons once removed, I shall carry all before me."

"Oh Walter, how you talk!" cried Milicent.—"She has far more pieces than you still."

"I intend to give you some trouble yet," said I; "and perhaps, sir, you will find yourself checkmated before you are aware. Look to your queen."

The combat deepened. The game *was* a long one, and I *did* give him some trouble: but he *was* a better player than I.

"What keen gamesters you are!" said Mr. Hattersley, who had now entered, and been watching us for some time. "Why, Mrs. Huntingdon, your hand trembles as if you had staked your all upon it! and Walter—you dog—you look as deep and cool as if you were certain of success,—and as keen and cruel as if you would drain her heart's blood!—But if I were you, I wouldn't beat her, for very fear: she'll hate you if you do—she will, by Heaven!—I see it in her eye."

"Hold your tongue, will you?" said I—his talk distracted me, for I was driven to extremities. A few more moves and I was inextricably entangled in the snare of my antagonist.

"Check,"—cried he: I sought in agony some means of escape—"mate!" he added, quietly but with evident delight. He had suspended the utterance of that last fatal syllable the better to enjoy my dismay. I was foolishly disconcerted by the event. Hattersley laughed; Milicent was troubled to see me so disturbed. Hargrave placed his hand on mine that rested on the table, and squeezing it with a firm but gentle pressure, murmured "Beaten—beaten!" and gazed into my face with a look where exultation was blended with an expression of ardour and tenderness yet more insulting.

"*No, never,* Mr. Hargrave!" exclaimed I, quickly withdrawing my hand.

"Do you deny?" replied he, smilingly pointing to the board.

"No, no," I answered, recollecting how strange my conduct must appear; "you have beaten me in that game."

"Will you try another, then?"

"No."

"You acknowledge my superiority?"

"Yes—as a chess-player."

I rose to resume my work.

"Where is Annabella?" said Hargrave, gravely, after glancing round the room.

"Gone out with Lord Lowborough," answered I, for he looked at me for a reply.

"And not yet returned!" he said seriously.

"I suppose not."

"Where is Huntingdon?" looking round again.

"Gone out with Grimsby—as you know," said Hattersley suppressing a laugh, which broke forth as he concluded the sentence.

Why did he laugh? Why did Hargrave connect them thus together? Was it true, then?—And was this the dreadful secret he had wished to reveal to me? I must know—and that quickly. I instantly rose and left the room to go in search of Rachel, and demand an explanation of her words; but Mr. Hargrave followed me into the ante-room, and before I could open its outer door, gently laid his hand upon the lock.

"May I tell you something, Mrs. Huntingdon?" said he, in a subdued tone, with serious, downcast eyes.

"If it be anything worth hearing," replied I, struggling to be composed, for I trembled in every limb.

He quietly pushed a chair towards me. I merely leant my hand upon it, and bid him go on.

"Do not be alarmed," said he: "what I wish to say is nothing in itself; and I will leave you to draw your own inferences from it. You say that Annabella is not yet returned?"

"Yes, yes—go on!" said I, impatiently, for I feared my forced calmness would leave me before the end of his disclosure, whatever it might be.

"And you hear," continued he, "that Huntingdon is gone out with Grimsby?"

"Well?"

"I heard the latter say to your husband—or the man who calls himself so—"

"Go on, sir!"

He bowed submissively, and continued, "I heard him say,—'I shall manage it, you'll see! They're gone down by the water; I shall meet them there, and tell him I want a bit of talk with him about some things that we needn't trouble the lady with; and she'll say she can be walking back to the house; and then I shall apologize, you know, and all that, and tip her a wink to take the way of the shrubbery. I'll keep him talking there, about those matters I mentioned, and anything else I can think of, as long as I can, and then bring him round the other way, stopping to look at the trees, the fields, and anything else I can find to discourse of.'" Mr. Hargrave paused, and looked at me.

Without a word of comment or further questioning, I rose, and darted from the room and out of the house. The torment of suspense was not to be endured: I would not suspect my husband falsely, on this man's accusation, and I would not trust him unworthily—I must know the truth at once. I flew to the shrubbery. Scarcely had I reached it, when a sound of voices arrested my breathless speed.

"We have lingered too long; he will be back," said Lady Lowborough's voice.

"Surely not, dearest!" was *his* reply, "but you can run across the lawn, and get in as quietly as you can: I'll follow in a while."

My knees trembled under me; my brain swam round: I was ready to faint. She must not see me thus. I shrunk among the bushes, and leant against the trunk of a tree to let her pass.

"Ah, Huntingdon!" said she reproachfully, pausing where I had stood with him the night before—"it was here you kissed that woman!" she looked back into the leafy shade. Advancing thence, he answered, with a careless laugh—

"Well, dearest, I couldn't help it. You know I must keep straight with her as long as I can. Haven't I seen you kiss your dolt of a husband, scores of times?—and do *I* ever complain?"

"But tell me, don't you love her still—a *little*?" said she placing her hand on his arm and looking earnestly in his face—for I could see them plainly, the moon shining full upon them from between the branches of the tree that sheltered me.

"Not *one bit*, by all that's sacred!" he replied, kissing her glowing cheek.

"Good heavens, I *must* be gone!" cried she, suddenly breaking from him, and away she flew.

There he stood before me; but I had not strength to confront him now; my tongue cleaved to the roof of my mouth,[1] I was well nigh sinking to the earth, and I almost wondered he did not hear the beating of my heart above the low sighing of the wind, and the fitful rustle of the falling leaves. My senses seemed to fail me, but still I saw his shadowy form pass before me, and through the rushing sound in my ears, I distinctly heard him say, as he stood looking up the lawn—

"There goes the fool! Run Annabella, run! There—in with you! Ah, he didn't see! That's right Grimsby, keep him back!" And even his low laugh reached me as he walked away.

"God help me now!" I murmured, sinking on my knees among the damp weeds and brushwood that surrounded me, and looking up at the moonlit sky, through the scant foliage above. It seemed all dim and quivering now to my darkened sight. My burning, bursting heart strove to pour forth its agony to God, but could not frame its anguish into prayer; until a gust of wind swept over me, which, while it scattered the dead leaves, like blighted hopes, around, cooled my forehead, and seemed a little to revive my sinking frame.[2] Then, while I lifted up my soul in speechless, earnest supplication,

---

1 This expression is used in Job 29:10, Psalm 137:6, and Ezekiel 3:26.

2 Helen's description of her wordless agony and subsequent experience of "some heavenly influence" could be a fictional explication of Romans 8:26: "Likewise the Spirit also helpeth our infirmities: for we know not what we should pray for as we ought: but the Spirit itself maketh intercession for us with groanings which cannot be uttered."

some heavenly influence seemed to strengthen me within: I breathed more freely; my vision cleared; I saw distinctly the pure moon shining on, and the light clouds skimming the clear, dark sky; and then, I saw the eternal stars twinkling down upon me; I knew their God was mine, and he was strong to save and swift to hear.[1] "I will never leave thee, nor forsake thee,"[2] seemed whispered from above their myriad orbs. No, no; I felt He would not leave me comfortless:[3] in spite of earth and hell I should have strength for all my trials, and win a glorious rest at last!

Refreshed, invigorated if not composed, I rose and returned to the house. Much of my newborn strength and courage forsook me, I confess, as I entered it, and shut out the fresh wind and the glorious sky: everything I saw and heard seemed to sicken my heart—the hall, the lamp, the staircase, the doors of the different apartments, the social sound of talk and laughter from the drawing-room. How could I bear my future life? In this house, among those people—oh, how could I endure to live! John just then entered the hall, and seeing me, told me he had been sent in search of me, adding that he had taken in the tea, and master wished to know if I were coming.

"Ask Mrs. Hattersley to be so kind as to make the tea, John," said I. "Say I am not well tonight, and wish to be excused."

I retired into the large, empty dining-room, where all was silence and darkness, but for the soft sighing of the wind without, and the faint gleam of moonlight that pierced the blinds and curtains; and there I walked rapidly up and down, thinking of[4] my bitter thoughts alone. How different was this from the evening of yesterday! *That* it seems, was the last expiring flash of my life's happiness. Poor, blinded fool that I was, to be so happy! I could now see the reason of Arthur's strange reception of me in the shrubbery: the burst of kindness was for his paramour, the start of horror for his wife. Now, too, I could better understand the conversation between Hattersley and Grimsby: it was doubtless of his love for *her* they spoke, not for me.

I heard the drawing-room door open: a light quick step came out of the ante-room, crossed the hall, and ascended the stairs. It was Milicent, poor

---

1 James 1:19–20: "Wherefore, my beloved brethren, let every man be swift to hear, slow to speak, slow to wrath: for the wrath of man worketh not the righteousness of God." This description of Helen's suffering and subsequent realization of God's presence and power is also reminiscent of Jane Eyre's when she has the vision of the moon "whisper[ing] in [her] heart—'my daughter, flee temptation,'" (411) and then later, when she has left Thornfield, appreciating God's omnipresence after looking up at the night sky (416).

2 Hebrews 13:5: "Let your conversations be without covetousness; and be content with such things as ye have: for he hath said, I will never leave thee, nor forsake thee."

3 John 14:18: "I will not leave you comfortless: I will come to you."

4 Brontë deletes the "of" in the AOC.

Milicent, gone to see how I was—no one else cared for me; but *she* still was kind. I had[1] shed no tears before, but now they came—fast and free. Thus she did me good, without approaching me. Disappointed in her search, I heard her come down—more slowly than she had ascended. Would she come in there, and find me out? No; she turned in the opposite direction and re-entered the drawing-room. I was glad, for I knew not how to meet her, or what to say. I wanted no confidant in my distress. I deserved none—and I wanted none. I had taken the burden upon myself: let me bear it alone.

As the usual hour of retirement approached, I dried my eyes, and tried to clear my voice and calm my mind. I must see Arthur tonight, and speak to him; but I would do it calmly: there should be no scene—nothing to complain or to boast of to his companions—nothing to laugh at with his lady love. When the company were retiring to their chambers, I gently opened the door, and just as he passed, I beckoned him in.

"What's to do with *you*, Helen?" said he. "Why couldn't you come to make tea for us? and what the deuce are you here for, in the dark? What ails you, young woman—you look like a ghost?" he continued, surveying me by the light of his candle.

"No matter," I answered—"to you—you have no longer any regard for me, it appears; and I have no longer any for you."

"Hal-low! what the devil is this?" he muttered.

"I would leave you tomorrow," continued I, "and never again come under this roof, but for my child"—I paused a moment to steady my voice.

"What in the devil's name *is* this, Helen?" cried he. "What can you be driving at?"

"You know, perfectly well. Let us waste no time in useless explanation, but tell me, will you—"

He vehemently swore he knew nothing about it, and insisted upon hearing what poisonous old woman had been blackening his name and what infamous lies I had been fool enough to believe.

"Spare yourself the trouble of forswearing yourself and racking your brains to stifle truth with falsehood," I coldly replied. "I have trusted to the testimony of no third person. I was in the shrubbery this evening, and I saw and heard for myself."

This was enough. He uttered a suppressed explanation of consternation and dismay, and muttering, "I *shall* catch it now!" set down his candle on the nearest chair, and, rearing his back against the wall, stood confronting me with folded arms.

"Well!—what then?" said he, with the calm insolence of mingled shamelessness and desperation.

---

1 Brontë added "had" in the AOC, importantly correcting the tense of this verb.

"Only this," returned I: "will you let me take our child and what remains of my fortune, and go?"

"Go where?"

"Anywhere, where he will be safe from your contaminating influence, and I shall be delivered from your presence—and you from mine."

"No—by *Jove* I won't!"

"Will you let me have the child then, without the money?"

"No—nor yourself without the child. Do you think I'm going to be made the talk of the country, for your fastidious caprices?"

"Then I must stay here, to be hated and despised.—But henceforth, we are husband and wife only in the name."

"Very good."

"I am your child's mother, and *your* housekeeper—nothing more. So you need not trouble yourself any longer, to feign the love you cannot feel: I will exact no more heartless caresses from you—nor offer—nor endure them either—I will not be mocked with the empty husk of conjugal endearments, when you have given the substance to another!"

"Very good—if *you* please. We shall see who will tire first, my lady."

"If I tire, it will be of living in the world with you; not of living without your mockery of love. When *you* tire of your sinful ways, and show yourself truly repentant, I will forgive you—and, perhaps, try to love you again, though that will be hard indeed."

"Humph!—and meantime, you will go and talk me over to Mrs. Hargrave, and write long letters to aunt Maxwell to complain of the wicked wretch you have married?"

"I shall complain to no one. Hitherto, I have struggled hard to hide your vices from every eye, and invest you with virtues you never possessed—but now you must look to yourself."

I left him—muttering bad language to himself, and went up stairs.

"You are poorly Ma'am," said Rachel, surveying me with deep anxiety.

"It is too true, Rachel!" said I, answering her sad looks rather than her words.

"I knew it—or I wouldn't have mentioned such a thing."

"But don't *you* trouble yourself about it," said I, kissing her pale, time-wasted cheek—"I can bear it—better than you imagine."

"Yes, you were always for 'bearing'—But if I was you I wouldn't bear it—I'd give way to it, and cry right hard!—and I'd talk too, I just *would*—I'd let him know what it was to—"

"I have talked," said I: "I've said enough."

"Then I'd cry," persisted she. "I wouldn't look so white and so calm, and burst my heart with keeping it in!"

"I *have* cried," said I, smiling in spite of my misery; "and I *am* calm now, really, so don't discompose me again, nurse: let us say no more about it—and *don't* mention it to the servants.—There, you may go now. Good night;—and don't disturb your rest for me: I shall sleep well—if I can."

Notwithstanding this resolution, I found my bed so intolerable that, before two o'clock, I rose, and, lighting my candle by the rushlight[1] that was still burning, I got my desk and sat down in my dressing-gown to recount the events of the past evening. It was better to be so occupied than to be lying in bed torturing my brain with recollections of the far past and anticipations of the dreadful future. I have found relief in describing the very circumstances that have destroyed my peace, as well as the little trivial details attendant upon their discovery. No sleep I could have got this night would have done so much towards composing my mind, and preparing me to meet the trials of the day—I fancy so, at least;—and yet, when I cease writing, I find my head aches terribly; and when I look into the glass I am startled at my haggard, worn appearance.

Rachel has been to dress me, and says I have had a sad night of it she can see. Milicent has just looked in to ask me how I was. I told her I was better, but to excuse my appearance admitted I had had a restless night.—I wish this day were over! I shudder at the thoughts of going down to breakfast—how shall I encounter them all?—Yet let me remember it is not *I* that am guilty: *I* have no cause to fear; and if *they* scorn me as the victim of their guilt, I can pity their folly and despise their scorn.

CHAPTER XXXIV
CONCEALMENT

EVENING. Breakfast passed well over, I was calm and cool throughout. I answered composedly all enquiries respecting my health; and whatever was unusual in my look or manner, was generally attributed to the trifling indisposition that had occasioned my early retirement last night. But how am I to get over the ten or twelve days that must yet elapse before they go? Yet why so long for their departure? When they *are* gone how shall I get through the months or years of my future life, in company with that man—my greatest enemy—for none could injure me as he has done? Oh! when I think how fondly, how foolishly I have loved him, how madly I have trusted him, how constantly I have laboured, and studied, and prayed, and struggled for his advantage; and how cruelly he has trampled on my love, betrayed my trust,

---

1   "A candle of feeble power made by dipping the pith of a rush in tallow or other grease" (*OED*).

scorned my prayers and tears, and efforts for his preservation—crushed my hopes, destroyed my youth's best feelings, and doomed me to a life of hopeless misery—as far as man can do it—it is not enough to say that I no longer love my husband—I HATE him! The word stares me in the face like a guilty confession, but it is true: I hate him—I hate him!—But God have mercy on his miserable soul!—and make him see and feel his guilt—I ask no other vengeance! If he could but fully know and truly feel my wrongs, I should be well avenged; and I could freely pardon all; but he is so lost, so hardened in his heartless depravity that, in this life, I believe he never will. But it is useless dwelling on this theme: let me seek once more to dissipate reflection in the minor details of passing events.

Mr. Hargrave has annoyed me all day long with his serious, sympathizing, and (as *he* thinks) unobtrusive politeness—if it were more obtrusive it would trouble me less, for then I could snub him; but, as it is, he contrives to appear so really kind and thoughtful that I cannot do so without rudeness and seeming ingratitude. I sometimes think I ought to give him credit for the good feeling he simulates so well; and then again, I think it is my *duty* to suspect him under the peculiar circumstances in which I am placed. His kindness may not all be feigned, but still, let not the purest impulse of gratitude to him, induce me to forget myself; let me remember the game of chess, the expressions he used on the occasion, and those indescribable looks of his, that so justly roused my indignation, and I think I shall be safe enough. I have done well to record them so minutely.

I think he wishes to find an opportunity of speaking to me alone: he has seemed to be on the watch all day, but I have taken care to disappoint him; not that I fear anything he could say, but I have trouble enough without the addition of his insulting consolations, condolences, or whatever else he might attempt; and, for Milicent's sake, I do not wish to quarrel with him. He excused himself from going out to shoot with the other gentlemen in the morning, under the pretext of having letters to write; and instead of retiring for that purpose into the library, he sent for his desk into the morning-room where I was seated with Milicent and Lady Lowborough. They had betaken themselves to their work; I, less to divert my mind than to deprecate conversation, had provided myself with a book. Milicent saw that I wished to be quiet, and accordingly let me alone. Annabella, doubtless, saw it too; but that was no reason why she should restrain her tongue, or curb her cheerful spirits: *she* accordingly chatted away, addressing herself almost exclusively to me, and with the utmost assurance and familiarity, growing the more animated and friendly, the colder and briefer my answers became. Mr. Hargrave saw that I could ill endure it; and, looking up from his desk, he answered her questions and observations for me, as far as he could, and attempted to transfer her social attentions from me to himself; but it would not do. Perhaps, she thought I had a headache and could not bear to talk—at any rate, she saw that her loquacious vivacity annoyed me as I could tell by the malicious pertinacity with which she persisted. But I checked it, effectually, by putting into her hand the book I had been trying to read, on the fly leaf of which I had hastily scribbled,—

"I am too well acquainted with your character and conduct to feel any real friendship for you, and, as I am without your talent for dissimulation, I cannot assume the appearance of it. I must, therefore, beg that hereafter, all familiar intercourse may cease between us; and if I still continue to treat you with civility, as if you were a woman worthy of consideration and respect, understand that it is out of regard for your cousin Milicent's feelings, not for yours."

Upon perusing this, she turned scarlet and bit her lip. Covertly tearing away the leaf, she crumpled it up and put it in the fire, and then employed herself in turning over the pages of the book and, really or apparently, perusing its contents. In a little while Milicent announced it her intention to repair to the nursery, and asked if I would accompany her.

"Annabella will excuse us," said she, "she's busy reading."

"No, I won't," cried Annabella, suddenly looking up and throwing her book on the table. "I want to speak to Helen a minute. You may go Milicent, and she'll follow in a while." (Milicent went.) "Will you oblige me, Helen?" continued she.

Her impudence astounded me; but I complied, and followed her into the library. She closed the door, and walked up to the fire.

"Who told you this?" said she.

"No one: I am not incapable of seeing for myself."

"Ah, you are suspicious!" cried she, smiling with a gleam of hope—hitherto, there had been a kind of desperation in her hardihood; now she was evidently relieved.

"If I *were* suspicious," I replied, "I should have discovered your infamy long before. No, Lady Lowborough, I do not found my charge upon suspicion."

"On what *do* you found it then?" said she, throwing herself into an armchair, and stretching out her feet to the fender, with an obvious effort to appear composed.

"I enjoy a moonlight ramble as well as you," I answered, steadily fixing my eyes upon her: "and the shrubbery happens to be one of my favourite resorts."

She coloured again, excessively, and remained silent, pressing her finger against her teeth, and gazing into the fire. I watched her a few moments with a feeling of malevolent gratification; then, moving towards the door, I calmly asked if she had anything more to say.

"Yes, Yes!" cried she eagerly, starting up from her reclining posture. "I want to know if you will tell Lord Lowborough?"

"Suppose I do?"

"Well, if you are disposed to publish the matter, I cannot dissuade you, of course—but there will be terrible work if you do—and if you don't, I shall think you the most generous of mortal beings—and if there is anything in the world I can do for you—anything short of—" she hesitated.

"Short of renouncing your guilty connection with my husband, I suppose you mean," said I.

She paused, in evident disconcertion and perplexity, mingled with anger she dared not show.

"I cannot renounce what is dearer than life," she muttered in a low, hurried tone. Then, suddenly raising her head and fixing her gleaming eyes upon me, she continued earnestly, "But Helen—or Mrs. Huntingdon, or whatever you would have me call you—*will* you tell him? If you are generous, here is a fitting opportunity for the exercise of your magnanimity: if you are proud, here am I—your rival—ready to acknowledge myself your debtor for an act of the most noble forbearance."

"I shall not tell him."

"You will not!" cried she delightedly. "Accept my sincere thanks, then!"

She sprang up, and offered me her hand. I drew back.

"Give me no thanks; it is not for *your* sake that I refrain. Neither is it an act of any forbearance: I have no wish to publish your shame. I should be sorry to distress your husband with the knowledge of it."

"And Milicent? will you tell her?"

"No, on the contrary I shall do my utmost to conceal it from her. I would not for much that she should know the infamy and disgrace of her relation!"

"You use hard words, Mrs. Huntingdon—but I can pardon you."

"And now Lady Lowborough," continued I, "let me counsel you to leave this house as soon as *possible*. You must be aware that your continuance here is excessively disagreeable to me—not for Mr. Huntingdon's sake," said I, observing the dawn of a malicious smile of triumph on her face—"you are welcome to him, if you like him, as far as *I* am concerned—but because it is painful to be always disguising my true sentiments respecting you, and straining to keep up an appearance of civility and respect towards one for whom I have not the most distant shadow of esteem; and because, if you stay, your conduct cannot possibly remain concealed much longer from the only two persons in the house who do not know it already. And, for your husband's sake, Annabella, and even for your own, I wish—I earnestly advise and *entreat* you to break off this unlawful connection at once, and return to your duty while you may, before the dreadful consequences—"

"Yes, yes, of course," said she, interrupting me with a gesture of impatience.—"But I cannot go, Helen, before the time appointed for our departure. What possible pretext could I frame for such a thing? Whether I proposed going back alone—which Lowborough would not hear of—or taking him with me, the very circumstance itself, would be certain to excite suspicion—and when our visit is so *nearly* at an end too—little more than a week—surely, you can endure my presence *so* long! I will not annoy you with any more of my friendly impertinences."

"Well! I have nothing more to say to you."

"Have you mentioned this affair to Huntingdon?" asked she, as I was leaving the room.

"How dare you mention his name to me!" was the only answer I gave.

No words have passed between us since, but such as outward decency or pure necessity demanded.

CHAPTER XXXV
PROVOCATIONS

NINETEENTH.—In proportion as Lady Lowborough finds she has nothing to fear from me, and as the time of departure draws nigh, the more audacious and insolent she becomes. She does not scruple to speak to my husband with affectionate familiarity in my presence, when no one else is by, and is particularly fond of displaying her interest in his health and welfare, or in anything that concerns him, as if for the purpose of contrasting her kind solicitude with my cold indifference. And he rewards her by such smiles and glances, such whispered words, or boldly spoken insinuations, indicative of his sense of her goodness and my neglect, as makes the blood rush into my face, in spite of myself—for I would be utterly regardless of it all—deaf and blind to everything that passes between them, since the more I show myself sensible of their wickedness, the more she triumphs in her victory, and the more he flatters himself that I love him devotedly still, in spite of my pretended indifference. On such occasions I have sometimes been startled by a subtle, fiendish suggestion inciting me to show him the contrary by a seeming encouragement of Hargrave's advances; but such ideas are banished in a moment with horror and self-abasement; and then I hate him tenfold more than ever, for having brought me to this!—God pardon me for it—and all my sinful thoughts! Instead of being humbled and purified by my afflictions, I feel that they are turning my nature into gall. This must be my fault as much as theirs that wrong me. No true Christian could cherish such bitter feelings as I do against him and her—especially the latter: him, I still feel that I could pardon—freely, gladly—on the slightest token of repentance; but *she*—words cannot utter my abhorrence. Reason forbids, but passion urges strongly; and I must pray and struggle long ere I subdue it.

It is well that she is leaving tomorrow, for I could not well endure her presence for another day. This morning, she rose earlier than usual. I found her in the room alone, when I went down to breakfast.

"Oh Helen! is it you?" said she, turning as I entered.

I gave an involuntary start back on seeing her, at which she uttered a short laugh, observing,—

"I think we are *both* disappointed."

I came forward and busied myself with the breakfast-things.

"This is the last day I shall burden your hospitality," said she, as she seated herself at the table. "Ah, here comes one that will not rejoice at it!" she murmured, half to herself, as Arthur entered the room.

He shook hands with her and wished her good morning: then, looking lovingly in her face, and still retaining her hand in his, murmured pathetically,—

"The last—last day!"

"Yes," said she with some asperity; "and I rose early to make the best of it—I have been here alone this half hour, and *you*, you lazy creature—"

"Well, I thought I was early too," said he—"but," dropping his voice almost to a whisper, "you see we are not alone."

"We never are," returned she. But they were almost as good as alone, for I was now standing at the window, watching the clouds, and struggling to suppress my wrath.

Some more words passed between them, which, happily, I did not overhear; but Annabella had the audacity to come and place herself beside me, and even to put her hand upon my shoulder and say softly,—

"You need not grudge him to me, Helen, for I love him more than ever you could do."

This put me beside myself. I took her hand and violently dashed it from me, with an expression of abhorrence and indignation that could not be suppressed. Startled, almost appalled, by this sudden outbreak, she recoiled in silence. I would have given way to my fury and said more, but Arthur's low laugh recalled me to myself. I checked the half-uttered invective, and scornfully turned away, regretting that I had given him so much amusement. He was still laughing when Mr. Hargrave made his appearance. How much of the scene he had witnessed I do not know, for the door was ajar when he entered. He greeted his host and his cousin both coldly, and me with a glance intended to express the deepest sympathy mingled with high admiration and esteem.

"How much allegiance do you owe to that man?" he asked below his breath, as he stood beside me at the window, affecting to be making observations on the weather.

"None," I answered. And immediately returning to the table, I employed myself in making the tea. He followed, and would have entered into some kind of conversation with me, but the other guests were now beginning to assemble and I took no more notice of him, except to give him his coffee.

After breakfast, determined to pass as little of the day as possible in company with Lady Lowborough, I quietly stole away from the company and retired to the library. Mr. Hargrave followed me thither, under pretence of coming for a book; and first, turning to the shelves, he selected a volume; and then, quietly, but by no means timidly, approaching me, he stood beside me, resting his hand on the back of my chair, and said softly,—

"And so you consider yourself free, at last?"

"Yes," said I, without moving, or raising my eyes from my book,—"free to do anything but offend God and my conscience."

There was a momentary pause.

"Very right," said he; "provided your conscience be not too morbidly tender, and your ideas of God not too erroneously severe; but can you suppose it would offend that benevolent Being to make the happiness of one who would die for yours?—to raise a devoted heart from purgatorial torments to a state of heavenly bliss when you could do it without the slightest injury to yourself or any other?"

This was spoken in a low, earnest, melting tone as he bent over me. I now raised my head; and, steadily confronting his gaze, I answered calmly,—

"Mr. Hargrave, do you mean to insult me?"

He was not prepared for this. He paused a moment to recover the shock; then, drawing himself up and removing his hand from my chair, he answered, with proud sadness,—

"That was not my intention."

I just glanced towards the door, with a slight movement of the head, and then returned to my book. He immediately withdrew. This was better than if I had answered with more words, and in the passionate spirit to which my first impulse would have prompted. What a good thing it is to be able to command one's temper! I must labour to cultivate this inestimable quality: God, only, knows how often I shall need it in this rough, dark road that lies before me.

In the course of the morning, I drove over to the grove with the two ladies, to give Milicent an opportunity for bidding farewell to her mother and sister. They persuaded her to stay with them the rest of the day, Mrs. Hargrave promising to bring her back in the evening and remain till the party broke up on the morrow. Consequently, Lady Lowborough and I had the pleasure of returning tête-à-tête in the carriage together. For the first mile or two, we kept silence, I looking out of my window, and she leaning back in her corner. But I was not going to restrict myself to any particular position for her: when I was tired of leaning forward, with the cold, raw wind in my face; and surveying the russet hedges, and the damp, tangled grass of their banks,

I gave it up, and leant back too. With her usual impudence, my companion then made some attempts to get up a conversation; but the monosyllables "yes," or "no," or "humph," were the utmost her several remarks could elicit from me. At last, on her asking my opinion upon some immaterial point of discussion, I answered,—

"Why do you wish to talk to me, Lady Lowborough?—you must know what I think of you."

"Well, if you *will* be so bitter against me," replied she, "I can't help it;—but *I'm* not going to sulk for anybody."

Our short drive was now at an end. As soon as the carriage door was opened, she sprang out, and went down the park to meet the gentlemen, who were just returning from the woods. Of course I did not follow.

But I had not done with her impudence yet:—after dinner, I retired to the drawing-room, as usual, and she accompanied me, but I had the two children with me, and I gave them my whole attention, and determined to keep them till the gentlemen came, or till Milicent arrived with her mother. Little Helen, however, was soon tired of playing, and insisted upon going to sleep; and while I sat on the sofa with her on my knee, and Arthur seated beside me, gently playing with her soft, flaxen hair,—Lady Lowborough composedly came and placed herself on the other side.

"Tomorrow, Mrs. Huntingdon," said she, "you will be delivered from my presence, which, no doubt, you will be very glad of—it is natural you should;—but do you know I have rendered you a great service?—Shall I tell you what it is?"

"I shall be glad to hear of any service you have rendered me," said I, determined to be calm, for I knew by the tone of her voice she wanted to provoke me.

"Well," resumed she, "have you not observed this salutary change in Mr. Huntingdon? Don't you see what a sober, temperate man he is become? You saw with regret the sad habits he was contracting, I know; and I know you did your utmost to deliver him from them,—but without success, until I came to your assistance. I told him, in few words, that I could not bear to see him degrade himself so, and that I should cease to—no matter what I told him,—but you see the reformation I have wrought; and you ought to thank me for it."

I rose, and rang for the nurse.

"But I desire no thanks," she continued, "all the return I ask is, that you will take care of him when I am gone, and not, by harshness and neglect, drive him back to his old courses."

I was almost sick with passion, but Rachel was now at the door: I pointed to the children, for I could not trust myself to speak: she took them away, and I followed.

"Will you, Helen?" continued the speaker.

I gave her a look that blighted the malicious smile on her face—or checked it, at least for a moment—and departed. In the ante-room I met Mr. Hargrave. He saw I was in no humour to be spoken to, and suffered me to pass without a word; but when, after a few minutes' seclusion in the library, I had regained my composure, and was returning, to join Mrs. Hargrave and Milicent, whom I had just heard come down stairs and go into the drawing-room,—I found him there still, lingering in the dimly lighted apartment, and evidently waiting for me.

"Mrs. Huntingdon," said he as I passed, "will you allow me one word?"

"What is it then?—be quick if you please."

"I offended you this morning; and I cannot live under your displeasure."

"Then, go, and sin no more,"[1] replied I, turning away.

"No, no!" said he hastily, setting himself before me—"Pardon me, but I must have your forgiveness. I leave you tomorrow, and I may not have an opportunity of speaking to you again. I was wrong, to forget myself—and you, as I did; but let me implore you to forget and forgive my rash presumption, and think of me as if those words had never been spoken; for, believe me, I regret them deeply, and the loss of your esteem is too severe a penalty—I cannot bear it."

"Forgetfulness is not to be purchased with a wish; and I cannot bestow my esteem on all who desire it, unless they deserve it too."

"I shall think my life well spent in labouring to deserve it, if you will but pardon this offence.—Will you?"

"Yes."

"Yes? but that is coldly spoken. Give me your hand and I'll believe you.— You won't? Then, Mrs. Huntingdon, you do *not* forgive me!"

"Yes—here it is, and my forgiveness with it: only—*sin no more.*"

He pressed my cold hand with sentimental fervour, but said nothing, and stood aside to let me pass into the room, where all the company were now assembled. Mr. Grimsby was seated near the door: on seeing me enter almost immediately followed by Hargrave, he leered at me, with a glance of intolerable significance, as I passed. I looked him in the face, till he sullenly turned away, if not *ashamed*, at least *confounded* for the moment. Meantime, Hattersley had seized Hargrave by the arm, and was whispering something in his ear—some coarse joke, no doubt, for the latter neither laughed nor spoke in answer, but, turning from him with a slight curl of the lip, disengaged himself and went to his mother, who was telling Lord Lowborough how many reasons she had to be proud of her son.

Thank Heaven, they are all going tomorrow.

---

1   John 8:11.

CHAPTER XXXVI
DUAL SOLITUDE

DECEMBER 20th, 1824.—This is the third anniversary of our felicitous union. It is now two months since our guests left us to the enjoyment of each other's society; and I have had nine weeks' experience of this new phase of conjugal life—two persons living together, as master and mistress of the house, and father and mother of a winsome, merry little child, with the mutual understanding that there is no love, friendship, or sympathy between them. As far as in me lies, I endeavour to live peaceably with him:[1] I treat him with unimpeachable civility, give up my convenience to his, wherever it may reasonably be done, and consult him in a business-like way on household affairs, deferring to his pleasure and judgment, even when I know the latter to be inferior to my own.

As for him: for the first week or two, he was peevish and low—fretting, I suppose, over his dear Annabella's departure—and particularly ill-tempered to me: everything I did was wrong; I was cold-hearted, hard, insensate; my sour, pale face was perfectly repulsive; my voice made him shudder; he knew not how he could live through the winter with me; I should kill him by inches. Again I proposed a separation, but it would not do: he was not going to be the talk of all the old gossips in the neighbourhood: he would not have it said that he was such a brute his wife could not live with him;—no; he must contrive to bear with me.

"I must contrive to bear with *you* you mean," said I, "for as long as I discharge my functions of steward and housekeeper, so conscientiously and well, without pay and without thanks, you cannot afford to part with me. I shall therefore remit these duties when my bondage becomes intolerable." This threat, I thought, would serve to keep him in check, if anything would.

I believe he was much disappointed that I did not feel his offensive sayings more acutely, for when he had said anything particularly well calculated to hurt my feelings, he would stare me searchingly in the face, and then grumble against my "marble heart," or my "brutal insensibility." If I had bitterly wept, and deplored his lost affection, he would, perhaps, have condescended to pity me, and taken me into favour for a while, just to comfort his solitude and console him for the absence of his beloved Annabella, until he could meet her again, or some more fitting substitute. Thank heaven, I am not so weak as that! I was infatuated once, with a foolish, besotted affection, that clung to him in spite of his unworthiness, but it is fairly gone now—wholly crushed and withered away; and he has none but himself and his vices to thank for it.

---

1   See Romans 12:18: "If it be possible, as much as lieth in you, live peaceably with all men."

At first, (in compliance with his sweet lady's injunctions, I suppose) he abstained wonderfully well from seeking to solace his cares in wine; but at length he began to relax his virtuous efforts, and now and then exceeded a little, and still continues to do so—nay, sometimes, not a little. When he is under the exciting influence of these excesses, he sometimes fires up and attempts to play the brute; and then I take little pains to suppress my scorn and disgust: when he is under the *depressing* influence of the after consequences, he bemoans his sufferings and his errors, and charges them both upon me; he knows such indulgence injures his health, and does him more harm than good; but he says I drive him to it by my unnatural, unwomanly conduct; it will be the ruin of him in the end, but it is all my fault;—and *then*, I am roused to defend myself—sometimes, with bitter recrimination. This is a kind of injustice I cannot patiently endure. Have I not laboured long and hard to save him from this very vice? Would I not labour still, to deliver him from it, if I could? But could I do so by fawning upon him and caressing him when I know that he scorns me? Is it *my* fault that I have lost my influence with him, or that he has forfeited every claim to regard? And should I seek a reconciliation with him, when I feel that I abhor him, and that he despises me?—and while he continues still to correspond with Lady Lowborough, as I know he does? No, never, never, never!—he may drink himself dead, but it is NOT my fault!

Yet I do my part to save him still: I give him to understand that drinking makes his eyes dull, and his face red and bloated; and that it tends to render him imbecile in body and mind; and if Annabella were to see him as often as I do, she would speedily be disenchanted; and that she certainly will withdraw her favour from him, if he continues such courses. Such a mode of admonition wins only coarse abuse for me—and indeed I almost feel as if I deserved it, for I hate to use such arguments, but they sink into his stupified heart, and make him pause, and ponder, and abstain, more than anything else I could say.

At present, I am enjoying a temporary relief from his presence: he is gone with Hargrave to join a distant hunt, and will probably not be back before tomorrow evening. How differently I used to feel his absence!

Mr. Hargrave is still at the Grove. He and Arthur frequently meet to pursue their rural sports together: he often calls upon us here, and Arthur not unfrequently rides over to him. I do not think either of these *soi-disant*[1] friends is overflowing with love for the other; but such intercourse serves to get the time on, and I am very willing it should continue, as it saves me some hours of discomfort in Arthur's society, and gives him some better

---

[1] "Calling oneself; would-be (usually with implication of pretense or deception)" (*OED*).

employment than the sottish indulgence of his sensual appetites. The only objection I have to Mr. Hargrave's being in the neighbourhood, is that the fear of meeting him at the Grove prevents me from seeing his sister so often as I otherwise should; for, of late he has conducted himself towards me with such unerring propriety that I have almost forgotten his former conduct. I suppose he is striving to "win my esteem." If he continues to act in this way, he *may* win it;—but what then? the moment he attempts to demand anything more, he will lose it again.

February 10th.—It is a hard, embittering thing to have one's kind feelings and good intentions cast back in one's teeth. I was beginning to relent towards my wretched partner—to pity his forlorn, comfortless condition, unalleviated as it is by the consolations of intellectual resources and the answer of a good conscience towards God—and to think I ought to sacrifice my pride, and renew my efforts once again to make his home agreeable and lead him back to the path of virtue; not by false professions of love, and not by pretended remorse, but by mitigating my habitual coldness of manner, and commuting my frigid civility into kindness wherever an opportunity occurred; and not only was I beginning to think so, but I had already begun to act upon the thought—and what was the result? No answering spark of kindness—no awakening penitence, but an unappeasable ill-humour and a spirit of tyrannous exaction that increased with indulgence, and a lurking gleam of self-complacent triumph, at every detection of relenting softness in my manner, that congealed me to marble again as often as it recurred; and this morning he finished the business:—I think the petrifaction[1] is so completely effected at last, that nothing can melt me again. Among his letters was one which he perused with symptoms of unusual gratification, and then threw across the table to me, with the admonition,—

"There! read that, and take a lesson by it!"

It was in the free, dashing hand of Lady Lowborough. I glanced at the first page; it seemed full of extravagant protestations of affection; impetuous longings for a speedy reunion; and impious defiance of God's mandates, and railings against his providence for having cast their lot asunder, and doomed them both to the hateful bondage of alliance with those they could not love. He gave a slight titter on seeing me change colour. I folded up the letter, rose, and returned it to him, with no remark but,—

"Thank you—I *will* take a lesson by it!"

My little Arthur was standing between his knees, delightedly playing with the bright, ruby ring on his finger. Urged by a sudden, imperative impulse to deliver my son from that contaminating influence, I caught him up in my arms and carried him with me out of the room. Not liking this abrupt

---

1 Turning something into stone.

removal, the child began to pout and cry. This was a new stab to my already tortured heart. I would not let him go; but, taking him with me into the library, I shut the door, and, kneeling on the floor beside him, I embraced him, kissed him, wept over him with passionate fondness. Rather frightened than consoled by this, he turned struggling from me and cried out aloud for his papa. I released him from my arms, and never were more bitter tears than those that now concealed him from my blinded, burning eyes. Hearing his cries, the father came to the room. I instantly turned away lest he should see and misconstrue my emotion. He swore at me, and took the now pacified child away.

It is hard that my little darling should love him more than me; and that, when the well-being and culture of my son is all I have to live for, I should see my influence destroyed by one whose selfish affection is more injurious than the coldest indifference or the harshest tyranny could be. If I, for his good, deny him some trifling indulgence, he goes to his father, and the latter, in spite of his selfish indolence, will even give himself some trouble to meet the child's desires: if I attempt to curb his will, or look gravely on him for some act of childish disobedience, he knows his other parent will smile and take his part against me. Thus, not only have I the father's spirit in the son to contend against, the germs of his evil tendencies to search out and eradicate, and his corrupting intercourse and example in after life to counteract, but already *he* counteracts my arduous labour for the child's advantage, destroys my influence over his tender mind, and robs me of his very love;—I had no earthly hope but this, and he seems to take a diabolical delight in tearing it away.

But it is wrong to despair; I will remember the counsel of the inspired writer to him "that feareth the Lord and obeyeth the voice of his servant, that *sitteth in darkness and hath no light*;—let him trust in the name of the Lord, and stay upon his God!"[1]

CHAPTER XXXVII
THE NEIGHBOUR AGAIN

DECEMBER 20th, 1825.—Another year is past; and I am weary of this life. And yet, I cannot wish to leave it: whatever afflictions assail me here, I cannot wish to go and leave my darling in this dark and wicked world alone, without a friend to guide him through its weary mazes, to warn him of its thousand snares, and guard him from the perils that beset him on every hand.

---

1   Isaiah 50:10: "Who is among you that feareth the Lord, that obeyeth the voice of his servant, that walketh in darkness, and hath no light? Let him trust in the name of the Lord, and stay upon his God."

I am not well fitted to be his only companion, I know; but there is no other to supply my place. I am too grave to minister to his amusements and enter into his infantile sports as a nurse or a mother ought to do, and often his bursts of gleeful merriment trouble and alarm me; I see in them his father's spirit and temperament, and I tremble for the consequences; and, too often, damp the innocent mirth I ought to share. That father on the contrary has no weight of sadness on his mind—is troubled with no fears, no scruples concerning his son's future welfare; and at evenings especially, the times when the child sees him the most and the oftenest, he is always particularly jocund and open-hearted: ready to laugh and to jest with anything or anybody— but me—and I am particularly silent and sad: therefore, of course, the child dotes upon his seemingly joyous, amusing, ever indulgent papa, and will at any time gladly exchange my company for his. This disturbs me greatly; not so much for the sake of my son's affection (though I do prize that highly, and though I feel it is my right, and know I have done much to earn it), as for that influence over him which, for his own advantage, I would strive to purchase and retain, and which for very spite his father delights to rob me of, and, from motives of mere idle egotism, is pleased to win to himself; making no use of it but to torment me, and ruin the child. My only consolation is, that he spends comparatively little of his time at home, and, during the months he passes in London or elsewhere, I have a chance of recovering the ground I had lost, and overcoming with good the evil he has wrought by his willful mismanagement.[1] But then it is a bitter trial to behold him, on his return, doing his utmost to subvert my labours and transform my innocent, affectionate, tractable darling into a selfish, disobedient, and mischievous boy; thereby preparing the soil for those vices he has so successfully cultivated in his own perverted nature.

Happily, there were none of Arthur's "friends" invited to Grassdale last autumn: he took himself off to visit some of them instead. I wish he would always do so, and I wish his friends were numerous and loving enough to keep him amongst them all the year round. Mr. Hargrave, considerably to my annoyance, did not go with him; but I think I have done with that gentleman at last.

For seven or eight months, he behaved so remarkably well, and managed so skillfully too, that I was almost completely off my guard, and was really beginning to look upon him as a friend, and even to treat him as such, with certain prudent restrictions (which I deemed scarcely necessary); when, presuming upon my unsuspecting kindness, he thought he might venture to overstep the bounds of decent moderation and propriety that had so long

---

1   Here, Helen is echoing Romans 12:21: "Be not overcome of evil, but overcome evil with good."

retained him. It was on a pleasant evening at the close of May: I was wandering in the park, and he, on seeing me there as he rode past, made bold to enter and approach me, dismounting and leaving his horse at the gate. This was the first time he had ventured to come within its enclosure since I had been left alone, without the sanction of his mother's or sister's company, or at least the excuse of a message from them. But he managed to appear so calm and easy, so respectful and self-possessed in his friendliness, that, though a little surprised, I was neither alarmed nor offended at the unusual liberty, and he walked with me under the ash trees and by the water-side, and talked, with considerable animation, good taste, and intelligence, on many subjects, before I began to think about getting rid of him. Then, after a pause, during which we both stood gazing on the calm, blue water; I revolving in my mind the best means of politely dismissing my companion, he, no doubt, pondering other matters equally alien to the sweet sights and sounds that alone were present to his senses,—he suddenly electrified me by beginning, in a peculiar tone, low, soft, but perfectly distinct, to pour forth the most unequivocal expressions of earnest and passionate love; pleading his cause with all the bold yet artful eloquence he could summon to his aid. But I cut short his appeal, and repulsed him so determinately, so decidedly, and with such a mixture of scornful indignation tempered with cool, dispassionate sorrow and pity for his benighted mind, that he withdrew, astonished, mortified, and discomforted; and, a few days after, I heard that he had departed for London. He returned however in eight or nine weeks—and, did not entirely keep aloof from me, but comported himself in so remarkable a manner that his quick-sighted sister could not fail to notice the change.

"What have you done to Walter, Mrs. Huntingdon?" said she one morning, when I had called at the Grove, and he had just left the room after exchanging a few words of the coldest civility. "He has been so extremely ceremonious and stately of late, I can't imagine what it is all about, unless you have desperately offended him. Tell me what it is, that I may be your mediator, and make you friends again."

"I have done nothing willingly to offend him," said I. "If he is offended, he can best tell you himself what it is about."

"I'll ask him," cried the giddy girl, springing up and putting her head out of the window; "he's only in the garden—Walter!"

"No, no, Esther! you will seriously displease me if you do; and I shall leave you immediately, and not come again for months—perhaps years."

"Did you call, Esther?" said her brother, approaching the window from without.

"Yes; I wanted to ask you—"

"Good morning, Esther," said I, taking her hand and giving it a severe squeeze.

"To ask you," continued she, "to get me a rose for Mrs. Huntingdon." He departed. "Mrs. Huntingdon," she exclaimed, turning to me and still holding me fast by the hand, "I'm quite shocked at you—you're just as angry, and distant, and cold as he is: and I'm determined you shall be as good friends as ever, before you go."

"Esther, how can you be so rude!" cried Mrs. Hargrave, who was seated gravely knitting in her easy chair. "Surely, you never *will* learn to conduct yourself like a lady!"

"Well mamma, you said, yourself—" But the young lady was silenced by the uplifted finger of her mamma, accompanied with a very stern shake of the head.

"Isn't she cross?" whispered she to me; but, before I could add my share of reproof, Mr. Hargrave reappeared at the window with a beautiful moss rose in his hand.

"Here, Esther, I've brought you the rose," said he, extending it towards her.

"Give it her yourself, you blockhead!" cried she, recoiling with a spring from between us.

"Mrs. Huntingdon would rather receive it from you," replied he in a very serious tone, but lowering his voice that his mother might not hear. His sister took the rose and gave it to me.

"My brother's compliments, Mrs. Huntingdon, and he hopes you and he will come to a better understanding by and by.—Will that do, Walter?" added the saucy girl, turning to him and putting her arm round his neck, as he stood leaning upon the sill of the window—"or should I have said that you are sorry you were so touchy? or that you hope she will pardon your offence?"

"You silly girl! you don't know what you are talking about," replied he gravely.

"Indeed I don't; for I'm quite in the dark."

"Now Esther," interposed Mrs. Hargrave, who, if equally benighted on the subject of our estrangement, saw at least that her daughter was behaving very improperly, "I must insist upon your leaving the room!"

"Pray don't, Mrs. Hargrave, for I'm going to leave it myself," said I, and immediately made my *adieux*.

About a week after, Mr. Hargrave brought his sister to see me. He conducted himself, at first, with his usual cold, distant, half-stately, half-melancholy, altogether injured air; but Esther made no remark upon it this time; she had evidently been schooled into better manners. She talked to me, and laughed and romped with little Arthur, her loved and loving playmate. He, somewhat to my discomfort, enticed her from the room to have a run in the hall; and, thence, into the garden. I got up to stir the fire. Mr. Hargrave asked if I felt cold, and shut the door—a very unseasonable piece of officiousness,

for I had meditated following the noisy playfellows, if they did not speedily return. He then took the liberty of walking up to the fire himself, and
asking me if I were aware that Mr. Huntingdon was now at the seat of Lord
Lowborough, and likely to continue there some time.

"No; but it's no matter," I answered carelessly; and if my cheek glowed
like fire, it was rather at the question than the information it conveyed.

"You don't object to it?" he said.

"Not at all, if Lord Lowborough likes his company."

"You have no love left for him, then?"

"Not the least."

"I knew that—I knew you were too high-minded and pure in your own
nature to continue to regard one so utterly false and polluted, with any feelings but those of indignation and scornful abhorrence!"

"Is he not your friend?" said I, turning my eyes from the fire to his face,
with perhaps a slight touch of those feelings he assigned to another.

"He *was*," replied he, with the same calm gravity as before, "but do not
wrong me by supposing that I could continue my friendship and esteem to
a man who could so infamously—so impiously forsake and injure one so
transcendently—well, I won't speak of it. But tell me, do you never think of
revenge?"

"Revenge! No—what good would that do—it would make him no better, and me no happier?"

"I don't know how to talk to you, Mrs. Huntingdon," said he smiling;
"you are only half a woman—your nature must be half human, half angelic.
Such goodness overawes me; I don't know what to make of it."

"Then sir, I fear you must be very much worse than you should be, if I, a
mere ordinary mortal, am by your own confession, so vastly your superior;—
and since there exists so little sympathy between us, I think we had better
each look out for some more congenial companion." And forthwith moving
to the window, I began to look out for my little son and his gay young friend.

"No, *I* am the ordinary mortal, I maintain," replied Mr. Hargrave. "I will
not allow myself to be worse than my fellows; but *you* Madame—I equally
maintain there is nobody like you. But are you happy?" he asked in a serious
tone.

"As happy as some others, I suppose."

"Are you as happy as you desire to be?"

"No one is so blest as that comes to, on this side eternity."

"One thing I know," returned he, with a deep, sad sigh; "you are immeasurably happier than I am."

"I am very sorry for you, then," I could not help replying.

"Are you *indeed*?—No—for if you were, you would be glad to relieve
me."

"And so I should, if I could do so, without injuring myself or any other."

"And can you suppose that I should wish you to injure yourself?—No; on the contrary, it is your own happiness I long for more than mine. You are miserable now, Mrs. Huntingdon," continued he, looking me boldly in the face. "You do not complain, but I see—and feel—and know that you are miserable—and must remain so, as long as you keep those walls of impenetrable ice about your still warm and palpitating heart;—and I am miserable too. Deign to smile on me, and I am happy: trust me, and you shall be happy also, for if you *are* a woman, I can make you so—and I *will* do it in spite of yourself!" he muttered between his teeth, "and as for others, the question is between ourselves alone: you cannot injure your husband, you know; and no one else has any concern in the matter."

"I have a son, Mr. Hargrave, and you have a mother," said I, retiring from the window, whither he had followed me.

"They need not know," he began, but before anything more could be said on either side, Esther and Arthur re-entered the room. The former glanced at Walter's flushed, excited countenance, and then at mine—a little flushed and excited too, I dare say, though from far different causes. She must have thought we had been quarrelling desperately, and was evidently perplexed and disturbed at the circumstance; but she was too polite, or too much afraid of her brother's anger to refer to it. She seated herself on the sofa, and putting back her bright, golden ringlets, that were scattered in wild profusion over her face, she immediately began to talk about the garden and her little playfellow, and continued to chatter away in her usual strain till her brother summoned her to depart.

"If I have spoken too warmly, forgive me," he murmured on taking his leave, "or I shall never forgive myself."

Esther smiled and glanced at me: I merely bowed, and her countenance fell. She thought it a poor return for Walter's generous concession, and was disappointed in her friend. Poor child, she little knows the world she lives in!

Mr. Hargrave had not an opportunity of meeting me again in private for several weeks after this; but when he did meet me, there was less of pride and more of touching melancholy in his manner than before. Oh, *how* he annoyed me! I was obliged, at last almost entirely to remit my visits to the Grove, at the expense of deeply offending Mrs. Hargrave and seriously afflicting poor Esther, who really values my society—for want of better, and who ought not to suffer for the fault of her brother. But that indefatigable foe was not yet vanquished: he seemed to be always on the watch. I frequently saw him riding lingeringly past the premises, looking searchingly round him as he went—or if *I* did not, Rachel did. That sharp-sighted woman soon guessed how matters stood between us, and, descrying the enemy's movements from her elevation at the nursery window, she would give me a quiet intimation, if she saw me preparing for a walk when she had reason to believe he was about, or to think it likely that he would meet or overtake me in the way I meant to traverse. I would then defer my ramble, or confine myself for that day to the park and gardens—or if the proposed excursion was a matter of importance, such as a visit to the sick or afflicted, I would take Rachel with me, and then I was never molested.

But one mild, sunshiny day, early in November, I had ventured forth alone, to visit the village school and a few of the poor tenants, and on my return, I was alarmed at the clatter of a horse's feet behind me approaching at a rapid, steady trot. There was no stile or gap at hand, by which I could escape into the fields: so I walked quietly on, saying to myself—

"It may not be he after all; and if it is, and if he *do* annoy me—it shall be for the last time—I am determined, if there be power in words and looks against cool impudence and mawkish sentimentality so inexhaustible as his."

The horse soon overtook me, and was reined up close beside me. It *was* Mr. Hargrave. He greeted me with a smile intended to be soft and melancholy, but his triumphant satisfaction at having caught me at last, so shone through, that it was quite a failure. After briefly answering his salutation and inquiring after the ladies at the Grove, I turned away and walked on; but he followed, and kept his horse at my side: it was evident he intended to be my companion all the way.

"Well! I don't much care. If you want another rebuff, take it—and welcome," was my inward remark. "Now sir, what next?"

This question, though unspoken, was not long unanswered: after a few passing observations upon indifferent subjects, he began, in solemn tones the following appeal to my humanity:—

"It will be four years next April since I first saw you, Mrs. Huntingdon,—*you* may have forgotten the circumstance, but *I* never can—I admired you then, most deeply, but I dared not love you: in the following autumn, I saw so much of your perfections that I could not fail to love you, though I dared not show it. For upwards of three years, I have endured a perfect martyrdom. From the anguish of suppressed emotions, intense and fruitless longings, silent sorrow, crushed hopes, and trampled affections,—I have suffered more than I can tell, or you imagine—and you were the cause of it—and not, altogether, the innocent cause. My youth is wasting away; my prospects are darkened; my life is a desolate blank; I have no rest day or night: I am become a burden to myself and others;—and you might save me by a word—a glance, and will not do it.—Is this right?"

"In the first place, I don't believe you," answered I: "in the second, if you will be such a fool, I can't hinder it."

"If you affect," replied he earnestly, "to regard as folly, the best, the strongest, the most godlike impulses of our nature,—*I* don't believe *you*—I know you are not the heartless, icy being you pretend to be—you had a heart once, and you gave it to your husband. When you found him utterly unworthy of the treasure you reclaimed it;—and you will not *pretend* that you loved that sensual, earthly minded profligate so deeply, so devotedly that you can never love another?—I know that there are feelings in your nature that have never yet been called forth—I know, too, that in your present neglected, lonely state you are, and *must* be miserable. You have it in your power to raise two human beings from a state of actual suffering to such unspeakable beatitude as only generous, noble self-forgetting love can give (for you *can* love me if you will; you may tell me that you scorn and detest me, but—since you have set me the example of plain speaking—I will answer that *I do not believe you!*), but you will not do it! you choose rather to leave us miserable; and you coolly tell me it is the will of God that we should remain so. *You* may call this religion, but *I* call it wild fanaticism!"

"There is another life both for you and for me," said I. "If it be the will of God that we should sow in tears, now, it is only that we may reap in joy, hereafter.[1] It is his will that we should not injure others by the gratification of our own earthly passions; and you have a mother, and sisters, and friends, who would be seriously injured by your disgrace; and I too have friends, whose peace of mind shall never be sacrificed to my enjoyment—or yours either, with my consent—and if I were alone in the world, I have still my God and my religion, and I would sooner die than disgrace my calling and break my faith with Heaven to obtain a few brief years of false and fleeting happiness—happiness sure to end in misery, even here—for myself or any other!"[2]

"There need be no disgrace—no misery or sacrifice in any quarter," persisted he. "I do not ask you to leave your home or defy the world's opinion."—But I need not repeat all his arguments. I refuted them to the best of my power; but that power was provokingly small, at the moment, for I was too much flurried with indignation—and even shame—that he should thus dare to address me, to retain sufficient command of thought and language to

---

1 See Psalm 126:5–6: "They that sow in tears shall reap in joy. He that goeth forth and weepeth, bearing precious seed, shall doubtless come again with rejoicing, bringing his sheaves with him."

2 Brontë again appears to be revising and responding to a crucial scene in *Jane Eyre*. After Jane has learned the truth about Bertha Mason, although tempted by Rochester, she responds by reminding him of her relationship with God, privileging her relationship with Him over human bonds: "The more solitary, the more friendless, the more unsustained I am, the more I will respect myself. I will keep the law given by God; sanctioned by man.... Laws and principles are not for the times when there is no temptation: they are for such moments as this, when body and soul rise in mutiny against their rigour: stringent are they; inviolate they shall be. If at my individual convenience I might break them, what would be their worth" (*Jane Eyre* 408).

enable me adequately to contend against his powerful sophistries. Finding, however, that he could not be silenced by reason, and even covertly exulted in his seeming advantage, and ventured to deride those assertions I had not the coolness to prove, I changed my course and tried another plan.

"Do you really love me?" said I seriously, pausing and looking him calmly in the face.

"Do I love you!" cried he.

"*Truly?*" I demanded.

His countenance brightened; he thought his triumph was at hand. He commenced a passionate protestation of the truth and fervour of his attachment which I cut short by another question:—

"But is it not a selfish love?—have you enough disinterested affection to enable you to sacrifice your own pleasure to mine?"

"I would give my life to serve you."

"I don't want your life—but have you enough real sympathy for my afflictions to induce you to make an effort to relieve them, at the risk of a little discomfort to yourself?"

"Try me, and see!"

"If you have—*never mention this subject again.* You cannot recur to it in any way, without doubling the weight of those sufferings you so feelingly deplore. I have nothing left me but the solace of a good conscience[1] and a hopeful trust in Heaven, and you labour continually to rob me of these. If you persist, I must regard you as my deadliest foe."

"But hear me a moment—"

"No, sir! you said you would give your life to serve me: I only ask your *silence* on one particular point. I have spoken plainly; and what I say I mean. If you torment me in this way any more, I must conclude that your protestations are entirely false, and that you hate me in your heart as fervently as you profess to love me!"

He bit his lip and bent his eyes upon the ground in silence for a while.

"Then I must leave you," said he at length looking steadily upon me, as if with the last hope of detecting some token of irrepressible anguish or dismay awakened by those solemn words. "I must leave you. I cannot live here, and be for ever silent on the all-absorbing subject of my thoughts and wishes."

"Formerly, I believe, you spent but little of your time at home," I answered: "it will do you no harm to absent yourself again, for a while—if that be really necessary."

---

1 Here, Helen is echoing biblical ideas about good conscience and hope for heaven. On good conscience see Acts 24:16, Hebrews 13:18, and 1 Peter 3:16. For passages on hopeful trust in heaven see Romans 8:24 and 12:12, Colossians 1:27, Titus 3:7 and 2:13, and Psalm 16.

"If that be really *possible*," he muttered—"and can you bid me go so coolly! Do you really wish it?"

"Most certainly I do. If you cannot see me without tormenting me as you have lately done, I would gladly say farewell and never see you more."

He made no answer, but, bending from his horse, held out his hand towards me. I looked up at his face, and saw, therein, such a look of genuine agony of soul that, whether bitter disappointment, or wounded pride, or lingering love, or burning wrath were uppermost, I could not hesitate to put my hand in his as frankly as if I bade a friend farewell. He grasped it very hard, and immediately put spurs to his horse and galloped away. Very soon after, I learned that he was gone to Paris, where he still is, and the longer he stays there the better for me.

I thank God for this deliverance!

CHAPTER XXXVIII
THE INJURED MAN

DECEMBER 20th, 1826.—The fifth anniversary of my wedding day, and I trust, the last I shall spend under this roof. My resolution is formed, my plan concocted, and already partly put in execution. My conscience does not blame me, but while the purpose ripens, let me beguile a few of these long winter evenings in stating the case for my own satisfaction—a dreary amusement enough, but having the air of a useful occupation, and being pursued as a task, it will suit me better than a lighter one.

In September, quiet Grassdale was again alive with a party of ladies and gentlemen (so called) consisting of the same individuals as those invited the year before last, with the addition of two or three others, among whom were Mrs. Hargrave and her younger daughter. The gentlemen and Lady Lowborough were invited for the pleasure and convenience of the host, the other ladies, I suppose for the sake of appearances; and to keep me in check and make me discreet and civil in my demeanour. But the ladies stayed only three weeks, the gentlemen, with two exceptions, above two months, for their hospitable entertainer was loath to part with them and be left alone with his bright intellect, his stainless conscience, and his loved and loving wife.

On the day of Lady Lowborough's arrival, I followed her into her chamber, and plainly told her that, if I found reason to believe that she still continued her criminal connection with Mr. Huntingdon, I should think it my absolute duty to inform her husband of the circumstance—or awaken his suspicions at least—however painful it might be, or however dreadful the consequences. She was startled at first, by the declaration, so unexpected, and so determinately yet calmly delivered; but rallying in a moment, she coolly replied that if I saw anything at all reprehensible or suspicious in her conduct, she would freely give me leave to tell his lordship all about it. Willing to be satisfied with this, I left her; and certainly I saw nothing thenceforth particularly reprehensible or suspicious in her demeanour towards her host; but then I had the other guests to attend to, and I did not watch them narrowly—for to confess the truth, I *feared* to see anything between them. I no longer regarded it as any concern of mine, and if it was my duty to enlighten Lord Lowborough, it was a painful duty, and I dreaded to be called to perform it.

But my fears were brought to an end, in a manner I had not anticipated. One evening, about a fortnight after the visitors' arrival, I had retired into the library to snatch a few minutes' respite from forced cheerfulness and wearisome discourse—for after so long a period of seclusion, dreary indeed, as I had often found it, I could not always bear to be doing violence to my feelings, and goading my powers to talk, and smile and listen, and play the attentive hostess—or even the cheerful friend:—I had just ensconced myself within the bow of the window, and was looking out upon the west where the darkening hills rose sharply defined against the clear amber light of evening, that gradually blended and faded away into the pure, pale blue of the upper sky, where one bright star was shining through, as if to promise—"When that dying light is gone, the world will not be left in darkness, and they who trust in God—whose minds are unbeclouded by the mists of unbelief and sin, are never wholly comfortless,"[1]—when I heard a hurried step approaching, and Lord Lowborough entered—this room was still his favourite resort. He flung the door to with unusual violence, and cast his hat aside regardless where it fell. What could be the matter with him? His face was ghastly pale; his eyes were fixed upon the ground; his teeth clenched; his forehead glistened with the dews of agony. It was plain he knew his wrongs at last!

Unconscious of my presence, he began to pace the room in a state of fearful agitation, violently wringing his hands and uttering low groans or incoherent ejaculations. I made a movement to let him know that he was not alone; but he was too preoccupied to notice it. Perhaps, while his back was towards me, I might cross the room and slip away unobserved. I rose to make the attempt, but then he perceived me. He started and stood still a moment; then wiped his streaming forehead, and advancing towards me, with a kind of unnatural composure, said in a deep, almost sepulchral tone—

---

1   This image echoes many parts of the Bible such as the Psalms and/or John. (See especially Psalm 112:4: "Unto the upright there ariseth light in the darkness: he is gracious, and full of compassion, and righteous.") Yet while Brontë could be referring to passages such as these, she could also be quoting a published sermon whose source is unknown to twenty-first-century readers.

"Mrs. Huntingdon, I must leave you tomorrow."

"Tomorrow!" I repeated, "I do not ask the cause."

"You know it then—and you can be so calm!" said he, surveying me with profound astonishment, not unmingled with a kind of resentful bitterness, as it appeared to me.

"I have so long been aware of—" I paused in time, and added, "of my husband's character, that nothing shocks me."

"But *this*—how long have you been aware of this?" demanded he, laying his clenched hand on the table beside him, and looking me keenly and fixedly in the face.

I felt like a criminal.

"Not long," I answered.

"You knew it!" cried he with bitter vehemence—"and you did not tell me! You helped to deceive me!"

"My lord, I did *not* help to deceive you."

"Then why did you not tell me?"

"Because, I knew it would be painful to you—I hoped she would return to her duty, and then there would be no need to harrow your feelings with such—"

"O God! how long has this been going on? how long has it been, Mrs. Huntingdon?—Tell me—I MUST know!" he exclaimed with intense and fearful eagerness.

"Two years, I believe."

"Great Heaven! and she has duped me all this time!" He turned away with a suppressed groan of agony, and paced the room again, in a paroxysm of renewed agitation. My heart smote me; but I would try to console him, though I knew not how to attempt it.

"She is a wicked woman," I said. "She has basely deceived and betrayed you. She is as little worthy of your regret as she was of your affection. Let her injure you no farther: abstract yourself from her, and stand alone."

"And you, Madam," said he sternly, arresting his walk and turning round upon me—"you have injured me too, by this ungenerous concealment!"

There was a sudden revulsion in my feelings. Something rose within me, and urged me to resent this harsh return for my heartfelt sympathy, and defend myself with answering severity. Happily, I did not yield to the impulse. I saw his anguish as suddenly smiting his forehead, he turned abruptly to the window, and, looking upward at the placid sky, murmured passionately, "O God, that I might die!"—and felt that to add one drop of bitterness to that already overflowing cup, would be ungenerous indeed. And yet, I fear there was more coldness than gentleness in the quiet tone of my reply:—

"I might offer many excuses that some would admit to be valid, but I will not attempt to enumerate them—"

"I know them," said he hastily, "you would say that it was no business of yours—that I ought to have taken care of myself—that if my own blindness has led me into this pit of hell, I have no right to blame another for giving me credit for a larger amount of sagacity than I possessed—"

"I confess I was wrong," continued I, without regarding this bitter interruption; "but whether want of courage or mistaken kindness was the cause of my error, I think you blame me too severely. I told Lady Lowborough two weeks ago, the very hour she came, that I should certainly think it my duty to inform you if she continued to deceive you: she gave me full liberty to do so if I should see anything reprehensible or suspicious in her conduct—I have seen nothing; and I trusted she had altered her course."

He continued gazing from the window while I spoke, and did not answer, but, stung by the recollections my words awakened, stamped his foot upon the floor, ground his teeth, and corrugated his brow, like one under the influence of acute physical pain.

"It was wrong—it was wrong!" he muttered, at length. "Nothing can excuse it—nothing can atone for it,—for nothing can recall those years of cursed credulity—nothing obliterate them!—nothing, nothing!" he repeated in a whisper whose despairing bitterness precluded all resentment.

"When I put the case to myself, I own it *was* wrong," I answered; "but I can only now regret that I did not see it in this light before, and that, as you say, nothing can recall the past."

Something in my voice or in the spirit of this answer seemed to alter his mood. Turning towards me and attentively surveying my face by the dim light, he said in a milder tone than he had yet employed,—

"You too have suffered, I suppose."

"I suffered much, at first."

"When was that?"

"Two years ago; and two years hence you will be as calm as I am now,—and far, far happier, I trust, for you are a man, and free to act as you please."

Something like a smile, but a *very* bitter one, crossed his face for a moment.

"You have not been happy lately?" he said with a kind of effort to regain composure, and a determination to waive the further discussion of his own calamity.

"Happy!" I repeated, almost provoked at such a question—"Could I be so, with such a husband?"

"I have noticed a change in your appearance since the first years of your marriage," pursued he: "I observed it to—to that infernal demon," he muttered between his teeth—"and he said it was your own sour temper that was eating away your bloom: it was making you old and ugly before your time, and had already made his fire-side as comfortless as a convent cell.—You smile Mrs. Huntingdon—nothing moves you. I wish my nature were as calm as yours!"

"My nature was not originally calm," said I: "I have learned to appear so by dint of hard lessons, and many repeated efforts."

At this juncture Mr. Hattersley burst into the room.

"Hallow, Lowborough!" he began—"Oh! I beg your pardon," he exclaimed on seeing me; "I didn't know it was a tête-à-tête. Cheer up, man!" he continued, giving Lord Lowborough a thump on the back, which caused the latter to recoil from him with looks of ineffable disgust and irritation. "Come, I want to speak with you a bit."

"Speak, then."

"But I'm not sure it would be quite agreeable to the lady, what I have to say."

"Then it would not be agreeable to me," said his lordship, turning to leave the room.

"Yes, it would," cried the other, following him into the hall. "If you've the heart of a man it would be the very ticket for you. It's just this, my lad," he continued, rather lowering his voice, but not enough to prevent me from hearing every word he said, though the half-closed door stood between us: "I think you're an ill-used man—nay, now, don't flare up—I don't want to offend you: it's only my rough way of talking. I must speak right out you *know*, or else not at all;—and I'm come—stop now! let me explain—I'm come to offer you my services, for though Huntingdon is my friend, he's a devilish scamp as we all know, and I'll be *your* friend for the nonce. I know what it is you want, to make matters straight: it's just to exchange a shot with him, and then you'll feel yourself all right again; and if an accident happens—why, that'll be all right too, I dare say, to a desperate fellow like you.—Come now! give me your hand, and don't look so black upon it. Name time and place, and I'll manage the rest."

"That," answered the more low, deliberate voice of Lord Lowborough, "is just the remedy my own heart—or the devil within it, suggested—to meet him, and *not to sever without blood*. Whether I or he should fall—or both, it would be an *inexpressible* relief to me, if—"

"Just so! Well then—"

"No!" exclaimed his lordship with deep, determined emphasis. "Though I hate him from my heart, and should rejoice at any calamity that could befall him—I'll leave him to God; and though I abhor my own life, I'll leave that too, to Him that gave it."

"But you see in this case," pleaded Hattersley—

"I'll not hear you!" exclaimed his companion, hastily turning away. "Not another word! I've enough to do against the fiend within me."

"Then you're a white livered fool, and I wash my hands of you," grumbled the tempter as he swung himself round and departed.

"Right, right, Lord Lowborough!" cried I, darting out and clasping his burning hand, as he was moving away to the stairs. "I begin to think the world is not worthy of you!"

Not understanding this sudden ebullition, he turned upon me with a stare of gloomy, bewildered amazement that made me ashamed of the impulse to which I had yielded; but soon a more humanized expression dawned upon his countenance, and, before I could withdraw my hand, he pressed it kindly, while a gleam of genuine feeling flashed from his eyes as he murmured,—

"God help us both!"

"Amen!" responded I; and we parted.

I returned to the drawing-room, where, doubtless, my presence would be expected by most, desired by one or two. In the ante-room was Mr. Hattersley, railing against Lord Lowborough's poltroonery[1] before a select audience, viz.[2] Mr. Huntingdon, who was lounging against the table exulting in his own treacherous villainy and laughing his victim to scorn, and Mr. Grimsby, standing by, quietly rubbing his hands and chuckling with fiendish satisfaction. At the glance I gave them in passing, Hattersley stopped short in his animadversions and stared like a bull calf, Grimsby glowered upon me with a leer of malignant ferocity, and my husband muttered a coarse and brutal malediction.

In the drawing-room I found Lady Lowborough, evidently in no very enviable state of mind, and struggling hard to conceal her discomposure by an overstrained affectation of unusual cheerfulness and vivacity, very uncalled for under the circumstances, for she had herself given the company to understand that her husband had received unpleasant intelligence from home, which necessitated his immediate departure, and that he had suffered it so to bother his mind that it had brought on a bilious headache, owing to which and the preparations he judged necessary to hasten his departure, she believed they would not have the pleasure of seeing him tonight. However, she asserted, it was only a business concern, and so she did not intend it should trouble *her*. She was just saying this as I entered, and she darted upon me such a glance of hardihood and defiance as at once astonished and revolted me.

"But I *am* troubled," continued she, "and vexed too, for I think it my duty to accompany his lordship, and of course I am very sorry to part with all my kind friends, so unexpectedly and so soon."

"And yet, Annabella," said Esther, who was sitting beside her, "I never saw you in better spirits in my life."

"Precisely so, my love; because I wish to make the best of your society, since it appears this is to be the last night I am to enjoy it, till Heaven knows

---

1   Cowardice.
2   Namely.

when; and I wish to leave a good impression on you all,"—she glanced round, and seeing her aunt's eye fixed upon her, rather too scrutinizingly, as she probably thought, she started up and continued,—"to which end I'll give you a song—shall I, aunt? shall I, Mrs. Huntingdon? shall I, ladies and gentlemen—all?—Very well, I'll do my best to amuse you."

She and Lord Lowborough occupied the apartments next to mine. I know not how *she* passed the night, but I lay awake the greater part of it listening to his heavy step pacing monotonously up and down his dressing-room, which was nearest my chamber. Once I heard him pause and throw something out of the window, with a passionate ejaculation; and in the morning, after they were gone, a keen-bladed clasp-knife was found on the grass-plot below; a razor, likewise was snapped in two and thrust deep into the cinders of the grate, but partially corroded by the decaying embers. So strong had been the temptation to end his miserable life, so determined his resolution to resist it.

My heart bled for him as I lay listening to that ceaseless tread. Hitherto, I had thought too much of myself, too little of him: now I forgot my own afflictions, and thought only of his—of the ardent affection so miserably wasted, the fond faith so cruelly betrayed, the—no, I will not attempt to enumerate his wrongs,—but I hated his wife and my husband more intensely than ever, and not for my sake, but for his.

"That man," I thought, "is an object of scorn to his friends and the nice-judging world. The false wife and the treacherous friend who have wronged him are not so despised and degraded as he; and his refusal to avenge his wrongs has removed him yet farther beyond the range of sympathy, and blackened his name with a deeper disgrace. He knows this; and it doubles his burden of woe. He sees the injustice of it, but he cannot bear up against it; he lacks that sustaining power of self-esteem which leads a man, exulting in his own integrity, to defy the malice of traducing foes and give them scorn for scorn—or, better still, which raises him above earth's foul and turbulent vapours, to repose in Heaven's eternal sunshine. He knows that God is just, but cannot see His justice now: he knows this life is short, and yet death seems insufferably far away; he believes there is a future state, but so absorbing is the agony of this that he cannot realize its rapturous repose. He can but bow his head to the storm, and cling, blindly, despairingly, to what he knows to be right. Like the shipwrecked mariner cleaving to a raft, blinded, deafened, bewildered, he feels the waves sweep over him, and sees no prospect of escape; and yet he knows he has no hope but this, and still, while life and sense remain, concentrates all his energies to keep it. Oh, that I had a friend's right to comfort him, and tell him that I never esteemed him so highly as I do this night!"

They departed early in the morning before any one else was down, except myself, and just as I was leaving my room, Lord Lowborough was descending to take his place in the carriage where his lady was already ensconced; and Arthur (or Mr. Huntingdon as I prefer calling him, for the other is my child's name) had the gratuitous insolence to come out in his dressing-gown to bid his "friend" good bye.

"What, going already, Lowborough!" said he. "Well, good morning." He smilingly offered his hand.

I think the other would have knocked him down, had be not instinctively started back before that bony fist quivering with rage and clenched till the knuckles gleamed white and glistening through the skin. Looking upon him with a countenance livid with furious hate, Lord Lowborough muttered between his closed teeth, a deadly execration he would not have uttered had he been calm enough to choose his words, and departed.

"I call that an unchristian spirit now," said the villain. "But I'd never give up an old friend for the sake of a wife. You may have mine if you like, and I call that handsome—I *can* do no more than offer restitution, can I?"

But Lowborough had gained the bottom of the stairs, and was now crossing the hall; and Mr. Huntingdon, leaning over the banisters, called out,— "Give my love to Annabella!—and I wish you both a happy journey," and withdrew laughing to his chamber.

He subsequently expressed himself rather glad she was gone: "She was so deuced imperious and exacting," said he: "now I shall be my own man again, and feel rather more at my ease."

I know nothing more of Lord Lowborough's subsequent proceedings but what I have heard from Milicent, who, though she is ignorant of the cause of his separation from her cousin, has informed me that such is the case; that they keep entirely separate establishments; that she leads a gay, dashing life in town and country, while he lives in strict seclusion at his old castle in the north. There are two children, both of whom he keeps under his own protection. The son and heir is a promising child nearly the age of my Arthur, and no doubt a source of some hope and comfort to his father; but the other, a little girl between one and two, with blue eyes and light auburn hair, he probably keeps from conscientious motives alone, thinking it wrong to abandon her to the teaching and example of such a woman as her mother. That mother never loved children, and has so little natural affection for her own that I question whether she will not regard it as a relief to be thus entirely separated from them, and delivered from the trouble and responsibility of their charge.

Not many days after the departure of Lord and Lady Lowborough, the rest of the ladies withdrew the light of their presence from Grassdale. Perhaps they might have stayed longer, but neither host nor hostess pressed them to prolong their visit—in fact, the former showed too plainly that he should be glad to get rid of them;—and Mrs. Hargrave retired with her daughters and her grand-children (there are three of them now) to the grove. But the gentlemen remained: Mr. Huntingdon, as I intimated before, was determined to keep them as long as he could; and, being thus delivered from restraint, they gave a loose to all their innate madness, folly, and brutality, and made the house night after night one scene of riot, uproar, and confusion. Who among them behaved the worst, or who the best, I can not distinctly say; for, from the moment I discovered how things would be, I formed the resolution of retreating upstairs or locking myself into the library the instant I withdrew from the dining-room, and not coming near them again till breakfast;—but this I must say for Mr. Hargrave, that from all *I* could see of him, he was a model of decency, sobriety, and gentlemanly manners *in comparison* with the rest.

He did not join the party till a week or ten days after the arrival of the other guests; for he was still on the continent when they came, and I cherished the hope that he would not accept the invitation. Accept it he did, however, but his conduct towards me, for the first few weeks, was exactly what I should have wished it to be—perfectly civil and respectful without any affectation of despondency or dejection, and sufficiently distant without haughtiness, or any of such remarkable stiffness or iciness of demeanour as might be calculated to disturb or puzzle his sister, or call forth the investigation of his mother.

CHAPTER XXXIX
A SCHEME OF ESCAPE

MY greatest source of uneasiness, in this time of trial, was my son, whom his father and his father's friends delighted to encourage in all the embryo vices a little child can show, and to instruct in all the evil habits he could acquire—in a word, to "make a man of him" was one of their staple amusements; and I need say no more to justify my alarm on his account, and my determination to deliver him at any hazard from the hands of such instructors. I first attempted to keep him always with me or in the nursery, and gave Rachel particular injunctions never to let him come down to dessert as long as these "gentlemen" stayed; but it was no use; these orders were immediately countermanded and over-ruled by his father: he was not going to have the little fellow moped to death between an old nurse and a cursed fool of a mother. So the little fellow came down every evening, in spite of his cross mamma, and learnt to tipple wine like papa, to swear like Mr. Hattersley, and to have his own way like a man, and sent mamma to the devil when she tried to prevent him. To see such things done with the roguish naïveté of that pretty little child and hear such things spoken by that small infantile voice,

was as peculiarly piquant and irresistibly droll to them as it was inexpressibly distressing and painful to me; and when he had set the table in a roar,[1]
he would look round delightedly upon them all, and add his shrill laugh to
theirs. But if that beaming blue eye rested on me, its light would vanish for
a moment, and he would say, in some concern,—"Mamma, why don't *you*
laugh? Make her laugh, papa—she never will."

Hence, was I obliged to stay among these human brutes, watching an
opportunity to get my child away from them, instead of leaving them immediately after the removal of the cloth, as I should always otherwise have
done. He was never willing to go, and I frequently had to carry him away
by force; for which he thought me very cruel and unjust; and sometimes his
father would insist upon my letting him remain;—and then, I would leave
him to his kind friends, and retire to indulge my bitterness and despair alone
or to rack my brains for a remedy to this great evil.

But here again, I must do Mr. Hargrave the justice to acknowledge that
I never saw *him* laugh at the child's misdemeanours, nor heard him utter a
word of encouragement to his aspirations after manly accomplishments. But
when anything very extraordinary was said or done by the infant profligate,
I noticed, at times, a peculiar expression in his face, that I could neither
interpret nor define—a slight twitching about the muscles of the mouth—a
sudden flash in the eye, as he darted a sudden glance at the child and then
at me; and then, I could fancy there arose a gleam of hard, keen, sombre
satisfaction in his countenance at the look of impotent wrath and anguish he
was too certain to behold in mine. But on one occasion, when Arthur had
been behaving particularly ill, and Mr. Huntingdon and his guests had been
particularly provoking and insulting to me in their encouragement of him,
and I particularly anxious to get him out of the room, and on the very point
of demeaning myself by a burst of uncontrollable passion—Mr. Hargrave
suddenly rose from his seat, with an aspect of stern determination, lifted the
child from his father's knee, where he was sitting half tipsy, cocking his head
and laughing at me, and execrating me with words he little knew the meaning of,—handed him out of the room, and setting him down in the hall, held
the door open for me, gravely bowed as I withdrew, and closed it after me.
I heard high words exchanged between him and his already half-inebriated
host as I departed, leading away my bewildered and disconcerted boy.

But this should not continue; my child must not be abandoned to this
corruption: better far that he should live in poverty and obscurity with a
fugitive mother, than in luxury and affluence with such a father. These guests

---

1   Hamlet, seeing Yorrick's skull, asks, "Where be your gibes now? your gambols? your
    songs? your flashes of merriment, that were wont to set the table on a roar?" (*Hamlet*
    V.i.183–85).

might not be with us long, but they would return again; and he, the most injurious of the whole, his child's worst enemy, would still remain. I could endure it for myself, but for my son it must be borne no longer: the world's opinion and the feelings of my friends must be alike unheeded here, at least, alike unable to deter me from my duty. But where should I find an asylum, and how obtain subsistence for us both? Oh, I would take my precious charge at early dawn, take the coach to M——, flee to the port of ——, cross the Atlantic, and seek a quiet, humble home in New England, where I would support myself and him by the labour of my hands. The palette and the easel, my darling playmates once, must be my sober toil-fellows now. But was I sufficiently skilful as an artist to obtain my livelihood in a strange land, without friends and without recommendation? No; I must wait a little; I must labour hard to improve my talent and to produce something worth while as a specimen of my powers, something to speak favourably for me, whether as an actual painter or a teacher. Brilliant success, of course, I did not look for, but some degree of security from positive failure was indispensable—I must not take my son to starve. And then I must have money for the journey, the passage, and some little to support us in our retreat in case I should be unsuccessful at first; and not too little either, for who could tell how long I might have to struggle with the indifference or neglect of others, or my own inexperience, or inability to suit their tastes?

What should I do then? Apply to my brother, and explain my circumstances and my resolves to him? No, no; even if I told him *all* my grievances, which I should be very reluctant to do, he would be certain to disapprove of the step: it would seem like madness to him, as it would to my uncle and aunt, or to Milicent. No; I must have patience and gather a hoard of my own. Rachel should be my only confidant—I thought I could persuade her into the scheme; and she should help me, first to find out a picture dealer in some distant town; then, through her means, I would privately sell what pictures I had on hand that would do for such a purpose, and some of those I should thereafter paint. Besides this, I would contrive to dispose of my jewels—not the family jewels, but the few I brought with me from home, and those my uncle gave me on my marriage. A few months' arduous toil might well be borne by me, with such an end in view; and in the interim, my son could not be much more injured than he was already.

Having formed this resolution, I immediately set to work to accomplish it. I might possibly have been induced to wax cool upon it afterwards, or perhaps, to keep weighing the pros and cons in my mind till the latter overbalanced the former, and I was driven to relinquish the project altogether, or delay the execution of it to an indefinite period,—had not something occurred to confirm me in that determination to which I still adhere, which I still think I did well to form, and shall do better to execute.

Since Lord Lowborough's departure, I had regarded the library as entirely my own, a secure retreat at all hours of the day. None of our gentlemen had the smallest pretensions to a literary taste, except Mr. Hargrave; and he, at present, was quite contented with the newspapers and periodicals of the day. And if, by any chance, he should look in here, I felt assured he would soon depart on seeing me, for, instead of becoming less cool and distant towards me, he had become decidedly more so since the departure of his mother and sisters, which was just what I wished. Here, then, I set up my easel, and here I worked at my canvass from daylight till dusk, with very little intermission saving when pure necessity, or my duties to little Arthur called me away—for I still thought proper to devote some portion of every day exclusively to his instruction and amusement. But contrary to my expectation, on the third morning, while I was thus employed, Mr. Hargrave *did* look in, and did *not* immediately withdraw on seeing me. He apologized for his intrusion, and said he was only come for a book; but when he had got it, he condescended to cast a glance over my picture. Being a man of taste, he had something to say on this subject as well as another, and having modestly commented on it, without much encouragement from me, he proceeded to expatiate on the art in general. Receiving no encouragement in that either, he dropped it, but did not depart.

"You don't give us much of your company, Mrs. Huntingdon," observed he, after a brief pause, during which I went on coolly mixing and tempering my colours; "and I cannot wonder at it, for you must be heartily sick of us all. I myself am so thoroughly ashamed of my companions, and so weary of their irrational conversation and pursuits—now that there is no one to humanize them and keep them in check, since you have justly abandoned us to our own devices—that I think I shall presently withdraw from amongst them—probably within this week—and I cannot suppose you will regret my departure."

He paused. I did not answer.

"Probably," he added, with a smile, "your only regret on the subject will be, that I do not take all my companions along with me. I flatter myself, at times, that though among them, I am not of them; but it is natural that you should be glad to get rid of me. I may regret this, but I cannot blame you for it."

"I shall not rejoice at *your* departure, for you *can* conduct yourself like a gentleman," said I, thinking it but right to make some acknowledgment for his good behaviour, "but I must confess I shall rejoice to bid adieu to the rest, inhospitable as it may appear."

"No one can blame you for such an avowal," replied he gravely; "not even the gentlemen themselves, I imagine. I'll just tell you," he continued, as if actuated by a sudden resolution, "what was said last night in the dining-room, after you left us—perhaps you will not mind it as you're so *very* philosophical on certain points," he added with a slight sneer. "They were talking about Lord Lowborough and his delectable lady, the cause of whose sudden departure is no secret amongst them; and her character is so well known to them all, that, nearly related to me as she is, I could not attempt to defend it.—God curse me," he muttered, *par parenthése*,[1] "if I don't have vengeance for this! If the villain *must* disgrace the family, must he blazon it abroad to every low-bred knave of his acquaintance?—I beg your pardon, Mrs. Huntingdon. Well, they were talking of these things, and some of them remarked that, as she was separated from her husband, he might see her again when he pleased."

"'Thank you,' said he; 'I've had enough of her for the present: I'll not trouble to see her, unless she comes to me.'

"'Then what do you mean to do, Huntingdon, when we're gone?' said Ralph Hattersley. 'Do you mean to turn from the error of your ways, and be a good husband, a good father, and so forth—as I do, when I get shut of you and all these rollicking devils you call your friends? I think it's time; and your wife is fifty times too good for you, you *know*—'

"And he added some praise of you, which you would not thank me for repeating—nor him for uttering; proclaiming it aloud, as he did, without delicacy or discrimination, in an audience where it seemed profanation to utter your name—himself utterly incapable of understanding or appreciating your real excellencies. Huntingdon meanwhile, sat quietly drinking his wine, or looking smilingly into his glass and offering no interruption or reply, till Hattersley shouted out,—

"'Do you hear me, man?'

"'Yes, go on,' said he.

"'Nay, I've done,' replied the other: 'I only want to know if you intend to take my advice.'

"'What advice?'

"'To turn over a new leaf, you double-dyed scoundrel,' shouted Ralph, 'and beg your wife's pardon, and be a good boy for the future.'

"'My wife! what wife? I have no wife,' replied Huntingdon, looking innocently up from his glass—'or if I have, look you gentlemen, I value her so highly that any one among you, that can fancy her, may have her and welcome—you may, by Jove and my blessing into the bargain!'

"I—hem—some one asked if he really meant what he said, upon which, he solemnly swore he did, and no mistake.—What do you think of that, Mrs. Huntingdon?" asked Mr. Hargrave, after a short pause, during which I had felt he was keenly examining my half-averted face.

"I say," replied I, calmly, "that what he prizes so lightly, will not be long in his possession."

---

1 Parenthetically.

"You cannot mean that you will break your heart and die for the detestable conduct of an infamous villain like that!"

"By no means: my heart is too thoroughly dried to be broken in a hurry, and I mean to live as long as I can."

"Will you leave him then!"

"Yes."

"When—and how?" asked he, eagerly.

"*When* I am ready, and *how* I can manage it most effectually."

"But your child?"

"My child goes with me."

"He will not allow it."

"I shall not ask him."

"Ah, then, it is a secret flight you meditate!—but with whom, Mrs. Huntingdon?"

"With my son—and, possibly, his nurse."

"Alone—and unprotected! But where can you go? What can you do? He will follow you and bring you back."

"I have laid my plans too well for that. Let me once get clear of Grassdale, and I shall consider myself safe."

Mr. Hargrave advanced one step towards me, looked me in the face, and drew in his breath to speak; but that look, that heightened colour, that sudden sparkle of the eye made my blood rise in wrath: I abruptly turned away, and, snatching up my brush, began to dash away at my canvass with rather too much energy for the good of the picture.

"Mrs. Huntingdon," said he with bitter solemnity, "you are cruel—cruel to me—cruel to yourself."

"Mr. Hargrave, remember your promise."

"I *must* speak—my heart will burst if I don't! I have been silent long enough—and you *must* hear me!" cried he boldly intercepting my retreat to the door. "You tell me you owe no allegiance to your husband; he openly declares himself weary of you, and calmly gives you up to any body that will take you; you are about to leave him; no one will believe that you go alone—all the world will say, 'She has left him at last, and who can wonder at it? Few can blame her, fewer still can pity him; but who is the companion of her flight?' Thus you will have no credit for your virtue (if you call it such): even your best friends will not believe in it; because, it is monstrous, and not to be credited—but by those who suffer from the effects of it, such cruel torments that they know it to be indeed reality.—But what can you do in the cold, rough world alone? you, a young and inexperienced woman, delicately nurtured, and utterly—"

"In a word, you would advise me to stay where I am," interrupted I. "Well, I'll see about it."

"By *all means*, leave him!" cried he earnestly, "but NOT alone! Helen! let *me* protect you!"

"Never!—while heaven spares my reason," replied I, snatching away the hand he had presumed to seize and press between his own. But he was in for it now; he had fairly broken the barrier: he was completely roused, and determined to hazard all for victory.

"I must not be denied!" exclaimed he vehemently; and seizing both my hands, he held them very tight, but dropped upon his knee, and looked up in my face with a half-imploring, half-imperious gaze. "You have no reason now: you are flying in the face of heaven's decrees. God has designed me to be your comfort and protector—I feel it—I know it as certainly as if a voice from heaven declared 'Ye twain shall be one flesh'[1]—and you spurn me from you—"

"Let me go, Mr. Hargrave!" said I sternly. But he only tightened his grasp.

"Let me go!" I repeated, quivering with indignation.

His face was almost opposite the window as he knelt. With a slight start, I saw him glance towards it; and then a gleam of malicious triumph lit up his countenance. Looking over my shoulder, I beheld a shadow just retiring round the corner.

"That is Grimsby," said he deliberately.

"He will report what he has seen to Huntingdon and all the rest, with such embellishments as he thinks proper. He has no love for you, Mrs. Huntingdon—no reverence for your sex—no belief in virtue—no admiration for its image. He will give such a version of this story as will leave no doubt at all, about your character, in the minds of those who hear it. Your fair fame is gone; and nothing that I or you can say can ever retrieve it. But give me the power to protect you, and show me the villain that dares to insult!"

"No one has ever dared to insult me as you are doing now!" said I, at length releasing my hands, and recoiling from him.

"I do not insult you," cried he: "I worship you. You are my angel—my divinity! I lay my powers at your feet—and you must and shall accept them!" he exclaimed impetuously, starting to his feet—"I *will* be your consoler and defender! and if your conscience upbraid you for it, say I overcame you and you could not choose but yield!"

---

1   A portion of the marriage service in the *Book of Common Prayer* that echoes the language of Matthew 19:5, Mark 10:8, and Ephesians 5:31. The marriage service reads, "He that loveth his own wife loveth himself: for no man ever yet hated his own flesh, but nourisheth and cherisheth it, even as the Lord the Church: for we are members of his body, of his flesh, and of his bones. For this cause shall a man leave father and mother, and shall be joined unto his wife; and they two shall be one flesh."

I never saw a man so terribly excited. He precipitated himself towards me. I snatched up my palette-knife and held it against him. This startled him: he stood and gazed at me in astonishment; I dare say I looked as fierce and resolute as he. I moved to the bell and put my hand upon the cord. This tamed him still more. With a half-authoritative, half-deprecating wave of the hand, he sought to deter me from ringing.

"Stand off, then!" said I. He stepped back—"And listen to me.—I don't like you," I continued, as deliberately and emphatically as I could, to give the greater efficacy to my words; "and if I were divorced from my husband—or if he were dead, I would not marry you. There now! I hope you're satisfied."

His face grew blanched with anger.

"I *am* satisfied," he replied with bitter emphasis, "that you are the most cold-hearted, unnatural, ungrateful woman I ever yet beheld!"

"Ungrateful sir?"

"Ungrateful."

"No, Mr. Hargrave; I am not. For all the good you ever did me, or ever wished to do, I most sincerely thank you: for all the evil you have done me, and all you would have done, I pray God to pardon you, and make you of a better mind."

Here the door was thrown open, and Messrs. Huntingdon and Hattersley appeared without. The latter remained in the hall, busy with his ram-rod and his gun; the former walked in, and stood with his back to the fire, surveying Mr. Hargrave and me, particularly the former, with a smile of insupportable meaning, accompanied as it was, by the impudence of his brazen brow and the sly, malicious twinkle of his eye.

"Well, sir?" said Hargrave interrogatively, and with the air of one prepared to stand on the defensive.

"Well, sir," returned his host.

"We want to know if you're at liberty to join us in a go at the pheasants, Walter," interposed Hattersley from without. "Come! there shall be nothing shot besides, except a puss[1] or two; *I'll* vouch for that."

Walter did not answer, but walked to the window to collect his faculties. Arthur uttered a low whistle, and followed him with his eyes. A slight flush of anger rose to Hargrave's cheek; but in a moment, he turned calmly round, and said carelessly—

"I came here to bid farewell to Mrs. Huntingdon, and tell her I must go tomorrow."

"Humph! You're mighty sudden in your resolution. What takes you off so soon, may I ask?"

---

1 Hare.

"Business," returned he, repelling the other's incredulous sneer with a glance of scornful defiance.

"Very good," was the reply; and Hargrave walked away. Thereupon, Mr. Huntingdon, gathering his coat laps under his arms, and setting his shoulder against the mantle-piece, turned to me, and, addressing me in a low voice, scarcely above his breath, poured forth a volley of the vilest and grossest abuse it was possible for the imagination to conceive or the tongue to utter. I did not attempt to interrupt him; but my spirit kindled within me, and when he had done, I replied—

"If your accusation were true, Mr. Huntingdon, how *dare you* blame me?"

"She's hit it, by Jove!" cried Hattersley, rearing his gun against the wall; and, stepping into the room, he took his precious friend by the arm, and attempted to drag him away. "Come, my lad," he muttered; "true or false, *you've* no right to blame her, you *know*—nor him either; after what you said last night. So come along."

There was something implied here that I could not endure.

"Dare you suspect me, Mr. Hattersley?" said I, almost beside myself with fury.

"Nay, nay, I suspect nobody. It's all right—it's all right. So come along Huntingdon, you blackguard."

"She can't deny it!" cried the gentleman thus addressed, grinning in mingled rage and triumph. "She can't deny it if her life depended on it!" and muttering some more abusive language, he walked into the hall, and took up his hat and gun from the table.

"I scorn to justify myself to you!" said I. "But you," turning to Hattersley, "if you presume to have any doubts on the subject, ask Mr. Hargrave."

At this, they simultaneously burst into a rude laugh that made my whole frame tingle to the finger's ends.

"Where is he? I'll ask him myself!" said I, advancing towards them.

Suppressing a new burst of merriment, Hattersley pointed to the outer door. It was half open. His brother-in-law was standing on the front without.

"Mr. Hargrave, will you please to step this way?" said I.

He turned and looked at me in grave surprise.

"Step this way, if you please!" I repeated, in so determined a manner that he could not, or did not choose to resist its authority. Somewhat reluctantly he ascended the steps and advanced a pace or two into the hall.

"And tell those gentlemen," I continued—"these *men* whether or not I yielded to your solicitations."

"I don't understand you, Mrs. Huntingdon."

"You *do* understand me, sir; and I charge you upon your honour as a gentleman, (if you have any), to answer truly. Did I, or did I not?"

"No," muttered he, turning away.

"Speak up sir; they can't hear you. Did I grant your request?"

"You did not."

"No, I'll be sworn she didn't," said Hattersley, "or he'd never look so black."

"I'm willing to grant you the satisfaction of a gentleman, Huntingdon," said Mr. Hargrave, calmly addressing his host, but with a bitter sneer upon his countenance.

"Go to the deuce!" replied the latter, with an impatient jerk of the head. Hargrave withdrew with a look of cold disdain, saying,—

"You know where to find me, should you feel disposed to send a friend." Muttered oaths and curses were all the answer this intimation obtained.

"Now Huntingdon, you see!" said Hattersley, "clear as the day."

"I don't care *what* he sees," said I, "or what he imagines; but you, Mr. Hattersley, when you hear my name belied and slandered, will you defend it?"

"I will. Blast me if I don't!"

I instantly departed, and shut myself into the library. What could possess me to make such a request of such a man? I cannot tell, but drowning men catch at straws: they had driven me desperate between them; I hardly knew what I said. There was no other to preserve my name from being blackened and aspersed among this nest of boon companions, and through them, perhaps into the world; and beside my abandoned wretch of a husband, the base, malignant Grimsby, and the false villain Hargrave, this boarish ruffian, coarse and brutal as he was, shone like a glow-worm in the dark, among its fellow worms.[1]

What a scene was this! Could I ever have imagined that I should be doomed to bear such insults under my own roof—to hear such things spoken in my presence—nay spoken *to* me and *of* me—and by those who arrogated to themselves the name of gentlemen? And could I have imagined that I should have been able to endure it as calmly, and to repel their insults as firmly and as boldly as I had done? A hardness such as this, is taught by rough experience and despair alone.

Such thoughts as these, chased one another through my mind, as I paced to and fro the room, and longed—oh, *how* I longed to take my child and leave them now, without an hour's delay! But it could not be: there was work before me—hard work, that must be done.

---

1   "Worms" was a way for the devout to refer to human beings; St John Rivers also refers to people as "feeble fellow-worms" in *Jane Eyre* (500). Similar to Anne Brontë's revision of Charlotte Brontë's pious Helen Burns with a much more realistic depiction of Christian faith in Helen Huntingdon, Anne Brontë's use of "fellow worms" here is also darker and lacks the hyperbole of St John Rivers's assessment of all humans as "worms."

"Then let me do it," said I, "and lose not a moment in vain repinings, and idle chafings against my fate, and those who influence it."

And conquering my agitation with a powerful effort, I immediately resumed my task, and laboured hard all day.

Mr. Hargrave did depart on the morrow; and I have never seen him since. The others stayed on for two or three weeks longer; but I kept aloof from them as much as possible, and still continued my labour, and have continued it, with almost unabated ardour, to the present day. I soon acquainted Rachel with my design, confiding all my motives and intentions to her ear, and much to my agreeable surprise, found little difficulty in persuading her to enter into my views. She is a sober, cautious woman, but she so hates her master, and so loves her mistress and her nursling, that after several ejaculations, a few faint objections, and many tears and lamentations that I should be brought to such a pass, she applauded my resolution and consented to aid me with all her might—on one condition, only—that she might share my exile: otherwise, she was utterly inexorable, regarding it as perfect madness for me and Arthur to go alone. With touching generosity, she modestly offered to aid me with her little hoard of savings, hoping I would "excuse her for the liberty, but really if I would do her the favour to accept it as a loan, she should be very happy." Of course I could not think of such a thing;—but now, thank Heaven, I have gathered a little hoard of my own, and my preparations are so far advanced, that I am looking forward to a speedy emancipation. Only let the stormy severity of this winter weather be somewhat abated, and then, some morning, Mr. Huntingdon will come down to a solitary breakfast-table, and perhaps be clamouring through the house for his invisible wife and child, when they are some fifty miles on their way to the western world—or it may be more, for we shall leave him hours before the dawn, and it is not probable he will discover the loss of both, until the day is far advanced.

I am fully alive to the evils that may, and must result upon the step I am about to take; but I never waver in my resolution, because I never forget my son. It was only this morning—while I pursued my usual employment, he was sitting at my feet, quietly playing with the shreds of canvass I had thrown upon the carpet—but his mind was otherwise occupied, for, in a while, he looked up wistfully in my face, and gravely asked—

"Mamma, why are you wicked?"

"Who told you I was wicked, love?"

"Rachel."

"No Arthur, Rachel never said so, I am certain."

"Well then, it was papa," replied he thoughtfully. Then, after a reflective pause, he added, "At least, I'll tell you how it was I got to know: when I'm with papa, if I say mamma wants me, or mamma says I'm not to do something that he tells me to do—he always says, 'Mamma be damned,'—and Rachel says it's only wicked people that are damned. So mamma, that's why I think you must be wicked—and I wish you wouldn't."

"My dear child, I am not. Those are bad words, and wicked people often say them of others better than themselves. Those words cannot make people be damned, nor show that they deserve it. God will judge us by our own thoughts and deeds, not by what others say about us. And when you hear such words spoken, Arthur, remember never to repeat them: it is wicked to say such things of others, not to have them said against you."

"Then it's papa that's wicked," said he, ruefully.

"Papa is wrong to say such things, and you will be very wrong to imitate him, now that you know better."

"What *is* imitate?"

"To do as he does."

"Does *he* know better?"

"Perhaps he does; but that is nothing to you."

"If he doesn't, you ought to tell him, mamma."

"I *have* told him."

The little moralist paused and pondered. I tried in vain to divert his mind from the subject.

"I'm sorry papa's wicked," said he mournfully, at length, "for I don't want him to go to hell." And so saying he burst into tears.

I consoled him with the hope that perhaps his papa would alter and become good before he died—but is it not time to deliver him from such a parent?

CHAPTER XL
A MISADVENTURE

JAN. 10th, 1827. While writing the above, yesterday evening, I sat in the drawing-room. Mr. Huntingdon was present, but, as I thought, asleep on the sofa behind me. He had risen however, unknown to me, and, actuated by some base spirit of curiosity, been looking over my shoulder for I know not how long; for when I had laid aside my pen, and was about to close the book, he suddenly placed his hand upon it, and saying—"With your leave, my dear, I'll have a look at this," forcibly wrested it from me, and, drawing a chair to the table, composedly sat down to examine it—turning back leaf after leaf to find an explanation of what he had read. Unluckily for me, he was more sober that night than he usually is at such an hour.

Of course I did not leave him to pursue this occupation in quiet: I made several attempts to snatch the book from his hands, but he held it too firmly for that; I upbraided him in bitterness and scorn for his mean and dishonour-able conduct, but that had no effect upon him; and, finally, I extinguished both the candles, but he only wheeled round to the fire, and raising a blaze sufficient for his purposes, calmly continued the investigation. I had serious thoughts of getting a pitcher of water and extinguishing that light too; but it was evident his curiosity was too keenly excited to be quenched by that, and the more I manifested my anxiety to baffle his scrutiny, the greater would be his determination to persist in it—besides it was too late.

"It seems very interesting, love," said he, lifting his head and turning to where I stood wringing my hands in silent rage and anguish; "but it's rather long; I'll look at it some other time;—and meanwhile, I'll trouble you for your keys, my dear."

"What keys?"

"The keys of your cabinet, desk, drawers, and whatever else you possess," said he, rising and holding out his hand.

"I've not got them," I replied. The key of my desk, in fact, was, at that moment, in the lock, and the others were attached to it.

"Then you must send for them," said he; "and if that old bitch, Rachel, doesn't immediately deliver them up, she tramps bag and baggage tomorrow."

"She doesn't know where they are," I answered, quietly placing my hand upon them, and taking them from the desk, as I thought, unobserved. "*I* know, but I shall not give them up without a reason."

"And *I* know, too," said he, suddenly seizing my closed hand and rudely abstracting them from it. He then took up one of the candles and relighted it by thrusting it into the fire.

"Now then," sneered he, "we must have a confiscation of property. But first, let us take a peep into the studio."

And putting the keys into his pocket, he walked into the library. I fol-lowed, whether with the dim idea of preventing mischief or only to know the worst I can hardly tell. My painting materials were laid together on the corner table, ready for tomorrow's use, and only covered with a cloth. He soon spied them out, and putting down the candle, deliberately proceeded to cast them into the fire—palette, paints, bladders,[1] pencils, brushes, varnish—I saw them all consumed—the palette knives snapped in two—the oil and turpentine sent hissing and roaring up the chimney. He then rang the bell.

"Benson, take those things away," said he, pointing to the easel, canvass, and stretcher;[2] "and tell the housemaid she may kindle the fire with them: your mistress won't want them any more."

---

1 A container for artist's paints that used to be made from animal bladders.

2 "A frame upon which an artist's canvas is spread and drawn tight by means of corner-pieces or wedges" (*OED*).

Benson paused aghast and looked at me.

"Take them away, Benson," said I; and his master muttered an oath.

"And this and all, sir?" said the astonished servant referring to the half-finished picture.

"That and all," replied the master; and the things were cleared away.

Mr. Huntingdon then went up stairs. I did not attempt to follow him, but remained seated in the arm-chair, speechless, tearless, and almost motionless, till he returned about half an hour after, and walking up to me, held the candle in my face and peered into my eyes with looks and laughter too insulting to be borne. With a sudden stroke of my hand, I dashed the candle to the floor.

"Hal-lo!" muttered he, starting back.—"She's the very devil for spite! Did *ever* any mortal see such eyes?—they shine in the dark like a cat's. *Oh*, you're a sweet one!" so saying, he gathered up the candle and the candlestick. The former being broken as well as extinguished, he rang for another.

"Benson, your mistress has broken the candle: bring another."

"You expose yourself finely," observed I as the man departed.

"I didn't say *I'd* broken it, did I?" returned he. He then threw my keys into my lap, saying,—"There! You'll find nothing gone but your money, and the jewels—and a few little trifles I thought it advisable to take into my own possession, lest your mercantile spirit should be tempted to turn them into gold. I've left you a few sovereigns in your purse, which I expect to last you through the month—at all events, when you want more you will be so good as to give me an account of how that's spent. I shall put you upon a small monthly allowance, in future, for your own private expenses; and you needn't trouble yourself anymore about my concerns; I shall look out for a steward, my dear; I won't expose you to the temptation. And as for the household matters, Mrs. Greaves must be very particular in keeping her accounts: we must go upon an entirely new plan—"

"What great discovery have you made *now*, Mr. Huntingdon? Have I attempted to defraud you?"

"Not in money matters, exactly, it seems, but it's best to keep out of the way of temptation."

Here Benson entered with the candles, and there followed a brief interval of silence—I sitting still in my chair, and he standing with his back to the fire, silently triumphing in my despair.

"And so," said he at length, "you thought to disgrace me, did you, by running away and turning artist, and supporting yourself by the labour of your hands, forsooth? And you thought to rob me of my son too, and bring him up to be a dirty Yankee tradesman, or a low, beggarly painter?"

"Yes, to obviate his becoming such a gentleman as his father."

"It's well you couldn't keep your own secret—ha, ha! It's well these women must be blabbing—if they haven't a friend to talk to, they must whisper their secrets to the fishes, or write them on the sand or something; and it's well too I wasn't over full tonight, now I think of it, or I might have snoozed away and never dreamt of looking what my sweet lady was about—or I might have lacked the sense or the power to carry my point like a man, as I have done."

Leaving him to his self-congratulations, I rose to secure my manuscript, for I now remembered it had been left upon the drawing-room table, and I determined, if possible, to save myself the humiliation of seeing it in his hands again. I could not bear the idea of his amusing himself over my secret thoughts and recollections; though, to be sure, he would find little good of himself therein indited, except in the former part—and oh, I would sooner burn it all than he should read what I had written when I was such a fool as to love him!

"And by the by," cried he as I was leaving the room, "you'd better tell that d—d old sneak of a nurse to keep out of my way for a day or two—I'd pay her her wages and send her packing tomorrow, but I know she'd do more mischief out of the house than in it."

And as I departed, he went on cursing and abusing my faithful friend and servant with epithets I will not defile this paper with repeating. I went to her as soon as I had put away my book, and told her how our project was defeated. She was as much distressed and horrified as I was—and more so than I was that night, for I was partly stunned by the blow, and partly excited and supported against it by the bitterness of my wrath. But in the morning, when I woke without that cheering hope that had been my secret comfort and support so long, and all this day, when I have wandered about restless and objectless, shunning my husband, shrinking even from my child—knowing that I am unfit to be his teacher or companion, hoping nothing for his future life, and fervently wishing he had never been born—I felt the full extent of my calamity—and I feel it now. I know that day after day such feelings will return upon me: I am a slave, a prisoner—but that is nothing if it were myself alone, I would not complain, but I am forbidden to rescue my son from ruin, and what was once my only consolation, is become the crowning source of my despair.

Have I no faith in God? I try to look to him and raise my heart to Heaven, but it will cleave to the dust:[1] I can only say—"He hath hedged me about, that I cannot get out: he hath made my chain heavy.[2] He hath filled

---

1   See Psalm 119:25: "My soul cleaveth unto the dust; quicken thou me according to thy word."

2   Lamentations 3:7.

me with bitterness, he hath made me drunken with wormwood:"[1]—I forget to add—"But though he cause grief, yet will he have compassion according to the multitude of his mercies. For he doth not afflict willingly nor grieve the children of men."[2] I ought to think of this; and if there be nothing but sorrow for me in this world, what is the longest life of misery to a whole eternity of peace? And for my little Arthur—has he no friend but me? Who was it said, "It is not the will of your Father which is in Heaven that one of these little ones should perish?"[3]

CHAPTER XLI
"HOPE SPRINGS ETERNAL IN THE HUMAN BREAST"[4]

MARCH 20th.—Having now got rid of Mr. Huntingdon for a season, my spirits begin to revive. He left me early in February; and the moment he was gone, I breathed again, and felt my vital energy return; not with the hope of escape—he has taken care to leave me no visible chance of that—but with a determination to make the best of existing circumstances. Here was Arthur left to me at last; and rousing from my despondent apathy, I exerted all my powers to eradicate the weeds that had been fostered in his infant mind, and sow again the good seed they had rendered unproductive. Thank Heaven, it is not a barren or a stony soil;[5] if weeds spring fast there, so do better plants. His apprehensions are more quick, his heart more overflowing with affection than ever his father's could have been; and it is no hopeless task to bend him to obedience and win him to love and know his own true friend, as long as there is no one to counteract my efforts.

I had much trouble at first in breaking him of those evil habits his father had taught him to acquire, but already that difficulty is nearly vanquished now: bad language seldom defiles his mouth, and I have succeeded in giving him an absolute disgust for all intoxicating liquors, which I hope not even his father or his father's friends will be able to overcome. He was inordinately fond of them for so young a creature, and, remembering my unfortunate father as well as his, I dreaded the consequences of such a taste. But if I had stinted him in his usual quantity of wine or forbidden him to taste it

---

1 Lamentations 3:15.

2 Lamentations 3:32–33.

3 Matthew 18:14.

4 Alexander Pope (1688–1744), *An Essay on Man* (1733), I, 95.

5 See the Parable of the Sower recounted in Matthew 13:18–23 and Mark 4:1–20 for the ideas and the extended metaphor of sowing that Helen uses here to describe educating her son.

altogether, that would only have increased his partiality for it, and made him regard it as a greater treat than ever. I therefore gave him quite as much as his father was accustomed to allow him—as much indeed, as he desired to have, but into every glass I surreptitiously introduced a small quantity of tartar-emetic[1]—just enough to produce inevitable nausea and depression without positive sickness. Finding such disagreeable consequences invariably to result from this indulgence, he soon grew weary of it, but the more he shrank from the daily treat the more I pressed it upon him, till his reluctance was strengthened to perfect abhorrence. When he was thoroughly disgusted with every kind of wine, I allowed him, at his own request, to try brandy and water and then gin and water; for the little toper[2] was familiar with them all, and I was determined that all should be equally hateful to him. This I have now effected; and since he declares that the taste, the smell, the sight of any one of them is sufficient to make him sick, I have given up teasing him about them, except now and then as objects of terror in cases of misbehaviour: "Arthur, if you're not a good boy I shall give you a glass of wine," or "Now Arthur, if you say that again you shall have some brandy and water," is as good as any other threat; and, once or twice, when he was sick, I have obliged the poor child to swallow a little wine and water *without* the tartar-emetic, by way of medicine; and this practice I intend to continue for some time to come; not that I think it of any real service in a physical sense, but because I am determined to enlist all the powers of association in my service:[3] I wish this aversion to be so deeply grounded in his nature that nothing in after life may be able to overcome it.

Thus, I flatter myself, I shall secure him from this one vice; and for the rest, if on his father's return I find reason to apprehend that my good lessons will be all destroyed—if Mr. Huntingdon commence again the game of teaching the child to hate and despise his mother and emulate his father's wickedness, I will yet deliver my son from his hands. I have devised another scheme that might be resorted to in such a case, and if I could but obtain my brother's consent and assistance, I should not doubt of its success. The old hall where he and I were born and where our mother died, is not now inhabited, nor yet quite sunk into decay, as I believe. Now if I could persuade him to have one or two rooms made habitable and to let them to me as a stranger, I might live there, with my child, under an assumed name, and still support myself by my favourite art. He should lend me the money to begin

---

1 A powder used to set dyes that was also used medically to induce vomiting or coughing.

2 "One who ... drinks a great deal" (*OED*).

3 Helen is using the principles of associationist psychology—the precursor to behaviorist psychology—to have Arthur hate alcohol by associating drinking it with the pain of illness.

with, and I would pay him back, and live in lowly independence and strict seclusion, for the house stands in a lonely place, and the neighbourhood is thinly inhabited, and he himself should negotiate the sale of my pictures for me. I have arranged the whole plan in my head; and all I want, is to persuade Frederick to be of the same mind as myself. He is coming to see me soon, and then I will make the proposal to him, having first enlightened him upon my circumstances sufficiently to excuse the project.

Already, I believe, he knows much more of my situation than I have told him. I can tell this by the air of tender sadness pervading his letters; and by the fact of his so seldom mentioning my husband, and generally evincing a kind of covert bitterness when he does refer to him; as well as by the circumstances of his never coming to see me when Mr. Huntingdon is at home. But he has never openly expressed any disapprobation of him or sympathy for me; he has never asked any questions, or said anything to invite my confidence. Had he done so, I should probably have had but few concealments from him. Perhaps, he feels hurt at my reserve. He is a strange being—I wish we knew each other better. He used to spend a month at Staningley every year, before I was married; but, since our father's death, I have only seen him once, when he came for a few days while Mr. Huntingdon was away. He shall stay many days this time, and there shall be more candour and cordiality between us than ever there was before, since our early childhood: my heart clings to him more than ever; and my soul is sick of solitude.

April 16th.—He is come and gone. He would not stay above a fortnight. The time passed quickly, but very, very happily, and it has done me good. I must have a bad disposition, for my misfortunes have soured and embittered me exceedingly: I was beginning insensibly to cherish very unamiable feelings against my fellow mortals—the male part of them especially; but it is a comfort to see there is at least one among them worthy to be trusted and esteemed; and doubtless there are more, though I have never known them—unless I accept poor Lord Lowborough, and he was bad enough in his day; but what would Frederick have been, if he had lived in the world, and mingled from his childhood with such men as these of my acquaintance? and what *will* Arthur be, with all his natural sweetness of disposition, if I do not save him from that world and those companions? I mentioned my fears to Frederick and introduced the subject of my plan of rescue on the evening after his arrival, when I presented my little son to his uncle.

"He is like you, Frederick," said I, "in some of his moods: I sometimes think he resembles you more than his father; and I am glad of it."

"You flatter me, Helen," replied he, stroking the child's soft, wavy locks.

"No,—you will think it no compliment when I tell you I would rather have him to resemble *Benson* than his father."

He slightly elevated his eyebrows, but said nothing.

"Do you know what sort of man Mr. Huntingdon is?" said I.

"I think I have an idea."

"Have you so clear an idea that you can hear, without surprise or disapproval, that I meditate escaping with that child to some secret asylum where we can live in peace and never see him again?"

"Is it really so?"

"If you have not," continued I, "I'll tell you something more about him"—and I gave a sketch of his general conduct, and a more particular account of his behaviour with regard to his child, and explained my apprehensions on the latter's account, and my determination to deliver him from his father's influence.

Frederick was exceedingly indignant against Mr. Huntingdon, and very much grieved for me; but still, he looked upon my project as wild and impracticable; he deemed my fears for Arthur disproportioned to the circumstances, and opposed so many objections to my plan, and devised so many milder methods for ameliorating my condition, that I was obliged to enter into further details to convince him that my husband was utterly incorrigible, and that nothing could persuade him to give up his son whatever became of me, he being as fully determined the child should not leave him, as I was not to leave the child; and that, in fact, nothing would answer but this, unless I fled the country as I had intended before. To obviate that, he at length consented to have one wing of the old Hall put into a habitable condition, as a place of refuge against a time of need; but hoped I would not take advantage of it, unless circumstances should render it really necessary, which I was ready enough to promise; for, though, for my own sake, such a hermitage appears like paradise itself compared with my present situation, yet for my friends' sakes—for Milicent and Esther, my sisters in heart and affection, for the poor tenants of Grassdale, and above all for my aunt—I will stay if I possibly can.

July 29th.—Mrs. Hargrave and her daughter are come back from London. Esther is full of her first season in town; but she is still heart-whole and unengaged. Her mother sought out an excellent match for her, and even brought the gentleman to lay his heart and fortune at her feet; but Esther had the audacity to refuse the noble gifts. He was a man of good family and large possessions, but the naughty girl maintained he was old as Adam, ugly as sin, and hateful as —— one who shall be nameless.

"But indeed, I had a hard time of it," said she: "mamma was very greatly disappointed at the failure of her darling project, and very, very angry at my obstinate resistance to her will,—and is so still; but I can't help it. And Walter, too, is so seriously displeased at my perversity and absurd caprice, as he calls it, that I fear he will never forgive me—I did not think he *could* be so unkind as he has lately shown himself. But Milicent begged me not to yield, and I'm sure, Mrs. Huntingdon, if you had seen the man they wanted to palm upon me, you would have advised me not to take him too."

"I should have done so whether I had seen him or not," said I. "It is enough that you dislike him."

"I knew you would say so; though mamma affirmed you would be quite shocked at my undutiful conduct—you can't imagine how she lectures me—I am disobedient and ungrateful; I am thwarting her wishes, wronging my brother, and making myself a burden on her hands—I sometimes fear she'll overcome me after all. I have a strong will, but so has she, and when she says such bitter things, it provokes me to such a pass that I feel inclined to do as she bids me, and then break my heart and say 'There mamma, it's all your fault!'"

"Pray don't!" said I. "Obedience from such a motive would be positive wickedness, and certain to bring the punishment it deserved. Stand firm, and your mamma will soon relinquish her persecution;—and the gentleman himself will cease to pester you with his addresses if he finds them steadily rejected."

"Oh, no! mamma will weary all about her before she tires herself with her exertions; and as for Mr. Oldfield, she has given him to understand that I have refused his offer, not from any dislike of his person, but merely because I am giddy and young, and cannot at present reconcile myself to the thoughts of marriage under any circumstances: but, by next season, she has no doubt, I shall have more sense, and hopes my girlish fancies will be worn away. So she has brought me home, to school me into a proper sense of my duty, against[1] the time comes round again—indeed, I believe she will not put herself to the expense of taking me up to London again, unless I surrender: she cannot afford to take me to town for pleasure and nonsense, she says, and it is not *every* rich gentleman that will consent to take me without a fortune, whatever exalted ideas I may have of my own attractions."

"Well Esther, I pity you; but still, I repeat, stand firm. You might as well sell yourself to slavery at once, as marry a man you dislike. If your mother and brother are unkind to you, you may leave them, but remember you are bound to your husband for life."[2]

"But I cannot leave them unless I get married, and I cannot get married if nobody sees me. I saw one or two gentlemen in London, that I

---

1   An obscure use of "against" here, meaning "by the time that" or "before" (*OED*).

2   The Matrimonial Causes Act of 1857 enabled women to get divorced, although it was still very difficult. Before that, however, one could only get a divorce by an Act of Parliament or through ecclesiastical courts. See Caroline Norton's *Letter* for more information about this (Appendix D2). See Sarah Lewis's *Woman's Mission* on the importance of making a wise choice in marriage (Appendix C3).

might have liked, but they were younger sons, and mamma would not let me get to know them—one especially, who I believe rather liked me, but she threw every possible obstacle in the way of our better acquaintance—wasn't it provoking?"

"I have no doubt you would feel it so, but it is possible that if you married him, you might have more reason to regret it hereafter, than if you married Mr. Oldfield. When I tell you not to marry *without* love, I do not advise you to marry for love alone—there are many, many other things to be considered. Keep both heart and hand in your own possession, till you see good reason to part with them; and if such an occasion should never present itself, comfort your mind with this reflection: that, though in single life your joys may not be very many, your sorrows, at least will not be more than you can bear. Marriage *may* change your circumstances for the better, but in my private opinion, it is far more likely to produce a contrary result."

"So thinks Milicent, but allow me to say, *I* think otherwise. If I thought myself doomed to oldmaidenhood, I should cease to value my life. The thoughts of living on, year after year at the Grove—a hanger-on upon mamma and Walter—a mere cumberer of the ground,[1] (now that I know in what light they would regard it), is perfectly intolerable—I would rather run away with the butler."

"Your circumstances are peculiar I allow; but have patience, love; do nothing rashly. Remember, you are not yet nineteen, and many years are yet to pass before any one can set you down as an old maid: you cannot tell what Providence may have in store for you. And meantime, remember you have a *right* to the protection and support of your mother and brother, however they may seem to grudge it."

"You are so grave, Mrs. Huntingdon," said Esther after a pause. "When Milicent uttered the same discouraging sentiments concerning marriage, I asked if she was happy: she said she was; but I only half believed her; and now I must put the same question to you."

"It is a very impertinent question," laughed I, "from a young girl to a married woman so many years her senior—and I shall not answer it."

"Pardon me, dear *madam*," said she, laughingly throwing herself into my arms, and kissing me with playful affection; but I felt a tear on my neck, as she dropped her head on my bosom and continued, with an odd mixture

---

1   Esther is echoing the language of the Parable of the Fig Tree, recounted in Luke 13:6–9, which "cumbereth [...] the ground." Esther is very aware of how, like the tree that was not bearing fruit, she could be perceived as useless, "a hanger-on." Brontë here is allying her text—and its commentary on the plight of "excess" women—with the message of the parable and the man who refused to cut the tree down until it had been well fertilized and given at least another year to bear fruit.

of sadness and levity, timidity and audacity,—"I know you are not so happy as I mean to be, for you spend half your life alone at Grassdale, while Mr. Huntingdon goes about enjoying himself where, and how he pleases.—I shall expect *my* husband to have no pleasures but what he shares with me; and if his greatest pleasure of all is not the enjoyment of my company— why—it will be the worse for him—that's all."

"If such are your expectations of matrimony, Esther, you must indeed, be careful whom you marry—or rather, you must avoid it altogether."

CHAPTER XLII
A REFORMATION

SEPT. 1st.—No Mr. Huntingdon yet. Perhaps he will stay among his friends till Christmas; and then, next spring, he will be off again. If he continue this plan, I shall be able to stay at Grassdale well enough—that is, I *shall* be able to stay, and that is enough; even an occasional bevy of friends at the shooting season, may be borne if Arthur gets so firmly attached to me—so well established in good sense and principles, before they come, that I shall be able, by reason and affection, to keep him pure from their contaminations. Vain hope, I fear! but still, till such a time of trial comes, I will forbear to think of my quiet asylum in the beloved old hall.

Mr. and Mrs. Hattersley have been staying at the Grove a fortnight; and as Mr. Hargrave is still absent, and the weather was remarkably fine, I never passed a day without seeing my two friends, Milicent and Esther, either there or here. On one occasion, when Mr. Hattersley had driven them over to Grassdale in the phaeton, with little Helen and Ralph, and we were all enjoying ourselves in the garden—I had a few minutes conversation with that gentleman, while the ladies were amusing themselves with the children.

"Do you want to hear anything of your husband, Mrs. Huntingdon?" said he.

"No, unless you can tell me when to expect him home."

"I can't.—You don't want him, do you?" said he with a broad grin.

"No."

"Well, I think you're better without him, sure enough—for my part, I'm downright weary of him. I told him I'd leave him if he didn't mend his manners—and he wouldn't; so I left him—you see I'm a better man than you think me;—and what's more, I have serious thoughts of washing my hands of him entirely, and the whole set of 'em, and comporting myself from this day forward, with all decency and sobriety as a Christian and the father of a family should do.—What do you think of that?"

"It is a resolution you ought to have formed long ago."

"Well, I'm not thirty yet: it isn't too late, is it?"

"No; it is never too late to reform, as long as you have the sense to desire it, and the strength to execute your purpose."

"Well, to tell you the truth, I've thought of it often and often before, but he's such devilish good company is Huntingdon, after all—you can't imagine what a jovial good-fellow he is when he's not fairly drunk, only just primed or half-seas-over[1]—we all have a bit of a liking for him at the bottom of our hearts, though we can't respect him."

"But should you wish yourself to be like him?"

"No, I'd rather be like myself, bad as I am."

"You can't continue as bad as you are without getting worse—and more brutalized every day—and therefore more like him."

I could not help smiling at the comical, half angry, half confounded look he put on at this rather unusual mode of address.

"Never mind my plain speaking," said I; "it is from the best of motives. But tell me, should you wish your sons to be like Mr. Huntingdon—or even like yourself?"

"Hang it, no."

"Should you wish your daughter to despise you—or, at least, to feel no vestige of respect for you, and no affection but what is mingled with the bitterest regret?"

"Oh, blast it, no! I couldn't stand that."

"And finally, should you wish your wife to be ready to sink into the earth when she hears you mentioned; and to loathe the very sound of your voice, and shudder at your approach?"

"She never will; she likes me all the same, whatever I do."

"Impossible, Mr. Hattersley! you mistake her quiet submission for affection."

"Fire and fury—"

"Now don't burst into a tempest at that—I don't mean to say she does not love you—she does, I know, a great deal better than you deserve—but I am quite sure, that if you behave better, she will love you more, and if you behave worse, she will love you less and less till all is lost in fear, aversion, and bitterness of soul, if not in secret hatred and contempt. But, dropping the subject of affection, should you wish to be the tyrant of her life—to take away all the sunshine from her existence, and make her thoroughly miserable?"

"Of course not; and I don't, and I'm not going to."

"You have done more towards it than you suppose."

"Pooh, pooh! She's not the susceptible, anxious, worriting creature you imagine: she's a little meek, peaceable, affectionate body; apt to be rather

---

1 Half drunk.

sulky at times, but quiet and cool in the main, and ready to take things as they come."

"Think of what she was five years ago, when you married her, and what she is now."

"I know—she was a little plump lassie then, with a pretty pink and white face: now, she's a poor little bit of a creature, fading and melting away like a snow-wreath[1]—but hang it!—by Jupiter, that's not my fault!"

"What is the cause of it then? Not years, for she's only five and twenty."

"It's her own delicate health, and—confound it, madam! what would you make of me?—and the children, to be sure, that worry her to death between them."

"No, Mr. Hattersley, the children give her more pleasure than pain: they are fine well dispositioned children—"

"I know they are—bless 'em!"

"Then why lay the blame on them?—I'll tell you what it is: it's silent fretting and constant anxiety on your account, mingled I suspect, with something of bodily fear on her own. When you behave well, she can only rejoice with trembling; she has no security, no confidence in your judgment or principles; but is continually dreading the close of such short-lived felicity: when you behave ill, her causes of terror and misery are more than any one can tell but herself. In patient endurance of evil, she forgets it is our duty to admonish our neighbours of their transgressions.[2]—Since you *will* mistake her silence for indifference, come with me, and I'll show you one or two of her letters—no breach of confidence, I hope, since you are her other half."

He followed me into the library. I sought out and put into his hands two of Milicent's letters; one dated from London and written during one of his wildest seasons of reckless dissipation; the other in the country during a lucid interval. The former was full of trouble and anguish; not accusing *him*, but deeply regretting his connection with his profligate companions, abusing Mr. Grimsby and others, insinuating bitter things against Mr. Huntingdon, and most ingeniously throwing the blame of her husband's misconduct on to other men's shoulders. The latter was full of hope and joy, yet with a trembling consciousness that this happiness would not last; praising his goodness to the skies, but with an evident, though but half expressed wish that it were based on a surer foundation[3] than the natural impulses of the heart, and a half

---

1   Snow drift.

2   See, for example, Zechariah 8:16, Ephesians 4:25, and Matthew 18:15–16.

3   This "surer foundation" is probably a Christian one, as outlined in 2 Timothy 2:19: "Nevertheless the foundation of God standeth sure, having this seal, The Lord knoweth them that are his. And, Let every one that nameth the name of Christ depart from iniquity."

prophetic dread of the fall of that house so founded on the sand,[1]—which fall had shortly after taken place, as Hattersley must have been conscious while he read.

Almost at the commencement of the first letter, I had the unexpected pleasure of seeing him blush; but he immediately turned his back to me and finished the perusal at the window. At the second, I saw him, once or twice, raise his hand and hurriedly pass it across his face. Could it be to dash away a tear? When he had done, there was an interval spent in clearing his throat and staring out of the window, and then, after whistling a few bars of a favourite air, he turned round, gave me back the letters and silently shook me by the hand.

"I've been a cursed rascal, God knows," said he as he gave it a hearty squeeze, "but you see if I don't make amends for it—G—d d—n me if I don't!"

"Don't curse yourself, Mr. Hattersley; if God had heard half your invocations of that kind, you would have been in hell long before now—and you *cannot* make amends for the past by doing your duty for the future, in as much as your duty is only what you *owe* to your Maker,[2] and you cannot do *more* than fulfill it—another must make amends for your past delinquencies.[3] If you intend to reform, invoke God's blessing, His mercy, and His aid; not His curse."

"God help me, then—for I'm sure I need it.—Where's Milicent?"

"She's there, just coming in with her sister."

He stepped out at the glass door, and went to meet them. I followed at a little distance. Somewhat to his wife's astonishment, he lifted her off from the ground and saluted her with a hearty kiss and a strong embrace; then, placing his two hands on her shoulders, he gave her, I suppose, a sketch of the great things he meant to do, for she suddenly threw her arms round him and burst into tears, exclaiming,—

"Do, do, Ralph—we shall be so happy! How very, very good you are!"

"Nay, not I," said he, turning her round and pushing her towards me. "Thank *her*, it's her doing."

---

1   See Matthew 7:24–27, where Jesus describes a "wise man, which built his house upon a rock. And [when] the floods came, and the winds blew, and beat upon that house; … it fell not: for it was founded upon a rock. And every one that heareth these sayings of mine, and doeth them not, shall be likened unto a foolish man, which built his house upon the sand" (24–26). Davies explains how this "allusion expresses the insecurity of the dependent state of wifehood, whose house is in a literal sense founded upon her husband's character and behaviour" (*PTWH* 528).

2   See Ecclesiastes 12:13: "Fear God, and keep his commandments: for this is the whole duty of man."

3   See Romans 3:21–26 for more information on how Jesus works "to declare [God's] righteousness for the remission of sins that are past" (3:25).

Milicent flew to thank me, overflowing with gratitude. I disclaimed all title to it, telling her her husband was predisposed to amendment before I added my might of exhortation and encouragement, and that I had only done what she might—and ought to[1]—have done herself.

"Oh, no!" cried she, "I couldn't have influenced him, I'm sure, by anything that I could have said. I should only have bothered him by my clumsy efforts at persuasion, if I had made the attempt."

"You never tried me, Milly," said he.

Shortly after, they took their leave. They are now gone on a visit to Hattersley's father. After that, they will repair to their country home. I hope his good resolutions will not fall through, and poor Milicent will not be again disappointed. Her last letter was full of present bliss and pleasing anticipations for the future; but no particular temptation has yet occurred to put his virtue to the test. Henceforth, however, she will doubtless be somewhat less timid and reserved, and he more kind and thoughtful.—Surely, then, her hopes are not unfounded; and I have one bright spot, at least, whereon to rest my thoughts.

CHAPTER XLIII
THE BOUNDARY PAST

OCTOBER 10th.—Mr. Huntingdon returned about three weeks ago. His appearance, his demeanour and conversation, and my feelings with regard to him, I shall not trouble myself to describe. The day after his arrival, however, he surprised me by the announcement of an intention to procure a governess for little Arthur: I told him it was quite unnecessary, not to say ridiculous, at the present season: I thought I was fully competent to the task of teaching him myself—for some years to come, at least: the child's education was the only pleasure and business of my life; and since he had deprived me of every other occupation, he might surely leave me that.

He said I was not fit to teach children, or to be with them: I had already reduced the boy to little better than an automaton, I had broken his fine spirit with my rigid severity; and I should freeze all the sunshine out of his heart, and make him as gloomy an ascetic as myself, if I had the handling of him much longer. And poor Rachel, too, came in for her share of abuse, as usual; he cannot endure Rachel, because he knows she has a proper appreciation of him.

---

1 This belief in a wife's duty to center her husband morally reached its height with Coventry Patmore's (1823–96) "The Angel in the House" (1854) later in the century.

I calmly defended our several qualifications as nurse and governess, and still resisted the proposed addition to our family; but he cut me short by saying, it was no use bothering about the matter, for he had engaged a governess already, and she was coming next week; so that all I had to do was to get things ready for her reception. This was a rather startling piece of intelligence. I ventured to inquire her name and address, by whom she had been recommended, or how he had been led to make choice of her.

"She is a very estimable, pious young person," said he; "you needn't be afraid. Her name is Myers, I believe; and she was recommended to me by a respectable old dowager—a lady of high repute in the religious world. I have not seen her myself, and therefore cannot give you a particular account of her person and conversation, and so forth; but, if the old lady's eulogies are correct, you will find her to possess all desirable qualifications for her position—an inordinate love of children among the rest."

All this was gravely and quietly spoken, but there was a laughing demon in his half-averted eye that boded no good I imagined. However, I thought of my asylum in ——shire, and made no further objections.

When Miss Myers arrived, I was not prepared to give her a very cordial reception. Her appearance was not particularly calculated to produce a favourable impression at first sight, nor did her manners and subsequent conduct, in any degree, remove the prejudice I had already conceived against her. Her attainments were limited, her intellect noways above mediocrity. She had a fine voice, and could sing like a nightingale, and accompany herself sufficiently well on the piano; but these were her only accomplishments. There was a look of guile and subtlety in her face, a sound of it in her voice. She seemed afraid of me, and would start if I suddenly approached her. In her behaviour, she was respectful and complaisant even to servility: she attempted to flatter and fawn upon me at first, but I soon checked that. Her fondness for her little pupil was over-strained, and I was obliged to remonstrate with her on the subject of over-indulgence and injudicious praise; but she could not gain his heart. Her piety consisted in an occasional heaving of sighs and uplifting of eyes to the ceiling, and the utterance of a few cant phrases. She told me she was a clergyman's daughter, and had been left an orphan from her childhood, but had had the good fortune to obtain a situation in a very pious family; and then she spoke so gratefully of the kindness she had experienced from its different members that I reproached myself for my uncharitable thoughts and unfriendly conduct, and relented for a time—but not for long; my causes of dislike were too rational, my suspicions too well founded for that; and I knew it was my duty to watch and scrutinize till those suspicions were either satisfactorily removed or confirmed.

I asked the name and residence of the kind and pious family. She mentioned a common name, and an unknown and distant place of abode, but told me they were now on the Continent, and their present address was unknown to her. I never saw her speak much to Mr. Huntingdon; but he would frequently look into the school-room to see how little Arthur got on with his new companion, when I was not there. In the evening, she sat with us in the drawing-room, and would sing and play to amuse him—or *us*, as she pretended—and was very attentive to his wants, and watchful to anticipate them, though she only talked to me—indeed, he was seldom in a condition to be talked to. Had she been other than she was, I should have felt her presence a great relief to come between us thus, except, indeed, that I should have been thoroughly ashamed for any decent person to see him as he often was.

I did not mention my suspicions to Rachel; but she, having sojourned for half a century in this land of sin and sorrow,[1] has learned to be suspicious herself. She told me from the first she was "down of[2] that new governess," and I soon found she watched her quite as narrowly as I did; and I was glad of it, for I longed to know the truth: the atmosphere of Grassdale seemed to stifle me, and I could only live by thinking of Wildfell Hall.

At last, one morning, she entered my chamber with such intelligence that my resolution was taken before she had ceased to speak. While she dressed me, I explained to her my intentions and what assistance I should require from her, and told her which of my things she was to pack up, and what she was to leave behind for herself, as I had no other means of recompencing her for this sudden dismissal, after her long and faithful service—a circumstance I most deeply regretted but could not avoid.

"And what will you do, Rachel?" said I—"will you go home, or seek another place?"

"I have no home, ma'm, but with you," she replied; "and if I leave you, I'll never go into place again as long as I live."

"But I can't afford to live like a lady, now," returned I: "I must be my own maid and my child's nurse."

"What *signifies!*" replied she in some excitement. "You'll want somebody to clean and wash, and cook, won't you? I can do all that; and never mind the wages—I've my bits o' savings yet, and if you wouldn't take me, I should

---

1 Although an expression for this world that was not uncommon, Brontë could be quoting Henry Martyn (1781–1812), a famous missionary believed to be one of the models for Charlotte Brontë's St John Rivers in *Jane Eyre*. See, for example, *Memoir of the Rev. Henry Martyn, B.D.: late Fellow of St. John's College, Cambridge and Chaplain to the Honourable East India Company*, ed. John Sargent (London: J. Hatchard and Son ... , 1820), and *Journals and Letters of the Rev. Henry Martyn, B.D. Late Fellow of St. John's College, Cambridge; and Chaplain to the Honourable East India Company*, ed. S. Wilberforce (London: Seeley and Burnside, 1837).

2 Suspicious, distrustful. See Partridge's *Dictionary of Historical Slang*, 275–76.

have to find my own board and lodging out of 'em somewhere, or else work among strangers—and it's what I'm not used to—so you can please yourself ma'am." Her voice quavered as she spoke, and the tears stood in her eyes.

"I should like it above all things, Rachel, and I'd give you such wages as I could afford—such as I should give to any servant of all work I might employ; but don't you see I should be dragging you down with me, when you have done nothing to deserve it?"

"Oh, fiddle!" ejaculated she.

"And besides, my future way of living will be so widely different to the past—so different to all you have been accustomed to—"

"Do you think, ma'am, I can't bear what my missis can?—surely I'm not so proud and so dainty as that comes to—and my little master too, God bless him?"

"But I'm young, Rachel; I shan't mind it; and Arthur is young too—it will be nothing to him."

"Nor me either: I'm not so old but what I can stand hard fare and hard work, if it's only to help and comfort them as I've loved like my own barns[1]—for all I'm too old to bide the thoughts o' leaving 'em in trouble and danger, and going amongst strangers myself."

"Then you shan't, Rachel!" cried I, embracing my faithful friend. "We'll all go together, and you shall see how the new life suits you."

"Bless you, honey!" cried she affectionately returning my embrace. "Only let us get shut of[2] this wicked house and we'll do right enough, you'll see."

"So think I," was my answer;—and so that point was settled.

By that morning's post, I despatched a few hasty lines to Frederick, beseeching him to prepare my asylum for my immediate reception—for I should probably come to claim it within a day after the receipt of that note,—and telling him in few words, the cause of my sudden resolution. I then wrote three letters of adieu: the first to Esther Hargrave, in which I told her that I found it impossible to stay any longer at Grassdale, or to leave my son under his father's protection; and, as it was of the last importance that our future abode should be unknown to him and his acquaintance, I should disclose it to no one but my brother, through the medium of whom I hoped still to correspond with my friends. I then gave her his address, exhorted her to write frequently, reiterated some of my former admonitions regarding her own concerns, and bade her a fond farewell.

The second was to Milicent; much to the same effect, but a little more confidential, as befitted our longer intimacy, and her greater experience and better acquaintance with my circumstances.

---

1 A variant of "bairns," children.

2 To get free from (dialect).

The third was to my aunt—a much more difficult and painful undertaking, and therefore I had left it to the last; but I must give her some explanation of that extraordinary step I had taken,—and that quickly, for she and my uncle would no doubt hear of it within a day or two after my disappearance, as it was probable that Mr. Huntingdon would speedily apply to them to know what was become of me. At last however, I told her I was sensible of my error: I did not complain of its punishment, and I was sorry to trouble my friends with its consequences; but in duty to my son, I must submit no longer; it was absolutely necessary that he should be delivered from his father's corrupting influence. I should not disclose my place of refuge even to her, in order that she and my uncle might be able, with truth, to deny all knowledge concerning it; but any communications addressed to me under cover to my brother, would be certain to reach me. I hoped she and my uncle would pardon the step I had taken, for if they knew all, I was sure they would not blame me; and I trusted they would not afflict themselves on my account, for if I could only reach my retreat in safety and keep it unmolested, I should be very happy, but for the thoughts of them; and should be quite contented to spend my life in obscurity, devoting myself to the training up of my child,[1] and teaching him to avoid the errors of both his parents.

These things were done yesterday: I have given two whole days to the preparation for our departure, that Frederick may have more time to prepare the rooms, and Rachel to pack up the things—for the latter task must be done with the utmost caution and secrecy, and there is no one but me to assist her: I can help to get the articles together, but I do not understand the art of stowing them into the boxes, so as to take up the smallest possible space; and there are her own things to do, as well as mine and Arthur's. I can ill afford to leave anything behind, since I have no money, except a few guineas in my purse;—and besides, as Rachel observed, whatever I left would most likely become the property of Miss Myers, and I should not relish that.

But what trouble I have had throughout these two days struggling to appear calm and collected—to meet him and her as usual, when I was obliged to meet them, and forcing myself to leave my little Arthur in her hands for hours together! But I trust these trials are over now: I have laid him in my bed for better security, and never more, I trust, shall his innocent lips be defiled by their contaminating kisses, or his young ears polluted by their words. But shall we escape in safety? Oh, that the morning were come, and we were on our way at least! This evening, when I had given Rachel all the assistance I could, and had nothing left me but to wait, and wish and tremble, I became

---

1 A secular iteration of Proverbs 22:6: "Train up a child in the way he should go: and when he is old, he will not depart from them."

so greatly agitated, that I knew not what to do. I went down to dinner, but I could not force myself to eat. Mr. Huntingdon remarked the circumstance.

"What's to do with you *now*?" said he, when the removal of the second course gave him time to look about him.

"I am not well," I replied: "I think I must lie down a little—you won't miss me much?"

"Not the least; if you leave your chair, it'll do just as well—better a trifle," he muttered as I left the room, "for I can fancy somebody else fills it."

"Somebody else *may* fill it tomorrow," I thought—but did not say. "There! I've seen the last of *you*, I hope," I muttered as I closed the door upon him.

Rachel urged me to seek repose, at once, to recruit my strength for tomorrow's journey, as we must be gone before the dawn, but in my present state of nervous excitement, that was entirely out of the question. It was equally out of the question to sit, or wander about my room, counting the hours and the minutes between me and the appointed time of action, straining my ears and trembling at every sound lest some one should discover and betray us after all. I took up a book and tried to read. My eyes wandered over the pages, but it was impossible to bind my thoughts to their contents. Why not have recourse to the old expedient, and add this last event to my chronicle? I opened its pages once more, and wrote the above account—with difficulty, at first, but gradually my mind became more calm and steady. Thus several hours have past away: the time is drawing near;—and now my eyes feel heavy, and my frame exhausted: I will commend my cause to God, and then lie down and gain an hour or two of sleep; and *then*!—

Little Arthur sleeps soundly. All the house is still: there can be no one watching. The boxes were all corded by Benson, and quietly conveyed down the back stairs after dusk, and sent away in a cart to the M—— coach-office. The name upon the cards was Mrs. Graham, which appellation I mean henceforth to adopt. My mother's maiden name was Graham, and therefore I fancy I have some claim to it, and prefer it to any other, except my own, which I dare not resume.

CHAPTER XLIV
THE RETREAT

OCTOBER 24th.—Thank Heaven, I am free and safe at last!—Early we rose, swiftly and quietly dressed, slowly and stealthily descended to the hall, where Benson stood ready with a light to open the door and fasten it after us. We were obliged to let one man into our secret on account of the boxes, &c. All the servants were but too well acquainted with their master's conduct, and either Benson or John would have been willing to serve me, but as the former was more staid and elderly, and a crony of Rachel's besides, I of course directed her to make choice of him as her assistant and confidant on the occasion, as far as necessity demanded. I only hope he may not be brought into trouble thereby, and only wish I could reward him for the perilous service he was so ready to undertake. I slipped two guineas into his hand, by way of remembrance, as he stood in the doorway, holding the candle to light our departure, with a tear in his honest grey eye and a host of good wishes depicted on his solemn countenance. Alas! I could offer no more: I had barely sufficient remaining for the probable expenses of the journey.

What trembling joy it was when the little wicket closed behind us, as we issued from the park! Then, for one moment, I paused, to inhale one draught of that cool, bracing air, and venture one look back upon the house. All was dark and still; no light glimmered in the windows; no wreath of smoke obscured the stars that sparkled above it in the frosty sky. As I bade farewell for ever to that place, the scene of so much guilt and misery, I felt glad that I had not left it before, for now there was no doubt about the propriety of such a step—no shadow of remorse for him I left behind: there was nothing to disturb my joy but the fear of detection; and every step removed us farther from the chance of that.

We had left Grassdale many miles behind us before the round, red sun arose to welcome our deliverance, and if any inhabitant of its vicinity had chanced to see us then, as we bowled along on the top of the coach, I scarcely think they would have suspected our identity. As I intend to be taken for a widow I thought it advisable to enter my new abode in mourning: I was therefore attired in a plain black silk dress and mantle, a black veil (which I kept carefully over my face for the first twenty or thirty miles of the journey), and a black silk bonnet, which I had been constrained to borrow of Rachel for want of such an article myself—it was not in the newest fashion, of course; but none the worse for that, under present circumstances. Arthur was clad in his plainest clothes, and wrapped in a coarse woollen shawl; and Rachel was muffled in a grey cloak and hood that had seen better days, and gave her more the appearance of an ordinary, though decent old woman, than of a lady's maid.

Oh, what delight it was to be thus seated aloft, rumbling along the broad, sunshiny road, with the fresh morning breeze in my face, surrounded by an unknown country all smiling—cheerfully, gloriously, smiling in the yellow lustre of those early beams,—with my darling child in my arms, almost as happy as myself and my faithful friend beside me; a prison and despair behind me, receding farther, farther back at every clatter of the horses' feet,—and liberty and hope before! I could hardly refrain from praising God aloud for my deliverance, or astonishing my fellow passengers by some surprising outburst of hilarity.

But the journey was a very long one, and we were all weary enough before the close of it. It was far into the night when we reached the town of L——, and still we were seven miles from our journey's end; and there was no more coaching—nor any conveyance to be had, except a common cart—and that with the greatest difficulty, for half the town was in bed. And a dreary ride we had of it that last stage of the journey, cold and weary as we were; sitting on our boxes, with nothing to cling to, nothing to lean against, slowly dragged and cruelly shaken over the rough, hilly roads. But Arthur was asleep in Rachel's lap, and between us we managed pretty well to shield him from the cold night air

At last we began to ascend a terribly steep and stony lane which, in spite of the darkness, Rachel said she remembered well: she had often walked there with me in her arms, and little thought to come again so many years after, under such circumstances as the present.

Arthur being now awakened by the jolting and the stoppages, we all got out and walked. We had not far to go; but what if Frederick should not have received my letter? or if he should not have had time to prepare the rooms for our reception; and we should find them all dark, damp, and comfortless; destitute of food, fire, and furniture, after all our toil?

At length the grim, dark pile appeared before us. The lane conducted us round by the back way. We entered the desolate court, and in breathless anxiety surveyed the ruinous mass. Was it all blackness and desolation? No; one faint red glimmer cheered us from a window where the lattice was in good repair. The door was fastened, but after due knocking and waiting, and some parleying with a voice from an upper window, we were admitted, by an old woman who had been commissioned to air and keep the house till our arrival,—into a tolerably snug little apartment, formerly the scullery of the mansion, which Frederick had now fitted up as a kitchen. Here she procured us a light, roused the fire to a cheerful blaze, and soon prepared a simple repast for our refreshment; while we disencumbered ourselves of our travelling gear, and took a hasty survey of our new abode. Besides the kitchen there were two bedrooms, a good sized parlour, and another smaller one, which I destined for my studio, all well aired and seemingly in good repair, but only partly furnished with a few old articles, chiefly of ponderous black oak—the veritable ones that had been there before, and which had been kept as antiquarian relics in my brother's present residence, and now in all haste, transported back again.

The old woman brought my supper and Arthur's into the parlour, and told me, with all due formality, that "The master desired his compliments to Mrs. Graham, and he had prepared the rooms as well as he could upon so short a notice, but he would do himself the pleasure of calling upon her tomorrow, to receive her further commands."

I was glad to ascend the stern-looking stone staircase, and lie down in the gloomy old-fashioned bed, beside my little Arthur. He was asleep in a minute; but, weary as I was, my excited feelings and restless cogitations kept me awake till dawn began to struggle with the darkness; but sleep was sweet and refreshing when it came, and the waking was delightful beyond expression. It was little Arthur that roused me, with his gentle kisses:—he was here, then—safely clasped in my arms, and many leagues away from his unworthy father!—Broad daylight illumined the apartment, for the sun was high in heaven, though obscured by rolling masses of autumnal vapour.

The scene, indeed, was not remarkably cheerful in itself, either within or without. The large bare room with its grim old furniture, the narrow, latticed windows, revealing the dull, grey sky above and the desolate wilderness below, where the dark stone walls and iron gate, the rank growth of grass and weeds, and the hardy ever-greens of preternatural forms, alone remained to tell that there had been once a garden,—and the bleak and barren fields beyond might have struck me as gloomy enough at another time, but now, each separate object seemed to echo back my own exhilarating sense of hope and freedom: indefinite dreams of the far past and bright anticipations of the future seemed to greet me at every turn. I should rejoice with more security, to be sure, had the broad sea rolled between my present and my former homes, but surely in this lonely spot I might remain unknown; and then, I had my brother here to cheer my solitude with his occasional visits.

He came that morning; and I have had several interviews with him since; but he is obliged to be very cautious when and how he comes: not even his servants, or his best friends must know of his visits to Wildfell—except on such occasions as a landlord might be expected to call upon a stranger tenant—lest suspicion should be excited against me, whether of the truth or of some slanderous falsehood.

I have now been here nearly a fortnight, and but for one disturbing care, the haunting dread of discovery, I am comfortably settled in my new home: Frederick has supplied me with all requisite furniture and painting materials: Rachel has sold most of my clothes for me, in a distant town, and procured me a wardrobe more suitable to my present position: I have a second-hand piano, and a tolerably well-stocked bookcase in my parlour; and my other room has assumed quite a professional, business-like appearance already. I am working hard to repay my brother for all his expenses on my account; not that there is the slightest necessity for anything of the kind, but it pleases me to do so: I shall have so much more pleasure in my labour, my earnings, my frugal fare, and household economy, when I know that I am paying my way honestly, and that what little I possess is legitimately all my own; and that no one suffers for my folly—in a pecuniary way at least.—I shall make him take the last penny I owe him, if I can possibly effect it without offending him too deeply. I have a few pictures already done, for I told Rachel to pack up all I had; and she executed her commission but too well, for among the rest, she put up a portrait of Mr. Huntingdon that I had painted in the first year of my marriage. It struck me with dismay, at the moment, when I took it from the box and beheld those eyes fixed upon me in their mocking mirth, as if exulting, still, in his power to control my fate, and deriding my efforts to escape.

How widely different had been my feelings in painting that portrait to what they now were in looking upon it! How I had studied and toiled to produce something, as I thought, worthy of the original! what mingled pleasure and dissatisfaction I had had in the result of my labours!—pleasure for the likeness I had caught; dissatisfaction, because I had not made it handsome enough. Now, I see no beauty in it—nothing pleasing in any part of its expression; and yet it is far handsomer and far more agreeable—far less repulsive I should rather say—than he is now; for these six years have wrought almost as great a change upon himself as on my feelings regarding him. The frame, however, is handsome enough; it will serve for another painting. The picture itself I have not destroyed, as I had first intended; I have put it aside; not, I think, from any lurking tenderness for the memory of past affection, nor yet to remind me of my former folly, but chiefly that I may compare my son's features and countenance with this, as he grows up, and thus be enabled to judge how much or how little he resembles his father—if I may be allowed to keep him with me still, and never to behold that father's face again—a blessing I hardly dare reckon upon.

It seems Mr. Huntingdon is making every exertion to discover the place of my retreat. He has been in person to Staningley, seeking redress for his grievances—expecting to hear of his victims, if not to find them there—and has told so many lies, and with such unblushing coolness, that my uncle more than half believes him, and strongly advocates my going back to him and being friends again; but my aunt knows better: she is too cool and cautious, and too well acquainted with both my husband's character and my own to be imposed upon by any specious falsehoods the former could invent. But he does not *want* me back; he wants my child; and gives my friends to understand that if I prefer living apart from him, he will indulge the whim and let me do so unmolested, and even settle a reasonable allowance on me, provided I will immediately deliver up his son. But, Heaven help me! I am not going to sell my child for gold, though it were to save both him and me from starving: it would be better that he should die with me, than that he should live with his father.

Frederick showed me a letter he had received from that gentleman, full of cool impudence such as would astonish any one who did not know him, but such as, I am convinced, none would know better how to answer than my brother. He gave me no account of his reply, except to tell me that he had not acknowledged his acquaintance with my place of refuge, but rather left it to be inferred that it was quite unknown to him, by saying it was useless to apply to him or any other of my relations for information on the subject, as it appeared I had been driven to such extremity that I had concealed my retreat even from my best friends; but that if he *had* known it, or should at any time be made aware of it, most certainly Mr. Huntingdon would be the last person to whom he should communicate the intelligence; and that he need not trouble himself to bargain for the child, for he (Frederick) fancied he knew enough of his sister to enable him to declare, that wherever she might be, or however situated, no consideration would induce her to deliver him up.

30th.—Alas! my kind neighbours will not let me alone. By some means they have ferreted me out, and I have had to sustain visits from three different families, all more or less bent upon discovering who and what I am, whence I came, and why I have chosen such a home as this. Their society is unnecessary to me, to say the least, and their curiosity annoys and alarms me: if I gratify it, it may lead to the ruin of my son, and if I am too mysterious, it will only excite their suspicions, invite conjecture, and rouse them to greater exertions—and perhaps be the means of spreading my fame from parish to parish, till it reach the ears of some one who will carry it to the lord of Grassdale Manor.

I shall be expected to return their calls, but if, upon enquiry, I find that any of them live too far away for Arthur to accompany me, they must expect in vain for a while, for I cannot bear to leave him, unless it be to go to church: and I have not attempted *that* yet, for—it may be foolish weakness, but I am under such constant dread of his being snatched away that I am never easy when he is not by my side; and I fear these nervous terrors would so entirely disturb my devotions, that I should obtain no benefit from the attendance. I mean, however, to make the experiment next Sunday, and oblige myself to leave him in charge of Rachel for a few hours. It will be a hard task, but surely no imprudence; and the vicar has been to scold me for my neglect of the ordinances of religion. I had no sufficient excuse to offer, and I promised, if all were well, he should see me in my pew next Sunday; for I do not wish to be set down as an infidel; and besides, I know I should derive great comfort and benefit from an occasional attendance at public worship, if I could only have faith and fortitude to compose my thoughts in conformity with the solemn occasion, and forbid them to be for ever dwelling on my absent child, and on the dreadful possibility of finding him gone when I return; and surely God in his mercy will preserve me from so severe a trial: for my child's own sake, if not for mine, He will not suffer him to be torn away.

November 3rd.—I have made some further acquaintance with my neighbours. The fine gentleman and beau of the parish and its vicinity (in his own estimation, at least), is a young ...

★ ★ ★ ★ ★

★ ★ ★ ★ ★

Here it ended. The rest was torn away. How cruel—just when she was going to mention me! for I could not doubt it *was* your humble servant she was about to mention, though not very favourably of course—I could tell that, as well by those few words as by the recollection of her whole aspect and demeanour towards me in the commencement of our acquaintance. Well! I could readily forgive her prejudice against me, and her hard thoughts of our sex in general, when I saw to what brilliant specimens her experience had been limited.

Respecting me, however, she had long since seen her error, and perhaps fallen into another in the opposite extreme; for if, at first, her opinion of me had been lower than I deserved I was convinced that now my deserts were lower than her opinion; and if the former part of this continuation had been torn away to avoid wounding my feelings, perhaps the latter portion had been removed for fear of ministering too much to my self-conceit. At any rate, I would have given much to have seen it all—to have witnessed the gradual change, and watched the progress of her esteem and friendship for me,—and whatever warmer feeling she might have—to have seen how much of love there was in her regard, and how it had grown upon her in spite of her virtuous resolutions and strenuous exertions to—but no, I had no right to see it: all this was too sacred for any eyes but her own, and she had done well to keep it from me.

CHAPTER XLV
RECONCILIATION

WELL Halford, what do you think of all this? and while you read it, did you ever picture to yourself what my feelings would probably be during its perusal? Most likely not; but I am not going to descant upon them now: I will only make this acknowledgement, little honourable as it may be to human nature, and especially to myself:—that the former half of the narrative was, to me, more painful than the latter; not that I was at all insensible to Mrs. Huntingdon's wrongs or unmoved by her sufferings, but, I must confess, I felt a kind of selfish gratification in watching her husband's gradual decline in her good graces, and seeing how completely he extinguished all her affection at last. The effect of the whole, however, in spite of all my sympathy for her and my fury against him, was to relieve my mind of an intolerable burden and fill my heart with joy, as if some friend had roused me from a dreadful nightmare.

It was now near eight o'clock in the morning, for my candle had expired in the midst of my perusal, leaving me no alternative but to get another, at the expense of alarming the house, or to go to bed and wait the return of daylight. On my mother's account, I chose the latter; but how *willingly* I sought my pillow, and how much sleep it brought me, I leave you to imagine.

At the first appearance of dawn I rose, and brought the manuscript to the window, but it was impossible to read it yet. I devoted half an hour to dressing, and then returned to it again. Now, with a little difficulty, I could manage; and with intense and eager interest, I devoured the remainder of its contents. When it was ended, and my transient regret at its abrupt conclusion was over, I opened the window and put out my head to catch the cooling breeze, and imbibe deep draughts of the pure morning air. A splendid morning it was; the half-frozen dew lay thick on the grass, the swallows were twittering round me, the rooks cawing and cows lowing in the distance; and early frost and summer sunshine mingled their sweetness in the air. But I did not think of that: a confusion of countless thoughts and varied emotions crowded upon me while I gazed abstractedly on the lovely face of nature. Soon, however, this chaos of thoughts and passions cleared away, giving place to two distinct emotions: joy unspeakable[1] that my adored Helen was all I wished to think her—that through the noisome vapours of the world's aspersions and my own fancied convictions, her character shone bright, and clear, and stainless as that sun I could not bear to look on; and shame and deep remorse for my own conduct.

Immediately after breakfast, I hurried over to Wildfell Hall. Rachel had risen many degrees in my estimation since yesterday. I was ready to greet her quite as an old friend; but every kindly impulse was checked by the look of cold distrust she cast upon me on opening the door. The old virgin had constituted herself the guardian of her lady's honour, I suppose, and doubtless she saw in me another Mr. Hargrave, only the more dangerous in being more esteemed and trusted by her mistress.

"Missis can't see any one today, sir—she's poorly," said she in answer to my enquiry for Mrs. Graham.

"But I must see her, Rachel," said I, placing my hand on the door to prevent its being shut against me.

"Indeed, sir, you can't," replied she, settling her countenance in still more iron frigidity than before.

"Be so good as to announce me."

"It's no manner of use, Mr. Markham; she's poorly, I tell you."

---

1 Again, Gilbert employs biblical phrases ("joy unspeakable") used to describe faith to articulate his worldly passion and faith in Helen. See 1 Peter 1:7–9.

Just in time to prevent me from committing the impropriety of taking the citadel by storm, and pushing forward unannounced, an inner door opened, and little Arthur appeared with his frolicsome playfellow the dog. He seized my hand between both his, and smilingly drew me forward.

"Mamma says you're to come in, Mr. Markham," said he, "and I'm to go out and play with Rover."

Rachel retired with a sigh, and I stepped into the parlour and shut the door. There, before the fireplace, stood the tall, graceful figure wasted with many sorrows. I cast the manuscript on the table, and looked in her face. Anxious and pale, it was turned towards me; her clear, dark eyes were fixed on mine with a gaze so intensely earnest that they bound me like a spell.

"Have you looked it over?" she murmured. The spell was broken.

"I've read it through," said I, advancing into the room,—"and I want to know if you'll forgive me—if you *can* forgive me?"

She did not answer, but her eyes glistened, and a faint red mantled on her lip and cheek. As I approached, she abruptly turned away, and went to the window. It was not in anger, I was well assured, but only to conceal or control her emotion. I therefore ventured to follow and stand beside her there,—but not to speak. She gave me her hand, without turning her head, and murmured, in a voice she strove in vain to steady,—

"Can *you* forgive *me*?"

It might be deemed a breach of trust, I thought, to convey that lily hand to my lips, so I only gently pressed it between my own, and smilingly replied,—

"I hardly can. You should have told me this before. It shows a want of confidence—"

"Oh, no," cried she, eagerly interrupting me, "it was not that! It was no want of confidence in you; but if I had told you anything of my history, I must have told you all, in order to excuse my conduct; and I might well shrink from such a disclosure, till necessity obliged me to make it. But you forgive me?—I have done very, very wrong, I know; but, as usual, I have reaped the bitter fruits of my own error,—and must reap them to the end."

Bitter indeed, was the tone of anguish, repressed by resolute firmness, in which this was spoken. Now, I raised her hand to my lips, and fervently kissed it again and again; for tears prevented any other reply. She suffered these wild caresses without resistance or resentment; then, suddenly turning from me, she paced twice or thrice through the room. I knew by the contraction of her brow, the tight compression of her lips, and wringing of her hands, that meantime a violent conflict between reason and passion, was silently passing within. At length she paused before the empty fireplace, and turning to me, said calmly—if that might be called calmness, which was so evidently the result of a violent effort—

"Now Gilbert, you must leave me—not this moment, but soon—and you must *never come again.*"

"Never again, Helen? just when I love you more than ever!"

"For that very reason, if it so, we should not meet again. I thought *this* interview was necessary—at least, I persuaded myself it was so—that we might severally ask and receive each other's pardon for the past; but there can be no excuse for another. I shall leave this place, as soon as I have means to seek another asylum; but our intercourse must end here."

"End here!" echoed I; and approaching the high, carved chimney-piece, I leant my hand against its heavy moldings, and dropped my forehead upon it in silent, sullen despondency.

"You must not come again," continued she. There was a slight tremor in her voice, but I thought her whole manner was provokingly composed, considering the dreadful sentence she pronounced. "You must know why I tell you so," she resumed; "and you must see that it is better to part at once:—if it be hard to say adieu for ever, you ought to help me." She paused. I did not answer. "Will you promise not to come ?—If you won't, and if you do come here again, you will drive me away before I know where to find another place of refuge—or how to seek it."

"Helen," said I, turning impatiently towards her, "I cannot discuss the matter of eternal separation, calmly and dispassionately as you can do. It is no question of mere expedience with *me*; it is a question of life and death!"

She was silent. Her pale lips quivered, and her fingers trembled with agitation, as she nervously entwined them in the hair chain to which was appended her small gold watch—the only thing of value she had permitted herself to keep. I had said an unjust and cruel thing; but I must needs follow it up with something worse.

"But Helen!" I began in a soft, low tone, not daring to raise my eyes to her face—"that man is *not* your husband: in the sight of Heaven he has forfeited all claim to—" She seized my arm with a grasp of startling energy.

"*Gilbert, don't!*" she cried, in a tone that would have pierced a heart of adamant. "For God's sake, don't *you* attempt these arguments! No *fiend* could torture me like this!"

"I won't, I won't!" said I, gently laying my hand on hers; almost as much alarmed at her vehemence, as ashamed of my own misconduct.

"Instead of acting like a true friend," continued she, breaking from me and throwing herself into the old arm chair—"and helping me with all your might—or rather taking your own part in the struggle of right against passion—you leave all the burden to me;—and not satisfied with that, you do your utmost to fight against me—when you know that I—" she paused, and hid her face in her handkerchief.

"Forgive me, Helen!" pleaded I, "I will never utter another word on the subject. But may we not still meet as friends?"

"It will not do," she replied, mournfully shaking her head; and then she raised her eyes to mine, with a mildly reproachful look that seemed to say, "You must know that as well as I."

"Then what *must* we do?" cried I, passionately. But immediately I added in a quieter tone—"I'll do whatever you desire;—only *don't* say that this meeting is to be our last."

"And why not? Don't you know that every time we meet, the thoughts of the final parting will become more painful? Don't you *feel* that every interview makes us dearer to each other than the last?"

The utterance of this last question was hurried and low, and the downcast eyes and burning blush too plainly showed that *she*, at least, had felt it. It was scarcely prudent to make such an admission, or to add—as she presently did—"I have power to bid you go, now: another time it might be different,"—but I was not base enough to attempt to take advantage of her candour.

"But we may write," I timidly suggested.—"You will not deny me that consolation?"

"We can hear of each other through my brother."

"Your brother!" A pang of remorse and shame shot through me. She had not heard of the injury he had sustained at my hands; and I had not the courage to tell her. "Your brother will not help us," I said: "he would have all communion between us to be entirely at an end."

"And he would be right, I suppose. As a friend of both, he would wish us both well; and every friend would tell us it was our interest, as well as our duty, to forget each other, though we might not see it ourselves. But don't be afraid, Gilbert," she added, smiling sadly at my manifest discomposure, "there is little chance of my forgetting you. But I did not mean that Frederick should be the means of transmitting messages between us, only that each might know, through him, of the other's welfare;—and more than this ought not to be; for you are young, Gilbert, and you ought to marry—and will some time, though you may think it impossible now:—and though I hardly can say I wish you to forget me, I know it is right that you should, both for your own happiness and that of your future wife;—and therefore I must and will wish it," she added resolutely.

"And you are young too, Helen," I boldly replied, "and when that profligate scoundrel has run through his career, you will give your hand to me— I'll wait till then."

But she would not leave me this support. Independently of the moral evil of basing our hopes upon the death of another, who, if unfit for this world, was at least no less so for the next, and whose amelioration would thus become our bane and his greatest transgression our greatest benefit,—she maintained it to be madness: many men of Mr. Huntingdon's habits had lived to a ripe though miserable old age;—"and if I," said she, "am young in years I am old in sorrow; but even if trouble should fail to kill me before vice destroys him, think, if he reached but fifty years or so, would you wait twenty or fifteen—in vague uncertainty and suspense—through all the prime of youth and manhood—and marry at last a woman faded and worn as I shall be—without ever having seen me from this day to that?—You would not," she continued interrupting my earnest protestations of unfailing constancy,—"or if you would you should not. Trust me, Gilbert; in this matter I know better than you. You think me cold and stony hearted, and you may, but—"

"I don't Helen."

"Well, never mind; you might if you would—but I have not spent my solitude in utter idleness, and I am not speaking now from the impulse of the moment as you do: I have thought of all these matters again and again; I have argued these questions with myself; and pondered well our past, and present, and future career; and, believe me, I have come to the right conclusion at last. Trust my words rather than your own feelings, now, and in a few years you will see that I was right—though at present I hardly can see it myself," she murmured with a sigh as she rested her head on her hand.—"And don't argue against me any more: all you can say has been already said by my own heart and refuted by my reason. It was bad enough to combat those suggestions as they were whispered within me; in your mouth they are ten times worse, and if you knew how much they pain me you would cease at once, I know. If you knew my present feelings, you would even try to relieve them at the expense of your own."

"I will go—in a minute, if *that* can relieve you—and NEVER return!" said I with bitter emphasis—"But, if we may never meet, and never hope to meet again, is it a crime to exchange our thoughts by letter? May not kindred spirits meet, and mingle in communion whatever be the fate and circumstances of their earthly tenements?"

"They may, they may!" cried she with a momentary burst of glad enthusiasm. "I thought of that too, Gilbert, but I feared to mention it, because I feared you would not understand my views upon the subject—I fear it even now—I fear any kind friend would tell us we are *both* deluding ourselves with the idea of keeping up a spiritual intercourse without hope or prospect of anything further—without fostering vain regrets and hurtful aspirations, and feeding thoughts that should be sternly and pitilessly left to perish of inanition—"

"Never mind our kind friends: if they can part our bodies, it is enough; in God's name, let them not sunder our souls!" cried I, in terror lest she should deem it her duty to deny us this last remaining consolation.

"But no letters can pass between us here," said she, "without giving fresh food for scandal; and when I departed, I had intended that my new abode should be unknown to you as to the rest of the world; not that I should doubt your word if you promised not to visit me, but I thought you would be more tranquil in your own mind if you knew you could not do it; and likely to find less difficulty in abstracting yourself from me if you could not picture my situation to your mind. But listen," said she, smilingly putting up her finger to check my impatient reply: "in six months you shall hear from Frederick precisely where I am; and if you still retain your wish to write to me, and think you can maintain a correspondence all thought, all spirit—such as disembodied souls or unimpassioned friends, at least, might hold,—write, and I will answer you."

"Six months!"

"Yes, to give your present ardour time to cool and try the truth and constancy of your soul's love for mine. And now, enough has been said between us.—Why can't we part at once!" exclaimed she almost wildly, after a moment's pause, as she suddenly rose from her chair with her hands resolutely clasped together. I thought it was my duty to go without delay; and I approached and half extended my hand as if to take leave, she grasped it in silence. But this thought of final separation was too intolerable: it seemed to squeeze the blood out of my heart; and my feet were glued to the floor.

"And must we never meet again?" I murmured in the anguish of my soul.

"We shall meet in Heaven. Let us think of that," said she in a tone of desperate calmness; but her eyes glittered wildly, and her face was deadly pale.

"But not as we are now," I could not help replying. "It gives me little consolation to think I shall next behold you as a disembodied spirit, or an altered being, with a frame perfect and glorious, but not like this!—and a heart, perhaps, entirely estranged from me."[1]

"No Gilbert, there is perfect love in heaven!"[2]

---

1 See, for example, Galatians 3:28, where Paul explains how in heaven, "There is neither Jew nor Greek, there is neither bond nor free, there is neither male nor female: for ye are all one in Christ Jesus." While this makes clear a heavenly equality among the faithful, many believe that these words also indicate a disembodied, nonsexual state. See also 1 Corinthians 15:50–52, where because "flesh and blood cannot inherit the kingdom of God" (15:50), "we shall all be changed" (15:51).

2 See 1 John 4:16–17: "God is love; and he that dwelleth in love dwelleth in God, and God in him. Here in is our love made perfect...."

"*So* perfect, I suppose, that it soars above distinctions,[1] and you will have no closer sympathy with me than with any one of the ten thousand thousand angels[2] and the innumerable multitude of happy spirits round us."

"Whatever I am, you will be the same, and therefore, cannot possibly regret it; and whatever that change may be, we know it must be for the better."

"But if I am to be so changed that I shall cease to adore you with my whole heart and soul, and love you beyond every other creature, I shall not be myself; and, though, if ever I win heaven at all, I must, I know, be infinitely better and happier than I am now, my earthly nature cannot rejoice in the anticipation of such beatitude, from which itself and its chief joy must be excluded."

"Is your love *all* earthly then?"

"No, but I am supposing we shall have no more intimate communion with each other, than with the rest."

"If so, it will be because we love them more and not each other less. Increase of love brings increase of happiness, when it is mutual, and pure as that will be."

"But can *you*, Helen, contemplate with delight this prospect of losing me in a sea of glory?"

"I own I cannot; but we know not that it will be so;—and I do know that to regret the exchange of earthly pleasures for the joys of heaven, is as if the groveling caterpillar[3] should lament that it must one day quit the nibbled leaf to soar aloft and flutter through the air, roving at will from flower to flower, sipping sweet honey from their cups or basking in their sunny petals.

---

1   Again, one can see how Gilbert's fears of heaven are connected to an understanding of Galatians 3:28, where the distinction of bodies does not exist.

2   An echo of Revelation 5:11–12: "And I beheld, and I heard the voice of many angels round about the throne and the beasts and the elders: and the number of them was ten thousand times ten thousand, and thousands of thousands; saying with a loud voice, Worthy is the Lamb that was slain to receive power and riches and wisdom, and strength, and honour, and glory, and blessing."

3   Although this metaphor of the caterpillar's metamorphosis into butterfly was not an altogether uncommon way of referring to the soul's eventual transformation in heaven, it seems to have struck a particular chord with all three Brontës. Both Charlotte and Emily wrote essays that explored this phenomenon when they studied in Belgium, titled "The Caterpillar" and "The Butterfly" respectively (Charlotte and Emily Brontë, *The Belgian Essays*, ed. and trans. Sue Lonoff [New Haven, CT: Yale UP, 1996], 176–85). An older run of the *Methodist Magazine* they likely read as one of the few reminders of their mother, also contains a remarkably similar essay analyzing the soul's heavenly conversion and is probably one of the more potent sources for all three sisters. (Anonymous, "Reflections on the Sloth or Sluggard and the Silk Worm," *Methodist Magazine* Vol. 34 [December 1811] 925–59.)

If these little creatures knew how great a change awaited them, no doubt they would regret it; but would not all such sorrow be misplaced? And if that illustration will not move you, here is another:—We are children now; we feel as children, and we understand as children;[1] and when we are told that men and women do not play with toys, and that our companions will one day weary of the trivial sports and occupations that interest them and us so deeply now, we cannot help being saddened at the thoughts of such an alteration, because we cannot conceive that as we grow up, our own minds will become so enlarged and elevated that we ourselves shall then regard as trifling those objects and pursuits we now so fondly cherish, and that, though our companions will no longer join us in those childish pastimes, they will drink with us at other fountains of delight, and mingle their souls with ours in higher aims and nobler occupations beyond our present comprehension, but not less deeply relished or less truly good for that,—while yet both we and they remain essentially the same individuals as before. But Gilbert, can you really derive no consolation from the thought that we may meet together where there is no more pain and sorrow, no more striving against sin, and struggling of the spirit against the flesh;[2] where both will behold the same glorious truths, and drink exalted and supreme felicity from the same fountain of light and goodness[3]—that Being whom both will worship with the same intensity of holy ardour, and whose pure and happy creatures both will love with the same divine affection? If you cannot, never write to me!"

"Helen, I can, if faith would never fail."

"Now, then," exclaimed she, "while this hope is strong within us—"

"We will part," I cried. "You shall not have the pain of another effort to dismiss me: I will go at once; but—"

I did not put my request in words: she understood it instinctively and *this* time she yielded too—or rather, there was nothing so deliberate as requesting or yielding in the matter: there was a sudden impulse that neither could resist. One moment I stood and looked into her face, the next I held her to my heart, and we seemed to grow together in a close embrace from which no physical or mental force could rend us. I whispered "God bless you!" and

---

1   See I Corinthians 13:11: "When I was a child, I spake as a child, I understood as a child, I thought as a child: but when I became a man, I put away childish things."

2   See Galatians 5:17: "For the flesh lusteth against the Spirit, and the Spirit against the flesh; and these are contrary one to the other: so that ye cannot do the things that ye would." Also see Romans 7:14–25 for more information on equating the body with "the law of sin" and with the struggle between spirit and flesh (7:25).

3   See Revelation 21:6: "I will give unto him that is athirst of the fountain of the water of life freely"; and Revelation 22:1: "And he showed me a pure river of water of life, clear as crystal proceeding out of the throne of God and of the Lamb."

"Go—go!" was all she said; but while she spoke, she held me so fast that, without violence, I could not have obeyed her. At length, however, by some heroic effort, we tore ourselves apart, and I rushed from the house.

I have a confused remembrance of seeing little Arthur running up the garden walk to meet me, and of bolting over the wall to avoid him—and subsequently running down the steep fields, clearing the stone fences and hedges as they came in my way, till I got completely out of sight of the old Hall and down to the bottom of the hill; and then of long hours spent in bitter tears and lamentations, and melancholy musings in the lonely valley, with the eternal music in my ears, of the west wind rushing through the over-shadowing trees, and the brook babbling and gurgling along its stony bed—my eyes, for the most part, vacantly fixed on the deep, checkered shades restlessly playing over the bright sunny grass at my feet, where now and then a withered leaf or two would come dancing to share the revelry, but my heart was away up the hill in that dark room where she was weeping desolate and alone—she whom I was not to comfort, not to see again, till years or suffering had overcome us both, and torn our spirits from their perishing abodes of clay.

There was little business done that day, you may be sure. The farm was abandoned to the labourers, and the labourers were left to their own devices. But one duty must be attended to: I had not forgotten my assault upon Frederick Lawrence; and I must see him to apologize for the unhappy deed. I would fain have put it off till the morrow; but what if he should denounce me to his sister in the mean time? No, no, I must ask his pardon today, and entreat him to be lenient in his accusation, if the revelation must be made. I deferred it however, till the evening, when my spirits were more composed and when—oh, wonderful perversity of human nature!—some faint germs of indefinite hopes were beginning to rise in my mind; not that I intended to cherish them after all that had been said on the subject, but there they must lie for a while, uncrushed though not encouraged, till I had learnt to live without them.

Arrived at Woodford, the young squire's abode, I found no little difficulty in obtaining admission to his presence. The servant that opened the door told me his master was very ill, and seemed to think it doubtful whether he would be able to see me. I was not going to be balked however. I waited calmly in the hall to be announced, but inwardly determined to take no denial. The message was such as I expected—a polite intimation that Mr. Lawrence could see no one; he was feverish and must not be disturbed.

"I shall not disturb him long," said I; "but I must see him for a moment: it is on business of importance that I wish to speak to him."

"I'll tell him sir," said the man. And I advanced farther into the hall and followed him nearly to the door of the apartment where his master was—for it seemed he was not in bed. The answer returned, was that Mr. Lawrence hoped I would be so good as to leave a message or a note with the servant, as he could attend to no business at present.

"He may as well see me as you," said I; and, stepping past the astonished footman, I boldly rapped at the door, entered, and closed it behind me. The room was spacious and handsomely furnished—very comfortably, too, for a bachelor. A clear, red fire was burning in the polished grate: a superannuated greyhound, given up to idleness and good living lay basking before it on the thick, soft rug, on one corner of which, beside the sofa, sat a smart young springer, looking wistfully up in its master's face; perhaps, asking permission to share his couch, or, it might be, only soliciting a caress from his hand or a kind word from his lips. The invalid himself looked very interesting as he lay reclining there, in his elegant dressing-gown, with a silk handkerchief bound across his temples. His usually pale face was flushed and feverish; his eyes were half closed, until he became sensible of my presence—and then he opened them wide enough;—one hand was thrown listlessly over the back of the sofa, and held a small volume with which, apparently, he had been vainly attempting to beguile the weary hours. He dropped it, however, in his start of indignant surprise as I advanced into the room and stood before him on the rug. He raised himself on his pillows and gazed upon me with equal degrees of nervous horror, anger, and amazement depicted on his countenance.

"Mr. Markham, I scarcely expected this!" he said; and the blood left his cheek as he spoke.

"I know you didn't," answered I; "but be quiet a minute, and I'll tell you what I came for." Unthinkingly I advanced a step or two nearer. He winced at my approach, with an expression of aversion and instinctive physical fear anything but conciliatory to my feelings. I stepped back however.

"Make your story a short one," said he, putting his hand on the small silver bell that stood on the table beside him,—"or I shall be obliged to call for assistance. I am in no state to bear your brutalities now, or your presence either." And in truth the moisture started from his pores and stood on his pale forehead like dew.

Such a reception was hardly calculated to diminish the difficulties of my unenviable task. It must be performed, however, in some fashion: and so I plunged into it at once, and floundered through it as I could.

"The truth is, Lawrence," said I, "I have not acted quite correctly towards you of late—especially on this last occasion; and I'm come to—in short, to express my regret for what has been done, and to beg your pardon.—If you don't choose to grant it," I added hastily, not liking the aspect of his face, "it's no matter—only, *I've* done *my* duty—that's all."

"It's easily done," replied he, with a faint smile bordering on a sneer: "to abuse your friend and knock him on the head, without any assignable cause, and then tell him the deed was not quite correct, but it's no matter whether he pardons it or not."

"I forgot to tell you that it was in consequence of a mistake," muttered I. "I should have made a very handsome apology, but you provoked me so confoundedly with your——. Well, I suppose it's my fault. The fact is, I didn't know that you were Mrs. Graham's brother, and I saw and heard some things respecting your conduct towards her, which were calculated to awaken unpleasant suspicions, that allow me to say, a little candour and confidence on your part might have removed; and at last, I chanced to overhear a part of a conversation between you and her that made me think I had a right to hate you."

"And how came you to know that I was her brother?" asked he in some anxiety.

"She told me herself. She told me all. *She* knew I might be trusted. But you needn't disturb yourself about *that*, Mr. Lawrence, for I've seen the last of her!"

"The last! is she gone then?"

"No, but she has bid adieu to me; and I have promised never to go near that house again while she inhabits it." I could have groaned aloud at the bitter thoughts awakened by this turn in the discourse. But I only clenched my hands, and stamped my foot upon the rug. My companion however, was evidently relieved.

"You have done right!" he said in a tone of unqualified approbation, while his face brightened into almost a sunny expression, "And as for the mistake, I am sorry for both our sakes that it should have occurred. Perhaps you can forgive my want of candour, and, remember, as some partial mitigation of the offence, how little encouragement to friendly confidence you have given me of late."

"Yes, yes, I remember it all: nobody can blame me more than I blame myself in my own heart—at any rate, nobody can regret more sincerely than I do the result of my *brutality* as you rightly term it."

"Never mind that," said he, faintly smiling; "let us forget all unpleasant words on both sides, as well as deeds, and consign to oblivion everything that we have cause to regret. Have you any objection to take my hand—or you'd rather not?" It trembled through weakness, as he held it out, and dropped before I had time to catch it and give it a hearty squeeze, which he had not the strength to return.

"How dry and burning your hand is Lawrence," said I. "You are really ill, and I have made you worse by all this talk."

"Oh, it is nothing: only a cold got by the rain."

"My doing, too."

"Never mind that—but tell me, did you mention this affair to my sister?"

"To confess the truth, I had not the courage to do so; but when you tell her, will you just say that I deeply regret it, and—"

"Oh, never fear! I shall say nothing against you, as long as you keep your good resolution of remaining aloof from her. She has not heard of my illness then, that you are aware of?"

"I think not."

"I'm glad of that, for I have been all this time tormenting myself with the fear that somebody would tell her I was dying, or desperately ill, and she would be either distressing herself on account of her inability to hear from me or do me any good, or perhaps committing the madness of coming to see me. I must contrive to let her know something about it, if I can," continued he reflectively, "or she will be hearing some such story. Many would be glad to tell her such news, just to see how she would take it; and then she might expose herself to fresh scandal."

"I wish I had told her," said I. "If it were not for my promise, I would tell her now."

"By no means! I am not dreaming of that;—but if I were to write a short note, now—not mentioning you, Markham, but just giving a slight account of my illness, by way of excuse for my not coming to see her, and to put her on her guard against any exaggerated reports she may hear,—and address it in a disguised hand—would you do me the favour to slip it into the post-office as you pass? for I dare not trust any of the servants in such a case."

Most willingly I consented, and immediately brought him his desk. There was little need to disguise his hand, for the poor fellow seemed to have considerable difficulty in writing at all, so as to be legible. When the note was done, I thought it time to retire, and took leave after asking if there was anything in the world I could do for him, little or great, in the way of alleviating his sufferings, and repairing the injury I had done.

"No," said he; "you have already done much towards it; you have done more for me than the most skilful physician could do; for you have relieved my mind of two great burdens—anxiety on my sister's account, and deep regret upon your own, for I do believe these two sources of torment have had more effect in working me up into a fever, than anything else; and I am persuaded I shall soon recover now. There is one more thing you can do for me, and that is, come and see me now and then—for you see I am very lonely here, and I promise your entrance shall not be disputed again."

I engaged to do so, and departed with a cordial pressure of the hand. I posted the letter on my way home, most manfully resisting the temptation of dropping in a word from myself the same time.

CHAPTER XLVI
FRIENDLY COUNSELS

I felt strongly tempted, at times, to enlighten my mother and sister on the real character and circumstances of the persecuted tenant of Wildfell Hall; and at first I greatly regretted having omitted to ask that lady's permission to do so; but, on due reflection, I considered that if it were known to them, it could not long remain a secret to the Millwards and Wilsons, and such was my present appreciation of Eliza Millward's disposition, that, if once she got a clue to the story, I should fear she would soon find means to enlighten Mr. Huntingdon upon the place of his wife's retreat. I would therefore wait patiently till these weary six months were over, and then, when the fugitive had found another home, and I was permitted to write to her, I would beg to be allowed to clear her name from these vile calumnies: at present I must content myself with simply asserting that I knew them to be false, and would prove it some day, to the shame of those who slandered her. I don't think anybody believed me: but everybody soon learned to avoid insinuating a word against her, or even mentioning her name in my presence. They thought I was so madly infatuated by the seductions of that unhappy lady that I was determined to support her in the very face of reason; and meantime I grew insupportably morose and misanthropical from the idea that every one I met was harbouring unworthy thoughts of the supposed Mrs. Graham, and would express them if he dared. My poor mother was quite distressed about me; but I couldn't help it—at least I thought I could not; though sometimes I felt a pang of remorse for my undutiful conduct to her, and made an effort to amend, attended with some partial success—and indeed I was generally more humanized in my demeanour to her than to any one else, Mr. Lawrence excepted. Rose and Fergus usually shunned my presence; and it was well they did, for I was not fit company for them, nor they for me, under the present circumstances.

Mrs. Huntingdon did not leave Wildfell Hall till above two months after our farewell interview. During that time she never appeared at church, and I never went near the house: I only knew she was still there by her brother's brief answers to my many and varied enquiries respecting her. I was a very constant and attentive visitor to him throughout the whole period of his illness and convalescence; not only from the interest I took in his recovery, and my desire to cheer him up and make the utmost possible amends for my former "brutality," but from my growing attachment to himself, and the increasing pleasure I found in his society—partly, from his increased cordiality to me, but chiefly on account of his close connection—both in blood and in affection—with my adored Helen. I loved him for it better than I liked to express; and I took a secret delight in pressing those slender, white fingers, so marvelously like her own, considering he was not a woman, and in watching the passing changes in his fair, pale features, and observing the intonations of his voice—detecting resemblances which I wondered had never struck me before. He provoked me at times, indeed, by his evident reluctance to talk to me about his sister, though I did not question the friendliness of his motives in wishing to discourage my remembrance of her.

His recovery was not quite so rapid as he had expected it to be: he was not able to mount his pony till a fortnight after the date of our reconciliation; and the first use he made of his returning strength, was to ride over by night to Wildfell Hall, to see his sister. It was a hazardous enterprise both for him and for her, but he thought it necessary to consult with her on the subject of her projected departure, if not to calm her apprehensions respecting his health, and the worst result was a slight relapse of his illness; for no one knew of the visit, but the inmates of the old Hall—except myself; and I believe it had not been his intention to mention it to me, for when I came to see him the next day, and observed he was not so well as he ought to have been, he merely said he had caught cold by being out too late in the evening.

"You'll *never* be able to see your sister, if you don't take care of yourself," said I, a little provoked at the circumstance on her account, instead of commiserating him.

"I've seen her already," said he, quietly.

"You've seen her!" cried I, in astonishment.

"Yes." And then he told me what considerations had impelled him to make the venture, and with what precautions he had made it.

"And how was she?" I eagerly asked.

"As usual," was the brief though sad reply.

"As usual—that is, far from happy and far from strong."

"She is not positively ill," returned he; "and she will recover her spirits in a while I have no doubt—but so many trials have been almost too much for her. How threatening those clouds look!" continued he, turning towards the window. "We shall have thunder showers before night, I imagine; and they are just in the midst of stacking my corn. Have you got yours all in yet?"

"No.—And Lawrence, did she—did your sister mention me?"

"She asked if I had seen you lately."

"And what else did she say?"

"I cannot tell you all she said," replied he with a slight smile, "for we talked a good deal, though my stay was but short; but our conversation was chiefly on the subject of her intended departure, which I begged her to delay till I was better able to assist her in her search after another home."

"But did she say no more about me?"

"She did not say much about you, Markham. I should not have encouraged her to do so, had she been inclined; but happily she was not: she only asked a few questions concerning you, and seemed satisfied with my brief answers; wherein she showed herself wiser than her friend—and I may tell you too, that she seemed to be far more anxious lest you should think too much of her, than lest you should forget her."

"She was right."

"But I fear *your* anxiety is quite the other way, respecting her."

"No, it is not: I wish her to be happy; but I don't wish her to forget me altogether. She knows it is impossible that I should forget *her*; and she is right to wish me not to remember her too well. I should not desire her to regret me *too* deeply; but I can scarcely imagine she will make herself very unhappy about me, because I know I am not worthy of it, except in my appreciation of her."

"You are neither of you worthy of a broken heart,—nor of all the sighs, and tears, and sorrowful thoughts that have been, and I fear will be wasted upon you both; but at present, each has a more exalted opinion of the other than, I fear, he or she deserves; and my sister's feelings are naturally full as keen as yours, and I believe *more* constant; but she has the good sense and fortitude to strive against them in this particular; and I trust she will not rest till she has entirely weaned her thoughts—" he hesitated.

"From me," said I.

"And I wish you would make the like exertions," continued he.

"Did she *tell* you that that was her intention?"

"No; the question was not broached between us: there was no necessity for it, for I had no doubt that such was her determination."

"To forget me?"

"Yes Markham! Why not?"

"Oh! well," was my only audible reply; but I internally answered,—"No, Lawrence, you're wrong there, she is *not* determined to forget me. It would be *wrong* to forget one so deeply and fondly devoted to her, who can so thoroughly appreciate her excellencies and sympathize with all her thoughts as I can do, and it would be wrong in me to forget so excellent and divine a piece of God's creation as she, when I have once so truly loved and known her." But I said no more to him on that subject. I instantly started a new topic of conversation, and soon took leave of my companion, with a feeling of less cordiality towards him than usual. Perhaps I had no right to be annoyed at him, but I was so nevertheless.

In little more than a week after this, I met him returning from a visit to the Wilsons; and I now resolved to do *him* a good turn, though at the expense of his feelings, and, perhaps, at the risk of incurring that displeasure which is so commonly the reward of those who give disagreeable information or tender their advice unasked. In this, believe me, I was actuated by no motives of revenge for the occasional annoyances I had lately sustained from him,—nor yet by any feeling of malevolent enmity towards Miss Wilson, but purely by the fact that I could not endure that such a woman should be Mrs. Huntingdon's sister, and that, as well for his own sake as for hers, I could not bear to think of his being deceived into a union with one so unworthy of him, and so utterly unfitted to be the partner of his quiet home, and the companion of his life. He had had uncomfortable suspicions on that head himself, I imagined, but such was his inexperience, and such were the lady's powers of attraction and her skill in bringing them to bear upon his young imagination, that they had not disturbed him long, and I believe the only effectual causes of the vacillating indecision that had preserved him hitherto from making an actual declaration of love, was the consideration of her connections, and especially of her mother, whom he could not abide. Had they lived at a distance, he might have surmounted the objection, but within two or three miles of Woodford, it was really no light matter.

"You've been to call on the Wilsons, Lawrence," said I as I walked beside his pony.

"Yes," replied he, slightly averting his face: "I thought it but civil to take the first opportunity of returning their kind attentions, since they have been so very particular and constant in their enquiries, throughout the whole course of my illness."

"It's all Miss Wilson's doing."

"And if it is," returned he, with a very perceptible blush, "is that any reason why I should not make a suitable acknowledgment?"

"It is a reason why you should not make the acknowledgment she looks for."

"Let us drop that subject if you please," said he in evident displeasure.

"No, Lawrence, with your leave we'll continue it a while longer; and I'll tell you something, now we're about it, which you may believe or not as you choose—only please to remember that it is not my custom to speak falsely, and that in this case, I can have no motive for misrepresenting the truth—"

"Well, Markham! what now?"

"*Miss Wilson hates your sister.* It may be natural enough that, in her ignorance of the relationship, she should feel some degree of enmity against her, but no good or amiable woman would be capable of evincing that bitter, cold-blooded, designing malice towards a fancied rival that I have observed in her."

"Markham!!"

"Yes—and it is my belief that Eliza Millward and she, if not the very originators of the slanderous reports that have been propagated, were designedly the encouragers and chief disseminators of them. She was not desirous to mix up *your* name in the matter, of course, but her delight was, and still is, to blacken your sister's character to the utmost of her power without risking too greatly the exposure of her own malevolence!"

"I cannot believe it;" interrupted my companion, his face burning with indignation.

"Well, as I cannot prove it, I must content myself with asserting that it *is* so to the best of my belief; but as you would not willingly marry Miss Wilson if it *were* so, you will do well to be cautious, till you have proved it to be otherwise."

"I never told you, Markham, that I *intended* to marry Miss Wilson," said he proudly.

"No, but whether you do or not, she intends to marry you."

"Did she tell you so?"

"No, but—"

"Then you have no right to make such an assertion respecting her." He slightly quickened his pony's pace, but I laid my hand on its mane, determined he should not leave me yet.

"Wait a moment, Lawrence, and let me explain myself; and don't be so very—I don't know what to call it—*inaccessible* as you are.—I know what you think of Jane Wilson; and I believe I know how far you are mistaken in your opinion: you think she is singularly charming, elegant, sensible, and refined: you are not aware that she is selfish, cold-hearted, ambitious, artful, shallow-minded—"

"Enough, Markham, enough."

"No; let me finish.—You don't know that, if you married her, your home would be rayless and comfortless; and it would break your heart at last to find yourself united to one so wholly incapable of sharing your tastes, feelings, and ideas—so utterly destitute of sensibility, good feeling, and true nobility of soul."

"Have you done?" asked my companion quietly.

"Yes;—I know you hate me for my impertinence, but I don't care if it only conduces to preserve you from that fatal mistake."

"Well!" returned he, with a rather wintry smile—"I'm glad you have overcome, or forgotten your own afflictions so far as to be able to study so deeply the affairs of others, and trouble your head, so unnecessarily, about the fancied or possible calamities of their future life."

We parted—somewhat coldly again; but still we did not cease to be friends; and my well-meant warning, though it might have been more judiciously delivered, as well as more thankfully received, was not wholly unproductive of the desired effect: his visit to the Wilsons was not repeated, and, though, in our subsequent interviews, he never mentioned her name to me, nor I to him,—I have reason to believe he pondered my words in his mind, eagerly though covertly sought information respecting the fair lady from other quarters, secretly compared my character of her with what he had himself observed and what he heard from others, and finally came to the conclusion that, all things considered, she had much better remain Miss Wilson of Ryecote Farm, than be transmuted into Mrs. Lawrence of Woodford Hall. I believe, too, that he soon learned to contemplate with secret amazement his former predilection, and to congratulate himself on the lucky escape he had made; but he never confessed it to me, or hinted one word of acknowledgment for the part I had had in his deliverance—but this was not surprising to any one that knew him as I did.

As for Jane Wilson, she, of course, was disappointed and embittered by the sudden cold neglect, and ultimate desertion of her former admirer. Had I done wrong to blight her cherished hopes? I think not; and certainly my conscience has never accused me, from that day to this, of any evil design in the matter.

CHAPTER XLVII
STARTLING INTELLIGENCE

ONE morning, about the beginning of November, while I was inditing[1] some business letters, shortly after breakfast, Eliza Millward came to call upon my sister. Rose had neither the discrimination nor the virulence to regard the little demon as I did, and they still preserved their former intimacy. At the moment of her arrival, however, there was no one in the room but Fergus and myself, my mother and sister being both of them absent, "on household cares intent;"[2] but *I* was not going to lay myself out for her amusement, whoever else might so incline: I merely honoured her with a careless salutation and a few words of course, and then went on with my writing, leaving my brother to be more polite if he chose. But she wanted to tease me.

"What a pleasure it is to find you at home, Mr. Markham!" said she, with a disingenuously malicious smile. "I so seldom see you now, for you never come to the vicarage. Papa is quite offended I can tell you," she added playfully, looking into my face with an impertinent laugh, as she seated herself, half beside and half before my desk, off the corner of the table.

---

1   "To put into words, compose" (*OED*).

2   A reference to Eve in Milton's (1608–74) *Paradise Lost* (1667): "She turns, on hospitable thoughts intent / What choice to choose for delicacy best, / What order, so contriv'd / as not to mix / Tastes, not well join'd, inelegant, but bring / Taste after taste upheld with kindliest change" (V.332–36). Gilbert uses *Paradise Lost* to humorously magnify the importance of what his mother and sister are doing, as the original quotation describes Eve preparing for the angel Raphael's visit.

"I have had a good deal to do of late," said I, without looking up from my letter.

"Have you indeed! Somebody said you had been strangely neglecting your business these last few months."

"Somebody said wrong, for, these last *two* months—especially, I have been particularly plodding and diligent."

"Ah! Well, there's nothing like active employment, I suppose, to console the afflicted;—and, excuse me, Mr. Markham, but you look so very far from well, and have been, by all accounts, so moody and thoughtful of late,—I could almost think you have some secret care preying on your spirits. *Formerly*," said she timidly, "I could have ventured to ask you what it was, and what I could do to comfort you: I dare not do it now."

"You're very kind, Miss Eliza. When I think you can do anything to comfort me, I'll make bold to tell you."

"Pray do!—I suppose I mayn't guess what it is that troubles you?"

"There's no necessity, for I'll tell you plainly. The thing that troubles me the most at present, is a young lady sitting at my elbow, and preventing me from finishing my letter, and thereafter, repairing to my daily business."

Before she could reply to this ungallant speech, Rose entered the room; and Miss Eliza rising to greet her, they both seated themselves near the fire, where that idle lad, Fergus, was standing, leaning his shoulder against the corner of the chimney-piece, with his legs crossed and his hands in his breeches pockets.

"Now, Rose, I'll tell you a piece of news—I hope you've not heard it before, for good, bad or indifferent, one always likes to be the first to tell.—It's about that sad Mrs. Graham——"

"Hush—sh—sh!" whispered Fergus, in a tone of solemn import. "'We never mention her; her name is never heard.'"[1] And glancing up, I caught him with his eye askance on me, and his finger pointed to his forehead; then, winking at the young lady with a doleful shake of the head, he whispered—"a monomania—but don't mention it—all right but that."

"I should be sorry to injure any one's feelings," returned she, speaking below her breath, "another time, perhaps."

"Speak out, Miss Eliza!" said I, not deigning to notice the other's buffooneries, "you needn't fear to say anything in my presence—that is *true*."

---

1   From Thomas Haynes Bayly (1797–1839): "Oh! no! we never mention her." The text continues with "My lips are now forbid to speak / That once familiar word." This poem/song was so popular that in the posthumous collection of his work, *Songs, Ballads and Other Poems*, (London: R. Bently, 1844), edited by his widow Helena Beecher Hayes Bayly, the German, Italian, French, and Spanish versions of the song are also given (Vol. 1, 100–01).

"Well," answered she, "perhaps you know already that Mrs. Graham's husband is not really dead, and that she had run away from him?" I started, and felt my face glow; but I bent it over my letter, and went on folding it up as she proceeded, "but perhaps you did *not* know that she is now gone back to him again, and that a perfect reconciliation has taken place between them? Only think," she continued, turning to the confounded Rose, "what a fool the man must be!"

"And who gave you this piece of intelligence, Miss Eliza?" said I, interrupting my sister's exclamations.

"I had it from a very authentic source, sir."

"From whom, may I ask?"

"From one of the servants at Woodford."

"Oh! I was not aware that you were on such intimate terms with Mr. Lawrence's household."

"It was not from the man himself, that I heard it; but he told it in confidence to our maid Sarah, and Sarah told it to me."

"In confidence, I suppose; and you tell it in confidence to us; but *I* can tell *you* that it is but a lame story after all, and scarcely one half of it true."

While I spoke, I completed the sealing and direction of my letters, with a somewhat unsteady hand, in spite of all my efforts to retain composure, and in spite of my firm conviction that the story *was* a lame one—that the supposed Mrs. Graham, most certainly, had not *voluntarily* gone back to her husband, or dreamt of a reconciliation. Most likely, she was gone away, and the tale-bearing servant, not knowing what was become of her, had *conjectured* that such was the case, and our fair visitor had detailed it as a certainty, delighted with such an opportunity of tormenting me. But it was possible—barely possible, that some one might have betrayed her, and she had been taken away by force. Determined to know the worst, I hastily pocketed my two letters, and muttering something about being too late for the post, left the room, rushed into the yard and vociferously called for my horse. No one being there, I dragged him out of the stable myself, strapped the saddle on to his back and the bridle on to his head, mounted, and speedily galloped away to Woodford. I found its owner pensively strolling in the grounds.

"Is your sister gone?" were my first words as I grasped his hand, instead of the usual enquiry after his health.

"Yes; she's gone," was his answer, so calmly spoken, that my terror was at once removed.

"I suppose I mayn't know where she is?" said I, as I dismounted and relinquished my horse to the gardener, who, being the only servant within call, had been summoned by his master, from his employment of raking up the dead leaves on the lawn, to take him to the stables.

My companion gravely took my arm, and leading me away to the garden, thus answered my question:—

"She is at Grassdale Manor, in ——shire."

"Where?" cried I, with a convulsive start.

"At Grassdale Manor."

"How was it?" I gasped. "Who betrayed her?"

"She went of her own accord."

"Impossible, Lawrence!! She *could* not be so frantic!" exclaimed I, vehemently grasping his arm, as if to force him to unsay those hateful words.

"She did," persisted he in the same grave, collected manner as before— "and not without reason," he continued, gently disengaging himself from my grasp: "Mr. Huntingdon is ill."

"And so she went to nurse him?"

"Yes."

"Fool!" I could not help exclaiming—and Lawrence looked up with a rather reproachful glance. "Is he dying then?"

"I think not, Markham."

"And how many more nurses has he?—How many ladies are there besides, to take care of him?"

"None: he was alone, or she would not have gone."

"Oh, confound it! this is intolerable!"

"What is? That he should be alone?"

I attempted no reply, for I was not sure that this circumstance did not partly conduce to my distraction. I therefore continued to pace the walk in silent anguish, with my hand pressed to my forehead; then suddenly pausing and turning to my companion, I impatiently exclaimed,

"Why did she take this infatuated step? What fiend persuaded her to it?"

"Nothing persuaded her but her own sense of duty."

"Humbug!"

"I was half inclined to say so myself, Markham, at first. I assure you it was not by my advice that she went, for I detest that man as fervently as you can do—except, indeed that his reformation would give me much greater pleasure than his death:—but all I did was to inform her of the circumstance of his illness (the consequence of a fall from his horse in hunting), and to tell her that that unhappy person, Miss Myers, had left him some time ago."

·"It was ill done! Now, when he finds the convenience of her presence, he will make all manner of lying speeches and false, fair promises for the future, and she will believe him, and then her condition will be ten times worse and ten times more irremediable than before."

"There does not appear to be much ground for such apprehensions at present," said he, producing a letter from his pocket: "from the account I received this morning, I should say—"

It was *her* writing! By an irresistible impulse, I held out my hand, and the words—"Let me see it," involuntarily passed my lips. He was evidently reluctant to grant the request, but while he hesitated, I snatched it from his hand. Recollecting myself, however, the minute after, I offered to restore it.

"Here, take it," said I, "if you don't want me to read it."

"No," replied he, "you may read it if you like."

I read it and so may you.

GRASSDALE, NOV. 4th.

Dear Frederick,

I know you will be anxious to hear from me: and I will tell you all I can. Mr. Huntingdon is very ill, but not dying, or in any immediate danger; and he is rather better at present than he was when I came. I found the house in sad confusion: Mrs. Greaves, Benson, every decent servant had left, and those that were come to supply their places were a negligent, disorderly set, to say no worse—I must change them again if I stay. A professional nurse, a grim, hard old woman, had been hired to attend the wretched invalid. He suffers much, and has no fortitude to bear him through. The immediate injuries he sustained from the accident, however, were not very severe, and would, as the doctor says, have been but trifling to a man of temperate habits; but with *him* it is very different. On the night of my arrival, when I first entered his room, he was lying in a kind of half delirium. He did not notice me till I spoke; and then, he mistook me for another.

"Is it you, Alice, come again?" he murmured. "What did you leave me for?"

"It is I, Arthur—it is Helen, your wife," I replied.

"My wife!" said he, with a start.—"For Heaven's sake, don't mention her!—I have none.—Devil take her," he cried, a moment after,—"and you too! What did you do it for?"

I said no more; but observing that he kept gazing towards the foot of the bed, I went and sat there, placing the light so as to shine full upon me; for I thought he might be dying, and I wanted him to know me. For a long time, he lay silently looking upon me, first with a vacant stare, then with a fixed gaze of strange, growing intensity. At last he startled me by suddenly raising himself on his elbow and demanding in a horrified whisper, with his eyes still fixed upon me,—"Who is it?"

"It is Helen Huntingdon," said I, quietly, rising, at the same time, and removing to a less conspicuous position.

"I must be going mad,"[1] cried he—"or something—delirious perhaps—but leave me, whoever you are—I can't bear that white face, and those

---

1   In the Brontë family's edition of John Thomas Graham's (1795?–1876) *Modern Domestic Medicine* (London: Simpkin & Marshall et al., 1826), their father, Patrick Brontë, has

eyes—for God's sake go, and send me somebody else, that doesn't look like that!"

I went, at once, and sent the hired nurse. But next morning, I ventured to enter his chamber again; and, taking the nurse's place by his bed-side, I watched him and waited on him for several hours, showing myself as little as possible, and only speaking when necessary, and then not above my breath. At first he addressed me as the nurse, but, on my crossing the room to draw up the window-blinds, in obedience to his directions, he said—

"No, it isn't nurse; it's Alice. Stay with me do! that old hag will be the death of me."

"I mean to stay with you," said I. And after that, he would call me Alice—or some other name almost equally repugnant to my feelings. I forced myself to endure it for a while, fearing a contradiction might disturb him too much: but when, having asked for a glass of water, while I held it to his lips, he murmured "Thanks, dearest!"—I could not help distinctly observing—"You would not say so if you knew me," intending to follow that up with another declaration of my identity, but he merely muttered an incoherent reply, so I dropped it again, till some time after, when, as I was bathing his forehead and temples with vinegar and water to relieve the heat and pain in his head, he observed, after looking earnestly upon me for some minutes—

"I have such strange fancies—I can't get rid of them, and they won't let me rest; and the most singular and pertinacious of them all, is your face and voice; they seem just like hers. I could swear at this moment, that she was by my side."

"She is," said I.

"That seems comfortable," continued he, without noticing my words; "and while you do it, the other fancies fade away—but this only strengthens. Go on—go on, till it vanishes too. I can't stand such a mania as this; it would kill me!"

"It never will vanish," said I distinctly, "for it is the truth."

"The truth!" he cried, starting as if an asp had stung him. "You don't mean to say that you are really she!"

"I do; but you needn't shrink away from me, as if I were your greatest enemy: I am come to take care of you, and do what none of *them* would do."

---

written in the margin under the entry "Of Insanity, or Mental Derangement," where Graham explains that the causes are sometimes due to "intoxication" (391). Patrick Brontë writes, "there is also 'delirium tremens', brought on, sometimes, by intoxica-tion—'the patient thinks himself haunted; by demons…'" (391); "if intoxication be left off this madness will generally diminish, &c" (392). No doubt some of this knowledge came from the painful witnessing of his son Branwell's alcoholism.

"For God's sake, don't torment me now!" cried he in pitiable agitation; and then he began to mutter bitter curses against me, or the evil fortune that had brought me there; while I put down the sponge and basin, and resumed my seat at the bed-side.

"Where are they?" said he—"have they all left me—servants and all?"

"There are servants within call, if you want them; but you had better lie down now and be quiet: none of them could or would attend you as carefully as I shall do."

"I can't understand it at all," said he, in bewildered perplexity. "Was it a dream that—" and he covered his eyes with his hand, as if trying to unravel the mystery.

"No Arthur, it was not a dream, that your conduct was such as to oblige me to leave you; but I heard that you were ill and alone, and I am come back to you. You need not fear to trust me: tell me all your wants, and I will try to satisfy them. There is no one else to care for you; and I shall not upbraid you now."

"Oh! I see," said he with a bitter smile, "it's an act of Christian charity, whereby you hope to gain a higher seat in Heaven for yourself, and scoop a deeper pit in hell for me."

"No; I came to offer you that comfort and assistance your situation required; and if I could benefit your soul as well as your body, and awaken some sense of contrition and——"

"Oh, yes; if you could overwhelm me with remorse and confusion of face,[1] now's the time. What have you done with my son?"

"He is well, and you may see him some time, if you compose yourself, but not now."

"Where is he?"

"He is safe."

"Is he here?"

"Wherever he is, you will not see him till you have promised to leave him entirely under my care and protection, and to let me take him away whenever and wherever I please, if I should hereafter judge it necessary to remove him again. But we will talk of that tomorrow: you must be quiet now."

"No, let me see him now. I promise, if it *must* be so."

"No——"

"I swear it, as God is in Heaven! Now then, let me see him."

"But I cannot trust your oaths and promises: I must have a written agreement, and you must sign it in presence of a witness—but not today, tomorrow."

---

1 "Confusion of face" means shame and/or blushing. The expression is used in Daniel 8:9 and Ezra 9:7 to describe the shame of having trespassed against God's laws.

"No, today—now," persisted he: and he was in such a state of feverish excitement, and so bent upon the immediate gratification of his wish, that I thought it better to grant it at once, as I saw he would not rest till I did. But I was determined my son's interest should not be forgotten; and having clearly written out the promise I wished Mr. Huntingdon to give upon a slip of paper, I deliberately read it over to him, and made him sign it in the presence of Rachel. He begged I would not insist upon this: it was a useless exposure of my want of faith in his word, to the servant. I told him I was sorry, but since he had forfeited my confidence, he must take the consequence. He next pleaded inability to hold the pen. "Then we must wait until you can hold it," said I. Upon which, he said he would try; but then, he could not see to write. I placed my finger where the signature was to be, and told him he might write his name in the dark, if he only knew where to put it. But he had not power to form the letters. "In that case, you must be too ill to see the child," said I; and finding me inexorable, he at length managed to ratify the agreement; and I bade Rachel send the boy.

All this may strike you as harsh, but I felt I must not lose my present advantage, and my son's future welfare should not be sacrificed to any mistaken tenderness for this man's feelings. Little Arthur had not forgotten his father, but thirteen months of absence, during which he had seldom been permitted to hear a word about him, or hardly to whisper his name, had rendered him somewhat shy; and when he was ushered into the darkened room where the sick man lay, so altered from his former self, with fiercely flushed face and wildly gleaming eyes—he instinctively clung to me, and stood looking on his father with a countenance expressive of far more awe than pleasure.

"Come here, Arthur," said the latter, extending his hand towards him. The child went, and timidly touched that burning hand, but almost started in alarm, when his father suddenly clutched his arm and drew him nearer to his side.

"Do you know me?" asked Mr. Huntingdon intently perusing his features.

"Yes."

"Who am I?"

"Papa."

"Are you glad to see me?"

"Yes."

"You're *not!*" replied the disappointed parent, relaxing his hold, and darting a vindictive glance at me.

Arthur, thus released, crept back to me and put his hand in mine. His father swore I had made the child hate him, and abused and cursed me bitterly. The instant he began I sent our son out of the room; and when he paused to breathe, I calmly assured him that he was entirely mistaken; I had never once attempted to prejudice his child against him.

"I did indeed desire him to *forget* you," I said, "and especially to forget the lessons you taught him; and for that cause, and to lessen the danger of discovery, I own I have generally discouraged his inclination to talk about you;—but no one can blame me for that, I think."

The invalid only replied by groaning aloud and rolling his head on a pillow in a paroxysm of impatience.

"I am in hell, already!" cried he. "This cursed thirst is burning my heart to ashes! Will *nobody*—"

Before he could finish the sentence, I had poured out a glass of some acidulated,[1] cooling drink that was on the table, and brought it to him. He drank it greedily, but muttered, as I took away the glass,—

"I suppose you're heaping coals of fire on my head[2]—you think."

Not noticing this speech, I asked if there was anything else I could do for him.

"Yes; I'll give you another opportunity of showing your Christian magnanimity," sneered he:—"set my pillow straight,—and these confounded bed-clothes." I did so. "There—now, get me another glass of that slop." I complied. "This is delightful! Isn't it?" said he with a malicious grin, as I held it to his lips—"you never hoped for such a glorious opportunity?"

"Now, shall I stay with you?" said I, as I replaced the glass on the table— "or will you be more quiet if I go, and send the nurse?"

"Oh, yes, you're wondrous gentle and obliging!—But you've driven me mad with it all!" responded he, with an impatient toss.

"I'll leave you then," said I, and I withdrew, and did not trouble him with my presence again that day, except for a minute or two at a time, just to see how he was and what he wanted.

Next morning, the doctor ordered him to be bled; and after that, he was more subdued and tranquil. I passed half the day in his room at different intervals. My presence did not appear to agitate or irritate him as before, and he accepted my services quietly, without any bitter remarks—indeed he scarcely spoke at all, except to make known his wants, and hardly then. But on the morrow—that is, today—in proportion as he recovered from the state of exhaustion and stupefaction—his ill-nature appeared to revive.

---

1 "To render sour or acid" (*OED*). The *OED* cites one edition of Graham's *Modern Domestic Medicine* as recommending adding vinegar to barley water or any other ordinary beverage of the patient (page 91 of the 1844 edition). The Brontës owned an earlier edition of this text (1826) that their father, Patrick Brontë, heavily annotated; see n. 1, page 356.

2 By referring to Proverbs 25:21–22—"If thine enemy be hungry, give him bread to eat; and if he be thirsty, give him water to drink: For thou shalt heap coals of fire upon his head and the Lord shall reward thee"—Arthur is implying that Helen's aid has a spiteful quality to it.

"Oh, this sweet revenge!" cried he, when I had been doing all I could to make him comfortable and to remedy the carelessness of his nurse. "And you can enjoy it with such a quiet conscience too, because it's all in the way of duty."

"It is well for me that I *am* doing my duty," said I, with a bitterness I could not repress, "for it is the only comfort I have; and the satisfaction of my own conscience, it seems, is the only reward I need look for!"

He looked rather surprised at the earnestness of my manner.

"What reward *did* you look for?" he asked.

"You will think me a liar if I tell you—but I *did* hope to benefit you; as well to better your mind, as to alleviate your present sufferings; but it appears I am to do neither—your own bad spirit will not let me. As far as *you* are concerned, I have sacrificed my own feelings, and all the little earthly comfort that was left me, to no purpose;—and every little thing I do for you is ascribed to self-righteous malice and refined revenge!"

"It's all very fine, I dare say," said he, eyeing me with stupid amazement; "and of course I ought to be melted to tears of penitence and admiration at the sight of so much generosity and superhuman goodness,—but you see I can't manage it. However, pray do me all the good you can, if you do really find any pleasure in it; for you perceive I am almost as miserable just now as you need wish to see me. Since you came, I confess, I have had better attendance than before, for these wretches neglected me shamefully, and all my old friends seem to have fairly forsaken me. I've had a dreadful time of it, I assure you: I sometimes thought I should have died—do you think there's any chance?"

"There's always a chance of death; and it is always well to live with such a chance in view."

"Yes, yes—but do you think there's any likelihood that this illness will have a fatal termination?"

"I cannot tell; but, supposing it should, how are you prepared to meet the event?"

"Why the doctor told me I wasn't to think about it, for I was sure to get better, if I stuck to his regimen and prescriptions."

"I hope you may, Arthur, but neither the doctor nor I can speak with certainty in such a case: there is internal injury, and it is difficult to know to what extent."

"There now! you want to scare me to death."

"No; but I don't want to lull you to false security. If a consciousness of the uncertainty of life can dispose you to serious and useful thoughts, I would not deprive you of the benefit of such reflections, whether you do eventually recover or not. Does the idea of death appal you *very* much?"

"It's just the only thing I can't bear to think of; so if you've any—"

"But it must come sometime," interrupted I; "and if it be years hence, it will as certainly overtake you as if it came today,—and no doubt be as unwelcome then as now, unless you—"

"Oh, hang it! Don't torment me with your preachments now, unless you want to kill me outright—I can't stand it, I tell you—I've sufferings enough without that. If you think there's danger, save me from it; and then, in gratitude, I'll hear whatever you like to say."

I accordingly dropped the unwelcome topic. And now, Frederick, I think I may bring my letter to a close. From these details, you may form your own judgment of the state of my patient, and of my own position and future prospects. Let me hear from you soon, and I will write again to tell you how we get on; but now that my presence is tolerated—and even required in the sick-room, I shall have but little time to spare between my husband and my son,—for I must not entirely neglect the latter: it would not do to keep him always with Rachel, and I dare not leave him for a moment with any of the other servants, or suffer him to be alone, lest he should meet them. If his father get worse, I shall ask Esther Hargrave to take charge of him for a time, till I have re-organized the household at least; but I greatly prefer keeping him under my own eye.

I find myself in rather a singular position: I am exerting my utmost endeavours to promote the recovery and reformation of my husband, and if I succeed what shall I do? My duty, of course,—but how?—No matter; I can perform the task that is before me now, and God will give me strength[1] to do whatever he requires hereafter.—Good bye, dear Frederick.

Helen Huntingdon.

"What do you think of it?" said Lawrence as I silently refolded the letter.

"It seems to me," returned I, "that she is casting her pearls before swine. May they be satisfied with trampling them under their feet, and not turn again and rend her![2] But I shall say no more against her: I see that she was actuated by the best and noblest motives in what she has done; and if the act is not a wise one, may Heaven protect her from its consequences! May I keep this letter, Lawrence?—you see she has never once mentioned me throughout—or made the most distant allusion to me; therefore, there can be no impropriety or harm in it."

"And therefore, why should you wish to keep it?"

---

1 Possibly a reference to Philippians 4:13: "I can do all things through Christ which strengtheneth me."

2 See Matthew 7:6: "Give not that which is holy unto the dogs, neither cast ye your pearls before swine, lest they trample them under their feet, and turn again and rend you."

"Were not these characters written by her hand? and were not these words conceived in her mind, and many of them spoken by her lips?"

"Well," said he. And so I kept it; otherwise, Halford, you could never have become so thoroughly acquainted with its contents.

"And when you write," said I, "will you have the goodness to ask her if I may be permitted to enlighten my mother and sister on her real history and circumstance, just so far as is necessary to make the neighbourhood sensible of the shameful injustice they have done her? I want no tender messages, but just ask her that, and tell her it is the greatest favour she could do me; and tell her—no, nothing more.—You see I know the address, and I might write to her myself, but I am so virtuous as to refrain."

"Well, I'll do this for you, Markham."

"And as soon as you receive an answer, you'll let me know?"

"If all be well, I'll come myself and tell you, immediately."

CHAPTER XLVIII
FURTHER INTELLIGENCE

FIVE or six days after this, Mr. Lawrence paid us the honour of a call; and when he and I were alone together—which I contrived as soon as possible, by bringing him out to look at my cornstacks—he showed me another letter from his sister. This one he was quite willing to submit to my longing gaze: he thought, I suppose, it would do me good. The only answer it gave to my message was this:—

"Mr. Markham is at liberty to make such revelations concerning me as he judges necessary. He will know that I should wish but little to be said on the subject. I hope he is well; but tell him he must not think of me."

I can give you a few extracts from the rest of the letter, for I was permitted to keep this also—perhaps, as an antidote to all pernicious hopes and fancies.

★ ★ ★ ★ ★

He is decidedly better, but very low from the depressing effects of his severe illness and the strict regimen he is obliged to observe—so opposite to all his previous habits. It is deplorable to see how completely his past life has degenerated his once noble constitution, and vitiated the whole system of his organization. But the doctor says he may now be considered out of danger, if he will only continue to observe the necessary restrictions. Some stimulating cordials he must have, but they should be judiciously diluted and sparingly used; and I find it very difficult to keep him to this. At first, his extreme dread of death rendered the task an easy one; but in proportion as he feels his acute suffering abating and sees the danger receding, the more intractable he becomes. Now also, his appetite for food is beginning to return; and here too, his long habits of self-indulgence are greatly against him. I watch and restrain him as well as I can, and often get bitterly abused for my rigid severity; and sometimes he contrives to elude my vigilance, and sometimes acts in open opposition to my will. But he is now so completely reconciled to my attendance in general that he is never satisfied when I am not by his side. I am obliged to be a little stiff with him sometimes, or he would make a complete slave of me: and I know it would be unpardonable weakness to give up all other interests for him. I have the servants to overlook and my little Arthur to attend to,—and my own health too, all of which would be entirely neglected were I to satisfy his exorbitant demands. I do not generally sit up at nights, for I think the nurse who has made it her business, is better qualified for such undertakings than I am; but still, an unbroken night's rest is what I but seldom enjoy, and never can venture to reckon upon; for my patient makes no scruple of calling me up at any hour when his wants or his fancies require my presence. But he is manifestly afraid of my displeasure; and if at one time he tries my patience by his unreasonable exactions, and fretful complaints and reproaches, at another, he depresses me by his abject submission and deprecatory self-abasement when he fears he has gone too far. But all this I can readily pardon; I know it is chiefly the result of his enfeebled frame and disordered nerves—what annoys me the most, is his occasional attempts at affectionate fondness that I can neither credit nor return; not that I hate him: his sufferings and my own laborious care have given him some claim to my regard—to my affection even, if he would only be quiet and sincere, and content to let things remain as they are, but the more he tries to conciliate me the more I shrink from him and from the future.

"Helen, what do you mean to do when I get well?" he asked this morning. "Will you run away again?"

"It entirely depends upon your own conduct."

"Oh, I'll be very good."

"But if I find it necessary to leave you, Arthur, I shall not 'run away:' you know I have your own promise that I may go whenever I please, and take my son with me."

"Oh, but you shall have no cause." And then followed a variety of professions, which I rather coldly checked.

"Will you not forgive me then?" said he.

"Yes,—I *have* forgiven you; but I know you cannot love me as you once did—and I should be very sorry if you were to, for I could not pretend to return it: so let us drop the subject, and never recur to it again. By what I *have* done for you, you may judge of what I *will* do—if it be not incompatible with the higher duty I owe to my son (higher, because he never forfeited his claims, and because I hope to do more good to him than I can ever do to you); and if you wish me to feel kindly towards you, it is *deeds* not *words* that must purchase my affection and esteem."

His sole reply to this was a slight grimace, and a scarcely perceptible shrug. Alas unhappy man! words, with him, are so much cheaper than deeds; it was as if I had said, "Pounds, not pence, must buy the article you want." And then he sighed a querulous, self-commiserating sigh, as if in pure regret that he, the loved and courted of so many worshippers, should be now abandoned to the mercy of a harsh, exacting, cold-hearted woman like that, and even glad of what kindness she chose to bestow.

"It's a pity, isn't it?" said I; and whether I rightly divined his musings or not, the observation chimed in with his thoughts, for he answered—"It can't be helped," with a rueful smile at my penetration.

★ ★ ★ ★ ★

I have seen Esther Hargrave twice. She is a charming creature, but her blithe spirit is almost broken, and her sweet temper almost spoiled, by the still unremitting persecutions of her mother, in behalf of her rejected suitor—not violent, but wearisome and unremitting like a continual dropping. The un-natural parent seems determined to make her daughter's life a burden if she will not yield to her desires.

"Mamma does all she can," said she, "to make me feel myself a burden and incumbrance to the family, and the most ungrateful, selfish, and undutiful daughter that ever was born; and Walter, too is as stern and cold, and haughty as if he hated me outright. I believe I should have yielded at once if I had known, from the beginning, how much resistance would have cost me; but now, for very obstinacy's sake, I *will* stand out!"

"A bad motive for a good resolve," I answered. "But however, I know you have better motives, really, for your perseverance: and I counsel you to keep them still in view."

"Trust me, I will. I threaten mamma sometimes, that I'll run away, and disgrace the family by earning my own livelihood, if she torments me any more; and then that frightens her a little. But I *will* do it, in good earnest, if they don't mind."

"Be quiet and patient awhile," said I, "and better times will come."

Poor girl! I wish somebody that was worthy to possess her would come and take her away—don't you, Frederick?

★ ★ ★ ★ ★

If the perusal of this letter filled me with dismay for Helen's future life and mine, there was one great source of consolation: it was now in my power to clear her name from every foul aspersion. The Millwards and the Wilsons should see with their own eyes, the bright sun bursting from the cloud—and they should be scorched and dazzled by its beams;—and my own friends too should see it—they whose suspicions had been such gall and wormwood[1] to my soul. To effect this, I had only to drop the seed into the ground, and it would soon become a stately, branching herb:[2] a few words to my mother and sister, I knew, would suffice to spread the news throughout the whole neighbourhood, without any further exertion on my part.

Rose was delighted; and as soon as I had told her all I thought proper— which was all I affected to know—she flew with alacrity to put on her bonnet and shawl, and hasten to carry the glad tidings to the Millwards and Wilsons—glad tidings I suspect, to none but herself and Mary Millward— that steady, sensible girl, whose sterling worth had been so quickly perceived and duly valued by the supposed Mrs. Graham, in spite of her plain outside; and who, on her part, had been better able to see and appreciate that lady's true character and qualities than the brightest genius among them.

As I may never have occasion to mention her again, I may as well tell you here, that she was at this time privately engaged to Richard Wilson—a secret, I believe to every one but their two selves. That worthy student was now at Cambridge, where his most exemplary conduct and his diligent persever-ance in the pursuit of learning carried him safely through, and eventually brought him with hard-earned honours and an untarnished reputation, to the close of his collegiate career. In due time, he became Mr. Millward's first and only curate—for that gentleman's declining years forced him at last to acknowledge that the duties of his extensive parish were a little too much for those vaunted energies which he was wont to boast over his younger and less active brethren of the cloth. This was what the patient, faithful lov-ers had privately planned, and quietly waited for years ago; and in due time they were united, to the astonishment of the little world they lived in, that had long since declared them both born to single blessedness; affirming it impossible that the pale, retiring bookworm should ever summon courage

---

1   See Lamentations 3:19: "Remembering mine affliction and my misery, the wormwood and the gall." While clearly a biblical reference, this expression was used colloquially to mean bitterness. (Wormwood is a plant [*Artemisia Absinthium*] known for its bitter taste.) Charlotte Brontë uses this expression when Jane Eyre significantly learns from Helen Burns not to infuse so much "gall and wormwood" into her story at Lowood school (135).

2   Gilbert is echoing the biblical language of Jesus' parable of the mustard seed in Mat-thew 13:31–32, where Jesus compares the kingdom of heaven to "a grain of mustard seed ... [w]hich indeed is the least of all seeds: but when it is grown, it is the greatest among herbs, and becometh a tree, so that the birds of the air come and lodge in the branches thereof."

to seek a wife, or be able to obtain one if he did, and equally impossible that the plain-looking, plain-dealing, unattractive, unconciliating Miss Millward should ever find a husband.

They still continued to live at the vicarage, the lady dividing her time between her father, her husband, and their poor parishioners,—and subsequently, her rising family; and now that the Reverend Michael Millward has been gathered to his fathers, full of years and honours,[1] the Reverend Richard Wilson has succeeded him to the vicarage of Lindenhope, greatly to the satisfaction of its inhabitants, who had so long tried and fully proved his merits, and those of his excellent and well-loved partner.

If you are interested in the after fate of that lady's sister, I can only tell you—what perhaps you have heard from another quarter—that some twelve or thirteen years ago, she relieved the happy couple of her presence by marrying a wealthy tradesman of L——; and I don't envy him his bargain. I fear she leads him a rather uncomfortable life, though, happily he is too dull to perceive the extent of his misfortune. I have little enough to do with her myself: we have not met for many years; but, I am well assured, she has not yet forgotten or forgiven either her former lover or the lady whose superior qualities first opened his eyes to the folly of his boyish attachment.

As for Richard Wilson's sister, she, having been wholly unable to recapture Mr. Lawrence or obtain any partner rich and elegant enough to suit her ideas of what the husband of Jane Wilson ought to be, is yet in single blessedness. Shortly after the death of her mother, she withdrew the light of her presence from Ryecote Farm, finding it impossible any longer to endure the rough manners and unsophisticated habits of her honest brother Robert and his worthy wife, or the idea of being identified with such vulgar people in the eyes of the world,—and took lodgings in —— the county town, where she lived, and still lives, I suppose, in a kind of closefisted, cold, uncomfortable gentility, doing no good to others and but little to herself; spending her days in fancy-work and scandal; referring frequently to her "brother the vicar" and her "sister the vicar's lady," but never to her brother the farmer and her sister the farmer's wife; seeing as much company as she can without too much expense, but loving no one and beloved by none—a cold-hearted, supercilious, keenly, insidiously censorious old maid.

---

1 Here, Brontë has combined two biblical passages describing the deaths of revered patriarchs: Abraham in Genesis 25:8: "Then Abraham gave up the ghost and died in a good old age, an old man and full of years; and was gathered to his people"; and David in 1 Chronicles 29:28: "And he died in a good old age, full of days, riches, and honour: and Solomon his son reigned in his stead."

CHAPTER XLIX

"The rain descended, and the floods came, and the winds blew,
and beat upon that house; and it fell: and great was the fall of it."[1]

THOUGH Mr. Lawrence's health was now quite re-established, my visits
to Woodford were as unremitting as ever; though often less protracted than
before. We seldom *talked* about Mrs. Huntingdon; but yet we never met
without mentioning her, for I never sought his company but with the hope
of hearing something about her, and he never sought mine at all, because he
saw me often enough without. But I always began to talk of other things, and
waited first to see if *he* would introduce the subject. If he did not, I would
casually ask, "Have you heard from your sister lately?" If he said, "No," the
matter was dropped: if he said "Yes," I would venture to enquire, "How is
she?" but never "How is her husband?" though I might be burning to know;
because, I had not the hypocrisy to profess any anxiety for his recovery, and
I had not the face to express any desire for a contrary result. Had I any such
desire?—I fear I must plead guilty: but since you have heard my confession,
you must hear my justification as well—a few of the excuses, at least, wherewith I sought to pacify my own accusing conscience:—

In the first place, you see, his life did harm to others, and evidently no
good to himself; and though I wished it to terminate, I would not have hastened its close if, by the lifting of a finger, I could have done so, or if a spirit
had whispered in my ear that a single effort of the will would be enough,—
unless, indeed, I had the power to exchange him for some other victim of the
grave, whose life might be of service to his race, and whose death would be
lamented by his friends. But was there any harm in wishing that, among the
many thousands whose souls would certainly be required of them[2] before
the year was over, this wretched mortal might be one? I thought not; and
therefore I wished with all my heart that it might please Heaven to remove
him to a better world, or if that might not be, still, to take him out of this, for
if he were unfit to answer the summons now, after a warning sickness, and

---

1 Ominously, this quotation is from Jesus' parable about the "foolish man which built
his house upon the sand" (Matthew 7:26; the quotation that heads the chapter is from
Matthew 7:27). Brontë uses this same parable earlier, in chapter 42, to comment on
how women's married lives were built upon their husbands' good or bad behavior (see
n. 1, page 322).

2 This expression echoes the language in Jesus' parable of a rich man who told his soul,
"thou hast much goods laid up for many years; take thine ease, eat, drink, and be merry.
But God said unto him, Thou fool, this night thy soul shall be required of thee: then
whose shall those things be which thou hast provided?" Luke 12:19–20; the entire parable is told in Luke 12:16–21.

with such an angel by his side, it seemed but too certain that he never would be—that, on the contrary, returning health would bring returning lust and villainy, and as he grew more certain of recovery, more accustomed to her generous goodness, his feelings would become more callous, his heart more flinty and impervious to her persuasive arguments—but God knew best. Meantime, however, I could not but be anxious for the result of His decrees; knowing, as I did, that (leaving myself entirely out of the question) however Helen might feel interested in her husband's welfare, however she might deplore his fate, still, while he lived, she *must* be miserable.

A fortnight passed away, and my enquiries were always answered in the negative. At length a welcome "yes" drew from me the second question. Lawrence divined my anxious thoughts, and appreciated my reserve. I feared at first, he was going to torture me by unsatisfactory replies, and either leave me quite in the dark concerning what I wanted to know, or force me to drag the information out of him, morsel by morsel, by direct inquiries— "and serve you right," you will say; but he was more merciful; and in a little while, he put his sister's letter into my hand. I silently read it, and restored it to him without comment or remark. This mode of procedure suited him so well that thereafter he always pursued the plan of showing me her letters at once, when I enquired after her, if there were any to show: it was so much less trouble than to tell me their contents; and I received such confidences so quietly and discreetly that he was never induced to discontinue them.

But I devoured those precious letters with my eyes, and never let them go till their contents were stamped upon my mind; and when I got home, the most important passages were entered in my diary among the remarkable events of the day.

The first of these communications brought intelligence of a serious relapse in Mr. Huntingdon's illness, entirely the result of his own infatuation in persisting in the indulgence of his appetite for stimulating drink. In vain had she remonstrated, in vain she had mingled his wine with water: her arguments and entreaties were a nuisance, her interference was an insult so intolerable that at length, on finding she had covertly diluted the pale port that was brought him, he threw the bottle out of the window, swearing he would not be cheated like a baby, ordered the butler, on pain of instant dismissal, to bring a bottle of the strongest wine in the cellar, and, affirming that he should have been well long ago if he had been let to have his own way, but she wanted to keep him weak in order that she might have him under her thumb—but by the Lord Harry, he would have no more humbug—seized a glass in one hand and the bottle in the other, and never rested till he had drunk it dry. Alarming symptoms were the immediate result of this "imprudence" as she mildly termed it—symptoms which had rather increased than diminished since; and this was the cause of her delay in writing to her brother. Every former feature of his malady had returned with augmented virulence: the slight external wound, half-healed, had broken out afresh; internal inflammation had taken place, which might terminate fatally if not soon removed. Of course, the wretched sufferer's temper was not improved by this calamity—in fact, I suspect it was well nigh insupportable, though his kind nurse did not complain; but she said she had been obliged, at last, to give her son in charge to Esther Hargrave, as her presence was so constantly required in the sick room that she could not possibly attend to him herself; and though the child had begged to be allowed to continue with her there, and to help her to nurse his papa, and though she had no doubt he would have been very good and quiet,—she could not think of subjecting his young and tender feelings to the sight of so much suffering, or of allowing him to witness his father's impatience, or hear the dreadful language he was wont to use in his paroxysms of pain or irritation.

"The latter," continued she, "most deeply regrets the step that has occasioned his relapse,—but, as usual, he throws the blame upon me. If I had reasoned with him like a rational creature, he says, it never would have happened; but to be treated like a baby or a fool, was enough to put any man past his patience, and drive him to assert his independence even at the sacrifice of his own interest—he forgets how often I had *reasoned* him 'past his patience' before. He appears to be sensible of his danger; but nothing can induce him to behold it in the proper light. The other night while I was waiting on him, and just as I had brought him a draught to assuage his burning thirst—he observed, with a return of his former sarcastic bitterness,—

"'Yes, you're mighty attentive *now*!—I suppose there's *nothing* you wouldn't do for me now?'

"'You know,' said I, a little surprised at his manner, 'that I am willing to do anything I can to relieve you.'

"'Yes, *now*, my immaculate angel; but when once you have secured your reward, and find yourself safe in Heaven, and me howling in hell-fire, catch you lifting a finger to serve me *then*!—No, you'll look complacently on, and not so much as dip the tip of your finger in water to cool my tongue!'[1]

"'If so, it will be because of the great gulf over which I cannot pass;[2] and if I *could* look complacently on in such a case, it would be only from the as-

---

1   In the parable of Lazarus and Dives (Luke 16:19–31), the rich man, now in hell, "cried and said, Father Abraham, have mercy on me, and send Lazarus, that he may dip the tip of his finger in water, and cool my tongue; for I am tormented in this flame. But Abraham said, Son, remember that thou in thy lifetime receivedst thy good things, and likewise Lazarus evil things: but now he is comforted, and thou art tormented" (Luke 16:24–25).

2   Helen's response echoes Father Abraham's: "And beside all this, between us and you there is a great gulf fixed: so that they which would pass from hence to you cannot; neither can they pass to us, that would come from thence" (Luke 19:26).

surance that you were being purified from your sins, and fitted to enjoy the happiness I felt.[1]—But are you *determined*, Arthur, that I shall not meet you in Heaven?'

"'Humph! What should I do there, I should like to know?'

"'Indeed, I cannot tell; and I fear it is too certain that your tastes and feelings must be widely altered before you can have any enjoyment there. But do you prefer sinking, without an effort, into the state of torment you picture to yourself?'

"'Oh, it's all a fable;'[2] said he, contemptuously.

"'Are you sure, Arthur? are you *quite* sure? Because if there is any doubt, and if you should find yourself mistaken after all, when it is too late to turn—'

"'It would be rather awkward, to be sure,' said he; 'but don't bother me now—I'm not going to die yet.—I can't and won't,' he added vehemently, as if suddenly struck with the appalling aspect of that terrible event, 'Helen, you *must* save me!' And he earnestly seized my hand, and looked into my face with such imploring eagerness that my heart bled for him, and I could not speak for tears."

★ ★ ★ ★ ★

The next letter brought intelligence that the malady was fast increasing; and the poor sufferer's horror of death was still more distressing than his impatience of bodily pain. *All* his friends had not forsaken him, for Mr. Hattersley, hearing of his danger, had come to see him from his distant home in the north. His wife had accompanied him, as much for the pleasure of seeing her dear friend, from whom she had been parted so long, as to visit her mother and sister.

Mrs. Huntingdon expressed herself glad to see Milicent once more, and pleased to behold her so happy and well. "She is now at the Grove," continued the letter, "but she often calls to see me. Mr. Hattersley spends much of his time at Arthur's bed-side. With more good feeling than I gave him credit for, he evinces considerable sympathy for his unhappy friend, and is far more willing than able to comfort him. Sometimes he tries to joke and laugh

---

1   Here, Helen alludes to the possibility of universal salvation, a belief that after "being purified from [one's] sins," one could get to heaven. See Brontë's letter to the Reverend David Thom for her "trembling hope at first, and … [her later] glad conviction of its truth" (Appendix A1), and her poem "A Word to the Elect" (Appendix A3), which also explores this belief.

2   Davies points out how this line evokes Christopher Marlowe's (1564–93) *Dr Faustus* (c. 1594), when he says "I think hell's a fable" (V.128) (*PTWH* 531).

with him, but that will not do: sometimes he endeavours to cheer him with talk about old times; and this, at one time, may serve to divert the sufferer from his own sad thoughts; at another, it will only plunge him into deeper melancholy than before; and then Hattersley is confounded, and knows not what to say,—unless it be a timid suggestion that the clergyman might be sent for. But Arthur will never consent to that: he knows he has rejected the clergyman's well-meant admonitions with scoffing levity at other times, and cannot dream of turning to him for consolation now.

"Mr. Hattersley sometimes offers his services instead of mine, but Arthur will not let me go: that strange whim still increases, as his strength declines—the fancy to have me always by his side. I hardly ever leave him, except to go into the next room, where I sometimes snatch an hour or so of sleep when he is quiet; but even then, the door is left ajar that he may know me to be within call. I am with him now, while I write; and I fear my occupation annoys him; though I frequently break off to attend to him, and though Mr. Hattersley is also by his side. That gentleman came, as he said, to beg a holiday for me, that I might have a run in the park, this fine, frosty morning, with Milicent, and Esther, and little Arthur, whom he had driven over to see me. Our poor invalid evidently felt it a heartless proposition, and would have felt it still more heartless in me to accede to it. I therefore said I would only go and speak to them a minute, and then come back. I did but exchange a few words with them, just outside the portico—inhaling the fresh, bracing air as I stood—and then, resisting the earnest and eloquent entreaties of all three to stay a little longer, and join them in a walk round the garden,—I tore myself away and returned to my patient. I had not been absent five minutes, but he reproached me bitterly for my levity and neglect. His friend espoused my cause:—

"'Nay, nay, Huntingdon,' said he, 'you're too hard upon her—she must have food and sleep, and a mouthful of fresh air now and then, or she can't stand it I tell you. Look at her, man, she's worn to a shadow already.'

"'What are her sufferings to mine?' said the poor invalid. 'You don't grudge me these attentions, do you, Helen?'

"'No, Arthur, if I could really serve you by them. I would give my life to save you, if I might.'

"'Would you *indeed*?—No!'

"'Most willingly, I would.'

"'Ah! That's because you think yourself more fit to die!'

"There was a painful pause. He was evidently plunged in gloomy reflections, but while I pondered for something to say, that might benefit without alarming him, Hattersley, whose mind had been pursuing almost the same course, broke silence with,—

"'I say, Huntingdon, I *would* send for a parson, of some sort.—If you didn't like the vicar, you know, you could have his curate, or somebody else.'

"'No; none of them can benefit me if *she* can't,' was the answer. And the tears gushed from his eyes as he earnestly exclaimed,—'Oh, Helen, if I had listened to you, it never would have come to this! And if I had heard you long ago—Oh, God! how different it would have been!'

"'Hear me now, then, Arthur,' said I, gently pressing his hand.

"'It's too late now,' said he despondently. And after that another paroxysm of pain came on; and then his mind began to wander, and we feared his death was approaching; but an opiate was administered, his sufferings began to abate, he gradually became more composed, and at length sank into a kind of slumber. He has been quieter since; and now Hattersley has left him, expressing a hope that he shall find him better when he calls tomorrow.

"'Perhaps, I *may* recover,' he replied, 'who knows?—this may have been the crisis. What do *you* think, Helen?'

"Unwilling to depress him, I gave the most cheering answer I could, but still recommended him to prepare for the possibility of what I inly feared was but too certain. But he was determined to hope. Shortly after, he relapsed into a kind of doze—but now he groans again.

"There is a change. Suddenly he called me to his side, with such a strange, excited manner that I feared he was delirious—but he was not. 'That *was* the crisis, Helen!' said he delightedly—'I had an infernal pain here—it is quite gone now; I never was so easy since the fall.—Quite gone, by Heaven!' and he clasped and kissed my hand in the very fullness of his heart; but, finding I did not participate his joy, he quickly flung it from him, and bitterly cursed my coldness and insensibility. How could I reply? Kneeling beside him, I took his hand and fondly pressed it to my lips—for the first time since our separation—and told him as well as tears would let me speak, that it was not *that* that kept me silent; it was the fear that this sudden cessation of pain was not so favourable a symptom as he supposed.—I immediately sent for the doctor. We are now anxiously awaiting him: I will tell you what he says. There is still the same freedom from pain—the same deadness to all sensation where the suffering was most acute.

"My worst fears are realized—mortification has commenced. The doctor has told him there is no hope—no words can describe his anguish—I can write no more."

★ ★ ★ ★ ★

The next was still more distressing in the tenor of its contents. The sufferer was fast approaching dissolution—dragged almost to the verge of that awful chasm he trembled to contemplate, from which no agony of prayers or tears could save him. Nothing could comfort him now: Hattersley's rough attempts at consolation were utterly in vain. The world was nothing to him:

life and all its interests, its petty cares and transient pleasures were a cruel mockery. To talk of the past, was to torture him with vain remorse; to refer to the future, was to increase his anguish; and yet to be silent, was to leave him a prey to his own regrets and apprehensions. Often he dwelt with shuddering minuteness on the fate of his perishing clay—the slow, piecemeal dissolution already invading his frame; the shroud, the coffin, the dark, lonely grave, and all the horrors of corruption.

"If I try," said his afflicted wife, "to divert him from these things—to raise his thoughts to higher themes, it is no better:—'Worse and worse!' he groans. 'If there be really life beyond the tomb, and judgment after death, how *can* I face it?'—I cannot do him any good; he will neither be enlightened, nor roused, nor comforted by anything I say; and yet he clings to me with un-relenting pertinacity—with a kind of childish desperation, as if *I* could save him from the fate he dreads. He keeps me night and day beside him. He is holding my left hand now, while I write; he has held it thus for hours: some-times quietly, with his pale face upturned to mine: sometimes clutching my arm with violence—the big drops starting from his forehead, at the thoughts of what he sees, or thinks he sees before him. If I withdraw my hand for a moment, it distresses him:—

"'Stay with me, Helen,' he says; 'let me hold you so: it seems as if harm could not reach me while you are here. But death *will* come—it is coming now—fast, fast!—and—Oh, if I *could* believe there was nothing after!'

"'Don't try to believe it, Arthur; there is joy and glory after, if you will but try to reach it!'

"'What, for *me*?' he said, with something like a laugh. 'Are we not to be judged according to the deeds done in the body?[1] Where's the use of a probationary existence, if a man may spend it as he pleases, just contrary to God's decrees, and then go to Heaven with the best—if the vilest sinner may win the reward of the holiest saint, by merely saying, 'I repent?'

"'But if you *sincerely* repent—'

"'I *can't* repent; I only fear.'[2]

"'You only regret the past for its consequences to yourself?'

"'Just so—except that I'm sorry to have wronged you Nel, because you're so good to me.'

---

1   In Romans 2:6, God is described as the one "Who will render to every man according to his deeds." In Revelations 20:12, a similar scene of judgment for deeds is described: "And I saw the dead, small and great, stand before God; and the books were opened: and another book was opened which is the book of life: and the dead were judged out of those things which were written in the books, according to their works."

2   Davies again reminds us of *Dr Faustus*, pointing out that Huntingdon's line is very similar to Faustus's when he says, "My heart is harden'd, I cannot repent" (VI.18) (*PTWH* 532).

"'Think of the goodness of God, and you cannot but be grieved to have offended Him.'

"'What *is* God—I cannot see Him or hear Him?—God is only an idea.'

"'God is Infinite Wisdom, and Power,[1] and Goodness—and LOVE;[2] but if this idea is too vast for your human faculties—if your mind loses itself in its overwhelming infinitude, fix it on Him who condescended to take our nature upon Him, who was raised to Heaven even in his glorified human body, in whom the fullness of the godhead shines.'[3]

"But he only shook his head and sighed. Then, in another paroxysm of shuddering horror, he tightened his grasp on my hand and arm, and groaning and lamenting, still clung to me with that wild, desperate earnestness so harrowing to my soul, because I know I cannot help him. I did my best to soothe and comfort him.

"'Death is so terrible,' he cried, 'I cannot bear it! *You* don't know, Helen—you can't imagine what it is, because you haven't it before you; and when I'm buried, you'll return to your old ways and be as happy as ever, and all the world will go on just as busy and merry as if I had never been; while I——' He burst into tears.

"'You needn't let *that* distress you,' I said; 'we shall all follow you soon enough.'

"'I wish to God I could take you with me now!' he exclaimed, 'you should plead for me.'

"'No man can deliver his brother, nor make agreement unto God for him,' I replied: 'it cost more to redeem their souls[4]—it cost the blood of an incarnate God,[5] perfect and sinless in himself, to redeem us from the bondage of the evil one:—let *Him* plead for you.'

---

1   See Psalm 147:5: "Great is our Lord, and of great power: his understanding is infinite."

2   See 1 John 4:8: "He that loveth not knoweth not God; for God is love"; and 1 John 4:16: "And we have known and believed the love that God hath to us. God is love; and he that dwelleth in love dwelleth in God, and God in him."

3   See Colossians 2:9: "For in [Christ] dwelleth all the fullness of the Godhead bodily."

4   "None of them can by any means redeem his brother, nor give to God a ransom for him: (For the redemption of their soul is precious, and it ceaseth for ever)" (Psalm 49:7–8).

5   Redemption through the blood of Christ is discussed in several places in the Bible. See especially Romans, where Christ is described as the one "whom God hath set forth to be a propitiation through faith in his blood, to declare his righteousness for the remission of sins that are past, through the forbearance of God" (Romans 3:25); "Much more then, being now justified by his blood, we shall be saved from wrath through him" (Romans 5:9). Lastly, Colossians 1:14 explains how "in [Christ] we have redemption through his blood, even the forgiveness of sins."

"But I seem to speak in vain. He does not now, as formerly, laugh these blessed truths to scorn: but still he cannot trust, or will not comprehend them. He cannot linger long. He suffers dreadfully, and so do those that wait upon him—but I will not harass you with further details: I have said enough, I think, to convince you that I did well to go to him."

★ ★ ★ ★ ★

Poor, poor Helen! dreadful indeed her trials must have been! And I could do nothing to lessen them—nay, it almost seemed as if I had brought them upon her myself, by my own secret desires; and whether I looked at her husband's sufferings or her own, it seemed almost like a judgment upon myself for having cherished such a wish.

The next day but one, there came another letter. That too was put into my hands without a remark, and these are its contents:—

DEC. 5th

He is gone at last. I sat beside him all night, with my hand fast locked in his, watching the changes of his features and listening to his failing breath. He had been silent a long time, and I thought he would never speak again, when he murmured, faintly but distinctly—

"Pray for me, Helen!"

"I do pray for you—every hour and every minute, Arthur; but you must pray for yourself."

His lips moved but emitted no sound;—then his looks became unsettled; and, from the incoherent half-uttered words that escaped him from time to time, supposing him to be now unconscious, I gently disengaged my hand from his, intending to steal away for a breath of air, for I was almost ready to faint; but a convulsive movement of the fingers, and a faintly whispered "Don't leave me!" immediately recalled me: I took his hand again, and held it till he was no more—and then I fainted; it was not grief; it was exhaustion that, till then, I had been enabled successfully to combat. Oh Frederick! none can imagine the miseries, bodily and mental, of that death bed! How could I endure to think that that poor trembling soul was hurried away to everlasting torment? It would drive me mad! But thank God I have hope[1]—not only from a vague dependence on the possibility that penitence and pardon might have reached him at the last, but from the blessed confidence that, through whatever purging fires the erring spirit may be doomed to pass—whatever

---

1   See Brontë's letter to the Reverend Thom (Appendix A1) and her poetry (Appendix A2–3) to learn more about her belief in universal salvation as the logical principle given an understanding of God as loving.

fate awaits it, still, it is not lost, and God, who hateth nothing that he hath made,[1] *will* bless it in the end!

His body will be consigned on Thursday to that dark grave he so much dreaded; but the coffin must be closed as soon as possible. If you will attend the funeral come quickly, for I need help.

HELEN HUNTINGDON.

CHAPTER L
DOUBTS AND DISAPPOINTMENTS

ON reading this, I had no reason to disguise my joy and hope from Frederick Lawrence, for I had none to be ashamed of. I felt no joy but that his sister was at length released from her afflictive, overwhelming toil—no hope but that she would in time recover from the effects of it, and be suffered to rest in peace and quietness, at least, for the remainder of her life. I experienced a painful commiseration for her unhappy husband (though fully aware that he had brought every particle of his sufferings upon himself, and but too well deserved them all), and a profound sympathy for her own afflictions, and deep anxiety for the consequences of those harassing cares, those dreadful vigils, that incessant and deleterious confinement besides a living corpse— for I was persuaded she had not hinted half the sufferings she had had to endure.

"You will go to her, Lawrence?" said I, as I put the letter into his hand.

"Yes, immediately."

"That's right! I'll leave you, then, to prepare for your departure."

"I've done that, already, while you were reading the letter, and before you came; and the carriage is now coming round to the door."

Inly approving his promptitude, I bade him good morning, and withdrew. He gave me a searching glance as we pressed each other's hands at parting; but whatever he sought in my countenance, he saw there nothing but the most becoming gravity, it might be, mingled with a little sternness in momentary resentment at what I suspected to be passing in his mind.

Had I forgotten my own prospects, my ardent love, my pertinacious hopes? It seemed like sacrilege to revert to them now, but I had not forgotten them.

---

1   The Collect for Ash Wednesday in *The Book of Common Prayer* describes God in this way: "Almighty and everlasting God, you hate nothing you have made and forgive the sins of all who are penitent." See also Ezekiel 33:11: "Say unto them, As I live, saith the Lord God, I have no pleasure in the death of the wicked; but that the wicked turn from his way and live: turn ye, turn ye from your evil ways; for why will ye die, O house of Israel?"

It was, however, with a gloomy sense of the darkness of those prospects, the fallacy of those hopes, and the vanity of that affection, that I reflected on those things as I remounted my horse and slowly journeyed homewards. Mrs. Huntingdon was free now; it was no longer a crime to think of her—but did she ever think of *me*?—not *now*—of course it was not to be expected—but would she, when this shock was over?—In all the course of her correspondence with her brother (our mutual friend, as she herself had called him), she had never mentioned me but once—and that was from necessity. This, alone, afforded strong presumption that I was already forgotten; yet this was not the worst: it might have been her sense of duty that had kept her silent, she might be only *trying* to forget; but in addition to this, I had a gloomy conviction that the awful realities she had seen and felt, her reconciliation with the man she had once loved, his dreadful sufferings and death, must eventually efface from her mind all traces of her passing love for me. She might recover from these horrors so far as to be restored to her former health, her tranquility, her cheerfulness even—but never to those feelings which would appear to her, henceforth, as a fleeting fancy, a vain, illusive dream; especially as there was no one to remind her of my existence—no means of assuring her of my fervent constancy, now that we were so far apart, and delicacy forbade me to see her or to write to her, for months to come at least. And how could I engage her brother in my behalf? how could I break that icy crust of shy reserve? Perhaps he would disapprove of my attachment now, as highly as before; perhaps he would think me too poor—too lowly born, to match with his sister. Yes, there was another barrier: doubtless there was a wide distinction between the rank and circumstances of Mrs. Huntingdon, the lady of Grassdale Manor, and those of Mrs. Graham the artist, the tenant of Wildfell Hall; and it might be deemed presumption in me to offer my hand to the former—by the world, by her friends—if not by herself—a penalty I might brave, if I were certain she loved me; but otherwise, how could I? And, finally, her deceased husband, with his usual selfishness, might have so constructed his will as to place restrictions upon her marrying again. So that you see I had reasons enough for despair if I chose to indulge it.

Nevertheless, it was with no small degree of impatience that I looked forward to Mr. Lawrence's return from Grassdale—impatience that increased in proportion as his absence was prolonged. He stayed away some ten or twelve days. All very right that he should remain to comfort and help his sister, but he might have written to tell me how he was,—or at least to tell me when to expect his return; for he might have known I was suffering tortures of anxiety for her, and uncertainty for my own future prospects. And when he did return, all he told me about her, was that she had been greatly exhausted and worn by her unremitting exertions in behalf of that man who had been the scourge of her life, and had dragged her with him nearly to the portals of the grave,—and was still much shaken and depressed by his melancholy end and the circumstances attendant upon it; but no word in reference to me—no intimation that my name had ever passed her lips, or even been spoken in her presence. To be sure, I asked no questions on the subject: I could not bring my mind to do so, believing, as I did, that Lawrence was indeed averse to the idea of my union with his sister.

I saw that he expected to be further questioned concerning his visit, and I saw too, with the keen perception of awakened jealousy, or alarmed self-esteem—or by whatever name I ought to call it—that he rather shrank from that impending scrutiny, and was no less pleased than surprised to find it did not come. Of course, I was burning with anger, but pride obliged me to suppress my feelings, and preserve a smooth face—or at least, a stoic calmness throughout the interview. It was well it did, for, reviewing the matter in my sober judgment, I must say it would have been highly absurd and improper to have quarrelled with him on such an occasion: I must confess too that I wronged him in my heart: the truth was, he liked me very well, but he was fully aware that a union between Mrs. Huntingdon and me would be what the world calls a mésalliance;[1] and it was not in his nature to set the world at defiance;—especially in such a case as this, for its dread laugh, or ill opinion, would be far more terrible to him directed against his sister than himself. Had he believed that a union was necessary to the happiness of both, or of either, or had he known how fervently I loved her, he would have acted differently; but seeing me so calm and cool, he would not for the world disturb my philosophy;[2] and though refraining entirely from any active opposition to the match, he would yet do nothing to bring it about, and would much rather take the part of prudence, in aiding us to overcome our mutual predilections, than that of feeling, to encourage them. "And he was in the right of it," you will say. Perhaps he was—at any rate, I had no business to feel so bitterly against him as I did; but I could not then regard the matter in such a moderate light; and, after a brief conversation upon indifferent topics, I went away, suffering all the pangs of wounded pride and injured friendship, in addition to those resulting from the fear that I was indeed forgotten, and the knowledge that she I loved was alone and afflicted, suffering from injured health and dejected spirits, and I was forbidden to console or assist her, forbidden even to assure her of my sympathy, for the transmission of any such message through Mr. Lawrence was now completely out of the question.

But what should I do? I would wait, and see if she would notice me— which of course she would not, unless by some kind message entrusted to

---

1   "Marriage with a person of inferior social position" (*OED*).

2   "The mental attitude or habit of a philosopher; serenity under disturbing circumstances; resignation; calmness of temper" (*OED*).

her brother, that, in all probability, he would not deliver, and then—dreadful thought!—she would think me cooled and changed for not returning it—or perhaps, he had already given her to understand that I had ceased to think of her! I would wait, however, till the six months after our parting were fairly passed (which would be about the close of February), and then I would send her a letter modestly reminding her of her former permission to write to her at the close of that period, and hoping I might avail myself of it, at least to express my heart-felt sorrow for her late afflictions, my just appreciation of her generous conduct, and my hope that her health was now completely re-established, and that she would, some time, be permitted to enjoy those blessings of a peaceful, happy life, which had been denied her so long, but which none could more truly be said to merit than herself,—adding a few words of kind remembrance to my little friend Arthur, with a hope that he had not forgotten me, and, perhaps, a few more in reference to by-gone times—to the delightful hours I had passed in her society, and my unfading recollection of them, which was the salt and solace of my life,—and a hope that her recent troubles had not entirely banished me from her mind.—If she did not answer this, of course I should write no more: if she did (as surely she would, in *some* fashion) my future proceedings should be regulated by her reply.

Ten weeks was long to wait in such a miserable state of uncertainty, but courage! it must be endured;—and meantime I would continue to see Lawrence now and then, though not so often as before, and I would still pursue my habitual enquiries after his sister—if he had lately heard from her, and how she was, but nothing more.

I did so, and the answers I received were always provokingly limited to the letter of the enquiry: She was much as usual: She made no complaints, but the tone of her last letter evinced great depression of mind:—She said she was better:—and, finally;—She said she was well, and very busy with her son's education, and with the management of her late husband's property and the regulation of his affairs. The rascal had never told me how that property was disposed, or whether Mr. Huntingdon had died intestate or not; and I would sooner die than ask him, lest he should misconstrue into covetousness my desire to know. He never offered to show me his sister's letters now; and I never hinted a wish to see them. February, however, was approaching; December was past, January, at length, was almost over—a few more weeks, and then, certain despair or renewal of hope would put an end to this long agony of suspense.

But alas! it was just about that time she was called to sustain another blow in the death of her uncle—a worthless old fellow enough, in himself, I dare say, but he had always shown more kindness and affection to her than to any other creature, and she had always been accustomed to regard him as a parent. She was with him when he died, and had assisted her aunt to nurse him during the last stage of his illness. Her brother went to Staningley to attend the funeral, and told me, upon his return, that she was still there, endeavouring to cheer her aunt with her presence, and likely to remain some time. This was bad news for me, for while she continued there, I could not write to her, as I did not know the address, and would not ask it of him. But week followed week, and every time I enquired about her she was still at Staningley.

"Where *is* Staningley?" I asked at last.

"In ——shire," was the brief reply: and there was something so cold and dry in the manner of it, that I was effectually deterred from requesting a more definite account.

"When will she return to Grassdale?" was my next question.

"I don't know."

"Confound it!" I muttered.

"Why, Markham?" asked my companion, with an air of innocent surprise. But I did not deign to answer him, save by a look of silent, sullen contempt, at which he turned away, and contemplated the carpet with a slight smile, half pensive, half amused; but quickly looking up, he began to talk of other subjects, trying to draw me into a cheerful and friendly conversation; but I was too much irritated to discourse with him, and soon took leave.

You see Lawrence and I somehow could not manage to get on very well together. The fact is, I believe, we were both of us a little too touchy. It is a troublesome thing Halford, this susceptibility to affronts where none are intended. I am no martyr to it now, as you can bear me witness: I have learned to be merry and wise, to be more easy with myself and more indulgent to my neighbours, and I can afford to laugh at both Lawrence and you.

Partly from accident, partly from willful negligence on my part (for I was really beginning to dislike him), several weeks elapsed before I saw my friend again. When we did meet, it was *he* that sought *me* out. One bright morning early in June, he came into the field where I was just commencing my hay harvest.

"It is long since I saw you, Markham," said he after the first few words had passed between us. "Do you never mean to come to Woodford again?"

"I called once, and you were out."

"I was sorry: but that was long since; I hoped you would call again; and now, *I* have called, and *you* were out—which you generally are, or I would do myself the pleasure of calling more frequently—but being determined to see you this time, I have left my pony in the lane, and come over hedge and ditch to join you; for I am about to leave Woodford for a while, and may not have the pleasure of seeing you again for a month or two."

"Where are you going?"

"To Grassdale first," said he, with a half-smile he would willingly have suppressed if he could.

"To Grassdale! Is she there, then?"

"Yes, but in a day or two she will leave it to accompany Mrs. Maxwell to F—— for the benefit of the sea air; and I shall go with them." (F—— was at that time a quiet but respectable watering place: it is considerably more frequented now).

Lawrence seemed to expect me to take advantage of this circumstance to entrust him with some sort of a message to his sister; and I believe he would have undertaken to deliver it without any material objections, if I had had the sense to ask him; though of course he would not *offer* to do so, if I was content to let it alone. But I could not bring myself to make the request; and it was not till after he was gone, that I saw how fair an opportunity I had lost;—and then, indeed, I deeply regretted my stupidity and my foolish pride; but it was now too late to remedy the evil.

He did not return till towards the latter end of August. He wrote to me twice or thrice from F——; but his letters were most provokingly unsatisfactory, dealing in generalities or in trifles that I cared nothing about, or replete with fancies and reflections equally unwelcome to me at the time,—saying next to nothing about his sister, and little more about himself. I would wait, however, till he came back: perhaps I could get something more out of him then. At all events, I would not write to her now, while she was with him and her aunt, who doubtless would be still more hostile to my presumptuous aspirations than himself. When she was returned to the silence and solitude of her own home it would be my fittest opportunity.

When Lawrence came, however, he was as reserved as ever on the subject of my keen anxiety. He told me that his sister had derived considerable benefit from her stay at F——, that her son was quite well, and—alas! that both of them were gone, with Mrs. Maxwell, back to Staningley;—and there they stayed at least three months. But instead of boring you with my chagrin, my expectations and disappointments, my fluctuations of dull despondency and flickering hope, my varying resolutions, now to drop it, and now to persevere—now to make a bold push, and now to let things pass and patiently abide my time,—I will employ myself in settling the business of one or two of the characters, introduced in the course of this narrative, whom I may not have occasion to mention again.

Sometime before Mr. Huntingdon's death, Lady Lowborough eloped with another gallant to the continent, where, having lived awhile in reckless gaiety and dissipation, they quarrelled and parted. She went dashing on for a season, but years came and money went: she sunk, at length, in difficulty and debt, disgrace and misery; and died at last, as I have heard, in penury, neglect, and utter wretchedness. But this might be only a report: she may be living yet for anything I, or any of her relatives or former acquaintances can tell; for they have all lost sight of her long years ago, and would as thoroughly forget her if they could. Her husband, however, upon this second misdemeanour, immediately sought and obtained a divorce, and, not long after, married again. It was well he did, for Lord Lowborough, morose and moody as he seemed, was not the man for a bachelor's life. No public interests, no ambitious projects, or active pursuits,—or ties of friendship even (if he had had any friends), could compensate to him for the absence of domestic comforts and endearments. He had a son and a nominal daughter, it is true, but they too painfully reminded him of their mother, and the unfortunate little Annabella was a source of perpetual bitterness to his soul. He had obliged himself to treat her with paternal kindness: he had forced himself not to hate her, and even, perhaps, to feel some degree of kindly regard for her, at last, in return for her artless and unsuspecting attachment to himself; but the bitterness of his self-condemnation for his inward feelings towards that innocent being, his constant struggles to subdue the evil promptings of his nature (for it was not a generous one), though partly guessed at by those who knew him, could be known to God and his own heart alone;—so also was the hardness of his conflicts with the temptation to return to the vice of his youth, and seek oblivion for past calamities, and deadness to the present misery of a blighted heart, a joyless, friendless life, and a morbidly disconsolate mind, by yielding again to that insidious foe to health, and sense, and virtue, which had so deplorably enslaved and degraded him before.

The second object of his choice was widely different from the first. Some wondered at his taste; some even ridiculed it—but in this their folly was more apparent than his. The lady was about his own age—i.e. between thirty and forty—remarkable neither for beauty nor wealth, nor brilliant accomplishments; nor any other thing that I ever heard of, except genuine good sense, unswerving integrity, active piety, warm-hearted benevolence, and a fund of cheerful spirits. These qualities however, as you may readily imagine, combined to render her an excellent mother to the children, and an invaluable wife to his lordship. *He*, with his usual self-depreciation (or *appreciation?*) thought her a world too good for him, and while he wondered at the kindness of Providence in conferring such a gift upon him, and even at her taste in preferring him to other men, he did his best to reciprocate the good she did him, and so far succeeded that she was, and I believe still is, one of the happiest and fondest wives in England; and all who question the good taste of either partner, may be thankful if *their* respective selections afford them half the genuine satisfaction in the end, or repay their preference with affection half as lasting and sincere.

If you are at all interested in the fate of that low scoundrel, Grimsby, I can only tell you that he went from bad to worse, sinking from bathos to bathos of vice and villany, consorting only with the worst members of his club and the lowest dregs of society—happily for the rest of the world—and at last met his end in a drunken brawl from the hands, it is said, of some brother scoundrel he had cheated at play.

As for Mr. Hattersley, he had never wholly forgotten his resolution to "come out from among them,"[1] and behave like a man and a Christian, and the last illness and death of his once jolly friend Huntingdon, so deeply and seriously impressed him with the evil of their former practices, that he never needed another lesson of the kind. Avoiding the temptation of the town, he continued to pass his life in the country immersed in the usual pursuits of a hearty, active country gentleman; his occupations being those of farming, and breeding horses and cattle, diversified with a little hunting and shooting, and enlivened by the occasional companionship of his friends (better friends than those of his youth), and the society of his happy little wife, (now cheerful and confiding as heart could wish) and his fine family of stalwart sons and blooming daughters. His father, the banker, having died some years ago and left him all his riches, he has now full scope for the exercise of his prevailing tastes, and I need not tell you that Ralph Hattersley, Esqr., is celebrated throughout the country for his noble breed of horses.

CHAPTER LI
AN UNEXPECTED OCCURRENCE

WE will now turn to a certain still, cold, cloudy afternoon about the commencement of December, when the first fall of snow lay thinly scattered over the blighted fields and frozen roads, or stored more thickly in the hollows of the deep cart ruts and footsteps of men and horses, impressed in the now petrified mire of last month's drenching rains. I remember it well, for I was walking home from the vicarage, with no less remarkable a personage than Miss Eliza Millward by my side. I had been to call upon her father,—a sacrifice to civility undertaken entirely to please my mother, not myself, for I hated to go near the house; not merely on account of my antipathy to the once so bewitching Eliza, but because I had not half forgiven the old gentleman himself for his ill opinion of Mrs. Huntingdon; for though now constrained to acknowledge himself mistaken in his former judgment, he still maintained that she had done wrong to leave her husband; it was a violation

---

[1] See 2 Corinthians 6:17–18: "Wherefore come out from among them, and be ye separate, saith the Lord, and touch not the unclean thing; and I will receive you, and will be a Father unto you, and ye shall be my sons and daughters, saith the Lord Almighty."

of her sacred duties as a wife, and a tempting of Providence by laying herself open to temptation; and nothing short of bodily ill-usage (and that of no trifling nature) could excuse such a step—nor even that, for in such a case she ought to appeal to the laws for protection. But it was not of him I intended to speak; it was of his daughter Eliza. Just as I was taking leave of the vicar, she entered the room, ready equipped for a walk.

"I was just coming to see your sister, Mr. Markham," said she; "and so if you have no objection, I'll accompany you home. I like company when I'm walking out—don't you?"

"Yes, when it's agreeable."

"That of course," rejoined the young lady, smiling archly. So we proceeded together.

"Shall I find Rose at home, do you think?" said she, as we closed the garden gate, and set our faces towards Linden-Car.

"I believe so."

"I trust I shall, for I've a little bit of news for her—if you haven't forestalled me."

"I?"

"Yes: do you know what Mr. Lawrence is gone for?" She looked up anxiously for my reply.

"*Is* he gone?" said I, and her face brightened.

"Ah! then he hasn't told you about his sister?"

"What of *her*?" I demanded, in terror lest some evil should have befallen her.

"Oh, Mr. Markham, how you blush!" cried she with a tormenting laugh. "Ha, ha, you have not forgotten her yet! But you had better be quick about it, I can tell you, for—alas, alas!—she's going to be married next Thursday!"

"No, Miss Eliza! That's false."

"Do you charge me with a falsehood, sir?"

"You are misinformed."

"Am I? Do you know better then?"

"I think I do."

"What makes you look so pale then?" said she, smiling with delight at my emotion. "Is it anger at poor me for telling such a fib? Well, I only 'tell the tale as 'twas told to me:'[1] I don't vouch for the truth of it; but at the same time, I don't see what reason Sarah should have for deceiving me, or her informant for deceiving her; and that was what she told me the footman told her:—that Mrs. Huntingdon was going to be married on Thursday, and Mr. Lawrence was gone to the wedding. She did tell me the name of the gentle-

---

1   Sir Walter Scott, *The Lay of the Last Minstrel* (1805), II.xxii: "I cannot tell how the truth may be; / I say the tale as 'twas said to me."

man, but I've forgotten that. Perhaps you can assist me to remember it. Is there not some one that lives near—or frequently visits the neighbourhood, that has long been attached to her? a Mr.—oh dear!—Mr.—"

"Hargrave?" suggested I, with a bitter smile.

"You're right!" cried she, "that was the very name."

"Impossible, Miss Eliza!!" I exclaimed in a tone that made her start.

"Well, you know, that's what they told me," said she, composedly staring me in the face. And then she broke out into a long shrill laugh that put me to my wits' end with fury.

"Really, you must excuse me," cried she: "I know it's very rude, but ha, ha, ha!—did you think to marry her yourself? Dear, dear, what a pity! ha, ha, ha!—Gracious, Mr. Markham! are you going to faint? O mercy! shall I call this man? Here, Jacob—" But checking the word on her lips, I seized her arm and gave it, I think, a pretty severe squeeze, for she shrank into herself with a faint cry of pain or terror; but the spirit within her was not subdued: instantly rallying, she continued, with well feigned concern—

"What can I do for you? Will you have some water—some brandy?—I dare say they have some in the public-house down there, if you'll let me run."

"Have done with this nonsense!" cried I sternly. She looked confounded—almost frightened again, for a moment. "You know I hate such jests," I continued.

"*Jests* indeed! I wasn't *jesting*!"

"You were laughing, at all events; and I don't like to be laughed at," returned I, making violent efforts to speak with proper dignity and composure, and to say nothing but what was coherent and sensible. And since you are in such a merry mood, Miss Eliza, you must be good enough company for yourself; and therefore I shall leave you to finish your walk alone—for, now I think of it, I have business elsewhere; so good evening."

With that I left her (smothering her malicious laughter) and turned aside into the fields, springing up the bank, and pushing through the nearest gap in the hedge. Determined at once to prove the truth—or rather the falsehood of her story, I hastened to Woodford as fast as my legs could carry me—first, veering round by a circuitous curse, but the moment I was out of sight of my fair tormentor, cutting away across the country, just as a bird might fly—over pasture-land and fallow, and stubble, and lane-clearing hedges and ditches, and hurdles, till I came to the young squire's gates. Never till now had I known the full fervour of my love—the full strength of my hopes, not wholly crushed even in my hours of deepest despondency, always tenaciously clinging to the thought that one day she might be mine—or if not that, at least that something of my memory, some slight remembrance of our friendship and our love would be for ever cherished in her heart. I marched up to the door, determined if I saw the master, to question him boldly concerning his sister, to wait and hesitate no longer, but cast false delicacy and stupid pride behind my back, and know my fate at once.

"Is Mr. Lawrence at home?" I eagerly asked of the servant that opened the door.

"No sir, master went yesterday," replied he, looking very alert.

"Went where?"

"To Grassdale, sir—wasn't you aware, sir? He's very close,[1] is master," said the fellow with a foolish, simpering grin. "I suppose, sir—"

But I turned and left him, without waiting to hear what he supposed. I was not going to stand there to expose my tortured feelings to the insolent laughter and impertinent curiosity of a fellow like that.

But what was to be done now? Could it be possible that she had left me for *that* man? I could not believe it. Me she might forsake, but *not* to give herself to him! Well, I would know the truth—to no concerns of daily life could I attend, while this tempest of doubt and dread, of jealousy and rage distracted me. I would take the morning coach from L—— (the evening one would be already gone), and fly to Grassdale, I *must* be there before the marriage. And why? Because a thought struck me, that *perhaps* I might prevent it—that if I did not, she and I might both lament it to the latest moment of our lives. It struck me that some one might have belied me to her: perhaps her brother—yes, no doubt her brother had persuaded her that I was false and faithless, and taking advantage of her natural indignation, and perhaps her desponding carelessness about her future life, had urged her, artfully, cruelly on, to this other marriage in order to secure her from me. If this *was* the case, and if she should only discover her mistake when too late to repair it—to what a life of misery and vain regret might she be doomed as well as me! and what remorse for me, to think my foolish scruples had induced it all! Oh, I *must* see her—she must know my truth even if I told it at the church door! I might pass for a madman or an impertinent fool—even she might be offended at such an interruption, or at least might tell me it was now too late—but if I *could* save her! if she *might* be mine—it was too rapturous a thought!

Winged by this hope, and goaded by these fears, I hurried homewards to prepare for my departure on the morrow. I told my mother that urgent business which admitted no delay, but which I could not then explain, called me away to —— (the last large town through which I had to pass). My deep anxiety and serious preoccupation, could not be concealed from her maternal eyes; and I had much ado to calm her apprehensions of some disastrous mystery.

That night there came a heavy fall of snow, which so retarded the progress of the coaches on the following day, that I was almost driven to

---

1   Secretive or closemouthed.

distraction. I travelled all night of course, for this was Wednesday: tomorrow morning, doubtless, the marriage would take place. But the night was long and dark; the snow heavily clogged the wheels and balled[1] the horses' feet; the animals were consumedly lazy, the coachmen most execrably cautious, the passengers confoundedly apathetic in their supine indifference to the rate of our progression. Instead of assisting me to bully the several coachmen and urge them forward, they merely stared and grinned at my impatience: one fellow even ventured to rally me upon it—but I silenced him with a look that quelled him for the rest of the journey;—and when, at the last stage, I would have taken the reins into my own hand, they all with one accord opposed it.

It was broad daylight when we entered M—— and drew up at the Rose and Crown. I alighted and called aloud for a post-chaise[2] to Grassdale. There was none to be had: the only one in the town was under repair. "A gig[3] then—a fly—car[4]—anything—only be quick!" There was a gig but not a horse to spare. I sent into the town to seek one; but they were such an intolerable time about it that I could wait no longer: I thought my own feet would carry me sooner, and bidding them send the confounded conveyance after me, if it were ready within an hour, I set off as fast as I could walk. The distance was little more than six miles, but the road was strange, and I had to keep stopping to enquire my way—hallooing to carters and clod-hoppers, and frequently invading the cottages, for there were few abroad that winter's morning,—sometimes knocking up[5] the lazy people from their beds, for where so little work was to be done—perhaps so little food and fire to be had, they cared not to curtail their slumbers. I had no time to think of *them*, however: aching with weariness and desperation, I hurried on. The gig did not overtake me: it was well I had not waited for it—vexatious, rather, that I had been fool enough to wait so long.

At length however, I entered the neighbourhood of Grassdale. I approached the little rural church—but lo! there stood a train of carriages before it—it needed not the white favours bedecking the servants and horses, nor the merry voices of the village idlers assembled to witness the show, to

---

1 The snow stuck in the horses' hoofs—the shape of their shoes and the inside of their hoofs would make a type of snowball underfoot.

2 "A travelling carriage, either hired from stage to stage, or drawn by horses so hired" (*OED*).

3 A small carriage with only two wheels, pulled by one horse.

4 Rosengarten explains how "'fly' usually designated a small one-horse carriage let out for hire; and 'car' was used to describe various forms of light two-wheeled carts" (*OTWH* 485).

5 Slang, to wake up.

apprize me that there was a wedding within. I ran in among them, demanding, with breathless eagerness, had the ceremony long commenced? They only gaped and stared. In my desperation I pushed past them, and was about to enter the church-yard gate, when a group of ragged urchins, that had been hanging like bees to the windows, suddenly dropped off and made a rush for the porch, vociferating in the uncouth dialect of their county, something which signified, "It's over—they're coming out!"

If Eliza Millward had seen me then, she might indeed have been delighted. I grasped the gate-post for support, and stood intently gazing towards the door to take my last look on my soul's delight, my first on that detested mortal who had torn her from my heart, and doomed her, I was certain, to a life of misery and hollow, vain repining—for what happiness could she enjoy with him? I did not wish to shock her with my presence now, but I had not power to move away. Forth came the bride and bridegroom. Him I saw not; I had eyes for none but her. A long veil shrouded half her graceful form, but did not hide it; I could see that while she carried her head erect, her eyes were bent upon the ground, and her face and neck were suffused with a crimson blush; but every feature was radiant with smiles, and, gleaming through the misty whiteness of her veil, were clusters of golden ringlets! O Heavens! it was *not* my Helen! The first glimpse made me start—but my eyes were darkened with exhaustion and despair—dare I trust them? Yes—it *is* not she! It was a younger, slighter, rosier beauty—lovely, indeed, but with far less dignity and depth of soul—without that indefinable grace, that keenly *spirituel* yet gentle charm, that ineffable power to attract and subjugate the heart—*my* heart at least. I looked at the bridegroom—it was Frederick Lawrence! I wiped away the cold drops that were trickling down my forehead, and stepped back as he approached; but his eye fell upon me, and he knew me, altered as my appearance must have been.

"Is that you Markham?" said he, startled and confounded at the apparition—perhaps, too, at the wildness of my looks.

"Yes, Lawrence—is that you?" I mustered the presence of mind to reply.

He smiled and coloured, as if half-proud and half-ashamed of his identity; and if he had reason to be proud of the sweet lady on his arm, he had no less cause to be ashamed of having concealed his good fortune so long.

"Allow me to introduce you to my bride," said he, endeavouring to hide his embarrassment by an assumption of careless gaiety. "Esther, this is Mr. Markham, my friend Markham, Mrs. Lawrence, late Miss Hargrave."

I bowed to the bride, and vehemently wrung the bridegroom's hand.

"Why did you not tell me of this?" I said reproachfully, pretending a resentment I did not feel (for in truth I was almost wild with joy to find myself so happily mistaken, and overflowing with affection to him for this and for the base injustice I felt that I had done him in my mind—he might have wronged me, but not to *that* extent; and as I had hated him like a demon for the last forty hours, the reaction from such a feeling was so great that I could pardon all offences for the moment—and love him in spite of them too).

"I *did* tell you," said he, with an air of guilty confusion, "you received my letter?"

"What letter?"

"The one announcing my intended marriage."

"I never received the most distant hint of such an intention."

"It must have crossed you on your way then—it should have reached you yesterday morning—it was rather late, I acknowledge. But what brought you here then, if you received no information?"

It was now *my* turn to be confounded; but the young lady, who had been busily patting the snow with her foot during our short, *sotto voce* colloquy, very opportunely came to my assistance by pinching her companion's arm and whispering a suggestion that his friend should be invited to step into the carriage and go with them; it being scarcely agreeable to stand there among so many gazers, and keeping their friends waiting, into the bargain.

"And so cold as it is too!" said he, glancing with dismay at her slight drapery, and immediately handing her into the carriage. "Markham, will you come? We are going to Paris, but we can drop you anywhere between this and Dover."

"No thank you. Good bye—I needn't wish you a pleasant journey; but I shall expect a very handsome apology, some time, mind, and scores of letters, before we meet again."

He shook my hand and hastened to take his place beside his lady. This was no time or place for explanation or discourse: we had already stood long enough to excite the wonder of the village sight-seers, and perhaps the wrath of the attendant bridal party; though, of course, all this passed in a much shorter time than I have taken to relate or even than you will take to read it. I stood beside the carriage, and, the window being down, I saw my happy friend fondly encircle his companion's waist with his arm, while she rested her glowing cheek on his shoulder, looking the very impersonation of loving, trusting bliss. In the interval between the footman's closing the door and taking his place behind, she raised her smiling brown eyes to his face, observing playfully—

"I fear you must think me very insensible, Frederick: I know it is the custom for ladies to cry on these occasions, but I couldn't squeeze a tear for my life."

He only answered with a kiss, and pressed her still closer to his bosom.

"But what is this?" he murmured. "Why, Esther, you're crying now!"

"Oh, it's nothing—it's only too much happiness—and the wish," sobbed she, "that our dear Helen were as happy as ourselves."

"Bless you for that wish!" I inwardly responded as the carriage rolled away—"and Heaven grant it be not wholly vain!"

I thought a cloud had suddenly darkened her husband's face as she spoke. What did *he* think? Could he grudge such happiness to his dear sister and his friend as he now felt himself? At *such* a moment it was impossible. The contrast between her fate and his *must* darken his bliss for a time. Perhaps too he thought of me: perhaps he regretted the part he had had in preventing our union, by omitting to help us, if not by actually plotting against us—I exonerated him from *that* charge, now, and deeply lamented my former ungenerous suspicions; but he *had* wronged us, still—I hoped, I trusted that he had. He had not attempted to check the course of our love by actually damming up the streams in their passage, but he had passively watched the two currents wandering through life's arid wilderness, declining to clear away the obstructions that divided them, and secretly hoping that both would lose themselves in the sand before they could be joined in one. And meantime, he had been quietly proceeding with his own affairs: perhaps his heart and head had been so full of his fair lady that he had had but little thought to spare for others. Doubtless he had made his first acquaintance with her—his first intimate acquaintance at least—during his three months' sojourn at F——, for I now recollected that he had once casually let fall an intimation that his aunt and sister had a young friend staying with them at the time, and this accounted for at least one half his silence about all transactions there. Now too I saw a reason for many little things that had slightly puzzled me before; among the rest, for sundry departures from Woodford, and absences more or less prolonged, for which he never satisfactorily accounted, and concerning which he hated to be questioned on his return. Well might the servant say his master was "very close." But why this strange reserve to *me*? Partly, from that remarkable idiosyncrasy to which I have before alluded; partly, perhaps, from tenderness to my feelings, or fear to disturb my philosophy by touching upon the infectious theme of love.

CHAPTER LII
FLUCTUATIONS

THE tardy gig had overtaken me at last. I entered it, and bade the man who brought it drive to Grassdale Manor—I was too busy with my own thoughts to care to drive it myself. I would see Mrs. Huntingdon—there could be no impropriety in that now that her husband had been dead above a year—and by her indifference or her joy at my unexpected arrival, I could soon tell whether her heart was truly mine. But my companion, a loquacious, forward fellow, was not disposed to leave me to the indulgence of my private cogitations.

"There they go!" said he as the carriages filed away before us. "There'll be brave doings on yonder *today*, as what come tomorra.—Know anything of that family, sir? or you're a stranger in these parts?"

"I know them by report."

"Humph!—There's the best of 'em gone anyhow. And I suppose the old misses is agoing to leave after this stir's gotten overed, and take herself off, somewhere, to live on her bit of a jointure; and the young 'un—at least the new 'un (she's none so very young) is coming down to live at the Grove."

"Is Mr. Hargrave married, then?"

"Ay sir, a few months since. He should a been wed afore, to a widow lady, but they couldn't agree over the money: she'd a rare long purse, and Mr. Hargrave wanted it all to his-self; but she wouldn't let it go, and so then they fell out. This one isn't quite as rich—nor as handsome either, but she hasn't been married before. She's very plain they say, and getting on to forty or past, and so, you know, if she didn't jump at this hopportunity, she thought she'd never get a better. I guess she thought such a handsome young husband was worth all 'at ever she had, and he might take it and welcome; but I lay she'll rue her bargain 'afore long. They say she begins already to see 'at he isn't not altogether that nice, generous, perlite, delightful gentleman 'at she thought him afore marriage—he begins a being careless, and masterful already. Ay, and she'll find him harder and carelesser nor she thinks on."

"You seem to be well acquainted with him," I observed.

"I am, sir; I've known him since he was quite a young gentleman; and a proud 'un he was, and a willful. I was servant yonder for several years; but I couldn't stand their niggardly ways—she got ever longer and worse did Missis, with her nipping and screwing, and watching and grudging; so I thought I'd find another place as *what* came."

And then he discoursed upon his present position as ostler[1] at the Rose and Crown, and how greatly superior it was to his former one, in comfort and freedom, though inferior in outward respectability; and entered into various details respecting the domestic economy at the Grove, and the characters of Mrs. Hargrave and her son,—to which I gave no heed, being too much occupied with my own anxious, fluttering anticipations and with the character of the country through which we passed, that, in spite of the leafless trees and snowy ground, had for some time begun to manifest unequivocal signs of the approach to a gentleman's country seat.

"Are we not near the house?" said I, interrupting him in the middle of his discourse.

---

1   "A phonetic spelling of hosteler, hostler, representing the historical pronunciation with *h* mute…. A stableman, a groom" (*OED*).

"Yes, sir; yond's the park."

My heart sank within me to behold that stately mansion in the midst of its expansive grounds—the park as beautiful now, in its wintry garb, as it could be in its summer glory; the majestic sweep, the undulating swell and fall, displayed to full advantage in that robe of dazzling purity, stainless and printless—save one long, winding track left by the trooping deer—the stately timber-trees with their heavy laden branches gleaming white against the dull, grey sky; the deep, encircling woods; the broad expanse of water sleeping in frozen quiet; and the weeping ash and willow drooping their snowclad boughs above it—all presented a picture, striking, indeed, and pleasing to an unencumbered mind, but by no means encouraging to me. There was one comfort however,—all this was entailed upon little Arthur, and could not under any circumstances, strictly speaking, be his mother's. But how was she situated? Overcoming with a sudden effort my repugnance to mention her name to my garrulous companion, I asked him if he knew whether her late husband had left a will, and how the property had been disposed of. Oh, yes, he knew all about it; and I was quickly informed that to her had been left the full control and management of the estate during her son's minority, besides the absolute, unconditional possession of her own fortune (but I knew her father had not given her much), and the small additional sum that had been settled upon her before marriage.

Before the close of the explanation, we drew up at the park gates. Now for the trial—if I should find her within—but alas! she might be still at Staningley: her brother had given me no intimation to the contrary. I enquired at the porter's lodge if Mrs. Huntingdon were at home. No, she was with her aunt in ——shire, but was expected to return before Christmas. She usually spent most of her time at Staningley, only coming to Grassdale occasionally, when the management of affairs, or the interest of her tenants and dependants required her presence.

"Near what town is Staningley situated?" I asked. The requisite information was soon obtained. "Now then, my man, give me the reins, and we'll return to M——. I must have some breakfast at the Rose and Crown, and then away to Staningley by the first coach for ——"

"You'll not get there today, sir."

"No matter, I don't want to get there today; I want to get there tomorrow, and pass the night on the road."

"At an inn, sir? You'd better by half stay at our house; and then start fresh tomorrow, and have the whole day for your journey."

"What, and lose twelve hours? not I."

"Perhaps, sir, you're *related* to Mrs. Huntingdon?" said he, seeking to indulge his curiosity since his cupidity was not to be gratified.

"I have not that honour."

"Ah! well," returned he with a dubious, sidelong glance at my splashed, grey trousers and rough pea jacket. "But," he added, encouragingly, "there's many a fine lady like that 'at has kinsfolks poorer nor what you are, sir, I should think."

"No doubt,—and there's many a fine gentleman would esteem himself vastly honoured to be able to claim kindred with the lady you mention."

He now cunningly glanced at my face. "Perhaps, sir, you *mean* to—"

I guessed what was coming, and checked the impertinent conjecture with,—"Perhaps you'll be so good as to be quiet a moment. I'm busy."

"Busy, sir?"

"Yes, in my mind, and don't want to have my cogitations disturbed."

"Indeed, sir!"

You will see that my disappointment had not *very* greatly affected me, or I should not have been able so quietly to bear with the fellow's impertinence. The fact is I thought it as well—nay better, all things considered, that I should not see her today,—that I should have time to compose my mind for the interview—to prepare it for a heavier disappointment, after the intoxicating delight experienced by this sudden removal of my former apprehensions; not to mention that, after travelling a night and a day without intermission, and rushing in hot haste through six miles of new-fallen snow, I could not possibly be in a very presentable condition.

At M—— I had time before the coach started to replenish my forces with a hearty breakfast, and to obtain the refreshment of my usual morning's ablutions, and the amelioration of some slight change in my toilet,—and also to dispatch a short note to my mother (excellent son that I was) to assure her that I was still in existence and to excuse my nonappearance at the expected time. It was a long journey to Staningley for those slow travelling days; but I did not deny myself needful refreshment on the road, nor even a night's rest at a way-side inn; choosing rather to brook a little delay than to present myself worn, wild, and weatherbeaten before my mistress and her aunt, who would be astonished enough to see me without that. Next morning, therefore, I not only fortified myself with as substantial a breakfast as my excited feelings would allow me to swallow, but I bestowed a little more than usual time and care upon my toilet; and, furnished with a change of linen from my small carpet-bag, well brushed clothes, well polished boots, and neat new gloves,—I mounted "the Lightning," and resumed my journey. I had nearly two stages yet before me, but the coach, I was informed, passed through the neighbourhood of Staningley, and, having desired to be set down as near the Hall as possible, I had nothing to do but to sit with folded arms and speculate upon the coming hour.

It was a clear, frosty morning. The very fact of sitting exalted aloft, surveying the snowy landscape and sweet, sunny sky, inhaling the pure, bracing air, and crunching away over the crisp, frozen snow, was exhilarating enough in itself; but add to this the idea of to what goal I was hastening, and whom I expected to meet, and you may have some faint conception of my frame of mind at the time—only a *faint* one—though, for my heart swelled with unspeakable delight, and my spirits rose almost to madness—in spite of my prudent endeavours to bind them down to a reasonable platitude by thinking of the undeniable difference between Helen's rank and mine; of all that she had passed through since our parting; of her long, unbroken silence; and, above all, of her cool, cautious aunt, whose counsels she would doubtless be careful not to slight again. These considerations made my heart flutter with anxiety, and my chest heave with impatience to get the crisis over, but they could not dim her image in my mind, or mar the vivid recollection of what had been said and felt between us—or destroy the keen anticipation of what was to be—in fact, I could not realize their terrors now. Towards the close of the journey, however, a couple of my fellow passengers kindly came to my assistance, and brought me low enough.

"Fine land this," said one of them, pointing with his umbrella to the wide fields on the right, conspicuous for their compact hedge-rows, deep, well-cut ditches, and fine timber-trees, growing sometimes on the borders, sometimes in the midst of the enclosure;—"*very* fine land, if you saw it in the summer or spring."

"Ay," responded the other—a gruff elderly man, with a drab great coat buttoned up to the chin and a cotton umbrella between his knees. "It's old Maxwell's I suppose."

"It *was* his, sir, but he's dead now, you're aware, and has left it all to his niece."

"All!"

"Every rood of it,—and the mansion-house and all,—every hatom of his worldly goods!—except just a trifle, by way of remembrance to his nephew down in ——shire and an annuity to his wife."

"It's strange, sir!"

"It is sir. And she wasn't his own niece neither; but he had no near relations of his own—none but a nephew he'd quarrelled with—and he always had a partiality for this one. And then his wife advised him to it, they say: she'd brought most of the property, and it was her wish that this lady should have it."

"Humph!—She'll be a fine catch for somebody."

"She will so. She's a widow, but quite young yet, and uncommon handsome—a fortune of her own, besides, and only one child—and she's nursing a fine estate for him in ——. There'll be lots to speak for her!—'fraid there's no chance for uz'—(facetiously jogging me with his elbow, as well as his companion)—"ha, ha, ha! No offence, sir, I hope?" (to me) "Ahem!—I should think, she'll marry none but a nobleman, myself. Look ye sir," resumed he, turning to his other neighbour, and pointing past me with his umbrella, "that's the hall—grand park, you see—and all them woods—plenty of timber there, and lots of game—hallo! what now?"

This exclamation was occasioned by the sudden stoppage of the coach at the park gates.

"Gen'leman for Staningley Hall?" cried the coachman; and I rose and threw my carpet-bag on to the ground, preparatory to dropping myself down after it.

"Sickly, sir?" asked my talkative neighbour, staring me in the face (I dare say it was white enough).

"No. Here, coachman."

"Thank'ee, sir.—All right!"

The coachman pocketed his fee and drove away, leaving me not walking up the park, but pacing to and fro before its gates, with folded arms and eyes fixed upon the ground—an overwhelming force of images, thoughts, impressions crowding on my mind, and nothing tangibly distinct but this:— My love had been cherished in vain; my hope was gone for ever; I must tear myself away at once, and banish or suppress all thoughts of her like the remembrance of a wild, mad dream. Gladly would I have lingered round the place for hours, in the hope of catching, at least one distant glimpse of her before I went, but it must not be: I must not suffer her to see me; for what could have brought me hither but the hope of reviving her attachment, with a view, hereafter to obtain her hand? And could I bear that she should think me capable of such a thing!—of presuming upon the acquaintance—the *love* if you will—accidentally contracted, or rather forced upon her against her will, when she was an unknown fugitive, toiling for her own support, apparently without fortune, family connections—to come upon her now, when she was re-instated in her proper sphere and claim a share in her prosperity, which, had it never failed her, would most certainly have kept her unknown to me for ever? and this too, when we had parted sixteen months ago, and she had expressly forbidden me to hope for a reunion in this world—and never sent me a line or a message from that day to this? No! The very idea was intolerable.

And even, if she should have a lingering affection for me still, ought I to disturb her peace by awakening those feelings? to subject her to the struggles of conflicting duty and inclination—to whichsoever side the latter might allure, or the former imperatively call her—whether she should deem it her duty to risk the slights and censures of the world, the sorrow and displeasure of those she loved, for a romantic idea of truth and constancy to me, or to sacrifice her individual wishes to the feelings of her friends and her own sense of prudence and the fitness of things? No—and I would not! I would go at once, and she should never know that I had approached the place of her abode; for though I might disclaim all idea of ever aspiring to her hand, or even of soliciting a place in her friendly regard, her peace should not be broken by my presence, nor her heart afflicted by the sight of my fidelity.

"Adieu then, dear Helen, for ever!—For ever adieu!"

So said I—and yet I could not tear myself away. I moved a few paces, and then looked back, for one last view of her stately home, that I might have its outward form, at least impressed upon my mind as indelibly as her own image, which alas! I must not see again—then, walked a few steps farther; and then lost in melancholy musings, paused again and leant my back against a rough old tree that grew beside the road.

CHAPTER LIII
CONCLUSION

WHILE standing thus, absorbed in my gloomy reverie, a gentleman's carriage came round the corner of the road. I did not look at it; and had it rolled quietly by me, I should not have remembered the fact of its appearance at all; but a tiny voice from within it roused me by exclaiming—

"Mamma, mamma, here's Mr. Markham!"

I did not hear the reply, but presently the same voice answered—

"It is indeed, mamma—look for yourself."

I did not raise my eyes, but I suppose mamma looked, for a clear, melodious voice, whose tones thrilled through my nerves, exclaimed—

"Oh, aunt! Here's Mr. Markham—Arthur's friend!—Stop, Richard!"

There was such evidence of joyous though suppressed excitement in the utterance of those few words—especially that tremulous, "Oh, aunt—" that it threw me almost off my guard. The carriage stopped immediately, and I looked up and met the eye of a pale, grave, elderly lady surveying me from the open window. She bowed and so did I, and then she withdrew her head, while Arthur screamed to the footman to let him out; but before that functionary could descend from his box, a hand was silently put forth from the carriage window. I knew that hand, though a black glove concealed its delicate whiteness and half its fair proportions, and quickly seizing it, I pressed it in my own—ardently for a moment, but instantly recollecting myself, I dropped it, and it was immediately withdrawn.

"Were you coming to see us, or only passing by?" asked the low voice of its owner, who, I felt, was attentively surveying my countenance from behind the thick, black veil which with the shadowing panels, entirely concealed her own from me.

"I—I came to see the place," faltered I.

"The *place*," repeated she, in a tone which betokened more displeasure or disappointment than surprise.

"Will you not enter it then?"

"If you wish it."

"Can you doubt?"

"Yes, yes! he *must* enter," cried Arthur running round from the other door; and seizing my hand in both his, he shook it heartily.

"Do you remember me, sir?" said he.

"Yes, full well, my little man, altered though you are," replied I, surveying the comparatively tall, slim young gentleman with his mother's image visibly stamped upon his fair, intelligent features, in spite of the blue eyes beaming with gladness, and the bright locks clustering beneath his cap.

"Am I not grown?" said he, stretching himself up to his full height.

"Grown! three inches upon my word!"

"I was *seven* last birthday," was the proud rejoinder. "In seven years more, I shall be as tall as you, nearly."

"Arthur," said his mother, "tell him to come in. Go on Richard."

There was a touch of sadness as well as coldness in her voice, but I knew not to what to ascribe it. The carriage drove on and entered the gates before us. My little companion led me up the park, discoursing merrily all the way. Arrived at the Hall door, I paused on the steps and looked round me, waiting to recover my composure, if possible—or at any rate, to remember my new formed resolutions and the principles on which they were founded; and it was not till Arthur had been for some time gently pulling my coat, and re-peating his invitations to enter, that I at length consented to accompany him into the apartment where the ladies awaited us.

Helen eyed me as I entered with a kind of gentle, serious scrutiny and politely asked after Mrs. Markham and Rose. I respectfully answered her en-quiries. Mrs. Maxwell begged me to be seated, observing it was rather cold, but she supposed I had not travelled far that morning.

"Not quite twenty miles," I answered.

"Not on foot!"

"No, Madam, by coach."

"Here's Rachel, sir," said Arthur, the only truly happy one amongst us, directing my attention to that worthy individual, who had just entered to take her mistress's things. She vouchsafed me an almost friendly smile of recognition—a favour that demanded, at least, a civil salutation on my part, which was accordingly given and respectively returned—she had seen the error of her former estimation of my character.

When Helen was divested of her lugubrious bonnet and veil, her heavy winter cloak &c. she looked so like herself that I knew not how to bear it. I was particularly glad to see her beautiful black hair unstinted still and unconcealed in its glossy luxuriance.

"Mamma has left off her widow's cap in honour of uncle's marriage," observed Arthur, reading my looks with a child's mingled simplicity and quickness of observation. Mamma looked grave and Mrs. Maxwell shook her head. "And aunt Maxwell is never going to leave off hers," persisted the naughty boy; but when he saw that his pertness was seriously displeasing and painful to his aunt, he went and silently put his arm round her neck, kissed her cheek, and withdrew to the recess of one of the great bay windows, where he quietly amused himself with his dog while Mrs. Maxwell gravely discussed with me the interesting topics of the weather, the season, and the roads. I considered her presence very useful as a check upon my natural impulses—an antidote to those emotions of tumultuous excitement which would otherwise have carried me away against my reason and my will, but *just then* I felt the restraint almost intolerable, and I had the greatest difficulty in forcing myself to attend to her remarks and answer them with ordinary politeness; for I was sensible that Helen was standing within a few feet of me beside the fire. I dared not look at her, but I felt her eye was upon me, and from one hasty, furtive glance, I thought her cheek was slightly flushed, and that her fingers, as she played with her watch chain, were agitated with that restless, trembling motion which betokens high excitement.

"Tell me," said she, availing herself of the first pause in the attempted conversation between her aunt and me, and speaking fast and low with her eyes bent on the gold chain—for I now ventured another glance—"Tell me how you all are at Lindenhope?—has nothing happened since I left you?"

"I believe not."

"Nobody dead? nobody married?"

"No."

"Or—or expecting to marry?—No old ties dissolved or new ones formed? no old friends forgotten or supplanted?"

She dropped her voice so low in the last sentence that no one could have caught the concluding words but myself, and at the same time turned her eyes upon me with a dawning smile, most sweetly melancholy, and a look of timid though keen enquiry that made my cheeks tingle with inexpressible emotions.

"I believe not," I answered—"Certainly not, if others are as little changed as I." Her face glowed in sympathy with mine.

"And you really did not mean to call?" she exclaimed.

"I feared to intrude."

"To intrude!" cried she with an impatient gesture—"What"—but as if suddenly recollecting her aunt's presence, she checked herself and turning to that lady continued—"Why aunt, this man is my brother's close friend and was my own intimate acquaintance (for a few short months at least), and professed a great attachment to my boy—and when he passes the house, so many scores of miles from his home, he declines to look in for fear of intruding!"

"Mr. Markham is over modest," observed Mrs. Maxwell.

"Over ceremonious rather," said her niece—"over—well, it's no matter." And turning from me, she seated herself in a chair beside the table, and pulling a book to her by the cover, began to turn over the leaves in an energetic kind of abstraction.

"If I had known," said I, "that you would have honoured me by remembering me as an intimate acquaintance, I most likely should not have denied myself the pleasure of calling upon you, but I thought you had forgotten me long ago."

"You judged of others by yourself," muttered she without raising her eyes from the book, but reddening as she spoke and hastily turning over a dozen leaves at once.

There was a pause of which Arthur thought he might venture to avail himself to introduce his handsome young setter and show me how wonderfully it was grown and improved, and to ask after the welfare of its father Sancho. Mrs. Maxwell then withdrew to take off her things. Helen immediately pushed the book from her and after silently surveying her son, his friend, and his dog for a few moments, she dismissed the former from the room under pretence of wishing him to fetch his last new book to show me. The child obeyed with alacrity; but I continued caressing the dog. The silence might have lasted till its master's return had it depended on me to break it, but, in half a minute or less, my hostess impatiently rose, and taking her former station on the rug between me and the chimney corner, earnestly exclaimed—

"Gilbert, what *is* the matter with you?—why are you so changed?— It is a very indiscreet question I know," she hastened to add: "perhaps, a very rude one—don't answer it if you think so—but I hate mysteries and concealments."

"I am not changed, Helen—unfortunately I am as keen and passionate as ever—it is not I, it is circumstances that are changed."

"What circumstances? *Do* tell me!" Her cheek was blanched with the very anguish of anxiety—could it be with the fear that I had rashly pledged my faith to another?

"I'll tell you at once," said I. "I will confess that I came here for the purpose of seeing you (not without some monitory misgivings at my own presumption, and fears that I should be as little welcome as expected when I came), but I did not know that this estate was yours, until enlightened on the subject of your inheritance by the conversation of two fellow passengers in the last stage of my journey; and then, I saw at once the folly of the hopes I had cherished and the madness of retaining them a moment longer; and though I alighted at your gates, I determined not to enter within them; I lingered a few minutes to see the place, but was fully resolved to return to M—— without seeing its mistress."

"And if my aunt and I had not been just returning from our morning drive, I should have seen and heard no more of you?"

"I thought it would be better for both that we should not meet," replied I as calmly as I could, but not daring to speak above my breath from conscious inability to steady my voice, and not daring to look in her face lest my firmness should forsake me altogether: "I thought an interview would only disturb your peace and madden me. But I am glad, now, of this opportunity of seeing you once more and knowing that you have not forgotten me, and of assuring you that I shall never cease to remember you."

There was a moment's pause. Mrs. Huntingdon moved away, and stood in the recess of the window. Did she regard this as an intimation that modesty alone prevented me from asking her hand? and was she considering how to repulse me with the smallest injury to my feelings? Before I could speak to relieve her from such a perplexity, she broke the silence herself by suddenly turning towards me and observing—

"You might have had such an opportunity before—as far I mean as regards assuring me of your kindly recollections, and yourself of mine, if you had written to me."

"I would have done so, but I did not know your address, and did not like to ask your brother, because I thought he would object to my writing—but this would not have deterred me for a moment, if I could have ventured to believe that you expected to hear from me, or even wasted a thought upon your unhappy friend; but your silence naturally led me to conclude myself forgotten."

"Did you expect me to write to *you* then?"

"No, Helen—Mrs. Huntingdon," said I, blushing at the implied imputation, "Certainly not; but if you had sent me a message through your brother, or even asked him about me now and then—"

"I did ask about you, frequently. I was not going to do more," continued she, smiling, "so long as you continued to restrict yourself to a few polite enquiries about my health."

"Your brother never told me that you had mentioned my name."

"Did you ever ask him?"

"No; for I saw he did not wish to be questioned about you, or to afford the slightest encouragement or assistance to my too obstinate attachment." Helen did not reply. "And he was perfectly right," added I. But she remained in silence looking out upon the snowy lawn. "Oh, I will relieve her of my presence!" thought I; and immediately I rose and advanced to take leave, with a most heroic resolution—but pride was at the bottom of it, or it could not have carried me through.

"Are you going already?" said she, taking the hand I offered, and not immediately letting it go.

"Why should I stay any longer?"

"Wait till Arthur comes, at least."

Only too glad to obey, I stood and leant against the opposite side of the window.

"You told me you were not changed," said my companion: "you *are*—very much so."

"No, Mrs. Huntingdon, I only *ought* to be."

"Do you mean to maintain that you have the same regard for me that you had when last we met?"

"I have, but it would be wrong to talk of it now."

"It was wrong to talk of it *then*, Gilbert; it would *not* now—unless to do so would be to violate the truth."

I was too much agitated to speak; but, without waiting for an answer, she turned away her glistening eye and crimson cheek, and threw up the window and looked out, whether to calm her own excited feelings or to relieve her embarrassment,—or only to pluck that beautiful half-blown Christmas rose that grew upon the little shrub without, just peeping from the snow, that had hitherto, no doubt, defended it from the frost, and was now melting away in the sun. Pluck it however, she did, and having gently dashed the glittering powder from its leaves, approached it to her lips and said,—

"This rose is not so fragrant as a summer flower, but it has stood through hardships none of *them* could bear: the cold rain of winter has sufficed to nourish it, and its faint sun to warm it; the bleak winds have not blanched it, or broken its stem, and the keen frost has not blighted it. Look, Gilbert, it is still fresh and blooming as a flower can be, with the cold snow even now on its petals.—Will you have it?"

I held out my hand: I dared not speak lest my emotion should overmaster me. She laid the rose across my palm, but I scarcely closed my fingers upon it, so deeply was I absorbed in thinking what might be the meaning of her words, and what I ought to do or say upon the occasion; whether to give way to my feelings or restrain them still. Misconstruing this hesitation into indifference—or reluctance even—to accept her gift, Helen suddenly snatched it from my hand, threw it out on to the snow, shut down the window with an emphasis, and withdrew to the fire.

"Helen! what means this?" I cried, electrified at this startling change in her demeanour.

"You did not understand my gift," said she,—"or, what is worse, you despised it: I'm sorry I gave it you; but since I did make such a mistake, the only remedy I could think of, was to take it away."

"You misunderstood me, cruelly," I replied, and in a minute I had opened the window again, leaped out, picked up the flower, brought it in, and presented it to her, imploring her to give it me again, and I would keep it for ever for her sake, and prize it more highly than anything in the world I possessed.

"And will this content you?" said she as she took it in her hand.

"It shall," I answered.

"There, then; take it."

I pressed it earnestly to my lips, and put it in my bosom, Mrs. Huntingdon looking on with a half sarcastic smile.

"Now, are you going?" said she.

"I will if—if I must."

"You *are* changed," persisted she—"you are grown either very proud or very indifferent."

"I am neither, Helen—Mrs. Huntingdon. If you could see my heart—"

"You *must* be one,—if not both. And why Mrs. Huntingdon?—why not Helen, as before?"

"Helen, then—dear Helen!" I murmured. I was in an agony of mingled love, hope, delight, uncertainty, and suspense.

"The rose I gave you was an emblem of my heart," said she; "would you take it away and leave me here alone?"

"Would you give me your hand too, if I asked it?"

"Have I not said enough?" she answered with a most enchanting smile. I snatched her hand and would have fervently kissed it, but suddenly checked myself and said,—

"But have you considered the consequences?"

"Hardly, I think, or I should not have offered myself to one too proud to take me, or too indifferent to make his affection outweigh my worldly goods."

Stupid blockhead that I was!—I trembled to clasp her in my arms, but dared not believe in so much joy, and yet restrained myself to say,—

"But if you *should* repent!"

"It would be your fault," she replied: "I never shall, unless you bitterly disappoint me. If you have not sufficient confidence in my affection to believe this, let me alone."

"My darling angel—my *own Helen*," cried I, now passionately kissing the hand I still retained, and throwing my left arm around her, "you never shall repent, if it depend on me alone.—But, have you thought of your aunt?" I trembled for the answer and clasped her closer to my heart in the instinctive dread of losing my new-found treasure.

"My aunt must not know of it yet," said she. "She would think it a rash, wild step, because she could not imagine how well I know you; but she must know you herself; and learn to like you. You must leave us now, after lunch, and come again in spring, and make a long stay, and cultivate her acquaintance; and I know you will like each other."

"And then you will be mine," said I printing a kiss upon her lips, and another, and another—for I was as daring and impetuous now as I had been backward and constrained before.

"No—in another year," replied she, gently disengaging herself from my embrace, but still fondly clasping my hand.

"Another year! Oh, Helen, I could not wait so long!"

"Where is your fidelity?"

"I mean I could not endure the misery of so long a separation."

"It would not be a separation: we will write every day; my spirit shall be always with you; and sometimes you shall see me with your bodily eye. I will not be such a hypocrite as to pretend that I desire to wait so long myself, but as my marriage is to please myself alone, I ought to consult my friends about the time of it."

"Your friends will disapprove."

"They will not greatly disapprove, dear Gilbert," said she, earnestly kissing my hand—"they cannot, when they know you—or if they could, they would not be true friends; I should not care for their estrangement.—Now are you satisfied?" She looked up in my face with a smile of ineffable tenderness.

"Can I be otherwise, with your love? And you *do* love me, Helen?" said I, not doubting the fact, but wishing to hear it confirmed by her own acknowledgment.

"If you loved as *I* do," she earnestly replied, "you would not have so nearly lost me—these scruples of false delicacy and pride would never thus have troubled you—you would have seen that the greatest worldly distinctions and discrepancies of rank, birth, and fortune are as dust in the balance compared with the unity of accordant thoughts and feelings, and truly loving, sympathizing hearts and souls."

"But this is too much happiness," said I, embracing her again; "I have not deserved it Helen—I dare not believe in such felicity: and the longer I have to wait, the greater will be my dread that something will intervene to snatch you from me—and think, a thousand things may happen in a year!—I shall be in one long fever of restless terror and impatience all the time. And besides, winter is such a dreary season."

"I thought so too," replied she gravely: "I would not be married in winter—in December, at least," she added with a shudder—for in that month had occurred both the ill-starred marriage that had bound her to her former husband and the terrible death that released her—"and therefore, I said another year in spring."

"*Next* spring."

"No, no—next autumn, perhaps."

"Summer, then."

"Well, the close of summer. There now! be satisfied."

While she was speaking, Arthur re-entered the room—good boy for keeping out so long.

"Mamma, I couldn't find the book in either of the places you told me to look for it," (there was a conscious something in mamma's smile that seemed to say, "No, dear, I knew you could not"), "but Rachel got it for me at last. Look, Mr. Markham, a natural history with all kinds of birds and beasts in it, and the reading as nice as the pictures!"

In great good humour, I sat down to examine the book and drew the little fellow between my knees. Had he come a minute before, I should have received him less graciously, but now I affectionately stroked his curling locks, and even kissed his ivory forehead: he was my own Helen's son, and therefore mine; and as such I have ever since regarded him. That pretty child is now a fine young man: he has realized his mother's brightest expectations, and is at present residing in Grassdale manor with his young wife, the merry little Helen Hattersley, of yore.

I had not looked through half the book, before Mrs. Maxwell appeared to invite me into the other room to lunch. That lady's cool, distant manners rather chilled me at first; but I did my best to propitiate her, and not entirely without success I think, even in that first short visit; for when I talked cheerfully to her, she gradually became more kind and cordial, and when I departed she bade me a gracious adieu, hoping erelong to have the pleasure of seeing me again.

"But you must not go till you have seen the conservatory, my aunt's winter garden," said Helen, as I advanced to take leave of her, with as much philosophy and self-command as I could summon to my aid.

I gladly availed myself of such a respite, and followed her into a large and beautiful conservatory, plentifully furnished with flowers considering the season—but of course, I had little attention to spare for them. It was not however for any tender colloquy that my companion had brought me there:—

"My aunt is particularly fond of flowers," she observed, "and she is fond of Staningley too: I brought you here to offer a petition in her behalf that this may be her home as long as she lives, and—if it be not our home likewise—that I may often see her and be with her; for I fear she will be sorry to lose me; and, though she leads a retired and contemplative life, she is apt to get low spirited if left too much alone."

"By all means, dearest Helen!—do what you will with your own. I should not dream of wishing your aunt to leave the place under any circumstances; and we will live either here or elsewhere as you and she may determine, and you shall see her as often as you like. I know she must be pained to part with you, and I am willing to make any reparation in my power. I love her for your sake, and her happiness shall be as dear to me as that of my own mother."

"Thank you, darling! you shall have a kiss for that. Good bye. There now—there Gilbert—let me go—here's Arthur, don't astonish his infantile brain with your madness."

★ ★ ★ ★ ★

But it is time to bring my narrative to a close—any one but you would say I had made it too long already; but for *your* satisfaction, I will add a few words more; because, I know you will have a fellow-feeling for the old lady, and will wish to know the last of her history. I did come again in spring, and agreeably to Helen's injunctions, did my best to cultivate her acquaintance. She received me very kindly, having been doubtless, already prepared to think highly of my character, by her niece's too favourable report. I turned my best side out of course, and we got along marvellously well together. When my ambitious intentions were made known to her, she took it more sensibly than I had ventured to hope. Her only remark on the subject, in my hearing, was—

"And so Mr. Markham, you are going to rob me of my niece I understand. Well! I hope God will prosper your union, and make my dear girl happy at last. Could she have been contented to remain single, I own I should have been better satisfied; but if she must marry again, I know of no one, now living and of a suitable age, to whom I would more willingly resign her than yourself, or who would be more likely to appreciate her worth and make her truly happy, as far as I can tell."

Of course I was delighted with the compliment, and hoped to show her she was not mistaken in her favourable judgment.

"I have, however one request to offer," continued she. "It seems I am still to look on Staningley as my home: I wish you to make it yours likewise, for Helen is attached to the place and to me—as I am to her. There are painful associations connected with Grassdale, which she cannot easily overcome; and I shall not molest you with my company or interference here: I am a very quiet person, and shall keep my own apartments and attend to my own concerns, and only see you now and then."

Of course I most readily consented to this; and we lived in the greatest harmony with our dear aunt until the day of her death, which melancholy event took place a few years after—melancholy, not to herself (for it came quietly upon her, and she was glad to reach her journey's end), but only to the few loving friends and grateful dependants she left behind.

To return, however, to my own affairs: I was married in summer, on a glorious August morning. It took the whole eight months, and all Helen's kindness and goodness to boot, to overcome my mother's prejudices against my bride elect, and to reconcile her to the idea of my leaving Linden-Car and living so far away. Yet she was gratified at her son's good fortune after all, and proudly attributed it all to his own superior merits and endowments. I bequeathed the farm to Fergus, with better hopes of its prosperity than I should have had a year ago under similar circumstances; for he had lately fallen in love with the vicar of L——'s eldest daughter, a lady whose superiority had roused his latent virtues and stimulated him to the most surprising exertions, not only to gain her affection and esteem, and to obtain a fortune sufficient to enable him to aspire to her hand, but to render himself worthy of her, in his own eyes, as well as in those of her parents; and in the end he was successful, as you already know. As for myself, I need not tell you how happily my Helen and I have lived and loved together, and how blessed we still are in each other's society, and in the promising young scions that are growing up about us. We are just now looking forward to the advent of you and Rose, for the time of your annual visit draws nigh, when you must leave your dusty, smoky, noisy, toiling, striving city for a season of invigorating relaxation and social retirement with us.

    Till then, farewell,

GILBERT MARKHAM

Staningley, June 10th, 1847.

THE END

Appendix A: Other Writings by Anne and Charlotte Brontë

1. Acton Bell [Anne Brontë], Letter to the Reverend David Thom, 30 December 1848 [Robert H. Taylor Collection, Department of Rare Books and Special Collections, Princeton University Library. Published with permission of the Princeton University Library.]

Sir,

Ill health must plead my excuse for this long delay in acknowledging your flattering communication; but, believe me, I am not the less gratified at the pleasure you have derived from my own and my relatives' works, and especially from the opinions they express. I have seen so little of controversial Theology that I was not aware the doctrine of Universal Salvation had so able and ardent an advocate as yourself; but I have cherished it from my very childhood—with a trembling hope at first, and afterwards with a firm and glad conviction of its truth. I drew it secretly from my own heart and from the word of God before I knew that any other held it. And since then it has even been a source of true delight to me to find the same views either timidly suggested or boldly advocated by benevolent and thoughtful minds; and I now believe there are many more believers than professors in that consoling creed. Why good men should be so adverse to admit it, I know not; —into their own hearts at least, however they might object to its promulgation among the bulk of mankind.

But perhaps the world is not ripe for it yet. I have frequently thought that since it has pleased God to leave it in darkness so long respecting this particular truth, and often to use such doubtful language as to admit of such a general misconception thereupon, he must have some good reason for it. We see how liable men are to yield to the temptations of the passing hour; how little the dread of future punishment—how still less the promise of future reward can avail to make them forbear and wait; and if so many thousands rush into destruction with (as they suppose) the prospect of Eternal Death before their eyes,—what might not the consequence be, if that prospect were changed for one of a limited season of punishment, far distant and unseen,— however protracted and terrible it might be?

I thankfully cherish this belief; I honour those who hold it; and I would that all men had the same view of man's hopes and God's unbounded goodness as he has given to us, if it might be had with safety. But does not that if require some consideration? Should we not remember the weak brother and the infatuated slave of satan, and beware of revealing these truths too hastily to those as yet unable to receive them?

But in these suggestions I am perhaps condemning myself, for in my late novel, "The Tenant of Wildfell Hall," I have given as many hints in support of the doctrine as I could venture to introduce into a work of that description. They are however <u>mere</u> suggestions, and as such I trust you will receive them, believing that I am well aware how much may be said in favour of boldly disseminating God's truth and leaving that to work its way. Only let our zeal be tempered with discretion, and while we labour, let us humbly look to God who is able and certain to bring his great work to perfection in his own good time and manner.

Accept my best wishes in behalf of yourself and your important undertakings, and believe me to remain with sincere esteem,

Yours truly,
Acton Bell

2. Anne Brontë, "To Cowper,"[1] *Poems by Currer, Ellis, and Acton Bell* (London: Aylott and Jones, 1846), 92–94

SWEET are thy strains, celestial Bard;
    And oft, in childhood's years,
I've read them o'er and o'er again,
    With floods of silent tears.

The language of my inmost heart,
    I traced in every line;
My sins, *my* sorrows, hopes, and fears,
    Were there—and only mine.

All for myself the sigh would swell,
    The tear of anguish start;
I little knew what wilder woe
    Had filled the Poet's heart.

---

1   William Cowper (1731–1800), a convert to evangelical Christianity, was a famous poet and writer of hymns. He was tormented by depression and wrote movingly about his religious fears, most famously in "The Castaway" (1803). Edward Chitham explains that "of the eighteenth-century influences on Anne Brontë Cowper is the most pervasive, both in tone and subject matter." *The Poems of Anne Brontë: A New Text and Commentary* (London: Macmillan, 1979), 41.

I did not know the nights of gloom,
    The days of misery;
The long, long years of dark despair,
    That crushed and tortured thee.

But, they are gone; from earth at length
    Thy gentle soul is pass'd,
And in the bosom of its God
    Has found its home at last.

It must be so, if God is love,
    And answers fervent prayer;
Then surely thou shalt dwell on high,
    And I may meet thee there.

Is he the source of every good,
    The spring of purity?
Then in thine hours of deepest woe,
    Thy God was still with thee.

How else, when every hope was fled,
    Couldst thou so fondly cling
To holy things and holy men?
    And how so sweetly sing,

Of things that God alone could teach?
    And whence that purity,
That hatred of all sinful ways—
    That gentle charity?

Are *these* the symptoms of a heart
    Of heavenly grace bereft:
For ever banished from its God,
    To Satan's fury left?

Yet, should thy darkest fears be true,
    If heaven be so severe,
That such a soul as thine is lost,—
    Oh! How shall *I* appear?

3. Anne Brontë, "A Word to the 'Elect,'"[1] *Poems by Currer, Ellis, and Acton Bell* (London: Aylott and Jones, 1846), 104–06

YOU may rejoice to think *yourselves* secure;
You may be grateful for the gift divine—
That grace unsought, which made your black hearts pure,
And fits your earth-born souls in Heaven to shine.

But, is it sweet to look around, and view
Thousands excluded from that happiness
Which they deserved, at least, as much as you,—
Their faults not greater, nor their virtues less?

And, wherefore should you love your God the more,
Because to you alone his smiles are given;
Because he chose to pass the *many* o'er,
And only bring the favoured *few* to Heaven?

And, wherefore should your hearts more grateful prove,
Because for ALL the Saviour did not die?
Is yours the God of justice and of love?
And are your bosoms warm with charity?

Say, does your heart expand to all mankind?
And, would you ever to your neighbour do—
The weak, the strong, the enlightened, and the blind—
As you would have your neighbour do to you?

And, when you, looking on your fellow-men,
Behold them doomed to endless misery,
How can you talk of joy and rapture then?—
May God withhold such cruel joy from me!

That none deserve eternal bliss I know;
Unmerited the grace in mercy given:

---

1   The idea of election was promulgated by John Calvin (1509–64), a major figure in the Reformation, whose beliefs were accepted by many different types of Protestants. The elect were those chosen by God to go to heaven, or as Calvin states, "Scripture clearly proves this much, that God by his eternal and immutable counsel determined once for all those whom it was his pleasure one day to admit to salvation, and those whom, on the other hand, it was his pleasure to doom to destruction" (*Institutes* [1559], Book III, Chapter 21, Section 7). Anne Brontë disagreed vehemently with this belief, as the poem powerfully illustrates.

But, none shall sink to everlasting woe,
That have not well deserved the wrath of Heaven.

And, oh! there lives within my heart
  A hope, long nursed by me;
(And, should its cheering ray depart,
  How dark my soul would be!)

That as in Adam all have died,
  In Christ shall all men live;
And ever round his throne abide,
  Eternal praise to give.

That even the wicked shall at last
  Be fitted for the skies;
And, when their dreadful doom is past,
  To life and light arise.

I ask not, how remote the day,
  Nor what the sinners' woe,
Before their dross is purged away;
  Enough for me, to know

That when the cup of wrath is drained,
  The metal purified,
They'll cling to what they once disdained,
  And live by Him that died.

4. From Currer Bell [Charlotte Brontë], "Biographical Notice of Ellis and Acton Bell," *Wuthering Heights and Agnes Grey* by Ellis and Acton Bell. A New Edition Revised, with a Biographical Notice of the Authors, a Selection of Their Literary Remains, and a Preface (London: Smith, Elder, and Co., 1850), vii–xvi

It has been thought that all the works published under the names of Currer, Ellis, and Acton Bell, were, in reality, the production of one person. This mistake I endeavoured to rectify by a few words of disclaimer prefixed to the third edition of *Jane Eyre*. These, too, it appears, failed to gain general credence, and now, on the occasion of a reprint of *Wuthering Heights* and *Agnes Grey*, I am advised distinctly to state how the case really stands.

Indeed, I feel myself that it is time the obscurity attending those two names—Ellis and Acton—was done away. The little mystery, which formerly yielded some harmless pleasure, has lost its interest; circumstances are changed. It becomes, then, my duty to explain briefly the origin and author-ship of the books written by Currer, Ellis, and Acton Bell.

About five years ago, my two sisters and myself, after a somewhat pro-longed period of separation, found ourselves reunited, and at home. Resident in a remote district where education had made little progress, and where, consequently, there was no inducement to seek social intercourse beyond our own domestic circle, we were wholly dependent on ourselves and each other, on books and study, for the enjoyments and occupations of life. The highest stimulus, as well as the liveliest pleasure we had known from child-hood upwards, lay in attempts at literary composition; formerly we used to show each other what we wrote, but of late years this habit of communica-tion and consultation had been discontinued; hence it ensued, that we were mutually ignorant of the progress we might respectively have made.

One day, in the autumn of 1845, I accidentally lighted on a [manuscript] volume of verse in my sister Emily's handwriting. Of course, I was not sur-prised, knowing that she could and did write verse: I looked it over, and something more than surprise seized me,—a deep conviction that these were not common effusions, nor at all like the poetry women generally write. I thought them condensed and terse, vigorous and genuine. To my ear, they had also a peculiar music—wild, melancholy, and elevating.

...

Meantime, my younger sister quietly produced some of her own compo-sitions, intimating that since Emily's had given me pleasure, I might like to look at hers. I could not but be a partial judge, yet I thought that these verses too had a sweet sincere pathos of their own.

We had very early cherished the dream of one day becoming authors. This dream, never relinquished even when distance divided and absorbing tasks occupied us, now suddenly acquired strength and consistency: it took the character of a resolve. We agreed to arrange a small selection of our po-ems, and, if possible, get them printed. Averse to personal publicity, we veiled our own names under those of Currer, Ellis, and Acton Bell; the ambiguous choice being dictated by a sort of conscientious scruple at assuming Chris-tian names positively masculine, while we did not like to declare ourselves women, because—without at that time suspecting that our mode of writing and thinking was not what is called "feminine"—we had a vague impression that authoresses are liable to be looked on with prejudice; we had noticed how critics sometimes use for their chastisement the weapon of personality, and for their reward, a flattery, which is not true praise.

...

Ill-success failed to crush us: the mere effort to succeed had given a wonderful zest to existence; it must be pursued. We each set to work on a prose tale: Ellis Bell produced *Wuthering Heights*, Acton Bell, *Agnes Grey*, and Currer Bell also wrote a narrative in one volume. These [manuscripts] were perseveringly obtruded upon various publishers for the space of a year and a half; usually, their fate was an ignominious and abrupt dismissal.

...

[*Wuthering Heights* and *Agnes Grey*] appeared at last. Critics failed to do them justice. The immature but very real powers revealed in *Wuthering Heights* were scarcely recognized; its import and nature were misunderstood; the identity of its author was misrepresented; it was said that this was an earlier and ruder attempt of the same pen which had produced *Jane Eyre*.... [Brontë continues to discuss the reception of *Wuthering Heights*, but makes no mention of *Agnes Grey*.]

...

The Tenant of Wildfell Hall by Acton Bell, had likewise an unfavourable reception. At this I cannot wonder. The choice of subject was an entire mistake. Nothing less congruous with the writer's nature could be conceived. The motives which dictated this choice were pure, but, I think, slightly morbid. She had, in the course of her life, been called on to contemplate, near at hand and for a long time, the terrible effects of talents misused and faculties abused; hers was naturally a sensitive, reserved, and dejected nature; what she saw sank very deeply into her mind; it did her harm. She brooded over it till she believed it to be a duty to reproduce every detail (of course with fictitious characters, incidents, and situations) as a warning to others. She hated her work, but would pursue it. When reasoned with on the subject, she regarded such reasonings as a temptation to self-indulgence. She must be honest; she must not varnish, soften, or conceal. This well-meant resolution brought on her misconstruction and some abuse, which she bore, as it was her custom to bear whatever was unpleasant, with mild, steady patience. She was a very sincere and practical Christian, but the tinge of religious melancholy communicated a sad shade to her brief, blameless life.

Neither Ellis nor Acton allowed herself for one moment to sink under want of encouragement; energy nerved the one, and endurance upheld the other. They were both prepared to try again; I would fain think that hope and the sense of power was yet strong within them. But a great change approached: affliction came in that shape which to anticipate is dread; to look back on, grief. In the very heat and burden of the day, the labourers failed over their work.

My sister Emily first declined. The details of her illness are deep-branded in my memory, but to dwell on them, either in thought or narrative, is not in my power. Never in all her life had she lingered over any task that lay before her, and she did not linger now. She sank rapidly. She made haste to leave us. Yet, while physically she perished, mentally, she grew stronger than we had yet known her. Day by day, when I saw with what a front she met suffering, I looked on her with an anguish of wonder and love. I have seen nothing like it; but, indeed, I have never seen her parallel in anything.

Stronger than a man, simpler than a child, her nature stood alone. The awful point was, that, while full of ruth for others, on herself she had no pity; the spirit was inexorable to the flesh; from the trembling hand, the unnerved limbs, the faded eyes, the same service was exacted as they had rendered in health. To stand by and witness this, and not dare to remonstrate, was a pain no words can render.

...

We thought this enough: but we were utterly and presumptuously wrong. She was not buried ere Anne fell ill. She had not been committed to the grave a fortnight, before we received distinct intimation that it was necessary to prepare our minds to see the younger sister go after the elder. Accordingly, she followed in the same path with slower steps, and with a patience that equaled the other's fortitude. I have said she was religious, and it was by leaning on those Christian doctrines in which she firmly believed, that she found support through her most painful journey. I witnessed their efficacy in her latest hour and greatest trial, and must bear my testimony to the calm triumph with which they brought her through. She died May 28, 1849.

What more shall I say about them? I cannot and need not say much more. In externals, they were two unobtrusive women; a perfectly secluded life gave them retiring manners and habits. In Emily's nature the extremes of vigour and simplicity seemed to meet. Under an unsophisticated culture, inartificial tastes, and an unpretending outside, lay a secret power and fire that might have informed the brain and kindled the veins of a hero; but she had no worldly wisdom; her powers were unadapted to the practical business of life; she would fail to defend her most manifest rights, to consult her most legitimate advantage. An interpreter ought always to have stood between her and the world. Her will was not very flexible, and it generally opposed her interest. Her temper was magnanimous, but warm and sudden; her spirit altogether unbending.

Anne's character was milder and more subdued; she wanted the power, the fire, the originality of her sister, but was well-endowed with quiet virtues of her own. Long-suffering, self-denying, reflective, and intelligent, a constitutional reserve and taciturnity placed and kept her in the shade, and covered her mind, and especially her feelings, with a sort of nun-like veil, which was rarely lifted. Neither Emily nor Anne was learned; they had no thought of filling their pitchers at the well-spring of other minds; they always wrote from the impulse of nature, the dictates of intuition, and from such stores of observation as their limited experience had enabled them to amass. I may sum up all by saying, that for strangers they were nothing, for superficial observers less than nothing; but for those who had known them all their lives in the intimacy of close relationship, they were genuinely good and truly great.

This notice has been written, because I felt it a sacred duty to wipe the dust off their gravestones, and leave their dear names free from soil.

CURRER BELL
September 19, 1850

5. Currer Bell [Charlotte Brontë], "Poems by Acton Bell," *Wuthering Heights and Agnes Grey* by Ellis and Acton Bell. A New Edition Revised, with a Biographical Notice of the Authors, a Selection of Their Literary Remains, and a Preface (London: Smith, Elder, and Co., 1850), 490–91

In looking over my sister Anne's papers, I find mournful evidence that religious feeling had been to her but too much like what it was to Cowper;[1] I mean, of course, in a far milder form. Without rendering her a prey to those horrors that defy concealment, it subdues her mood and bearing to a perpetual pensiveness: the pillar of a cloud[2] glided constantly before her eyes: she ever waited at the foot of a secret Sinai,[3] listening in her head to the voice of a trumpet sounding long and waxing louder.[4] Some, perhaps, would rejoice over these tokens of sincere though sorrowing piety in a deceased relative; I own, to me they seem sad, as if her whole innocent life had been passed under the martyrdom of an unconfessed physical pain: their effect, indeed, would be too distressing, were it not combated by the certain knowledge that in her last moments this tyranny of a too tender conscience was overcome; this pomp of terrors broke up, and, passing away, left her dying hour unclouded. Her belief in God did not then bring to her dread, as of a stern Judge,—but hope, as in a Creator and Saviour: and no faltering hope was it, but a sure and steadfast conviction; on which, in the rude passage from Time to Eternity, she threw the weight of her human weakness, and by which she was enabled to bear what was to be borne, patiently—serenely—victoriously.

---

1 William Cowper (1731–1800) was a writer whose most famous poem, "The Castaway," articulates his profound religious fears. Anne Brontë responds to his doubts in her poem "To Cowper" (see Appendix A2, above).

2 See Exodus 13:21-22, describing how God led the Jews out of Egypt: "And the Lord went before them by day in a pillar of cloud, to lead them the way; and by night in a pillar of fire, to give them light; to go by day and night: He took not away the pillar of the cloud by day, nor the pillar of fire by night, from before the people." See also Numbers 14:14; Nehemiah 9:12, 9:19; Psalm 99:7.

3 Anne is compared here to the people who waited for Moses to come down from Sinai.

4 "And when the voice of the trumpet sounded long, and waxed louder and louder, Moses spake and God answered him by a voice" (Exodus 19:19).

Appendix B: Contemporary Reviews

1. Unsigned Review, *Athenaeum* No. 1080 (8 July 1848): 670–71

THE three Bells, as we took occasion to observe when reviewing *Wuthering Heights* [*Athenaeum*, No. 1052] ring in a chime so harmonious as to prove that they have issued from the same mould. The resemblance borne by their novels to each other is curious. *The Tenant of Wildfell Hall* must not hope to gain the popularity of her elder sister *Jane Eyre*,— but the blood of the family is in her veins. A short extract will sufficiently prove this.... Acton Bell, like Ellis and Currer, knows the nooks of the north of England well. As the opening scene will sufficiently testify.— [Quotes "the day I last ... stack of chimneys" (50–52).]

The reader is by this time curious to get a peep of "the tenant" of such a wild abode: being convinced that, since

Vague mystery hangs about these desert places,[1]

She must be a Lady with "a history." But not a line or passage of this shall be divulged in the *Athenaeum*,—however tempted to lengthen our lecture on family likeness. With regard to one point, however, we cannot remain silent:— The Bells must be warned against their fancy for dwelling upon what is disagreeable. The brutified estate of Mr. Huntingdon might have been displayed within a smaller compass in place of being elaborated with the fond minuteness of a Jan Steen.[2] The position of the wife with regard to her husband's paramour is, on the other hand, treated with a sort of hard indifference,— natural enough, it may be, but not in harmony with the impressions of the Lady which we have been invited to entertain. Were the metal from this Bell foundry of baser quality than it is, it would be lost time to point out flaws and take exceptions. As matters stand, our hints may not be without their use to future "castings:" nor will they be unpalatable, seeing that they are followed by our honest recommendation of *Wildfell Hall* as the most interesting novel which we have read for a month past.

---

1 A quotation from "Vyvyan's" "The Novelist: A Legend of the Hartz," *The Mirror of Literature, Amusement, and Instruction* 12.338 (1 Sept. 1828): 227.

2 A Dutch painter (1626[?]–79), known, in part, for the detail of his paintings, as the text implies.

2. Unsigned Review, *The Examiner* No. 2113 (29 July 1848): 483–84

THE authors of *Jane Eyre*, *Wuthering Heights*, *Agnes Grey*, and *The Tenant of Wildfell Hall*, are evidently children of the same family. They derive their scenes from the same country; their associations are alike; their heroines are for the most part alike, three being thrown upon their own talents for self-support, and two of them being all-enduring governesses; and their heroes also resemble each other, in aspect and temper, almost in habits. We have, once or twice, entertained a suspicion that all the books that we have enumerated might have issued form the same source; sent forth at different seasons, in different states of mind or humour, or at different periods or elevations of the intellect,— *Jane Eyre* having been achieved at the culminating point. At all events, the writers are of the same stock, have undoubted marks of family resemblance, and are, in fact,

> Matched in *mouth* like BELLS,
> Each under each.[1]

The Bells are of a hardy race. They do not lounge in drawing rooms or boudoirs. The air they breathe is not that of the hot-house, or of perfumed apartments: but it whistles through the rugged thorns that shoot out their prickly arms on barren moors, or it ruffles the moss on the mountain tops. Rough characters, untamed by contact with towns or cities; willful men, with the true stamp of the passions upon them; plain vigorous Saxon words, not spoiled nor weakened by bad French or school-boy Latin; rude habits; ancient residences—with Nature in her great loneliness all around;—these—with the grey skies or sunset glories above—are the elements of their stories, compounded and reduced to shape, in different moods and with different success.

From all this, it will be observed that Currer, Acton, and Ellis Bell, whatever may be their defects otherwise, are not common-place writers. Their characters are not faint or tawdry copies of other characters which have already wearied us, and which have oppressed the pages of novelists, month after month, for the last thirty years. They have bone and sinew about them; animal life peeps out in every form; and the phraseology, although sometimes tedious enough, is rarely conventional. On these accounts, we are disposed to give a full and overflowing measure of praise to writers, who in assuming to portray nature have been wise and sincere enough to go back to their

---

1 Part of Theseus' description of his hunting hounds from Shakespeare's *A Midsummer Night's Dream* (IV.i.122–23).

original; and we earnestly recommend them as examples to other labourers in the same path.

The story called *The Tenant of Wildfell Hall* is very inartificially construct-ed. The main part of the tale consists of a recital or journal made by a certain Mrs. Graham, the mysterious tenant for the time being of the Hall, and the subject of innumerable slanderous hints and innuendos on the part of the restless gossips of a remote village. The lady herself, whose charms have dis-turbed the tranquility of a very rough Cymon,[1] by name Gilbert Markham, turns out to be a Mrs. Huntingdon, and to be unhappily married; and it is not until the author very judiciously kills the first husband that the fortune of Gilbert the hero emerges out of the troubles which have hung about him, and his happiness is finally consummated.

There are two distinct series of character in the book: the one being the inhabitants of the village in the neighbourhood of Wildfell Hall; the other, less rural and far more ambitiously sketched, the friends and acquaintance who surround the heroine in her native county, and tend to illustrate her conduct in the earlier and later portions of her life. For she is "Tenant of Wildfell Hall" during some months only, when she has been forced to fly from a drunken, vicious, and tyrannical husband; and there is in fact no con-nection whatever between the two sets of *dramatis personae*, except the very slender link which the heroine herself presents, by passing from one place to the other.

To say the truth, there is no very intense excitement in any part of the book. Just at the time when we begin to feel some interest about Markham and the lady, we are thrown back upon her previous history, which occupies a full half of the three volumes before us. This is a fatal error: for, after so long and minute a history, we cannot go back and recover the enthusiasm which we have been obliged to dismiss a volume and half before.

Nevertheless, there are some distinct markings of character. In the village, besides the ordinary gabble of women who have nothing else to do but to slander their neighbour, there is an outline of a pompous parson, who seems drawn from life. The ladies are less original; and the general tone of all the conversations in this part of the story—except only when the willfulness or ferocity of the hero intervenes—are tedious and commonplace. We are reminded occasionally of the minute gossip in which Miss Austen[2] occasion-ally indulged, but with less of that particular quality which her dialogues invariably possessed, of illustrating the characters of the speakers.

---

1 Cymon is the name of a shepherd, who falls in love with a goddess, Iphigenia, and transforms himself from a humble rustic into an educated courtier (from Boccaccio's [1313–75] *Decameron* [1353]).

2 Jane Austen (1775–1817).

Owing to the faulty construction of the tale, it is scarcely possible to analyze it, for the information of the reader. We must content ourselves with stating that Helen Lawrence (the heroine), a young lady of small fortune, but of considerable beauty and spirit, after having been persecuted by the adoration of two venerable lovers, casts herself in to the arms of Mr. Arthur Huntingdon, a person with no very attractive superficies, and a blackguard of undoubted quality. As this person is preceded by a tolerably bad reputation, and as his pretensions are discountenanced by the uncle and aunt of Helen, and supported simply by mean and impudent conduct on his own part, it is difficult to understand his success. But the lady is a little willful, and has been worried and irritated by an old man's love; and as we all know, it is sometimes the weakness of our adversary that enables us to conquer.

The following extracts will put the reader in possession of all that it is necessary for him to know respecting Mr. Arthur Huntingdon. [Quotes "It was the portrait ... he looked no fool" (71); "A gentleman stood ... not anger me" (135); and "How will he greet ... I love him" (151–52).]

She eventually marries this vulgar coxcomb, who introduces her to some of his male associates,—a set of drunken savages, such as we do not remember to have heard of as having been tolerated for many years, within the pale of civilized society. Of these, Grimsby is a sordid blackleg;[1] Hattersley, a wild beast (partially tamed at last by love and pity for a suffering wife); Lord Lowborough, the victim, and Hargrave, The Joseph Surface,[2] of the party. There is something touching in the renovation of Lord Lowborough, who rises from his ruin, and abandons himself, heart and soul, to a heartless beauty, one Annabella Wilmot, who on her part despises and deserts him for the more ostentatious Huntingdon, already the husband of Helen. The infidelity of the parties is discovered by the heroine, who overhears a conversation between them, and who thereupon withdraws herself from the society of her husband (whose excesses of all sorts increase daily), and finally flies, with her child, from his residence, to seclude herself at Wildfell Hall, under the assumed name of Mrs. Graham.

At this period of the tale she makes the acquaintance of Gilbert Markham, a sort of gentleman farmer in the neighbourhood; and the consequence is a violent and avowed attachment on his part, and an evident liking on hers. Owing to some suspicious circumstances he becomes jealous of a Mr. Lawrence, who turns out to be her brother, and striking him down senseless, induces the so-called Mrs. Graham to entrust to him a written recital of her history. Markham and Helen part; she returns to the house of her husband,

---

1   Slang for swindler.

2   A hypocritical character in Richard Brinsley Sheridan's (1751–1816) *School for Scandal* (1777).

who is apparently dying, and who in the end actually dies, leaving Helen free to bestow herself on the man of her heart, which she accordingly does, and they "all live happy afterwards."

The volumes afford few extracts. Here is a description, however, of Wildfell Hall, which is not very unlike the house inhabited by the wild people in *Wuthering Heights*. [Quotes "I left the more frequented ... its departed occupants" (50–51).]

There is a drunken scene of considerable power in the second volume, but we do not know that we should edify any of our readers by extracting it. We therefore forbear, and turn to gentler matters. The husband of Helen dies, as we have said, but Markham is ignorant of the sentiments of the beautiful widow, respecting whom he has received no tidings; and therefore, restless and unhappy, he wanders about her residence—hears of her great wealth—and, poor himself, is too proud to announce himself to her. They meet, however, by accident, and, after a few of those little misunderstandings which only enhance the happiness that succeeds and clears them away, the lovers are united, and the narrative ends. Here is a short love passage; and with this we must conclude our extracts. [Quotes "She remained in silence ... my worldly goods" (401–03).]

3. [Charles Kingsley], *Fraser's Magazine for Town and Country* (April 1849): 423–26

A people's novel of a very different school is *The Tenant of Wildfell Hall*. It is, taken altogether, a powerful and an interesting book. Not that it is a pleasant book to read, nor, as we fancy, has it been a pleasant book to write; still less has it been a pleasant training which could teach an author such awful facts, or give courage to write them. The fault of the book is coarseness—not merely that coarseness of subject which will be the stumbling-block of most readers, and which makes it utterly unfit to be put into the hands of girls; of that we do not complain. There are foul and accursed undercurrents in plenty, in this same smug, respectable, whitewashed English society, which must be exposed now and then; and Society owes thanks, not sneers, to those who dare to show her the image of her own ugly, hypocritical visage. We must not lay Juvenal's[1] coarseness at Juvenal's door, but at that of the Roman world which he stereotyped in his fearful verses.

But the world does not think so. It will revile Acton Bell for telling us, with painful circumstantiality, what the house of a profligate, uneducated country squire is like, perfectly careless whether or not the picture be true, only angry at having been disturbed from its own self-complacent doze—just as it has reviled gallant 'S.G.O.' for nasty-mindedness, and what not, be-

---

1 A Roman satirist of the late first and early second century.

cause, having unluckily for himself a human heart and eyes, he dared to see what was under his nose in the bedrooms of Dorsetshire labourers.[1]

It is true, satirists are apt to be unnecessarily coarse. Granted; but are they half as coarse, though, as the men whom they satirise? That gnat-straining, camel-swallowing Pharisee,[2] the world, might, if it chose, recollect that a certain degree of coarse-naturedness, while men continue the one-sided beings which they are at present, may be necessary for all reformers, in order to enable them to look steadily and continuously at the very evils they are removing. Shall we despise the surgeon because he does not faint in the dissecting-room? Our Chadwicks[3] and Southwood Smiths[4] would make but poor sanitary reformers if their senses could not bid defiance to sulphuretted hydrogen[5] and ammonia. Whether their nostrils suffer or not, ours are saved by them: we have no cause to grumble. And even so with 'Acton Bell.'

But taking this book as a satire, and an exposure of evils, still all unnecessary coarseness is a defect,—a defect which injures the real usefulness and real worth of the book. The author introduces, for instance, a long diary, kept by the noble and unhappy wife of a profligate squire; and would that every man in England might read and lay to heart that horrible record. But what greater mistake, to use the mildest term, can there be than to fill such a diary with written oaths and curses, with details of drunken scenes which no wife, such as poor Helen is represented, would have the heart, not to say the common decency, to write down as they occurred? Dramatic probability and good feeling are equally outraged by such a method. The author, tempted naturally to indulge her full powers of artistic detail, seems to have forgotten that there are silences more pathetic than all words.

---

1   Lord Sidney Godolphin Osborne (1808–89), a philanthropist whom the *Dictionary of National Biography* describes as "of a militant and almost ferocious type," lived and worked in Dorset from 1841–75. He was particularly knowledgeable about agricultural laborers.

2   A reference to Matthew 23:24, where Jesus is expressing frustration with the hypocritical Pharisees' obsessive attention to biblical laws: "Ye blind guides, which strain at a gnat, and swallow a camel." The biblical passage underscores the reviewer's frustration at other critics who have been overly distressed at the "coarseness" of *The Tenant of Wildfell Hall*.

3   Edwin Chadwick (1800–90) was a Victorian reformer who worked on the problems of poverty and sanitation. He published the influential *Report ... on an Enquiry into the Sanitary Condition of the Labouring Population of Great Britain* in 1842.

4   Thomas Southwood-Smith (1788–1861) was a doctor who worked on sanitation reform and poverty. His *Treatise on Fever* (1830) made the connection between the unsanitary living conditions of the poor and the spread of infectious disease.

5   This toxic gas smells like rotten eggs, is formed from decaying animal matter, and can often be found in swamps and sewers. We now refer to it as hydrogen sulfide.

A cognate defect, too, struck us much; the splenetic and bitter tone in which certain personages in the novel are mentioned, when really, poor souls, no deeds of theirs are shown which could warrant such wholesale appellations as "brute" and "demon." One is inclined sometimes to suspect they are caricatures from the life, against whom some private spite is being vented; though the author has a right to reply, that the whole novel being the autobiography of a young gentleman farmer, such ferocities are to be charged on him, not on her. True, but yet in his mouth as much as in any one's else they want cause for them to be shown, according to all principles of fiction; and if none such exists on the face of the story, it only indicates a defect in the youth's character which makes his good fortune more improbable. For the book sets forth how the gallant Gilbert wins the heart, and after her husband's death, the hand of the rich squire's well-born and highly-cultivated wife.

Now we do not complain of the "impossibility" of this. *Ne me dites jamais ce bête de mot,*[1] as Mirabeau[2] said. Impossible? Society is full of wonders: our worst complaint against fiction-mongers is, that they are so tame, so common-place, so shamefully afraid of wonders, of ninety-nine hundredths of what a man may see every day of the week by putting his head out of his own window. You old whited sepulcher of a world![3] There are dead men's bones enough inside you, of which you could give but an ugly account! It was but the other day, for instance, we heard a true story of piracy and parricide, of ill-gotten wealth, worse than heathen barbarity, and God's awful judgments, transacted among scenery of such romantic horror, physical and spiritual, as would make Mr. Ainsworth's fortune.[4] We would offer now to sell him the story for twenty pounds, as the best investment he ever made in his life, were it not so fearfully true and recent, that its publication would wantonly wound the hearts of many innocent people now living. So much for improbabilities. But the novelist, especially when he invents a story, instead of merely giving dramatic life to one already made, which is the Shakespearian, and, as we suspect, the higher path of art, must give some internal and spiritual probability to his outward miracles; and this, we think, Acton Bell has in this

---

1   "Don't ever call/speak of me by that bad name" (literally "beast of a name").

2   Honoré Gabriel Riqueti, comte de Mirabeau (1749–91), a French politician who recommended using Britain's constitutional monarchy as a model for the French during the Revolution.

3   Another biblical reference to Jesus' frustration with the Pharisees. "Woe unto you, scribes and Pharisees, hypocrites! For ye are like unto whited sepulchers, which indeed appear beautiful outward, but are within full of dead men's bones, and of all uncleanness" (Matthew 23:27).

4   William Harrison Ainsworth (1805–82) was a popular Victorian novelist who wrote historical romances.

case failed to do. We cannot see any reason why Gilbert Markham, though no doubt highly attractive to young ladies of his own caliber, should excite such passionate love in Helen, with all her bitter experiences of life, her painting, and her poetry, her deep readings and deep thoughts—absolutely no reason at all, except the last one in the world, which either the author or she would have wished, namely, that there was no other man in the way for her to fall in love with. We want to see this strange intellectual superiority of his to the general run of his class (for we must suppose some such); and all the characteristics we do find, beyond the general dashing, manful spirit of a young farmer, is a very passionate and somewhat brutal temper, and, to say the least, a wanton rejection of a girl to whom he has been giving most palpable and somewhat rough proofs of affection, and whom he afterwards hates bitterly, simply because she rallies him on having jilted her for a woman against whose character there was every possible ground for suspicion. This is not to be counterbalanced by an occasional vein of high-flown sentimentalism in the young gentleman (and that, too, not often) when he comes in contact with his lady-love. If the author had intended to work out the noble old Cymon and Iphigenia[1] myths, she ought to have let us see the gradual growth of the clown's mind under the influence of the accomplished woman; and this is just what she has not done. Gilbert Markham is not one character oscillating between his old low standard and his higher new one, according as he comes in contact with his own countrified friends or his new lady-love, but two different men, with no single root-idea of character to unite and explain the two opposite poles of his conduct. For instance, Mr. Markham is one day talking to Helen in the following high-flown vein....
[Quotes "It gives me ... spirits around us" (340–41) and "My [unenviable] task must ... Mrs. Graham's brother" (344–45).]

Quantum mutatus ab illo Hectore![2] To us, this and many other scenes seem as vulgar and improbable in conception, as they are weak and disgusting in execution. The puffs[3] inform us that the book is very like *Jane Eyre*. To us it seems to have exaggerated all the faults of that remarkable book, and retained very few of its good points. The superior *religious* tone in which alone it surpasses *Jane Eyre* is, in our eyes, quite neutralized by the low *moral* tone which reigns throughout.

Altogether, as we said before, the book is painful. The dark side of every body and every thing is dilated on; we had almost said, reveled in. There are a very few quite perfect people in the book, but they are kept as far out of sight

---

1   See Appendix B2, above, n.1, page 420.

2   "How changed from that earlier Hector," a quotation from Virgil's *Aeneid* II.274–75.

3   "Undue or inflated praise or commendation, uttered or written in order to influence public estimation; an extravagantly laudatory advertisement or review of a book...." (*OED*).

as possible; they are the "accidentals," the disagreeable people, the "necessary" notes of the melody; and the "timbre" of the notes themselves is harsh and rough. The author has not had the tack which enabled Mr. Thackeray, in *Vanity Fair*[1] to construct a pleasing whole out of most unpleasing materials, by a harmonious unity of parts, and, above all, by a tone of tender grace and solemn ironic indignation, in the midst of all his humour, spreading over and softening down the whole;—that true poetic instinct, which gives to even the coarsest of Fielding's[2] novels and Shakespeare's comedies, considered as wholes, a really pure and lofty beauty. The author has not seen that though it is quite fair to write in a melancholy, or even harsh key, and to introduce accidental discords, or even sounds in themselves disagreeable, yet that this last must be done only to set off by contrast the background of harmony and melody, and that the key of the whole must be a correct and a palpable one; it must not be buried beneath innumerable occasional flats and sharps; above all, we must not, as in *The Tenant of Wildfell Hall*, with its snappish fierceness, be tortured by a defective chord, in which one false note is perpetually recurring; or provoked by a certain flippant, rough staccato movement throughout, without softness, without repose, and, therefore, without dignity. We advise the author, before the next novel is taken in hand, to study Shakespeare somewhat more carefully and see if she* cannot discover the secret of the wonderful harmony with which he, like Raphael,[3] transfigures the most painful, and, apparently, chaotic subjects.

4. Unsigned Review, *The Literary World: A Journal of American and Foreign Literature, Science, and Art* III.28 (12 August 1848): 544–46

THERE is no longer a doubt that the public is threatened with an infinite series of novels of a new class, which will be strung on, like the knotted tail of a kite, to the popular work *Jane Eyre*. That book has been already sufficiently discussed, and we purpose here confining our remarks to the crude though powerful productions named at the head of this article [*The*

---

*   We have spoken of the author in the feminine gender, because, of whatever sex the name "Acton Bell" may be, a woman's pen seems to us indisputably discernible in every page. The very coarseness and vulgarity is just such as a woman, trying to write like a man, would invent,—second-hand and clumsy, and not such as men do use; the more honour to the writer's heart, if not to her taste.

---

1   William Makepeace Thackeray's (1811–68) famous satire, *Vanity Fair*, first published serially from 1847–48, also called attention to social problems.

2   Henry Fielding (1707–54) was a dramatist and novelist. His *The History of the Adventures of Joseph Andrews* (1742) parodies Samuel Richardson's *Pamela* (1740), a novel that some believe influenced *Tenant*.

3   An Italian painter of the high Renaissance, known in part for the sensitive and innovative interpretations of the scenes he was commissioned to paint (1483–1520).

Tenant of Wildfell Hall by Acton Bell]. The mind that conceived them is one of great strength and fervor, but coarse almost to brutality. Its owner may be descended from a jarl[1] or a sea-king; but though his name be written on the roll of Battle-Abbey,[2] there is a leaven of intense vulgarity in his very fibre that no washings of heraldry can ever efface. But we mean not to be offensively severe on this trait—we only want his American readers to recognize it while doing just homage to his genius. The *reality* of these writings makes them seize upon the public mind; and already there is the liveliest discussion about their principles, when in fact the danger from their diffusion lies much nearer the surface. For good taste supplies the *antennae* or feelers as to what is right with half the world, and if that be perverted the weaker part at least are sure to go wrong.

Let us illustrate. The delightful tales of Hogg,[3] the Ettrick shepherd, are full of grossness; but these tell for nothing with the reader of education. 'Tis a man of genius whom he knows to have been originally low in his associations, describing scenes of social life through his own peculiar appointed medium of viewing them. But in the novels of Acton Bell the public mind is fixed as yet only upon the *genius* of the writer: his pictures of nature are unsurpassed, and his pictures of life being almost equally vivid, we take his delineations of the better classes of society in the north of England with the same confidence that we accord to his delineations of scenery. And yet what a set of boorish cubs, nauseating profligates, and diabolical ruffians, does he present us, as specimens of the social life, whether immediately around him, or among the gay and far-descended, with whose habits and peculiarities he claims to be more or less familiar! In *Wuthering Heights*, all his far-descended demi-noblesse of the north of England would be out of place in a decent American kitchen. And in his last book the beautiful tenant of Wildfell Hall, the heiress of parks and villas, and the belle of a London season, marries a boor, whom the writer describes as lacking either spirit, generosity, or language to make a full apology to her invalid brother, whom he has nearly beaten to death by mistake; and this caitiff[4] ditcher,[5] who should have been

---

1 "Originally 'a man of noble birth' hence used as the title of hereditary Norse and Danish chieftains; later of the royal liegemen next in rank to the king whom they followed. An old Norse or Danish chieftain or under-king" (*OED*).

2 Allegedly the list of families who fought victoriously with William the Conqueror (c. 1028–87) in 1066 at the Battle of Hastings during the Norman invasion of England.

3 James Hogg (1770–1835) was a Scottish writer and a frequent contributor to magazines such as *Blackwood's Edinburgh Magazine*, where he wrote under the name "The Ettrick Shepherd."

4 "Expressing contempt and often involving strong moral disapprobation: A base, mean, despicable 'wretch,' a villain" (*OED*).

5 "One who makes and repairs ditches" (*OED*).

passed out of the window with a farm-yard fork, the writer makes his hero; because he can talk sentiment, and criticize pictures, loves poetry, and has something more than a peasant's meteorological observation of the influence of the weather on the landscape.

But it may be said, "there is a good deal of human nature about the whole thing." There is the blindness of the critic! It is the writer's genius which makes his incongruities appear natural. When or where was there such a state of society, such a jumble of character and manners as he describes. His London Buck, Mr. Huntingdon, belongs to the squirearchy period of Smollet and Fielding's novels[1]—the wife of the profligate to the sentimental, progress women of the present era. His "Gilbert Markham" has the intelligence of a country gentleman that might have flourished in some pleasant hamlet on the North river; but he commits an assault and battery upon "the squire" that would have wrought an indictment wherever our country squires are to be found; while his very apology, if it did not provoke a call for pistols and coffee in the party outraged, would have insured his being set ashore from a Mississippi steamboat as unfit to associate with the cabin passengers. Such gross incongruities of character do undoubtedly exist in individuals the world over; but can this sort of half-civilization, half-brutification, be characteristic of English society in any portion of that highly artificial country? Is it customary to find the combination of the boor and the bravo (both male and female by the way) in hereditary possession of long-descended estates like Wuthering Heights? Is it characteristic of "English Respectabilities"—the landlords, common law men, or gig-keeping[2] classes—to unite manners and principles like those of Huntingdon to property and position like his—or intelligence and taste like that of Markham to his clownishness?

We shrewdly suspect these books to be written by some gifted and retired woman, whose principle notions of men are derived from other books; or who, taking some walking automaton of her native village for a model, throws in certain touches of rascality, of uncouthness or boisterousness, to make her lay figures animated and, as she thinks, masculine. If any one chooses to study her male characters, it will be found that all that is good or attractive about them is or might be womanish, while all that is bad relishes either of the flash English novel, or of the melodrama of Kotzebue's day.[3]

But what, then, do we leave this writer as the secret of her power?—It is comprised in vigor of thought, freshness and naturalness of expression, and remarkable reality of description. No matter how untrue to life her scene

---

1 Tobias George Smollet (1721–71) was a Scottish writer; Henry Fielding (1707–54) was a dramatist and novelist.

2 A gig was a light, two-wheeled carriage, pulled by one horse.

3 August von Kotzebue (1761–1819), a German dramatist.

or character may be, the vividness and fervor of her imagination is such that she instantly *realizes* it. And herein lies the undoubted test—the distinctive power—the often sad gift of genius, viz. the thorough sympathy with, the living in, the intense realization of the creations of its own fancy. There are many thoroughly matter of fact scenes in these books so literally depicted that we read them only as faithful transcripts of the writer's experience; yet these very scenes are not unlikely to originate just as much in the conceptions of fancy as any others. You cannot detect the *joining* on of the real to the unreal, in a writer of genius, from the simple fact that the images of the latter are often more vivid to his own mind than the actual pictures drawn by the former. But you may trace his identities through the medium of his tastes, natural or conventional. If these are coarse he will certainly betray himself at some time, like the cat who, endowed as a princess, instinctively betrayed the royal dignity, when a mouse at the foot of the throne called out her feline propensities.

The work before us, although infinitely inferior to, yet in some respects greatly resembles *Jane Eyre*: not alone in manner of thinking but in the execution. Like its predecessor, it is an autobiography. One-half of it consists of letters from Gilbert Markham to his brother-in-law, giving an account of his career; the remainder, of a journal kept by Helen Graham (we hate to give her any other name than the one we knew her by) of her own life. Here is the argument. Helen Lawrence is wooed and won by Arthur Huntingdon, a fascinating, profligate scoundrel, of good family and fortune. Shortly after marriage, he returns to his wonted scenes of vice and debauchery, and wickedness generally, and his brutality towards his wife gradually eradicates every feeling of her heart, in which he has a place, save that of utter loathing and hatred. In fact, one of the chief improbabilities of the book consists in the absurdity of supposing any community or family in England would tolerate such a household as Mr. Huntingdon's among them. In this world men do not maltreat their wives, seduce openly other men's, and beat their brothers-in-law with impunity. In our American world, at least, some friendly bullet would rapidly cure such disagreeable habits. At length, however, things reach such a pass at Grassdale, that either the wife or the mistress must yield precedency; and in this crisis the former flies, with her little boy, to Wildfell Hall, her family's seat, where she remains unknown to any of her friends save her brother, earning a scanty support by her pencil; for, like Jane Eyre, she was a skillful artist. Long unoccupied, the Hall was very ruinous, and her retreat was unsuspected by her persecutors: but to make herself more secure she assumes the name of Graham, and passes for a widow among the inhabitants of the neighborhood.

We cite a description of Wildfell Hall and its fair tenant. [Quotes "about two miles ... its departed occupants" (51); ... "I beheld ... amiable temper"

(47).] And afterwards, we learn that "her eyes were full of soul, large, clear, and nearly black—not brown, but very dark grey" (84).

As may be surmised, Mr. Gilbert Markham soon becomes madly enamored of the soi-disant[1] Helen Graham; nor is his passion unreturned. Principle, however, and a firm sense of virtuous rectitude, triumph in Helen's bosom, as it did in that of Jane Eyre, and her lover is peremptorily dismissed. As usual with lovers, Gilbert enacts the usual quantity of fantastic freaks before high heaven, and goes through the customary agonies of hope, jealousy, despair, and settled triumphant happiness, all of which are well portrayed by our author, Mr. Huntingdon being on his deathbed, his wife returns to him to smooth his dying pillow; and after his happy (to her) departure, becomes suited to the man of her post-nuptial choice.

In all this the reader will discover a strong family likeness to the plot of *Jane Eyre*, which purports to be written by a brother of the author. It may be curious to point out some few additional proofs of this resemblance. In both, the heroines, so soon as troubles thicken around them, take to the open country under an assumed name, like Rosalind and Celia, in the Forest of Arden,[2] where they keep themselves concealed, and suffer hardships. Certainly, they ought to have had a legal advisor to show them the use of their country's laws. And so in style does this likeness exist. Every one remembers, in *Jane Eyre*, how beautifully, in a few words, a whole landscape is presented to the reader—aye, and more than that—how cunningly or how magically the author conveys the scene he (or she) describes to the mind's eye, so as not only to impress it with the mere view, but to speak, as it were, to the imagination, to the inner sense, as is ever the case with the Poetry as the Painting of real genius. This same mysterious word-painting is one of the features of the present tale. How plainly, how distinctly, do the following pictures present themselves to us, and with what a mystic language do they appeal to our hearts.

[Quotes "a pretty sketch of Lindenhope ... dull beclouded sky above" (70).]

[After declaring "... no other pencil painted it than the one which, guided by the little fingers of Jane Eyre," the reviewer quotes two other passages from *Tenant*: "At length our walk ... these were far away" (83) and "My heart sank ... means encouraging to me" (393), before closing.]

We have yet a few remarks to add before taking leave of these works. We have at the opening of this article expressed our sense of the author's views of life and society in sufficiently decided terms. But after placing him (or her) in about the same social position as the rarely endowed author of *The Queen's*

---

1 From the French, *soi* oneself; *disant* saying. Thus, so called or claimed by oneself.

2 Shakespeare, *As You Like It*.

Wake;[1] and accounting for many coarsenesses upon the same score that every one excuses them in the prose tales of the Ettrick Shepherd,[2] we do not believe one word in the charge of immorality so often brought against these books. An aberration of taste, an ignorance of society, must by no means be confounded with a departure from principle. But still further, while we hold the writer responsible at the bar of criticism for painting life and manners as they really exist—yet as to the correctness of his characters in the abstract, we assuredly do not mean to hold him or any other author responsible.

We consider him here solely as an artist. Who holds Moses accountable for the conduct of the children of Korah? Or pardons the morals of Tom Moore, because sweet Fanny of Timmol resisted the devil in a stage coach?[3] Why must an author father all the sins committed in his books? Yet, after all, no such apology or defense is here necessary. In tracing her career, the heroine tells truthfully everything that would interest the reader, however much the cool head of worldly calculation or of self-complacent inexperience may sneer at or condemn it. Who does not cry Amen to the indignant malison[4] Jane Eyre denounces against her devilish aunt? Alas for poor human nature! Who can justly discriminate between the glow of triumph at the ruin of Helen Graham's persecutors, and the recognition of the mysterious hand of Providence in their downfall? To speak for ourselves, we cannot. *Homo sum; nihil humanum a me alienum puto.*[5] ... [The reviewer then discusses Helen Burns's death in *Jane Eyre* before returning to his discussion of *The Tenant of Wildfell Hall.*]

To pursue further the ideas that call forth the censure of some estimable judges of character against them. We are told that no woman, unless divested of all those finer sensibilities that constitute the chief graces of her heart, could possibly comport herself towards any man as do the heroines before us, Helen and Jane. Again we doubt all this. Utterly inexperienced as we are

---

1   Immensely popular poem by James Hogg, first published in 1813, with a revised, fifth edition in 1819.

2   A reference to Hogg; see n. 3, page 427.

3   Thomas Moore (1779–1852), a popular poet whose work influenced all of the Brontës. Anne Brontë even has Gilbert quote his "Let Erin Remember the Days of Old" (75). "Fanny of Timmol. A Mail-Coach Adventure" is a sexually frank poem about a man's attraction to a young woman with whom he rode in a "close little carriage" (2) whose "dear little lips, to their destiny true, / Seem'd to know they were born for the use of another" (5–6). By the end of the work, she leaves him to return to Timmol, apparently still a virtuous woman despite what transpired in the coach. It was published in *The Poetical Works of the Late Thomas Little Esq.* (1801; Oxford and New York: Woodstock Books, 1990): 92–94.

4   Curse.

5   "I am a man [human]; I consider nothing human [to be] alien to me," a quotation from the Roman poet Terence (c. 190–159 BCE), *Heauton Timorumenos*, 77.

in the labyrinthine intricacies of the heart of woman, we may err in our conceptions of its nature. But still, we contend that it was not possible for Jane Eyre, loving as she did with all the nervous tension of which the heart is capable, to act otherwise than she did. The affections of a woman are like the tendrils of a vine; in their infancy they are tender and susceptible, but when for a time they have encircled the limb in their grasp, and have been exposed as well to the cold winds of Spring as to the hot suns of Summer, they become obdurate and hard; and then is the object of her affection "grappled to her soul with hooks of steel."[1] It is contrary to the very spirit of Love to sit in judgment on every little peccadillo of his votaries. How could anyone mould her heart to love one whom she had never seen, solely on grounds of esteem? If such were the case, if reason alone dictated in such matters, a man might marry his grandmother as likely as any one else. No, cold, deliberate calculation can never originate, though it may control love. The mariner who loosens his sails to the gale, may as well seek to make the wind blow from what quarter he listeth.

Like Dian's kiss, unasked, unsought,
Love gives itself, but is not bought;
Nor voice nor sound betrays
Its deep impassioned gaze.

It comes—the beautiful, the free
The crown of all humanity—
In silence and alone
To seek the elected one.[2]

It is sheer nonsense to say that because the ceremonials of society—that wholesome framework of conventionality which makes the common sense of the many in times past and present, the stay and support against which the weak and the bewildered may always lean with safety.—It is sheer nonsense to say that these useful but arbitrary rules for discreet guidance, must always *inevitably* interfere between the earthly—perhaps the eternal happiness of two beings whose destiny is wound up in each other! Prims and Prudes may decry passages exhibiting the heart as it is, but as honest Jack Falstaff says, "Is not the truth the truth;"[3] what more can we say? However objectionable

---

1 A slightly rephrased version of Thomas de Quincey's (1785–1859) description of Samuel Taylor Coleridge's (1772–1834) relationship to truth: "[H]e grappled [truth] to his soul with hooks of steel."

2 Henry Wadsworth Longfellow (1807–82), "Endymion," *Ballads and Other Poems* (1842): lines 14–20.

3 Shakespeare, *Henry IV, Part I* (II.iv.230–31).

these works may be to crude minds which cannot winnow the chaff of vulgarity from the rich grain of genius which burdens them, very many, while enjoying their freshness and vigor, will gladly hail their appearance, as boldly and eloquently developing blind places of wayward passion in the human heart, which it is far more interesting to trace than all the bustling lanes and murky alleys through which the will-o'-wisp genius of Dickens has so long led the public mind.*

5. Unsigned Review [E.P. Whipple], *North American Review* No. 141 (October 1848): 355–60

THE first three novels on our list are those which have proceeded from the firm of Bell & Co. Not many months ago, the New England States were visited by a distressing mental epidemic, passing under the name of the "Jane Eyre fever," which defied all the usual nostrums of the established doctors of criticism. Its effects varied with different constitutions, in some producing a soft ethical sentimentality, which relaxed all the fibres of conscience, and in others exciting a general fever of moral and religious indignation. It was to no purpose that the public were solemnly assured, through the intelligent press, that the malady was not likely to have any permanent effect either on the intellectual or moral constitution. The book which caused the distemper would probably have been inoffensive, had not some sly manufacturer of mischief hinted that it was a book which no respectable man should bring into his family circle. Of course, every family soon had a copy of it, and one edition after another found eager purchasers....

...

[...] The truth is, that the whole firm of Bell & Co. seem to have a sense of the depravity of human nature peculiarly their own. It is the yahoo, not the demon, that they select for representation; their Pandemonium[1] is of mud rather than fire.

---

* Note.—At the risk of being esteemed hypocritical, we wish to point out a little anachronism of our author. It is in October, 1827, that Wildfell Hall receives its tenant. About the time of the harvest moon in the ensuing summer (1828) Gilbert is attracted by a volume upon her table that he had not seen before. It was Sir Humphrey Davy's *Consolations in Travel, or the Last Days of a Philosopher* (Chapter XV). With all respect for Mr. Bell, he must have had uncommonly good eyes if he had seen it before: inasmuch as it was not even written, and probably not imagined, at the time he mentions. It was written at Rome, in the winter of 1828–9 [?], and the first edition published not before January 6 [?], 1830.

---

1 Originally a reference to the capital of Hell in John Milton's (1608–74) *Paradise Lost* (1667) I:755–56; during the Victorian era, it meant a hellish or lawless place.

This is especially the case with Acton Bell, the author of *Wuthering Heights*, *The Tenant of Wildfell Hall*, and, if we mistake not, of certain offensive but powerful portions of *Jane Eyre*. Acton, when left altogether to his own imaginations, seems to take a morose satisfaction in developing a full and complete science of human brutality. In *Wuthering Heights* he has succeeded in reaching the summit of this laudable ambition. He appears to think that spiritual wickedness is a combination of animal ferocities, and has accordingly made a compendium of the most striking qualities of tiger, wolf, cur, and wild-cat, in the hope of framing out of such elements a suitable brute-demon to serve as the hero of his novel....

The Tenant of Wildfell Hall is altogether a less unpleasing story than its immediate predecessor, though it resembles it in the excessive clumsiness with which the plot is arranged, and the prominence given to the brutal element of human nature. The work seems a convincing proof, that there is nothing kindly or genial in the author's powerful mind, and that, if he continues to write novels, he will introduce into the land of romance a larger number of hateful men and women than any other writer of the day. Gilbert, the hero, seems to be a favorite with the author, and to be intended as a specimen of manly character; but he would serve as the ruffian of any other novelist. His nature is fierce, proud, moody, jealous, revengeful, and sometimes brutal. We can see nothing good in him except a certain rude honesty; and that quality is seen chiefly in his bursts of hatred and his insults to women. Helen, the heroine, is doubtless a strong-minded woman, and passes bravely through a great deal of suffering; but if there be any lovable or feminine virtues in her composition, the author has managed to conceal them. She marries a profligate, thinking to reform him; but the gentleman, with a full knowledge of her purpose, declines reformation, goes deeper and deeper into vice, and becomes at last as fiendlike as a very limited stock of brains will allow. This is a reversal of the process carried on in *Jane Eyre*; but it must be admitted that the profligate in *The Tenant of Wildfell Hall* is no Rochester. He is never virtuously inclined, except in those periods of illness and feebleness which his debaucheries have occasioned, thus illustrating the old proverb,—

"When the devil was sick, the devil a monk would be,
When the devil was well, the devil a monk was he."[1]

---

1 A version of "The Devil was sick, the Devil a saint would be; the Devil was well, the Devil a saint was he!" "A colloquial use of *devil* expressing strong negation. The last section means that when the Devil was well, he was nothing like the saint [or monk] he promised to be." *The Concise Oxford Dictionary of Proverbs*, 2nd ed. (Oxford: Oxford UP, 1992): 62–63.

He has almost constantly by him a choice coterie of boon companions, ranging from the elegant libertine to the ferocious sensualist, and the reader is favored with exact accounts of their drunken orgies, and with numerous scraps of their profane conversation. All the characters are drawn with the great power and precision of outline, and the scenes are as vivid as life itself. Everywhere is seen the tendency of the author to degrade passion into appetite, and to give prominence to the selfish and malignant elements of human nature; but while he succeeds in making profligacy disgusting, he fails in making virtue pleasing. His depravity is total depravity, and his hard and impudent debauchees seem to belong to that class of reprobates whom Dr. South[1] considers "as not so much born as damned into the world." The reader of Acton Bell gains no enlarged view of mankind, giving a healthy action to his sympathies, but is confined to a narrow space of life, and held down, as it were, by main force, to witness the wolfish side of his nature literally and logically set forth. But the criminal courts are not the places in which to take a comprehensive view of humanity, and the novelist who confines his observation to them is not likely to produce any lasting impression, except of horror and disgust.

6. Unsigned Review, *Rambler* Vol. III (September 1848): 65–66

THE names of Acton Bell, Currer Bell, and Ellis Bell, are now pretty generally recognized as mere *noms de guerre*[2] in the literary world. The novels lately published by these supposed individuals, or at least those which have the names of the first two of the three, are too palpably the work of one hand to deceive even the unpracticed critic; while few people would doubt that the hand belonged to a woman, and, as we suspect, a Yorkshirewoman. *Jane Eyre* is the best known of all the tales bearing the *Bell* designation; and the last that has come forth from the same source is the story whose title is *The Tenant of Wildfell Hall*. These two are, indeed, so strikingly alike in sentiment, style, and general modes of thought, that the criticisms which apply to one of them are almost equally applicable to the other.

That the author is a clever and vigorous writer, the popularity of *Jane Eyre* is a fair proof. She has also a certain marked tone of mind, which has impressed itself upon her books, and rendered them more individual and characteristic than the ordinary run even of clever novels. And for the sake of the morals of the novel-reading public, we hope that this their peculiar

---

1 Likely Robert South (1634–1716), an Anglican preacher and writer with Calvinist tendencies, whose works (sermons, poems, etc.) were published several times in the nineteenth century.

2 Pseudonyms.

feature has been the real cause of their attractiveness to many readers; and not that truly offensive and sensual spirit which is painfully prominent both in *Jane Eyre* and in the tale now before us. We should be sorry to believe that sympathy with the authoress's personages, or approval of her principles, had any thing to do with the interest which her books are calculated to excite in those who are wearied with the cloying monotonousnesses of the average run of novels, and who are fascinated with every thing and any thing that is new.

Jane Eyre is, indeed, one of the coarsest books which we ever perused. It is not that the *professed* sentiments of the writer are absolutely wrong or forbidding, or that the odd sort of religious notions which she puts forward are much worse than is usual in popular tales. It is rather that there is a certain perpetual *tendency* to relapse into that class of ideas, expressions, and circumstances, which is most connected with the grosser and more animal portion of our nature; and that the detestable morality of the most prominent character in the story is accompanied with every sort of palliation short of unblushing justification. The heroine, who tells the story, and who certainly is made to paint herself and her companions with very considerable force and skill, is as utterly unattractive and unfeminine a specimen of her sex as the pen of novelist ever drew.

The Tenant of Wildfell Hall is also a species of autobiography. One third of the story is told by the hero, a kind of gentleman farmer, whose morals, religion, cultivation, and talents, are about on a par with those of Jane Eyre herself; and the other two thirds consist of the diary of the lady with whom he falls in love, not knowing that, though living in solitude, she is really married to a living husband. Throughout the whole book, there does not appear a single character who has the power to interest the sympathies of the reader. All are commonplace, vulgar, rough, brusque-mannered personages, whatever their supposed station in life; while the scenes which the heroine relates in her diary are of the most disgusting and revolting species. She is married to a man of family and fortune, to whom she chose to link herself against the wishes of her friends, and who speedily turns out a sensual brute of the most intolerable kind, and treats her with every indignity, insult, and ill-usage which can be conceived, short of actual personal violence. Her diary is the record of what she endured at his hands, and details with offensive minuteness the disgusting scenes of debauchery, blasphemy, and profaneness, in which, with a herd of boon companions, he delighted to spend his days. By and by, of course, he dies, and the authoress gives us one of those pictures of a death-bed which are neither edifying, nor true to life, nor full of warning to the careless and profligate. In the end, the hero and heroine marry, after a courtship conducted with that peculiar bluntness and roughness of conduct and language which is the characteristic of all this writer's creations.

Nevertheless, on the whole, we should say that *The Tenant of Wildfell Hall* is not so *bad* a book as *Jane Eyre*. There is not such a palpable blinking of the abominable nature of the morality of its most prominent characters. The hero and heroine are people of decent intentions; and though the same offensive element of interest (so to call it) occurs in both of the tales, and in each our sympathies are unwittingly engaged for an attachment formed by a married person before death had dissolved the first contracted bond; yet the subject of this second passion in the last published story is more conscious of its real nature than in its predecessor. The religious sentiments which the authoress puts into the mouth of her heroine are either false and bad, or so vague and unmeaning as to add to the unreality of the scenes, without in any way redeeming their blots, as uncalled-for and unhealthy representations of the viler phases of human life. In a word, unless our authoress can contrive to refine and elevate her general notions of all human and divine things, we shall be glad to learn that she is not intending to add another work to those which have already been produced by her pen.

We hardly know where to find an extract suitable for quotation, by way of illustration of our criticisms, and shall content ourselves with a sketch of one of the least disagreeable individuals who figure in the story. [Quotes "The Reverend Michael Millward ...was all fancy" (48–49).]

7. Unsigned Review, *Sharpe's London Magazine: A Journal of Entertainment and Instruction for General Reading*, Vol. 7 (August 1848): 181–84

SEVERAL novels have lately appeared before the public, purporting to be written by three brothers, Currer, Ellis, and Acton Bell. Of these works, *Jane Eyre*, by Currer Bell, is the best known, and deservedly the most popular. We say deservedly, for though it has great faults, it has still greater merits. Such is by no means the case with the work now before us; indeed, so revolting are many of the scenes, so coarse and disgusting the language put into the mouths of some of the characters, that the reviewer to whom we entrusted it returned it to us, saying it was unfit to be noticed in the pages of *Sharpe*; and we are so far of the same opinion, that our object in the present paper is to warn our readers, and more especially our lady-readers, against being induced to peruse it, either by the powerful interest of the story, or the talent with which it is written. Did we think less highly of it in these particulars, we should have left the book to its fate, and allowed it quietly to sink into the insignificance to which the good taste of the reading public speedily condemns works disfigured by the class of faults we have alluded to; but, like the fatal melody of the Siren's song, its very perfections render it more dangerous, and therefore more carefully to be avoided. Yet we consider the evils which render the work unfit for perusal (for we go that length in regard to it,) to arise from a perverted taste and an absence of mental refinement in the writer, together with a total ignorance of the usages of good society, rather than from any systematic design of opposing the cause of religion and morality. So far from any such intention being apparent, the moral of the tale is excellent, and the author we should imagine a religious character, though *he* (for, despite reports to the contrary, we *will* not believe any woman could have written such a work,) holds one doctrine, to which we shall more particularly allude hereafter, for which we fear he can find no sufficient authority in Scripture.

As we are unable to support our strictures by adducing extracts, (for we must not fall into a fault somewhat too common with reviewers, and, by polluting our pages with coarse quotations, commit the very sin we are inveighing against,) we will proceed to give a slight sketch of the story, and leave our readers to judge whether scenes such as we shall glance at, where each revolting detail is dwelt with painful minuteness, each brutal or profane expression chronicled with hateful accuracy, can be fit subject matter for the pages of a work of fiction, a popular novel to be obtruded by every circulating library-keeper upon the notice of our sisters, wives, and daughters.

[The reviewer then summarizes the novel and quotes "The sufferer was fast ... did well to go to him" (373–76).]

The only thing which in the slightest degree affords Helen consolation under these harrowing circumstances, is her belief (which, from the way in which it is mentioned, we cannot but conclude to be that of the writer also,) in the doctrine of universal salvation—the wicked are to pass through purifying penal fires, but all are to be saved at last. The dangerous tendency of such a belief must be apparent to any one who gives the subject a moment's consideration; and it becomes scarcely necessary, in order to convince our readers of the madness of trusting to such a forced distortion of the Divine attribute of mercy, to add that this doctrine is alike repugnant to Scripture, and in direct opposition to the teaching of the Anglican Church.

One word as to the authorship of this novel. At the first glance we should say, none but a man could have known so intimately each vile, dark fold of the civilized brute's corrupted nature; none but a man could make so daring an exhibition as this book presents to us. On the other hand, no man, we should imagine, would have written a work in which all the women, even the worst, are so far superior in every quality, moral and intellectual, to all the men; no man would have made his sex appear at once coarse, brutal, and contemptibly weak, at once disgusting and ridiculous. There are, besides, a thousand trifles which indicate a woman's mind, and several more important things which show a woman's peculiar virtues. Still there is a bold coarseness, a reckless freedom of language, and an apparent familiarity with the sayings and doings of the worst style of *fast* men, in their worst moments, which would induce us to believe it impossible that a woman could have written it. A possible solution of the enigma is, that it may be the production of an authoress assisted by her husband, or some other *male* friend: if this be not the case, we would rather decide on the whole, that it is a man's writing.

In taking leave of the work, we cannot but express our deep regret that a book in many respects eminently calculated to advance the cause of religion and right feeling, the moral of which is unimpeachable and most powerfully wrought out, should be rendered unfit for the perusal of the very class of persons to whom it would be most useful, (namely, imaginative girls likely to risk their happiness on the forlorn hope of marrying and reforming a captivating rake,) owing to the profane expressions, inconceivably coarse language, and revolting scenes and descriptions by which its pages are disfigured.

8. Unsigned Review, *The Spectator* Vol. 21 (8 July 1848): 662–63

THE volumes of fiction that some time since appeared under the name of Bell, with three several praenomens,[1] had such a generic resemblance to one another that several reviewers remarked it. The first and most striking affinity was of substance. Each of the Bells selected the singular both in character and incident. The persons were such as are formed by a natural peculiarity of disposition, influenced by an equal peculiarity of circumstances, or produced by strong passions running their course unrestrained in the freedom of a remote country place, at a time which permitted greater liberty to individual will or caprice than is vouchsafed even to brutal and isolated squireens[2] in these days. The composition—not mere diction, but the arrangement of the incidents and persons, as well as the style of the things themselves—was extreme and wild; seeking to base effects on the startling, without much regard either to probability or good taste. A rough vigour characterized the whole batch of Bells; but Currer Bell, the author or editor of *Jane Eyre*, exhibited rather the most cultivated taste and decidedly the most literary skill. Nearly one half of *The Tenant of Wildfell Hall*, by Acton Bell, seems a sort of setting to the main story, and is pitched in a more natural key than the author's previous novel, though not without occasional roughness. In escaping from his extreme and violent manner, however, he loses somewhat of his strength and interest. There is nature, undoubtedly; but it is of a common kind. The daily life of a young and self-sufficient gentleman farmer and his family, with the characters and gossip of his neighbourhood, are scarcely enough to sustain the reader for a volume, even with the addition of the aforesaid farmer's love for the mysterious tenant of Wildfell Hall.

---

1 First or Christian names.
2 "A petty squire; a small landowner or country gentleman" (*OED*).

The tale of this lady, which she has written down apparently for her lover to read, is a story of suffering in married life, arising from the licentiousness, drunkenness, and downright blackguardism[1] of her husband and his associates. She is provoked by his profligacy, disgusted by his habits, and surrounded by tempting gallants; and scenes founded on such subjects form the narrative of the tale, till she secretly escapes, and takes refuge near her brother; whom Gilbert Markham, the farmer lover, has mistaken for a favoured swain, and ferociously assaulted. In due time Mr. Huntingdon the husband dies: his widow's possession of property causes a considerable delay in the denouement; but it comes at last.

The Tenant of Wildfell Hall, like its predecessor, suggests the idea of considerable abilities ill applied. There is power, effect, and even nature, though of an extreme kind, in its pages; but there seems in the writer a morbid love for the coarse, not to say the brutal; so that his level subjects are not very attractive, and the more forcible are displeasing or repulsive, from their gross, physical, or profligate substratum. He might reply, that such things are in life: and probably glimpses of such a set as Huntingdon and his friends are occasionally caught in Doctors Commons cases,[2] and tradition pictures such doings as not very rare in the early part of George the Third's reign,[3]—although Mr. Bell paints them as contemporary. Mere existence, however, as we have often had occasion to remark, is not a sufficient reason for a choice of subject: its general or typical character is a point to consider, and its power of pleasing must be regarded, as well as its mere capabilities of force or effect. It is not only the subject of this novel, however, that is objectionable, but the manner of treating it. There is a coarseness of tone throughout the writing of all these Bells, that puts an offensive subject in its worst point of view, and which generally contrives to dash indifferent things.

From the nature of the work, any scene from *The Tenant of Wildfell Hall* will be of rather a broad kind. The following exhibits a Mr. Hargrave, having worked himself up to a phrensy in making love to Mrs. Huntingdon, suddenly surprised by the husband and friend.

[Quotes "I never saw ... if I don't" (305–07).]

---

1 "Brutally vicious or scurrilous" behavior (*OED*).

2 The Doctors Commons, established in 1511, was a group of lawyers who practiced civil and ecclesiastical law. As such, they worked with divorce cases, among others.

3 George III (1738–1820) reigned from 1760–1820, although his son ruled as Prince Regent from 1811–20 because of George III's insanity.

Appendix C: Women's Education

1. From Mary Wollstonecraft, *A Vindication of the Rights of Woman: with Strictures on Political and Moral Subjects* (1792), in *The Vindications: The Rights of Men The Rights of Woman*. Ed. D.L. Macdonald & Kathleen Scherf (Peterborough, ON: Broadview, 1997), 109–14; 254–55

[The footnotes in brackets are those added by Macdonald and Scherf; the footnotes without brackets are Mary Wollstonecraft's.]

[From the Introduction:]

... I have turned over various books written on the subject of education, and patiently observed the conduct of parents and the managements of schools; but what has been the result?—a profound conviction that the neglected education of my fellow-creatures is the grand source of the misery I deplore; and that women, in particular, are rendered weak and wretched by a variety of concurring causes, originating from one hasty conclusion. The conduct and manners of women, in fact, evidently prove that their minds are not in a healthy state; for, like the flowers which are planted in too rich a soil, strength and usefulness are sacrificed to beauty; and the flaunting leaves, after having pleased a fastidious eye, fade, disregarded on the stalk, long before the season when they ought to have arrived at maturity.—One cause of this barren blooming I attribute to a false system of education, gathered from the books written on this subject by men who, considering females rather as women than human creatures, have been more anxious to make them alluring mistresses than affectionate wives and rational mothers; and the understanding of the sex has been so bubbled by this specious homage, that the civilized women of the present century, with a few exceptions, are only anxious to inspire love, when they ought to cherish a nobler ambition, and by their abilities and virtues exact respect.

In a treatise, therefore, on female rights and manners, the works which have been particularly written for their improvement must not be overlooked; especially when it is asserted, in direct terms, that the minds of women are enfeebled by false refinement; that the books of instruction, written by men of genius, have had the same tendency as more frivolous productions; and that, in the true style of Mahometanism, they are treated as a kind of subordinate beings, and not as a part of the human species, when improveable reason is allowed to be the dignified distinction which raises men above the brute creation, and puts a natural sceptre in a feeble hand.

Yet, because I am a woman, I would not lead my readers to suppose that I mean violently to agitate the contested question respecting the equality or inferiority of the sex; but as the subject lies in my way, and I cannot pass it over without subjecting the main tendency of my reasoning to misconstruction, I shall stop a moment to deliver, in a few words, my opinion.—In the government of the physical world it is observable that the female in point of strength is, in general, inferior to the male. This is the law of nature; and it does not appear to be suspended or abrogated in favour of the woman.[1] A degree of physical superiority cannot, therefore, be denied—and it is a noble prerogative! But not content with this natural pre-eminence, men endeavour to sink us still lower, merely to render us alluring objects for a moment; and women, intoxicated by the adoration which men, under the influence of their senses, pay them, do not seek to obtain a durable interest in their hearts, or to become the friends of the fellow creatures who find amusement in their society.

...

My own sex, I hope, will excuse me, if I treat them like rational creatures, instead of flattering their *fascinating* graces, and viewing them as if they were in a state of perpetual childhood, unable to stand alone. I earnestly wish to point out in what true dignity and human happiness consists—I wish to persuade women to endeavour to acquire strength, both of mind and body, and to convince them that the soft phrases, susceptibility of heart, delicacy of sentiment, and refinement of taste, are almost synonymous with epithets of weakness, and that those beings who are only the objects of pity and that kind of love, which has been termed its sister, will soon become objects of contempt.[2]

Dismissing then those pretty feminine phrases, which the men condescendingly use to soften our slavish dependence, and despising that weak elegancy of mind, exquisite sensibility, and sweet docility of manners, supposed to be the sexual characteristics of the weaker vessel, I wish to shew that elegance is inferior to virtue, that the first object of laudable ambition is to obtain a character as a human being, regardless of the distinction of sex; and that secondary views should be brought to this simple touchstone.

...

The education of women has, of late, been more attended to than formerly; yet they are still reckoned a frivolous sex, and ridiculed or pitied by the writers who endeavour by satire or instruction to improve them. It is acknowledged that they spend many of the first years of their lives in ac-

---

1   [Cf. Catherine Graham Macaulay, *Letters on Education. With Observations on Religious and Metaphysical Subjects* (London: C. Dilly, 1790. Rpt. New York: Garland, 1974): 206.]

2   [Cf. *Original Stories; The Works of Mary Wollstonecraft.* Ed. Janet Todd and Marilyn Butler. Asst. Emma Rees-Mogg. 7 vols. (London: William Pickering, 1989) 4:381.]

quiring a smattering of accomplishments;[1] meanwhile strength of body and mind are sacrificed to libertine notions of beauty, to the desire of establishing themselves,—the only way women can rise in the world,—by marriage. And this desire making mere animals of them, when they marry they act as such children may be expected to act:—they dress; they paint, and nickname God's creatures.[2]—Surely these weak beings are only fit for a seraglio!—Can they be expected to govern a family with judgment, or take care of the poor babes whom they bring into the world?

If then it can be fairly deduced from the present conduct of the sex, from the prevalent fondness for pleasure which takes place of ambition and those nobler passions that open and enlarge the soul; that the instruction which women have hitherto received has only tended, with the constitution of civil society, to render them insignificant objects of desire—mere propagators of fools!—if it can be proved that in aiming to accomplish them, without cultivating their understandings, they are taken out of their sphere of duties, and made ridiculous and useless when the short-lived bloom of beauty is over,[3] I presume that *rational* men will excuse me for endeavouring to persuade them to become more masculine and respectable.

Indeed the word masculine is only a bugbear: there is little reason to fear that women will acquire too much courage or fortitude; for their apparent inferiority with respect to bodily strength, must render them, in some degree, dependent on men in the various relations of life; but why should it be increased by prejudices that give a sex to virtue, and confound simple truths with sensual reveries?

Women are, in fact, so much degraded by mistaken notions of female excellence, that I do not mean to add a paradox when I assert, that this artificial weakness produces a propensity to tyrannize, and gives birth to cunning, the natural opponent of strength, which leads them to play off those contemptible infantine airs that undermine esteem even whilst they excite desire. Let men become more chaste and modest, and if women do not grow wiser in the same ratio, it will be clear that they have weaker understandings. It seems scarcely necessary to say, that I now speak of the sex in general.

---

1   [Cf. *Original Stories*; *Works* 4:435; and Macaulay, *Letters* 61–62.]

2   [Shakespeare, *Hamlet* 3.1.142–46. Cf. Edmund Burke, *A Philosophical Enquiry into the Origin of our Ideas of the Sublime and Beautiful*. Ed. Adam Phillips. (Oxford: Oxford UP, 1990): 100 (3.9); Macaulay, *Letters* 48.]

3   A lively writer, I cannot recollect his name, asks what business women turned of forty have to do in the world? [Wollstonecraft may be thinking of a remark made by Lord Merton, a character in Frances Burney (1752–1840), *Evelina; or, The History of a Young Lady's Entrance into the World* (1778), ed. Edward A. Bloom (London: Oxford UP, 1968) 275; Vol. 3, letter 1.]

Many individuals have more sense than their male relatives; and, as nothing preponderates where there is a constant struggle for an equilibrium, without it has naturally more gravity, some women govern their husbands without degrading themselves, because intellect will always govern.

...

[From Chapter VII:]

[...] Purity of mind, or that genuine delicacy, which is the only virtuous support of chastity, is near akin to that refinement of humanity, which never resides in any but cultivated minds. It is something nobler than innocence, it is the delicacy of reflection, and not the coyness of ignorance. The reserve of reason, which, like habitual cleanliness, is seldom seen in any great degree, unless the soul is active, may easily be distinguished from rustic shyness or wanton skittishness; and, so far from being incompatible with knowledge, it is its fairest fruit. What a gross idea of modesty had the writer of the following remark! "The lady who asked the question whether women may be instructed in the modern system of botany, consistently with female delicacy?—was accused of ridiculous prudery: nevertheless, if she had proposed the question to me, I should certainly have answered—They cannot."[1] Thus is the fair book of knowledge[2] to be shut with an everlasting seal! On reading similar passages I have reverentially lifted up my eyes and heart to Him who liveth for ever and ever, and said, O my Father, has Thou by the very constitution of her nature forbid Thy child to seek Thee in the fair forms of truth? And, can her soul be sullied by the knowledge that awfully calls her to Thee?

I have then philosophically pursued these reflections till I inferred that those women who have most improved their reason must have the most modesty—though a dignified sedateness of deportment may have succeeded the playful, bewitching bashfulness of youth.[3]

And thus have I argued. To render chastity the virtue from which unsophisticated modesty will naturally flow, the attention should be called away from employments which only exercise the sensibility; and the heart made to beat time to humanity, rather than to throb with love. The woman who has dedicated a considerable portion of her time to pursuits purely intellectual, and whose affections have been exercised by humane plans of usefulness, must

---

1 [John Berkenhout (1730?–91), *A Volume of Letters to his Son at the University* (Cambridge, 1790), 307. Berkenhout's point is that the Linnaean system of botany, popularized in Erasmus Darwin's poem *The Loves of the Plants* (1789), classified plants according to their sexual organs.]

2 [Milton, *Paradise Lost* 3.47.]

3 Modesty, is the graceful calm virtue of maturity; bashfulness, the charm of vivacious youth.

have more purity of mind, as a natural consequence, than the ignorant beings whose time and thoughts have been occupied by gay pleasures or schemes to conquer hearts.[1] The regulation of the behaviour is not modesty, though those who study rules of decorum are, in general, termed modest women. Make the heart clean, let it expand and feel for all that is human, instead of being narrowed by selfish passions; and let the mind frequently contemplate subjects that exercise the understanding, without heating the imagination, and artless modesty will give the finishing touches to the picture.

She who can discern the dawn of immortality, in the streaks that shoot athwart the misty night of ignorance, promising a clearer day, will respect, as a sacred temple, the body that enshrines such an improvable soul. True love, likewise, spreads this kind of mysterious sanctity round the beloved object, making the lover most modest when in her presence.[2] So reserved is affection that, receiving or returning personal endearments, it wishes, not only to shun the human eye, as a kind of profanation; but to diffuse an encircling cloudy obscurity to shut out even the saucy sparkling sunbeams. Yet, that affection does not deserve the epithet of chaste, which does not receive a sublime gloom of tender melancholy, that allows the mind for a moment to stand still and enjoy the present satisfaction, when a consciousness of the Divine presence is felt—for this must ever be the food of joy! [...]

2. From Hannah More, *Strictures on the Modern System of Female Education with a View of the Principles and Conduct Prevalent among Women of Rank and Fortune* (1799; New York: Evert Duyckinck Inc, 1813), vol. 2, ch. 13, 3–4

The chief end to be proposed in cultivating the understandings of women, is to qualify them for the practical purposes of life. Their knowledge is not often like the learning of men, to be reproduced in some literary composition, nor ever in any learned profession; but it is to come out in conduct. A lady

---

1 I have conversed, as man with man, with medical men, on anatomical subjects; and compared the proportions of the human body with artists—yet such modesty did I meet with, that I was never reminded by word or look of my sex, of the absurd rules which make modesty a pharisaical cloak of weakness. And I am persuaded that in the pursuit of knowledge women would never be insulted by sensible men, and rarely by men of any description, if they did not by mock modesty remind them that they were women: actuated by the same spirit as the Portugueze ladies, who would think their charms insulted, if, when left alone with a man, he did not, at least, attempt to be grossly familiar with their persons. Men are not always men in the company of women, nor would women always remember that they are women, if they were allowed to acquire more understanding.

2 Male or female; for the world contains many modest men.

studies, not that she may qualify herself to become an orator or a pleader; not that she may learn to debate, but to act. She is to read the best books, not so much to enable her to talk of them, as to bring the improvement which they furnish, to the rectification of her principles, and the formation of her habits. The great uses of study are to enable her to regulate her own mind, and to be useful to others.

To woman therefore, whatever be her rank, I would recommend a predominance of those more sober studies, which, not having display for their object, may make her wise without vanity, happy without witnesses, and content without panegyrists; the exercise of which will not bring celebrity, but improve usefulness. She should pursue every kind of study which will teach her to elicit truth; which will lead her to be intent upon realities; will give precision to her ideas; will make an exact mind; every study, which, instead of stimulating her sensibility, will chastise it; which will give her definite notions; will bring the imagination under dominion; will lead her to think, to compare, to combine, to methodise; which will confer such a power of discrimination, that her judgment shall learn to reject what is dazzling if it be not solid; and to prefer, not what is striking, or bright, or new, but what is just. That kind of knowledge which is rather fitted for home consumption than foreign exportation, is peculiarly adapted to women.

It is because the superficial nature of their education furnishes them with a false and low standard of intellectual excellence, that women have sometimes become ridiculous by the unfounded pretensions of literary vanity: for it is not the really learned but the smatterers, who have generally brought their sex into discredit by absurd affectation, which has set them on despising the duties of ordinary life. There have not indeed been wanting (but the character is not now common) *precieuses ridicules*,[1] who, assuming a superiority to the sober cares which ought to occupy their sex, have claimed a lofty and supercilious exemption from the dull and plodding drudgeries

Of this dim speck called earth!

---

1 Literally "ridiculous precious ones," a reference to Molière's (1622–73) *Les Précieuses Ridicules*, a play that mocked the *précieuses*, a group of women who gathered at the salon of the Marquise de Rambouillet (1588–1665) to talk and write. They are known for their fairy tales today. "The celibate ideal of the précieuses—to enjoy *tendresse* with men of equal intelligence and similar inclinations without the yoke of arranged marriages, their concomitant rejection of the economic basis of alliances, their argument for an end of the double standard which permitted male adultery but disgraced adulteresses—made them profoundly subversive, anomalous women within the social order of the *ancien régime*" (Marina Warner, *From the Beast to the Blonde: On Fairy Tales and their Tellers* [New York: The Noonday Press, Farrar, Straus and Giroux, 1994], 169).

who have affected to establish an unnatural separation between talents and usefulness, instead of bearing in mind that talents are the great appointed instruments of usefulness; who have acted as if knowledge were to confer on woman a kind of fantastic sovereignty, which should exonerate her from female duties; whereas it is only meant the more eminently to qualify her for the performance of them. For a woman of real sense will never forget, that while the greater part of her proper duties are such as the most moderately gifted may fulfill with credit, (since Providence never makes that to be very difficult, which is generally necessary,) yet the most highly endowed are equally bound to fulfill them; and the humblest of these offices, performed on Christian principles, are wholesome for the minds even of the most enlightened, and tend to be the casting down of those high imaginations which women of genius are too much tempted to indulge.

3. From Sarah Lewis, *Woman's Mission* (1839; Boston: William Crosby & Co., 1840), 74–78

Let no sober-minded person be startled at the deduction hence drawn, that it is foolish to banish all thoughts of love from the minds of the young. Since it is certain that girls will think, though they may not read or speak, of love; and that no early care can preserve them from being exposed, at a later period, to its temptations, might it not be well to use here the directing, not the repressing, power? Since women will love, might it not be as well to teach them to love wisely? Where is the wisdom of letting the combatant go unarmed into the field, in order to spare him the prospect of a combat? Are not women made to love, and to be loved; and does not their future destiny too often depend upon this passion? And yet the conventual prejudice which banishes its name subsists still.

...

Examine the first choice of a young girl. Of all the qualities which please her in a lover there is, perhaps, not one which is valuable in a husband. Is not this the most complete condemnation of all our systems of education? From the fear of too much agitating the heart, we hide from women all that is worthy of love, all the depth and dignity of that passion when felt for a worthy object;—their eye is captivated, the exterior pleases, the heart and mind are not known, and after six months union, they are surprised to find the beau ideal metamorphosed into a fool or a coxcomb; this is the issue of what are ordinarily called love-matches, because they are considered as such; "Cupid is indeed often blamed for deeds in which he has no share."[1] In the

---

1 Maria Edgeworth (1767–1849), "Mademoiselle Panache," *Moral Tales for Young People* (1801).

opinion of the wise, the mischief is occasioned by the action of vivid imaginations upon minds unprepared by previous reflection on the subject, *i.e.*, by the entire banishment of all thoughts of love from education. We should endeavour, then, to engrave on the soul a model of virtue and excellence, and teach young women to regulate their affections by an approximation to this model. The result would not be an increased facility in giving the affections, but a greater difficulty in so doing: for women, whose blindness and ignorance now make them the victims of fancied perfections, would be able to make a clear-sighted appreciation of all that is excellent, and have an invincible repugnance to a union not founded upon that basis. Love, in the common acceptation of the term, is a folly,—love, in its purity, its loftiness, its unselfishness, is not only a consequence, but a proof of our moral excellence;—the sensibility to moral beauty, the forgetfulness of self in the admiration engendered by it, all prove its claim to be a high moral influence; it is the triumph of the unselfish over the selfish part of our nature.

What is meant by educating young women to love wisely is simply this, that they be taught to distinguish true love from the false spirit which usurps its name and garb; that they be taught to abstract from it the worldliness, vanity, and folly, with which it has been mixed up. They should be taught that it is not to be the amusement of an idle hour, the indulgence of a capricious and greedy vanity, the ladder, by the assistance of which they may climb a few steps higher in the grades of society; in short, that except it owe its origin to the noble qualities of heart and mind, it is nothing but a contemptible weakness, to be pitied perhaps, but not to be indulged or admired.

When the mighty influence of this passion is considered, the important relations and weighty responsibilities to which it gives rise, we have reason to be astonished at the levity with which the subject is treated by the world at large, and the unconsciousness and indifference with which those responsibilities are assumed. It is like the madman who flings about firebrands and calls it sport. The remedy for this evil must begin with the sex who have in their hands that powerful influence, the liberty of rejection. Let them not complain that liberty of choice is not theirs; it would only increase their responsibilities without adding to their happiness or to their usefulness. The liberty which they do possess is amply sufficient to ensure for them the power of being benefactors of mankind. As soon as the noble and elevated of our sex shall refuse to unite on any but moral and intellectual grounds with the other, so soon will a mighty regeneration begin to be effected; and this end will, perhaps, be better served by the simple liberty of rejection than by liberty of choice. Rejection is never inflicted without pain, it is never received without humiliation, however unfounded, (for simply to want the power of pleasing can be no disgrace,) but in the existence of this conventional feeling we find the source of a deep influence. If women would, as by one common league and covenant, agree to use this powerful engine in defense of morals, what a change might they not effect in the tone of society? Is it not a subject that ought to crimson every woman's cheek with shame, that the want of moral qualifications is generally the very last cause of rejection? If the worldly find the wealth, and the intellectual the intelligence, which they seek in a companion, there are few who will not shut their eyes in willful and convenient blindness to the want of such qualifications. It is a fatal error which has bound up the cause of affection so intimately with worldly considerations; and it is a growing evil. [...]

4. John Cowie, "Noble Sentiments on the Influence of Women, from the Introductory Address to the Edinburgh Mechanics' Institution,"[1] in "The Weekly Record of Facts and Opinions Connected with General Interests and Popular Progress" a Separate Section within *Howitt's Journal* 1.13 (March 1847): 21

["The Weekly Record" is found between pages 154 and 155 of the journal proper and has its own pagination.]

THIS Institution will offer facilities for the instruction of our female friends and sisters as well as of our brethren; and it is the imperative and bounden duty of every member of this Institution to encourage the visits of females. Woman's mission and influence constitute a subject of the most imperative and vital interest. Her position and relations are the most important and attractive in life. The mind of the young generation is moulded by her plastic hand; she is the source and directress of the elemental statesmen, poets, philosophers, philanthropists, and producers of futurity; and it has become an axiom that there are few great men who do not owe their intellectual or moral excellence to their mothers. It is on the knee and at the fireside that we imbibe the bias of afterlife. It is from the hearth that we bear away the strongest and most lasting of our early impressions....

The cultivation of the sentiments, then, and of the social virtues, is solely dependent upon woman. I do not speak of her as the companion and soother of man, so much as I do of her as the mother of man. In the former capacity she is weak and gentle, clinging to man for protection, and seeking shelter in his heart and beneath his arm. Ignorant brutal man has taken ad-

---

1 Mechanics Institutes were established to give educational opportunities for workers in the nineteenth century; for example, one could attend lectures there, or use their lending libraries. Many people benefited from them. In fact, the Brontës borrowed books from the Keighley Mechanics Institute.

vantage of this weakness, and has made her a slave to the perpetuation of his own ignorant brutality. But viewed as the mother of man, how her position alters! She is then the source of all human power and dignity. If she is weak, one who will yet be strong is nurtured on her lap. If she is prescribed to the possession of noble sentiments and a sphere of household action, she can yet transfuse her sentiments into one who will bear them abroad to the world. What is the man of action but the delegate of thoughtful woman? Where is barbarity most inveterate and debasing but where woman is most debased? I tremble when I contemplate the position into which society has been wrested through the illegitimate assumptions of man as the representative of brute force. He has denuded woman of her responsibility as an agent of progress, and has destroyed her moral grandeur, with her liberty and equality. Sent to be a companion and guide, she has been made a toy and nonentity. Made with a mind equal to man's in every respect, perhaps superior in the gentler attributes, she has been hitherto treated as if the doctrine of the Mussulman[1] were true. Young men seldom attempt to engage in serious or instructive conversation in promiscuous assembles; they seem to have studied inane twaddle and frivolous disgusting repartee, that they might insult the intellect and perpetuate the subjugation of woman.

Shall this continue to mock and chide our social polity? Shall the companion, the instructress, and the mother of man, be still confined to her present condition of ignorance? *It is* in the power of man to raise and exalt her. She is the half of the human economy, equal in all things, save strength, to the male half; and if she is degraded man is her tyrant.

I need hardly reiterate, that with men rests the cause of women. They are man's companions in the concert-room to hear sweet sounds discoursed; they are solicited to join with him in the comparative frivolities of the ball; at the theatre or arena they are at his side; they accompany him to all the sight-seeings which allure the idle or excite the giddy—but they are seldom or never to be found in the lecture room. Why is this; Is it not the fault of men? They are the arbiters for woman? She has seldom any other power save that of *negation*. If man can prevail upon her to seek the scene where her feet alone are to be educated, can he not inspire her with nobler motives, and induce her to bear him company to the place where the noblest faculties are cultivated? Where there is a will there is a way; and if man would only lead woman more into the elevating atmosphere of moral and intellectual culture than into the assemblies of his pastimes and frivolities, society would be the gainer, and he individually would not be the loser.

Is it supposed that women are less capable than men, or less attached to intellectual pursuits? Let a hundred protests against such a supposition be

---

1   Muslim.

heard from the Miss Edgeworths, Mary Howitts, Mrs. Nortons, Harriet Martineaus, Mrs. Hemans, Mrs. Johnstones, and Lydia Childs, of this age.[1] They had a Mary Wollstonecraft to preach their rights, and an Elizabeth Fry[2] to canonize them as of the true race of heroines; but an idea has hitherto been their tyrant, and that idea has been nurtured and supported by man.

It has often been asserted that the women of our class "*had no use*" (I use the hackneyed phrase) for any elements of education, save reading; and I know that many of the antiquated preachers of this almost obsolete blasphemy still mumble it in their coteries. And is it not a rag of such false idea that still denies her the position that man has educationally assumed? Is it not a shred of such a prejudice that perpetuates an aversion to the blue stocking,[3] yet tolerates the male pedant? Is it not a lingering after the dominion which physical man assumes over woman, his slave, to the material retardation of that progress which must elevate her into the true companion and equal of intellectual man? I fear that it is; and consequently, for the sake of the rising generation, and for woman's especial sake, I hail with joy the formation of Mechanics' Institutions.

---

1 Maria Edgeworth (1767–1849), an Irish novelist; Mary Howitt (1799–1888), a poet, who along with her husband William founded *Howitt's Journal*; Caroline Norton (1808–77) a poet and novelist who agitated for reform on divorce and custody laws and women's rights (see Appendix D2, below); Harriet Martineau (1802–76), writer, philosopher and social reformer; Felicia Hemans (1793–1835), poet; Christian Isobel Johnstone (1781–1857), a Scottish novelist and cookbook author who, after working at several significant periodicals, became the editor of *Tait's Edinburgh Magazine*; Lydia Maria Child (1802–80) an American writer and abolitionist.

2 A Quaker who worked on prison reform (1780–1845). Mary Wollstonecraft (1759–97), writer and philosopher; see Appendix C1, above, for an example of her prose.

3 Initially a derogatory term for learned or literary women. The term originated from one of the supporters of their salons who wore gray or blue wool stockings, instead of fancier black silk stockings.

Appendix D: Wives

1. From Hannah More, *Coelebs in Search of a Wife, Comprehending Observations on Domestic Habits and Manners, Religion and Morals* (1808; New York: David Carlisle, 1809), 88–92

"You know," resumed Mr. Stanley, "they married not only without any inclination on either side, but on her part with something more than indifference, with a preference for another person. *She* married through an implicit obedience to her mother's will, which she had never in any instance opposed; *he*, because his father had threatened to disinherit him if he married any other woman; for as they were distant relations, there was no other way of securing the estate in the family."

"What a motive for a union so sacred and so indissoluble!" exclaimed I,[1] with an ardour which raised a smile in the whole party. I asked pardon for my involuntary interruption, and Mr. Stanley proceeded.

"She had long entertained a partiality for a most deserving young clergyman much her inferiour in rank and fortune. But though her high sense of filial duty led her to sacrifice this innocent inclination, and though she resolved never to see him again, and had even prevailed on him to quit the country, and settle in a distant place, yet Carlton was ungenerous and inconsistent enough to be jealous of her without loving her. He was guilty of great irregularities, while Mrs. Carlton set about acquitting herself of the duties of a wife, with the most meek and humble patience, burying her sorrows in her own bosom and not allowing herself even the consolation of complaining.

"Among the many reasons for his dislike, her piety was the principal. He said religion was of no use but to disqualify people for the business of life; that it taught them to make a merit of despising their duties, and hating their relations; and that pride, ill-humour, opposition and contempt for the rest of the world, were the meat and drink of all those who pretend to religion.

"At first she nearly sunk under his unkindness; her health declined, and her spirits failed. In this distress she applied to the only sure refuge of the unhappy, and took comfort in the consideration that her trials were appointed by a merciful Father to detach her from a world which she might have loved too fondly had it not been thus stripped of its delights.

"When Mrs. Stanley, who was her confidential friend, expressed the tenderest sympathy in her sufferings, she meekly replied, 'remember who are they whose robes are washed white in the kingdom of glory, *it is they who*

---

1 Coelebs is the narrator of the novel; he is listening to a story about the Carltons, told to him by Mr. Stanley.

come out of great tribulation.[1] I endeavour to strengthen my faith with a view of what the best Christians have suffered, and my hope with meditating on the shortness of all suffering. I will confess my weakness,' added she: 'of the various motives to patience under the ills of life, which the Bible presents, though my reason and religion acknowledge them all, there is not one which comes home so powerfully to my feelings as this—*the time is short.*'[2]

"Another time Mrs. Stanley, who had heard of some recent irregularities of Carlton, called upon her, and lamenting the solitude to which she was often left for days together, advised her to have a female friend in the house, that her mind might not be left to prey upon itself by living so much alone. She thanked her for the kind suggestion, but said she felt it was wiser and better not to have a confidential friend always at hand, 'for of what subject should we talk,' said she, 'but of my husband's faults? Ought I to allow myself in such a practice? It would lead me to indulge a habit of complaint which I am labouring to subdue. The compassion of my friend would only sharpen my feelings, which I wish to blunt. Giving vent to a flame only makes it rage the more: if suppressing cannot subdue it, at least the consciousness that I am doing my duty will enable me to support it.—When we feel,' added she, 'that we are *doing* wrong, the opening [of] our heart may strengthen our virtue; but when we are *suffering* wrong, the mind demands another sort of strength; it wants higher support than friendship has to impart. It pours out its sorrows in prayer with fuller confidence, knowing that he who sees can sustain; that he who hears will recompense; that he will judge not our weakness but our efforts to conquer it; not our success but our endeavours; with him endeavour is victory.

"'The grace I most want,' added she, '—is humility. A partial friend, in order to support my spirits, would flatter my conduct: gratified with her soothing, I should, perhaps, not so entirely cast myself for comfort on God. Contented with human praise I might rest in it. Besides having endured the smart, I would not willingly endure it in vain. We know who has said, "if you suffer with me, you shall also reign with me."[3] It is not, however, to mere suffering that the promise is addressed, but to suffering for his sake, and in his spirit.' Then turning to the Bible which lay before her, and pointing to the sublime passage of St. Paul, which she had just been reading "our light

---

1 A slightly rephrased version of Revelation 7:14.
2 See 1 Corinthians 7:29. The idea of time being short has two meanings here: first, that their lives are short; second, that there is not much time before the second coming of Christ. Both understandings of this phrase would make Mrs. Carlton mindful of the importance of eternal goals such as salvation, not worldly ones—or even suffering.
3 A version of 2 Timothy 2:12, "If we suffer, we shall also reign with him; if we deny him, he also will deny us."

affliction which is but for a moment, worketh for us a far more exceeding and eternal weight of glory."[1] 'Pray,' said she, 'read this in connection with the next verse which is not always done. *When* is it that it works for us this weight of glory? *Only*, "while we are looking at the things which are not seen?"[2] Do admire the beauty of this position, and how the good is weighed against the evil, like two scales differently filled; the affliction is light and but for a moment; the glory is a *weight* and it is for *ever*. Tis a feather against lead, a grain of sand against the universe, a moment against eternity. Oh, how the scale which contains this world's light trouble kicks the beam, when weighed against the glory which shall be revealed.'

"At the end of two years she had a little girl; this opened to her a new scene of duties, and a fresh source of consolation. Her religion proved itself to be of the right stamp by making her temper still more sweet, and diffusing the happiest effect through her whole character and conversation. When her husband had stayed out late, or even all night, she never reproached him. When he was at home, she received his friends with as much civility as if she had liked them. He found that his house was conducted with the utmost prudence, and that while she maintained his credit at his table, her personal expenses were almost nothing: indeed self seemed nearly annihilated in her. He sometimes felt disappointed, because he had no cause of complaint, and was angry that he had nothing to condemn.

"As he has a very fine understanding, he was the more provoked, because he could not help seeing that her blameless conduct put him continually in the wrong. All this puzzled him. He never suspected there was a principle, out of which such consequences could grow, and was ready to attribute to insensibility, that patience which nothing short of Christian piety could have inspired. He had conceived of religion, as a visionary system of words and phrases, and concluded that from so unsubstantial a theory, it would be a folly to look for practical effects.

"Sometimes, when he saw her nursing his child, of whom he was very fond, he was almost tempted to admire the mother, who is a most pleasing figure; and now and then when his heart was thus softened for a moment, he would ask himself, what reasonable ground of objection there was either to her mind or person?

"Mrs. Carlton, knowing that his affairs must necessarily be embarrassed, by the extraordinary expenses he had incurred, when the steward brought her usual year's allowance, she refused to take more than half, and ordered

---

1   2 Corinthians 4:17.

2   "While we look not at the things which are seen, but at the things which are not seen: for the things which are seen are temporal; but the things which are not seen are eternal" (2 Corinthians 4:18).

him to employ the remainder on his master's account. The faithful old man was ready to weep, and could not forbear saying, 'Madam you could not do more for a kind husband. Besides, it is but a drop of water in the ocean.' 'That drop,' said she, 'it is my duty to contribute.' When the steward communicated this to Carlton, he was deeply affected, refused to take the money, and again was driven to resort to the wonderful principle, from which such right but difficult actions could proceed."

...

Mr. Stanley went on. "Mrs. Carlton frequently sat up late, reading such books as might qualify her for the education of her child, but always retired before she had reason to expect Mr. Carlton, lest he might construe it into upbraiding. One night, as he was not expected to come home at all, she sat later than usual, and had indulged herself with taking her child to pass the night in her bed. With her usual earnestness she knelt down and offered up her devotions by her bed-side, and in a manner particularly solemn and affecting, prayed for her husband. Her heart was deeply touched, and she dwelt on these petitions in a strain peculiarly fervent. She prayed for his welfare in both worlds, and earnestly implored that she might be made the humble instrument of his happiness. She meekly acknowledged her own many offences; of his she said nothing.

"Thinking herself secure from interruption, her petitions were uttered aloud; her voice often faltering, and her eyes streaming with tears. Little did she suspect that the object of her prayers was within hearing of them. He had returned home unexpectedly, and coming softly into the room, heard her pious aspirations. He was inexpressibly affected. He wept, and sighed bitterly. The light from the candles on the table fell on the blooming face of his sleeping infant, and on that of his weeping wife. It was too much for him. But he had not the virtuous courage to give way to his feelings. He had not the generosity to come forward and express the admiration he felt. He withdrew unperceived, and passed the remainder of the night in great perturbation of spirit. Shame, remorse, and confusion, raised such a conflict in his mind, as prevented him from closing his eyes; while she slept in quiet, and awoke in peace.

"The next morning, during a very short interview, he behaved to her with a kindness which she had never before experienced. He had not resolution to breakfast with her, but promised, with affection in his words and manner to return to dinner. The truth was, he never quitted home, but wandered about his woods to compose and strengthen his mind. This self-examination was the first he had practiced; its effects were salutary."

...

[After eating a dinner Mrs. Carlton specially prepared for him,] "Tears of gratitude rushed into Carlton's eyes, and tears of joy overflowed those of the old domestic, when his master, rising from the table, tenderly embraced his wife, and declared he was unworthy of such a treasure. 'I have been guilty of a public wrong, Johnson,' said he to his servant, 'and my reparation shall be as public. I can never deserve her, but my life shall be spent in endeavouring to do so.'

"The little girl was brought in, and her presence seemed to cement this new formed union. An augmented cheerfulness on the part of Mrs. Carlton, invited an increased tenderness on that of her husband. He began every day to discover new excellencies in his wife, which he readily acknowledged to herself, and to the world. The conviction of her worth had gradually been producing esteem, esteem now ripened into affection, and his affection for his wife was mingled with a blind sort of admiration of that piety which had produced such effects. He now began to think home the pleasantest place, and his wife the pleasantest companion."

2. From Caroline Norton, *A Letter to the Queen on Lord Chancellor Cranworth's Marriage and Divorce Bill*[1] (London: Longman, Brown, Green and Longmans, 1855), 8–16

A married woman in England has *no legal existence*: her being is absorbed in that of her husband. Years of separation or desertion cannot alter this position. Unless divorced by special enactment in the House of Lords, the legal fiction holds her to be "*one*" with her husband, even though she may never see or hear of him.

She has no possessions, unless by special settlement; her property is *his* property. Lord Ellenborough[2] mentions a case in which a sailor bequeathed "all he was worth" to a woman he cohabited with; and afterwards married, in the West Indies, a woman of considerable fortune. At this man's death it was held,—notwithstanding the hardship of the case,—that the will swept away from his widow, in favour of his mistress, every shilling of the property. It is now provided that a will shall be revoked by marriage: but the claim of *the husband* to all that is his wife's exists in full force. An English wife has no legal right even to her clothes or ornaments; her husband may take them and sell them if he pleases, even though they be the gifts of relatives or friends, or bought before marriage.

---

1   Robert Monsey Rolfe, First Baron of Cranworth (1790–1868), was the Lord Chancellor from 1852–58; the Marriage and Divorce Act was passed in 1857. This act enabled people to get divorces legally (rather than through a special act of Parliament). Significantly, it also began to dismantle laws of coverture. See the Introduction for more information on Victorian women's legal status (pages 20–21).

2   Edward Law, First Baron Ellenborough (1750–1818), was Lord Chief Justice from 1802–18.

An English wife cannot make a will. She may have children or kindred whom she may earnestly desire to benefit; —she may be separated from her husband, who may be living with a mistress; no matter: the law gives what she has to him and no will she could make would be valid.

An English wife cannot legally claim her own earnings. Whether wages for manual labour, or payment for intellectual exertion, whether she weed potatoes, or keep a school, her salary is *the husband's*; and he could compel a second payment, and treat the first as void, if paid to the wife without his sanction.

An English wife may not leave her husband's house. Not only can he sue her for "restitution of conjugal rights," but he has a right to enter the house of any friend or relation with whom she may take refuge, and who may "harbour her,"—as it is termed,—and carry her away by force, with or without the aid of the police.

If the wife sue for separation for cruelty, it must be "cruelty that endangers life or limb," and if she has once forgiven, or, in legal phrase, "*condoned*" his offences, she cannot plead them; though her past forgiveness only proves that she endured as long as endurance was possible.

If her husband take proceedings for a divorce, she is not, in the first instance, allowed to defend herself. She has no means of proving the falsehood of his allegations. She is not represented by attorney, nor permitted to be considered a party to the suit between him and her supposed lover, for "damages." Lord Brougham[1] affirmed in the House of Lords: "*in that action the character of the woman was at immediate issue, although she was not prosecuted. The consequence not unfrequently was, that the character of a woman was sworn away; instances were known in which, by collusion between the husband and a pretended paramour, the character of the wife has been destroyed. All this could take place, and yet the wife had no defence; she was excluded from Westminster-hall, and behind her back, by the principles of our jurisprudence, her character was tried between her husband and the man called her paramour.*"

If an English wife be guilty of infidelity, her husband can divorce *her* so as to marry again; but she cannot divorce the husband *a vinculo*,[2] however profligate he may be. No law court can divorce in England. A special Act of Parliament annulling the marriage, is passed for each case. The House of Lords grants this almost as a matter of course to the husband, but not to the

---

1   Henry Peter Brougham (1778–1868) was Lord High Chancellor of Great Britain, presiding in the House of Lords, from 1830–34, where he passed the Reform bill of 1832 and the Slavery Abolition Act of 1833. Significantly for Norton, he was appointed attorney general in 1820 to Caroline, Princess of Wales, and helped her during divorce proceedings from her husband, the Prince of Wales, who later became King George IV.

2   Latin "from the bond." A divorce *a vinculo* dissolves the marriage tie.

wife. In only four instances (two of which were cases of incest), has the wife obtained a divorce to marry again.

She cannot prosecute for a libel. Her husband must prosecute; and in cases of enmity and separation, of course she is without a remedy.

She cannot sign a lease, or transact responsible business.

She cannot claim support, as a matter of personal right, from her husband. The general belief and nominal rule is, that her husband is "bound to maintain her." That is not the law. He is not bound to *her*. He is bound to his country; bound to see that she does not cumber the parish in which she resides. If it be proved that means sufficient are at her disposal, from relatives or friends, her husband is quit of his obligation, and need not contribute a farthing: even if he have deserted her; or be in receipt of money which is hers by inheritance.

She cannot bind her husband by any agreement, except through a third party. A contract formally drawn out by a lawyer,—witnessed, and signed by her husband,— is *void in law*; and he can evade payment of an income so assured, by the legal quibble that "a man cannot contract with his own wife."

Separation from her husband by consent, or for his ill usage, does not alter their mutual relation. He retains the right to divorce her *after* separation,—as before,—though he himself be unfaithful.

Her being, on the other hand, of spotless character, and without reproach, gives her no advantage in law. She may have withdrawn from his roof knowing he lives with "his faithful housekeeper": having suffered personal violence at his hands; having "condoned" much, and being able to prove it by unimpeachable testimony: or he may have shut the doors of her house against her: all this is quite immaterial: the law takes no cognizance of which is to blame. As *her husband*, he has a right to all that is hers: as *his wife*, she has no right to anything that is his. As her husband, he may divorce her (if truth or false swearing can do it): as his wife, the utmost "divorce" she could obtain, is permission to reside alone,—married to his name. The marriage ceremony is a civil bond for him,—and an indissoluble sacrament for her; and the rights of mutual property which that ceremony is ignorantly supposed to confer, are made absolute for him, and null for her.

Of course an opposite picture may be drawn. There are bad, wanton, irreclaimable women, as there are vicious, profligate, tyrannical men: but the difference is *this*: that to punish and restrain bad wives, there are laws, and very severe laws (to say nothing of social condemnation); while to punish or restrain bad husbands, there is, in England, no adequate law whatever. Indeed, the English law holds out a sort of premium on infidelity; for there is no doubt that the woman who is divorced for a lover and marries him, suffers less (except in conscience) than the woman who *does not deserve to suffer at all*—the wife of a bad husband, who can inflict what he pleases, whether she remain in her home, or attempt to leave it.

Such, however, is "the law": and if anything could add to the ridicule, confusion, and injustice of its provisions, it would be the fact, that though it is law for the rich, it is not law for the poor; and though it is the law in England, it is not the law in Scotland!

It is not the law for the poor.

Since the days of King Henry VIII, for whose passions it was contrived, our method of divorce has remained an indulgence sacred to the aristocracy of England. The poorer classes have no form of divorce amongst them. The rich man makes a new marriage, having divorced his wife in the House of Lords: his new marriage is legal; his children are legitimate; his bride occupies, in all respects, the same social position as if he had never previously been wedded. The poor man makes a new marriage, *not* having divorced his wife in the House of Lords; his new marriage is null; his children are bastards; and he himself is liable to be put on his trial for bigamy: the allotted punishment for which crime, at one time was hanging, and is now imprisonment. Not always offending knowingly,—for nothing can exceed the ignorance of the poor on this subject; they believe a Magistrate[1] can divorce them; that an absence of seven years constitutes a nullity of the marriage tie; or that they can give each other reciprocal permission to divorce: and among some of our rural populations, the grosser belief prevails, that a man may legally *sell* his wife, and so break the bond of union! They believe anything,—rather than what is the fact,—viz. that *they* cannot do legally, that which they know is done legally in the classes above them; that the comfort of the rich man's home, or the indulgence of the rich man's passions, receives a consideration in England which the poor need not expect to obtain.

It is not the law of Scotland. In your Majesty's kingdom, nothing but

> "The rapid running of the silver Tweed"[2]

divides that portion of the realm where women are protected by law,—from that portion where they are *un*protected, though living under the same Sovereign and the same government!

When, In Queen Anne's reign,[3] the legislative union of Scotland was completed, the laws relating to trade, customs, and excise, were assimilated

---

1 Judge.

2 The River Tweed runs, in part, between the border of Scotland and England.

3 Queen Anne (1665–1714) ruled from 1702–14. Under her reign, England and Scotland were united as Great Britain with the Act of Union (1707).

to those of England; but other laws remained untouched; and in nothing is there a larger difference than in all matters relating to marriage, divorce, and legitimation of children.

In Scotland, the wife accused of infidelity defends herself as a matter of course, and as a first process,—instead of suffering by the infamous English action for "damages," where she is not allowed to interfere, though the result may be to ruin her.

In Scotland, the property of the wife is protected; rules are made for her "ailment" or support; and her clothes and "paraphernalia" cannot be seized by her husband.

In Scotland, above all, the law *has* power to divorce *a vinculo* so as to enable *either* party to marry again; and the right of the wife to apply for such divorce is equal with the right of the husband; that license for inconstancy, taken out under the English law by the English husband,—as one of the masculine gender,—being utterly unknown to the Scottish courts.

Appendix E: Childrearing

1. From Hannah More, *Strictures on the Modern System of Female Education with a View of the Principles and Conduct Prevalent among Women of Rank and Fortune* (1799; New York: Evert Duyckinck Inc, 1813), vol.1, 27–28

It is far from being the object of this slight work to offer a regular plan of female education, a task which has been often more properly assumed by far abler writers; but it is intended rather to suggest a few remarks on the reigning mode, which, though it has had many panegyrists, appears to be defective, not only in a few particulars, but as a general system. There are indeed numberless honourable exceptions to an observation which will be thought severe; yet the author questions if it be not the natural and direct tendency of the prevailing and popular system to excite and promote those very defects, which it ought to be the main end and object of Christian education to remove; whether, instead of directing this important engine to attack and destroy vanity, selfishness, and inconsideration, that triple alliance in league against female virtue; the combined powers of instruction are not sedulously confederated in confirming their strength and establishing their empire?

If indeed the *material* substance, if the body and limbs with the organs and senses, be really the more valuable objects of attention, then there is little room for animadversion and improvement. But if the immaterial and immortal mind; if the heart, "out of which are the issue of life"[1] be the main concern; if the great business of education be to implant ideas, to communicate knowledge, to form a correct state and a sound judgment, to resist evil propensities, and, above all, to seize the favourable season for infusing principles and confirming habits; if education be a school to fit us for life, and life be a school to fit us for eternity; if such, I repeat it, be the chief work and grand ends of education, it may then be worth inquiring how far these ends are likely to be effected by the prevailing system.

Is it not a fundamental error to consider children as innocent beings, whose little weaknesses may perhaps want some correction, rather than as beings who bring into the world a corrupt nature and evil dispositions which it should be the great end of education to rectify? This appears to be such a foundation truth, that if I were asked what quality is most important in an instructor of youth, I should not hesitate to reply, *such a strong impression of the corruption of our nature, as should insure a disposition to counteract it; together*

---

1 Proverbs 4:23: "Keep thy heart with all diligence; for out of it are the issues of life."

with such a deep view and thorough knowledge of the human heart, as should be necessary for developing and controlling its most secret and complicated workings. And let us remember that *to know the world,* as it is called, that is, to know its local manners, temporary usages, and evanescent fashions, is not to *know human nature:* and where this prime knowledge is wanting, those natural evils which ought to be counteracted will be fostered.

2. From John S.C. Abbott, *The Mother at Home; or the Principles of Maternal Duty Familiarly Illustrated* (Boston: Crocker and Brewster, 1833), 15–17

Byron[1] had a mother just the reverse of lady Washington;[2] and the character of the mother was transferred to the son. We cannot wonder then at his character and conduct, for we see them to be the almost necessary consequence of the education he received, and the scenes he witnessed in his mother's parlor. She would, at one time, allow him to disobey with impunity; again she would fly into a rage and beat him. She thus taught him to defy all authority, human and divine; to indulge, without restraint, in sin; to give himself up to the power of every maddening passion. It was the mother of Bryon who laid the foundation of his pre-eminence in guilt. She taught him to plunge into that sea of profligacy and wretchedness, upon whose agitated waves he was tossed for life. If the crimes of the poet deserve the execration of the world,—the world can not forget, that it was the mother, who fostered in his youthful heart, those passions, which made the son a curse to his fellow men. Had Byron and Washington exchanged cradles, during the first month of their infancy, it is very certain that their characters would have been entirely changed; and it is by no means improbable, that Washington might have been the licentious profligate, and Byron the exemplar of virtue and the benefactor of nations.

There are, it is true, innumerable causes incessantly operating in the formation of character. A mother's influence is by no means the only influence which is exerted. Still it may be the most powerful; for, with God's ordinary blessing, it may form, in the youthful mind, the habits, and implant the principles, to which other influences are to give permanency and vigor.

A pious and faithful mother *may have* a dissolute child. He may break away from all restraints, and God my leave him to "eat of the fruit of his own devices."[3] The parent, thus afflicted and broken hearted, can only bow before

---

1 Romantic poet George Gordon, Lord Byron (1788–1824).
2 George Washington's (1732–99) mother, Mary Ball Washington (1708–89).
3 Proverbs 1:31: "Therefore shall they eat of the fruit of their own way, and be filled with their own devices."

the sovereignty of her Maker, who says, "be still, and know that I am God."[1]
The consciousness, however, of having done one's duty divests this affliction
of much of its bitterness. And besides, such cases are rare. Profligate children
are generally the offspring of parents, who have neglected the moral and religious education of their family. Some parents are themselves profligate, and
thus not only allow their children to grow up unrestrained, but by their own
example lure them to sin. But there are others, who are very upright, and
virtuous, and even pious themselves, who do, nevertheless, neglect the moral
culture of their children, and as a consequence, they grow up in disobedience
and sin. It matters but little what the cause is, which leads to this neglect.
The neglect itself will ordinarily be followed by disobedience and self will.

Hence the reason that children of eminent men, both in church and state,
are not unfrequently the disgrace of their parents. If the mother is unaccus-
tomed to govern her children, if she look to the father to enforce obedience,
and to control;—when *he* is absent all family government is absent, and the
children are left to run wild; to learn lessons of disobedience; to practice
arts of deception; to build, upon the foundation of contempt for a mother,
a character of insubordination and iniquity. But if the children are under
the efficient government of a judicious mother, the reverse of this is, almost
invariably the case. And since, in nearly every instance, the early years of life,
are entrusted to a mother's care, it follows that maternal influence, more than
any thing else, forms the future character.

3. From John S.C. Abbott, *The Child at Home; or the Principles of Filial Duty* (Boston: Crocker and Brewster, 1834), 76–78

Sometimes you will see a son who will not be obedient to his mother. He
will have his own way, regardless of his mother's feelings. He has grown
up to be a stout and stubborn boy, and now the ungrateful wretch will
by his misconduct break the heart of that very mother, who for months
and years watched over him with a care which knew no weariness. I call
him a *wretch*, for I can hardly conceive of more enormous iniquity. That
boy, or that young man, who does not treat his affectionate mother with
kindness and respect, is worse than I can find language to describe. Perhaps
you say, your mother is at times unreasonable. Perhaps she is. But what of
that? You have been unreasonable ten thousand times ten thousand, and she
has borne with you and loved you. And even if your mother be at times
unreasonable in her requirements, I want to know with what propriety you
find fault with it? Is she to bear with all your cries in infancy, and all your
fretfulness in childhood, and your ingratitude and wants till you arrive at

1   Psalms 46:10.

years of discretion, and then because she wishes you to do some little thing which does not exactly meet your views, are you to turn upon her like a viper and sting her to the heart? The time was when you were a little infant, your mother brought paleness to her own cheek, and weakness to her own frame, that she might give you support. You were sick, and in the cold winter night she would sit lonely by the fire, denying herself rest that she might lull her babe to sleep. You would cry with pain, and hour after hour she would walk the floor, carrying you in her arms till her arms seemed ready to drop, and her limbs would hardly support her through excess of weariness. The bright sun, and the cloudless sky would invite her to go out for health and enjoyment, but she would deny herself the pleasure, and stay at home to take care of you her helpless babe. Her friends would solicit her to indulge in the pleasures of the social evening party, but she would refuse for your sake, and in the solitude of her chamber, she would pass weeks and months watching all your wants. Thus have years passed away in which you have received nothing but kindness from her hands, and can you be so hard hearted, so ungrateful as now to give her one moment of unnecessary pain? If she have faults can you not bear with them, when she has so long borne with you? Oh if you knew but the hundredth part of what she has suffered for your sake, you could not, *could not* be such a wretch as to requite her with ingratitude. A boy who has one particle of generosity glowing in his bosom, will cling to his mother with an affection which life alone can extinguish. He will never let her have a single want which he can prevent. And when he grows to be a man, he will give her the warmest seat by his fireside, and the choicest food upon his table. If necessary he will deprive himself of comforts, that he may cheer her declining years. He will prove by his actions, which can not be misunderstood, that he feels a gratitude for a mother's love, which shall never, never leave him. And when she goes down to the grave in death, he will bedew her grave with the honorable tears of manly feeling. The son who does not feel thus, is unworthy of a mother's love; the frown of his offended Maker must be upon him, and he must render to Him an awful account for his ungrateful conduct.

4. From Sarah Lewis, *Woman's Mission* (1839; Boston: William Crosby & Co., 1840), 25–31

The fate of society is more particularly affected by [maternal] power, because it is more especially influential on the character of men. Most great men have had extraordinary mothers, and it seems as though by some peculiar influence, the nature of the mother acts upon the son. It may be really so, but if this doctrine be objected to as fanciful, let us try to account for it in a more philosophical manner. It is as notorious as it is unfortunate, that the maternal influence is almost the only moral influence to which boys in their early training are subjected. In the education of girls, no one would dare to assume that absolute indifference to moral results, which has been not only permitted, but authorized in the instructors of boys. Neither are they to be blamed, for provided the power of conveying the requisite instruction in Latin and Greek was proved, who ever inquired into the capabilities of a schoolmaster as a moral trainer of youth? Nay, most persons entered on the office without the slightest notion that they were expected to be such. The idea is quite a novel one! so novel, that even now it is most difficult for conscientious parents to find a school in which the moral and religious training of boys is not left at an awful distance behind the intellectual. [...]

But even those who do take some heed to preserve boys from the contaminating influence, which makes them an easy prey to flagrant immorality, seem to have no conception that it is their place to watch over the minor points of character, which, though they may not affect a man's good fame, and hinder his worldly advancement, materially influence his happiness and his virtue. The regulation of temper, the repression of selfishness, the examination of motive—how seldom do they form any part of the training of boys! The neglect has a most fatal effect on their happiness, and the happiness of all connected with them. We may see it illustrated in that curious popular paradox, which allows a man to be by his unregulated temper the torment of all around him, and yet retain the name of a "thoroughly good-hearted fellow." —How far the good heart brings forth good fruits, may be read in the anxious looks of the timid wife—the unchild-like, and joyless manners of frightened children—the obsequious but unloving obedience of domestics—all fearing to awake the lion's wrath. A woman with such a temper is deservedly called a vixen, but a man is "a good-hearted fellow;" except it can be proved that there is a different moral code for the two sexes, it is very puzzling to simple-minded people to know why that which excites merited dislike in a woman, is so leniently passed over in a man: nay, of the two, we should say that the ill temper of a man has less excuse than that of a woman, because he has more power to escape from domestic annoyances. The error here is in the fundamental principle, which makes the regulation of temper no part of the education of boys; such neglect is the greatest possible cruelty, for it adds tenfold difficulty to that internal conflict, which all must sustain, who are anxious to improve their own character. Violence of temper is so easily corrected in early childhood, that judicious early training may almost always save this trouble in after years.*

---

* The force of these strictures is enhanced by the fact, that nine tenths of those engaged in the education of boys in this country, are professedly ministers of the gospel of Christ—the gospel of purity—of unselfishness—of love.

Again, men are said to be more selfish than women. How can they help it? no pains are taken in their education to make them otherwise. That pugnacity which is so admired as a proof of *spirit*, is the very embodiment of the selfish principle—a fighting for their *own* rights—an assertion of their *own* superiority. They are taught at school to despise the weak, and practise the lesson at home in petty domestic torments to the weak of their circle—their sisters; receiving, at the same time, from those very sisters a thousand little services, without consciousness and without gratitude. Is it astonishing that these boys should hereafter be selfish husbands and tyrannical fathers? Considering how little the moral training of boys has, (even in profession,) formed a part of their education, the only subject of astonishment is, that any should escape the evil effects of such a system, and not that many fall victims to it.

A reflecting mind will have no difficulty in acknowledging the bearing of these well-known facts upon the point under discussion; viz., the importance of maternal influence on the character of boys. As there is a great chance that, except they receive religious and moral principles from their mother, their whole life may pass without any attempt to impress them with such,—does it not become of unspeakable importance, that they be detained as long as possible under maternal influence? Yet the very contrary is usually the case, and boys are removed even sooner than girls from the beneficial atmosphere of purity and love, with which family affection, and, above all, maternal affection environs them. And then men are blamed as cold, and hard, and selfish! It would be as natural to feel surprise, that the plant exposed to the constant action of a petrifying spring loses its vegetable characteristics and turns to stone. Till the intellectual will condescend to become likewise the moral trainers of youth—for heaven's sake, let them imbibe as long as possible that pure and beneficent influence which may be their soul's preservative in the midst of moral danger. [...]

Oh, why are mothers in such haste to delegate to others the delightful task which Providence has assigned to them? Why do they hasten to intrust the unformed mind—the unsettled principles of their sons to the ungenial influence of scholastic establishments? Do they thereby hope to lessen the weighty sense of responsibility? it is a vain hope. They, as the guardian angels of man's infancy are charged with a mission—to them is committed the implanting that heavenly germ to which God must indeed give the increase; but for the early culture of which they are answerable. The importance of early impressions—of *home* impressions—is proved by the extreme difficulty of eradicating or counteracting them if bad. Conscientious teachers of youth can bear ample testimony to this fact. They have often occasion to lament with grief and humiliation the powerlessness of their most devoted endeavors to remove early bad impressions—or to do any thing more than just palliate the effects of unfavorable domestic influences—of an unhealthy domestic atmosphere. It is the mother who, as the source of moral influence, is the former of the moral atmosphere. ... *Moral* contagion is more dangerous than physical, by far—would that the horror with which the one is regarded could be, in any degree, extended to the other! [...]

5. From Berthold Auerbach, "Every-day Wisdom, Plucked from the Garden of Childhood," *Howitt's Journal* III.53 (January 1848): 13–14

THE destruction of things, is often the means by which the child shows its earliest activity. You return from the town where you have been making good bargains; you wish to give your child some pleasure at home, and you bring him a pretty play-thing. But scarcely is the first joy of surprise and wonder over, then the child begins to make some alteration in the present you have made him. To play at bowls with it, and to throw it about, until in a few days, the play-thing is all to pieces and destroyed.

...

Very probably this spirit of destruction in the child makes you angry, and you will not give him anything more, or else you take away from him that which you gave, and lock it up in a closet. If you go and talk to some learned person about this propensity of the child, ten to one but he will say to you, "all this proceeds from original sin, which shows itself thus early in this passion for destruction in the child."—Thus say very many of those persons who, from one year's end to another, preach about love, and who are always praising the supreme wisdom of God, for the arrangements of creation, and yet whenever you take council of them, they immediately invite the devil to be godfather.

...

This impulse of activity; this pleasure in trying the strength and impressing the will upon something, shows itself early and powerfully in the child. Give it a play-thing; to your little daughter that she may amuse herself with it, a doll to dress and undress, to lay in the cradle and to rock (and in that also, very soon is the principle of action seen); your son will immediately tie on his whip-lash, or saddle his wooden horse differently; roll about his wagon or pull it entirely to pieces. Do not scold him if he have very soon destroyed your present; he did not mean to destroy it, but only to make something new out of it. The cause of your gift being spoiled, is only owing to the inexperience of the youthful mind, and is something very different from evil propensity and love of destruction.

Neither is it *the inborn spirit of evil working in the child which causes the tender little hand to destroy that which has been carefully put together, but a natural and proper impulse to do and to make something.*

Regard the soul of a child always as a sacred temple, and you will discover that the principles of his action are holy and blameless.

Give the child something upon which he may exercise his strength in a harmless manner, and out of which he can make something; a ball, wooden bricks, and such like, and you will soon see his enduring pleasure therein.

And yet, now also, you may see something which you may be disposed to regard as naughtiness, and love of destruction. ... How he exults in the rattling and crashing down of all the individual pieces, and thinks no longer on the downfallen magnificence. Is that only the influence of the Evil One and the love of destruction? Certainly not; it is much rather astonishment, the delight of altering that which was made, and the unconscious thought of being able at a touch, to do so much all at once, which is the true foundation of the joy. Nothing bad is intended thereby. For the human soul is by nature, good and noble; wickedness is an aberration. Therefore I repeat it, *always regard the soul of a child as a sacred temple, and you will soon discover that the principles of his action, are holy and blameless.*

[The article goes on to discuss many different aspects of childrearing: from ideas about the importance of surrounding the child with other children to teaching children how to do their duty and obey their parents. It closes with musings on the importance of being kind to children.]

6. From Anonymous, "The Moral Discipline of Children," *British Quarterly Review* 27 (April 1858): 383–413 [This extract is from 407–11]

Do not expect from a child any great amount of moral goodness. During early years every civilized man passes through that phase of character exhibited by the barbarous race from which he is descended. As the child's features— flat nose, forward-opening nostrils, large lips, wide-apart eyes, absent frontal sinus, &c.—resemble for a time those of the savage, so, too, do his instincts. Hence the tendencies to cruelty, to thieving, to lying, so general among children—tendencies which, even without the aid of discipline, will become more or less modified just as the features do. The popular idea that children are "innocent," while it may be true in so far as it refers to evil *knowledge*, is totally false in so far as it refers to evil *impulses*; as half-an-hour's observation in the nursery will prove to any one. Boys when left to themselves, as at a public school, treat each other far more brutally than men do; and were they left to themselves at an earlier age their brutality would be still more conspicuous.

Not only is it unwise to set up a high standard for juvenile good conduct, but it is even unwise to use very urgent incitements to such good conduct. Already most people recognize the detrimental results of intellectual precocity; but there remains to be recognized the truth that there is a *moral precocity* which is also detrimental. Our higher moral faculties, like our higher intellectual ones, are comparatively complex. By consequence they are both comparatively late in their evolution. And with the one as with the other, a very early activity produced by stimulation will be at the expense of the future character. Hence the not uncommon fact that those who during childhood were instanced as models of juvenile goodness, by-and-by undergo some disastrous and seemingly inexplicable change, and end by being not above but below par; while relatively exemplary men are often the issue of a childhood by no means so promising.

Be content, therefore, with moderate measures and moderate results. Constantly bear in mind the fact that a higher morality like a higher intelligence must be reached by a slow growth; and you will then have more patience with those imperfections of nature which your child hourly displays. You will be less prone to that constant scolding and threatening, and forbidding, by which many parents induce a chronic domestic irritation, in the foolish hope that they will thus make their children what they should be.

This comparatively liberal form of domestic government, which does not seek despotically to regulate all the details of a child's conduct, necessarily results from the system for which we have been contending. Satisfy yourself with seeing that your child always suffers the natural consequences of his actions, and you will avoid that excess of control in which so many parents err. Leave him wherever you can to the discipline of experience, and you will so save him from that hothouse virtue which over-regulation produces in yielding natures, or that demoralizing antagonism which it produces in independent ones.

By aiming in all cases to administer the natural reactions to your child's actions you will put an advantageous check upon your own temper. The method of moral education pursued by many, we fear by most, parents, is little else than that of venting their anger in the way that first suggests itself. The slaps and rough shakings, and sharp words, with which a mother commonly visits her offspring's small offences (many of them not offences considered intrinsically) are very generally but the manifestations of her own ill-controlled feelings—result much more from the promptings of those feelings than from a wish to benefit the offenders. While they are injurious to her own character, these ebullitions tend, by alienating her children and by decreasing their respect for her, to diminish her influence over them. But by pausing in each case of transgression to consider what is the natural consequence, and how that natural consequence may best be brought home to the transgressor, some little time is necessarily obtained for the mastery of yourself: the mere blind anger first aroused in you settles down into a less vehement feeling, and one not so likely to mislead you.

Do not, however, seek to behave as an utterly passionless instrument. Remember that besides the natural consequences of your child's conduct which the working of things tends to bring round on him, your own approbation or disapprobation is also a natural consequence, and one of the ordained agencies for guiding him. ... Beware, however, of the two extremes; not only in respect of the intensity, but in respect of the duration of your displeasure. On the one hand, anxiously avoid that weak impulsiveness, so general among mothers, which scolds and forgives almost in the same breath. On the other hand, do not unduly continue to show estrangement of feeling, lest you accustom your child to do without your friendship, and so lose your influence over him. The moral reactions called forth from you by your child's actions, you should as much as possible assimilate to those which you conceive would be called forth from a parent of perfect nature.

Be sparing of commands. Command only in those cases in which other means are inapplicable, or have failed. ... As in primitive societies a breach of law is punished, not so much because it is intrinsically wrong as because it is a disregard of the king's authority—a rebellion against him; so in many families, the penalty visited on a transgressor proceeds less from reprobation of the offence than from the anger at the disobedience. ... As Richter[1] remarks—"The best rule in politics is said to be '*pas trop gouverner:*'[2] it is also true in education." And in spontaneous conformity with this maxim, parents whose lust of dominion is restrained by a true sense of duty, will aim to make their children control themselves wherever it is possible, and will fall back upon absolutism only as a last resort.

But whenever you *do* command, command with decision and consistency. If the case is one which really cannot be otherwise dealt with, then issue your fiat, and having issued it, never afterwards swerve from it. ... Let your penalties be like the penalties inflicted by inanimate nature—inevitable. The hot cinder burns a child the first time he seizes it; it burns him the second time; it burns him the third time; it burns him every time; and he very soon learns not to touch the hot cinder. If you are equally consistent—if the consequences which you tell your child will follow certain acts, follow with like uniformity, he will soon come to respect your laws as he does those of Nature. And this respect once established will prevent endless domestic evils. ... Better even a barbarous form of domestic government carried out consistently, than a humane one inconsistently carried out. Again we say, avoid coercive measures whenever it is possible to do so; but when you find despotism really necessary, be despotic in good earnest.

---

1 Eugen Richter (1838–1906), German writer and politician, one of the founders of liberalism.

2 "Do not govern/rule too much."

Bear constantly in mind the truth that the aim of your discipline should be to produce a *self-governing* being; not to produce a being to be *governed by others*. Were your children fated to pass their lives as slaves, you could not too much accustom them to slavery during their childhood; but as they are by-and-by to be free men, with no one to control their daily conduct, you cannot too much accustom them to self-control while they are still under your eye. ... All periods of transition are dangerous; and the most dangerous is the transition from the restraint of the family circle to the non-restraint of the world. Hence the importance of pursuing the policy we advocate; which, alike by cultivating a child's faculty of self-restraint, by continually increasing the degree in which it is left to its self-restraint, and by so bringing it, step by step, to a state of unaided self-restraint, obliterates the ordinary sudden and hazardous change from externally-governed youth to internally-governed maturity. [...]

Appendix F: Temperance

1. From Joseph Entwisle, "On Drinking Spirits," *The Methodist Magazine* Vol. 27 (July 1804): 320–24

VARIOUS are the snares and temptations,[1] to which professors of religion, in the present age, are exposed; insomuch that the best men are in continual danger of being drawn or driven from the path of duty and holy obedience. Every man therefore has need of line upon line, and of admonition upon admonition. And some persons, in circumstances peculiarly dangerous, have need of the most faithful and pointed cautions.

...Will you allow me ... with candor and tenderness, yet with the utmost plainness, to deliver my sentiments on a subject of high importance to the cause of religion and morality, viz. "*The abuse of Spirituous Liquors?*" My apology for proposing the insertion of such a paper in your Magazine, is, the *evident necessity* of it, in this age of commerce, and of increasing riches and luxury.

Our ancestors knew little, comparatively, of the use or abuse of Spirituous Liquors, for they seldom had recourse to them. But *now*, they are in almost general use; nor is it uncommon for *sober*, and even *religious* persons to bring them to their tables, from motives of hospitality to their friends. Hence the most temperate and conscientious have need to be upon their guard. I should be sorry to give you pain, for one moment, by *undue* severity, in speaking of the frequent use of such liquors: but the *abuse* is so common, and there is so much danger of it spreading, that great plainness ought to be used in speaking on the subject.

I wish ... that particular notice may be taken of the term *abuse*; for it must be admitted that ardent spirits have their *use*; and in some cases it may become a duty to apply them. Such cases, however, seldom occur; and when they do, the greatest caution should be observed.

It will be difficult, perhaps, precisely to fix any general standard by which persons may be directed as to this point. But an unprejudiced person may form a correct judgment for himself.

It cannot be doubted for a moment, whether those persons are guilty of the evil in question, who drink *at any time* till they are intoxicated. Who does not know that drunkenness is a sin; a sin against God and against the community? But many, who are never seen in a state of intoxication, *are in a considerable degree culpable.* This remark will apply to *most* who are in the habit of drinking spirits, either pure or mixed with water, *day by day.* I say, *to most:*

---

1 Although often used by the faithful as an expression, this appears to have its roots in 2 Timothy 1:9: "But they that will be rich fall into temptation and a snare, and into many foolish and hurtful lusts, which drown men in destruction and perdition."

for there may be some exceptions. Here and there one, for physical reasons, takes a portion of this mixture as his daily beverage, and, perhaps, measures it with as much caution as he would any dangerous ingredient in the composition of medicine. Such a person must be exculpated from blame; though it is questionable, whether the CONSTANT use of *such a medicine*, for so we must term it, answer any valuable purpose. "There is no medicine I know of," saith Dr. Cadogan, "that, taken every day, will not cease to act entirely, or by acting do much harm."[1] Cad[ogan] on the Gout.

Notwithstanding the above concessions, impartial men will not deem it uncharitable to assert, that such as from *mere custom*, out of compliance to others, or for their own sensual gratification, indulge themselves in the daily use of Spirituous Liquors cannot be exculpated.

In some parts of the Kingdom, it is not uncommon to give spirits, very freely, to sick persons, sometimes mixed with water, and sometimes even unmixed. The design of this is to cheer their spirits. The patient, at first, probably, takes the potion reluctantly, but by degrees acquires a relish for it, and fancies he cannot do without it. This is an awful abuse indeed. It frequently accelerates the dissolution of the unhappy person so treated; and, at the same time, indisposes, nay more, *incapacitates* him to prepare for his important change.

Another instance must not be unnoticed. Some persons are in the habit of pressing Spirituous Liquors upon others, particularly their guests; compelling them, by their importunities, to take more than they are disposed to take; often urging, as if conscious they were doing wrong, "I hope it will not hurt you!!"

It is scarcely necessary to consider the force, or rather the *weakness* of arguments in favour of a daily and habitual use of Spirituous Liquors. Many never think of any reasons for it. It is *agreeable* to them; and long custom has induced a habit, which renders it so necessary that they cannot be easy without it.

They who are questioned by others, or whose own minds are, at times, uneasy, endeavour to find out reasons for a continuance of the practice; which, if examined, will appear to have no force at all. One uses spirits to *promote digestion*!! Another to *cheer his mind*!! A third *to keep out the cold*!! and a fourth, because he wants something to *nourish and strengthen him*!! These commonplace arguments can have no weight but on uninformed minds, or on persons who wish to find an excuse for a conduct they are resolved to pursue.

You will perceive ... the design of this Letter, is, to dissuade from and guard against the *daily use* of strong Liquors, which, (admitting very few exempt cases) is, as I contend, an *abuse* of them. Were arguments necessary to enforce this advice, they might be multiplied. The following may suffice.

---

1   Dr William Cadogan (1711–97) was a writer of several popular pamphlets on medicine.

[Entwisle continues to discuss how "the use of Spirituous Liquors occasions unnecessary expense[;] ... is injurious to health[;] ... [and] is hurtful to the soul."]

...

It would be uncharitable to suppose that the evil, we wish to remove, or prevent, is *very common* amongst professors of religion. Yet its existence cannot be denied; and the danger is great and increasing. And if it do not meet with a firm resistance from *religious men, who* shall stem the torrent? "If the salt have lost its savour, wherewith shall it be seasoned?"[1]

Should this paper be the effectual mean of caution to a single individual, and in any degree answer the design of the writer, by *producing in the minds of professors a resolution to avoid the appearance of evil,* he will rejoice. And if any should blame him for the liberty he has taken, and find fault with the manner of his address, he will still enjoy the satisfaction which arises from a conscientious discharge of his duty. [...]

2. A Lecture Delivered by Mr. J.P. Parker [about Temperance and Slavery] on 19 April 1847 at the Star of Temperance Hall, Reprinted in "The Weekly Record of Facts and Opinions Connected with General Interests and Popular Progress," a Separate Section within *Howitt's Journal* Vol. 1 (24 April 1847): 33

["The Weekly Record" is found between pages 238 and 239 of the journal proper and has its own pagination.]

To the Members of the Temperance Societies in the United States of America.

DEAR Friends, and Fellow Workers in the cause of Temperance.—We, the undersigned members of Temperance Societies in London, respectfully address you on a most important subject. We have long laboured in our respective hemispheres in the promulgation of our excellent and self-denying principles. We have exerted ourselves on behalf of those who were ready to perish, and for whom no man seemed to care. We have brought liberty to the captive, and we have opened the prison doors of those who were bound. Thousands have been made to rejoice, who once were sad and sorrowing. Thousands have become respectable and respected members of society, who once were outcasts, the offscouring of all things.

We have stood forward firmly and fearlessly, in the face of difficulty and danger, boldly and zealously seeking to emancipate the White Slave—the self-made bondman. In the pursuit of our noble object, we have "known no man after the flesh,"[2] but have sacrificed time, money, and even reputation, in the calm confidence of a conscience void of offence in the sight of God. We have

---

1   A slightly rephrased version of Matthew 5:13.

2   2 Corinthians 5:16.

been rewarded for our pains and privations. Almighty God has blessed our exertions, and crowned them with abundant success; and we are at this time looking forward, with a hope that is sure and steadfast, that our principles will ultimately be universally acknowledged, and universally reduced to practice.

We were favoured with the presence of a large body of American citizens, who, in your name, appeared at our World's Temperance Convention as your delegates and representatives. We rejoiced to meet them in our fatherland, and we doubt not that they on their return informed you that we received and parted from them as dear friends and brethren.

But we have been informed that a large body of Americans who with ourselves have long practiced the healthy and invigorative system of total abstinence from all intoxicating liquors, did not avail themselves of that opportunity to unite with us in presenting a great moral spectacle to the world; and we have been told that these were not represented at our Temperance Convention, because they feared lest, the colour of their skin being different to ours, we should not have received them as dear brethren. We regret that such should have been the case; we should have hailed their appearance with joyful acclamation; we should have received them with fraternal affection, and have listened to their statements or suggestions with profound respect. With us there is no respect of persons, whether white, or black, or red, or yellow; all men with us are brethren, children of the same Almighty Parent, the offspring of the same common father.

There came with one of the delegates from your highly favoured land a man who had been, as we were informed, a slave in one of your southern states—his name is Frederick Douglass.[1] He stood on our Temperance platforms at our largest places of assembly, and we rejoiced to hear him speak of what our principles had done for his coloured brethren. We recognized in him a triumphant refutation of that vile calumny which had declared the Negro to be an unintellectual and inferior being. He stood, a man distinguished by his talents and eloquence, among men long acknowledged by us as talented and eloquent, and from them and from us he received the respectfully and cordially offered right hand of fellowship and affection.

Our ministers, our statesmen, our men of literature and learning, our merchants and mechanics, men of every class and grade in society, came around that noble specimen of coloured humanity, and with united voice declared him to be one of nature's aristocracy.

And now, dear brethren, we have a friendly controversy with you. We are told that in your land, the land of liberty as we have often called it, there are thousands of such men held in the bonds of slavery. Men created in the image of God, but treated as the brutes that perish. Men whose birthright is freedom, but whose natural rights have been forcibly torn from them. Men

---

1 An American former slave, who became a speaker, writer, and publisher (1817?–95).

who have hearts to love, but whose hearts' affections have been sported with and blighted. Men who have been taught that for them the Saviour died, and who have been placed upon the auction block with this commendation to enhance their value—that they were Christians.

Brethren, are these things true? Are men and women united together among you in the holy bands of matrimony, and then, at the caprice of their fellow men, torn from each other never to meet again? Are men and women to be found among you, whose backs have been torn and lacerated by the whip—whose faces have been branded by the burning iron—whose limbs have been hacked and maimed? Brethren, are these things true? Is the husband torn from the wife—the child from the parent—the suckling from the mother's breast—and sold like cattle in the public market? Dear brethren, are these things true, and have you not the power to alter this? If you have not, we feel that you have a right to our deepest sympathies; we sincerely regret your inability.

But if you have the means, if you have the power, to crush this system of iniquity, we beg you to employ those means with all the energy and earnestness that the case demands.

As Englishmen, our boast is this:—Our fathers sanctioned slavery; our fathers trafficked in human flesh and blood; our fathers bought and sold their sable brethren;—but we, thank God, are wiser than our fathers; we, thank God, have seen our duty clearly; and we rejoice to say that he who plants his foot on British ground remains a slave no longer.

Brethren, will you not join us in one loud cry of "Perish Slavery—let all men be free?" Will you not unite with us to carry out that heavenly precept, "Whatsoever ye would that men should do unto you, do ye also unto them?"

Brethren, let us hear from you that, while the drunkard or the moderate drinker may be base enough to hold his fellow man in slavery's bonds, with you the name of Temperance is synonymous with freedom—freedom from strong drink—freedom from the degrading traffic in human beings, God's dear children equally with ourselves.

We are, most affectionately,

Yours in the Temperance cause,

J.P. Parker ... [and] A.F. Pridgeon ... Honorary Secretaries

3. From Anonymous, "Temperance and Teetotal Societies," *Blackwood's Edinburgh Magazine* Vol. 73, No. 450 (April 1853): 389–410

We are not about to commit the folly of proving by argument that drunkenness is an evil of great magnitude—that it is a sin; nor to deny that it is most praiseworthy, nay, a Christian duty, to suppress it. On the contrary, we think the good to be obtained by judicious efforts so great, that we

grieve to see the foolish and the designing making themselves the prominent, or, where not prominent, the really moving agents. We have read
many of their publications; we have seen in them, often in subtle disguise,
disaffection to the institutions of our country, disloyalty, and dissent. Where
these are, we expect to find more hatred than love, and a lamentable lack of
that charity which "thinketh no evil,"[1] and is the "bond of peace."[2] Under
an affected philanthropy, a universal pity, for all who are not like themselves,
we see sweeping and severe condemnations—denunciations against all who
dare to combat the most problematical of their opinions. We are sorry to
say that there is the coarseness of a vulgar hatred in their very commiseration; and we have no doubt they would—that is, the more virulent of
them—after putting down their weaker brethren, establish, if they could,
in this our land, an Inquisition as detestable as any which religious bigotry
has inflicted upon mankind. Even now, they will not let man or woman die
quietly in their beds without a sitting in inquest, and branding the character
of even the drinkers of "so small a thing as small beer" with the infamy of
drunkards. [...]

...

[...] Heaven's bounty is not to be denied, because it may be abused. Is
all wine a poison, as they pronounce it to be, because too much of it will
intoxicate? So then is every good given to us. A man may eat beef like a
glutton, and fall down in a fit of apoplexy, but is beef therefore a poison?
Is the butcher to be indicted for murder, because his neighbor Guttle[3] has
stuffed himself with veal into the undertaker's hands? There are such outrages
upon common-sense, that we can only wonder they can ever be seriously
entertained. It seems quite a satire on the credulity and folly of mankind to
bring them to the proof of argument; the only argument, however, must
be *argumentum ad absurdum*.[4] The world at large can never assent to such
nonsense, and is more likely to put down temperance and teetotal societies,
than to be put down by them. These societies are really, by their absurdities,
marring the good they might do. If any should use soberness of speech and
conduct, surely they are the professors of temperance; whereas, they are the
perpetual scolds wherever they plant themselves. They proclaim war against
the innocent, as against the guilty. If you drink anything but water, you are a
drunkard; and should any accident befall you, let your loving relatives—wife,
husband, children, brothers, sisters—dread the epitaph that will be found
of you (mayhap the drinker of a glass of poor small-beer, on the day or the
day before your death) in that awful obituary published monthly in these

---

1   1 Corinthians 13.
2   Ephesians 4:3.
3   A personification of greedily devouring or gorging.
4   An absurd argument where the logic has become senseless.

Chronicles and Advocates, which gloat upon your infamy, and delight to suspend you over the limbo-lake of drunkards. Nay, these most intolerant of men will not tolerate each other, if there is the slightest suspicion of a shade of difference among them. [...]

...

[...] Fanaticism, of whatever kind, is of the nature of intoxicating gas—whoever takes it, though the meekest of the earth, throws about his pugnacious arms ferociously. It is the real "Devil's drink" which makes humanity fiendish.

...

[...] Moderation is the rule of all happiness, not a lonely abstinence. Teach all to be religious, to be "temperate in all things;"[1] let them receive, as blessings to be thankfully and piously used, the gifts of God in meats and drinks, and we venture to say the proper cure for drunkenness, for excess of any kind, will be applied. ... Use and not abuse, should be the law to every rational being, and to every thankful being. It is good to be thankful, and in order to be so, it is well to have a few things for which the poorest may be especially thankful. Grace before meat, and after even wholesome drink, is no evil custom. The pleasure for which we may be thankful is not of the nature of a sin. Whatever sweetens life improves the man; whatever sours it degrades him. It tends to make him unthankful. He looks around him, sees how beautiful nature is; he knows that, by industry, he can obtain such share as it pleased his Maker he should have. We were not intended to sit down at a perpetual Barmecide feast.[2] ... Moderation is the measure both of life and of its pleasures. But this serious reasoning is unnecessary; common-sense wants it not, and fanaticism has but a deaf ear.

...

[...] Nay, we (always meaning, by this usual plural, the individual writer) belong ourselves to a Temperance Society—be not surprised, good reader—yes; a Temperance Society, and, as we believe, the best in the kingdom—The Church of England. There is no teaching there, in her old-fashioned beautiful catechism, of a religion that is of a Babel-confusion of tongues, intermingled with notions of "kingcraft and priestcraft,"[3] and controversial hatreds, in place of charity and patient love. Where that catechism is taught, scholars cannot say they are not warned against drunkenness. It does not, it is true, teach total abstinence from anything, but from evil. It is a safeguard, in

---

1   A portion of 1 Corinthians 9:25: "And every man that striveth for the mastery is temperate in all things...."
2   Imaginary feast.
3   The writer is quoting a pro-temperance piece he cites earlier in this article that finds the church guilty of promoting drink in its communion service.

education, as far as teaching can go, against drunkenness, against every vice, against every crime. [...]

We most seriously and earnestly, nay, solemnly, warn all people against this new tuition [temperance] as a substitute for the old. No good can come of it; and we entreat the very societies on whose doings we have so freely commented, to take a calm review of their own proceedings, and not to think every one an enemy who tells them a truth, however severely, or however unpalatable to them. ... We have thought it our imperative duty to employ every argument, and use every vein, of seriousness or of ridicule. A great evil is to be put down, and we unhesitatingly use every legitimate weapon in the warfare. We contend not for a moment against the good the societies do, but against the manifest evils which fearfully preponderate over the good. ... Let Temperance Societies wisely direct their movements, and they shall have our best wishes and support.

4. Thomas Buchanan Read, "What a Word May Do," *The Poetical Works of Thomas Buchanan Read* Vol. III (Philadelphia: J.B. Lippincott & Co, 1868): 401–02

ONE day, as we sat at a generous board,
Where wine with a liberal hand was poured,
I heard a beautiful lady say,
Whose lord had sometimes gone astray,
Just as the sparkling cup was raised,
   That one too much for a social dinner—
A rebuke, I am sure, the angels praised—
    "I *hate* the sin, but I *love* the sinner."

Down went the cup to the snowy cloth,
Brimming and laughing with creamy froth,
That quickly flattened below the brim,
While the master's eye with a haze grew dim,
And ever after, the wine at his side,
Wooed him in vain as it sparkled and died;
And though he should sit at the board of a duke,
   'Mid the kingliest wines of a princely dinner,
He would still remember that sweet rebuke,
    "I *hate* the sin, but I *love* the sinner."

Appendix G: Women and Art

1. Anonymous, "Let Us Join the Ladies," *Punch* Vol. 33 (July 1857): 27

THOSE who are fond of "the Society of Ladies" will rush to No. 315, Oxford Street, and there enjoy an exhibition that is the result of female handiwork. It is not an exhibition of stitching or embroidery, such as shirts made at home, or anti-macassars, or floral smoking caps, or butterfly braces, or sporting slippers with a series of foxes running helter-skelter over the toes. It is not an exhibition of Berlin-wool work[1] or potichomanie,[2] or any other mania that occasionally seizes hold of young ladies' fingers, and makes them, for the time being, excessively sticky to squeeze, as though you were shaking hands with a Sub-Editor, in the full agony of paste and scissors. It is not an exhibition of jams, or jellies, or marmalades, or preserves, or much less, pickles. You must not expect you are about to be invited to a choice collection of pies, or tarts, or cakes, or puddings, of a most marvelous sweetness, such is generally imparted by white-looking hands that are more in the habit of playing with the keys of a piano than the keys of the store-room. Nor is it wax-work with its mossy baskets of blooming fruit, such as would certainly tempt birds to come and peck at them, nor vases of paper flowers, so faithfully rendered as actually to cause maid-servants to water them. It is nothing to eat, nothing to play with, nothing to wear, nothing that you can adorn your magnificent person with. It is simply a collection of 358 works of art, that have been contributed exclusively by the talent and genius of English Ladies. A Frenchman would nickname the Exhibition: *Les Femmes peintes par elles-mêmes*[3]—though it must not be surmised that the painting is in the ungallant sense that a Frenchman would satirically convey. If cheeks are delicately coloured—if lips are strung into the precise shape of Cupid's bow—if eyebrows are splendidly arched into so many *Arcs de Triomphe*—if eyelashes are artistically penciled—the penciling and the painting are not upon their own fair features, but on the faces of others; and there is no law as yet laid down, we believe, by the tyranny of Man, that a Lady, though she may not colour her own adorable physiognomy, is forbidden to paint the face of another.

---

1 "A fine dyed wool used for knitting, tapestry, and the like" (*OED*).

2 "The craze for imitating Japanese or other porcelain by covering the inner surface of glass vessels, etc., with designs on paper or sheet gelatine; the process of doing this" (*OED*).

3 A joke, as this translates with a double meaning: "the women, painted by themselves" or "the painted women [slang for prostitutes] by themselves."

The Society, to which we have just introduced the reader, numbers none but Ladies. The only doubt of that fact is the extraordinary silence that reigns round the room; though, in opposition to that ungenerous sneer, we can state that the likenesses of the ladies are all so perfectly true to their sex, that every one of them is a speaking likeness![1] Thus, there is a compensating balance in all things, which, *en passant*,[2] makes us only regret that there is not one at our banker's. But away with regrets in the presence of such delightful company! You are communing with the works of ANNA, JULIA, KATE, AGNES, FLORENCE, FRANCES, and fifty other pretty names. Not a man's ugly cognomen is to be found in the whole catalogue. It is a *Book of Beauty*, into which the admission of the whiskered sex is rigidly prohibited. The visitor involuntarily takes his hat off before so much unknown loveliness. That *Brigand*, who is taking your fancy captive, first reared his musket in the Byronic imagination of HARRIET. Stand with respectful awe before that tender *Brigand*, for who knows, HARRIET may one day be your wife? That *Bivouac in the Desert*, which is glowing before you with the crimson light of a hundred blazing Havannahs,[3] was encamped originally in the snug parlour of LOUISA—that very same LOUISA, that probably you flirted with last week at a picnic at Birnam Beeches; halt and warm your hands lovingly before that *Bivouac*, and admire it, if it is only for the primrose glove you stole on that occasion. Be careful of your remarks. Drop not an ugly word, lest you do an injury to the memory of some poetic creature, who at some time or other handed you a cup of tea, or sang you the songs you loved, or conferred on you some bright fleeting happiness that for the moment deluged your heart with Italian sunshine. With GEORGIANA on your right, MARIA on your left; with EMMA gazing from her gorgeous frame right at you, and SOPHIA peeping from behind that clump of moon-silvered trees over your shoulder, be tender, be courteous, be complimentary, be everything that is gentle, and devoted, and kind. Not that there is any necessity for courtesy or compliments; but still, we fancy, that every gentleman, who goes to an Exhibition, carries always a little bit of the RUSKIN[4] with him, and fancies he is "nothing," unless he is "critical."

There is an Emigrant Ship of Mrs. [McTAN's], that many a R.A.[5] would have been proud to have launched into fame. There are some Teneriffe [sic][6]

---

1   A true or faithful rendering of their sex.
2   "In passing."
3   Cigars, from Havana, the capital of Cuba.
4   John Ruskin (1819–1900), writer, painter, and critic.
5   The coveted initials members of the Royal Academy could put after their names on their paintings, also shorthand for members of the RA.
6   One of the Canary Islands.

views by MRS. MURRAY,[1] that are so beautiful, and seem so true, that you may almost swear for the remainder of your life, and maintain stoutly too, without suspecting even you are committing perjury, that you have been to Teneriffe, and know it thoroughly, from its curious-coloured houses, its hanging vineyards, its luxuriant fruit down to the rich tawny gipsy-looking beauties that sell them. How you hate the unpicturesque applewomen and orange girls when you come into Oxford Street afterwards!

There are, also, water-colours, and copies from the Old Masters, and a Tennysonian picture by MRS. WARD[2] and a *genre* subject by MISS BREAD-STREET, and wonderful portraits of lace collars and Crinoline dresses (look at the HON. MRS. RASHLEIGH! No. 180), that would send our *Châlons* and *Dubufes*[3] into fits of envy; and oil paintings, large and small, modest and ambitious, and such suctorious birds'-eggs and glorious odoriferous flowers by MRS. HARRISON,[4] that you suspect she must have borrowed the palette and brushes of HUNT[5] to have painted them! Besides these, there are little pieces of sculpture, and an infinity of agreeable pictures, the majority of which are ticketed in the corner, "Sold." And, for a picture, many consider the height of criticism is to be "Sold!" and, in truth, but few artists go beyond it, while hundreds of poor struggling fellows never get so far. However, we must reluctantly leave the "Society of Ladies." Agree with us, reader, that as in most societies of the same kind (and it always is kind), that there is plenty to admire, plenty to praise, and very little to condemn.

However, we have one great fault to find. We do strongly object to the Secretary and the Checktakers. We have nothing to say against those gentlemen, excepting that they are gentlemen. They should have belonged to the opposite sex. That round collar, that black coat, those Wellington boots, have no right to be in a room that, as they write over railway carriages, is "Engaged for Ladies." They are an intrusion, a living anachronism, two black spots on the uniform beauty of the picture. Away with them! Turn them out!

---

1   This is likely Mrs. Eliza Dundas Murray, who specialized in sea pieces, and exhibited in London from 1859–90. *Dictionary of Artists Who Have Exhibited Works in the Principal London Exhibitions from 1760–1893*, 3rd ed., compiled by Algernon Graves (1901; first edition 1895; reprinted New York: Burt Franklin, 1970), 200.

2   Mrs. Edward Matthew Ward, née Henrietta Ward (1832–1924), who exhibited from 1849–93, specialized in historical paintings. *Dictionary of Artists* 292.

3   Châlon is either John James Châlon (1778–1854) or Alfred Edward Châlon (1780–1860), famous Swiss painters of French descent who were members of the Royal Academy; Claude-Marie DuBufe (1790–1864) or Louis-Edouard Dubufe (1819 or 1820–83), French father and son portrait artists.

4   Mrs. Harrison, née Mary P. Rossiter (1788?–1875), specialized in flowers and exhibited in London from 1833–75. *Dictionary of Artists* 129

5   William Henry Hunt (1790–1864), a famous water colorist and painter of still lifes.

This is the "Ladies'" debût in the artistic world. Of course, they will go on improving (if any improvement is possible in the sex!) year after year. And, who knows, but in time the Royal Academy may have a female President? Not so very improbable either, considering that Sir Charles Eastlake's[1] predecessor was well known to be a Shee![2]

2. From Ellen C. Clayton, "Mrs. Carpenter" and "Mrs. Harrison," *English Female Artists*, Vol. I (London: Tinsley Brothers, 1876), 386–414

Margaret Sarah Carpenter was one of the most distinguished portrait painters of England. The daughter of Captain Alexander R. Geddes, she was born 1793, in Salisbury. The Geddes family counted among its members some men of considerable professional and literary reputation. In her early youth, Miss Geddes received instruction in figure drawing and painting from a resident master at Salisbury. Lord Radnor[3] gave her permission to copy in his gallery at Longford Castle,[4] and by his advice she sent pictures three successive years to the Society of Arts.[5] On each of these occasions she received a public acknowledgment of her talent and industry…. From that time [1814] up to 1866, she rarely failed, year by year, to exhibit portraits and fancy subjects, all admirably painted, and treated with brilliant power.

…

Personally, Mrs. Carpenter was genial and amiable. Her death [in 1872] was deplored by a large circle of friends. Two of her children—Mr. W. and Miss Henrietta Carpenter—have become artists. The former is especially well known.

It was a matter of indignation that so eminent and able an artist should have been debarred the honour of becoming an Academician. The *Art Journal* made some severe, but justifiable, remarks on the subject. "Had the Royal Academy abrogated the law which denies a female admission to its ranks, Mrs. Carpenter would most assuredly have gained, as she merited, a place in

---

1 Sir Charles Lock Eastlake (1793–1865) was an English painter who became president of the Royal Academy in 1850. Significant for Brontë scholars is his marriage in 1849 to Elizabeth Rigby (1809–93), whose review of *Jane Eyre* in 1848 denounced it as "an anti-Christian composition" (see *Quarterly Review* 84.167 [Dec. 1848]: 153–85).

2 Martin Archer Shee (1769–1850), an Irish painter, studied at the Royal Academy and was its president from 1830–50.

3 Likely William Pleydell-Bouverie, the third Earl of Radnor (1779–1869).

4 The family seat of the Earl of Radnor; Longford Castle is known for its fine collection of eighteenth-century art and furniture.

5 Founded in 1754, this organization benefited both art and science; it later shifted its focus from fine art to industrial design.

them; but we despair of ever living to see the rights of women vindicated in this respect; the doors of the institution are yet too narrow for such to find entrance." It cannot be denied that since the days of Angelica Kauffman and Mary Moser,[1] and the female honourary members of the same period, the Academy has studiously ignored the existence of women artists, leaving them to work in the cold shade of utter neglect. Not even once has a helping hand been extended, not once has the most trifling reward been given for highest merit and industry. Accident made two women Academicians— the accident of circumstances, and the accident of birth.[2] Accident opened the doors to girl students—accident aided by courage and talent. In other countries, women have the prizes fairly earned quietly placed in their hands, and can receive them with dignity. In free, unprejudiced, chivalric England, where the race is said to be to the swift, the battle to the strong, without fear or favour, it is only by slow, laborious degrees that women are winning the right to enter the lists at all, and are then viewed with half contemptuous indulgence.

...

Landscape painting was not a favourite study, apparently, with ladies during the earlier years of this century. [...]

Flower and fruit painting, so eminently suited to the delicacy and the then narrowed range of study of women, was high in favour.

...

One of the most graceful flower painters of modern times was Mary Harrison.[3] She was born at Liverpool, about 1788; her father was Mr. Rossiter, a hat manufacturer of Stockport. As it was not the fashion at that period for young ladies to be taught the accomplishments of painting and music, her parents rather discouraged the early love she showed for those arts. She was allowed to draw only "when she had been very good at her lessons," but she might use a slate; and she has amused her children and grandchildren by describing the sort of dramatic pictures she used to make when six or seven years old. First, she would draw a scene of some famed story, then rub it out to make room for a second, and so go on with a little imaginative history, like a story-book. Being at a loss for pencils to paint with, she cut bits from her hair, to fasten in a quill, while all her pennies were lavishly expended in

---

1 Angelica Kauffman (1741–1807), Swiss painter who was one of the founding members of the Royal Academy in 1768 along with Mary Moser (1744–1819).

2 Kauffman was close friends with Sir Joshua Reynolds (1723–92), one of the founders and the first president of the Royal Academy; Moser was trained by her father, George Michael Moser (1706–83), a famous artist, who was also one of the founders of the RA.

3 See the sarcastic mention of her in *Punch* (Appendix G1, above).

gamboges[1] and common dry colour for blue. She used to beg from the servants the stuff employed in the laundry, and by repeated experiments found out the different tints made by mixing her compounds. The greatest pleasure she ever knew in her childhood was when her father gave her a little book of common coloured prints, which she regarded as the perfection of artistic beauty. To the end of her life she vividly remembered the first plate she ever copied. It was a man getting over a stile. She put in with bold hand a pink coat, yellow face, and blue stockings, and used to gaze at this work with more admiration than subsequently she felt in contemplating a renowned Titian.[2] Having an invalid mother and sister for many years, she found little leisure to devote to painting, and in the year 1814 married Mr. Harrison, a gentleman in easy circumstances, with whom she went to the Continent to spend the honeymoon. The allied armies were then in France.[3] Napoleon was at Elba. In the midst of all the hubbub and excitement, the bride contrived to obtain an order from count Denon[4] to copy in the Louvre—thus being, it is believed, the first English lady who had ever painted there. Just before the battle of Waterloo, the young couple returned to England.

Some fifteen years elapsed. Mr. Harrison, who possessed a tolerable fortune in landed property, unfortunately entered into disastrous business speculations, and lost the greater part of his income. Mrs. Harrison then endeavoured to assist him in the maintenance of the family—a serious responsibility, as there were twelve children. The poor gentleman fell into an utterly hypochondriacal state. Mrs. Harrison rose superior to adversity: she cultivated her talent for painting, and removed to London, when she joined some artist friends in establishing a new Society of Painters in Water Colours—now the Institute,[5] of which she remained a member to the day of her death.

As at that time there were few flower painters, and she had been accustomed to paint chiefly roots of wild flowers surrounded by grasses, moss, and dead leaves, Mrs. Harrison fixed upon that branch of art, which, being a novelty, was much admired. In birds' nests, and detached groups of fruit, too, she succeeded very well. Her art was simple, but delicate and refined;

---

1   A yellow pigment.

2   Tiziano Vecelli or Vecellio (1488–90 to 1576), known as Titian, a Renaissance painter.

3   The French Wars (1792–1815).

4   Baron Dominique Vivan Denon (1747–1825), French artist and one of the founders of the Louvre Museum.

5   The Royal Institute of Painters in Water Colours was founded in 1831 as the Society of Painters in Water Colours, competing with the Royal Water Colour Society, founded in 1804. Significantly, the Institute allowed non-members to exhibit their work. These societies were created, in part, because the Royal Academy did not believe water color was suitable for high art.

charming, even if slightly prim. Her subjects were remarkable for taste, feeling, and fond love of nature. Sometimes she would delineate cut sprigs of garden flowers, or a branch of blackberry blossom lying near a bird's nest—violets, cowslips, crocuses, primroses, snowdrops, roses. Her careful hand was happy in picturing a wild bank. Her painting was always a great delight to her, and she rejoiced to find all her children imbued with the same taste. Two of her daughters gained reputation—Maria and Harriet.

In France, during the reign of Louis Philippe,[1] when she met with Madame Sand[2] and many celebrities, she was much sought after, and called the Rose and Primrose Painter. [...]

---

1   Louis Philippe (1773–1850) reigned from 1830–48.
2   George Sand (1804–76), French novelist and feminist.

Select Bibliography

Barker, Juliet. *The Brontës*. New York: St Martin's, 1994.

Berry, Laura C. "Acts of Custody and Incarceration in *Wuthering Heights* and *The Tenant of Wildfell Hall*." *Novel* 30.1 (Fall 1996): 32–55.

Carnell, Rachel K. "Feminism and the Public Sphere in Anne Brontë's *The Tenant of Wildfell Hall*." *Nineteenth-Century Literature* 53.1 (June 1998): 1–24.

Chitham, Edward. *The Poems of Anne Brontë: A New Text and Commentary*. London: Macmillan, 1979.

Clapp, Alisa M. "The Tenant of Patriarchal Culture: Anne Brontë's Problematic Female Artist." *Michigan Academician* 28 (1996): 113–22.

Davies, Stevie, ed. Introduction. *The Tenant of Wildfell Hall*. By Anne Brontë. London: Penguin Books, 1996. vii–xxx.

Frawley, Maria H. "The Female Saviour in *The Tenant of Wildfell Hall*." *Brontë Society Transactions* 20.3 (1991): 133–43.

Gordon, Jan B. "Gossip, Diary, Letter, Text: Anne Brontë's Narrative *Tenant* and the Problematic of the Gothic Sequel." *ELH* [*English Literary History*] 51.4 (Winter 1989): 719–45.

Gruner, Elizabeth Rose. "Plotting the Mother: Caroline Norton, Helen Huntingdon, and Isabel Vane." *Tulsa Studies in Women's Literature* 16.2 (Fall 1997): 303–26.

Hargreaves, G.D. "Incomplete Texts of *The Tenant of Wildfell Hall*." *Brontë Society Transactions* 16.82 (1972): 113–17.

——. "Further Omissions in *The Tenant of Wildfell Hall*." *Brontë Society Transactions* 17.87 (1977): 115–21.

Jackson, Arlene M. "The Question of Credibility in Anne Brontë's *The Tenant of Wildfell Hall*." *English Studies: A Journal of English Language and Literature* 63.3 (June 1982): 198–206.

Jacobs, Naomi. "Gender and Layered Narrative Technique in *Wuthering Heights* and *The Tenant of Wildfell Hall*." *Journal of Narrative Technique* 16.3 (Fall 1986): 204–19.

Langland, Elizabeth. "The Voicing of Feminine Desire in Anne Brontë's *The Tenant of Wildfell Hall*." *Gender and Discourse in Victorian Literature and Art*. Ed. Antony H. Harrison and Beverly Taylor. Dekalb: Northern Illinois UP, 1992. 111–23.

Losano, Antonia. "The Professionalization of the Woman Artist in Anne Brontë's *The Tenant of Wildfell Hall*." *Nineteenth-Century Literature* 58.1 (2003): 1–41.

McMaster, Juliet. "'Imbecile Laughter' and 'Desperate Earnest' in *The Tenant of Wildfell Hall.*" *Modern Language Quarterly* 43.4 (Dec 1982): 352–68.

Nash, Julie, and Barbara A. Suess, eds. *New Approaches to the Literary Art of Anne Brontë.* Aldershot, UK: Ashgate, 2001.

O'Toole, Tess. "Siblings and Suitors in the Narrative Architecture of *The Tenant of Wildfell Hall.*" *Studies in English Literature,* 39.4 (Autumn 1999): 715–31.

Rosengarten, Herbert, ed. Introduction. *The Tenant of Wildfell Hall.* By Anne Brontë. Oxford: Clarendon P, 1992. xi–xxxvi.

Ruff, William. "First American Editions of the Brontë Novels." *Brontë Society Transactions* VIII (1934): 143–50.

Shires, Linda M. "Of Maenads, Mothers, and Feminized Males: Victorian Readings of the French Revolution." *Rewriting the Victorians: Theory, History, and the Politics of Gender.* Ed. Linda M. Shires. New York: Routledge, 1992. 147–65.

Smith, Margaret, ed. *The Letters of Charlotte Brontë: with a selection of letters by family and friends.* Vol. II: 1848–51. Oxford: Oxford UP, 1995.

——. Introduction. *The Tenant of Wildfell Hall.* By Anne Brontë. Oxford: Oxford UP, 1998. ix–xxiv.

Talley, Lee A. "The Case for Anne Brontë's Marginalia in the Author's Own Copy of *The Tenant of Wildfell Hall.*" *Brontë Studies* 32 (July 2007): 132–37.

Thormählen, Marianne. "The Villain of *Wildfell Hall*: Aspects and Prospects of Arthur Huntingdon." *Modern Language Review* 88.4 (Oct 1993): 831–42.

——. *The Brontës and Religion.* Cambridge: Cambridge UP, 1999.

Wheeler, Michael. *Heaven, Hell, and the Victorians.* Cambridge: Cambridge UP, 1994.

Wright, Danaya C. "The Crisis of Child Custody: A History of the Birth of Family Law in England." *Columbia Journal of Gender and Law* 11 (2002): 175–270.